In bed later, Molly stared at the ceiling. She knew Christian was very attractive. He was athletic and intelligent, unattached—so was she. There was no reason on earth why she would not go to bed with him.

Other than that he was the wrong man. They all were.

Because Molly, half horrified, admitted to herself when she was being really honest that she was not interested in anyone except her brother. The knowledge appalled but excited her. . . . Many times, alone in her bed, she remembered herself across his lap, his strong hands holding her, the wind against her bare legs. Molly kept the fantasy locked away in a secret, multicolored box, bound in her imagination with a ribbon . . . but late at night, in the darkness, the ribbon slithered open—sometimes involuntarily, sometimes at her own tremulous tugging—a slow, pleasurable prelude to the release of the fantasy itself. . . .

Molly O'Brian was torn between burning passion and chilling premonition . . . drawn to the arms of a man she could neither have nor resist . . . a man who would soon make her his, body and soul. . . .

"Beautifully crafted . . . a gripping love story."
—*Sunday Tribune*

"A Pandora's Box of writing talent!"
—*Irish Independent*

COMING IN MAY

"An important and revolutionary book."
—Barbara Ehrenreich, *Mirabella*

"Neither women nor marriage will ever be
the same."—Gloria Steinem

THE EROTIC SILENCE OF
THE AMERICAN WIFE

Dalma Heyn

This riveting book shatters the silence about married
women and extramarital sex today. Based on hundreds
of intimate, in-depth interviews with married women
who have had affairs, this insightful book may startle
you. The stories these women tell challenge every myth
about women's sexuality. "Another silence broken—it's
about time women gave voice to all their dimensions,
including the erotic, without shrinking in guilt."

—Gail Sheehy

A PLACE
OF STONES

Deirdre Purcell

A SIGNET BOOK

SIGNET
Published by the Penguin Group
Penguin Books USA Inc., 375 Hudson Street,
New York, New York 10014, U.S.A.
Penguin Books Ltd, 27 Wrights Lane,
London W8 5TZ, England
Penguin Books Australia Ltd, Ringwood,
Victoria, Australia
Penguin Books Canada Ltd, 10 Alcorn Avenue,
Toronto, Ontario, Canada M4V 3B2
Penguin Books (N.Z.) Ltd, 182–190 Wairau Road,
Auckland 10, New Zealand

Penguin Books Ltd, Registered Offices:
Harmondsworth, Middlesex, England

Published by Signet, an imprint of New American Library, a division of
Penguin Books USA Inc. Previously published in a somewhat different version in the United Kingdom by Pan Books.

First Printing, May, 1993
10 9 8 7 6 5 4 3 2 1

For my mother, Maureen

ACKNOWLEDGMENTS

The poem "Tarantella" by Hilaire Belloc (1870–1953) is reprinted by permission of the Peters Fraser and Dunlop Group Ltd.

I should like to thank Dr. Aidan Nulty, Joe Lennon, and Harry Snyder for their meteorological and aviation advice; Pat Brennan and Frank Byrne for reading the manuscript; Michael Legat and Jane Wood for their editorial skills; Vincent Browne and the *Sunday Tribune* for their understanding and encouragement.

I thank my agents, Treasa Coady and Charles Pick, for pushing me into doing this in the first place and the Tyrone Guthrie Centre, Annaghmakerrig, for giving me a room with a view.

Last but most, I should like to thank my family and friends, particularly Kevin, Adrian, and Simon, for putting up with me while I wrote.

A PLACE
OF STONES

1

The DC3 was loading up. Through the dirty window of the operations room at Midway, her captain, Tucker Thompson, studied her as her newly washed frame and the cowlings of her Pratt and Whitney engines glinted under the Chicago sun. Although it was still early, the air in the room was heavy, acrid with the smell of kerosene. The electric fan placed on a filing cabinet gave little relief, barely elevating the red and blue plastic streamers attached to its bent frame; the fan's orbiting hinge needed oiling and its rhythmic creaking was getting on Tucker's nerves. Even the clicking of teletypes was bothering him this morning.

Pulling at his shirt collar where it cut into dewlaps of flesh, Tucker watched the relaxed activity on the tarmac around the plane as she was fueled and provisioned for the long flight ahead: in her captain's sour view, the modifications had turned this good workhorse of a plane into the equivalent of a flying couch. Yet despite the extra tanks fitted behind a false bulkhead when she was modified after the war, the DC3's limited range meant they had to make the journey in a series of hops, from Midway to Bangor, Maine, to Goose Bay, to Prince Christian in Greenland, to Reykjavik, to Shannon and then to London. Well at least the forecast was favorable, he thought gloomily—tailwinds. At a steady 150 knots, the trip should not be too demanding.

He looked again at the manifest and it did not improve his mood. These Smiths, like all rich people, toted a huge amount of luggage. Three trunks and seven suitcases, weighing a total of nearly twelve hundred pounds. All for three adults and a baby! he thought, swatting irritably at a fly buzzing against the streaked windowpane.

Tucker, an ex-ferry pilot, one of the brave, somewhat

reckless breed who flew war supplies to Europe on the transAtlantic run, had never married. He was squat and built somewhat like a miniature bison, with a powerful neck supporting a shaggy, jowled head. His face was creased and leathered, and he viewed the world through hooded, cynical eyes of faded brown. All through the war, Tucker had made plans for afterward—his own airline maybe, or even chief pilot in someone else's airline; but here it was 1953 and he was still jobbing at charter work.

He sighed and looked toward the briefing table, his eyes falling on the dark head bent over the spread of documents. Damn it, he thought, noticing the smooth apple cheeks of his copilot for the trip, they seemed to be getting younger and younger. This one was little more than a child.

The boy looked up and smiled as his superior joined him, but Tucker did not smile back. By long tradition, captains kept their distance from copilots, and chumminess, at least in front of operations and weather men, was not appropriate.

"Heard anything about these Smiths?" Tucker asked, flicking at a paper clip.

" 'Fraid not, Captain!" The boy's voice was light and eager. "All I know is that they're in brewing. You know— Blue Mountain? Smoky Mountain? They're both made by McKennon's, and I believe the Smiths are the people who own and run it now."

Tucker did know the brands—from a brewery whose marketing pitch was independence and quality of product—but he merely grunted and took the clutch of forecast telexes from the meteorologist, a man he knew only slightly and who also seemed to be only half his age. He studied the telexes and TAF's—Terminal Area Forecasts—for London and for each stop en route: it was CAVOK everywhere—Ceiling and Visibility OK. The telexes also showed that they could expect overcast conditions between two and ten thousand feet. Since Tucker had planned a cruising altitude of ten thousand, that posed no problems. He lowered his head over the charts with their swirling lines and triangular symbols denoting Warm and Cold Fronts.

There was an Anti-Cyclone marked in, about one

thousand miles southwest of Ireland, and a long Cold Front was drawn a couple of degrees south of the polar regions, its leading edge crossing Spitzbergen and moving southwestward. Along its length, the meteorologist had crosshatched a long, scalloped ovoid around the abbreviations ISOL CB and MOD ICE.

"Moderate ice, Captain, and only isolated cumulonimbs!" The copilot's young, eager voice irritated Tucker still further. "Thank you for that, son!" he snapped and then, when he saw the copilot redden, felt sorry: "I've seen a lot of charts like this," he said in a more conciliatory tone, "and you don't teach your grandmother to suck eggs." The boy moved away from the table.

With an index finger, Tucker traced the line of the Cold Front all along its length, and the meteorologist, who was picking at his nails, answered the question before it was asked: "Slow-moving," he drawled. "No problem. Not expected to reach your latitudes until at least this time tomorrow."

In the wooded suburb of Evanston, north of the city, the Smiths' Cadillac was humming quietly outside the entrance of the family's mansion. Greentrees, substantial, pillared but discreet, was a square red-brick house built just before the Great Depression. It had changed hands many times, being acquired by Malcolm Smith on his accession to the presidency of the brewery twenty years ago.

There was a small van backed up against the front steps, the driver of which, assisted by the Cadillac's chauffeur, was loading into its maw the last of three heavy trunks. The doors were closed and the van sped off, spraying gravel as it turned out through the tall iron gateway onto the street outside.

Inside the house, Malcolm had almost finished his breakfast. On this warm day, the French doors to the lawn stood open and the dining room was flooded with light reflected from the mirror of Lake Michigan. The president of McKennon's brewery always breakfasted alone, and the servants knew not to come near him.

He gazed on the expanse of bright water, which this morning glittered and danced as far as the eye could see.

Today, he thought, was going to be a hot one. "Yes, a hot one!" he said aloud.

When sitting in his chair, a worn museum piece with wings, Malcolm frequently voiced the tail ends of his thoughts or finished imaginary conversations. At first, when it began to happen and he heard his own voice drop into the morning stillness, he would start in the chair and look around, afraid that someone else might have heard. But that was years ago.

Malcolm was a man on whom the years lay well. An immigrant from Wales who remained grateful to his Maker for the gift of his fortune, he was known in the brewery and amongst his associates as a fair man who drove his workers hard but who rewarded loyalty and dedication. He also cultivated orderliness in all things, in his household, in his brewery, and in his person. His wife was fond of saying that in the unlikely event of a Chicago earthquake, Malcolm would be surprised but his routine would survive. Cordelia, whose grandfather had founded the brewery and who actually owned most of its stock, was one of the few people in Chicago who took no notice of her husband's outward puritanism.

On this particular Saturday at the end of April, he had risen as usual at 6:45, but unusually, had not been the first to stir. As he had padded down the back staircase toward the kitchen, he had heard movement from the adjoining bedrooms occupied by his son, Cal, and his daughter-in-law, Maggie. Cal, he saw, had already put a suitcase outside his door for collection.

Taking a last, satisfying swig out of his coffee as he finished his breakfast, Malcolm reached into his breast pocket for his cigar and cutter, but was interrupted by the arrival into the room of his granddaughter and her nanny.

Susanna, a sunny, placid baby, cried out in delight and stretched out her arms when she saw him. She was almost one year old now, and from the moment she was born, her grandfather had been besotted by her. He hated the fact that she was going to Europe for a month with her parents.

"It's okay, Rosemary." He addressed the English nanny, but had eyes only for the baby, "I'll take her."

The nanny, a pale, fair-haired woman in her early

twenties, smiled. "Mind you don't get Mr. Smith all dirty now, Susanna!" she said, handing the child over.

Malcolm waited until the nanny left the room, then he stroked the baby's blond head. "Aren't you the little doll!"

Susanna giggled. "Oll!" she said, or so it sounded to her grandfather's enchanted ears.

"Did you hear that!" he exclaimed to the empty room. "Did you *hear* that? She distinctly said 'doll'!" He raised her in the air high above his head and she screamed with delight. "Doll, Susanna!" he said. "Say it again, you little charmer. You're a *doll*!"

But Susanna kicked her legs and batted the air with small fat fists.

"Happy birthday for tomorrow, sweetie!" Malcolm whispered it into her soft hair and then he took her out onto the lawn, where the sprinklers were already turning in slow hissing arcs, flashing miniature rainbows in the sunshine. Susanna wriggled to be put down, and her grandfather stooped and placed her gently upright on wobbly legs. She clung on to his trousers for a second; then the legs gave way and she plonked onto the grass.

"Oooh, no!" Malcolm put her on her feet again. "Grass wet! Mommy wouldn't like you to sit on the grass in your lovely new dress." He scooped her up again and she allowed it without demur, patting Malcolm's cheek and smiling coyly. Delighted all over again, he chuckled back at her. "Oh, you little doll!"

In her bedroom, which was in disarray, Malcolm's daughter-in-law, Maggie, sat in front of her dressing table, fastening a string of pearls around her neck. Dressed expensively and plainly in a gray dress, she was the type who would look as good at sixty as she did at thirty, large but not fleshy, with wide shoulders and high cheekbones.

Gazing at herself in the mirror, she tried once again to infuse herself with courage. She must have been mad to agree to this trip. She dreaded it, dreaded the next half hour when she would have to say good-bye to Christian.

She heard her husband moving around in his own room next door. He was whistling.

She looked at her watch. No more dithering.

She went along the corridor to Christian's room, but

the door was open and his bed was empty. She went downstairs, her feet silent on the thick carpeting of the staircase. There was no one in the dining room, but the doors were open, and from outside there was the faint sound of laughter. Her heels clicking on the parquet, Maggie walked across to the doors and saw her father-in-law about fifty yards away. He had Susanna in his arms and was picking leaves from a shrub, throwing them in the air so that they fell like confetti around their heads.

She watched for a few seconds as Susanna, reaching for the leaves with both hands, teetered forward to the point of overbalancing, trusting absolutely that she would be safely held by her grandfather. Maggie smiled. If only the men on the floor of the brewery could see the behavior of their taskmaster now.

She went through to the kitchen, where the housekeeper was tidying up after Malcolm's breakfast. "Have you seen Christian, Bridie?"

The housekeeper dried her hands on her apron, and rolling her eyes sympathetically to the ceiling, inclined her head in the direction of the pantry.

The small room was dim, but pausing inside the doorway to allow her eyes to adjust, Maggie did not turn on the light. Within a few moments, her son's small shape materialized, folded into a corner under a shelf that held Bridie's supplies of flour, sugar, and salt.

She waited another moment or two, then called softly: "Christian? Come on out, honey—don't you want to say good-bye?"

He stayed still as a cat.

Maggie hunkered down where she stood. "Sweetheart, come out, please. You don't *have* to come out. But please, I want to talk to you, to say good-bye. I'll be very, very sorry to have to go away without saying good-bye . . ."

She thought she saw his eyes move. "Christian?"

"What?" The voice was sullen.

"Will you come outside with me? I have something very important to tell you."

No answer, no movement.

"You'll like it, I promise you. . . ."

Still no answer.

"Have I ever broken a promise to you? I *promise* you, you will like what I have to tell you."

She held her breath.

"What?" he said again. The voice was still belligerent, but there was a flicker of interest.

"I can't tell you in here, it's too dark. You know how I hate the dark!"

There was a pause. Then he scrambled out from under the shelf. "What is it?"

She stood up. "Come on into the dining room and I'll tell you there." She put out her hand to take his, but he darted past her, holding his arm across his body as if fearful of contamination.

When they were in the dining room, he stood away from her, poised for flight and eyeing her with something approaching hatred.

Maggie's heart nearly broke. So young, only ten years old, and so much he could not understand, could not be told. For a second or two, she stared away from him and out through the doors. Although it was still so early, two sailboats, small as toys, tacked across the glistening water; Malcolm and the baby still played on the grass. No, it was not fair to take the baby and to leave Christian behind. She had fought but had been defeated by Cal, who had insisted, not unreasonably, that while the baby would be no distraction, being cared for by her nanny, a ten-year-old boy certainly would.

She took a deep breath. "Now listen, honey, I want you to do me a favor . . ."

He stared at her through impassive blue eyes, forcing her to plunge on, improvising. "You know that old pile of wood in the garage that Grandpa wouldn't let Sam throw out? Well, I want you to get that pile of wood—" She paused for effect. "And I want you to build a kennel out of it."

"A kennel?" he asked, still sullen, but to her relief she saw a spark in his eyes. He would not give in easily, however, and looked away. "What's the point of a kennel when I don't have a dog?"

"You can have a dog, Christian!"

"You mean you're going to let me have a dog?" He had been badgering them for a puppy since he was seven years old, but Cal had refused to allow it. Maggie had now decided that she was overruling Cal. Even if there was going to be an argument about it, it was worth it, she thought, just to see the blaze on Christian's face as he looked at her. "Oh, Mom, can I pick it out myself?"

"Yes, honey, you can," she said, "but don't tell Dad just yet. For now it can be our secret. Okay?"

She made their sign, which they used to one another when they had a special secret, an "O" formed between finger and thumb and held up in front of the face.

Christian ran his fingers through his hair. The cowlick that defeated all ministrations of comb, brush, or barber stood even more untidily at the crown of his head. Maggie walked across to him and hugged him. He had still not capitulated completely, but he allowed himself to be embraced. "I'll call the puppy Bluey," he said, muffled against her breast. She laughed and hugged him tighter. "Well, wait until you get him. He might be yellow or black or even patched or spotty. You never know."

She held him away from her and stroked his unruly hair. "Will you help me bring down my bags?" she asked. He dashed off and she had to fight the tears as she watched his sturdy little body, athletic like his father's, take the stairs two at a time ahead of her. *I will never, ever, leave this child again!* she thought fiercely.

When they got back to the entrance hallway, she saw that a small group had gathered around the Cadillac. Malcolm had brought the baby out and she was being handed in to the nanny, who was already sitting in the backseat of the automobile. With his height and erect carriage, thought Maggie fondly, her father-in-law might be taken for a distinguished actor. He heard her approach and turned around.

"Good morning, Maggie."

She threw her arms around his neck. "I'll miss you, Dad!" From the day she had first been introduced to him, Maggie, unlike most people, had never been in awe of Malcolm. And her matter-of-fact ignoring of his crustiness had worked in her favor, making communication and affection between them a two-way street. Now, after a second's hesitation, he hugged her back and muttered something she could not catch.

"What did you say, Dad?" She stood away from him.

He cleared his throat: "Nothing. Just—just take care of yourself and come back safely to us."

"I will," she promised, and turned to look at Cal as he came down the steps two at a time. Resentment at her husband's high spirits flapped angrily in her throat like a trapped crow, but she managed to hide it and turned back to her father-in-law as Malcolm addressed Christian: "Everything okay, Chris?"

She saw that although Christian might have mended fences with her, he was not giving in easily in general. He refused to meet his grandfather's eyes and looked stubbornly at the ground.

"Christian! Your grandpa's asked you a question!" Maggie spoke more sharply than she intended and the boy's blue eyes blazed accusingly at her for a second before he looked away across the lawn. Maggie took a step toward him, but Malcolm restrained her: "Would you like a sourball, son?" He rooted around in a pocket.

"No, thank you, Grandpa." Christian continued to look off into the distance.

"Yes, well, I'd better get your grandma . . ." The old man turned away and went back into the house. "Delia! Delia! They're leaving now!"

Maggie pulled Christian tightly to her side and after a moment's resistance, felt Christian's small body cave in.

She could not bear much more of this, she thought. She wanted to be spirited away—now, right now; failing that, all clocks should stop, relieving her of the necessity of leaving her son.

Although she held onto him and he to her as though their bodies were one, the fatal minute did come and she did have to kiss him, to leave him standing outside the car as she climbed inside.

Half blinded, she risked a backward glance as the Cadillac turned out of the driveway. He was standing between his grandmother and grandfather, and even at a distance of fifty yards, she could make out the jaunty "O" he had formed with the index finger and thumb of his small right hand, held in the air above his head.

"Let me take your coats," offered the stewardess as the passengers boarded the DC3. She was petite and dark-eyed, and beside her Maggie felt like a big, bony horse.

Cal, she noticed wryly, did not react to the girl's vitality as once he might have. *Maybe he's losing his touch,* she thought, *or maybe I am!*

Still wrung out after the parting from Christian, she flopped into her seat and looked around the aircraft. For once, she decided, Cal had been right to insist that they charter a plane instead of taking any of the new, scheduled services from B.O.A.C. or PanAm. The cabin was luxurious, fitted with thick carpet in olive-green; its eight passenger seats, wide, deeply padded, and upholstered in velvet of paler green, reclined fully for sleeping; there was a small lounge area in front of the bulkhead, with two ottomans and a coffee table stacked with newspapers and current copies of *Photoplay, Look,* and *Life,* all held to the surface of the table with specially designed brass clips.

"Would you like a drink before we take off?" Having put the coats away and helped the nanny to organize the baby, the stewardess opened a cabinet in the lounge area, fitted with brass racks of bottles, decanters, and crystal glasses. Maggie accepted a vermouth and attempted to relax for the first time that morning. Having poured a bourbon for Cal and a seltzer for the baby's nanny, the stewardess then went behind the bulkhead into the cockpit.

"How do you feel?" Cal leaned toward his wife, scanning her face for clues, his own face anxious.

"I'm fine, Cal." She smiled.

"Looking forward to the trip?"

"Yes . . ."

He caught the hesitation. "But what, Maggie?"

"But nothing, Cal . . ."

The propellers outside the window turned once and roared into life, distracting him and, to Maggie's relief, precluding further conversation of any intimacy. She lay back in her seat as the plane roared down the runway and took off. But then, as the ground fell slowly away, Maggie decided that there was no minute like the present one to start feeling positive. She was here, she had come on the trip, there was no point in being silly.

She leaned out to look across her husband and out of the window and was immediately engaged. From this height, the housescape was dotted with so many swim-

ming pools she had the impression they was being
watched by dozens of little turquoise eyes; what's more,
she had never before realized quite how full of trees and
parkland the city was. She was able to pick out the curve
of Sheridan Road where it fringed the northern suburbs,
Evanston, Wilmette, Winnetka, Glenview, Highland
Park, Lake Forest . . .

Christian was down there, along the lake, she thought,
and wondered how he was and what he was doing. She
stopped that line of thought. Positive. She had to be positive. She took another mouthful of her vermouth.

By the time lunch was served in the cabin, an hour
after takeoff, the passengers had had several drinks and
the atmosphere was easy. Cal had had little to say, but at
least, thought Maggie, the tension seemed to have been
defused. She finished her own lunch, took the baby from
the nanny, and while Cal leafed methodically through the
newspapers, she fed Susanna with a spoon from the supplies of baby food they had brought with them. Susanna
had taken happily to flying and had spent most of the
first hour crawling along the aisle of the aircraft, pulling
herself upright on the seats, playing peek-a-boo with the
stewardess.

When the baby had finished feeding and had been taken
away by the nanny for a change of diaper, Maggie slept
a little. She came awake with the realization that the engine note of the plane had changed in frequency. They
were making their descent into Bangor.

While his mother and father were stretching their legs
in Bangor, Maine, Christian was on his way to Wrigley
Field with his grandpa Malcolm. They were going to a
doubleheader between the Cubs and the Cardinals.
Christian was not all that interested in baseball, but, uneasy in the sole presence of his grandfather and unsure
of his right to refuse, he had acquiesced to the outing.

He saw they were nearly there. The Cadillac was nos-
ing its way through the chaos, the clogged hooting traffic
and jaywalkers at Sheridan and Irving Park. He and his
grandfather had not spoken much and Christian wondered if he could trust Malcolm with the secret about the
puppy. It was burning a hole in his tongue. He had to
tell *someone*. . . .

"Grandpa, can you keep a secret?"

Malcolm, who was leaning forward in his seat, looking ahead through the glass partition over the shoulder of the chauffeur, answering without looking at him: "Of course I can, Chris."

"Guess what Mom told me I can have when she gets back from Europe!"

"I don't know, son, what? A new bicycle?" Malcolm drummed his fingertips impatiently on the glass and Christian almost did not have the courage to continue.

"No, Grandpa," he said, "something much better than that."

"Speak up, son! Can't hear you with this din—hey!" He snapped his head to the right and yelled at a pedestrian who had almost bumped into the side of the car. "Did you see that?" he said. "Stupid fool!" He turned to Christian, moderating his tone: "Now what's this we were talking about?"

"Nothing," muttered Christian. "It doesn't matter."

"Of course it matters. A secret. Now, wasn't that what all this was about?" He frowned, but Christian could see that it was a pretend frown and that his grandfather was making a determined effort to be agreeable. "Let me guess," said Malcolm, putting a finger to his temple. "Your mom's going to bring you back a duck-billed platypus!"

Despite himself, Christian giggled. "Grandpa, this is *serious*. A serious secret!"

"Oh, dear, all right, Chris, I give up. Here, Morgan!" Malcolm tapped the glass between himself and the driver. "You can let us off here. See you again when the game's over."

"A puppy!" said Christian. "She's going to let me have a puppy. We're going to get it from Orphans of the Storm."

At least he had managed to gain his grandfather's full attention. "Well, well!" he said, clearly astonished. "Does your dad know?"

"Not yet. But Mom says—"

"Yes, well, I'm sure if your mom says it's okay, your dad will think so too. Now, here we are, son," he said, holding open the door.

"I'm going to call the puppy Bluey," said Christian,

getting out, but his words were lost in the din of the crowd outside the ballpark.

Once inside, Christian cheered up. It was never the baseball game itself he liked, but the general air of good humor, the feel of the warm sun on the back of his neck. He even sang along with the crowd as they all gave voice to "Let's Go Out to the Ballgame." Just before the Cubs walked onto the field, he tugged at his grandfather's sleeve: "Can I have a hot dog?"

"Sure, son." Malcolm smiled down at him. Now that they were here and inside, he seemed to have relaxed, and Christian relaxed beside him. He asked for the works on the hot dog.

For the rest of the afternoon, his grandfather did not say a harsh word to him, even when a fat globule of multicolored goo—ketchup, mustard, chopped onion, and picalilli—oozed out of both sides of the bun enclosing his third hot dog and fell on his shirt. When it happened, he looked up nervously, but Malcolm merely passed him a handkerchief.

All in all, it turned out to be a great afternoon. The Cubs even won the doubleheader.

Five thousand miles away, on the west coast of Ireland, Conor O Briain, twelve years old, burned with shame.

It was dinnertime at St. Kevin's School for Boys, and in the refectory, the pupils were eating boiled beef, cabbage, and potatoes. They ate at uncovered deal tables, twenty to each one, in what was supposed to be silence but was in reality a cacophony of tin on delph as the boys wolfed their food from their plates with cheap cutlery. Outside the refectory, the stony Connemara landscape was dark with drizzle and the lights had been switched on, five bare bulbs swinging from the mottled ceiling on wires frayed with age. The bulbs were opaque with the fine mist of steam that rose from the cabbage on each plate—and also from the boys' breath, visible in the damp air. The smell was strong, a mingling of cabbage, damp, and the sweetish, unpleasant scent of imperfectly washed adolescent bodies.

The boys ate under the watchful eye of Brother Patrick, a sandy-haired giant, who patrolled slowly among the tables, his leather belt cutting the bulge of his stomach into half moons under his soutane, his hands, as big as half hams, behind his back. Brother Patrick, it was said, had been a boxer in his youth.

Conor was a scholarship boy from the Aran island of Inisheer off the coast of County Galway. Because there were no secondary schools on the islands, the government paid automatically for all Aran Islands children to attend school on the mainland. Although this was well-known among the other boys at St. Kevin's, scholarship boys tended to be the butt of teasing and Conor hated his status, never more so than today.

He was not eating with the others but was kneeling on the platform at the top of the long room, facing his schoolmates. He was big for his age, loose-jointed, with large hands and feet; his black hair had been cut in the pudding-bowl manner so that seen from the front, it came only halfway down his ears and made his long face seem longer still. But he had extraordinary eyes, fringed with long, thick lashes. The eyes were large, deepset but wide open, of a gradated blue. Around the pupils, the irises were pale, but the blue grew darker toward the outside until the rims were deep gray, almost black. The eyes were wide now, staring, but entirely expressionless, fixed somewhere above the heads of the other boys. Most of these, out of a sense of collegial decency—or at least the knowledge that tomorrow it could be one of them—kept their own eyes averted. But a few, the bullies and the types who gained savage satisfaction from the misfortunes of others, stared openly, and when they were sure they were unobserved by Brother Patrick, elbowed each other in the ribs and sniggered. Amongst these was Conor's brother, Brendan, two years older than Conor, whose seat was quite close to the platform. The family resemblance was slight. Although Brendan was of the same height as his younger brother, his eyes were pale blue, his hair was fair, his frame was thinner and more round-shouldered; and because of untreated adenoids, his mouth hung permanently open.

Currying favor, anxious to be one of the gang, Brendan now nudged the boy next to him and snickered and the boy snickered back.

The sequence that had led to Conor's humiliation had begun the previous evening. He had been having his tea when the brother on duty had handed him a letter from home, as usual already open and preread. The news from his mother appalled him. His baby sister, Molly, had pneumonia: a cold, caught in the wet depths of February, had persisted and now she was critically ill, with a high fever. He had looked across the refectory and seen that Brendan, too, had received a letter, but Brendan had just read his as though there were nothing untoward in it.

Perhaps there had not. Although Conor's family was small by island standards, it was neatly divided. Conor was close to his mother and to his baby sister, while Brendan had, since an early age, aligned himself with their father, Micheál. The brothers, thrown together for companionship while they were younger, had, with some relief, fallen into separate social circles as soon as Brendan went away to school. Now, except when actually in the cottage together on Inisheer, they had little to do with one another.

After he had read his mother's letter, Conor had folded it carefully and had put it in his pocket, his hands shaking. Saying he was not hungry, he had passed the bread off his own plate to that of his neighbor, a bespectacled, fat child named Seán Lyons, who was adept at wriggling out of trouble by bringing on one of his asthma attacks. Places at table and in the dormitory were allocated by the brothers on the first day of school, and Seán and Conor had struck up a sort of friendship, in which proximity took a larger role than liking.

At Recreation that evening, while some of his class squabbled over the use of the pitted table-tennis table in the recreation hall and while others listened to céilidhe music on the radio, Conor stole away to the chapel, which was the only place in the school where, during Recreation, a boy was permitted to go without permission.

He settled into a pew at the very back and stared at the altar where, in the faint red glow cast by the sanctuary lamp, the studs gleamed in the fat Easter candle.

The only other person in the chapel was one of the oldest brothers in the community. Long retired from teaching and therefore harmless, this brother spent his days either sitting here at his *prie-Dieu*, answering the back door to tradesmen and tinkers, or feeding the fowl in the small hen-run beside the stream at the boundary of the school property. Apart from the sanctuary lamp, the only other illumination in the chapel came from the single, shaded wall lamp above the brother's *prie-Dieu*. Despite his inner turmoil, Conor forced himself to sink into the peace of the place, and as the stir made by his own arrival subsided, he became gradually aware of small sounds he never noticed when the chapel was full: the rustling of a mouse in the choir loft above his head, the settling of wood, the crack of the iron radiator beside him as someone elsewhere in the house brushed against it.

He fixed his eyes on a golden sliver of the Tabernacle that shone through a gap in the satin curtain that covered it, and tried to pray. But he could not concentrate. He took the letter out of his pocket and read it again, seeing his mother in the kitchen as she wrote it, the oil lamp turned up to its fullest. The letter rustled as he crushed it between his fingers and the brother looked around from his *prie-Dieu*, his eyes trying to focus over the tops of his glasses. Conor lowered his head in an attitude of prayerful meditation, stuffing his fingers into the inner corners of his eyes to stem the wetness.

When he had composed himself, he got up, genu-flected in the aisle, and left the chapel. He got back to the recreation hall just before the bell and filed with the others into the study hall. But while all around him nibs scratched and pages turned, he could not concentrate on his geometry theorems. The lines kept blurring.

Later, in bed, he could not sleep.

Molly would not die. She could not die. God would not allow it. Fiercely, daring God, he tossed himself over on to his stomach and the bedsprings groaned loudly.

"Who's that?" called out Brother Patrick from his cu-bicle in the corner.

Conor's heart sank. "It's me, Brother."

"Who's me—the cat?"

Conor could hear some of the other boys in the dor-mitory stifling giggles at the sarcasm. He forced himself to sound calm. "It's Conor O Briain, Brother."

"What are you at, O Briain?"

"Nothing, Brother."

"I'll give you nothing! Are you out of your bed?"

"No, Brother . . ."

"Well, stop disturbing others and go to sleep, or you'll taste something you won't forget in a hurry!"

Conor lay rigid for a long time, but eventually he drifted into sleep.

In the morning, when Brother Patrick rang the bell at ten past seven, he sprang out of bed—there were fines and penalties for being late for Mass—but the cold air hit him around the legs more keenly than usual. On examination, he discovered, to his horror, that his pajamas were wet and so was his bottom sheet. He had wet his bed.

It could not have happened on a worse day, because on Saturday mornings there was dormitory inspection after breakfast. On any normal day, the boys had to strip and remake their beds before going down to Mass, but on Saturdays, they left them stripped, for airing. Conor ripped off the stained sheet and placed his bedspread on top of it over his chair. He was afraid he would burst into tears like a crybaby.

At Mass, while the others around him shuffled and coughed, fiddled with their missals, or, their heads resting comfortably in their hands, caught forty winks while pretending to be meditating, Conor prayed despairing, desperate adolescent prayers. He assaulted Heaven. He bored with his eyes through the chasubled back of the priest, through the ornate door of the Tabernacle and right inside it as though he would force its Occupant to accede. He divided his prayers between his two intentions, each more urgent than the other.

O Jesus, please, please, please, don't let them find out. Please, Jesus, I promise you that I'll be a priest. I'll help Brendan with his schoolwork. I'll never talk back to my father again . . . And please, Jesus, help Mam and Molly. Please make Molly well again. Please, Jesus, don't let her die . . .

But please, Jesus, O Sacred Heart, Immaculate mother, St. Ciaran, please please, don't let them find out. . . .

After Holy Communion, he battered Jesus with wild promises. He had no money to light candles or to make offerings, but he promised that for the rest of the term he would Keep Silence until lunchtime every day. That was allowed, except in class, if you explained that it was for a special intention. And he promised that during the school holidays, he would make a visit to the Blessed Sacrament in the island church twice a day . . .

During breakfast, despite the sick, tight feeling in his stomach, he spooned up every last trace of the porridge on his plate, not wanting to draw on himself a scintilla of attention. He prayed all through breakfast, all the way up to the dormitory afterward.

But they were all in vain, all the prayers and the promises. Because Brother Patrick noticed the yellow stains, still damp, on the sheet. "What's this?" Exaggeratedly fastidious, he picked it up with the tips of spatulate, tobacco-stained fingers. "What's this, O Briain?" He held the sheet up to the weak light from the window of the dormitory. The other boys suspended operations around their own beds and watched, half fascinated, half horror-struck.

Conor, mortified, could not speak.

"Take it!" The brother flung the sheet at Conor, then caught his ear and paraded him, bent double, to the bathroom, where he stood over him while Conor held the stained part under a running faucet. After a minute or so, without waiting for the boy to wring out the sopping fabric, Brother Patrick took the ear again—so hard that Conor yelped—and led him back down the dormitory toward the window. An irregular river trailed behind them on the varnished floorboards.

The brother paused when they reached the window. "This boy is a bed-wetter," he announced. "We'll have to make a man out of this baby, won't we, boys?" Then, when there was no answer: "Won't we, boys?" roared so loudly over his shoulder that the round-eyed juniors were shocked into answering. "Yes, Brother," they said, but some were so frightened that no sounds came from their mouths and the chorus was ragged and feeble.

The brother regarded them contemptuously, then turned back to Conor. He pushed up the sashed window, indicating that the sheet should be hung out to dry on the windowsill.

Conor obeyed, pushing the bundle of cold, wet fabric out through the opening. Too fast. He failed to hold onto a corner of it as he let it out and the wind caught it, filling it like a sail. It went ballooning across the grass in front of the school, flapping and turning until it sank to rest about a hundred yards into a field, snagged against a thorn bush.

The brother's thick neck reddened with rage. ''Now look what you've done, you stupid, asinine cretin! Stupid, stupid cretin!''

He knuckled Conor hard, bringing the knuckles down on the back of the boy's head. Instinctively Conor ducked, raising his arms to protect himself. This enraged the brother even more, and not pausing to unbuckle his leather strap from where it hung on his belt, with one hand he caught hold of Conor's thick hair and with the other swung at him indiscriminately with the short length of the strap that hung free. Because it was still attached to his belt, he could get no purchase and the strap did little damage, but the energy and sound of the assault was terrifying.

One of the other boys began to snivel. Brother Patrick swung around on him. ''And what's wrong with *you*, me bucko? You shut up or you'll get some of the same!'' He turned back to the cowering Conor, a handful of whose hair he still grasped, and swiped at him again. Then he let go and straightened up, panting. ''Now you, go and get that sheet and bring it down to the line in the orchard. You'll pay for this at dinner.''

Conor did not obey at once but stood, holding his head where the brother's hand had been entangled in his hair. His left ear, the target of many blows from the strap, glowed crimson.

As he hesitated, the brother's rage erupted again. *''Did you hear me, you idiotic, oversized sheep! Get out of my sight!''*

Conor fled, his heavy shoes skidding on the wet floor.

Later, at the beginning of dinner and as the boys stood for Grace Before Meals, Conor did not take his place but walked in front of Brother Patrick to the platform. He did not look right or left and knelt without being told to do so.

He had now been kneeling for about twenty minutes and his knees were beginning to hurt. But he saw that his ordeal was nearly over. The boys were lining up, in order of class seniority, at the big serving table near the door, where, from stainless steel vats, two prefects were doling out dollops of stewed apple and watery custard.

After the meal, the boys filed out of the refectory in a decorous double line, but as they were released through the door, the lines broke up and they thundered along the stone-floored corridor toward the cloakroom, where their outdoor boots were stored in rows of numbered cubbyholes. Saturday was a half-day, with only the morning spent in classes. After dinner, they were all required to play games: Gaelic football or hurling, basketball or handball.

Conor heard the thunder of the boys' departure subside and assumed his punishment was over. But he did not dare to move until formally released.

He saw Brother Patrick walking toward him up the room. The platform was only two feet high and their eyes were level. This time, Conor did not flinch. He stared, not into the hard eyes, but at the brother's mouth, noticing that in both corners, adhering to tiny red cracks, there were encrustations of yellow flakelets. Brother Patrick smoked Sweet Afton.

He saw that the brother, for once, appeared nonplussed and had the obscure feeling that for once he had the upper hand. "Get down off there," the brother said gruffly, after a few seconds. "Go into the kitchen and get your dinner." He turned and swept toward the door, snapping off all the light switches on a wall panel before disappearing from Conor's view.

Conor waited until he could no longer hear the swish of his soutane. Then he stood and rubbed his aching knees. Stiffly, he walked down the echoing room and into the adjoining kitchen. Two local girls labored over the dinner dishes in sinks full of greasy water. On a draining board beside one of the sinks was a plate of congealed potatoes, cabbage, and scraps of grayish mutton.

He took the unappetizing plate and brought it out into the empty refectory, sitting in his allocated place at one of the tables. But although he had thought himself to be hungry, he found he could not stomach more than a few mouthfuls.

It was during the DC3's fourth stop, at Reykjavik, when the trip was more than halfway through, that Tucker Thompson became worried. He could not say why. The aircraft had behaved impeccably throughout the journey so far, and although the wind had come up slightly during the hours of darkness, the sky was still clear. Yet some sixth sense warned him to be careful. All good fliers trusted their hunches and Tucker was well aware that the difference between being successful as a captain and being unsuccessful depended not only on skill, but on separating hunches from emotions.

In the spartan waiting room, Cal dozed in a chair and Maggie walked up and down, soothing the baby made fretful by rude awakening, but outside on the tarmac, Tucker stood back a little from the plane looking critically at the mass of its silvery outline, etched against the stars. Was there something he was missing? Like a horse, he raised his head and sniffed the cold breeze. He got a flashlight and prowled around the fuselage, checking rivets on the wings, examining the undercarriage and the radio aerials. He ran the flashlight carefully along each of the propeller blades, moving them slightly, watching for minute fractures or cracks, but they seemed sound. He took a ladder, mounted it, swung the rudder back and forth and peered closely at the ailerons and flaps. He went inside the cabin and checked the fuel tanks behind the false bulkhead. No leaks. No untoward smells.

In the ops room, the weather forecast for their route showed little development from what they had been given at their last stop in Greenland, yet he was still uneasy. He rechecked the telexes. Everything looked fine. So what was bothering him?

He concentrated on the large area map. The Anti-Cyclone was still stationary, about a thousand miles southwest of Ireland. Tucker traced his finger along the length of the Cold Front, which had moved but not significantly, since he saw it first at Midway. Its present position now stretched, northwest to southeast, from just south of the 35-miles-long volcanic island of Jan Mayen in the Arctic Ocean, southwestward into the center of Norway.

"Are you absolutely sure about the speed of this thing?" he asked the duty meteorological officer, "any chance of a push from polar air?"

Not often, but frequently enough to give cause for worry, a sudden influx of freezing gales from inside the Arctic Circle collided with the rear of a Cold Front, causing it to accelerate rapidly and—because of the relatively warm and humid air the Front was pushing ahead of it—churning it up internally.

The meteorologist shook his head. "Not so far as we know," he said, "although, as you know, we can't be a hundred per cent certain." Tucker saw the man suppress a sigh and knew what he was thinking. All meteorologists hated being pushed. And in a way it was unfair, since there was always a paucity of hard information from the polar regions.

He weighed up the possibilities. Many of the problems faced by pilots over the Atlantic, where they were out of contact with Air Traffic Control, involved icing of the engine or airframe. Because of this ever-present danger, the leading edges of the wing and tail sections of the DC3—the most vulnerable parts of the airframe—were covered with rubber boots. If the pilot suspected icing, he could, by means of a timer-controlled pump, force a large volume of air into these boots through a valve and when they swelled, the accretions of ice broke off harmlessly. Tucker had paid particular attention to these boots during his visual inspection, but they were sound and unpunctured.

He also knew that his carburetor de-icing equipment was working perfectly and decided he was being over-fussy. He thanked the duty officer and headed back to his plane, from which the refueling nozzle was just being removed. He went on to the flight deck to go through his preflight-check procedures for the fifth time that day.

While everyone else slept, Conor O Briain lay awake, fully clothed under his pajamas. He was planning to run away.

He had no money at all and the school was a long way from Galway and the ferry to Inisheer. But there was late rising—eight o'clock—on a Sunday. He knew that if he managed to slip out in the very early morning, just before dawn, he could probably make it to the main Galway road and maybe get a lift toward the city from someone going on the road to a creamery or to early Mass. He would be well on his way before anyone missed him. Then, when he got to the ferry dock, he was sure to meet

one or more of his Inisheer neighbors, who would lend
him the fare.

He had planned his escape the previous afternoon,
while he was kneeling on the platform during his punishment and had later made rudimentary preparations. Un-
seen during the activity on the playing pitch later in the
afternoon, he had hidden his outdoor boots under a bush
by the main gates. And during supper, on the pretext of
going to the lavatory, he had managed to smuggle six
thick slices of bread out of the refectory, hiding them
under his jumper. His heart in his mouth, he had raced
up to the dormitory, to which access was forbidden during the day, and had hidden the bread behind the sponge
bag in his bedside locker, getting back to the refectory
just as the bell was rung for Grace After Meals. The
bread, wrapped in his spare shirt, now lay at his feet,
just under the edge of the mattress. He had to keep his
knees bent so it would not be too squashed.

He listened hard for untoward noises in the dormitory
but all seemed to be well. His neighbor, the asthmatic
Seán Lyons, snorted and wheezed satisfactorily in the
bed beside him. After some consideration, Conor had
taken Seán into the plot. Round-eyed with the importance of the task entrusted to him and the daring of it all,
Seán had agreed to have one of his asthma attacks after
Mass, just before breakfast. The plan was that the brother
on duty would be distracted into looking after him and
bringing him to the infirmary, and in the confusion, Con-
or's absence from the refectory during breakfast might
not be noticed. Even if it was, the prefects would probably assume that he had accompanied Seán to the infirmary.

The night seemed endless. Conor craned his neck to
see the big clock above the window at the end of the
dormitory. He had tried to keep count of the time and
reckoned it must now be close to three o'clock. He could
see the glass on the clockface, reflecting blue from the
votive lamp in front of the statue of Our Lady below it
on the windowsill, but to his frustration he could not see
the hands. He was afraid he might nod off and miss the
crucial departure time. There was no point in making his
bid too early, however. He had to be patient.

Moving as slowly and as quietly as he could, he retrieved one of his slippers from under the bed and eased it under the small of his back. It had lumpy blanket stitching along the seams, so even if he did doze, the discomfort should wake him up again.

On the flight deck of the DC3, the pilot and first officer drank black coffee. The night was moonless, and as they flew on, that special, womblike peace of night flying enveloped the dimly lit cockpit. They seemed to float in the blue-blackness, suspended between the quilt of stars and the luminous floor of cloud which stretched beneath them like an undulating carpet of softest white wool. Reacting, they lowered their voices.

Both kept an eye on the instruments that flickered in front of them, needles quivering slightly, the half-circle of the artificial horizon quite stable. When they were about three and a half hours out of Reykjavik, Tucker handed control of the aircraft to the younger man so he could snatch forty winks. The aircraft was rock steady, and with the friendly tailwinds, they were ahead of schedule. Before he closed his eyes, he glanced at the log. If this kept up, they would be landing at Shannon in less than two hours.

In the passenger cabin, the nanny was sound asleep and Cal and Maggie continued to converse quietly over the head of the sleeping baby, whose bassinet Maggie had placed on the floor in front of them. They had each slept a little, but they were now wakeful. Lulled by the steady, unvarying drone of the engines outside the windows, they were in a rare state of peace with one another.

They had been talking of the trip to come and of the places they would see. But deliberately, it seemed to Maggie, they had skirted the past pain, the disillusionments, the aridity of their relationship over the past few years. Then Cal, leaning over to grab her hand, suddenly brought the problems out into the open. "Maggie," he said, "you know I've changed. I promise you it'll be different from now on."

"Look," said Maggie, "can't we just leave it?" She was feeling no rancor or urgency and was unwilling to disturb the soothing, somnolent feeling in which the cabin of the aircraft was bathed. "We're here, aren't we? I'm here—I came with you. Let's see what develops, okay?"

She gave his hand a squeeze and extricated her own, but he took it again: "All I can ask of you is to trust me just one last time," he said passionately. "Give us this chance, please, for all our sakes. I promise you won't regret it. . . ."

"I wouldn't have come at all if I didn't think it was worth one more try."

Almost to her surprise, Maggie found that she meant it. She really was going to put the past away and make a real effort. What was it all about, after all? So her husband took a few drinks? So he was not the most faithful person in the world? So what? She was not the first wife nor would she be the last to have suffered from a husband's weaknesses. The affairs, such as they were, never lasted long, and she knew in her heart of hearts that they were as unimportant as last year's snow. And to give Cal his due, in the last few months he really had made an effort to cut down on excessive drinking. She looked across at his beautiful face. In the soft, warm light from the overhead lamp, his skin was childlike and unlined. Immature or not, she thought, she had taken this man for better or for worse. . . .

As though he sensed her softening, he adopted his most winning expression. "I promise you won't regret it," he repeated.

"I won't, I'm sure." She smiled at him and lay back in her seat. Yet, despite her resolve and the soft words, it was an effort to allow him to keep her hand. His felt inanimate, dry as rice paper, and she found herself wondering how soon she could decently drop it.

She found herself wondering also about the ephemerality of physical attraction. There was a time when she and Cal could not keep their hands off one another. Now his touch left her, quite literally, cold. She and Cal had not made love, or even slept in the same bed, for nearly fifteen months now.

On the other hand, seen objectively, Cal Smith was still a very attractive man. How many times had she seen the way women of all ages lit up like comets when he entered a room?

So why did he not excite her anymore? Was it her fault too? And would she be able to reexcite herself to the

extent of making love with him in London, Paris, or
Rome?

As if to save her mother from further thoughts of this
nature, Susanna stirred in her sleep and then whimpered.
She was clearly about to wake. Maggie looked behind
her, and seeing that the nanny was still fast asleep, decided not to wake the young woman. In any event, feeding the baby would be a legitimate counter-activity in the
face of Cal's attentions. She picked up the baby and
rooted around in the carryall to find a bottle of formula.
Susanna, her face rosy, snuffled and nuzzled into her
mother's shoulder.

Maggie cradled her, then offered her the milk. Susanna
fastened on to the bottle with both hands and clamped
her mouth around the teat, sucking contentedly. After a
while, one of her hands moved to Maggie's face and she
kept it there while she fed, her fingers lightly stroking
Maggie's cheek.

The aircraft bumped slightly.

In the cockpit, Tucker jolted awake, instantly alert.
The motion of the plane had not altered appreciably, but
he had felt, rather than heard, his copilot's gasp. He
looked out the window ahead of him and saw what had
caused the copilot's reaction. Towering ahead, at about
four kilometers and stretching from left to right as far as
the eye could see, an ominous wall of cloud soared upward like an unbroken wall of skyscrapers, blocking out
all the stars.

"Damn!" said Tucker. The copilot's gasp was apt: any
child could see that this one was a biggie. Some of these
cumulo-nimbus systems extended for hundreds of miles,
with a depth of up to fifty. And Tucker knew that inside
that baby, rapidly coming closer, were huge storm systems of freezing rain, hail, ice, and God knew what else.

He had no doubts about his own or his plane's ability
to handle the storms, but he had the passengers to think
about. Telling the second officer to plot a triangular
course, one which would take them first on a south-
southwesterly backtrack, followed by one heading due
east and then, when the danger was over, one which
would take them north-northeast and back on course, he
took over the controls and, bringing the plane's nose

down slightly, hauled the aircraft around. Their ETA would be delayed, but that could not be helped. He had plenty of fuel. He checked the gauges. One of the tanks was showing almost empty. He switched to a full one, snapped on the PA, and asked his passengers to fasten their seat belts.

In the cabin, the sound of the PA shattered the calm. Susanna dropped her bottle and began to cry, and the stewardess came down the aisle, sat, and took her while the others struggled to get their seats upright and their seat belts fastened. The baby made a strange sound and stretched her arms out to her mother, but before Maggie could take her back, they were caught in the storm and were bucketing around, making the transfer impossible.

Up front, Tucker's mind had clicked into overdrive. "Tighten your harness," he barked at his junior officer, "and lower your seat as far as it will go."

"Why?"

"You'll see . . ."

The copilot obeyed until his seat rested almost on the floor.

Tucker turned his cockpit lights up to full power to counter the flash-blindness that occurs after lightning. Then, eyes moving swiftly over his controls, he made sure his de-icing systems were on and synchronized the direction indicator with the magnetic compass. The turn-and-run maneuver had failed. The front was on them. No choice. Too late. Nothing to do now but ride this one . . .

Almost as a reflex, he turned on his landing lights and immediately wished he hadn't. Twin spears, they bounced against a monstrous acropolis of *son et lumière*, twisting yellow pillars of vapor, illuminated from within by flashing displays of dirty lightning. He turned off his lights again and braced himself for the noise.

Experienced though he was, Tucker still hated the noise of thunder at such close quarters; abrupt and shocking, it always felt as if it were exploding right inside his head with no warning buildup or cushioning echo.

After one mighty crash, he glanced across at the copilot, whose face was ashen but whose eyes, sensibly, were fixed on the wildly dancing needles on the instruments in front of him. It was one of the first tricks Tucker had learned. As long as eyes were below the eye level of the windscreen and fixed on the instruments and not on what was happening outside, a pilot could exist in some semblance of normality.

Tucker's hands felt as though they were welded to the stick; he was a strong man and pushed at it with all his might to keep the plane's nose down; yet the altimeter showed that the plane was rising like a cork on a geyser. "Hold tight!" he shouted to the copilot, a split second before the Dak, having reached the apex of the upward current, began to plunge downward as if over the face of a waterfall.

Out of the corner of his eye, he saw that the copilot was using all his strength on his own controls, mimicking Tucker's own actions, having recognized correctly that the captain's aim was to keep the line on the artificial horizon as straight as possible and to allow the storm itself to dictate the altitude. But at one point, as the plane again began its stomach-churning descent, he panicked and jammed his feet hard on to the rudder. The aircraft began to slew like a crazed bronco and Tucker had to fight harder than ever for control. "Get your feet off that!" he yelled. "Do you want to break us up!"

"Sorry!" the copilot yelled back.

"Go with it!" shouted Tucker. "Corrections as small and as smooth as you can!" Although Tucker did not now have time to go into the niceties, he made a mental note that as soon as this was over, he would ram into this kid's head the fact that more aircraft disintegrated inside a system like this through pilot panic and overcorrection—which put intolerable stress on the airframe—than from any other cause. But the kid was not doing too badly. "You okay?" he called.

The kid nodded, white-faced but calm.

The sweat was now pouring down Tucker's face, getting into his eyes, but he dared not take his hands off the controls long enough to brush it away. Instead, he blinked constantly and once or twice dashed at it by bringing shoulder and eye together.

How long more?

"Get on the radio," he shouted. "Try to see if there's anything out there!"

The copilot nodded, and holding his right forearm steady with his left hand, he operated the high-frequency radio which had a range of a thousand miles, trying to contact any other aircraft or ships in the area. The attempt was futile. All he heard in his headset was a deafening torrent of static and crackling. He persisted for about five minutes. "Nothing, Captain," he shouted over the din.

Tucker nodded. It had been a long shot anyway. They were on their own.

There was chaos in the passenger cabin as Susanna continued to scream. Maggie tried to leave her seat to take her from the stewardess, but as she unbuckled her belt, the aircraft gave a terrific jolt and she was bowled right across the plane to the far wall, slamming into it and hurting her shoulder.

Seeing her mother being shot across the floor, the baby doubled the volume of her screams.

With great difficulty, Maggie crawled back to her seat, holding her hurt arm at an awkward angle. She hoped she had not done it any great damage. For the first time since the storm had hit she was frightened, but she had always had the ability to postpone the full extent of her panic until a crisis was over. She stayed calm now as, one-armed, she buckled herself into her seat.

There was no point in her giving way to her fear. It was only by keeping herself in control that she could be of help to the others. As her arm began to throb, she hoped she still could.

In the radar room of Shannon airport, slumped in front of his flickering screen, the operator on the evening shift rubbed his eyes and then, for the umpteenth time that night, looked at his watch. It was coming up to midnight and knocking-off time, thank God. It had been an exceptionally boring shift and he had just logged the latest arrival on his screen—it was, he reckoned, about 180 miles out. He consulted the file of active flight plans. Like all flights he had logged that evening, she was early.

He updated his logs, ready to hand them over to the man who was to succeed him, but when he looked again, the blip, which should have moved farther in, had in fact fallen outward toward the perimeter of his screen; instead of progressing southeasterly, it now seemed to be taking a southwesterly course. If they continued that way, he thought, he'd lose them off his screen altogether, as his range was only two hundred miles. He picked up the flight plan again. They were definitely off course—or had changed course. Poor buggers, he thought. Probably caught in the storm which had passed overhead about forty minutes earlier . . .

He logged the changed direction and, sure enough, when he raised his eyes again to the screen, the blip had disappeared. He logged that too, then, yawning, he glanced at the door, impatient to be off home. This night man, he thought irritably, would be late for his own funeral.

The blip had not reappeared by the time the night man, a weedy individual with a cadaverous face, pushed open the door, panting. He was briefed by his younger colleague as he was still removing his woolen coat and the bicycle clips from around his ankles. When the door slammed behind the other man, the night man placed the clips on the top of a wooden cupboard beside his paper-wrapped sandwiches and lemonade bottle filled with milk. Keeping an eye on the screen, he moved the one-bar electric fire as close to the desk as its wire would allow, aiming its puny heat at his shins. Then he sat down, the logs in front of him. Still no sign of that Dak.

Susanna continued to cry, despite the stewardess's best efforts and iron grip. Her screams reached a new crescendo as her head was snapped sideways, cracking against the rim of the window beside the seat. The stewardess examined her as best she could and ascertained that the baby was not really injured.

She looked at her watch. The rest of the passengers seemed to be coping well enough, she thought—or had been, up to the moment when the nanny, who had had her eyes closed, risked a look out of her porthole. To her horror, she had seen a jagged blue halo of flame dancing around the port engine like an ethereal pinwheel. Then she too had opened her mouth and had begun to scream, terrifying the baby even more. In vain, the stewardess tried to make her voice heard, yelling at the nanny that the phenomenon was harmless. "It's only St. Elmo's fire," she shouted again and again, but to no avail.

The turbulence was so severe that the stewardess was powerless to do anything except stay locked in her seat. She concentrated her efforts on the baby. How long could they all put up with this before someone snapped and did something really silly?

There was worse to come. As they shot upward on one of their dizzy ascents, they seemed to cannon through a solid wall which disintegrated around them in a fusillade of what sounded like machine-gun fire. The wall they had hit was made of hail.

Cal began to retch, the vomit skewing around him. Maggie, ignoring the pain in her arm, gripped the armrests of her seat and continued to tell herself that at present, as there was nothing she could do for anyone else, her duty was to concentrate on *not* being sick, *not* to add to the general chaos. She closed her eyes tightly and held on to the determination to remain fit. It would be up to her to help the others. When they got out of this.

But conditions were so bad up front that Tucker had failed to notice that the aircraft was not responding to his handling as it should. He became alert to this only when he realized that for the second time in five minutes, he had had to open the throttle to maintain engine revs. The plane was using far too much fuel. His brain flicked along a checklist:

Rudder? Seemed okay . . .

Carburetor? No, the engine revs were steady and there was no roughness, as far as he could tell in this turbulence.

Icing? His de-icing systems were on. He risked opening a side window for an instant to look back at the wing. Water and hail poured into the cockpit, blinding and drenching him, but he held his nerve for a few seconds and managed to see that the shape of the nacelle was regular and the wing was clean, or so it seemed; no telltale bulge on the leading edge. He crossed opaque rime ice off his problem list. This would have shown as a fast-growing and ungainly bulge which wreaks havoc with aerodynamics.

One of the few remaining possibilities was rain ice. On such a short visual inspection in these conditions, there was no way of knowing for sure, as this invisible insidious substance flows and freezes and flows again, glacierlike, along vulnerable surfaces, rendering impotent the deicing boots that inflate and deflate uselessly inside it. In fact, the equipment actually worsens the problem as it pushes the ice farther along the wing, allowing it to add exponentially to the weight of the aircraft.

Tucker looked at his controls again. No help there, but watching his airspeed indicator dropping alarmingly near stalling speed and having to open his throttle further, his hunch was that the problem was, indeed, rain ice.

Somehow, they had to get below the altitude where the rain ice was forming. Tucker gripped the stick with all his strength and gritted his teeth . . .

There was a tremendous crash from the galley, followed by a second one, which temporarily eclipsed the rattling and banging that was going on inside the fitted bar. The doors of the washroom and the closet were swinging open and shut in counterpoint. Even the walls of the cabin were creaking and straining. Maggie continued to grip the armrests of her seat, wishing that she was near enough to the nanny to slap her as the young woman continued to scream on a long, sustained note, broken only when she paused to draw breath. Maggie exchanged a glance with the stewardess, who managed to smile professionally, although Maggie could see that like herself, there was little she could do, strapped in as she was and restraining the struggling, hysterical baby. Maggie reached over to touch Cal, who sat, almost catatonic, streaked in his own vomit. He was rigid with fright, his face gray and his hair plastered to his head with perspiration. He did not respond to her touch, and then she was jolted sideways again away from him and had to look to her own equilibrium.

Tucker, aided by the copilot, had managed to get down to a median level of about four thousand feet. Not long now, he thought, feeling gratefully by the way it was handling that the plane was lightening. Either the deicing system was now working again, or the ice was coming off under the flood of rain which obscured his windscreen and which was so heavy it leaked a little through the seals of the side windows. His fingers felt as though they would never again unclasp from the stick as he fought to control the aircraft, which still bounced around like a paper cup tossed into a torrent of white water.

Then, just as suddenly as it had begun, it was over, and after a few minor bumps, they were into relatively clear air. Tucker looked across at his copilot. The younger man was pale, but had borne up well.

"You okay, kid?" asked the captain.

"Yeah, I'm fine. Hope they're all right down the back. That one was really a doozy."

"You take over, will you? I'm going down to see how things are." But he had to peel his fingers off the stick one by one with his free hand before he could stand up, and he had difficulty unstrapping his harness.

"Want me to get our bearings?" asked the copilot, who did not have the presumption to ask if his captain needed any help.

"Yeah," said Tucker, who, to his shame, felt that his knees were weak.

The night man at Shannon was not yet seriously worried. According to the flightplan she had filed, the DC3 was only now due within range. He accepted that his predecessor's theory was probably correct—that the pilot had changed course to avoid the storm. In that case, the DC3 should be due on his screen within five minutes. Although it was still early on his shift he weakened, as he did every night, and extracted a tomato sandwich from the greasy brown paper bag he had brought in with him. He promised himself he would eat only one. As he munched the limp sandwich, soggy with juice, he tracked the overflight of two U.S. military aircraft and watched for the DC3. Then he reached for a second sandwich.

As best he could, Tucker had calmed down his passengers. The English girl was in a really bad state. She had stopped screaming but had wrapped herself completely in her blanket and tears coursed down her white face as she shivered uncontrollably in her seat. He could get no sense from the man and left him to the ministrations of the stewardess.

But he saw that the mother had come through well

enough. At present she was engaged in soothing the hiccuping baby. Aiming his words at her, he reassured them all that there should be no further problems, although they would now be late arriving at Shannon since they were flying, not with friendly tailwinds, but against quite a heavy headwind which had followed the storms. Giving what he hoped was a generally reassuring smile, he turned on his heel and went back to the cockpit.

As soon as he had left, Cal, white-faced, asked the stewardess, who was cleaning him up with soda water and tissue, if he could have some brandy.

Maggie, dandling the baby, who was settling down, also accepted a drink. She took a deep draft and then hummed gently into Susanna's ear. Quite soon the baby pillowed her head on her mother's shoulder and dropped off again to sleep.

The DC3 plowed on as though nothing had happened.

But something had.

In the cockpit, Tucker's disbelieving eyes checked and double-checked his fuel gauges. He had been so busy fighting the storm that he had not realized the extent of the icing, and the aircraft, carrying perhaps more than an extra ton and a half of weight, had gobbled the fuel.

"Have you figured out where we are yet?" He spoke gruffly.

"Just about," answered the copilot, who, now that the sky was clear again, had been able to use the directional gyro, aimed at Sirius.

The news was not good. They were eighty miles south and seventy west off their planned course.

Tucker checked his fuel gauges again and made calculations. With the throttles full open, the Dak could make speed of only 130 knots in this headwind. Even by the most optimistic forecasts, they did not have enough fuel to make Shannon.

He thought swiftly. There was no cargo, nothing on board he could dump to lighten the load—except, he remembered, the passengers' luggage. Twelve hundred pounds. It would have to go. He told the copilot to bring the plane slowly down to two thousand feet and went back into the passenger cabin.

The appearance of the cabin was returning to normal

as the stewardess tidied up, rehanging the coats in the closets. But two of the glasses had smashed and hundreds of crystal fragments crunched under the soles of Tucker's ankle boots as he entered the compartment. He sat in one of the seats opposite the couple and, on instinct, decided to address Maggie again. Keeping his eyes on her, he explained the situation as calmly and encouragingly as he could.

The husband began to bluster. "I refuse to allow this! There are thousands and thousands of dollars' worth of clothes and equipment in that luggage . . ." Tucker ignored him, keeping his eyes fixed on the woman. She held his eyes with her own, quite steady.

"How bad is it?" she asked finally.

Tucker thought fast. There really was not much point in fudging. "Put it this way, Mrs. Smith," he said. "If we lighten the load sufficiently, we have a fighting chance. If we don't, we will run out of fuel. It's as simple as that."

The gray eyes flickered, but she made no other movement.

"We are still making calculations," he went on, "and you can be sure we're not alone in this part of the Atlantic. There are ships around and we are already mobilizing Shackletons from the RAF as escorts. We'll be okay. . . ."

Cal butted in again. "This is preposterous!" he began.

Tucker cut him off. "I don't want to frighten you," he said, still addressing Maggie, "but every second we carry that extra weight is a second extra of fuel burned. Your luggage is replaceable, I'm sure . . . and there's insurance." He put an emphasis on the word "luggage" and let the implication sink in. To her credit, he thought, the woman still did not blink.

"Can I get a few things out of one of the trunks?" she asked finally. The only hint of distress was a small quiver in her voice.

"I'm afraid there isn't time," said Tucker. And with that, he stood up and made his way back to the cockpit. He took over the controls and sent the copilot to do the job.

He knew from his controls what was happening. With

each dislodgement of luggage, the plane jumped slightly. And with each jump, the airspeed indicator crept up a few knots. He decided to stay low, at two thousand feet, because the winds at this level would not be so strong—and their chances for a visual sighting of a ship or large fishing trawler were better. When the copilot came back, Tucker ordered him to plot the most direct route to Shannon and to search on his HF for contacts.

But no matter how the sums were done, they came out the same. Ireland was still just under two hours' flying time away. At best estimates, they had fuel for one hour and forty-five minutes. He began to call on his radio.

As Tucker well knew, a pilot's priority during an emergency was to deal with it as expeditiously as possible. It was only when he had done all he could to safeguard his aircraft and load that he would call for assistance. The acronym in that case was PACER—he radioed Position, Altitude, Conditions, Estimate of next contact, and a Request for whatever it was he required.

Over and over again, Tucker's junior colleague called these out, but there was no response.

At last! Fifteen minutes later, the night man at Shannon caught the blip on the side of his screen. He had become concerned at the nonappearance of the DC3, but there it was, about 190 miles out.

He checked the log. The time they had left Reykjavik indicated that they should have been landing at Shannon within the next half hour, but at their present rate they could not make it for at least seventy minutes. He took a gulp of his dark brown tea and wondered if he should make a few inquiries.

Better be safe than sorry, that was his motto. He lifted the telephone and contacted Shannon's air-sea rescue center, asking for the duty officer. "Hello, Séamus," he said, when the officer came on. "Listen, it may be nothing to worry about, but have you had any calls about a DC3? She's behind time, the storm, I think, and I was wondering if anyone had picked up anything. . . ."

He listened for a minute and nodded. "Well, I'm just wondering about her endurance. Seven people on board." He nodded again. "Okay. Well, I'll keep you posted."

He replaced the receiver and, taking a wedge of fruitcake out of his paper bag, chewed it thoughtfully as he watched the screen in front of him.

The copilot was still calling on the radio, moving his frequencies. Miraculously, there was an answer at last, from Shannon air-sea rescue. Quickly he gave his location, altitude, course, and estimated flying time left on the fuel. Forty-five minutes—at most fifty.

"Roger," said the faint voice in his earpiece. "We have you on radar at Shannon. Don't worry. Keep in contact. We'll get in touch with the RAF to intercept and escort."

Tucker set his propellers at low revs—said by engineers to conserve fuel, although he had his doubts about it—and had his copilot plot a slightly new course which would take them more broadside than head on into the wind. By searching for a friendlier airstream, he was going to try to outmaneuver the headwind.

The copilot called in the new course to Shannon.

"Roger," said the voice on the other end. "Got that. We're sending the troops. Keep in touch. . . ."

Tucker looked at his hands for a long minute, then made up his mind. "Take over," he said to his colleague. "Time to tell the truth." Then he opened the door into the passenger cabin and beckoned to the stewardess to join him.

Maggie watched the stewardess and the captain coming toward her. The hefty measure of brandy had calmed her nerves—and the warm weight of the baby lying cradled in her arms was additionally soothing. But the set expression on Captain Thompson's face shot alarm into the back of her throat. "What is it?" she said quietly, before he could say anything.

Cal, who had been dozing, sat up.

"We've a major problem, ma'am," said Tucker.

"What! What now?" Cal's voice was high.

"Stop it, Cal!" said Maggie sharply. "Go on, Mr. Thompson."

"The simple fact is that we have not got enough fuel on board to reach our destination. Or any land," he added.

Cards all on the table, face up.

His words did not wholly sink into Maggie's brain. They seemed outlandish, indecipherable. The cabin of this plane was their bounded world. It had kept them safe through storm and wind and hail and lightning. It was cozy and quiet, a secure moonlet moving quietly under the stars. And they had agreed to dump their luggage. They had already made their sacrifice to safety. She began to stroke Susanna's sleeping head. "What are you saying, Mr. Thompson?"

"What I'm saying, Mrs. Smith, is that there is every possibility that we may have to set the aircraft down on the sea." Tucker hoped his own voice matched hers. For obvious reasons, there was no "live" training for ditching, it was all done with models and tanks. Pilots learned the theory, but very few lived to talk about the actual test, which was entirely unpredictable. And the only thing consistent about ditching in the open sea was that the results were inconsistent.

"I see." She was still stroking the baby's head.

"Now, look here. Thompson—" Cal's voice had risen in pitch.

"*Shut up,* Cal!" The violence of her response startled even herself. She turned to the Captain again. "How much longer—I mean, how soon?"

"At our present speed and heading, I would say about forty-five minutes," said Tucker. "But may I point out that it is not all bad news. We have been in touch with Shannon air-sea rescue center and they have, in turn, been in touch with the RAF. There is already a Shackleton reconnaissance aircraft in the air, en route to intercept us."

Privately, he hoped there was. He waited as she thought for a moment. "How will they find us in the dark?"

"We have flares and rockets—and we will be in constant touch by radio."

Again Tucker waited. The husband seemed about to open his mouth again, but his wife put a restraining hand on his arm. "Right, Captain. You just tell us what to do and we'll do it. . . ."

"Well, when the time comes, about ten minutes beforehand I'll tell the stewardess here and she will tell you what to do. That should be"—he looked at his watch—"in about thirty minutes from now."

She nodded and he stood up. He stood in front of her for a second in admiration, not knowing what to say. This was some lady. He saw her rubbing her shoulder, across the body of the sleeping baby. "Is your arm okay?" he asked.

"Fine, fine!" said Maggie, "I just gave it a knock. It's absolutely fine."

In a strange way, thought Maggie, watching the retreat of Tucker's wide back, she was not afraid. She felt detached. She looked down at the peaceful baby and then across at Cal, who was again rigid, jaws working. She decided there and then that if they survived this, she would divorce him. Her brain felt like an abacus, clicking away, simple and crystal-clear. Her priorities were Susanna and Christian and finally herself. She had been floundering around, trying to please too many people.

It was now her responsibility to get them all safely through the next few hours. She had a baby to look after and a small child to get back to.

"Take the baby." Without meeting his eyes, she handed Susanna to Cal, who, responding to the note of quiet authority in her voice, took his daughter without saying a word. Then Maggie went over to the sleeping nanny, shaking her awake. The young woman's eyes fluttered open, bloodshot and red-rimmed from her earlier tears. "Yes, Mrs. Smith?" She struggled upright. Keeping her voice as calm as she could, Maggie briefly explained the situation.

The nanny's eyes widened, but Maggie put both hands on her shoulders, willing her to be quiet. "We will be rescued, Rosemary," she said, every word firm and emphatic. "We will be rescued by the British air force. They are already on the way."

Rosemary's eyes filled with tears and she clapped her hand over her mouth. "Oh, Mrs. Smith—"

The last thing Maggie wanted or needed was another bout of hysterics. "Now, Rosemary, pull yourself together," she said. "It's only by being calm that we will all survive this thing. I'm sure everything is going to turn out okay. We will all have specific tasks. I want you to take charge of Susanna. We have about half an hour before things start to get busy around here. . . .

"Here is a life jacket," she went on slowly and calmly,

handing over the Mae West she had taken from the stewardess. "Now, I want you to wrap Susanna in a blanket and then tie this on over it," she said. "Be very careful with the straps. Tie it around her with her arms inside it, so she can't struggle. Okay? If you have any difficulty, call me. She can have her pacifier in her mouth; that should help."

The nanny gave a little sob, but nodded. She took the life jacket and went over and took the baby from Cal.

Maggie went to the galley. "Now tell me," she said to the stewardess, "what *exactly* is going to happen."

For the next twenty minutes, Maggie refused to let herself think of anything but how to deal with this situation. She was gentle with Cal, patting his shaking hand. "Oh, Maggie, if only we had it all to live over again—" he started, but she cut him short, like a kindly nurse. "Now, Cal, there's no time for that."

He asked then for another brandy, but she refused to let him have it. "We're all going to have to have our wits about us."

Before binding on the Mae West, the nanny had followed Maggie's instructions and had swaddled the baby tightly in her blanket. Susanna, like a strange little orange larva, responded to the air of calm and purpose and made no sound but sucked quietly at her pacifier while the nanny rocked her. Maggie sat upright in her own seat, every nerve alert.

All too soon, the stewardess was in front of her with a Mae West. "Don't inflate it inside the aircraft," she instructed. She gave life jackets to Cal and the nanny, then pulled an orange life raft from its bin and placed it in readiness near the door. She explained how they should brace themselves for the impact, bent double in their seats, one arm behind their necks, the other across their chests.

Her voice was crisp. "After we ditch, there will only be a matter of a minute or two for us all to get out of the aircraft." She turned to the nanny. "I want you to go first." Then, looking across at Maggie, "Next you, Mrs Smith. I will hand the baby to you when you are safely on the raft. Make sure that you pull the string to inflate the baby's lifejacket the moment she gets to you. And don't forget your own.

"You go next, Mr. Smith," she continued. "The captain and copilot and I will follow you."

In the cockpit, while his copilot continued to broadcast their coordinates, Tucker was watching the altimeter, bringing the aircraft gently up to six thousand feet. His plan was not to wait until the fuel had entirely run out, but to have some left to assist the ditching. The theory was that the plane should be brought down, nose kept as high as possible, on the upward face of a large swell. But as far as he had been able to in the darkness, he had seen that the sea was choppy, with large swells and whitecaps, and secondary waves and cross-wavelets which broke the symmetry of the surface. This was not going to be easy, and he wanted enough fuel left to rise again on full power if his first, second, or even his third attempt to ditch proved too dangerous.

He looked at his gauges. About enough for ten minutes. Right, this was it. He told the copilot to give, over the passenger PA, the order to brace, then turned on his landing lights and brought the DC3 in a long, slow descent toward the heaving black water.

At fifty feet he eased back the throttle and the plane began to sink, but in the split second before he hit, a curling whitecap rose, rearing upward against the twin beams of his light, and Tucker's automatic reaction was to pull on the stick and to open the throttle fully. The plane shuddered and jerked and some of the water splashed up over the nose, but like the Trojan she was, she gathered herself and surged upward at an angle of 45 degrees, roaring into the sky.

Tucker's mouth was dry and his heart was thudding painfully against his ribs. He looked at his instruments and gauges again. Three thousand feet and still climbing; the overuse of the throttle meant only two minutes left in the tank. The next attempt had to succeed.

He forced himself to think calmly and fast. Even as he set the plane into a shallow dive once again, he recreated the moments he had almost come in contact with the water. He had registered that although the waves were not tremendously high, they were choppy, with no discernible pattern. It would be a matter of luck.

The last seconds ticked away. First the port, then the starboard engine, sputtered and died. Then there was silence, eerie after the hours of droning, broken only by the rushing wind outside and the sound of the copilot's voice still calling continuous Mayday into the HF, repeating it like a mantra. "November-Two-Three, Mayday, Mayday, November-Two-Three we are ditching, Mayday, we are ditching, November-Two-Three, Mayday . . ." Each time he gave his latitude and longitude, about sixty-five miles off the west coast of Ireland.

In the last few precious seconds Tucker flattened out, searching ahead for a friendly wave. There was no more time. His height was zero.

In the cabin the sound of the impact was like a small explosion, and despite herself, Maggie cried out.

There was a skidding, tearing, ten-second interval while the fuselage vibrated along the wave tops until finally, like an ungainly powerboat whose engine had been suddenly cut, the Dak skidded to a violent halt. Miraculously, she stayed afloat and the lights stayed on.

The moment the plane stopped, the stewardess unstrapped herself and pushed open the door. Water began to pour into the cabin. Within seconds it was a foot deep. Maggie unstrapped her own belt and waded over to the door, helping the stewardess to shove the folded orange raft out into the darkness, keeping a tight hold on its rope. They could see that as soon as it hit the water outside, it expanded to its full size. The stewardess grabbed the baby's bassinet and wedged it into the opening, so that it acted as a temporary if inefficient barrier against the water, which poured in a new flood each time the aircraft lurched to the side as it rose and fell on the waves.

"Cal! Rosemary!" screamed Maggie at the other two.

Both appeared to be riveted to their seats. Both were still bent double—the nanny's head was pillowed on the baby in her lap—and neither answered.

So far they had been in the water for seventeen seconds.

The bulkhead door opened and Tucker and his copilot came through.

"Help them!" screamed Maggie, indicating the two still in their seats as she saw the pilots appear. The water continued to wash in. It was very cold. The wind outside howled.

The stewardess continued to hang on to the raft's mooring rope while she stuggled to keep the bassinet wedged against the door.

Tucker extricated the baby from the nanny and passed her, whimpering but still sucking her pacifier, to her mother. Then he unsnapped the nanny's seat belt and pulled her to her feet, manhandling her through the rising water toward the door.

Meanwhile the copilot, having undone Cal's seat belt, was pulling with all his might at the man's shoulders, trying to dislodge him. But Cal was strong and determined and wouldn't budge, his face like a rock. The young pilot slapped his face over and over again, but it was useless. The older man did not try to avoid the blows, just closed his eyes.

They had been in the water for thirty seconds. They had a maximum of a minute to go before they sank. Maybe less, for at that moment the plane lurched to starboard and the water washed the bassinet back into the cabin on a great curling wave.

"Leave him!" screamed Maggie as the copilot continued to harry Cal. She waded over to the nanny and helped the captain push her toward the door.

The water was now above their knees.

The stewardess had managed to keep hold of the tethering rope to the raft. With her free hand, she helped Maggie bundle the nanny out the door and tumble her onto the raft, which rocked dangerously but stayed upright.

The tail of the DC3 was caught by a wave and the aircraft swung around about 30 degrees. The stewardess fell backward, almost losing her grip on the rope, but she was steadied by Maggie.

The water was now up to their thighs and they were plunged into darkness as all the lights went out. The aircraft was rocking and being buffeted in the swell and it was difficult to keep their footing.

Maggie groped for Susanna, found her in Tucker's arms, and took her from him, and while the stewardess strained on the rope to bring the raft back to the door of the aircraft, Maggie managed to pass the baby out to her nanny.

There was another inrush of water which beat all three of them back from the door, now half submerged. This time it was Maggie who lost her footing and who fell backward. She disappeared under the water, cracking her head hard against the corner of the brassbound bar. A tide of green and black rose before her eyes and her head was bleeding badly when she was fished out by Tucker, but although she was dizzy, she assisted him as much as possible as he half carried her toward the door. The stewardess helped her through the opening and then pushed her so she tumbled, headfirst, onto the raft, landing on top of the nanny and the baby.

The stewardess hesitated at the door. They had maybe fifteen seconds left.

Tucker saw her looking toward the husband. The water was up to their armpits so they could feel the suction as the sea pulled at them. "Forget him, that's an order!" he snapped. *"Get into that raft!"*

She obeyed, passing the rope to him, half swimming, half climbing through the door. From the raft outside, Maggie could see her head and then her arms, thrashing strongly in the water.

The DC3 was going down fast. All that remained above water now was the fin and starboard wing.

The stewardess made it to the raft and Maggie pulled her on. Then, as the three women on the raft looked in horror, the water surged and the plane slipped under the waves. Even in the darkness, Maggie could see the wide circle of swirling white that its plunge left on the dark surface.

The raft, already rising and falling alarmingly on the waves that came from all sides, reared upward then spun crazily over the swell.

Against the white water, an arm appeared and then a head. It was Cal. He was not wearing a life jacket, but somehow, in the last moments, he had swum or been washed out of the fuselage. The stewardess threw him a rope and he caught it, but as if he were a participant in a horrific slow-motion water ballet, he was rolled across the surface, then pulled under by the suction created by the DC3 as it sank.

He did not let go of the rope, and the raft, weighted by him, teetered dangerously, one side clear out of the water. A large swell rose under this raised side and pushed the whole vessel over, heeling its human cargo into the sea.

Maggie struggled under the surface. The freezing temperature shocked her into full consciousness. Her life jacket was only partially inflated, but she kicked strongly and with the help of its buoyancy, managed to break the surface.

Something brushed her feet and then surfaced beside her. It was the small figure of Susanna, a compact orange bundle. The baby's eyes were closed and her mouth was slack. Maggie grabbed on to her and struggled to keep them both afloat.

A short distance away, maybe thirty feet, the raft had righted itself.

Maggie, despite shock and the injuries to her shoulder and head, was strong and healthy and a good swimmer. Keeping her injured arm tightly wrapped around the baby, she struck out with the other to where she saw the raft appear and disappear intermittently between the waves that rose all around her.

Several times she and the baby were swamped and her mouth filled with water, but each time, with grim strength, she spat and surfaced and continued her one-armed progress until she reached the side of the raft. It was rising and falling with the waves, but still listing hard to one side, one edge almost under the water. Cal was obviously still attached to the rope.

It was his last service to his family, because Maggie was exhausted now and would have found it very difficult to get the baby and herself on board if the raft had been riding high. With a huge effort, she heaved Susanna ahead of her—the baby had not made a sound or moved—and dragged herself on board after her. She lay beside her daughter, panting and spluttering on the listing floor as the waves washed over the sunken edge. Then she roused herself to her knees and forced her numb fingers into action. She took one of the straps that trailed free from the baby's life jacket and tied it to the rope that ran around the inside of the raft. She did not know whether her daughter was alive or dead.

She blew on her fingers and then started to untie the rope that kept them bound to Cal. But she miscalculated. The knot opened faster than she had bargained for and the raft, relieved of Cal's weight, bounced level as she was still leaning forward and off-balance. She fell forward from her knees and instinctively thrust her hands out. The momentum carried her over the edge and she fell back into the sea. This time, she did not struggle.

The raft was light now, buoyant and free, with only the baby on board. Maggie watched, almost dreamily, as it drifted fast away from her. Her head really hurt, but the water did not seem so cold. It was soft, in fact. Soft kind water. Underneath the waves there was peace. No sound after the din. Even the pain was quietened. Quiet soft water. Blessed quiet dark water. Soft black cradle.

The raft was now several hundred yards away, tipping briskly along on the restless lacy surface.

2

It was nearly time. Conor's bed was second-last in a long double row in the dormitory. He lay awake, barely daring to breathe, as the sky outside the window at the far end of the room turned gradually from black to pearl. Knowing that by bumping into something he could wake Brother Patrick or a prefect, he had not wanted to make his move until there was some light.

At one time during the long night, a violent storm had crashed and rattled at the roof and windows of the dormitory and he had thought he might have to abort his mission. Now it seemed to be dry and calm outside. Maybe, he thought, God was on his side after all. . . .

It was definitely getting lighter. He counted out the seconds: *one-and-two-and-three-and-four* . . . Now, at last, he could differentiate solid objects from shadows.

He could postpone his move no longer.

Inch by inch, heart thumping, he stole out of his bed, timing his movements to the loud snores of Seán Lyons in the bed beside his. He eased the shirt-wrapped bread out from under the mattress, then, one agonising step after the other, crept out of the dormitory, avoiding the boards he knew were the creakers. On the small landing outside the door, he paused for a moment and exhaled, realizing that his chest was hurting from holding his breath for so long. He had a strong urge to go to the toilet, but did not dare. Instead, he started to move carefully down the worn stone steps that opened on to the front corridor. Once there, progress was easier. Although the corridor was a long one and was lit only by a window at each end, there were religious statues in niches all along the walls facing the classrooms, and in front of each one burned a votive lamp, little lighthouses of red and blue in the passage toward the door. As he crept

along, he was conscious of an overwhelming smell of
floor polish.

Down a further flight of steps, along another corridor,
and he was into the front hall, tiled with squares of marble. His stomach jumped with relief. There was a key in
the iron lock of the front door—it was the one thing he
had not been able to check in advance. He turned it and,
well-oiled, it gave easily. Then he took a deep breath and
unlatched the door. The click resounded so loudly that
he froze. He waited for a full minute, straining his ears,
but the only sounds were his own fast breathing and the
thudding of his heart as it banged against his ribcage. He
slipped outside into the lightening day, not daring to pull
the door shut after him. It was heavy, made of oak and
impossible to close without making a substantial thump.
He knew that when it was discovered to be open, there
would be a hue and cry, but he could not help that.

Keeping close to the walls of the house, his breath
misting, he moved like a shadow along the damp grass
which was cold and slippery under his bare feet, which,
to his dismay, he saw were leaving clear imprints. Well,
that could not be helped. Now what mattered was putting
as much distance as possible between himself and the
school. Bending low, ignoring the discomfort as the
stones cut into the soles of his feet, he crossed the grav-
eled driveway in front of the school.

When he reached the playing fields in front of the
school he felt very exposed and remained doubled over,
making himself as small as possible. To keep the grass
under control, the brothers allowed a local farmer to
graze sheep on the playing fields. The flock was resting,
wooly bodies seeming to float above the drifting ground-
fog. As Conor's humped shape approached, the nearest
ewe struggled up on dainty hooves and trotted away from
him, followed by her two lambs. One of the lambs bleated
shrilly and Conor froze again in his tracks, risking a look
over his shoulder at the gray bulk of the school building.
Some of the windows on the upper stories glowed faintly, lit by votive lamps or nightlights, but none was fully
lit, and although he watched for a few moments, no lights
snapped on.

So far so good.

He reached the big iron gates and, finding his boots

where he had left them, sat on the grass to lace them on, first putting on the socks that he had carried with him in the breast pocket of his pajama jacket. Then, having forgotten to take off his pajama bottoms before putting on the boots, he had to force the garment over the boots, ripping the worn cotton along the seams.

Quickly rolling both bottoms and jacket into a compact ball, he shoved them under a bush, and taking one last look behind him, he set off at a run along the laneway toward the main road. Coatless and therefore conspicuous in his school uniform, he had a story ready for any carter or farmer who might pick him up. He was a prefect, he would say, and had been sent by the superior into Galway on an important errand.

As he trotted along between the furze and hawthorn hedges that bordered the laneway, the cool air of the May morning felt sharp and clean against his cheek and he began to feel almost lighthearted. Again he rehearsed his arrival at Inisheer: his mother would be surprised to see him; she would be afraid for him too; but he knew that deep down, she would be glad. His place was at home at a time like this and he would deal with the consequences later.

To catch his breath, he stopped for a few seconds beside a five-barred gate, his boots sinking into the quagmire churned up around its base by livestock. Seeing him, an old sway-backed donkey raised her ears and then trotted across to the gate, butting at him through the bars. Conor stroked the donkey, loving the soft velvety feel of her nose. He had always been fascinated by the busy lives led by animal, insect, and bird and now, despite his hurry, he could not resist watching and listening to the beginning of the new day.

Like the tentative tuning of an orchestra, the birds were warming up. Somewhere in the hedge, a blackbird tested his throat, competing for airtime with the growing cacophany from a crowd of sociable crows in the branches of a horse-chestnut tree nearby. On the other side of the gate, two heifers huffed rhythmically as they tore at the new growth between clumps of sedge and reeds in the boggy field. Far away, from the depths of the bog, a curlew called once, twice. . . .

Conor felt his panic subside. He was tempted to linger,

to search for the voles, shrews, and field mice he knew
he would find in the ditches only yards from where he
stood, but he also knew that any further delay would be
foolish. He gave the donkey a final pat and looked toward
the main road. From where he stood, he could see the cop-
pice of rowans planted by the brothers around the Lourdes
grotto at the junction of their laneway to the school. He
scraped the soles of his boots on the lowest rung of the
gate and set off again.

While on the mainland his son hurried toward the Galway road, Micheál O Briain lifted his tired body from
where he had sat most of the night. The chair legs scraped
on the stone floor of the hearth as he stood up. He
dragged his feet a few steps to the window of his kitchen
to look out across the stone landscape of the island. It
was a clear dawn. His bones ached with the stiffness of
the long night, but he must have dozed for a small while
at least, because looking back, he noticed that the fire
was nearly out. He took four sods of turf from the creel
in the chimney corner and threw them onto the heap of
white ashes, rising a shower of sparks.

He leaned against the chimneypiece and looked across
at the other side of the hearth where his wife, Sorcha,
was still rocking the child. Her head was low and resting
on Molly's fair, lifeless head. The baby, just a year old,
had been unconscious for hours.

Micheál was more angry than sorrowful, railing, as he
frequently did, against his grubbing, mean life. He was
not really surprised that his only daughter was so ill. He
watched as the sods of turf caught. It was no consolation
that nearly every family on the island was in a similar
position to his own, scratching a living from the rocks,
getting a few shillings from the government in faraway
Dublin, watching the post for the money-bearing letters
from the relatives in Boston or Birmingham or Coventry.
Micheál and his brother shared a currach and a few lobster pots which they set each night; but the money they
got for the lobsters paid only for a few basic groceries.

Only the rhythmic tapping of Sorcha's chair leg against
an uneven part of the flags disturbed the quietness of the
kitchen and Micheál suddenly felt dislocated, as though
he were not in full control of his own thoughts. Although

he rarely indulged in such foolishness, memories of his courtship and wedding stormed into his mind.

He had first encountered Sorcha Ní Choirreáin, a gentle girl from the neighboring island of Inishmaan, at a céilidhe in that island's hall. With her sister as partner, she had been parading gravely around the dance floor, one of the large circle of couples taking part in The Stack of Barley. He knew her from previous céilidhes, but up to now, she being as light on her feet as a fairy and himself as heavy as a clodhopper, he had never been able to summon up enough courage to ask her up.

But this night, emboldened by porter, he had cut in on her and the sister: " 'Tis not right for two girls to be dancing together. . . ."

"Is it not now!" the sister had been pert. Sorcha had said nothing but had stood with eyes cast down. So he had addressed her directly, offering his arm. "Will we go, so?"

"All right." She had taken the arm and they had carried on around the room, leaving the sister to drag another young fellow onto the floor.

Somehow, that night he had managed not to trip or to walk on her feet, which even though shod in cheap plastic sandals, were as small and delicate as the feet of a princess. Afterward, he had asked her if he could walk her home across the unlit island, but she had refused: "I'll be going with my sisters."

Flushed with the success of the dance, he had persisted. "Will you be coming to the pattern on Inisheer?"

"I might."

"Will I see you there?"

"You might."

"Will you come, so?"

"I told you, I might." And with that he had had to be content.

But she did come to the pattern and they began a long, slow courtship.

He knew that what he had for her was his height and his dark looks, and during the time they walked out, he curbed his drinking and managed to keep his temper well under control. Also in his favor was the priceless asset of a free house. Since he was the eldest son of his family and both his parents were dead, he had control of the house and a couple of perches of land—and what's more, the house would be free of a mother-in-law.

To him, she was warmhearted and clever and acquiescent. She could cook. She was modest but attractive too, and on summer evenings that first year, he had preened as other boys and men joshed him about his stewardship of her on the Inishmaan pier or on the launching points on Inisheer, as one or other of them embarked for home across the stretch of water between their islands, appropriately named *Bealach Na Fearbhach*, Foul Sound.

But that courtship had proven to be the high point of their lives together. After marriage, he found her fearful and prudish in bed and knew to his chagrin that she found him coarse and brutal. But they had no vocabulary to discuss such things, so her fear and his resentment blossomed between them like weeds, so deeply rooted they spread across the daylight.

He looked across to where she cradled their daughter. It was odd he was thinking such thoughts at a time like this. On the other hand, perhaps it was not all that unusual. Perhaps the immediate problems had stirred up the long-term ones too.

Looking at his wife's worn face, Micheál realized with unaccustomed clarity that if he was disappointed, Sorcha must be doubly so. He hated himself for that. It was not that he meant to be violent, but sometimes a red tide rose before his eyes. Sorcha's long-suffering silence did not help. If she would only retaliate sometimes . . .

That thought grew and grew. Why didn't Sorcha hit back? Some of it was her fault. She provoked him. Now, as she rocked and rocked, the child's hand covered in her own, the little face held into her shoulder, he felt the rage coming, waking up, scrabbling like a cold black beetle in his blood.

He threw another sod on the fire. The worst of it all was that he knew she was afraid of him and so were his children. If they could only talk together . . .

"Táim a' dul amach," he said gruffly, stamping toward the door in his heavy boots. Sorcha made no answer and he looked at her with something approaching hatred. She was a living reproach to him.

Almost tearing the latch off its screws, Micheál went outside, slamming the door shut behind him. The family's collie dog, black and white, emerged from the lean-to that housed their turf. She stretched, yawned, and shook herself, then, head low and keeping well out of range of her master's boot, she came toward him with a tentative wagging of her tail.

For once she need not have worried. Micheál's attention was caught by the sight of a small can of milk, covered with a saucer, on the windowsill of the cottage. Yet another offering for the child from a neighbor, placed there after darkness to avoid offense. The tact of the gesture enraged Micheál still further. He picked up the can, swung it around his head, and threw it with all his strength down the hill. Like a comet trailing a tail of milk, the can sailed high over the limestone, clattered to a halt against a wall, and rolled down the hill over and over until, badly dented, it came to rest against a boulder. Its destruction gave Micheál a sort of satisfaction. He looked around at the landscape and took a deep breath to calm himself. The air felt fresh and cool after the stuffiness of the kitchen.

The O Briains' cottage was high on the island, about half a mile above the shore. The whole island was a single fissured rock, flat limestone, gray on gray, crisscrossed by a latticework of low walls and pocked with minute fields of forced grass. The sky was black to the west, where the next landfall was America, but across on the mainland, about nine miles to the east, the sun had raised tentative fingers of pink and gold above the horizon, brightening Inisheer and giving it texture. It was that still period before the day when the wind had all but died and only the sound of the sea filled the air.

Micheál looked back at his house, which had been his father's, where he had brought a wife, where his children had been born, and where he would presumably die. He saw that the thatch on the roof needed patching after the storm.

Three rooms and an outside water closet. A few sticks of furniture and a bit of delph Sorcha had brought with her when they got married. That was the sum total of a lifetime's work. His fury of a few minutes before had ebbed away and was now replaced by deep depression. Why him? Why them? Consumption in an infant was not

all that unusual on the island. But Sorcha had been a good
mother and he had worked his fingers to the bone . . .

The ache in his joints eased out as, followed at a safe
distance by the collie, he clumped downhill between the
waist-high walls. As far as he could see, the island was
deeply asleep and he and the dog were the only moving
creatures on the island; two donkeys slept, nose to tail,
in the lee of a wall; Marcus O Braonáin's bony cow sat
dozing in her tiny field.

Micheál himself had helped with that field, backbreak-
ingly created around the cracks of limestone by three
generations. They had cleared the loosest of the rocks,
using them to build the walls, and then had hauled huge
loads of seaweed and sand from the seashore, spreading
the material across the rock, adding it to the precious
filaments of soil that they dug out of the crevices in the
limestone. As a result of this, the O Braonáins had been
able to plant enough grass to graze a single cow.

Looking at the cow now, her head curled on to her
hind legs, Micheál's heart leapt with jealousy. He would
never own a cow. His own handkerchief of land supported enough soil for two short drills of potatoes and
that was all. If he had had a cow, maybe his daughter
need not have got consumption. Even if he had been
born, not on Inisheer but on Inishmore, the biggest of
the three islands, where the land was warmer . . .

It was too late now to be thinking such things. Not all
the good milk or warm land in the world could save his
daughter now. Only a miracle could do that. Micheál
wished he could pray, but prayer was gone from him a
long time.

He realized he had reached the beach. Innocent of last
night's storm, long, gentle breakers, tipped with the gold
of the rising sun, poured like cream along the edge of a
crescent of fine, opalescent sand. Although he rarely noticed such things, it occurred to Micheál that this morning this beach was as untouched and untainted as it must
have been fifteen hundred years ago, fifteen thousand
years ago. At the beginning of the world.

Who could he say this to? Who would understand?

The collie, sensing his mood, bellied up to him and
shoved an ingratiating nose into his hand.

He patted her.

* * *

Christian could not get to sleep. His room was at the front of the house and every time he was just on the point of dropping off another car seemed to scrunch in or out of the driveway. And if that was not enough, the downstairs telephones rang constantly.

He raised himself in the bed and clicked on his bedside lamp, illuminating the colorful, ordered chaos of his own small world. Christian was a hoarder and did not allow anyone to throw out any of his outgrown possessions. Neatly ranged on a shelf, there were teddy bears and stuffed animals from his babyhood; some of the carpeted floor was taken up with a Hornby train set imported from England, still laid out but unused for a number of years. In one corner, a junior trampoline shared space with a handmade rocking horse with mane and tail of real hair; in another, on his custom-made toybox was so full the lid did not close properly, and beside it, a half-sized pool table was stacked high with outgrown sets of building blocks and other toys. His Davy Crockett hat, Indian headdresses, and Stetsons decorated the length of one entire wall, and above his homework desk, specially fitted shelves brightly painted in bold shades of primary red and blue held his collection of exotic seashells and his books, leather-bound sets of children's classics, fairy tales and encyclopaedias, dog-eared Marvel comics and well-thumbed novels. It was for this section that he headed. On top was an illustrated version of *Huckleberry Finn*, so often read that it was falling apart, but there was an even tattier book underneath: in Christian's opinion, the best book of all, Anna Sewell's *Black Beauty*. He retrieved it carefully, trotted back to bed, and snuggled down again under his striped quilt.

The book fell open naturally at the passage where the old war horse, Captain, tells Beauty of his experiences in the Crimean War.

> I, with my noble master, went into many actions together without a wound; and though I saw horses shot down with bullets, pierced through with lances and gashed with fearful sabre-cuts; though we left them dead on the field, or dying in the agony of their wounds, I don't think I feared for myself. . . .

In all the books he owned, this was Christian's favorite passage. His mind used it as a launching pad; after reading it, he rode his own charger into mighty battles, always with the addition of a canine companion called Shep or Blue or Rusty running faithfully by his side. Christian's imagination brought him to exotic places with names familiar from his atlases and encyclopaedias: Afghanistan, India, Timbuktu, Mexico, the Congo. He and his animal companions fought battles in China and Mongolia and Spain. They charged up the slopes of Mount Everest and fought for their lives in flash floods on the Amazon. Tonight it was Christian's new puppy, Bluey, who accompanied him and his charger. It had been a good day at the ballpark, and as a result, the trio of adventurers journeyed to Wales.

From time to time, when he was in a good mood, Christian's grandpa had told him stories about his childhood in the villages and coal pits of Wales and how, tragically, his grandpa's dad and two brothers had been killed underground in a big explosion.

So tonight, Christian and his animal friends dashed to the site of an explosion in the Welsh valley, and while Bluey dug through the rubble, Christian and his charger got busy dragging huge rocks from the collapsed mouth of the pit. Then, when they had unblocked an opening big enough for them to get through, they were able to rescue the battered, black-faced miners, taking them out one at a time on his saddle. Christian, Bluey, and Captain, the charger, became heroes in the valley and the grateful villagers put up a statue to the three of them.

Downstairs, Christian heard the doorbell ring for the umpteenth time that night. His grandma and grandpa must be having a party, he decided, although it was strange he had not been told about it, nor had he heard any music or laughter. He was tempted to get out of bed to investigate, but he was too snug. He switched off his lamp and closed his eyes. Christian's last waking thought was of his puppy and whether it should be a big brave one, able to do battle, or a small floppy one he could carry around with him in a special carrier on his bicycle.

Half an hour later, his bedroom door opened and his grandparents stood framed in the light from the landing outside. "Let him sleep," said Cordelia Smith to Mal-

colm. "He's only a baby. He'll know soon enough . . ."
She crossed the room and picked up from the floor beside
the bed an ancient stuffed rabbit, barely recognizable as
such because it was earless, one-eyed, and bald. Carefully, she placed it on the pillow.

And while two RAF Shackletons flew wide, coordi-
nated sweeps over the area of sea from which the DC3
had made its last radio call, Christian slept on and
dreamed of brave horses and fleet, valorous dogs.

Four hours later, on the dockside in Galway city, Conor
O Briain stood dejectedly while the wind blew off the
Claddagh and rocked the hookers and fishing boats tied
up alongside the jetties. He had achieved his objective.
But he had forgotten that on Sundays, there was no ferry
service to the Aran Islands.

There was no point in hanging around and he was cold.
Behind him the city rang with church bells, so he decided
to go to Mass; the church would be warm, it would lend
him time to think.

He followed the sounds of the bells, which led him
across a bridge over the fast-flowing Corrib. The nearer
he got to the church the bigger the converging crowd
became. The men, compressed into suits and ties, looked
uncomfortable, the boys' knees were red from scrubbing
and their hair was artificially flat with Brylcreem; the
girls, on the other hand, wore smug expressions and ribbons in their ringlets, while their big sisters, aunts, and
mothers were happily decked out in Easter finery only a
few weeks old, wearing hats or carrying mantillas and
clicking along on high heels. Conor shoved his shirt-
wrapped bread under his jumper and held his hands in
front of the bulge in an effort to hide it. As he walked,
he made efforts to shine first one shoe, then the other, on
the back of his school trousers.

When he reached it, the church was tall and echoing,
with long stained-glass windows depicting the tortures
and triumphs of various saints and martyrs. There were
big sprays of lilies on the altar, where the priest had already begun the *Confiteor*. Conor sat at the back of the
church and joined in the familiar responses when the
priest turned around to face the congregation.
Dominus Vobiscum—

Et cum spirituo tuo . . .

The familiar, soporific responses were comforting and quieting, and little by little he felt his spirits rise. But his relief proved short-lived. For when the time came, fearing he was too conspicuous in his school uniform, he did not dare take Communion. On the other hand, when everyone else had gone up to the altar, snaking along the aisles in two long lines, he wished he had because, alone in his pew, he fancied he was the butt of all attention and speculation. He was sure everyone else in the church was wondering if he had broken his fast, or what heinous crime he had committed that kept him from the rails. He buried his head in his hands and tried to project an aura of exceptional holiness like the boy Saint Tarcisius whose breast concealed the Holy Host from the attentions of murderous Roman centurions. But after a few minutes, that particular image proved less than comforting as Connor remembered that Tarcisius had been captured and martyred.

When the Mass ended and the congregation spilled out into the fresh air, Conor left the church with the others, but once outside, had no idea what to do next. So he hung around, first looking expectantly into the distance as if waiting for someone, then turning to study the church notices on the porch. The crowd for the next Mass was already gathering, so when the church was nearly full, Conor slipped inside again.

He attended three Masses and a baptism, staying well to the rear of the church for the latter. Throughout the ceremony, the baby cried: a lusty, full-blown shriek. Conor hated the sound. Inevitably, it reminded him of his baby sister and increased his feelings of helplessness and frustration. He became aware of a more urgent physical problem, however, he was now ravenously hungry and his stomach was rumbling so loudly he was sure the baptism party could hear it.

When the ceremony was over, the congratulations made and all the snaps taken, the sacristan snuffed out the altar candles. Besides himself, Conor saw that the only other person left in the church, suddenly so dusky and quiet, was an old lady, dressed all in black, walking and genuflecting her way around the stations of the Cross. Still pretending to pray, he was afraid to leave his bolt-hole, but his stomach was not only rumbling but actually in pain. At about this time, he thought with longing, the boys in St. Kevin's were sitting down to dinner. Sundays meant bacon and marrowfat peas and extra potatoes.

His fear of being discovered and exposed struggled with his hunger, and hunger won. He went outside and after some hesitation, walked around the back of the church, where there were no overlooking houses. Leaning on a set of railings, he unwrapped his bread and devoured all six slices, one after the other. Then, feeling thoroughly ashamed, he urinated into a gutter at the end of a downpipe and went back into the church again. It seemed the only option. By now he would have certainly been missed from the school. He had already spotted a place where, on a Sunday afternoon, he could probably stay for a while without being detected. He went over to a dim side chapel dominated by a large statue of Our Lady and curled up on one of the pews. Within minutes, he was asleep.

He was still asleep at about six o'clock when he was found by the curate, Father Tom Hartigan, a little man whose most obvious feature was a large, hooked nose. Before waking him, the curate stood looking down at him for a few seconds, contemplating the dark, pudding-bowled head, the too-small uniform, the bony wrists protruding from the sleeves. It was quite dark in the alcove, but the guttering bank of candles in front of the Virgin's statue softened the long face and created shadows under the twin crescents of dark lashes.

Conor, whose sleep was not deep, came awake at once when he felt his shoulder being shaken. Opening his eyes, he found himself face-to-face with a small priest who was squatting on the floor in front of him talking gently: "Son, son, wake up. You shouldn't be here."

He sat up, instantly alert, heart thumping. "Sorry, Father . . ."

The curate removed his glasses and, standing up, cocked his head to one side. "What are you doing here, son? What's your name?"

Conor hung his head.

"Come on now, son, I'm a priest. You know you can tell anything to a priest! Even your name . . ." He chuckled, but to Conor the sound that came out was one of the strangest he had ever heard from a human, half snuffle, half snort. Despite his embarrassment and fear, an answering laugh escaped his mouth. Then he caught himself. Anyone in a soutane was suspect. Again he hung his head.

The priest was not deterred. "If you tell me your name," he coaxed, "I'll bring you over to the house and we can have a bite to eat and a bit of a chat . . ."

Conor was as ravenous as ever and the offer was very tempting. He wavered: "I don't know, Father, but thanks anyway. I'd best be getting home . . ."

"Come on now," said the priest, and Conor knew he was not deceived. "I've a housekeeper over there makes the best apple tart in the county," he continued. "How's about it, son?"

That was more than flesh could bear. "All right, Father . . ."

"So what's your name?" the priest asked again as they crossed the church grounds toward the two-story presbytery.

"Conor O Briain."

"Where from?"

"Inisheer."

"And what are you doing here?"

Conor struggled to answer, but the words would not come. The priest's kindness broke through the last reserves of his composure and self-control, and at last he gave way to all the emotions of the past thirty-six hours.

"Don't worry, son," said the curate, patting his shoulder, "whatever it is, we'll sort it out. You'll feel better after a bite to eat and a cup of tea, and then I'll help you sort it out."

Before they sat down to eat, Conor went to the priest's bathroom to wash his face and hands. But when he buried his face in a towel to dry it, the enormity of his predicament hit him fully. What was he going to do? Authority, in the shape of a priest, waited downstairs. He had no money to run any farther, no way to get to Inisheer. He did not care contemplate the scene that faced him if he made his way back to St. Kevin's. He had got through most of his life without getting into trouble. Now here he was, in such serious trouble there was no way out.

When he got back downstairs, the priest was sitting in

a fireside chair in a small, overfurnished parlor off the
kitchen of the house. A coal fire burned in the grate, and
from a Bakelite radio on a trolley in the corner came the
soothing tones of an announcer introducing a piece of
music. Right in front of the fireplace, a small table had
been laid with the promised apple tart and the tea things.

"There you are," said the priest as Conor, pink from
washing, recent tears, and embarrassment, came shyly
into the room. "Sit down there now, till I get the tea,"
he continued. "It's already wet and drawing. How do
you like it? Strong or weak?"

Conor was entirely unused to being consulted about
how he liked his tea. "A-any way at all, Father . . ." he
stammered.

"Right," answered the priest, "it should be ready by
now." He got up from the chair and went into the
kitchen. "Inisheer," he called from there, "is that where
you said you were from?"

Conor, who was sitting in the second fireside chair,
tensed even more than he had already. "Yes, Father."

"I know Inisheer quite well. Which part are you
from?"

This was dangerous. Inisheer housed fewer than four
hundred inhabitants on its sparse fourteen hundred acres.
Why did this priest want to pin him down? But before he
could gather his wits about him, the curate was back.
"Which part did you say?"

"Near Cashel, Father."

"O Briain, O Briain," mused the priest as he poured
the tea, "I'm afraid I've never come across any O Briains
in those parts . . ."

Conor's surge of relief was still tempered by caution.
He watched the priest begin the work on the apple tart.
"My name is Tom Hartigan, by the way," the priest said
then. "I'm not from around here at all. I'm from Dublin.
Have you ever been to Dublin?"

"No, Father." Conor's eyes were on the viscous juice
that bubbled out of the pastry case as the priest wielded
the knife. "Dublin's a great city," the priest continued.
"A great place for a boy to grow up in. I like Galway
too, of course, but where a man grows up is always the
place he wants to live—wouldn't you say?"

"Yes, Father." Conor did not care where the priest

wanted to live or didn't want to live. If he had been alone, Conor would have, there and then, stuffed the entire apple tart into his mouth. The priest served him a large slice, about a third of the whole, and Conor managed—barely—to eat it one mouthful at a time. When he had finished it, the priest placed another huge slice on his plate. "Now, Conor," he said, sitting back in his chair, "why don't you tell me, really tell me, what brings you here?"

Conor swallowed a mouthful of apple tart. "I'm trying to get home, Father."

"That's a St. Kevin's uniform. Did something happen to you in school? Is that why you're going home?"

Still Conor could not trust anyone in a black soutane. "No, Father, school is fine. . . ." Then, seeing the priest's encouraging expression, he hesitated. "It's just, it's just that my little sister is sick, very sick and I want to see her before—" His voice wobbled and he stopped.

The priest poured some more tea and, unasked, put three spoonfuls of sugar into Conor's cup. "Are you afraid your little sister is going to die? "The tears welled again in Conor's eyes, but luckily, the priest seemed busy with the tea and didn't see. "Yes, Father," he managed, "I am."

At last Father Hartigan looked directly at him, with such a kind face that for once, Conor was not ashamed of being such a baby. "Drink your tea, son," he said, "and then we'll see what we can do for you."

They ate the rest of their little meal in silence. Although the tears continued to run down his face, making the apple tart taste salty, Conor finished everything on his plate. When he had swallowed the last of his tea, Father Hartigan spoke again. "Listen, Conor, the first thing we have to do is to let the brothers know you're all right. They probably have the guards out for you at this stage . . ."

Conor's heart turned over with fear and he must have showed it, because the priest leaned forward, gripping his wrist. "It's all right, son, it'll be all right. I know the head brother there. I'll ring him up and tell him you're with me. You can stay here tonight and then, in the morning, we'll organize a boat for you to Inisheer. All right?"

Conor was not convinced. His treacherous body started

to shake with fear and tension. The priest never let go his grip on his wrist. "What is it, son? You can tell me what you're afraid of! I promise, I promise, I swear on my mother's grave, that I won't tell anyone what you tell me—"

"Nothing, Father."

"Son, I know it's something. Please trust me, you can trust me. As God is my judge, you can. . . ."

Finally Conor risked it. "It's Brother Patrick, Father," he whispered. "He'll kill me."

"I see." Father Hartigan waited a bit and Conor did not dare look up to see his expression. Then he felt his chin being taken. "Look at me now, Conor," the priest said.

Although Conor was still afraid to raise his eyes, he could feel Father Hartigan's insistence. At last he looked directly into the priest's eyes. They showed nothing but concern. "That's better, son," Father Hartigan said, and Conor was at last sure he could trust him. "No one, Brother Patrick, or *no one,* is going to kill you," the priest continued. "I promise. I'll bring you back to the school myself when you get back from Inisheer, and I'll make sure that nothing happens to you."

Conor closed his eyes.

"Do you believe me, son?"

Conor did believe him, but even if he had not, he felt he now had no option. At least he was not alone with the huge trouble anymore. He nodded slowly and the priest released him. "All right, son. Now, I'd better get on the telephone before the guards arrest me for kidnapping!"

But Conor was too emotionally exhausted to smile at the joke, and after a moment or two, Father Hartigan left the room and went into the hall, from where Conor heard him dialing a number.

Christian was confused. Sunday mornings were predictable in his house—early-morning bustle, big breakfast—but this morning, he woke up by himself. He saw by the clock on the wall above his bookshelf that it was after nine o'clock. Not only had he not been woken up for his breakfast, but there was hardly any noise in the house. He looked out the window. The driveway was empty. The car should have been there by now, to take them to church.

He put on his bathrobe and slippers and went downstairs. There was no one in any of the rooms, not even a maid. He found Bridie in the kitchen, but there was no smell of food, no roast in the oven. Bridie was sitting at the big table. Her eyes were red and she was crying, wiping the tears away with her apron. Christian became seriously alarmed. "What's wrong, Bridie? Where's everyone? Where's Grandma and Grandpa?"

Bridie did not answer him. She let out a great sob and went to the refrigerator to get the milk for his cereal. "Bridie, what's wrong?" Christian's heart began to hammer.

The housekeeper waved her hands in the air but still did not say anything. Christian reassured himself that Bridie was well known in the house for crying—weddings, mushy films on television—Bridie cried at them all. But this crying seemed different, far more real, somehow . . . "Is someone sick, Bridie?" he asked helplessly, this time addressing Bridie's ample back, which still shook with sobs as she stirred the milk in a pot on the big gas stove. He felt his own tears starting in sympathy with Bridie, but he tried not to let them out. "Will I get to see Grandma, Bridie? he asked. "Where's Grandma?" He really wished his mom was not away. She'd know how to deal with this.

"Your grandma and grandpa had to go out early." Bridie managed to gasp out the words before the next onslaught of tears.

Christian now felt embarrassed at all this emotion and could not wait to get out of the kitchen. "Bridie, I'm not very hungry this morning," he said. "I think I'll skip breakfast . . ." And before she could turn around, he had fled from the kitchen.

He sat in his room on his bed and tried to puzzle things out. There was definitely something wrong in the house, it felt wrong. He picked up *Black Beauty* from the floor where it had fallen when he had gone to sleep the night before, but for once the words failed to hold his interest.

He decided to get dressed. He was still worried, but his mom always said that work and activity were the best ways to fight worry. He would make a start on building his kennel.

Forty-five minutes later he was absorbed in his task. He had managed to join together two sides of the kennel, using two small angle irons he found in the gardener's toolbox. The third side was proving more tricky and he was beginning to get frustrated. Then he sensed there was someone else in the garage.

He looked around. The chauffeur was standing behind him. "Hello, Jim," he chirped, "I'm just building a kennel here—see? Mom said I could have a puppy when she gets back from Europe and I want everything to be ready for him when I get him . . . ."

Something about the chauffeur struck him as odd. The man was not dressed in his uniform but in a suit. The only other time Christian had seen the chauffeur in a suit was when he and his grandpa had met him by chance on the sidewalk when they were paying a visit to his grandpa's Auntie Mamie on the south side.

But before he could ask the chauffeur about this, the man spoke. "I know all about the puppy, Christian— your grandpa told me."

Christian was flabbergasted. "He wasn't supposed to tell *anyone*! It was a *secret*!"

"Yes, but he told me because he says we're to go get the puppy now. . . ."

"Now? Today?"

"Yes, Christian." The chauffeur's voice was level. "He wants me to drive you to Orphans of the Storm where we can pick out whatever puppy you like. That's by far the best place to get a puppy, you know, because all the puppies there have been abandoned and have no homes. So you can do a good deed, save one and give it a nice home here. And it's open on a Sunday . . . ."

Christian looked doubtful. "Are you sure, Jim? Mom said she would come with me when they got home from Europe. Are you sure she won't mind?"

"Yes, Christian, I'm absolutely sure she won't mind. Your grandpa's sure she won't mind." The chauffeur rubbed at something in his eye.

Christian ran into the house to fetch his jacket and when he came out again, he took the entrance steps three at a time but was so excited he almost tripped and fell.

"Sorry about that, Jim," he said as he hopped into the front of the Cadillac. "Nearly ruined my good pants!" He giggled. Christian loved surprises. The only bad thing about the puppy had been that he would have had to wait for it until his mom came back. Now everything was perfect. "This is terrific, Jim," he said as the car glided away from the house. "Do we need money? How much do we need? Should I go back and get my savings box?"

"It's okay, Christian," said the chauffeur, "I have all we need. Your grandpa gave me money."

All the way to Riverwoods, Christian bubbled over with plans for his puppy. And as they traveled through the suburb of Deerfield, he spotted a woman being hauled along the sidewalk by a Saint Bernard. "I wonder will I get a big one?" he asked the chauffeur. "What do you think, Jim?"

"Well, it's up to you, of course, Christian, but I think one that big would be a bit difficult. How big is your kennel going to be?"

Christian nodded. "You're probably right. Maybe one not so big . . ." He thought for a bit. Although he had always wanted a dog, he suddenly began to doubt his own ability to manage one. And suppose he and the dog didn't hit it off? That had never occurred to him before. "Do you think the puppy will love me right away?" he asked anxiously. "How will I know which one to pick, Jim?"

"It'll love you. You don't have to worry about that," answered the chauffeur. "Dogs love anyone who loves them."

Christian was not so sure of that. "Maybe," he said doubtfully.

As it was still morning, there were very few customers at Orphans of the Storm. The girl tending the reception desk took them out to the yards, where Christian's eyes widened with pity. The cats were in rows of raised hutches, about three feet square. Most of them ignored all efforts to attract their attention, but one or two mewed loudly and stuck a forepaw through the wire grille on the front of their cages, in an effort to make contact with humans. Christian wished he could take them all home. Maybe he should change his mind and take a cat or a kitten?

But then they came to the dog runs. The dogs displayed

an entirely different attitude to their potential rescuers. Wildly hopeful, most of them barked and whined with excitement as he approached, rushing up and down their runs, pressing up against the wire gates, climbing over one another. "Take me home, take me home, me, me!" each one seemed to plead with Christian, and he became quite upset at the thought that he could only take one.

He couldn't make up his mind between an excited young golden labrador which bounced around, trying desperately to lick him through the bars, and a very sad black and white mongrel which hung back at the rear of its run as if it knew that there was no point in asking any favours in such glamorous company. It sat, a resigned expression on its intelligent face, looking away from Christian, but darting occasional glances of query at him while he dithered. After a while, it flopped down and put its head on its feathery paws, seeming to give up.

Christian could not resist such sorrow. "I'll take that one," he said to the chauffeur, pointing to the mongrel, which seemed to sense the decision, because it got up on its forepaws and wagged its tail, but only at the very tip, as though not wanting to count any chickens until it had supervised them all safely out of their shells.

The formalities were easy. Christian and the chauffeur selected a collar and a leash and two bowls, one for feeding and one for water. Then the girl went to get the dog.

When it was brought out it was transformed, wagging its tail until its whole body was in motion, ears pricked, panting happily. It jumped up at Christian, licking his face and then his hands, licking the chauffeur too, as if to thank both of them. The chauffeur made his donation and they went back to the car. The dog had no hesitation in leaping through the open door onto the backseat.

"Where'll we keep him?" worried Christian. "I don't have his kennel ready yet."

"Don't worry about it," said the chauffeur. "Your grandpa will probably let you keep him in your room for a little while, until you have the kennel ready."

The kennel was never completed. The dog, which Christian named Flash because of the white streak on its black muzzle, moved in to Christian's room that night and slept there until it died six years later. Because that afternoon, not long after he and Flash returned from their first walk together, Christian was told by his grandparents that his mother, father, and sister were missing after an air crash.

They were waiting for him when he let himself back into the house. His grandmother met him in the hall and he saw immediately there was something seriously wrong, because her face was puffy. She had definitely been crying. He remembered Bridie that morning and his heart began to hammer again. "What's wrong, Grandma?" he asked, afraid of the answer.

"Christian, darling," said his grandmother, "will you come into the breakfast room?" She took his hand. "Your grandpa and I have something very sad to tell you."

Malcolm was sitting in his wing chair, but it was turned away from the lake and facing the door. His face also looked all funny. Christian realized that his grandpa, too, had been crying. His heart seemed to shrink in his chest.

His grandpa held out his arms to Christian, who still had Flash on the leash. The dog, picking up the tension and fearful of the feel of the polished parquet under his paws, strained backward against the leash, his paws splayed. Christian dragged him forward toward Malcolm and the dog's nails scratched along the floor. Christian was afraid to look at his grandpa's blotchy face.

He heard Malcolm's voice as though it were coming from the bottom of one of the Welsh pit shafts he was always talking about. "Christian," the voice said, "I don't know how to tell you this, but there's been an air crash . . ."

Christian said nothing, but kept his eyes fixed on Flash, who, tail between his legs, was still straining away from him toward the door.

"Do you understand, Christian?" the voice asked. "Your mom and dad and Susanna have been in an air crash . . ."

The world stopped for Christian. He felt himself growing smaller and smaller until he was a little dot. The only real thing in the room was Flash. "How do you know it was the right plane?" he asked eventually. His voice sounded as small as himself.

"Christian," said the voice, "we've checked and

checked. We were up all night. We've been to the police station. There's no mistake.''

Christian kept his eyes on Flash. He saw that one of the dog's ears was higher than the other. ''How do you know they crashed? Dad said they were flying over Greenland, he showed it to me on the atlas. They could've just landed in Greenland and nobody's found them yet . . .''

''Christian, that would be impossible because they took off from Iceland in the plane all right, but they never reached Ireland. And a life raft from the plane was found washed up on some island off Ireland's west coast. Christian, it was empty.''

Christian concentrated on the dot that was himself. He was afraid it would disappear altogether. ''That doesn't mean anything,'' he insisted. ''Even if the plane did crash, you said they were only missing. They were picked up by a ship. I just know they were.''

He looked fiercely at his grandpa, but his grandpa just put his head in his hands. Christian felt he had to keep holding tightly on to his still-shrinking self, just as tightly as he was holding his dog's leash. He glanced at his grandma, but she too had her hands up to her face so that only her eyes were visible. Her eyes were brimming over with tears. He noticed the tears running down the backs of her splayed hands, and watched the way they ran through the big freckles on them, like little streams through brown rocks. ''Can I go now?'' he asked. ''They're on a ship, Grandma,'' he said as definitely as he could. ''I know they're on a ship.''

''I'll come up in a minute, Christian,'' said his grandma.

Christian walked quietly out of the room and toward the staircase, the dog trotting alongside him. When he got to the foot of the stairs he looked back through the open door into the breakfast room.

His grandpa was still sitting in his chair and he could see just the tip of his grandma's foot. The sun blazed in from the lake. In Christian's brain, the scene shrank until it had the size and texture of a painting.

Flash was reluctant to climb the stairs, but he ignored the dog's fretful whining. Pulling savagely at the leash, he dragged him upward and into his room. Once inside, he closed the door and dropped the leash and Flash immediately crawled on his belly into the nearest corner, fitting his back as tightly as possible into its vee.

The room did not seem familiar to Christian. It was larger, emptier—despite the clutter and confusion of his possessions—than he was used to. He crossed to the bed and sat on its side and noticed that the lace on one of his sneakers had come undone. He bent down and re-tied it, moving slowly and carefully, making the action last as long as possible. They were on a ship.

They had definitely been picked up by a ship.

A picture of his mom flashed up. In a gray dress. He remembered being hugged by her in a gray dress as she said good-bye to him. She had pearls on. That was only yesterday.

He finished tying his lace and sat upright again. It could not have been yesterday. It was too far away to have been yesterday.

He remembered the feeling of the pearls as they made a dent in his cheek when she hugged him. They were warm from her skin. What happened to the pearls . . . ?

He wouldn't think of that. His mom was on a ship.

Christian banged his head against the wall above his bedstead. He banged it over and over again. It hurt and the tears came, but he couldn't hurt it enough.

Conor woke early. For the first few moments he did not know where he was; the bed was softer than he was used to and he was in a room by himself. He crept out of bed and looked out of the window. The sun, not long risen, danced along the empty street beyond the churchyard and made a chandelier of the white lilac in the garden of the house opposite. The birds were going crazy; blackbirds and crows, starlings and sparrows, all shouted together, creating a ruckus which would have woken him if the bell had not.

He longed to be on Inisheer.

Immediately, his heart sank. Who knew what faced him over there? How was Molly? Was she dead? How would he cope?

He went back to bed, to try to sleep some more until he was called by someone in authority.

At last, at seven-thirty, the priest's housekeeper

knocked on his door. He got up immediately, washed and
dressed, and went downstairs. The housekeeper fussed
over him, serving him with rashers and eggs and thick
fried bread. Starving as usual, he wolfed the food and
was finished eating before Father Hartigan joined him,
having celebrated early Mass in the church.

The housekeeper left them to it and went upstairs to
do her work, and because it was still too early to telephone the island, time slowed down and passed by one
dragging tick after another.

While he ate his own breakfast, Father Hartigan started
to ask him about his studies. Conor could see that the
priest was trying to distract him from his worries and
was as forthcoming with his answers as his reserve and
peculiar situation allowed. He admitted that his favorite
subject in school was geography.

Father Hartigan seemed immediately interested. "Why
do you like geography?"

"I don't know, Father." It was the standard answer to
an authority figure if questions went too deep. But this
priest would not be put off. "Come on now," he joshed,
his face friendly and smiling, "if it's your favorite subject, you must know why you like it. . . ."

Just as he was unused to being consulted about his
likes and dislikes, Conor was totally unused to conversation on an equal footing with an adult. And here was
someone, a priest at that, actually interested in what he
felt. Hesitantly, he tried to be as honest and as truthful
as he could. "I don't really know, Father. I like to imagine what it must be like in other countries. Hot countries," he added. It was the first time this had occurred
to him, Amazed, he realized it was true. He was attracted to the notion of warm climates, tropical breezes.
The antithesis of Inisheer.

"What hot countries have you imagined?" asked
Father Hartigan.

"Places like Africa or Mexico or India. There are exotic animals in those places, Father, and huge plants—
because of the heat, you see—and you can grow anything
you like. In fact, if you put something in the ground you
can see it growing up the next day. The best thing about
living there is you're always warm and you don't have to
wear a lot of clothes, Father. God," he said passionately,

"they must have great freedom—" He stopped dead. He had overstepped the mark. Anyone in authority—any priest or brother—would object to someone his age talking so freely. Especially about subjects like freedom. he tensed for a lecture.

But to his astonishment, this priest didn't seem to think he had notions or had said anything above his station. "And what do you mean by freedom, Conor?" he asked, helping himself to a slice of toast.

"I don't know, Father," answered Conor. He had never actually thought this through. It was just something that had popped out.

"Oh, come now!" said the priest, joshing. "You must know what you mean when you use the word 'freedom.' Don't be afraid to tell me. It's not a trick question, I'm just interested. I have a definition of freedom that you might not have. Everyone has his own definition of freedom. Maybe you can give me yours and then I'll give you mine and we can learn from each other."

Conor considered. "I think," he said slowly, "that to be free might mean not to be responsible to anyone or for anyone else, only for yourself. That's if you're not married and don't have children," he added hastily, in case Father Hartigan might think him selfish.

"In other countries, they have all different tribal customs and different religions and they don't all believe the same thing. But they don't get punished for not behaving the same as everyone else. At least I don't think they do."

Then he amended that too, trying to be fair. "Well, I suppose they do in some places, places where there are dictators and so on, but I think in general, in places like America, for instance, or in the Sahara Desert, there's great freedom."

The priest finished his piece of toast. "I think," he said, "that you have something there, Conor. But would you not take it down to the personal level, and when you do that, would you not think that only when you subjugate yourself to God are you totally free?"

Conor frowned, trying to work that one out, but it was too deep for him. He glanced at the priest but Father Hartigan did not seem to be trying to trap him. As he waited for an answer, the priest still looked open, quite friendly. Conor found to his surprise he was actually enjoying this discussion. He risked a counter-question. "Why do *you* think that, Father?"

"We're taught it by all the great masters of theology. We're taught that to bend our imperfect wills to the will of God is the only way to liberate our imperfect souls."

Again Conor wrinkled his forehead in concentration, trying to grasp the concept. "But in these other countries, Father, like America and India, there are millions and millions of people who don't believe in God—or who believe in other gods. Can they not be free because they don't believe in God? How come millions and millions of people are wrong and only those who believe in God and obey Him the way we are taught to do are free? If there is a God, surely He wouldn't let all those millions and millions of people not be free? He's not omnipotent or all-just then, is He, if He lets that happen? And to tell you the truth, Father, I think that when you *have* to do something, like go to Mass, or fast in Lent, or not eat meat on Fridays, and if it's a mortal sin if you don't, then you're definitely not free. If God wants us to be free why does He order us around like that?" In the passion of the argument, Conor had leaned forward across the edge of the table, and now found himself gazing directly into the priest's eyes. To his amazement, what he saw there was not the usual expression he found in the eyes of authority figures—barely concealed irritation—but real interest and humor. And then the priest said something absolutely extraordinary: "To tell you the truth, Conor, I don't know the answer to that!"

Before Conor could respond, the telephone rang. "Saved by the bell!" said Father Hartigan, and then his face imploded with that extraordinary sound which in him, passed for a laugh. He patted Conor on the shoulder as he got up from the table to go to answer the call.

From inside, Conor could tell that the call was from St. Kevin's. He heard only one side of the conversation and the priest said very little. But after he put down the receiver, Father Hartigan bounced back into the kitchen. "Great news, son! We won't need any boat after all! Your little sister took a turn for the better during the night and she's on the mend. She'll still have to be nursed for a while more, but everything's going to be all right. So now! What do you think of that? Our prayers are answered!''

Conor felt giddy with relief and then half disappointed—he would not now be going out to the island. His disappointment hardened into alarm: he would now have to go back to the school. He noticed the priest was watching him closely and attempted to smile. But Father Hartigan, serious now, put a hand on his shoulder: ''Now look, Conor,'' he said, ''I'm going to drive you back to St. Kevin's in the car. And you're not to worry. Nobody, I mean *nobody,* is going to harm you. I promise.''

Conor looked at his shoes. He was not convinced. But the priest persisted. ''If there ever is any problem,'' he went on, ''you can rely on me. And if you like, I'll come to visit you from time to time. Not every visiting day, mind, but sometimes. That'll keep Brother Patrick in line, if he knows you have a friend who's a priest. Even the brothers are afraid of the priests!''

Conor looked up at him. For the first time he actually believed help might be at hand. He smiled and Father Hartigan dropped the hand from his shoulder. ''That's better!'' Then he stepped back a little. ''Christ, Conor,'' he said, ''but you'd want to see the difference a smile makes to that long gob of yours! Now listen, son, if you and I are to be friends, and I hope we are, I'll want to see a lot more of that smile. Less of the other. All right? No messing now. All right?'' He punched Conor's shoulder.

''No messing, Father!''

''Hot countries indeed!'' said Father Hartigan as the two of them got into his car.

When they were on their way, he told Conor a little bit about himself. He was an only child and his parents were dead: ''So unlike most of the fellas I met in Maynooth, I've no nephews or nieces to take out and give presents to. Poor me!'' he snorted. ''All alone in the world. I'm not even anyone's favorite uncle!'' But they were getting closer and closer to the school, and knots of tension were forming in Conor's shoulders and stomach, preventing him from laughing in response. Father Hartigan, seeming not to notice, continued in the same vein: ''That's right,'' he said again, ''poor me! Sure, maybe you were sent!'' he suggested, glancing across at his silent passenger. "Maybe we can help each other. You need protection, I need a nephew. Voilà! The Lord moves in mysterious ways, eh?"

Suddenly, so unexpectedly that Conor was thrown against the window, he swerved the car off the road. "Sorry," he said as they bumped along a pitted, twisting boreen. "So long as we're passing, I just thought I'd take the opportunity of paying a call on someone I haven't seen for a while. You don't mind?"

Conor shook his head. Mind? On the contrary. Anything to postpone the arrival at St. Kevin's.

The yard into which they drove was black, slimy with neglect. "Doesn't look great, does it?" The priest turned off the ignition. "You've got to make allowances, though," he said, "Francey's a bachelor. I don't suppose he feels he needs to keep up appearances. Come on in with me," he invited as he got out of the car.

Conor followed him to the open door of the farmhouse. Hearing their approach, fawning and smiling, a scrawny greyhound bitch, obviously nursing, ran out of the house to meet them. Conor tickled the animal under the chin and she blew with pleasure, rolling over on her back, bicycling her paws in the air. "Anyone home?" called the priest through the door opening.

Peering over Father Hartigan's shoulder, Conor saw the chaos of the kitchen and felt his stomach heave. Seeing Conor and the priest, a hen that had been pecking at the food debris under the table, squawked and flapped away into a corner. The greyhound's three piebald puppies were wriggling in a jumble of torn newspapers in front of the range; piles of blackened saucepans and food-encrusted dishes spilled over from the sink onto a draining board that held dozens of opened food cans, animal syringes, a basin full of pig swill, and a glass jug containing what was, based on the smell coming from it, rotten milk. Unwashed plates, mugs, and cutlery covered the kitchen table. "Francey!" the priest called, and when there was no reply, he turned to Conor: "He must be down in the fields. I'll call again on the way back."

Conor was very glad to get back out to the open air and readily acceded to the suggestion that they take a walk. "Are you sure you want to come?" The priest's eyes were mischievous. "Maybe you're in a desperate hurry to get back to Brother Patrick?"

Conor smiled. He did not know what to expect next from this unpredictable cleric. Up to now, his personal experience with men of the cloth had been almost entirely negative.

As they walked across the bright hard fields, for a while, St. Kevin's seemed very far away. And then Father Hartigan brought it crashing back again. "Tell me about Brother Patrick," he said.

Conor, who had been two paces ahead of the priest, sensed something beneath the question, but when he looked back, Farther Hartigan was intent on examining a piece of fungus on the bark of a dead ash tree. "What do you want to know, Father?" he asked cautiously.

"Well, maybe I shouldn't tell you this," said the priest, "but I know a lot about the brother. He and I go back a long way. We're the same age, you know, and we studied in the junior seminary together. I don't think anything you tell me would surprise me."

Conor told him then, all about the ritual humiliations, the physical and verbal abuse. Once he started he could not stop, and the words flooded from him as if a dam had opened. By the time he had finished, he was scarlet with embarrassment.

All Father Hartigan said when he was finished with the story was: "I see," in a quiet, casual sort of way, making Conor feel even more embarrassed. He had gone too far, said much too much.

They were just about to cross a drain between two fields and he jumped it ahead of his companion, again moving a few paces ahead. They had taken a route that led them in a wide circle, and ahead of him he could now see the house. Head low, in despair that he had made a fool of himself—that the priest would consider him to be an immature crybaby who could not take his knocks—he walked at a pace that he knew taxed the priest's stamina. And behind him he could actually hear Father Hartigan's chest wheezing as he struggled to keep up.

But when they were still about a hundred yards away from the house, the curate caught up with him and took his arm. Conor went rigid. If Father Hartigan noticed Conor's tension, he did not show it. "Listen to me now,

Conor,'' he said, ''do you remember the promise I made you back at the presbytery? That you would have nothing to fear from Brother Patrick?'' Conor nodded. He could feel his cheeks burning and was still furious with himself. Then he was flummoxed by the priest's next words. ''Well, I think I can guarantee,'' said Father Hartigan, ''that as from today, you will never have to suffer at his hands like that again.''

''How are you going to do that, Father?''

''That's for me to know, Conor,'' said Father Hartigan, ''that's private. But I give you my personal word. All right?''

In his deepest heart, Conor felt that the priest was overstepping the mark. What could anyone do to protect anyone from Brother Patrick? But when Father Hartigan extended his hand, he shook it. ''All right so,'' he said. For the first time, he realized he was taller than his new friend.

They encountered no one on the long driveway into the school, and when they pulled up in front of the facade, it was as lifeless as if this Monday morning fell in the middle of the school holidays. As they got out of the car, however, Conor heard through the open windows the familiar sounds of unison chanting, faint notes of a piano scale, the clatter he recognized as some brother threw a duster against the blackboard. His heart started to thump.

The door was answered by the school principal himself. ''Morning, Brother Camillus!'' said Father Hartigan cheerfully.

''Thought it would be you!'' replied the principal. He was bespectacled and rotund and permanently harassed, but the boys in St. Kevin's, while treating him with the wary respect due his status, acknowledged amongst themselves that he was not the worst of them. ''Come on in,'' he said now, taking the priest's hand. ''How're you keeping, Tom?'' He closed the big door behind them. ''This man here gave us a fright. Just as well it was yourself that found him.'' He talked about Conor as though he were a package gone astray in a railway station.

The three of them stood for an awkward second. Conor was again aware of the overpowering smell of floor polish, at this time of day overlaid with the aroma of cooking cabbage.

"I'd like a word with you in private, Aidan," said Father Hartigan, breaking the awkwardness. To Conor, the use of the brother's given name gave him a humanity he and the other boys rarely considered. "Sure thing, sure thing, sure thing!" the brother replied, flinging open the door to the parlor. "Wait you out here, O Briain," he said over his shoulder as he cantered into the room. "Yeah," said Father Hartigan before he closed the parlor door, "you wait out here, son." And although Conor could not be certain, he thought he saw a wink.

He strained to discern individual words in the murmur of voices that came through the heavy parlor door, but he could not distinguish anything and did not have the courage to go any closer. He whiled away the time by counting the number of black and white squares in the floor tiles but was too nervous to concentrate and kept losing count. He was examining the two pictures in the hall, one, a gloomy portrait of the school's founder, the other a garish photograph of Pius XII, when he heard the door of the parlor reopen. Father Hartigan came out first. He walked across the hall and took Conor's arm. "Right!" he said. "Come on. Walk me to my car."

Conor looked for permission at the head brother, who was rocking on the balls of his feet and fidgeting with something in his cassock pocket. He could not interpret the principal's expression, but as he hesitated, the brother waved him out the door. "Go on, go on, go on, go on!"

When they got to the car, Farther Hartigan opened the door and then turned to the boy. His face was deadly serious. "Now listen, Conor. If you mind your P's and Q's and do your work, you'll have no more trouble in this school."

"What—what did you say to him?" Conor stammered.

"What I said is neither here nor there. I told you before that Brother Patrick and I go back a long way—and I know Camillus well enough too. That's all you need to know—except this—"

Taking a crumpled envelope out of his pocket he rummaged around in the glove compartment of the car, extracting a ballpoint pen. He scribbled something on the envelope and handed it to Conor. "That's my telephone

number. If you need me for anything—I mean *anything*—
you telephone me, all right? I've told Brother Camillus
that I'm giving you this permission and he will arrange
that you get to the telephone.''

Conor looked at him in stupefaction.

"Take that look off your face!'' The priest gave him a
friendly thump on the bicep. "Now, I don't expect you
to ring me when you fancy the need for a bar of chocolate. But do ring me if you need to talk. All right?''

Still dumbstruck, Conor nodded.

The priest hopped into the car and started the engine,
roaring off down the driveway.

It was not until that night, in the dormitory, that Conor,
while transferring the telephone number from the back
of the envelope to his writing case, found that the envelope contained a five-pound note. He was putting the
writing case away in his locker when he heard Brother
Patrick's heavy tread on the boards of the dormitory floor.
The curtains of his cubicle swished open and the brother
stood framed huge in the opening. Conor's immediate
instinct was to cower, but instead, he got out of bed and
stood as tall as he could. Brother Patrick and he stared
at one another. In the semi-darkness he could see that
the brother's fists were bunched at his sides.

"The big fella!'' said the brother. "Look at the big
fella!'' A gob of spittle shot out of his mouth and rested
on his chin as he spoke, but Conor was able to resist
staring at it. The stand-off continued for what seemed
like an eternity, but it was the brother who retired first.

A week after Conor's return to school, Micheál O
Briain and his brother, Seán, were stranded by weather
on Inishmaan, the middle island. They were not the only
ones from Inisheer; two of their neighbors were stranded
too and so were several of the Inishmore men. The drink
in the pub that night was recently landed and in great
condition, so the pub was full and raucous. Micheál had
gone outside to relieve himself and Seán was minding his
own business in a corner when, from behind him, he
heard a sudden explosion of talk more furious than the
rest. There was a loud crack, a tinkle of glass, and then
a silence as all the talk edged away.

He looked around. The two Inisheer men were on their

feet and had been joined by his brother, who held a broken bottle, jagged edge pointed at one of the men from Inishmaan. Seán, slightly addled from drink but not yet drunk, had no idea what the row was about but immediately got up off his chair and went to stand shoulder-to-shoulder with his brother and neighbors. The four of them, packed tightly together, presented a belligerent unit which drew four of the other Inishmaan men to stand with their own man, still being threatened by Micheál's bottle.

Five to four, the two groups stood facing one another, necks stretched like stalking dogs, and for a full minute the pub was as still as a tomb. Then the woman of the house, who had been away from behind the bar, came back and saw what was happening. With the base of a pint glass, she banged the bar loudly and shouted at them to ease off, to sit down or to get out.

Stiff-legged, the men from Inisheer backed out through the door. When they were outside in the darkness, Seán turned to his brother. *"Cad a thárla?"*

He saw that Micheál was reluctant to tell him what had led to the incident, so he turned to one of the other men. *"Tada, tada!"* muttered the neighbor, but Seán did not believe it was nothing. The man seemed about to say something else, but Micheál turned on him, catching him threateningly by the lapels of his jacket. The man had had enough: "Leave me go, you!" he shouted.

"Leave him go!" Seán stepped in between the two of them and pulled them apart. While Micheál stood glowering, the neighbor, keeping an eye on him, brushed off his lapels and told Seán that the man from Inishmaan had made insulting remarks about recent goings-on in Inisheer.

"About what?" Seán was genuinely puzzled.

The neighbor pulled his collar around his throat. "Nothing, nothing. Loose talk. Changelings. That sort of talk."

"Nobody will say that about me and my house!" Seán and the other two barely managed to restrain Micheál as he rushed again toward the door of the pub. The struggle to subdue him took the combined strength of the other three.

"Let's go home!" Seán gasped when at last the melee

had subsided and Micheál had calmed sufficiently. Then for a minute it looked as though the fight would flare up all over again. "I don't want to go home!" Micheál roared. "Nobody says that about my house. I'll get those fuckers!"

It was not the first time there had been allegations about changelings on the island. Many of the older people on all three islands and even on the mainland, still believed that an unexpected recovery from illness by a really sick child could be attributed to the fairies. The fairies, it was said, snatched the sick child and substituted one of their own.

The four men from Inisheer walked in silence to where their currachs were tied up. Although it was still raining, the wind had calmed while they had been drinking, and faintly across the Sound, they could see a pinpoint of light where some wife had set an oil lamp in the window to guide her husband home.

Seán and Micheál said nothing as they got into their currach and set off. But when they were halfway across, Seán, who was sitting in front of his brother, heard Micheál repeat to himself that no one would get away with connecting his house with changelings.

3

Christian, long-legged in tennis whites, took the front stairs two at a time, Flash bounding by his side. Although still far off his adult height, the boy was beautiful, with an athletic, wide-shouldered body and clear, healthy eyes.

The sudden noise was an island of life in the dead house, and although he was very conscious of making a disturbance, Christian did not care. He was sick to the teeth of living in this mausoleum. He was fourteen years old, it was a Saturday, and he couldn't wait to get on over to Dick's house to have a bit of *fun*.

Flash panting happily beside him. he flung open the door of his room and surveyed the chaos. Although she did vacuum the rug, the housemaid was under orders not to pick up after him, and his grandfather had made Christian's allowance dependent on his keeping his room tidy himself. Today was allowance day and the room was a disaster. He had better move fast.

He tore into the task, starting the clean up by flinging armloads of laundry into the chute in his bathroom. The pace proved to be a mistake; Flash responded by rushing around him in frenzied circles, snatching socks and T-shirts from the floor and running into corners with them so Christian had to fight him for possession. "Down, Flash!" he ordered again and again, but Flash took no notice. Eventually, Christian aimed an exasperated kick at the dog, who crept away into "his" corner of the room.

Thus freed, and not bothering to be too meticulous in sorting of clean from dirty, or by actually hanging anything in his closets, Christian got through the clothes and the rest of the tidying in double-quick time.

He straightened the coverlet on the bed and then took a breather while he surveyed the room. He had refused to allow anything from his childhood to be thrown out, and his possessions, augmented yearly as he moved from childhood to adolescence, threatened to overwhelm the room. Large though it was, it was now a cross between Aladdin's cave and a crammed five-and-dime store; annually, there was more to keep tidy and less room in which to maneuver.

Everything seemed in order and he called to the dog. Flash dropped something he had been chewing and wagged his tail. On investigating, Christian discovered that what Flash had been worrying was his stuffed rabbit, comfort of his childhood: "Give, Flash!" he shouted but his voice, which had begun to break, cracked and swooped alarmingly. Doubly irritated, as the dog picked up the rabbit again to give it to him, he pulled the toy from Flash's teeth, ripping the threadbare covering so that some of the kapok spilled out on the floor. "Now look what you've done!" he said crossly and, to his horror, found he was dangerously close to tears. He picked up some of the kapok and stuffed it back inside the shell, but the rabbit, beyond repair, drooped in his hands like a limp and mangled sausage. Embarrassed about his attachment to the wretched thing, he was returning the rabbit to its customary place on one of the shelves when from below, he heard Bridie's voice, calling him down to lunch.

His grandmother was as usual presiding at the small lunch table at one end of the dining room; his grandfather was in his usual chair to her left.

Everything was as usual and Christian could have screamed. Just once he wished they could do something out of the ordinary in this house, even something as mundane as changing places at the table or even changing tables. The massive table that ran down the center of the room had not been used for years.

Christian's grandfather looked up from that morning's *Tribune*. "Room clean?" Even the question never varied from one Saturday to the next and always grated on Christian's nerves. Nevertheless, he did not dare give an overtly smart-alec answer, contenting himself with injecting as much insolence into his reply as he dared: "Yes, it is, *as usual*, Grandpa," he said, but as far as he could tell, the subtlety was wasted on his grandfather, who had already returned to his newspaper.

Christian slipped into his chair and his grandmother passed the butter to him. "I see Lew Hoad won Wimbledon again, Chris." He loved his grandmother, but more and more lately, he was finding that he despised her pathetic little attempts to pick subjects that might engage him in conversation. "Uh-huh!" he said, his mouth full of bread.

Noisily, Malcolm folded his newspaper. "Don't talk with your mouth full, Christian."

"I didn't!" Christian spluttered indignantly, but his grandmother cut in, "Leave it, leave it now, you two!" She turned to her husband. "The boy's right this time, Malcolm, he didn't actually say any words." Further conversation or argument was cut short by the housekeeper's arrival with the soup. She served it in silence, and for the next few minutes, the only sound in the room was the clattering of spoons on plates.

Christian's grandmother spoke again when they were all finished. "Would you like to go to the ballgame this afternoon, Chris? Grandpa thinks he might go."

"No, thank you," said Christian, reaching for another roll. He spoke politely but kept his eyes fixed firmly on the roll. His grandfather made an effort. "It's the Cubs and the Pirates. Should be a good one . . ."

"No, thank you," Christian repeated, "I have other plans."

"Oh?" His grandmother took up the running. "That's nice! So what are you doing this afternoon, Christian?"

"Going to Dick's." Christian spread butter on his roll so liberally that it made little slopes at the edges. He bit hard into it, concentrating on the way it oozed between the cracks in his teeth. "Here's a good idea," said his grandmother. "Maybe Dick could go with you?" Again she looked at his grandfather: "That'd be okay with you, wouldn't it, Malcolm?"

"Certainly," said Malcolm. "That's if Christian will deign to come. He has not been all that keen lately on his family's company."

Christian did not reply. He masticated slowly and obviously, swallowing every few seconds. The ploy worked. With satisfaction, he noted the mottled flush rising from his grandfather's neck to suffuse his face. "Sorry, Grandpa," he said sweetly when he had followed the last morsel, "but I didn't want to talk with my mouth full. No offense about the ballgame, but not today, thank you. Dick and me might *watch* it all right—"

"Dick and I!" corrected his grandfather immediately.

"Sorry! Well, as I was saying, Dick *and I* might watch the game on TV. We haven't decided yet. We'll see."

"Suit yourself." Abruptly, his grandfather changed the subject. "You know, Cordelia," he said, "I've been watching Bridie lately. Can you believe she's been with us more than thirty years? Time we were thinking of her future?"

"You mean let her go?" Christian forgot the subtleties of the game he was playing. He was genuinely outraged. Bridie Loftus meant a great deal to him and he could not envisage Greentrees without her warm, bosomy presence. "Oh, now," said his grandmother hastily, "nothing like that, Chris! What your grandfather means is some sort of honorable retirement. Isn't that right, Malcolm? Bridie is getting on a bit, you know. She must be tired. She must have considered such a thing herself . . ."

Further discussion was cut off as the subject arrived with a platter of roast beef and vegetables. Christian was fuming. How could they, how could *he*—of course, his grandmother would never dream of being so callous— how could they even *think* of getting rid of Bridie?

"Thank you, Bridie," he said loudly as he was served. His tone drew a curious look from the housekeeper. "What's up with you, Christian?" she asked.

"Oh, nothing!" said Christian. "Nothing much. Just the usual."

"Mind your manners!" said Malcolm sharply; then, picking up his spoon, "That'll be all. Bridie. We'll ring if we need you."

"Yes, Bridie," echoed Christian, glaring at his grandfather, "we'll ring if we need you!"

"Yerra whisht outa that!" Bridie smiled. She had lived too long in this house to be upset by its internal ripples.

Malcolm waited until she had left the room. "Christian, I won't have that!"

"What, Grandpa? You won't have what?"

"Any more of this behavior. That's what I won't have. You apologize this instant!"

"For what?" Christian appealed to his grandmother. "What did I do, Grandma?"

"Please, Malcolm, just drop it now, will you? The boy means no harm."

"Oh, yes he does. He's constantly picking arguments. His tone of voice while he addressed me in that way in front of Bridie was nothing short of disgraceful." Malcolm's color was heightened again and the fork trembled in his hand.

"Please, please." Cordelia's tone was soothing. "Come on now, Malcolm, just eat your lunch. You too, Christian. For goodness' sake, will the two of you stop behaving like geese . . ."

"If he says one more impertinent word, he goes without his allowance."

"I'm sure he won't. Now, let's all eat our lunch. It's getting cold, and after all Bridie's trouble . . ."

Christian bent his head to his meal, bolting it down without tasting a single mouthful. The most awful thing in the world was dependence, he thought savagely. And dependence on such a measly allowance, too! Lately he had begun to question his grandfather's right to use money as a bartering tool for good behavior. He knew his allowance was drawn off income from a trust fund set up for him after his parents' death and thought the present system deeply unfair. It was his money, damn it, he thought, using his knife on his meat as though it were a hacksaw. His grandfather had no right to dole it out as if every dime were being wrenched from somewhere deep in his own soul.

The tension spread across the table, so dense that even Cordelia could not penetrate it. Now Christian deliberately made noise, scraping gravy over his vegetables, chinking his glass against his plate. Someday, he thought . . . Someday he'd get even.

"How's the track going?" asked Cordelia, again trying to normalize the situation. Christian was well on his way to becoming a star on his high school athletics team, and she knew that this was one subject on which he could be drawn out.

But today he would not. "Fine!" he muttered.

"Answer your grandmother this instant!"

"I did! I did answer her!"

"Malcolm—" Cordelia began again, but this time the old man would not be mollified.

"I'm sick, sore, and teed off with this, Cordelia. I won't have it in my own house, I'm telling you—I won't be responsible for my actions."

"*Now* what have I done?" Christian appealed to his grandmother.

"Your grandmother asked you a civil question. She asked you how you were getting on in track. Answer her this instant!"

Christian felt almost exultant. He was certainly winning this one; his grandfather was almost apoplectic. "Sorry, Grandma," he said. "I'm getting along fine at track. Coach says if I keep it up I might make the nationals." He left a pause and then turned to his grandfather. "Will that do, Grandpa?"

"Young pup!" Malcolm put down his knife and fork. "Pity you can't apply some of this energy to your grades . . . If I'd had my way you'd be at school in the East. That would have straightened you out. But your grandmother wouldn't have any of it."

"I *told* you, Grandpa, those grades weren't finished ones. I *told* you that the finals will be better." Christian had no inclination to open up, once again, the thorny subject of his academic achievement—or nonachievement. "Could I be excused?" He turned to his grandmother.

"Not waiting for dessert?" she replied. "I smelled Bridie's apple pie."

Christian, who would not have deliberately hurt his grandmother for the world, was sorry that she was so evidently distressed, but the situation had progressed too far for appeasement. All he wanted was to get out of there. "No, thank you," he said through tight lips, "may I go now?"

When his grandmother nodded, he got up and left the room without a backward glance, closing the door with exaggerated care.

Molly Ní Bhriain's day-to-day life on Inisheer was that of any little girl; as soon as she was big enough, she learned to fasten her petticoat, to tie her laces; she helped her mother with the chores; on fine days she played outside with the collie, which she had named Beauty; on days that were too cold or wet to go out, she learned her prayers, her numbers, and her letters from her mam at the kitchen table. Molly was looking forward to going to school and was a willing learner because her mam had told her over and over again how much of an advantage it would be to equal to the other pupils on her first day.

But today, the 26th of May, was going to be a big day, maybe the biggest in her life, Molly thought when she woke up. She was exactly five years, three months and twenty-six days old, and on this day she was going to the mainland for the very first time.

It was always easy to know exactly how old she was, because her mam had taught her the calendar and she could count from her birthday on the first of February, *La 'le Bhríde*, the feast of St. Brigid, patron saint of Ireland. It was a good day to have your birthday, her mam always said, because it was the first day of spring. Molly was a bit doubtful about that at first, because each year, when she looked out of the window on her birthday, it was usually very cold and wet and stormy. But her mam had told her that on this day, under the ground, all the plants started to uncurl their leaves, getting ready to push them up into the fresh air. Molly felt privileged then. And she pitied anyone who had a birthday on any ordinary old date.

For weeks she had been counting off the days, marking them in pencil on the calendar on the kitchen wall. Now that she was nearly five and a half, her mam said she was old enough not to get lost and that was why she was taking her. And what's more, she and her mam were going to make a real outing of it and stay in a real lodging house for the night. Molly had never spent a night anywhere but in her own bed.

Today she woke early, with a lovely fluttery feeling all over, and the first thing she saw, hanging on the big nail in the wall over her bed, was the blue silk frock. She knelt up on the bed now and touched it; it must be just about the most beautiful dress in the whole world, she thought. It had yellow teddy bears chasing each other all around the hem and a yellow sash which tied in a big bow at the back; when she had tried it on, it had felt cool and sort of slippy against her bare legs and made a rustling noise when she moved. There was a real foreign smell off it too, not surprising, of course, because it had come in a parcel from America, not to them—they had no relatives in America—but to the Ketts up the road. The parcel had come from the Ketts' auntie in Boston, but Aine Kett was still too small to wear it and her mother had loaned it to Molly's mam so Molly could look respectable for her first trip to Galway.

She hopped out of bed and went to the window. The sun was shining already, but there was nobody else up. She wondered if it was too early to get dressed and strained her ears, listening for the first signs that her mam might be stirring. She knew not to go into her mam's bedroom to wake her up; her dadda would be annoyed and would shout. There were only the three of them in the house now. Conor was still at school in Galway and Brendan was away in Birmingham working at a job, which meant he could send home money. Her mam kept the money in a big jar on the mantel and used it to buy things she had never before been able to afford, like jam and a cloth for the table and knitting wool and Sunday shoes for Molly. They even had curtains on the kitchen window now.

She put her ear right up against the closed door of her bedroom but could hear no sounds in the rest of the house. If only she knew what time it was! Maybe she would ask Santy for a clock for Christmas. Or maybe she would buy one today in Galway . . .

Molly climbed back into bed and put in the time by watching a line of sunshine crawling along her wall. It started with a shape like a pencil, right beside her window. Then, slowly, the top of the shape stretched out and stretched out, pulling the rest with it until there was another window on her wall, bright yellow, just like the teddy bears on the dress.

At last! There was the door of her mam's room opening!

She jumped out of bed and ran into the kitchen. Her mam, who was ladling water from the can into the kettle, scolded her. "Molly! You'll catch your death. Put something on. . . ."

Molly ran back into her bedroom and put a jumper on over her nightdress. Then she took her porridge bowl from the dresser and sat in her place at the table, swinging her legs. She was disappointed that her mam was not yet dressed in her good clothes, just in her old house skirt and shawl. She watched impatiently while her mam raked the embers in the fire and then stirred the porridge in the skillet over it.

"Cathain a bhfuil muid ag imeacht?" she asked. She knew better than to start annoying her mam right away about how long it would be until they would be going, but she couldn't help herself, the words just burst out.

Her mam did not answer, just threw her eyes to heaven.

Molly finished her breakfast in jig time and then wished she hadn't, because the hours just slowed down and slowed down until they were only crawling. And still it wasn't time to go yet.

Then she had to endure being washed. Molly hated with all her heart being washed. When, on Saturday nights her Mam took out the galvanized bath and set the kettles to boil, she always got a sick feeling in her tummy; sometimes she could not help crying, especially when the water was being poured over her head. At least, she thought, grateful for small mercies, she was not getting a bath today; just an ordinary wash with the face cloth. She screwed up her eyes and tried not to wriggle. After the wash, her mam combed her hair then—finally!—helped her into the frock and tied the sash.

When she was all dressed, she did a twirl, and her mam stood back and told her she looked like a little princess. So she twirled again. She certainly did feel like a little princess.

She picked up the new patent leather shoes with the strap across the instep—each shoe stuffed with a new white sock. *"Anois?"* she pleaded, but her mam would not allow her to put on the shoes yet, in case she would scuff them.

So she busied herself by checking, for the hundredth time, the contents of her new white plastic handbag. The handbag had a lovely sharp new smell off it, but the gilt clasp kept springing open because she had put too much in it: her money, the sandwiches for the journey—made with ''shop'' marmalade—her clean hanky, and two

brown paper bags. These were for her shopping. She had
a whole pound she had been saving since Christmas.

When she could think of nothing more to do, she went
outside into the sunshine to wait.

The *Naomh Eanna* was already at anchor in the deep
water out in the bay, her cranes busy. When at last Molly's mam came out, carrying her shopping bag and two
old hens tied together inside a lobster pot, Molly almost
cheered and her heart began to beat with excitement and
nerves. It was really here; the adventure was really starting.

She knew they were hoping to sell the hens in the market around the Spanish church; it all sounded very exotic
and exciting since Molly had never been to a market and
the only church she had ever seen was the little chapel
on the island. As her mam went back inside to make sure
she hadn't forgotten anything, Molly peered closely at
the hens and couldn't help feeling a bit sorry for them.
Bundled so close together in the lobster pot that they
seemed to be one big hen with two heads, they looked
really surprised and bewildered.

Her mam came back out: *"Ar aghaidh linn!"* and they
were off.

Beauty trotted in front of them as they walked down
the hill from their house. Molly had seen the *Naomh
Eanna* lots of times before, but this time it was different
and she was a bit nervous. The steamer looked huge, as
big as a castle, especially beside the currachs that were
moving in the water all around her, taking her cargo.

She watched as the men on the ship unloaded a cow
and two heifers. They fastened the animals into special
slings attached to the cranes on the ship and then swung
them high, out over the water, lowering them into the sea
where the men in the currachs caught them and towed
them the fifty yards into the shallows. Several small boys
dashed into the waves then and hooshed the cattle, water
running like rivers off their backs, safely on to dry land.
Molly didn't help today, of course, because today she had
to keep herself tidy.

The last loads came ashore, cartons of tinned groceries, dusty bags of cement, planks of wood and barrels
of porter, fresh bread, eggs, a side of bacon to be cut
into rashers, a big piece of beef, tomatoes, newspapers,

and mail. There were two chimney pots for a house being built by Marcus O Briain, one of Molly's cousins, a second-hand bicycle for a distant relative of her mother's; an eiderdown for a double bed, several coils of shiny new rope, a gross of scholars' copybooks, and a box of tungsten light bulbs for the island houses that had the electric light. Any other time, Molly would have been rooting around with the other children, checking on everything, but today she couldn't care less what the ship brought in.

Eventually she was able to climb with her mam into one of the currachs to be rowed out. She held tightly to her mam's hand; the sea, as it got deep, frightened her; she felt she had nothing under her feet and that she was already falling in. She could just imagine what it must be like to fall in, how cold it would be and how dark, how she would smother . . .

And when they came alongside the steamer, the deck seemed so high as to be on top of a mountain, but she was helped on to the boarding ladder by one of the men. Another man took her hand as she climbed onto the deck. From up here the sea was not so frightening, although she did keep a wary distance from the rail. There were bars, but there was a big gap between them and she felt it would be very easy to fall through.

The *Naomh Eanna* sounded her horn and made Molly jump. But then there was a sort of grinding noise. That was the anchor coming up, her mam said. The engines roared, sending an exciting feeling through the soles of Molly's feet, and then they were really on their way.

Out in the open water the ship started to roll a bit from side to side, but Molly, sitting so close beside her mam, felt safe enough. She watched over the stern as Inisheer got smaller and smaller until she couldn't even see her house. When she couldn't see it anymore, she leaned back and looked up at the sky, but quite soon she had to stop that; it was like the sky and the clouds were moving very fast and gave her a funny, sick feeling in her tummy. So instead she concentrated on watching the gulls which were following them across to Galway.

It was ages and ages before they got to the quayside and Molly was even getting a bit bored, but at last they were there.

Then Molly couldn't believe her eyes and ears. The

noise and bustle and the crowds and crowds of people!
More people than she could ever have imagined there
were in the whole world! Awestruck, she held tight to
her mam's tweed skirt as they came down the gangway
and went into the streets, gazing at the pavements and
the tall houses—all crammed together side by side—all
the shops and horses and motor cars and money changing
hands and people speaking English. It was all too much
all together.

They went to the market right away, and although the
hens were haggled over and bought immediately by a
tinker woman, Molly was disappointed with the Spanish
Church. It was huge all right but made only of ordinary
gray stone and not some sort of red Spanish stuff as she
had imagined.

When they left the market, they walked as far as a huge
open space her mam said was called Eyre Square. They
sat in the sun for a while, eating their sandwiches and
washing them down with a bottle of milk they had bought
from a shop, and Molly was so full of questions and chat
that her mam got tired of them and told her to hush. But
in a nice way. Molly could see she wasn't really annoyed.

When they had finished their meal, they set off all
around the town, and soon her mam's shopping bag was
nearly filled to the top with string and candles and par-
affin wicks, matches, white bandages, cough linctus,
baking powder, sweet cake, apples, more shop marmalade, Cadbury's chocolate, new boots for Molly's dadda,
a ribbon for her hair . . .

After a couple of hours her new shoes hurt, but the
best part was still to come. She still had not spent her
pound.

At long last her mam brought her to a very special
shop. It was huge, packed with treasure: tons and tons
of sweets, little bottles and brushes and pencils and tubes
that her mam said were for coloring ladies' faces, birthday cards and writing pads and big rolls of brown wrapping paper; there were sparkling necklaces made with
diamonds; there were rows of books and comic books.
And everything was laid out on little platforms so you
didn't have to ask the shop girl to show you anything but
could pick it up yourself. Molly's eyes were out on stalks
and she had a terrible time deciding what to select.

Then her mam brought her to a special place at the back of the shop. It was like toyland, filled with all the colors of the rainbow; she saw not only dolls and coloring books, but beautiful little doll carriages and go-cars and cars, train sets and hoops and spinning tops and a heap of tiny little donkeys on round stands. Her mam showed her how to work them: when you pressed the stand, the donkey's legs collapsed. Molly fell in love with this and nearly bought it.

Then she forgot the donkey and fell in love with a bright red kite. The Ketts had had a kite once, but the wind on Inisheer had been too strong for it and it had broken loose and flown away over the sea.

After changing her mind a dozen times, Molly finally settled for a doll with real curly hair; the doll, which was dressed in a lovely satin dress, was a sleeping doll—her blue eyes closed when you put her on her back.

Even after buying the doll, she still had more than ten shillings left. So she bought a book in English called *Dancing Star* because she liked the picture of the lady in it. The lady's name was Anna Pavlova and she was from Russia and was a very famous ballerina. Her mam said she would read a bit of it to her that night in bed and would explain the English words.

She bought a pair of shoelaces for her dadda and a lovely goldy tiepin for Conor. She bought a toy watch for Aine Kett to thank her for the frock and then, because she couldn't decide what to buy for Brendan, went back and bought him a pair of shoelaces too.

And then, while her mam was busy looking at something else, Molly sneaked up to where the jewelry was and picked out a bracelet studded with huge glittering diamonds, white and blue and green. She gave the bracelet to her mam, who was absolutely thrilled, tearing open the bag and putting on the bracelet right then and there. Molly spent the rest of her money on sweets, enough sweets, which the girl shoveled into a big paper bag, to last her for weeks.

When they were finished shopping, they went to a photographer's studio. Molly was very frightened by the bright light and the man's brusque manner and the loud popping sound made by the flashbulb when it went off as he was photographing her mam. She sat on the floor, dreading her own turn. And when it came, it turned out that it was all right. But although the photographer told her to smile and she tried her best, she just couldn't make herself do it.

The two of them said good-bye to the photographer, then went to have a cup of tea in a restaurant. They stayed at their table until the restaurant closed and then, because it was still too early to go to the lodging house, went back to Eyre Square for a bit of a rest. They sat on a bench and her mam put an arm around her and Molly felt so comfortable she dozed off. When she woke up the sun was just setting and it was time to go.

She was a bit disappointed, though, when she saw the lodging house; she had expected a sort of palace, but when she and her mam got into their room, it was very small, even smaller than her own bedroom at home. And the walls were a horrible color, brown, with dark stains along the top; and when she climbed into it, the bed was lumpy and there was a funny smell off the blankets.

But she did love the cozy snug feeling she got as she watched her mam brushing out her own hair, which she usually wore fastened in a knot at the back of her head. The hairbrush made a soft, shushing sound; the hair was sort of faded now, like old hay, but Molly knew—because her mam had told her, that when she had been young it had been as blonde as Molly's own.

They were too tired to start reading *Dancing Star* so they just snuggled up together in the narrow bed, warm and safe. Across the room, on a chest of drawers, Peggy, Molly's new doll, seemed to smile at her.

Such a day!

Christian parked his bicycle against the stoop of Dick's home, one in a row of almost identical brick-and-clapboard houses built alongside the railroad tracks in what his friend's father cheerfully called the low rent area of Evanston. Christian had brought over a brand-new Elvis record, and something else, a bulky brown envelope. He took them off the carrier of the bike, being careful with the record which he had padded with a teeshirt.

Dick was the eldest of seven; his father was a desk sergeant in the Evanston police department, and as Christian came level with the screen door, he could al-

ready hear the hubbub from inside. In Dick's house people competed for ear space and there were always at least
two people talking together, raising their voices against
the radio and the recently acquired television. The decibel level was one of the things that attracted Christian
and why, given a choice, he would have spent all of his
time in Dick's home rather than in the elegant but dismal
spaciousness of his own.

He could never see Greentrees through Dick's eyes. To
him, his grandfather's house was as oppressive as a cemetery and just about as much fun. More and more since
his parents' death, he seemed to live at Dick's. He pulled
open the screen door. ''Hi!'' he said to the room in general.

Two of Dick's little brothers, three and four, were
wrestling with one another, rolling around on the floor;
one of their sisters, six years old and therefore in a position of authority, was standing over them, hands on
hips, ordering them to ''stop it! stop it this instant!''
They took as little notice of her as they did of Christian's
arrival.

Another sister, eleven years old, was holding a baby,
feeding it from a bottle while watching the flickering
black and white images of an old Fred Astaire movie.
She, at least, acknowledged Christian's arrival with a
terse ''Hi!''

He walked through to the kitchen, picking up one of
the two kittens that were chasing one another around the
floor. ''Hi Mrs. Spielberg!'' he said to Dick's mother,
who was stirring something in a mixing bowl at the sink.

She turned with a start. ''Oh, hello, Christian,'' she
answered, ''how nice to see you.'' It was what Christian
had expected her to say; it was what she always said,
even though she might have seen him only the previous
night or even within the previous few hours. But somehow, although sameness and routine irked him at home,
here he found it comforting. Putting down the kitten, he
crossed to the refrigerator and opened it: laden down
with food, most of it still edible, it exhaled a strong
breath of garlic.

Christian prospected through the bowls and pots of
leftovers—Mrs. Spielberg was a very good, if erratic,
cook—the half-filled jars of peanut butter, jelly, bowls of

Jello, containers of baby formula, opened packets of bologna, liverwurst, snack crackers, and selected the larger of two half-eaten hot dogs. Mrs. Spielberg, having watched the selection, turned back to her mixing bowl. "Why don't you make yourself a sandwich, Christian?" she asked, turning on the radio set on a little shelf over the sink. The kitchen was filled with the voice of Perry Como, and Dick's mother raised the volume.

"Naw, that's okay, Mrs. Spielberg," said Christian, having to raise his voice to compete with the music, "I just ate. Where's Dick?"

"In the basement—I think!"

"Thanks!" Christian stepped over a bundle of magazines at the top of the stairs down to the basement, picking his way down by the greenish light that came from the half-window near the ceiling. He threaded his way toward Dick, dark-haired and already inclining to fat, through an obstacle course of broken furniture, suitcases, cases of soda, and heaps of laundry, and flopped down on an old car seat beside his friend, who was absorbed in a *Spiderman* comic book. "Hi!" said Dick, without lifting his eyes from the page. "Wanna watch the ballgame?"

"I don't mind," answered Christian. "I brought 'All Shook Up.' "

"Seventy-eight or L.P.?"

"Seventy-eight. Wanna hear it?"

"Later," said Dick, turning a page, but Christian knew his friend was impressed. 'All Shook Up' was the new Number One. He selected a comic book from the heap beside Dick and began to read.

"Dad agreed to get me a new camera," said Dick, still without lifting his eyes, but his voice betrayed his excitement. Six months previously, he had been given an ancient box Brownie by one of his father's colleagues and had developed a passion for photography, a passion that so far had left his friend cold. "How nice!" answered Christian.

"Shut up! It's important to *me*!"

"*Sorry.*"

After a few minutes, Christian threw his comic book aside. "I brought something else . . ."

"What?" Again Dick did not raise his eyes from the comic book.

"This . . ." Christian picked up the brown envelope and held it out. Something about his voice at last caught Dick's attention. "What is it?" he asked, looking at it.

"I was up in the attic of the house looking for my old baseball glove and I found it in a trunk, with other papers and a pile of old books."

"Yes, but what is it?"

"Why don't you open it and see?"

Dick took the envelope, which was not sealed, and shook out the contents, which proved to be a pile of yellowing newspaper cuttings. He leafed through them. "I've seen most of these before," he said without surprise. "They're all about the crash . . ."

"Yeah, but there's stuff in there about my dad." Christian felt his heart speed up. "They must have kept those ones away from me at the time."

"What kind of stuff?"

"Here, I'll show you—" Christian leaned over and took the pile of cuttings. He searched through them and selected three, handing them back without comment.

His forehead knitted, Dick read the cuttings. Christian watched; he had debated whether or not he should reveal his discovery about his father to Dick—or to anyone. But the discovery had been churning, going through and through his mind, until this morning it had all become too much and he felt he had to talk to someone.

In the immediate aftermath of the crash, it seemed some of the newspapers had dug more than a little into the family background. The three unfamiliar cuttings contained a lot of biographical data about Malcolm Smith, the self-made man, about the tragedies that had continued to dog his life; about his marriage to the beautiful brewery heiress. None of this was news to Christian.

What was news was the biographical sketch of Cal, Christian's father, and Malcolm's difficulties with him. Apparently Cal had nursed early ambitions to become an actor, but all attempts in this direction had failed. He was characterized in all three clippings as a drifter, a borderline alcoholic who dabbled in drugs and gambling and who moved from job to job as frequently as other people ate dinners.

Eighteen months before the air crash, the brewery, engaged in diversification, had acquired a small Midwest cinema chain. Malcolm Smith had placed his son in charge of this subsidiary, hoping that since it had tenuous connections with show-business, Cal might enjoy the work and might settle down. And at first that had seemed to be the case. In his first year, Cal had persuaded the parent company to expand the chain, building three brand-new houses, all of which opened, in the fall of 1952 within two months of each other.

But after Cal's death, when a new man was placed in charge of the chain, he discovered within six weeks that the accounts were in shambles and that the chain itself was almost bankrupt, with letters and demands from creditors, including contractors and building firms, bundled away in the back of a drawer in a filing cabinet. Cal, with the unwitting help of a friend in a local branch of Illinois Trust who had fallen for his charm, had apparently manipulated the money at his disposal and had borrowed more, paying staff but not paying creditors, getting deeper and deeper into trouble; Malcolm Smith had not discovered any of this until three months after his son's death, when the new man, trying to unscramble the mess, was visited by a representative of a gambling syndicate downtown. The representative held promissory notes which showed that Cal had tried to bet and borrow his way out of trouble.

Dick read the clippings one after the other. He made no comment and Christian could not divine his reaction. "What do you think?" he asked when Dick had replaced the three articles on top of the others.

"I don't know what to say . . ." Although Dick looked him directly in the eye, Christian could see he was uncomfortable.

"Pretty terrible things to learn about your dad, don't you agree?"

"But you don't remember him like that, do you? You know what newspapers are like—"

"Don't try to excuse him!" Christian was scornful of any attempts to minimize the enormity of what he had found out.

"I'm not! And don't yell at me. I've done nothing to you."

"Sorry."

"It's okay. I'm sorry too—about this, I mean." Dick indicated the cuttings.

The ceiling creaked and pounded above their heads as another wrestling match—or possibly two—erupted. Both boys raised their eyes. After an interval, Christian said, "What am I going to do, Dick?" His unreliable voice cracked and he put his hand to his throat as though to control it.

"What can you do? Would you look at that!" As a result of the overhead activity, the bulb in the light socket had started to sway on its wire. As Christian watched the bulb, fierce anger against his dead father, against his grandfather, against the world welled up inside him. It was as if sharing the information had set it bubbling. "I dunno," he said, clenching his fists, "but I sure want to do something."

"Like what?" Dick's voice betrayed his discomfort at discussing this situation at all. "That ceiling's going to come down if those little guys don't put a sock in it," he said. Then, after a pause, hesitantly: "If I were you I'd put those cuttings away and forget I'd ever read them."

"How can I?" Christian vented the anger. "Easy enough for you to say. You have everything!"

"Whaddya mean, everything. What do I have that you don't have?" Dick's placid nature was outraged.

"A family, for one thing!" There was a particularly loud thump from upstairs and both of them looked up again. "I'd give anything to have a family like yours, Dick," said Christian in a softer tone. "Even half your family. Anyway, could you do that?"

"Do what?" Dick was still in a snit.

"Sorry I shouted at you," said Christian. "You've been very good. So's your family. It's just that—"

"Don't worry about it," answered Dick, "it's all right."

"Well, could you?" Christian went back to the original question. "I mean, if it was your dad, could you put those clippings away and forget you'd ever read them?"

"Naw," said Dick slowly, "I suppose not."

The noises upstairs stopped abruptly. In the silence, Christian picked up the pile of clippings and fitted them back into their envelope. "I can't stand it, Dick. It's not

fair. And on top of everything else my grandfather—''
Some of the clippings would not fit neatly and he stuffed
them in willy-nilly, almost hoping they would tear.

He looked at his friend. ''Sometimes I wish I was
dead.''

Conor was due home from school about ten days after
Molly's trip to the mainland. On the day he was to arrive,
Molly, escorted by Beauty, left the house very early in
the morning to go down to the beach to watch for the
Naomh Eanna, even though her mam had told her it
would be hours yet.

The sun warmed her face as she stepped outside the
door, and loving the feel of the warm stone under her
bare feet, she sat down immediately on the rock pavement outside her front door to take off her pampooties.
Putting them on the windowsill to keep them safe, she
stood up again and, straining her eyes, looked out to sea.
As often happened when Inisheer baked like this, it was
raining on the mainland only nine miles away. She could
see the rain, slanting down from the sky to the ground,
so gray and dark that behind it, she could barely see the
peaks of The Twelve Bens.

She walked down to the beach, stepping carefully along
the center strand of grass that marked the middle of the
boreen so she would not cut her feet on the stones, stopping now and then to pick a celandine or a few dandeli-
ons from the tufts that pushed out between and under the
stones of the boundary walls. It was so still and silent,
that when she pulled the flowers, she could hear the stalks
snapping. A sparrow landed on a wall near where she
studied the shape of one of her flowers, and when the
bird took off again, the whirring of its wings startled her.
Even the larks, which flooded the sky with song, seemed
higher up than usual today.

She searched the horizon when she got to the beach,
but only a little breeze, puffing up patterns along its surface, moved on the empty glittering sea. Keeping one
eye out for any other movement, she passed the time by
riffling through the sand with her fingers, searching for
the shells of sea snail and little pink cowries.

When she tired of this, she wandered down on to the
harder sand over which the tide would travel soon, stop-

ping now and then to jump on it with all her strength, making sure to come down hard on her heels, then stepping aside to watch the water well up into her footprints.

Was that a line of smoke? She shaded her eyes in the direction of the mainland.

But it wasn't. She would have to have patience.

She scooped out little hollows in the sand and inserted her feet into their coolness. Then, her eyes steadily fixed on the horizon, she sat down, curled her arms around her knees, and settled down to wait.

In Galway, the *Naomh Eanna* had not yet cast off. Conor was being seen off at the dockside by Father Hartigan. The two of them, collars up, stood beside Father Hartigan's battered old Volkswagen under the priest's black umbrella. Absorbed in watching the loading of the steamer, they did not speak. The rain drummed on the stretched fabric and Father Hartigan dragged deeply on a Craven A, holding it—lethal and untipped—cupped in his hand so the glowing tip was millimeters from his palm. Abruptly he bent double, coughing as though he would turn his gut inside out.

"Listen, Father," said Conor when the paroxysm had passed, "if you don't give up those coffin nails, you're going to die on me!"

"I know, I know," gasped the priest, tears running down his face, "but a man has to have some vices! Do you want me to start running with loose women?"

Conor smiled. Although still only sixteen, he was a good twelve inches taller than the little priest now. Their relationship had progressed through the years since Father Hartigan had first found him to the point where he took his clerical friend almost for granted; their conversations and discussions, frequently heated, were conducted as though they were equals. Because of his friendship with Father Hartigan, Conor had gained immeasurably in self-confidence and no one in the school, boy or brother, could dent it. "Do you think you might come out, so, Father?" he asked as the steamer's crane boom swung out yet again, taking on a pallet. Although Father Hartigan continued to nag him, the one intimacy he could not adopt was to drop the "Father."

"I will if I can get away, Conor," the priest answered.

"As a matter of fact, I'm almost sure I will. There's a conference I have to go to in Maynooth, but other than that and a few weddings, the summer is fairly clear."

"That'll be great." Conor really was looking forward to the visit. The previous summer they had spent almost a week together on Inisheer. Father Hartigan stayed with the local curate, but since he was on holiday he had no pastoral duties, and he and Conor had spent most of their time walking the island, fishing for mackerel, or swimming in the clean, cold sea. Father Hartigan did not object when Molly tagged along, as she frequently did.

Conor had enjoyed displaying his knowledge of the local flora and fauna. He was aware of a certain amount of sniggering and muttered comments about them as they walked the roads together or bent to examine a gentian, or picked dog roses, or pulled handfuls of wild garlic to bring home with them. But the sidelong glances and half-mocking salutes from the small groups of men they encountered at various crossroads on the island did not bother Conor a whit and he put them down to jealousy.

His mam and dadda could not understand the friendship, he knew that. But he got the feeling, from a few things his mam said especially, that she was secretly proud that a priest would take such interest in her son.

It was nearly time to board. "I'll write to let you know what my plans are, never fear," said Father Hartigan.

"All right, so, Father," said Conor.

"Have you got the magazines?" asked the priest.

"Yes, safe in the bag," replied Conor, patting his battered suitcase. In the past year, Father Hartigan had taken out a postal subscription to *National Geographic* and after reading them himself, passed them on, usually three or four at a time.

"Don't forget to write to Brother Patrick now!"

Conor just grinned, and in farewell, Father Hartigan patted him on the shoulder. He walked up the gangway into the steamer. Ignoring the rain, which streamed off his hair and down under his collar, he leaned on the rail. Father Hartigan was already getting into his Beetle. He slammed the door without looking back and the car began to move. Conor watched until it had gone out of sight around a corner of a building. A faint cloud of blue smoke hung in the air where it had turned.

The weather cleared up when they were about a mile off the Galway coast and the journey was pleasant, over a brisk, choppy sea that halfway across the sound flattened out and became completely calm.

Conor identified Molly on the beach, long before the *Naomh Eanna* was within shouting distance. Her tiny figure, distinctive with its blonde head, jumped up and down, waving frantically with both arms. He waved back, although he doubted if, at that distance, she could pick him out on the deck.

It was half an hour before the vessel anchored and the currachs left the shore to come out. By that time Sorcha had joined Molly on the beach. She did not often wear the Aran shawl, but she had it on now, Conor saw, crisscrossed on her breast, in honor of his homecoming. He was the first to disembark. When the currach he was in got within six feet of the shore, he jumped overboard into the thigh-deep water, not caring that his school shoes and trousers got wet, and humping his suitcase on his back, splashed in to the beach, holding out his free arm to his little sister.

Molly, squealing with joy, danced on the sand, just in front of the breaking wavelets, holding out both of her own arms. When he got to her, Conor flung the suitcase up the beach and swept her off her feet, whirling her around and around in the air. *"Mo chailín, mo chailín! Féach chomh fásta 's ata tu!"* She had definitely grown. Such a big girl now and so lovely. Boys were not supposed to cry, so Conor squeezed his eyes shut and held Molly in the crook of one arm while he hugged his mother with the other. The collie skittered around their heels.

Then the three of them set out for the house.

Micheál was out collecting the lobster pots and Conor was just as glad. He threw his suitcase behind the settle in the kitchen and, ripping off his school uniform, changed into his home clothes, thick tweed trousers and a báinín sweater he would wear all summer.

His ankles stuck out from the turn-ups like the boles of young trees, and Sorcha laughed. "I'll have to let down those trousers—again!" But after she had examined the hems she shook her head in sorrow. "No letting-down left . . ."

"Doesn't matter, Mam!" Conor could not have cared less about his appearance. "These are fine."

Molly stood before him, her hands held shyly behind her back. "What's wrong, a *stóirín*?" he asked, squatting in front of her. She brought her hand out, offering the cheap gilt tiepin. "Ohhh! Look at this. Real gold!" Conor was moved all over again. She nodded. "I got it in Galway when Mam and me went to the mainland."

He fastened the tiepin into the collar of his shirt: "Now I'll have to get a real tie, Molly. When I leave school, *I'll* bring you to the mainland and you can help me buy a proper tie to go with this . . ."

She nodded again gravely, and his heart was flooded with love. It was the first present she had ever given him bought with her own money, and she was so full of grown-up importance. He gave her a hug and then sat at the table where Sorcha had set a meal for him, good bacon and sweet little potatoes all washed down with plenty of milk. Molly climbed into her chair at one end of the table and sat watching him eat, her chin in her hands.

When he was finished, he swung her onto his shoulders and they were off on their travels around the island.

Molly held tight to her brother's head, burying her fists in his black hair. First he brought her to the puffing hole beside the cliff. He had brought her there once before when the sea was running, and each time the white spout of water spumed high into the air through the opening, she had been scared and excited all at once. But it was quiet today, so quiet that Conor let her lie on her belly, holding her feet so she could look straight down into it, to where the green sea heaved like liquid glass far below.

In another place he found primroses in little crevices in the rocks; hidden from the burning light of the sun, they were still blooming despite the lateness of the year. And he showed her where, in a few weeks' time, she would be able to pick harebells. They listened for the cuckoo then and scanned the high sky for a peregrine falcon, one of a pair they had seen last summer, but the falcon, if she was still around, was not hunting today.

And finally, when she was tired, he found a little hollow, sheltered under the rim of a cliff, where they could rest. The hollow was soft with couch grass and she curled up beside him. His side was warm against her cheek, but not as soft as her mam's. He told her he was going to recite a poem for her, one he had learned this term in school. "It's a poem about a place far away from here, Molly, a lovely place where there are high mountains and there is snow in winter and where the cows wear bells around their necks so that even from the cities, the mountains sound like a faraway piano . . ."

The piano in Molly's school had five notes missing and did not sound at all like tinkling bells, but she wrinkled up her forehead and imagined what faraway mountains would sound like, ringing with little bells.

"I'll take you there someday," continued Conor, throwing back his head to look up at the drifting sky. "We'll go there together. The poem is in English, Molly, so pay attention. Don't worry if you don't understand. Just listen to the sounds."

And he began to recite, emphasizing the consonants:

"Do you remember an Inn,
  Miranda?
  Do you remember an Inn?
  And the tedding and the spreading.
  Of the straw for a bedding,
  And the fleas that tease in the high Pyrenees
  And the wine that tasted of the tar?
  And the cheers and the jeers of the young muleteers
  (Under the vine of the dark verandah)?
  Do you remember an Inn, Miranda,
  Do you remember an Inn?
  And the cheers and the jeers of the young muleteers
  Who hadn't got a penny,
  And you weren't paying any,
  And the hammer at the doors and the Din?"

He did not finish the poem, his attention caught by a pair of gulls wheeling lazily above him, screaming on the wind.

Molly was disappointed when he stopped. She had listened intently, and although she understood very few of the words, she responded to their rhythm. She had recognized one line and pulled at his sleeve. "I haven't got a penny either," she said.

He turned on his side and got up on one elbow, "Molly! You understood! How clever you are. You're going to be the scholar of the family. And I'll give you loads and loads of pennies when I get the big job in Dublin!" He tried to tickle her but she was too fast for him, getting away before he could catch her. So he gave up the chase and flopped on his back again to watch the sky.

As she crept in again beside him, she decided that her brother was definitely the most wonderful person in the whole world. But then she felt disloyal to her mam. Her mam was the most wonderful person in the world too. She couldn't sort out whom she loved the most, Conor or her mam.

That whole summer was magical for Molly, at least until the awful day after the céilidhe.

And ironically the day before, the day she and her mam and Conor went across to the Inishmaan céilidhe, was one of the best days of all.

Brendan was home on holidays from his job in Birmingham, but Molly was not surprised that he would not go. He had always been cranky, but he seemed to have become even more so since he had left the house. Because he was a man now and earning, he was given Molly's room while he was home and she had to sleep on the settle bed in the kitchen while Conor slept on the other bed beside the fire. Brendan never emerged from the room until nearly dinnertime.

For the time he was home, Conor and Molly stayed out of his way as much as they could, and although their mam tried all the time to coax him into a better humor, he seemed to want only their dadda's company, frequently going out with him and their uncle in the currach to set the pots—and going down with them afterward to the public house.

Sorcha was longing to see her sisters on Inishmaan, and the céilidhe was a great opportunity, for there would be many boats going from Inisheer. She asked Conor if he would go with her, as Micheál would never have dreamt of taking her, and she would not have gone on her own. "I'll go," Conor had replied, swinging Molly off her feet and above his head, "if I can take my girlfriend with me!'' It was settled then that Micheál's brother, Seán, would take the three of them.

Céilidhes on Inishmaan never got under way properly until nearly midnight, and they would have to stay overnight. So for a whole day beforehand, Molly had to help her mam get ready. The blue silk frock was borrowed again from the Ketts and ironed and folded carefully. Sorcha took her own good dress out of its tissue paper and washed it, hanging it out to dry in the fresh wind. Then, late in the evening, Sorcha, helped by Molly, cooked bacon and made soda bread, making sure there was enough food to feed Brendan and Micheál while they were away.

The next morning the three of them and Seán O Briain set off in his currach, which had a small outboard engine. Seán held the tiller at the stern; Sorcha, surrounded by her bundles and parcels, sat in the bow; and Molly sat proudly beside Conor on the plank seat in the center of the boat. They bounced along on a choppy, bottle-green sea, the spray wetting their faces. Molly, whose uneasiness about the sea had abated only a little as a result of her trip to the mainland, held tight to Conor and licked the spray off her mouth; it tasted cold and salty.

When they were halfway across Foul Sound, they were joined by a school of dolphins.

Dolphins and porpoises, even small whales, were common in the waters around Aran, and Molly had frequently seen them from the shore, but this was her first experience of the animals up close. When the first one rose, she got a terrible fright and gave a little scream, but Conor tightened his arm around her shoulder so she felt safe.

Even their uncle, who was well used to dolphins, got caught up in the excitement and slowed the engine. The school churned up the surface of the sea all around their little craft, in ones and twos and sometimes threes; they made great leaps clear of the water, gazing across at the occupants of the boat each time they leaped. Molly thought their mouths were laughing. She clapped her hands and saw that in the bow, Sorcha too was clapping her hands, laughing with exhilaration. Sorcha's headscarf had slipped down the back of her head and her hair, caught by the strong sea breeze, had come loose.

One of the dolphins, more curious than the rest, kept pace right alongside the currach, traveling only about ten feet away. Each time it surfaced, dark and shiny with water pouring off its back, it smiled directly at Molly, one large eye looking straight into her own. And each time it splashed back into the water she saw hundreds of little rainbows caught in the droplets that fell after the dolphin.

The school stayed with them for about five minutes, and just before it moved off, Molly's dolphin raised itself upright and danced perpendicularly on its tail for a second or two. When it dropped back it raised a wall of spray, so big that some of the water landed on the boat, drenching its occupants.

After that, the rest of the journey was tame. But Sorcha's sisters met the boat at the Inishmaan pier and brought them to the house of the sister who had the biggest cottage, where, in great excitement, they told the story of the dolphins and dried themselves off in front of the range.

All the sisters were there, with their husbands and their children, and they all crowded around the kitchen table, adults sitting, children standing, while they ate a big meal of fish and bacon, with Bird's jelly and custard for dessert. The children were sent out to play then, so the men could smoke and the women could gossip over cups of tea.

Although she had met them before, Molly was shy with her cousins and hung back from the game of hopscotch and skipping. But Conor was involved in discussions with the big boys, and if she was not to be alone, she had no choice but to join in.

As the dusk stole in from the sea, the sisters all started titivating in preparation for the céilidhe. Molly and her mam were squeezed into a bedroom with two of the children of the house. They would be sleeping in the bed, while the two children had been put on a mattress on the floor. It was difficult to move around in the tiny room, but eventually they were all ready. Everyone admired Molly in her princess frock and all the adults remarked on what a big girl she was for her age and how lovely and silky was her blonde hair.

At last, a party of twenty, they all set out for the hall

where the céilidhe was being held. The building was on
a height, and when she was still some distance away,
Molly could see the light streaming from the open door
and could hear, drifting across the tiny fields and stone
walls, the faint sounds of music. She wondered if this
was how it sounded when the mountains in the high Pyrenees rang with bells but was afraid to walk up to Conor
to ask. He was walking ahead with the boy cousins, three
lads bigger than himself and two smaller, absorbed in a
masculine world she knew she could not enter.

Although it was nearly midnight, it was not yet pitch-
dark, and far out to sea, to the west, Molly could see a
streak of pale blue above the horizon. And as she walked
between her mother and one of her aunts, Molly could
see, bobbing like groups of fireflies on the web of boreens all around her, the pinpricks of light cast by scores
of flashlights as people moved toward the hall.

At last they were there. Coming in from outside, Molly
was dazzled and stunned by the level of light and noise.
A great wall of conversation rose over the music being
played by seven musicians, five local men and two stars
on melodeon and flute brought in specially from the big
island. And the smells! Of drink and sweat and worsted
wool as they pushed their way in to the hall through a
crowd of men and boys who were packed three-deep
around the door, of cologne from the women, of cigarette
and pipe smoke, of shellac from the polished floor.

As soon as they got inside the hall, the women called
to her mam; twin-setted and wearing Sunday skirts, they
sat in a beaming row on chairs set against one wall and
made a great fuss over Molly when Sorcha introduced
her. One of them got up immediately and went to bring
her a glass of lemonade.

While she sipped her drink, Molly, fascinated, listened
to the talk, which was all about days and dances long
ago. She watched as the dancers, all ages from three to
eighty, stamped loudly with one foot or both and twirled
and swung.

Then Conor came and lifted her out. She did not know
how to dance, but he whirled her around and around anyway, and then another boy came and took her away from
Conor and whirled her again, so hard that her feet swung
off the floor. When the set ended, Conor took her back

to her mam, but Sorcha was already getting out of the chair, asked up to dance by an old man whose back was humped. The hump did not hinder him and he was as light on his feet as a fairy. Her mother's face was light too, and laughing, and Molly thought she looked beautiful, just as she had when she was laughing at the dolphins in the boat. When the old man brought her back he bowed and stamped his two feet and let out a big "hurrooo!" and said to Molly he hoped she knew that her mother was the best dancer in Ireland.

But as the night wore on, Molly got very sleepy; she had never, except when she was sick, been awake so late. So Conor made a little nest for her out of a bundle of coats and she curled up in a corner of the hall where her mam could check on her from time to time. There were other children sleeping there already, two little boys and another girl, not more than about two, Molly thought. As she drifted off, to the strains of an old-time waltz, her mother, dancing with one of her sisters, passed her by and Molly thought how lucky she was to be the daughter of the best dancer in Ireland.

She did not remember being brought back to the cottage of her aunt, and when she woke up her mam was already getting ready for the trip back to Inisheer. They were leaving early so Sorcha could be home in time to make dinner for Micheál and Brendan.

The trip across Foul Sound was uneventful this time. No dolphins came to ride with them on the calm sea, and above them only a single gull, very white against the slaty gray of the sky, floated lazily, as though it could not be bothered to flap its wings. They were very tired, all four of them. Molly could hardly keep her eyes open.

There was no one on the beach to meet them, but Conor jumped out and dragged the currach up on the beach so Molly and Sorcha did not have to get wet. Then he and Seán turned the vessel over and, balancing it on their heads, carried it above the waterline to where it would be safe. They all said good-bye to Seán and trekked up the hill to the house.

Brendan was nowhere to be seen, but Molly's dadda was sitting by the fireplace. The fire was out. "You took your time!" he said as they came in. Then he stomped out the door and away down the road.

Conor glowered after him, but Sorcha merely sighed and sent Molly out to fetch some turf, while she raked the ashes and set a bit of kindling to start the fire again. She sent Conor to the well for water as the creamery can they used to store it in was nearly empty.

Micheál came back after about an hour and the four of them took their dinner in silence. Brendan was still nowhere in sight, but such was Micheál's mood that none of them dared asked about him.

Molly's dadda sat in his place, stabbing at the food with his fork, never raising his eyes. There was no meat today, only a few salted herrings Sorcha's sister had given her as a gift. Like most of their neighbors, the family ate very little fish, but neither Molly nor Conor made any comment today as they chewed the tough, stringy flesh.

It was a relief when the meal was over. Micheál pushed his chair back from the table without a word, went to the mantelpiece, and took some of the money out of Sorcha's jar. The rain had started while they were eating, and he took his oilskin from its hook behind the door, shrugged himself into it, and went out. As soon as the door banged shut behind him, the other three relaxed. Molly helped her mam clear the plates and mugs off the table and cleaned down the scrubbed surface. Conor took a book out of the bag behind his bed and carried a chair to the window so he could read.

The rain cleared up about teatime and Sorcha sent Molly outside to sit on the wall and report to her when she saw her father and brother coming home. It was nearly seven o'clock by the time she saw them walking up the hill.

Brendan was staggering. Micheál was not so bad, but there was an unsteadiness in his gait and a belligerent thrust to his chin.

The table was already laid for their tea, for just the two of them. The other three had already eaten.

"Let you go away out, Conor," begged Sorcha urgently when Molly reported they were coming and what state they were in. "Slip out and up by the chapel till I get them settled. They'll be better when they've had their tea."

"Mam," Conor answered quietly, "I'll go nowhere.

I'm doing no harm here and neither is anyone else. We'll all just rest easy . . .''

Molly heard and understood this exchange, because when Micheál had drink on him there was usually a row. She wished Conor would go and she would go with him. But when he took up his book again by the window, she crept into a corner of the kitchen and made herself as small as she could.

The two men came through the door. Brendan swayed against the wall and would have fallen if Micheál had not caught him under the arm. Sorcha moved to the table. "The tea's ready, Micheál," she said. Molly's dadda helped Brendan to the table and the two of them sat down. Sorcha poured the tea and made sure the bread was within their reach.

Brendan, however, was too far gone to eat; he sat, head bobbing unsteadily on his neck, reaching out to the food and then changing his mind and letting his hands drop again.

Micheál, on the other hand ate and drank fast, slurping great drafts of tea and stuffing bread into his mouth. After a bit, looking up as he reached for the butter, his eye caught Conor's. "What are *you* looking at!" he bellowed so loudly that small pieces of half-chewed bread sputtered out of his mouth. One piece stuck to his stubbled chin.

Before he could smother it, a nervous laugh escaped from Conor. Micheál sprang to his feet and his chair clattered to the stone-flagged floor as he made a lunge across the kitchen. "You young pup!" he roared, "I'll teach you to laugh at your father!"

Sorcha ran to intervene, trying to place herself in front of Conor, but Micheál pushed her aside so violently that she lost her balance and fell against the dresser.

"Dadda!" Molly screamed from her corner. "Please, Dadda, don't!"

Conor screamed too. "Dadda, I'm sorry, please, please, Dadda, I'm sorry . . .''

Maddened, Micheál swung, open-palmed, but Conor ducked and the impetus of the swing carried the older man onward so that he crashed into the wall of the kitchen. He clutched his shoulder as if he had hurt it.

Conor ran to the door in an attempt to escape, but the door opened inward and Micheál, making a renewed charge, managed to grab him from behind. The two of them fell, struggling, to the ground. Conor was big and strong, but no match for his much heavier and stronger father. Nevertheless he fought wildly, using his knees and fists.

Molly was so terrified she could not even scream. She flattened herself against the wall as her father and brother rolled around the floor, upsetting chairs and crashing into the legs of the table so it almost tipped over. Sorcha had picked herself up and was attempting to claw at Micheál's back, but he brushed her off and she stumbled and fell again on one knee. All the time, Molly's dadda was roaring and cursing, in Irish and English, swear words, "You fucking little bastard . . ." even some words Molly had never heard before. He managed to get a lock on Conor, pinning one of his son's arms to his side, and rising, pulled him up after him. He dragged him across the floor and into Molly's room and slammed the door.

The sounds of the struggle continued, with Conor's voice now raised to pitch Molly thought would shatter her ears. "Please, Dadda, I'm sorry, please please! Please don't. I'm sorry, Dadda, I'm sorry!"

Brendan continued to sit at the table, his mouth slack, barely aware of what was going on. Sorcha could bear no more. Sobbing, she took her shawl from the hook and ran out the door; Molly ran out after her, but her mother's flight was too fast and Sorcha was fifty yards up the hill before Molly rounded the corner of the house. She could hear her mother's sobs, carried across the walls, while from the house, the sounds of Conor's screaming continued. Two men going along the road stopped and looked after Sorcha and then at each other and Molly nearly died with terror, shame, and sorrow.

She ran in under the lean-to roof over the turf stack, where the collie usually slept on a bed of dried seaweed. Creeping in beside the little dog, she buried her head in the warm fur and covered her ears to the sounds still coming from the house. Instead, she concentrated on hearing the beat of the collie's heart. The dog was

afraid too—she trembled and licked Molly's bare elbow.

After a little while, she did not know how long, Molly
uncovered her ears. There was quiet. No screaming, no
crying, no shouting.

Slowly, still terrified, she tiptoed back around the corner of the house. She would have looked in the window,
but it was too high for her. So, getting up her nerve, she
went as far as the open door and peered in.

The kitchen was empty. All the chairs were upset and
lying around the table. The shards of what had been a
bowl lay on the floor in front of the dresser; there were
broken eggshells everywhere; and the whites and yolks
of the eggs had spread in a glutinous slick over a wide
area of the flagstones.

She stepped carefully around the mess and, afraid of
what she might find, opened the door of her room. This
room, too, bore signs of the huge struggle. The blankets
were mostly off the bed and an alarm clock, brought
home from Birmingham by Brendan, lay on the floor, the
glass on its face broken, its tick, however, still loud.

Conor was lying on the bed, his back to her. He was
seminaked. His trousers were down around his ankles
and his shirt was ripped to shreds. There were bruises
already showing all over his body, particularly on his
buttocks and back, and long red weals, where his father
had thrashed him with a belt, had begun to rise. There
were welts on his arms as well.

His hands were tied behind his back with baler twine.

When he saw her come in he turned his head to the
wall. Molly ran to the dresser in the kitchen and opened
one of the drawers. She took out the big knife her mother
used when she was preparing fowl and ran back into the
bedroom. She found it difficult to cut the twine and sawed
at it, for ages it seemed, but Conor assisted her by flexing
his wrists, putting pressure on the twine, stretching it as
much as he could. When at last the twine gave and he
was free, he pulled his trousers up to hide his nakedness.
Then he looked at Molly, an expression in his eyes Molly
had never seen before, and she was afraid all over again.
But the expression went away and Conor's eyes filled with
tears. He held out his arms to her and she climbed up
beside him on the bed, curling in against his chest like a

little kitten. His skin, she found, smelled sour as he tightened his arms around her: *"La amhain!"* He whispered into her hair. "One day, Molly. One day I'll get him. One day . . ."

4

The whispering in the school dormitory rose to a pitch where it could not be called whispering at all; as well as the customary Friday-night feeling, tomorrow was the beginning of the summer holidays and normal discipline had been relaxed.

Molly's bed was beside the window; one side of her cubicle was not curtained, but faced out over the lawn of the school toward the lake. Being beside the window was of doubtful privilege in winter, when the battering of the rain kept her awake and drafts, like robbers, crept in through cracks in the putty.

But now it was high summer and she had a grandstand view as the sun, orange in a cloudless sky, sank behind the mountains which slid into the lake along the western shore. Propped up on her pillow, she watched as the water slowly darkened, as the dome of the sky took on the opalescence of mother-of-pearl. While she watched, she daydreamed of what might happen this summer.

The curtain dividing her bed from the one beside her twitched and was pulled aside. Kathleen Agnes's curly head appeared around the edge. "Molly!"

Molly and Kathleen Agnes had been friends since First Year. Within a week of their arrival at the convent, they had discovered that their birthdays were on the same day—at present they were both almost sixteen and a half—and from that day on, Kathleen Agnes, who dabbled in astrology, was convinced that they were destined to be soulmates. Always watchful of "special" friendships, the nuns had separated them earlier in the present year, but had allowed them back together again when Kathleen Agnes, flashing her dimples, had persuaded them that Molly *needed* her because she was so shy; that Molly, being the only boarder from the island, was lonely; that without Kathleen Agnes, she would have no friends at all.

In most respects, Kathleen Agnes's plea had been valid. Kathleen Agnes was as bouncy as Molly was reserved and the two could not have been more dissimilar in background, appearance, or temperament. Kathleen Agnes's father was a farmer, with a hundred and fifty acres of flat land in Limerick; and whereas Molly was blonde and had always been tall for her age, her friend was tiny, covered with freckles, and sported a mop of bright red curls which she hated with deep passion.

The two friends planned to visit one another in August and this was what Kathleen Agnes wanted now to discuss. "Are you sure you'll be let?" she whispered.

"I've told you over and over again," replied Molly, "that I've already written to my mam. They'll be delighted to get rid of me! Last summer I was really bored over there by the end of the holidays. I hope you won't be bored," she added anxiously. "I don't know why you want to come out at all. There's nothing to do. It could be cat." "Cat" was a mainland expression Molly had picked up from her friend. To Kathleen Agnes, everything was either "fabulous" or "cat" and there was no middle ground.

"Ah, for Christ's sake!" said Kathleen Agnes, "we've been over this and over this, Molly. Shut up about it now. Here's her Royal Bleddy Highness . . ." She dropped the curtain as a rattle of beads announced the arrival of a nun to give out the rosary.

Molly joined in the communal murmurs as the girls responded, but her mind was not on her prayers. Although she was looking forward to the trip to Limerick, she was genuinely worried about Kathleen Agnes coming to Inisheer on the reciprocal visit.

Having always been self-sufficient, she did not really believe that island life was boring, but she was fearful that Kathleen Agnes, accustomed to opulence and material wealth, might find it so. She worried about how her friend would react to the simplicity of the cottage and the choice of entertainment on hand, which would boil down to either walking or swimming. And suppose the weather was foul and they had to confine themselves to the cottage kitchen? How would Kathleen Agnes react to her dadda's outbursts? She had tried to prepare her friend for that, but out of loyalty, had been unable to bring herself to say how bad they could be. Now she worried that this had been a mistake and she had been too subtle; Kathleen Agnes had not seemed to take the warnings seriously.

At least, she thought, Conor would be there at the time of Kathleen Agnes's visit. That would be a blessing. Conor was good-looking and—with his job in Dublin—very sophisticated; Molly was banking on Kathleen Agnes's romantic heart being temporarily smitten and thereby distracted from the shortcomings of life in Inisheer.

The rosary was finishing. Fervently she concentrated on the 'Hail Holy Queen', offering it up that her dadda wouldn't be too bad for the duration of Kathleen Agnes's visit.

"Good night, girls!" called the nun, "straight to sleep now! No more messing." Her voice sounded young, like a real person's, thought Molly. Even the nuns seemed to be infected with the holiday mood. "Good night, Mother!" she chorused with the rest of the girls.

"Don't let the fleas bite!" A lone voice, from the other side of the big room, cracked up at its own daring.

Her curtain was pulled aside again. "Good night, sweetheart!" Kathleen Agnes's eyes were merry. "Good night, you too!" Molly snuggled down and closed her eyes.

She didn't mind school, in fact she liked it quite well. And she was really looking forward to going home, to seeing her mam again—and later on, Conor. Even as a sister, she could see that Conor was gorgeous: Kathleen Agnes would have no chance, no chance at all. All in all, she thought, life had turned out well for her. Even her dealings with her dadda were a bit easier. Anyway, he was not there all that much; before she went asleep, she offered an additional decade of the rosary that her dadda would be peaceful during Kathleen Agnes's visit.

When she woke next morning, there was already a subdued buzz of activity up and down the dormitory. There was no talking, but the girls were ignoring the rule that decreed they should not get up before the bell and were moving in and out of the bathrooms. Locker doors

opened and shut and she could hear suitcases being
dragged along the floor.

The arrangement for her was that she would be driven
into Galway with the others who were to catch trains and
buses, but in case there was bad weather and the *Naomh
Eanna* should be delayed or canceled, a lay sister would
travel with her and stay with her until the ship pulled
away. Looking through her window at the morning sky,
she had no worries. The sun was high; it was going to
be a fine day.

She hopped out of bed, washed herself, gasping at the
coldness of the water against her warm cheeks, and then
took her basin into the bathroom to empty the slops down
one of the sinks. She was back beside her bed, squeezing
her sponge bag into her suitcase, when the bell rang.

Breakfast was a gala affair, cornflakes instead of porridge. There were no classes, of course. Even the Inter
and Leaving Cert girls were engaged purely in supervised revision. So after breakfast, she and Kathleen Agnes, whose father was driving from Limerick to collect
her, strolled down to the shores of the lake across the
lawn. "Wouldn't you think the nuns'd cut those daisies!"
Kathleen Agnes kicked at a clump of the little flowers
that starred the grass. "Oh, no!" Molly protested. "I'm
glad they've let them grow, they're lovely."

"My mother's a Tartar for daisies!" Kathleen Agnes
warned. "She'll have the two of us out with the mower.
You mark my words!"

Molly laughed affectionately. "Oh, I won't mind a bit.
But that's one advantage we have over you. No grass—
no daisies!"

"Can't wait!" Kathleen Agnes gave her friend a one-
armed hug, having to reach mightily to get her arm
around Molly's shoulder. "I just hate being so tall!"
Molly returned the hug and then looked gloomily at the
way her wrists stuck out of her blouse, then at her exposed knees. "Look at this uniform, I'm a show!" Tall
though she had been at the beginning of the year, she
had put on a further three inches during the school year,
and the hem of her gym skirt was an inch above her
knees.

"For goodness' sake, stop moaning!" Kathleen Agnes
was never one to mince her words. "Mother Josephine

told me she thought that with your looks, you could be a model or a film star.''

"That's not true and you know it!'' Although Molly was grateful for her friend's support, she knew that Kathleen Agnes was embroidering. "At the time, what you *said* she said was that she'd never seen such a tall woman coming from Aran. That's not the same thing at all . . .''

"That was another time!'' Kathleen Agnes insisted. "She said that too. It's just that I didn't tell you about the film star bit. I didn't want you to get a swelled head.''

"I haven't got a swelled head.''

"No fault of mine. I'm always telling you you're fabulous. And anyway, why shouldn't you be a film star? It isn't only me. Everyone says you were brilliant in *Hamlet* . . .''

As part of the end-of-term festivities, the Fifth Years had put on a condensed half-hour version of the play for the entertainment of the rest of the school. Molly had somewhat of a track record—being the tallest, she was always cast as a man—and because she had always been successful, at least by the lights of the standards in the convent, latterly she always got to play the leads.

"I liked it all right,'' she admitted. "I suppose it went okay . . .''

"Okay? I tell you you were *fabulous*! Everyone said it. Even Mother Provincial. I tell you, you could *definitely* be an actress. And when you're a famous film star and living in Hollywood with your swimming pool, don't forget your friends!'' Kathleen Agnes picked up a stone and flung it into the lake. "If I had your looks and your height,'' she said in a more serious tone, "there is no way in the world I'd come back to this kip next year just to do my stupid Leaving Cert. I'd be off to London.''

"Kathleen Agnes, you're *beautiful*! I wish I was petite like you. I really do! And the Leaving Cert is *essential*. It's all about choices later in life,'' Molly said, echoing the nuns.

"I couldn't give a shit about choices.'' Kathleen Agnes tossed her red curls. To Molly, one of the revelations of boarding school had been the colorful language. She was thinking up some suitable reply when Kathleen Agnes, staring out across the lake, put her hands on her hips. "I'm going to marry a rich man,'' she announced, "*not* a farmer, they're cat! I'm definitely going to have only two children. I'm going to have my own car and my own social life and the hell with everybody!''

"I hope it keeps fine for you." Molly smiled. She was well used to Kathleen Agnes's definite opinions and plans. She had not the faintest idea herself what she wanted to do after she left school. Imbued with the religious ambience of the convent, she had thought vaguely about becoming a nun, a thought she would not have dreamed of confiding to anyone, even Kathleen Agnes.

She had entertained fantasies about becoming an actress. Throughout her school career, the elocution teacher had entered her in the local *feiseanna,* which was in reality a glorified talent competition, and somewhat to her own surprise, Molly frequently won. Now her collection of silver cups and certificates was proudly displayed in the school's gloomy entrance hall.

But it wasn't the verse-speaking she enjoyed, rather it was the plays; the sense of self-containment, of drawing on emotions and feelings that would not normally be sanctioned at the school or at home.

The nights of actual performance were always the best, the tummy-fluttering, the peeping through the holes in the ancient, musty stage curtain in the school hall as the audience, parents, day girls, pupils not involved in the play, ranged themselves on rows of wooden chairs. The front two rows always stayed empty until the very last moment, when all the nuns, led by the Reverend Mother, filed in. A symbolic throne—the only chair with arms—was reserved right in the center for Mother Provincial, whose arrival was the signal for the performance to begin.

And after the performance started, Molly always felt a heightened sense of awareness of herself. She loved the way the lights blotted out all faces beyond the edge of the stage and warmed her own, creating a capsule world around her as her character moved and spoke through her. On performance nights, Molly felt as secure as an oyster in a shell.

Arm in arm, she and Kathleen Agnes ambled back to the school, and when the time came to leave, said good-bye to one another on the gravel outside the front door of the school. "Write *immediately!*" ordered Kathleen Agnes as she slammed the door of the nuns' minibus which Molly was sharing with seven other girls, the driver, and the lay sister.

"I will!" promised Molly. Through the open window of the vehicle, Kathleen Agnes then passed in a folded holy picture. Molly opened it as the minibus moved away from the school; it proved to be an image of Saint Maria Goretti, the young girl canonized for choosing to be stabbed to death rather than to give in to the sexual demands of a man. Molly turned it over. *Better be safe than sorry!* her friend had written in her distinctive, expansive hand.

Molly, suppressing a giggle, kept an eye on the lay sister as she shoved the picture deep into the pocket of her uniform. Kathleen Agnes was the best, the funniest, the most outrageous friend anyone could have.

The *Naomh Eanna,* which today was calling first at Kilronan, on the big island, before going on to Inisheer and then to Inishmaan, was crowded with day-trippers and summer tourists. Molly said goodbye to the lay sister and boarded, hefting her suitcase with one hand, holding the hem of the offending gym skirt with the other to keep it from blowing up in the breeze. She stood on the starboard side, looking beyond the port; now that she was actually on her way, she was impatient to be off. Her mother, she knew, would be on the beach to meet her; the thought of Sorcha brought happy tears to her eyes.

"Its' going to be a fine summer, please God . . ." Molly started at the sound of the voice and looked around. Just behind her, puffing clouds of smoke from a pipe, a priest sat on a suitcase. Uncertain as to whether he had been addressing her or not, she looked around, but most of the other passengers were on the port side, watching the final preparations for departure. "Yes, Father," she said. Molly's social experience with priests was not large. On the island, her house was not one that was frequented by the clergy; at school, the chaplain kept a pair of springer spaniels and liked to hunt with them, and Molly, influenced by Conor to respect and love all living things, passionately disapproved of hunting.

She leaned over the rail and pretended to be fascinated by what she saw in the water, but then she felt the breeze lift her gym skirt and had to grab at the hem. She was mortified. Had he seen anything?

After a bit, he spoke again: "I don't know you, do I? Are you going to Kilronan?"

"No, Father, I'm for Inisheer." she said, still gazing out toward the sea. "That's where I'm going too," he said, and she had to turn around so he wouldn't think she was being rude. She saw he was smiling. "It's only my second trip there," he continued. "Father Naughton is going on holidays and I'm filling in for two weeks. I'm sure we'll see each other." He stuck out his hand. "I'm Pat Moran."

"How do you do, Father. My name is Molly Ní Bhriain."

"Not related to Conor, by any chance?"

"He's my brother!" Molly was wide-eyed at the co-incidence.

"I don't know him all that well," he said then, "but I've met him a couple of times through another friend of mine, Father Hartigan. Do you know Tom Hartigan?"

Of course, thought Molly. "Sure I do, Father," she said. "Father Hartigan was over on the island last summer. I thought he was very nice."

"He is that," agreed the priest. He stood up from his perch. "It's breezy enough up here, Molly," he said. "Maybe we should go back a bit?"

"All right, Father . . ." She was nonplussed at being included in his plans.

Near the stern, Father Moran found a spot that was sheltered by the steamer's infrastructure. Molly smiled at him while she searched desperately for a suitable topic of conversation. "That's amazing that you should know my brother," she said, knowing as soon as it was out of her mouth that it sounded a bit lame.

But he did not seem to notice her conversational shortcomings. "Not really," he said. "Sure Tom Hartigan and I are about the same age and there aren't that many of us in the diocese. Not like the old days!" he added, and smiled again.

"I suppose so," she said and then, to her relief, the steamer blasted its horn and started disengaging from the dockside.

"You're not doing the Leaving?" he asked when they were about five minutes out into the bay.

"No, Father, next year."

"And what then?" She looked closely at him, but it didn't seem as though he was interrogating her. He wasn't even looking at her, but out across the water. She relaxed a little: "I don't know, Father," she said, then because half the class thought they might be nurses, added, "I might go into nursing . . ."

"That's wonderful, Molly, Nursing is a great profession. I thought once I might like to be a doctor!"

"Did you, Father?" She was definitely feeling a little easier with him. Always curious about other people's lives, she was also genuinely interested.

"Yes, but unfortunately it didn't work out."

"Why not, Father?"

"Well, in those days, people like me didn't become doctors. That was for the gentry and the sons of big farmers."

"So how did you become a priest?" She regretted the stupid question as soon as it was out of her mouth.

But he didn't seem to think it was stupid. "Are you really interested?" he asked. He had a peculiar expression on his face. For a moment, Molly thought he looked as though he might be afraid of something. "Sure, Father," she said, "of course I'm interested."

They were having to shout to make themselves heard above the noise of the steamer's engines and the swishing sea. But she listened intently as he told her about the poor farm he was brought up on in County Mayo, about his mother's scrimping so he could go to secondary school, and about the glamorous missionary who had come around in Fifth Year, asking for volunteers to go on the African missions as soldiers for Christ. "It seemed like a great escape from the bogs and the slavery on the farm," he said. "And the missionary order was going to pay for everything, so my mother wouldn't have to worry about university fees or anything like that."

Molly was so astonished that she forgot her shyness. She had always thought that priests' vocations began with blinding suddenness; in her imagination she saw them, terrified in their beds in the middle of the night as a shaft of light hit them and deep somewhere in their souls they heard the real voice of God as He called to them. "And did you actually go to Africa, Father?" she asked. "Was it very exciting and strange?"

"Well, no . . ." he said, "I never got to Africa. As it happened, I didn't stay with the missionaries." She nearly asked why not, but just in time, remembered her manners. "I had two years of theology done," he went on, "so I was accepted in Maynooth for the diocese. That's how it happened." He seemed about to say more, but instead took a box of matches out of his pocket and concentrated on relighting his pipe, making a little cup from his hands to shelter the match flame from the wind.

When the pipe was going to his satisfaction, again he looked off into the distance. "So that's it, and here I am on the way to Inisheer! Inisheer is a lovely place, Molly, you're lucky to live there. My own village where I grew up is like a ghost town now. We used to have a cobbler and a blacksmith working in two workshops side by side when I was a boy. Even a mill. All closed up, Molly, all gone. We have no butcher now, no chemist, no dispensary, no doctor—only the public nurse who comes around in her little car. It's all very sad." He puffed on his pipe.

Molly finally decided that she liked him. He was certainly very easy to talk to.

She found herself volunteering information about Kathleen Agnes, about how she hoped to go to visit Limerick later in the summer. "Her father's really rich, Father. They have a motor car and horses and their own telephone, and Kathleen Agnes says she'll teach me to ride . . ."

"That'll be nice."

"Yes," Molly went on, "I'm really looking forward to that. I've never been on a horse before, but Kathleen Agnes says there's nothing to it and that I have the build for it."

"I'd say you have that!" Molly was looking ahead toward the big island and did not notice the look, almost of pain, that crossed the priest's face. "There's Inishmore!" she said. "You can see it really clearly now. Do you ride yourself, Father?" she asked.

"I've been known to, yes."

"Kathleen Agnes says it's fabulous," she said eagerly, "that there's nothing like it, the power of the horse under you, the wind in your hair." Thinking she was getting carried away, she glanced at him apologetically. "Sorry! Kathleen Agnes is a bit dramatic."

"Your friend is right."

Molly noticed that suddenly there seemed to be something wrong with the priest; his eyes looked somehow as though he was suffering. But since it would be rude to ask him directly, she continued with her eulogy of Kathleen Agnes's home: "And they have *two* televisions, Father!" To her relief, that provoked a laugh.

She laughed too. "They really have, Father. I told you they're rich."

"Do you watch much television?" he asked.

"Only saw it once in my life, Father. That was in a shop in Galway. The nuns were taking me to the dentist." She smiled at him, but the suffering look came back and he turned away. "I think I'll take a turn around the deck . . ."

"Sure thing, Father. It was nice to meet you."

Although she saw him in the distance, they did not speak again until he came alongside her just as they were maneuvering into the pier at Kilronan. He stood right beside her at the rail; was it her imagination or did she smell whiskey off him? She certainly hadn't noticed it before . . .

Molly decided she was being stupid. She was probably smelling a particular brand of tobacco.

But she did notice that he certainly was not as relaxed as he had been when they had first started to talk. He seemed stiff and agitated and once or twice, as they watched the unloading and reloading operation, she caught him looking at her, again with that peculiar expression of pain on his face. What was it? Did she remind him of someone? It certainly made her feel uncomfortable. "Soon be off now, Father," she said after intercepting one such look.

"Yes," he said, "That's right, Molly . . ." Then she noticed his hands were shaking a little. She had been very stupid. He was probably suffering from some illness or other. She smiled at him sympathetically and then immediately regretted it, for he turned away. Clearly, he didn't want anyone to know or even to guess.

The steamer took on very little, just a few crates of fish, and then they were on their way to Inisheer. A couple of miles ahead of them they could see the island, an unmistakable hump of land against the horizon. Then, as they got closer, Molly was able to make out the forlorn lines of the *Plassy,* the steamship wrecked in March of 1960 and now rusting quietly away above the waterline. She forgot about Father Moran and his odd looks and shaking hands.

She was nearly home.

There were strange things happening to Father Moran as the *Naomh Eanna* steamed slowly toward the bay at Inisheer. His pulse was racing and he could not get out of his head the vision she had presented to him of herself astride one of Kathleen Agnes's horses. The picture was making smithereens of his carefully constructed and maintained defenses against sexual attraction to women.

All his priestly life he had managed to steer a shaky but faithful celibate path through the obstacle course women threw up in his path. But this young girl was different; he had found that he was overtly trying to interest her, had heard his own voice adopt an unusually vivacious tone.

To his horror, Father Moran had heard himself flirting.

He was appalled. She could not be more than sixteen or seventeen and he was over fifty. He felt as though he were twelve. He had thought that at his age he had survived the storms of sex and had sailed into the more peaceful waters of middle age, battle-scarred but victorious. Now he found that he could not have been more wrong. Now here he was. No fool like an old fool.

He hung back when the steamer anchored, letting Molly go ahead of him in a different currach to his own. A woman, her mother, no doubt, met her on the beach. She turned and waved as she walked with the woman up the hill.

''There's no harm done,'' he told himself that night as he knelt beside his bed in the curate's house to say his prayers. ''*Yet!*'' answered his treacherous heart.

Father Moran's lust for Molly Ní Bhriain hit him like a lightning bolt. He had never believed in the romantic foolishness of love at first sight; but this girl was everything he had dreamed about all his life.

He burrowed down in the bed and prayed desperately for deliverance from the torment of her. He took every remedial action he could think of, recited the Litany of

Our Lady, thought about the Seven Circles of Dante, tried to remember the exact words of the opening of the Book of Genesis, wrestled with gargantuan algebraic problems. But her face, her body, her hair, her scent, engulfed him as though she were physically present with him under the bedcovers.

Over and over again, he reran the three hours he had spent with her on the *Naomh Eanna,* everything she said, every expression that had crossed her face, every gesture and smile, every line of her beautiful young body. Her gym skirt had been too short, tantalizing him occasionally by blowing upward in the breeze so he could see her long, straight thighs. Once, as she was leaning over the rail and he was behind her, the wind had raised the garment sufficiently to allow a glimpse of the seat of her white cotton panties.

That glimpse was the greatest torture of all. Despite strenuous efforts, Father Moran could not stop that picture from recreating itself as over and over in his mind he visualized the cleft between the two round white hummocks; he imagined himself stroking those hummocks, the softness of the cotton, the firmness underneath; he imagined himself slowly removing the panties . . .

He got out of bed and went on his knees on the cold linoleum, saying an Act of Contrition, begging God for help.

But when he got back into bed the pictures rose before him again. Those and more; the young just-swelling breasts pushing at the sexless pleats of the gym skirt . . . He pictured how his hands might cup them, how they would feel, like velvety, sun-warmed peaches . . .

Just before dawn, Father Moran got out of bed and retrieved the silver hip flask from the inside pocket of his jacket, unscrewed the cap, and without bothering to pour the whiskey into it, put the flask directly to his lips. The alcohol hit his stomach like a tongue of fire; he took another swig, recapped the flask and feeling a little steadier and calmer, climbed back into the curate's lumpy spare bed. The first rays of the sun were shafting through the east-facing window of the bedroom when at last he dropped into exhausted sleep.

Red-eyed and slightly nauseated from fatigue, he found it difficult to concentrate on the Mass the next morning.

Knowing that she had to be somewhere in the body of the congregation, he steadfastly kept his eyes within the sanctuary.

But there was no avoiding her when the time came for Holy Communion. Long before she got to him, he saw her in the queue, her bright head shining in the sunlight that infused the small chapel. It took a supreme effort not to watch her as she came closer and closer; then, too soon, she was in front of him, eyes reverently closed, hands folded. He hoped that no one could see that the hand that placed the Host on her outstretched tongue was shaking.

As he disrobed in the sacristy after Mass he fought the urge to flee, to pretend he was sick and to get a boat and go back to the mainland. But he already knew he would not do anything of the sort. He ricocheted between three desires: his desire to run away, his desire to be true to his vows—and his overwhelming desire to see her.

That evening and the following day, he tramped around the island on long walks, trying to fool himself into believing that he was doing it for the good of his health. But his heart was not fooled. Inisheer was such a small island, only two square miles, that unless she stayed in her house all of the time, he was bound to run into her sooner or later.

She came out just after ten on the second day.

Knowing full well he was behaving like a moonstruck schoolboy, Father Moran was sitting on a wall bordering a road above and behind her house. It had not been difficult to find out where she lived; a few comments about Conor had elicited the information, and, pretending to admire the view out to sea, he had adopted his vantage point a half-hour before she appeared. His breviary rested on the wall beside him and from time to time he had picked it up and tried to concentrate on its well-worn pages, but the print swam before his eyes and he might as well have been trying to read an Arabic Koran. It seemed, he thought, that he had lost the power to direct his own actions.

When at last he saw her, his heart began to thump and his breath ran short for a few seconds. But out of the corner of his eye, he saw she had started up the hill toward him, and pulling himself together he slipped off the wall. Keeping as casual a pace as he could manage, he strolled up the boreen, stopping after a minute or two to examine the fossils on the surface of the limestone pavement. He thought his heart might suffocate him as he sensed her coming closer.

"Hello, Father!"

"Why, hello, Molly," he said, shooting upright as though she had surprised him, hoping his voice and face did not betray him, "I'm just out for a walk."

Stupid, inane, stupid . . .

But she did not seem to think anything was wrong. She was wearing a longish skirt of red wool and a báinín sweater, the rough textures emphasizing the pearliness of her skin. Her blonde hair was blowing loose in the breeze. As he looked at her, Father Moran felt almost physically ill with desire. To cover his confusion, he squatted again on the pavement. "See what I've found?" Pointing to the delicate coils of the fossils: "I wonder what these are, now?"

She hunkered down beside him. She smelled of soap. "They're crinoids, Father," she said. "The other name for them is sea lilies. Conor—that's my brother—oh, of course you know him! Sorry! Well, he has made a study of all the island. He knows every stone on it."

They both stood up. "My, my!" said the priest too heartily. "Did you ever!" Then: "Do you see that big boulder over there in the middle of the field, the pinkish-colored one. Do you know what kind of rock it is?"

He could have kicked himself for his fatuousness.

"Oh, yes, Father." She fell in step beside him as they walked up the hill. "The rock is granite; it was carried here by the glaciers of the Ice Age, but if you go close to it you'll see that the rock is really gray. It's the crystals of feldspar that make it look pink. Do you know what that is?"

The physical-geography classes in primary school where everything had to be learned by rote came to his rescue. He adopted a singsong, recitation voice: "Feldspar-is-a-mineral-deposit-containing-aluminum-and-other-silicates." That earned another smile and he felt ludicrously like shouting high into the sky. Instead he said, "It's wonderful you know so much about the island, Molly. Any chance you'd have a bit of spare time

to show me more? Might as well use my time here con-
structively.'' And then he laughed.

*Stop laughing, You sound crazed. False and crazed.
She has to notice . . .*

He felt nervous sweat begin to gather on his palms and
in his armpits. But she merely gazed around the landscape. ''Certainly, Father,'' she said, ''it's just a pity
that Conor isn't here yet, He's coming in the middle of
August. He would be much better than me to show you
around. But I'll be happy to.''

He pushed his luck. ''Are you on your way somewhere, or have you a bit of time now?''

''I was just going up to the chapel for a visit.''

''That's fine, Molly. We'll make a visit together and
then we'll set off.''

They knelt beside one another in the plain, white-
painted chapel. Father Moran bent his head but again
could not pray. She was so near that the clean scent of
her skin assaulted him. He remembered the blowing gym
skirt and what was underneath.

Leaving her to her prayers, he got up and walked out
of the chapel, and by the time she joined him, he had
himself again under some semblance of control. As they
moved along, he tried to concentrate on the little lectures
she gave him, about the fact that while there were no
rivers on this or on either of the other two islands, there
were good springs. ''And many centuries ago, Father''—
she pointed at a pair of dwarf hazels which clearly had
to struggle to survive—''Aran was covered in trees and
was fertile enough. But our ancestors didn't know about
conservation and they overgrazed and overcultivated the
land and cut down the trees, and this was the result . . .''
Unconsciously she was speaking like a schoolteacher.

They were standing on the highest point of the island
and the rock fell away from them toward the sea,
emerald-colored in the sunshine. ''I wish I was able to
paint!'' the priest said, overcoming his obsession with
her for a few moments, marveling at the clearness of the
light which seemed to be reflected back at the sky off the
flat limestone pavements.

But then she unmanned him all over again with that
smile of hers. ''Sure why don't you have a go, Father!
You never know till you try!'' And he forgot about sea

and sky and light and it took all his strength not to take
her in his arms there and then. Instead, he walked away
from her, staying a little way ahead until they got to a
crossroads. He was sufficiently composed to thank her.
"That was wonderful, Molly. You're a wonderful guide."

"I wish Conor was here. He knows everything."

"I'm sure he does, but he can be proud of you. Could
we do it again, tomorrow, maybe?"

She hesitated and then glanced at the sky: "Sure why
not, Father. The weather'll stay fine, they say, and I
haven't all that much to do in the house these days."

"Same time, same place?" Had he really said that?
Had he really said that?

"Sure thing, Father. About half ten. *Slán!*" And she
was away down the hill toward her house. He watched
her until she vanished around the side of the house.

Although on his bare head the sun was hot enough to
crack an egg, walking back to his own lodgings Father
Moran felt as gay and as light as Gene Kelly in *Singin'
in the Rain*.

Molly took Father Moran out again on the following
day. This time she had given a little thought to the tour,
and because he was a priest, gave it a clerical flavor.
They visited the ruins of Cill na Seacht n-Inín (the Church
of the Seven Daughters) built during monastic times on
the site of a much older stone fort. They went then to the
ruins of the tenth-century church of St. Cavan and she told
him how the little church fights bravely against the ma-
rauding sandhill which frequently all but covers it and
how it is kept in sight only by frequent excavation.

Molly's pupil seemed already to know of the islanders'
devotion to St. Cavan and of their belief in the saint's
miraculous intercessions. He certainly knew all about the
pattern to be held at his church on his feastday in a few
days' time. "Do you believe in miracles, Molly?" he
asked her as they walked along the beach, away from the
tiny church. "I suppose I do, Father," she replied, although if she was honest, she didn't really, despite the
gospels and all the rest of it. She couldn't have said why
not. Everyone else believed in them, Kathleen Agnes and
everyone.

Then Father Moran said a funny thing: "I think I do too!"

Molly thought that very odd. Priests were supposed to believe completely in miracles. They preached about miracles all the time, didn't they?

They climbed the island and she found for him several species of alpine flora, sea-pinks, saxifrage, a couple of ferns; then she discovered an old wren's nest in one of the fissures in the limestone pavement. "Did you know wrens can swim, Father?"

"I certainly did *not* know that!"

"Well, they can. Conor says they can . . ."

They walked along the clifftops and she explained that the cliffs were mainly too sheer and too smooth to provide good nesting for seabirds, but out on the water, they did spot three puffins and a pair of black-throated divers to which he responded enthusiastically.

But as she got to know him better, Molly was beginning to wonder more and more about Father Moran. He was definitely a little odd. For instance, he laughed at things she said when they weren't even remotely funny. And twice he stopped to look out to sea, pointing in wonder but asking about perfectly ordinary things like a mallard drake and two currachs pulling along beside each other. She couldn't help but suspect that he was sort of artificially keeping things going.

Then she remembered the shaking hands. Of course! He was probably suffering from strain and his bishop had sent him over here for a bit of rest and fresh air. Molly castigated herself for her intolerance. She would have to be extra nice to him if he was suffering from strain. "Are you all right, Father?" she asked as they reached the top of a hill and she noticed he was panting a little. "You're not too tired? I'm not going too fast for you?"

"Not at all, Molly," he said. But he did ask to sit down for a while. She sat down beside him and they gazed out over the island and to Inishmaan beyond.

She racked her brain as to what she could do with him next. She judged that they had been crisscrossing Inisheer for the best part of two hours, and between today and yesterday, they had covered almost everything she could think of.

She was saved by the first drops of rain. The air, so

warm the day before, had turned cold, and out to the west the clouds were piling up, so it was not just a shower they were in for. "I suppose we'd better make a run for it, Father," she suggested. "Anyway, I'd better be going home. I have to help my mam with the tea . . ."

"You've been very good to me, Molly." He stood up and brushed a few grains of the sandy soil off his trousers. "Not at all, Father," said Molly, "I enjoyed it. Maybe we'll do it again—although I think I've shown you every single thing there is to be seen here!" She laughed and he laughed too. "So!" he said then, as they walked back down the hill, "we'll run into each other again anyway . . ." Again her quick ear picked up that strange heartiness in his voice, and, strain or no strain, she was just as glad her duty with him was done "Oh, I'm sure we will, Father," she said, quickening her pace.

"Sure I'm not leaving for a week or so yet!" He kept in step with her.

"That's right, Father. Of course we'll see each other."

He hit the side of his head with his open palm. "And there's the pattern, of course. You'll be there?"

She nodded. "The whole island'll be there that day, Father . . ." She put her hands over her head. "We'd better run, this rain is getting heavy!"

Instead of running, however, he stopped dead: "And sure we'll see each other again later on in the summer . . ."

They had come as far as the crossroads where, unless he was going to come right to her door, their paths should have parted. "When will you be over again?" Molly asked, taking a few backward steps down her own road.

"I don't know, probably in August." He was staring at her and now she felt a little uncomfortable. "Oh, I hope Conor's here by that time. As I've told you, he's much better than me at telling all about the island. He's fabulous at it."

"I'm sure he is, Molly, but he couldn't be as good as you." The rain was really bucketing now, but he was holding out his hand and she had to go back to shake it. "Cheerio now, Father," she said.

"Cheerio, Molly."

At last she was free to run home. Her impressions about Father Moran were confusing. She glanced back toward the crossroads as she went in through the front door of the cottage, and to her astonishment he was still standing there. He must be getting drenched, poor man.

On the whole he was a nice man, she decided, but definitely a little odd, definitely suffering from strain. Probably to do with him being a priest.

The Lincoln convertible, top down in deference to the warm evening, progressed regally along the Outer Drive; its maroon paintwork shone, its white leather upholstery gleamed with polishing, but it was not the car itself—common enough in the area—that caused heads to turn in nearby automobiles, but the glamour and beauty of the Lincoln's four occupants.

Christian's grandfather was driving with Christian beside him; Christian's grandmother and his wife sat together in the backseat. Individually, any one of the four would have attracted attention. Together, resplendent in evening dress and traveling in the magnificent Lincoln, they presented a picture of the American dream: two generations of beautiful people, rich and successful, on their way to the social event of the season.

"Are you warm enough, my dear?" Malcolm Smith turned around and glanced back at his wife, who smiled and nodded. "How about you, Jo-Ann?" he continued, "you okay?"

Christian's wife nodded too, but her smile, in contrast to Cordelia's, was tight. Blonde and blue-eyed, with high cheekbones and a long, graceful neck graced with drop earrings of diamonds and gold, her demeanor, nevertheless, was tense.

Throughout the exchange, Christian kept his eyes firmly fixed to his left and on the lake. He wished with all his heart that he was elsewhere.

Anywhere.

Timbuktu, Tibet, anywhere but on his way to the goddamned Chicago Opera House. But his grandmother, as usual, had gotten her way. Tonight's concert was for one of her charities, and for her sake he had not kicked up too much of a fuss when she had asked him and Jo-Ann to join her and his grandfather.

Now he was bitterly sorry he had been so soft. Jo-Ann was in one of her moods and Malcolm, as usual, would be glowering at him, blaming him for everything.

Christ, he thought, what he wouldn't give for a drink.

"Nearly there, Christian!" His grandmother, obviously sensing his discontent, tapped him on the shoulder. "Sure, Grandma," he said, tugging at the tight collar of his dress shirt. He realized he had sounded churlish and turned around to flash her a smile.

As he did so, he caught Jo-Ann's eye and the smile froze.

He turned back again to his contemplation of the lake. She was obviously determined to play the bitch tonight. Well, let her, he thought. Why should he do all the work in the relationship? Put up with all the nonsense and mood swings? Any seriously objective person would be on his side in the present situation; his so-called crime, what she was in such a snit about, was the heinousness of his having a few drinks before they left their apartment.

It was all right for her, Miss Perfect, but she knew very well how much he dreaded socializing with his grandfather. Why couldn't she just understand that and be on his side, be supportive, like a real wife, instead of going on and on at him as if she were a goddamn temperance worker.

He realized his temper was rising and, for his grandmother's sake, tried to calm down. He inhaled deeply three times. That's what Dick always did. And it always worked for a while. He tried to forget the fight and concentrated on the scene around him.

Christian always loved this time of the evening in Chicago, particularly at this season of year before summer had wilted the streets. He felt energized as the city snapped from business to pleasure, with cabs ferrying people dressed in party clothes and streetlights coming on to compete with the evening haze rolling in from the lake. Ahead of them now, he could see the aggressive shape of the Hancock Center as it thrust itself protectively above the city like a latter-day Minotaur, brandishing the twin horns of its antennae at the sky.

They joined the snarl of traffic along Michigan Avenue, crossing the Chicago River which flowed between the Wrigley Building and its almost-twin which housed the *Sun-Times*. Automatically Christian looked downriver toward the building which contained his own newspaper, the *Sentinel*. If he had been up with the game, he thought irritably, he could have organized it with his editor to be on assignment tonight and could have avoided all this hassle.

Covertly he glanced at his grandfather's profile. His grandfather was the only fly in the ointment of his job satisfaction. Christian liked and enjoyed his job with the newspaper—and he knew he was good. But Malcolm rarely let him forget that the job had been given to him as a result of his intervention; the paper's owner was on the board of McKennon's Breweries.

The knowledge that he had not been able to get a decent job on his own merits still rankled with Christian. Although his grades at journalism school had been good—eventually, when he settled down after a few lost years—he never performed well at job interviews. Something about the person asking the questions always struck deep into Christian's anti-authoritarian soul, and no matter how much he had wanted the job in the first place, he always found himself becoming arrogant and scornful as the interview progressed.

Again he glanced across at his grandfather's patrician profile. In his heart of hearts, he had to admit that in practical terms, Malcolm had stood by him through the drunken escapades, the failures, the more unsavory side of Christian's school career, but now that he was on his feet and making out for himself, he was sick and tired of Malcolm always making him feel beholden.

He and his grandfather could never be in the same ten square feet of space without a row breaking out. The old man was constantly criticizing his clothes, his spending habits, his life-style, his supposed neglect of Jo-Ann. Naturally, he thought bitterly, his grandfather would take Jo-Ann's side in any rows. Well, his marriage was none of his grandfather's business, and Christian was sick of his interference and of Jo-Ann's whining.

He saw they were almost at the Opera House and looked at his watch. Good. Still twenty minutes to curtain. There would be time for a drink.

"I've waited a long time to hear Carreras!" Despite his bad humor, Christian made an effort to join in his grandmother's gentle enthusiasm. "Well, tonight's the night, Grandma!" he said over his shoulder as Malcolm pulled the Lincoln into the curb. "You go ahead, Grandpa," he added to Malcolm, "I'll park the car."

Malcolm looked at him, irritating Christian all over again with the surprise written on his face. "You offering to do something all by yourself?"

For his grandmother's sake, Christian gritted his teeth. "Yes, Grandpa. You three go on . . ."

Malcolm got out and Christian moved across into his seat. "See you in a few minutes," he called after them as they joined the perfumed crowds milling around on the sidewalk outside the theater.

As he drove to a parking garage, Christian was sorely tempted not to come back at all, to hit the road west, to keep driving until he got to a place where there was no Jo-Ann, no grandfather, no rich and industrious tradition to keep up. But then, immediately, he thought of all he would miss, particularly his job. And Dick.

Although Dick's parents could not afford to send him to college, the two had remained friends all through Christian's own checkered college career. Dick had continued with his photography and while Christian was stumbling his way through college, Dick quietly got on with his own life, turning professional and getting a job in the photographers' pool at the *Sun Times*. Then, a year after Christian's assignment to the foreign desk at the *Sentinel*, Dick had transferred to that newspaper, and now the two of them worked a great deal together. They had become a sort of roving international conscience for the paper, covering atrocities in Central America, apartheid in South Africa, floods and poverty in Asia and South America and injustice and corruption anywhere and in any sphere it occurred. In that context, it gave Christian great satisfaction to know that his pieces on issues close to home were frequently discussed unfavorably at his grandfather's country club.

He parked the car at the entrance to the garage and gave the attendant a generous tip. "Careful with that baby, we like her a lot!"

The attendant whistled: "You bet, man!" But even as he walked away, Christian heard the squeal of the Lincoln's tires as the attendant enjoyed himself on the ramps. He shook his head. If anything happened to the car, it would be simply something else for his grandfather to nag on about.

Malcolm and the two women were waiting for him in the lobby of the Opera House, so he had no chance to take a quick trip to the bar.

"Everything all right?" Malcolm's tone was conciliatory but Christian refused to accept the olive branch. "Sure!" he said, looking into the crowd over Malcolm's shoulder. "What do you think? I crashed between here and LaSalle?"

"Let's go!" Malcolm started up the stairs.

"Anyone feel like a drink?" Christian tried to make his voice light and jocular and addressed the two women.

"No time, Christian!" Jo-Ann was using her snippy voice. He was about to snap back when Malcolm cut across him; he had recognized the backs of a pair of country-club acquaintances who were ascending the staircase just ahead of them. "Hello, Sam. Hi, Dave!"

The two men turned and pumped Malcolm's hand. "You know my wife? My grandson's wife, Jo-Ann? My grandson, Christian?" He performed the introductions.

The one called Dave raked Jo-Ann's lithe body with his puffy eyes. "How do you do? Pleased to meetja! Where's this guy been hiding you?"

Christian stepped in: "Sorry, didn't catch your name?" he said, and before the man could answer, stuck out his hand. "I'm Christian Smith, this lady's husband."

Dave's smile vanished. "Yeah, the reporter," he said, looking Christian up and down. "The guy who turns over all those rocks!"

Christian smiled. "Depends on who's under them," he said smoothly, and had the satisfaction of seeing the man's eyes twitch.

The one called Sam introduced the two men's wives, both artificially tanned. On being introduced to Christian, Dave's wife, the smaller and darker of the two women, looked up at him with a directness which he recognized instantly. Although she was not his type, he was so pissed off with her husband that he gave her his most dazzling smile and saw the appraisal turn to frank admiration. She stepped a little toward him and took his hand. "Hello there!"

He kept her hand only long enough to show he was

mildly interested and then walked ahead of the rest of the company toward the balcony of the theater. The night wasn't wasted after all.

On the day Conor was expected, Molly was down early on the beach to watch for the steamer just as she had done as long as she remembered. Today the ship was exactly on time and as she watched him being rowed ashore in the currachs with the other passengers and tourists, she could not help but mourn the early days when he bounded through the waves to swing her off her feet. Nevertheless, her heart lifted at the sight of him; these times she only saw him at Christmas and during the summer holidays and every time she saw him it was as if they had been apart for years. As the currach approached, she stood at the very edge of the water, as close as she could without getting her feet wet.

He climbed out of the boat, threw his bag on the sand, and rushed over to her, hugging her strongly. "My God!" he said then, holding her away from him. "You've changed so much. You're not my little sister anymore— you're my huge *big* sister!"

"Shut up, Conor," she said, hating to have her height referred to.

"All right, all right. You're my little sister all over again. How's my little sister?"

"Shut up!" But she was laughing.

She broached the subject of Kathleen Agnes to him within the first minute. "Listen, Conor, my friend, Kathleen Agnes Dwyer—you know my friend?"

He nodded. "I know, the one with the two televisions."

"Well, she's coming here to visit next week for the whole week and then I'm going back to Limerick for a holiday at her house when she leaves here."

"Yeah," said Conor, "you've told me that. I got your last letter."

Molly ignored the sarcasm. "Now, the reason I'm telling you this, Conor, is that I'm a bit worried that there'll be nothing much for her to do here. She's used to telephones and cars and television. So will you be nice to her, Conor? Will you show her around and take her places and be *nice* to her?"

"Whoa!" he said, "not so fast. I'm here on *my* holidays. I'm not here to entertain your friends, you know."

She stopped dead. "*Please,* Conor."

"For goodness' sake, I'm only joking. Of course I'll be nice to your friend." She laughed happily and linked her arm in his and the two of them continued up the boreen to the house. "Oh, it's great to see you again, Conor, it really is!"

"Me too." He squeezed his elbow tightly against the arm underneath it.

She was very proud of him. Twenty-seven years old now, he had been a junior lecturer at the National Botanic Gardens in Dublin for the past five years. He had won a scholarship to train at the Gardens but his career had a lot to do with Sorcha, who despite Micheál's frequent raids on the jar on the mantelpiece, had managed to squirrel enough money away to pay for Conor's keep in Dublin during his studies.

The first few days he was home, Molly and her brother could not get out much. The weather was stormy and Conor spent a lot of time reading, keeping well out of Micheál's way. Worried, thinking ahead to Kathleen Agnes's visit, Molly watched the silent sparring between the two of them. Part of the difficulty was that Micheál, whose bad humor had become permanent over the years, thought Conor's job not a proper job at all.

To avoid trouble, Conor tried, with Sorcha's collusion, to eat separately from his father, but sometimes this was impossible; those times, when they were forced to sit captive within feet of one another were the worst for the household. Conor did not rise to Micheál's muttered goading, however, and the fragile equilibrium between them was maintained for a time.

Toward the end of the week, the weather improved at last and Conor and Molly set out to walk around their old haunts. They stopped for a rest, flopping in a little hollow. "Do you remember the first time I brought you here?" he asked after they had been sitting in companionable silence for a few minutes.

"I do," answered Molly happily, and began to recite the Belloc poems she now knew herself:

* * *

"Do you remember an Inn,
  Miranda?
  Do you remember an Inn?
  And the tedding and the spreading
  Of the straw for a bedding,
  And the fleas that tease in high Pyrenees . . ."

"Uh-oh, said Conor. "Mistake!"

"What mistake?" she was surprised.

"It's not 'in high Pyrenees'—it's 'in *the* high Pyrenees' . . ."

"It is not. It's 'in high Pyrenees.' That's the way *we* learned it . . ."

"Well, you learned wrong."

"We did not!"

"You did so!"

"We did not, Conor O Briain. It was your rotten school that taught *you* wrong!"

"What did you say, Miss Molly Ní Bhriain? Rotten school? I'll show you rotten . . ."

He reached out as though to pull her hair. But she was up and away, too fast for him. He got to his feet and chased her around the soft grass. They were both laughing as she danced away from him, always a little out of his reach.

"Come here to me!" he yelled. "I'll spiflicate you!"

"You'll have to catch me first!" she yelled back, dodging and twisting.

He caught her, and although she struggled and fought, he managed to drag her as far as a rock. She kicked all the way against his attempts to pull her down across his knees. "I'll teach you how to recite poetry!" he cried, panting.

He proved too strong for her, and suddenly she felt the breeze on her thighs as he raised her skirt and started to spank her. The spanking did not really hurt, although she squealed and protested, half laughing, half in earnest. Abruptly, however, after he had given her half a dozen rapid smacks, he stopped and tumbled her off his lap onto the grass. He stood up. "That'll do," he said gruffly.

She looked up at him in astonishment and then scrambled to her feet. Her buttocks tingled where he had spanked her but not unpleasantly, and she felt the tingling spread to her blood. "Conor?" she said uncertainly.

He was standing with his back to her. "I'm sorry I smacked you," he said in that strange, gruff voice.

"That's all right, you didn't hurt me . . ."

"Let's go home. It's getting late."

She mulled it over in her head as they walked back to the house together. Something new had happened. She stole a sideways glance at him as he loped along, his head sunk and his face inscrutable. They were walking as far apart as the narrow boreen would allow, and for the first time she saw that he was more than her ally and her lovely, gentle brother—he was a man.

This new truth struck new sensations and she was more aware than ever of the tingling on her bottom. The truth was that she had liked being spanked. And she was aware that in some way it was forbidden, which made it all the more exciting. "Conor?" she said.

"Yes?" For the first time since he had taken her across his knees, he looked at her directly. She was relieved, but she could not fathom the look in his eyes. He obviously also knew something had changed. But what did he feel about it?

"I'm sorry I said your school was rotten." She knew it was weak.

"It's all right, Molly, you were quite right. It was a rotten school."

She kept quiet then. A little later, as they were still wreathed in silence, she saw the steamer had anchored in the bay, the currachs bobbing around her. Her arrival three times a week was the main event in the life of the island and people clustered on the shore in groups of three and four. Two tractors with trailers waited for the loads.

"Let's go down to the beach, Conor." Molly was very anxious to put right whatever had gone wrong between them. Again she was relieved when he nodded. She would give it a little time. It was how she humored Micheál; Brendan too, before he had gone off to work in England.

The first currach had already deposited four people on the sand by the time they got there. Molly saw that one of them was Pat Moran. "Oh, look, Conor," she said with excitement, "it's Father Moran, I'm so glad he's come, you'll be able to show him so much more than I did. Come on, let's go and meet him.''

The priest was walking up the beach with a small suitcase in his hand.

Father Moran had spotted her distinctive blond head as his currach was being rowed ashore, and his heart started to thump so sickeningly that he had to breathe fast in order to breathe at all. She was even more beautiful than he remembered, although he had thought of little else for weeks.

He had no sisters and his mother had been a silent woman. At the age of twelve, Pat Moran had gone from primary school into a single-sex secondary school, which was also a preparatory seminary. And from there he had gone straight into his six years' study for the priesthood.

In his summer holidays from the seminary and through all the years since ordination, Father Moran had sustained mild, secret crushes on various girls and women who came within his ambit, but, well warned and well trained, he had always managed, like most of his confreres, to recognize them as unavoidable aberrations in his vocation to celibacy. He avoided "occasions of sin," by ensuring that he was never alone with one of these aberrations. A relationship between a man and a woman had been up to now, in Pat Moran's imagination, always in soft focus, like a film—an affair of utter rapture, filled with soft delights—he looked up at Molly, hurrying to meet him—not this urgent, tearing passion full of pain . . .

He had never in his life kissed a woman.

He saw there was a man with her, and although the two had not met for years, recognized him immediately as Molly's brother, Conor. He had his face schooled by the time he came close enough to talk to them. Molly, clearly delighted to be the bearer of good news, smiled at him: "Hello, Father. Back again? You remember Conor? You know you met him with Father Hartigan? He's the botanist, as I told you. This man, Father," she announced like a magician unveiling the woman in the box, "knows every plant and bird on this island!" She smiled and stepped back to leave the two of them at it. She looked so beautiful that Father Moran wanted to fall on his face to worship her.

Instead, with the help of God, he managed some semblance of normality: "It's been a long time, Conor. And you have a good agent here. I've been hearing all about you."

Conor was far more reserved than his sister: "How do you do, Father, nice to see you again." The two men shook hands and then Father Moran turned again to Molly. He had to look at her. "And how are you since, Molly?"

"Oh, I'm fine, Father. Looking forward to going on my own holidays. Do you remember I told you about going to visit my friend, Kathleen Agnes?"

Father Moran did. The one with the horses. Molly astride . . .

"Isn't this great?" she said happily, looking from one to the other. She seemed different since his last visit, he thought, brighter, much more alive.

He allowed Conor to take his bag and set off with the two of them. The boreen was just wide enough to accommodate the three of them abreast and Molly, walking between them, was so near he imagined he could feel the heat coming from her body. But super-sensitized as he was, he felt the tension in the brother, some of it, he was sure, directed toward himself. Molly seemed absolutely oblivious to it, chattering on about her plans for Kathleen Agnes.

"Are you home for long, Conor?" he asked, when Molly seemed to run out of steam.

"Another few days."

"I see."

He felt a huge surge of an emotion which, to his despair, he recognized as jealousy. This brother was taking up her time, could come and go in her house, could touch her if he wanted to . . .

The silence as they walked along became almost unbearable for him, and he was relieved when they got as far as her house and the two of them went inside, leaving him to walk alone as far as the house where he was to stay.

To Molly's surprise, Micheál was sitting by the fire when she got inside the house. He looked up when she came in: *"Cá raibh tusa?"* Molly was used to being asked to account for her movements but, adept at interpreting the intonations of his voice, heard that the question was rhetorical. Her father, unusually, was in a mellow frame of mind. *"Thánaig an Naomh Eanna, Dadda."* She told him Father Moran had arrived on the steamer, this time not as locum, but for a holiday. *"Cupán tae, Dadda?"* she asked then and when he nodded that he would indeed like a cup of tea, she busied herself with the kettle and the teapot. As he took the cup and saucer from her, he hesitated as if he wanted to say something. But he merely nodded again at her and drank the tea, pouring it into the saucer and sucking at it.

He was so rarely present in the middle of the afternoon that Molly wondered if he was ill. She was also at a loss as to how to deal with him on her own, particularly in his present quiescent state. She was seldom alone with him, since Sorcha left the house only to go to the chapel or for short periods to visit a neighbor. When Micheál was present in the house, Molly was accustomed to being watchful and placatory; to find him sitting solitary and quiet like this, was unnerving.

His silence, she thought, was sort of different this afternoon, and his eyes seemed to be following her as she moved around the kitchen. Molly formed the vivid impression that her father had somehow been imprisoned behind a sheet of glass and was trying to break out. She hovered nervously, ready to refill his teacup, trying to bridge the gap between them. Many, many nights, particularly if he had been sharp with her or after one of the vicious rows between himself and Conor, she had lain in her bed, beating into her pillow that she hated him, hated him. But today, as she watched him sucking his tea, she felt an odd tenderness. She saw for the first time that without her noticing it, he had become old. If they had had a different relationship, she might have hugged him. But reticence and wariness in Micheál's presence were habits of a lifetime.

"If you go out that door, don't come back!" The living room of the apartment was large and echoed with the challenge.

Christian stood up from his chair, slow rage rising like a tide: "I'll come and go any goddamn hour of the day or night I choose. It's my goddamn apartment and don't you forget it!''

''*Your* apartment!'' Jo-Ann's scorn dripped like acid from a mouth distorted with derision. ''That's rich! Oh, that's really rich! It's *your* apartment now. For Christ's sake, Christian, you couldn't scrape enough money together to keep a—a—'' She hesitated. ''A *gerbil*!'' she finished triumphantly. ''If it wasn't for your precious grandfather we'd be out on the side of the street.''

''You leave my grandfather out of this.''

''You bring him up often enough. How often have I had to listen to you moaning on and on and on about the terrible, the frightful atrocities committed by your grandfather against your own lily-white self? How often—''

Christian brushed past her, rushing toward the front door of the apartment. ''I've had enough of this, I have to go to work.''

''Yes!'' Screaming, she followed him into the entrance hallway, ''work! I forgot about work. You mean, of course, *work,* as in the Shamrock Lounge Bar?''

''I mean work, as in the *Chicago Sentinel.*'' He was so angry that he pushed over a coatstand and kicked it. ''Or have you forgotten, my dearest darling honeybun, that my *work* is what pays the bills around here? Bills run up by you and your trollopy friends on quiet little lunches and expeditions to Field's.''

Her outrage reached heights even he had never seen before. ''How dare you!'' she screamed. ''Who was it who ran over the limit in the charge account at Field's? On the gas charge card? On American Express? That wasn't me or my so-called trollopy friends, my darling! And speaking of *trollops* . . .''

All the steam seemed to evaporate out of Christian. he sat heavily on a small antiqued chaise longue and put his head in his hands. ''Look, Jo-Ann, this can't go on, day after day, night after night. We're killing each other. Why don't we just call it a day?''

Shocked at last into speechlessness, she stood quivering in front of him. ''What?'' she whispered at last. ''What did you say?''

''You heard me. Don't pretend you haven't thought of it many times.''

''You mean divorce?''

"What else?"

"You're wrong, I've never thought of divorce."

"Don't be silly." He felt utterly weary. Rarely a day went by now without some sort of fight. "Of course you've thought of divorce, I've seen it in your face when you look at me. Be honest. You hate me, Jo-Ann."

"That doesn't mean I'd want to divorce you!"

The absurdity of the statement struck them simultaneously and they burst out laughing. But the laughter died away as quickly as it had arisen and she sat beside him on the chaise. "I love you, honey, I really do. What are we going to do?"

"I'm serious. I don't think we've any choice. I meant it when I said we're killing each other."

"But I love you." She attempted to embrace him, rubbing her breasts against his chest, but he found the gesture repugnant. "Stop it, don't make a fool of yourself, of both of us . . ." Her eyes widened and she was about to protest, but she caught his mood and contented herself with another plea. "We could try again, go to a counselor?"

"What would he tell us that we don't know ourselves?"

"If we love each other enough—"

"Love is not enough and you know it!"

"But we're great in bed. You know we are. We give each other a great time. You love my body."

"You've got a great body, all right. Nobody's saying you don't have a great body. But there's more to a relationship than that."

"Come on, let's go to bed, right now, Christian. I love you, Christian, let's go to bed now, right now. You can do anything you like to me, you know you turn me on, so much—" She was pulling at him, attempting to place his hand around her waist, and in that moment he really knew he had to divorce her. He hated her in that moment, hated what she was doing to herself and to what they used to have. She was using their sex, which had always been electric, as cheap currency.

She saw she was getting nowhere with him and changed tack, using a wheedling, ingratiating tone which grated on his already raw nerves. "Christian," she said softly, "why don't you give up alcohol? At least give it a try?

I'd help you, I really would.'' She attempted to take his hand, but he snatched it out of her reach: ''That subject is closed. Fini. I've told you I won't discuss that. It's too facile to put our problems down to my drinking. That's your answer to everything, I give up drink and hey! everything's hunky-dory . . .'' He stood up and righted the coat stand. ''Will you grow up? Try to think like an adult instead of a teenager?''

''*Me* think like an adult? Me?''

He raised his eyes to heaven: ''Here we go again.''

''Well, you started it—why won't you go to see a marriage counselor, what's wrong with that? And suppose we did and he advised you to give up drinking. Would you do it then?''

He looked down at her, so beautiful and so stupid. He wanted to strangle her. ''That's what you really want, isn't it, Jo-Ann?''

Strangle her. In his own ears his voice sounded like a strangler's. ''A nice, tame, dry little pet who'll stay home every night and stroke you and tell you you're beautiful.''

''That's not fair. That's not what I want and you know it . . .''

''Oh, shut it, Jo-Ann!'' He reached for the catch of the door, but she darted in front of him and spread her arms across it, barring his way. ''Where are you going?''

He clenched his fists by his sides. ''Out.''

''Out where?''

''I said shut it.''

Her beautiful eyes filled with tears. ''Please, Christian,'' she begged, ''please don't go. We can work something out, we really can. I'm sorry I shouted.'' Her pleading was piercing him, goading him, feeding his rage; he thought he was angrier than he had ever been in his life. ''I can't stand this,'' he said through clenched teeth, ''I'm warning you, I really can't stand it. Get out of the way or I'll have to do something really stupid.''

''Like what?'' She was taunting him now. He could see she did not believe he would do anything violent.

''Like hit you, goddamn it!'' Christian had never hit her and did not want to do so now, but he was having great difficulty in controlling the rage that boiled and bubbled somewhere between his chest and his throat.

"Hit me? Oh—hit me? Wife beating?" She widened her eyes almost provocatively. "Is that what we've come to now?"

He couldn't help himself; almost of its own volition, his open right hand raised itself and cracked across her beautiful, porcelain face. The sound it made was shocking to him and he could not bear to watch the porcelain crumple and redden.

The rage boiled over and spilled into his eyes, making him half blind. "Now look what you've made me do!" Before she could recover or do anything to stop him, he wrenched open the door and ran out of the apartment.

They were on the second floor of the building, and the sound of hysterical weeping floated after him as he pounded down the stairs.

By teatime, the August heat had conquered the island and the midges swarmed densely outside the cottage. In contrast to his earlier mood, Micheál came home from the pub in truculent form. He sat at the head of the table, drumming his fingers irritably while Sorcha hovered around the new bottled gas cooker, waiting anxiously for the bread she had baked to be ready. Conor sat at the other end of the table, very still. The hot oven intensified the heat until it stifled the air and every ticking second was like a quarter of an hour.

At last Sorcha picked up the loaf in a dish towel and carried it toward the dresser to cut it on the breadboard, but Molly, in her haste to help, intercepted her mother and took it. The dish towel slipped and the crust of the loaf, still hot from the hob, burned her hand. She gave a little scream and dropped the loaf on the floor.

"*Mhuire's trua*! You stupid bitch!" Micheál banged the table, making the crockery jump.

"You leave her alone!" Conor's voice was like a whiplash. His face was white and his hands in front of him on the table were balled into fists. Molly looked at him fearfully: she had never seen such rage and frustration on his face before.

"What did you say?" Micheál's voice matched his son's.

"I said, you . . . leave . . . her . . . alone!"

"Who'll make me?" Micheál tucked in his chin and

looked at his son from under his eyebrows. He held his head forward on his neck like a bull about to charge.

"If necessary, I will," said Conor, his own head forward now, his voice dangerously soft. "I hope it won't be necessary."

"Micheál, Micheál, he doesn't mean it *a stór* . . . You don't mean it, sure you don't. Conor." Sorcha moved forward automatically, but Micheál jumped up, and as he had so often before, pushed her out of the way. He tore off his jacket. "By God, we'll settle this once and for all."

"If you say so, Dadda." Conor was still cool, but his eyes glittered. He too stood up: "Where would you like it to be, Dadda? Here? Would you like to wreck the furniture again?" His voice rose throughout this speech, but he was still in control. Micheál stared at him, temporarily stupefied.

"What's keeping you, Dadda? Perhaps you need time to fetch your twine?" Conor's voice oozed with hatred.

Micheál exploded and lunged at him. "You fuckin' shit! Speaking to your father like that . . . ! I'll kill you—"

Conor stepped aside, too quick for him. "Oh, no, you won't. I won't let you. But I'm going to beat the shit out of you for all the shit you beat out of me." Lightfooted, he stepped outside into the heat. Micheál followed him at a lumbering run.

Molly and Sorcha ran into the back room and shut the door. Molly flung herself facedown on the bed and covered her ears. Sorcha lay beside her. She held Molly tightly and both their bodies shook with fear and weeping and shame that the fighting was to be seen by neighbors who, they knew, would not be long in gathering to watch the sport.

Despite the closed door and their own distress, they could hear faint sounds of the struggle outside. It went on, augmented by shouts from the small crowd that had gathered, for a good five minutes. Then abruptly the roaring stopped. Sorcha sat up on the bed and Molly uncovered her ears. "What is it, Mam?"

"I don't know, child. Something's happened." Neither of them moved. They hardly dared breathe.

There was a clatter in the kitchen and the door of the bedroom crashed open. It was Conor, bloody, with a torn shirt. The blood poured from both his eyebrows, from his nose, and from a split lip. He seemed dazed and held on to the door for support. "Mam, Mam. Come quick." His voice was bewildered. "Dadda's fallen and I think he's hurt . . ."

Sorcha pulled herself up from the bed and walked outside. Molly followed.

The little group of neighbors clustered around the door parted respectfully as Sorcha emerged. The men took off their caps. One of the old women blessed herself. After the shouting, the quiet was eerie.

Everything was very clear and slow. Micheál lay on the gray pavement. One of his fists was still bunched, the knuckles grazed and purpling. But the other hand lay open-palmed, like a baby's, and Molly noticed the scarring and deep lines that scored it. Her feet were bare and she noticed how warm the pavement was under the soles. She saw that Micheál's sightless eyes were open and that there was a trickle of blood out of the corner of one of them. As she watched, more blood came. It came from his mouth. Sluggish. Like water filled with red seaweed.

Micheál was dead.

Conor came out of the house and stood at the back of the crowd. Still there was silence. The day was overcast and humid and the earlier brightness of the afternoon had turned to gray. More and more neighbors were gathering around the body. A boy had been sent for the priest, and Father Moran came running down from the priest's house, his stole flapping. They all knelt down in a ragged little circle around Micheál while the last rites were administered.

Conor continued to stand at the back, but no one paid him any attention. He fixed his gaze on his father's face. He noticed that two flies were buzzing around the blood which was congealing on the forehead.

The crowd began to recite the rosary and Conor backed slowly into the house and then, moving quietly, packed the few clothes he could lay his hands on easily into his bag.

The crowd was still on the fourth Mystery when he came back out into the heat. They watched Conor as he walked away toward the beach, but no one attempted to stop him, and although their voices quietened somewhat, they did not interrupt the rhythm of the prayer.

He looked back at them from the beach. He could see them, many of them, standing silently now, watching his departure. Irrelevantly, the thought struck him that the rosary must have finished. He turned and continued to walk toward the water but looked back once more and his resolve to flee almost faltered. Molly, too, had come to watch him. He could pick out her distinctive blond head, a little apart from the rest of the crowd. She held one arm peculiarly, above her head, forearm resting on the crown.

As he hesitated, he saw Sorcha come to stand beside her.

His resolve hardened. He must not cause them any more trouble.

Turning his back, he took his uncle's currach. It was awkward to handle for one man, but he managed successfully to launch it in the calm sea. He threw his bag in and climbed in after it and began to row.

Even out here on the sea, there was a profound August silence, and the plashing of the oars was loud. He could still see the crowd watching him from the front of his house; in return, he watched them until he could no longer pick them out as individuals. He strained his eyes, keeping them fixed on Molly and his mother until the heat haze caused them to waver and finally to disappear. He closed his eyes and rowed and rowed, rhythmically beating the awful deed out of his shoulders.

Halfway across to Doolin, he felt his strength nearly gone, and the temptation was strong to curl up on the floor of the boat, to let the wind and the currents take him where they might. Every bone in his body ached and his hands were badly blistered. He had never rowed so far alone. Inisheer lay low to his face, but when he turned around, the mainland was still miles away.

He shipped his oars and, slumping in defeat on the seat, let the currach drift. The boat rocked gently on the swell; a pair of seagulls, which had been following in the hope of scraps, settled in the water twenty yards away and watched him with bright, knowing eyes.

After five minutes or so, he became aware of the faint throb of diesels from somewhere across the water and, alarmed, looked around for the source. A small trawler, half a mile from him, was moving briskly northwestward, too far away for him to read her name but he assumed from her course and the attendant gulls and seabirds that she was motoring homeward to Inishmore with her catch. He could not see if anyone on board had noticed him—but if they had, the trawler did not change course.

The sight of the trawler galvanized him. He realized the cuts on his face were stinging as badly as the blisters on his hands and, ripping off his torn and bloody shirt, he bathed his hands in the sea and then, taking care that he would not overbalance the boat, scooped the cooling water over his head and face.

Again and again he cleansed himself. The cold water ran down over his chest and back, and the shock of its coldness gave him courage. When he felt strong enough, he began to row again.

But the sun was setting as he neared the shore, and half dead from exhaustion, he could barely manage to beach the currach at Doolin. The only person about was an old man mending nets about a hundred yards away.

Conor turned the boat and took his bag and his torn shirt and sat on the shingle beach. His legs were trembling and his whole body felt as though it had been put through a mincer. Although all he wanted to do was to crawl into the soft grass behind him, he knew he had to keep moving. The moving was everything.

He looked over his shoulder to see if the old netmender was watching him and as far as he could tell he was not. He opened the bag, took out a clean shirt, and put it on. For the first time he noticed that Micheál's blood, or perhaps his own, had stained his trousers as well as his shirt. He eased them off and replaced them with a clean pair. Then, bundling up the discarded clothing, he placed it in the bag and pulled himself to his feet.

He had to find a telephone.

Molly stood away from the neighbors and watched the currach pull away on the flat sea until it was almost impossible to see it anymore. Her heart felt like lead. She could not cry, although she knew she probably should.

Behind her, she heard some of the neighbors carrying Micheál inside.

When she could no longer distinguish the figure in the currach, she turned away from the sea and went quietly into the kitchen of the house, where she found that the neighbors already had the situation under control. She sat beside Sorcha and accepted a cup of tea while the women washed Micheál and dressed him in his Sunday suit and put clean sheets on his bed. One neighbor brought in two beeswax candles to put on each side of the bedhead; another lent a white candlewick bedspread; a third supplied a linen pillowcase to cover the pillow.

It was only when he was properly laid out and decent, the candles lit and another decade of the rosary said, that it was decided to send word to the doctor on the big island to get the death certificate.

There was an argument then about whether the police should be fetched along with the doctor, with many of the men objecting, saying that this was the doctor's business if he saw fit. It was nothing at all to do with them, they said. But others argued that if they did not send for the police, the police would bother everyone on the island for weeks. This was the argument that prevailed in the end.

It was after dark when the doctor and the sergeant arrived. The sergeant spoke to everyone in the house, but no one, not one man or woman present, could throw light on what had happened to Micheál. No one had seen anything. They were polite and helpful: "Would he have fallen, d'you think?" asked Marcus O Braonáin.

"He might have tripped on the pavement, 'tis treacherous out there with all them cracks!" offered Seán Bán Nóra, Molly's second cousin.

" 'Tis that. Dangerous entirely. The government should do something about it!" snapped a widow woman from the far side of the island. "These days we're not safe outside our own front doors!"

The sergeant wrote everything down and then went into the bedroom to examine the body with the doctor. He had his notebook open still when he came out of the bedroom. "There's one son in Birmingham; where's the other son, Conor, is it?" he asked the general company.

The crowd looked at one another. Seán Bán was the

one who spoke. He said the last he had seen of Conor was when he went to the beach for a walk. "Aye, a walk. He might be back shortly, Sergeant," he said, looking around the company for confirmation, and everyone nodded in agreement.

The sergeant spoke to Sorcha, doffing his cap out of respect for her bereavement. "Sorry for your trouble, ma'am. Is that the truth, ma'am? Did your son go to the beach for a walk?"

Sorcha nodded and several of the neighbors joined in, saying they too had seen Conor go to the beach.

"Well, if he went for a walk, it's a long walk." The Sergeant looked around the circle of serious faces. "Where is he now?"

"Maybe he's gone to the big island?" suggested a man who had come with the widow woman from the other side of the island. Another man agreed with that, saying that he heard that Conor had plans to go to Inishmore. "Something to do with a trawler, maybe," said a third, cracking his knuckles and then taking a gulp of tea.

"A trawler," said the Sergeant.

"A trawler, aye!" agreed a chorus of the men.

"He has a lot of money now, d'you see, from Dublin," said the man who was first to say he heard Conor might be gone to Inishmore.

Molly felt nothing at all as she sat beside her mother. It was as if she were not present at the scene. But in her detachment, various pieces of detail engaged her attention. For instance, as he spoke to her mother, she noticed the way the oil lamp shone on the sergeant's silver buttons, turning them to gold.

Now the policeman was standing in front of her. "And what about you, miss? Did you see anything?"

She shook her head.

"I see." The sergeant snapped his notebook shut and looked around. "Nobody here saw nothing. Is that the case?"

The company murmured, each looking right and left to his or her neighbors.

"Well, ye'll all be called for the inquest. And if Conor O Briain comes back from his *walk* or from his *trawler* anytime in the near future, be sure to let us know. We'd like to have a word!"

He put his cap back on and stooped through the door.

"A right runner!" muttered one of the men, and a general snigger ran around the room. They all knew the sergeant was from the midlands.

Christian found himself in Rogers Park, heading toward Evanston. His agitation was such that after his exit from the apartment, his automobile had seemed almost of its own accord to take the road toward Greentrees. What was he thinking about? His grandfather's house was the last place he should go—or wanted to go. Sheridan Road at that point was wide and relatively traffic-free, so after a quick glance in his rearview mirror, he pulled the vehicle, tires squealing, through a violent U-turn and accelerated back toward the center of the city.

Almost at once a siren started up behind him. Shit! He might have known. Everything always happened to him. He could get away with nothing.

The policeman was polite but distant: "Can I see your driver's license, sir?" For once in his life, Christian managed to control his tongue; he handed over his license without comment and then sat, fuming but silent, as the officer wrote out the ticket.

The police car stayed behind him for several blocks, ensuring that he did not dare exceed the speed limit. He was tempted to slow down to a provocative crawl, but his survival instincts dictated prudence and he drove at a steady twenty-five until he saw the police car turn off at the Clark intersection.

He did not dare tempt fate again and kept within legal limits all the way along the Outer Drive. Although he did not normally favor classical music, he kept the car radio tuned to WFMT, which was broadcasting an hour of Schubert. After a while the relaxed, easy pace of the music and the low hiss of the automobile's air-conditioning combined to soothe him.

He tried to sort out his emotions as he continued to drive aimlessly, swinging right at Cermak and drifting along through an area of warehouses and used-car lots. At the junction with Western Avenue, a group of kids had opened a fire hydrant and were running, half naked and screaming, in and out of the gush of water. A woman, obviously the mother of one of them, unleashed a tirade of abuse at them from the other side of the street, while trying to control a perambulator and a toddler bent on running across the busy junction to join in the fun. Utterly detached, Christian watched the little scene as though the people involved were actors in a movie.

Then, in and out of the movie, flashed the scene with Jo-Ann. But each time it appeared, his brain, refusing absolutely to watch it, banished it again.

He forced his brain to remember the images. The tears, the distorted face, the slap. Despite the air conditioning, he went hot. The slap. What were they doing to each other? He would have to divorce her. There was no other way.

He was deeply unhappy and he could see that so was she.

His flirting and one-night stands did not make him happy; nothing made him happy anymore. The sex between him and Jo-Ann had been so powerful, so all-consuming, that for a time he had *thought* himself happy. But now he recognized that this had been an illusion, just the emotions being kept at bay with the busyness of the senses. At base, his happiness had been as unreal as the movie of the mothers and children he was now watching through the tinted glass of his windshield.

A few drinks, which used to help, no longer made him happy either.

In fact, the only thing right with his life was his work.

The light changed and he moved off, still not knowing where he was headed. Two blocks later he pulled over to the curb and looked around to get his bearings. Work. Although he was officially on a day off, he would go in to work. He and Dick were due to go again to Central America in ten days; there would be plenty to keep him occupied in the library.

He pulled out again into the light traffic, this time with purpose. And one thing was very clear. He would definitely divorce Jo-Ann.

The wind whistled through the broken glass in the telephone box, but Conor, oblivious to the discomfort, gripped the handset. The telephone at the other end rang and rang and he was just about to hang up in despair when there was a click and Tom Hartigan came on the line: "Hello?" The voice sounded frail.

The operator came on the line: "One shilling and eightpence, please."

There was an agonizing delay while Conor pressed the coins into the slot one by one. He pressed Button A and finally he was through: "Hello, Father."

"Conor!" The priest sounded pleased. "Is that you?"

"Yes, Father. Listen, I've not time to explain now, I'll be cut off and I've no more change. But I have a huge favor to ask of you . . ."

"What is it, Conor?"

"I'm telephoning you from just outside Doolin. I know this is a terrible imposition, and I wouldn't ask you except there's no one else I can turn to, but is there any chance you would come down here and pick me up? There's no transport out of here at this time of the evening and I don't want to hitch. I could wait for you in Lahinch."

"Sure, Conor," The priest didn't hesitate. "I've nothing on this evening anyway. Be glad to."

"And could I stay with you tonight?"

"You know you're always welcome here."

"Thanks, Father. I know it's a tall order, but I'll explain on the way."

"No problem," said Father Hartigan. "Where'll we meet?"

"I'll wait in The Sheaf," said Conor, mentioning a pub in the town. They hung up.

Conor welcomed the walk into Lahinch as a chance to clear his thoughts. The mugginess of the day had released the scents of the hedgerows and despite his distress and confusion, he was conscious of the smell of honeysuckle and wild thyme. It was a fine evening and there were a lot of people around, young people on bicycles and with packs on their backs, local families out taking the air. Not wanting to appear strange, he returned their greetings.

He tried to sort out his feelings. When his father fell, he had waited for a second or two for him to get up, rage and the heat of battle still flushing through his blood. But Micheál had not moved, and it was one of the neighbors who had moved forward and checked for a pulse.

Conor's first reaction had been one of bewilderment. He had looked stupidly at the body and then at the little crowd of now-silent neighbors. Then he had rushed in to get his mother. She had been lying on the bed with Molly.

Molly. The memory of the episode earlier in the afternoon, the surge of lust for her as Molly's long legs kicked and he cracked his palm on her bottom, washed over him like a wave, competing with the image of his dead father. He had been staggered when it happened and was staggered now. Whatever resulted from this day, nothing could ever be the same again between himself and Molly.

Never one for self-pity, Conor faced the inevitable: it would be better for all concerned if he disappeared. He looked out to sea. The long blue twilight had darkened the water and he could no longer see Inisheer. It was probably just as well. The sight of it might weaken his resolve. He turned his back and forced his aching legs to carry on toward Lahinch.

It was almost dark when he dragged himself into the town. His travel bag, so light when he arrived at Inisheer so few days before, felt as though it had tripled in weight. The sea shushed quietly and the promenade along the beach was still populated with strollers, but he made straight for the pub. It was crowded but mostly with vacationers, and to his relief, there was no one he recognized amongst the locals. He ordered a pint and sat at a table, pretending to watch two young men playing a fierce game of bar billiards.

The priest arrived at the pub less than an hour later, when Conor was halfway through his second pint. He stood up from his table: "I'd offer you a drink, Father, but I'm anxious to get going out of here."

They went out to the car. Father Hartigan had long ago disposed of his battered Beetle and now drove an equally battered Ford Escort. "Nothing could survive long on these roads," he commented as they bumped along through the darkness, but when Conor made no response, he did not continue the conversation.

They were approaching Ballyvaughan when he spoke again. He kept his eyes on the road as he said, "Suppose you tell me what happened."

* * *

Two days later, after Micheál's funeral, Father Moran was the last to leave the house following the customary meal. It had been a terrible day for him emotionally, conducting Molly's father's funeral, seeing her remote, beautiful face at every hand's turn. She was wearing unrelieved black, which contrasted starkly with her creamy skin and light hair.

He found it difficult to behave as a priest should during the obsequies, although the rubrics helped, leading him along familiar pathways which did not require too much concentration.

He had not, of course, referred at all to the manner of Micheál's death. No one had. It was as if a great silence had descended on all the island. The familiar phrases were passed around the mourners outside the church and in the graveyard:

He was a fine man . . .
A fine fisherman . . .
He had it hard . . .
He was a good man, he was . . .

To an outsider it would have seemed that Micheál O Briain had died in his bed.

The most difficult part of the day for Father Moran was the meal in the dead man's house after he was buried. Molly had been so near then, serving him his food and drink, moving around him in the crowded kitchen, so close that sometimes he could have touched her by merely shifting his position in his chair.

At last it was over and he could leave. He saw he was the last.

He stood up, and automatically the brother, Brendan, stood up too. From time to time throughout the day, Father Moran had noticed Brendan, home for the funeral from Birmingham. He was large and strong, like Conor, but there was a subtle difference. Brendan held himself slightly crooked, as if always waiting for someone to hit him.

Father Moran walked the few steps across the kitchen and shook hands with the man—who would not meet his eyes—and had a final word with Sorcha, who sat with her four sisters at the kitchen table. But although he mouthed the right words, the time-worn clichéd words about God's comfort and God's will, all the time he was conscious of Molly, sitting in an upright chair in front of the hearth.

He steeled himself to say good-bye to her, but just as he turned toward her, she got up from her chair to see him to the door.

She stepped outside with him into the blue evening.

Before he could stop himself the words were out and he had asked her to take a turn around the island.

She hesitated and looked back into the house. He saw she was going to refuse: "I don't know if I should leave Mam and Brendan," and he was almost relieved. "Of course, of course! I'll see you some other time." Then, to his amazement, she looked out over the sea and spoke again. "The aunties are all there, she'll be all right for a while. I think I would like a walk after all."

The day, like the day Micheál had died, had been overcast but not hot and humid, and the evening was soft with the lingering warmth. There was no wind, and in unspoken consent they walked down toward the shore where they would get the coolest air. As they walked slowly along just a few inches apart, and not wanting to break the spell of her presence, Father Moran, delirious at being alone with her, was afraid to open his mouth. He was afraid if he did, he would blurt something foolish which would shock or frighten her.

On the other hand, he could not understand why she did not feel the danger and run from him as fast as she could. His every sense was sharp as though newly born. He could smell her cleanness and could hear each step of her feet.

In expiation for what he was doing, he reassured himself that he had not planned this walk; if she had refused to come as at first she seemed about to do, he would have walked away. But her compliance seemed to him an omen.

They got to the beach and walked along it, their feet scrunching the shells concealed in the sand. She bent and picked up a piece of dried bladderwrack, popping its bubbles as children do for entertainment. The sound of the popping seemed overloud. Maddened with desire, watching those delicate fingers, Father Moran saw them playing, not with seaweed, but with himself . . . In an effort to maintain the vestige of his self-control, he walked a little ahead, but he was still acutely aware of her exact physical position relative to his own.

They came to the end of the beach and continued out of the sand into the dunes. The sea washed gently against the rocks beside them. They came to a little hill of grass. It was nearly dark.

"Let's sit down awhile, Molly, it's peaceful here." He couldn't help himself. He was embarking on something he could not control. A voice inside him wanted to warn her: *Don't. Don't sit down!*

She did sit down against the hill and spread one hand on the marram grass that pushed up through the sand, combing the rough blades between her fingers.

He sat down beside her. *This is madness . . .*

But he could not have moved away from her if his life depended on it.

She spoke then, for the first time; "Thank you, Father . . ."

"For what?" He was hoarse.

"For being so good to us."

He took her hands in his. "Oh, Molly, darling, darling Molly . . ."

She seemed taken aback but not excessively, and the words were out before he could stop them: "Can I kiss you?"

She continued to look at him and he could almost see her thoughts. He was a priest, after all, a pillar of celibacy and respectability. "I—I don't know, Father." She sounded puzzled, but still not alarmed.

He threw caution and self-control to the winds. He pulled her to him strongly, feeling against his chest the round young breasts. He kissed her hungrily, pinioning her body with urgent hands while he covered her face and throat with his inexperienced mouth and tongue. The pressure of his weight pushed her under him and for the first time in his life, Father Moran lay full-length on a woman's body. He was tensed for her to struggle, but she lay under him, quiescent; he pulled back a little, searching her face for signals. It was still and expressionless, staring up at him with large, surprised eyes. He kissed her again and heard his own throat make little moaning sounds. He unbuttoned the blouse she wore and, allowed at last to worship, lifted her breasts to his lips. They were smooth, ineffably smooth and pliant. Her skirt had but-

tons too but before he undid the first one, he looked at
her face again.

Now her eyes were closed. She had slipped from the
little hillock, and the movement had spread her hair out
behind her, a pale halo, paler than the sand.

The buttons slipped through his fingers, the skirt fell
away on either side, and her long legs and belly were
exposed to him. In the deepening darkness, her body
seemed to shine. Father Moran almost wept with joy and
desire.

When he began to pull down her panties she gave a
little cry, but he soothed her with soft kisses on her stomach; under his lips it had the feel of warm, downy silk.
His Molly, his beautiful young Molly. His lovely long-
limbed scented Molly . . .

Then, out of the blue, he was struck with panic. He
was fumbling desperately at the zipper of his fly when
the voice of some long-forgotten mentor boomed in his
brain, some canon in a country pulpit, or a Redemptorist
missionary raining perdition and brimstone on a congregation of terrified parishioners.

Pictures swirled: His mother's grave. His own body
prostrate on the ground at his ordination.

Frightening, gory pictures from his childhood: St. Se-
bastian pierced with arrows. Hellfire . . . An avenging,
terrible God with flaring white beard and thunderbolts
for fingers . . .

He looked at this luminous, unquestioning creature
spread beneath him, and luridly, she too seemed like a
picture from his childhood, an angel, an unblemished
martyr, St. Maria Goretti, the sixteen-year-old virgin at
the Annunciation: The Little Flower . . .

Father Moran pulled himself off her and ran away,
stumbling and tripping in the soft sand of the dunes, until
he got as far as the sea. Fully dressed, he plunged into
the water, surging forward until it had reached his waist.
He beat the water with his hands and bathed his face with
it as though its coldness could wash away his sin and his
lust . . .

Molly lay on her back and stared up at the sky. She
could already see two stars. He was a priest. No harm

could ever come to her with a priest. It would be the end of the world if you couldn't trust priests.

But she supposed now she could not be a nun.

She listened to the frenzied sounds in the water a few yards away. What was happening to her? Why wasn't she upset? She should be upset. Sex was the worst sin anyone could commit.

But it was all somehow like a dream, part of the last three days, fragmenting in half-seen, half-remembered snatches: her father's dead face, Conor in the boat, the open grave, the aunties' worried faces—it was all pictures. She had seen Father Moran unbuttoning her and it was like she herself were six feet above the two of them, looking down at him doing it. And when he took her breasts in his hands she half liked it, although somewhere deep inside she knew she shouldn't.

One Saturday afternoon about eighteen months ago, she and Kathleen Agnes had gone down to the nuns' orchard and kissed each other just to see what kissing felt like. Kathleen Agnes kissing her had been nothing like this kissing; Father Moran's mouth was hard and rough and yet at the same time, when he had kissed her nipples, she felt the same sort of sensations she felt while Conor was smacking her bottom.

Realization as to what had actually happened poured abruptly down over her like winter rain and she sat bolt upright, pulling her clothes around her. She should not have let him do that. He shouldn't have done it, any of it, but most of it was her fault. She hadn't stopped him, she had led him on.

She was an occasion of sin.

She was guilty of tempting a priest.

She became aware that the sounds in the sea had stopped. Oh, God! He was coming back . . .

Panic-stricken, Molly rebuttoned her blouse and skirt, her fingers clumsy in their haste. What was she going to do? What was she going to say to him? He loomed up before her before she had finished dressing and she jumped up guiltily, feeling as though she had been caught doing something dreadfully wrong. Father Moran's wet clothes clung to him and he had his hands over his face: "Oh, my God, Molly," he said in a voice she could barely hear, "what will you think of me, what can I say?" To her horror, she realized that he was weeping.

"It's all right, Father, it's all my fault, really . . ." While he couldn't see her, she continued the struggle with the buttons, but then he uncovered his face and took her hand. Molly felt paralyzed. She left her hand in his but it felt like limp pastry. His was as cold as a fish just taken from the nets. The tears were really streaming down his face and she was horribly embarrassed. "Please, Father, please," she begged, "don't . . ."

He bent his head over her hand: "Oh, my darling, darling, Molly, can you ever forgive me? I'm so sorry, I'm so, so sorry. You're the last person I'd want—"

Molly nodded desperately, hoping against hope he'd stop. "Please don't be upset, Father, it's all right, Father, it really is . . ."

He seized her other hand. "Molly, priests are human beings as well as priests and they fall in love just like other men . . ."

"Yes, Father," she said again. She was about to say a little prayer but remembered that it would be no use. She was now in mortal sin.

"Do you forgive me? The awful thing is, Molly, that I love you. I can't stand to be near you and yet I can't stand not to be. I know I shouldn't be saying any of this, but I've got to say it or I feel I will burst. It's not fair to say it to you, Molly, it's not fair, but I have to, I have to . . ."

"Please, Father," she begged again. She gave her hands a little tug and he let them go immediately. "I know you'll never want to clap eyes on me for the rest of your life," he cried, "but there's one thing you've got to believe, Molly—Molly, listen to me!" Now it was her face he took between his hands: "I love you very, very much, and what happened between us is all my responsibility. It's all my fault. You had nothing to do with it, Molly, don't ever believe that. You're a good, wonderful, pure person. It's just that I love you so much—" His voice cracked and she thought he was going to break down completely. She wished the ground would open up and swallow her. His eyes, only inches from her own, were blazing through the tears.

After a second or two he gained a semblance of control

and let her go. "You have your whole life ahead of you, Molly, and you must put this behind you." She stood very still. She felt that if she didn't move one single muscle that all this might go away. "I promise," he went on, "on my mother's grave I promise that I will never, ever bother you like this again. Please believe me."

"Of course I do, Father." She tried to move only her mouth and not her face or any other part of her body as she spoke. "I'm sorry too," she added, because she really was.

"Please try to remember me a bit kindly . . ." He seemed about to say something else but abruptly, he turned away and left her, running fast away from her across the dunes. She did not dare move until she could no longer hear the squelching of his shoes.

As she walked slowly back to the cottage, Molly decided that she would never reveal the events in the dunes to anyone, not even to Kathleen Agnes or Conor. She tried to think clearly.

A priest was in love with her. She hated the feeling, and it had nothing at all to do with Father Moran himself. It just did not feel right to have a priest fall in love with her. And there definitely must be something wrong with her. Priests just didn't fall in love with young girls. It just didn't happen unless there was some serious flaw in the girl.

She couldn't even go to confession about it. Priests stuck together.

He had promised he would not bother her again—and she believed he was sincere—but it was inevitable that if she stayed here they would run into one another over and over again.

She would have to leave.

The cottage was just ahead of her, light spilling out onto the pavement through the open door. She stopped and looked at it long and hard. How would she feel about leaving it?

Molly had said her real good-byes to the cottage and to Inisheer on the day she had left for the mainland boarding school. It would be hard on her mam, but she would send her money and keep in touch and would come home frequently—when she was sure that Father Moran was not on the island. She would have to devise some method of checking this out. Maybe she would have to confide in Conor after all—he could find out about Father Moran's movements through Father Hartigan.

But she discarded that idea. She knew instinctively that if he knew what had happened in the dunes, Conor would want to kill the priest.

Molly suddenly felt old. She checked that all her buttons were fastened properly before she let herself into the cottage. Her mother and the aunts were still sitting at the kitchen table, chatting quietly. Molly felt that her crime was probably written all over her face but none of the women seemed to notice anything unusual. She offered them a last cup of tea, but they all declined, so she said good night and went into her room.

She did not undress immediately, but sat on the side of her bed. She would tell her mam in the morning.

She would expiate her sins. The picture of Conor's dark, dishevelled figure, pulling strongly on the oars of the currach, swam into vision. Immediately she banished it. For now, that was a part of herself she refused to explore. She had enjoyed her brother spanking her. There was definitely something wrong with her.

She stood up decisively, undressed, and got into bed, turning on her side to try for sleep. Attempt as she might to keep it out, the picture of Conor pulling away in the currach kept coming into her brain; it kept getting mixed up with pictures of her dadda's corpse, of the priest's tearful face, of his lips on her nipples, of Conor's hand on her bottom . . .

For the first time since her dadda's death, she wept. She could not separate all the reasons for her tears. She wept for her dadda's death, her mother's sorrow, and Brendan's white, anxious face. She wept because Conor was gone. She wept because the priest was in love with her. She wept because she had grown up now.

When she woke next morning, it was broad daylight and Brendan was standing at the foot of her bed.

"I'll be going, Molly," he said awkwardly.

She sat up. "Where are you going, Brendan?"

"I think I'll be going back to Birmingham . . ."

"But it's still very early! The steamer won't be here until this afternoon." He shuffled his feet. "I know! Seán Bán said he'd take me to Inishmore." He looked at her with what she could see was an appeal. She understood. Brendan had to get away from this house of mourning and of women.

She told him to wait a few minutes and when he left the room, unquestioning, got dressed. She took her suitcase down from the top of her wardrobe and put her everyday clothes into it and her sponge bag and the whole lot came to only halfway up the inside of the case. Then she took her money from the drawer of her dresser. She had about eighteen pounds. She always saved her birthday and Christmas money from Brendan and Conor, because on Inisheer there was hardly anything to spend it on.

Her writing case was also in the dresser drawer. It was a long time before she started to write. When she did, she wrote fast; she knew if she hesitated at all, she would not carry out her plan. When she was finished, she picked it up and reread it:

> Dear Mam,
> I hope you'll understand this, but I have to leave the island and go to Dublin for a while.
> I hope you will be all right and that Aintín Móna and Aintín Moya will be able to stay with you a little while longer so you won't be too lonely. I'm only going for a week or two and I'll be home before the end of the summer, so don't worry.
> I will be fine in Dublin. I have the telephone numbers of the two girls in my class who live in Dublin and they have invited me to stay with them anytime. So I'll ring them just as soon as I arrive.
> Again, I hope you won't be too lonely, but don't forget, I'll be home soon. And I'll write just as soon as I arrive.
> Lots and lots of love,
>
>   Molly

The invitations from the Dublin friends were figments of her imagination, but she did actually have the telephone numbers and the more she thought about it, the more she thought contacting the two girls to be a realistic idea. Certainly the possession of the telephone numbers had increased her courage and determination.

She put the note into an envelope and addressed it.

When she went out into the kitchen, Brendan was sitting by the fireplace, staring into its cold depths. "Won't be a minute, Brendan," Molly called, propping the letter against a milk jug on the dresser. She put on her school gaberdine, too small for her, but the only coat she owned.

Brendan took her suitcase as well as his own and it occurred to her that he had not once asked her where she was going or why or what their mother would say. She supposed that if she lived to be a hundred, she would never fully understand this brother, so different from Conor.

They walked down toward the beach in silence, greeting neighbors they met along the way. There was no sign yet of Seán Bán Nóra. Molly had no idea what her brother's plans were but she intended to take the *Naomh Eanna*, which was not due to call at Inisheer today, from Inishmore.

She sat on her suitcase on the beach and looked out to sea. Brendan paced up and down the sand, scanning the roads of the island for first sight of Seán Bán. "I wonder should I go to his house?" he asked Molly after a few minutes, frowning.

"Give him another little while," she said. "It's still early." She looked over her shoulder to see if there was any sign of him.

Sorcha was running down the road toward the beach. Molly stood up. The sight of her mother running pierced her strange detachment.

Her mother's hair was loose and her feet were bare. When she was still a few yards away, she stopped.

"Hello, Mam," said Molly.

One of her mother's hands went up to her throat; "Molly . . ."

Molly saw that in her other hand, her mother carried her letter and another envelope. Sorcha took a few steps until she was within reach and held out the second envelope, so old that the folds were opaque, like old cotton. It was thick and she knew it contained money. Molly hesitated, but Sorcha pressed it into her hand.

"Oh, Mam!" Molly had deliberately left without saying good-bye. She had not thought she could bear it. She and Sorcha faced each other now while Brendan stood a little way off.

"What time are you going?" Sorcha asked, her hand still at her throat.

"Seán Bán Nóra is taking us to Inishmore. He'll be here any minute." Sorcha nodded and Molly could see she was trying to look businesslike. "Don't forget to write!" she said.

"I won't, Mam." Molly thought her heart might break, but she kept her tears in check.

"And if you see Conor . . ." Her mother looked away and tightened the hand on her throat. "Here's Seán Bán now," she said. "God bless."

She muttered good-bye to Brendan, then turned and walked back up the beach.

As the two men launched the currach, Molly opened the envelope. There were eighty pounds in it. She knew that it must be the money for Sorcha's funeral. All the women on the island put small sums of money aside throughout their lifetimes to pay for the boards for their coffins and supplies for the wake.

5

Y ou're welcome, I'm sure!'' Christian was past caring whether or not the caller noticed the sarcastic inflection.

Rubbing his eyes under his reading glasses, he replaced the receiver. He was doubling up, looking after his own copy and also helping out with the city-desk phones which had been hopping all night with calls which had been, from the desk's point of view, entirely unproductive. Most had come from concerned citizens in the suburbs who wanted to know if it would be safe for their little darlings to go downtown. How on earth did the city reporters handle all this crap without losing their tempers?

He got back to his profile of Tom Hayden, studying transcripts of the most recent speeches made by the New Left activist. Like flies to a feast, the Democratic Convention had drawn them all, a coalition of oddballs and radicals, Hayden and Abbie Hoffman, the Yippie Jerry Rubin, the poet Allen Ginsberg; the Reverend Ralph Abernathy was just about to arrive with his mule train and his Poor People; even the French playwright Jean Genet had popped up. In Christian's view, however, the convention in the Amphitheater and in the boiling streets and parks came down to a single contest: Mayor Daley versus The Rest.

He fiddled around with his opening paragraph, trying to frame the words so that they were trenchant but not opinionated. Given his very strong views on the way Mayor Daley ran Chicago, the task was difficult. It might well have been the Middle Ages and not 1968, he thought, with Richard Daley behaving as though the city were his own personal fiefdom. Tear gas, mace, and head-bashing outside; ructions amongst the delegates inside; but overall, astride Chicago and the Democratic party, the mayor had a single clear vision: Things His Way.

But things were not going all his way this week, and there were rumors all around town that Daley would make use of the National Guard.

For the fifth time, he tore the flimsy out of his type-writer and inserted a fresh sheet. Christian had a degree of sympathy for the radicals. He himself had escaped the draft and Vietnam only because, absurdly, he had been discovered to have flat feet and defective vision in one eye. If it had not been for this good fortune, he might now be a statistic. And as the war dragged on and on, the more useless and wasteful it appeared to him.

Professionally, however, he was required to be neutral. The owners of the newspaper were Republicans, but the *Sentinel's* editorial line was firmly nonpartisan about the war—although along with all the other newspapers in the city, it had called on the mayor to grant permits for the demonstrators.

It was more than Christian's job was worth to betray his personal opinions in his pieces. Foreign wars and famines were much easier, he thought glumly as he again attempted to start his piece. He wished this week was over and he could escape from the city desk, on which he was helping out simply because all spare bodies were required. The telephone rang again. He bent his head over a flurry of typing and ignored it.

"Nearly finished?" He looked up. Dick, festooned with cameras and laminated passes, was standing in front of him. "Yeah, another ten minutes!" The hell with it. He'd mulled over this long enough. He'd just write the goddamn thing and be done with it.

"I think I've one or two good shots of Hayden in to-night's stuff," said Dick, "I'm going in to develop them now. Want to see them when I'm done?"

"Sure."

"It's murder out there. You should go and see for your-self."

"Yeah, maybe later . . ."

The telephone rang again and this time he picked it up. It was a reporter from England, wanting to know if he could use the newspaper's morgue. Christian knew that at present the librarian was run off his feet with requests for clippings from the newspaper's own staff, but his sympathy was with the reporter. He had often been in such a position himself—strange city, knowing no one, needing information fast. "Yeah, that's okay," he said, "just come along to the front desk." He replaced the receiver. "How long will you be until you're clear?" he asked Dick.

"About an hour," answered his friend, already moving toward the darkroom.

"Want one?"

Dick hesitated, then: "Okay. See you in the Shamrock."

Christian, distracted from his copy, watched his best friend's progress through the newsroom. He had noticed Dick's hesitation about joining him in the bar. All right, so he took a few too many now and then, but that was his own business, not Dick's. Christ, he thought, returning to the typewriter and attacking the keys, was he never to get a bit of peace? Dick seemed to be taking over where Jo-Ann had left off.

As it happened, he and Dick did not make it to the Shamrock Bar that evening.

Just as Christian was finishing his piece, the switchboard of the *Sentinel* received a tip-off about possible trouble in Lincoln Park, and the pair of them went down to investigate.

An hour later Christian was wondering if the tip-off might not have been a little premature—although the number of pressmen and media crews present indicated that somebody, somewhere, was expecting something. But it had been dark for more than an hour and so far there had been no incidents.

On the other hand, the tension in the air was as sharp as the blade of a knife. The demonstrators, mostly long-haired and nearly all kids as far as he could tell, were determined not to be moved away from this grassy patch between North Clark and La Salle Drive. The police, he knew, were just as determined to move them. But as far as he could tell, neither side seemed to want to make any sudden moves.

Many of the kids, occasionally passing joints to one another, sat cross-legged in little groups, but their posture was straight-backed and alert; more of them milled restlessly around, talking in low, urgent voices. Christian, accustomed to picking up words here and there and lacing them together, realized they were expecting a police charge. Indeed, as he watched, some of them began building a crude barricade with benches, tables, branches of trees, garbage, twigs—anything they could find.

The police cars prowled nearby, quietly, not making much of a fuss, although the crackle of the radios was constant and several of the cops muttered into walkie-talkies. The police cars were not sounding their sirens, but the blue and white roof lights revolved in the darkness, giving a surreal cast to the people nearby.

The impending trouble laced the air between the two sides like a bad smell.

Members of the press corps, which included Christian and Dick, were hanging around in a little wooded area. Christian had done all the interviews he needed for his piece. He had quotes from Genet and the American writer William Burroughs and acres of crazy, idealistic prose from the kids. But he could not leave until after the trouble. All the other reporters waited too. No one wanted anyone else to have exclusive action. To pass the time, they talked about expenses.

A girl who was part of a group near Christian was handing out jars of Vaseline from an embroidered Indian bag and the group began to smear the petroleum jelly all over their faces and hands. Christian strolled over. "Excuse me," he said, "I'm from the *Chicago Sentinel*. Could you tell me what you're doing?" The girl, he saw, could not be more than seventeen, with a fragile, gentle face. "It's to protect our skin from the mace." she said. "That stuff really burns, you know, and if they get your eyes, you're in deep shit!" Her voice shook.

Christian, in the interest of color for his story, watched her, noting mentally that some of her long, fine hair was sticking to her cheek.

Then all hell broke loose.

It started when a police car drove at speed toward the barricade and smashed it. After the calm, the tearing and grinding and gunning of the engine was shocking. For a split second the girl sat, frozen, with the open jar of Vaseline in her hand. Then she leaped to her feet. "Pig! Fascist pig!" she screamed, her face contorted with hate.

She threw the tiny jar in the direction of the police car, but it landed just twenty or thirty feet away from her.

The action of the police car acted as some sort of signal, unleashing individual action. For a few seconds Christian's instincts as a reporter deserted him. He watched in horror as the police raced toward the demonstrators, swinging their clubs at random, cracking them on the youngsters' unprotected heads.

Then the kids counter-attacked, pulling at the cops with bare hands and makeshift weapons, sticks, anything they could find; Christian snapped to. He switched on his tape recorder and began a steady commentary on the action; dictating continuously, he backed away toward the wooded area and the safety of the newsmen's phalanx.

But then, as the television crews, big burly men, walked resolutely toward the action and into the thick of it, he walked back with them. All around him sounded the screams of the outraged and the wounded; a girl who could not have been more than sixteen ran around and around in erratic circles, screaming obscenities; an elderly man, his long, stringy hair matted with blood, sat alone and untended. As the action swirled around him, he held out a hand, begging for assistance from anyone who would give it. Everyone, including the reporters, ignored him.

A policeman went down and was set upon by a group of demonstrators who congealed around him into a snarling, hate-ridden mob; the man's colleagues rushed to his aid and brought their batons down indiscriminately on backs, on shoulders, on any unprotected part of a human body they could reach.

The screaming rose to a pitch that shocked and sickened Christian, but his adrenaline was pumping now, and staying with one particularly robust TV crew, he switched his brain into a gear that automatically registered all the sounds, smells, and sights while his voice continued to record the detail of the incidents around him into his tape recorder.

He realized he had temporarily lost sight of Dick and looked around for him. He spotted him almost immediately, kneeling on the grass to photograph a boy in a poncho who seemed to be unconscious, blood pouring out of a wound high on his cheekbone. Christian was just about to shout to him when, from the wooded part of the park, a pack of police, badges and name-plates removed, came surging out from the cover, swinging at the photographers and snatching at their cameras.

"Dick! Dick!" screamed Christian, but his voice was lost in the mayhem. Dick, intent on his work, was not watching what was going on behind him and did not see that one of the pack, nightstick in the air, was bearing down fast on him.

Before he could think, Christian sprinted to intercept the cop, who he could see was intent on his target and did not notice him coming in from the side. Christian managed to get to him a split second before the baton arced at Dick's unprotected head. He threw himself bodily at the cop, catching him in a football tackle and knocking him over so the policeman, carried by his own momentum, cannoned over his back as though he were a vaulting horse.

Christian managed to scramble instantly to his feet and put out a hand to help Dick get up, but then, inside his head, there was a huge explosion, wheeling with bright lights and colors and shocking pain.

He woke in Henrotin Hospital, his head pounding. Dick was sitting beside him and so was one of the night editors from the newspaper.

"How are you feeling?" asked the editor.

"What happened?" The muscles in Christian's face hurt when he moved his mouth to speak.

"You were clubbed," said Dick, "but don't feel bad! You weren't the only one. Seventeen newsmen. Even the networks."

Christian closed his eyes. He felt giddy.

"Sorry to have to ask you this," said the editor after a pause, "but I don't suppose you know where your notes are?"

Christian shook his head, or tried to. "Tape recorder?" he managed faintly.

"They took the cassette," said Dick, "and my film. All of it."

Despite the pain, Christian felt the rage well up from his toes. "Don't need notes," he said. "My clothes . . ."

"You can't leave here. You've had a bad concussion."

But the editor's voice lacked conviction. They had already missed the first edition and they weren't covered.

Christian, fueled by his fury, was feeling stronger. "Dick," he said, "get me out of here."

"Are you sure?"

"I'm sure."

Against the doctors' explicit advice, Christian signed himself out of Henrotin. He felt groggy and the pain still split his skull, but his rage was stronger than the pain. He was going to get the bastards, he told himself. When he had the story written he could think about rest and sleep.

The newsroom was frantic with telephones. Christian sat at his typewriter and took a deep breath, trying consciously to bite back his fury so he would use nothing but the facts. He started to type, forcing himself to write only exactly what he had seen, but even as the words flowed, he knew exultantly that this would be the best thing he had ever done. The story poured like molten steel, hardening precisely on the pages.

It took only forty minutes to write and the night editor, who stood by Christian's desk and took the pages one by one as they were finished, changed not a single comma. When the last page was off his desk, Dick drove Christian home to his apartment in Old Town, but Christian waved away his offers of help. He let himself into the apartment and went straight for the refrigerator in the kitchen.

Jo-Ann had pinned a note to the door: *Gone to Mary-Ann's.*

Jo-Ann's mother had been called Ann and all her sisters were Something-Anns. When he had first met her, Christian had thought it cute; now he thought it just plain cutesy.

He crumpled the note and put it in the trash can under the sink and took a fresh bottle of Scotch from a cupboard. He put a large quantity of ice into a tall glass and poured in a generous measure of the whiskey, loving the crackling sound it made as it came in contact with the cubes. Then he carried the drink into the bedroom and without bothering to undress, got into bed.

The next day he woke around noon, his head throbbing as though it had been put through a mincer. But at least, he thought, flexing his arms and legs, he did not any longer feel he was going to die. In his bathroom, he shook four aspirins into his hand and gulped them down with a glass of water, then padded into his kitchen and made himself a cup of strong black coffee, into which he poured another tot of the Scotch. He lay down on his bed again, but within half an hour he was feeling a little better and from the telephone on his night table put a call through to the newsdesk.

"Hi, Christian," said the news editor, "there's a message for you—by the way, congratulations on your story—Morton wants to see you." Morton was the newspaper's editor-in-chief.

"What's it about?" Christian was always suspicious of summonses to the inner sanctum.

"Have no idea," said the news editor. "Why don't you call him?"

"Okay," said Christian. As soon as he had hung up, he dialed the newspaper again and was put through at once to the editor's office. "That was a fine story from the park, Mr. Smith," said the editor, who called all his staff by their surnames.

"Thank you, sir . . ."

"The wires picked it up and I believe you were quoted on BBC television news in London." The editor, like most newsmen all over the world, have very high regard for the standards of British broadcasting.

"That's great, sir."

"Yes, well, just wanted to say that. By the way, how's your head?"

"Getting better, sir. No lasting damage."

"Yes, good, good. If you feel up to it, Smith, maybe you could do a follow-up? The action isn't over yet, you know . . ."

"Yes, sir." Christian's customary attitude to all bosses was one of barely concealed truculence, but the editor's tone was conversational, man to man, and made him feel uncomfortable. "Yes, sir," he repeated, "I'll go down to the mayor's office and see what's what there . . ."

"Good man!" said the editor, then, before he broke the connection, added a succinct: "Bastards!"

Christian replaced the receiver. That was good. Maybe a raise or a bonus in that . . . He should get started on the story.

He sat up in the bed and his head swam; his hands were shaking too. Better have a drink, he thought.

Kingsbridge Station in Dublin was bedlam and Molly had to fight hard to control her feelings of panic. Her suitcase at her feet, she stood on the platform, trying to get her bearings while the streams of disembarking passengers flowed around her. The noise was awful too; beside her, the throbbing of the diesel locomotive seemed to vibrate right inside her head and, the stream of loudspeaker announcements booming through the struts of the iron roof was completely unintelligible.

Everyone except herself seemed to have a purpose, to know exactly where to go; everyone else seemed to have friends meeting them, jostling behind a barrier at the end of the platform. No one gave her a second glance and the impulse to turn right around and to take the next train back to Galway was very strong.

But she must not be a coward. She had come this far and there was no going back now.

She picked up her suitcase and joined the throng hurrying toward the barrier. At least she had a definite plan and enough money to last her for a bit. She planned that for the first night at least, she could afford to stay in a hotel. She would be safe and it would give her a breathing space.

When she got outside, she had no idea whether to turn right or left. The only place-names in Dublin with which she was familiar were O'Connell Street and the G.P.O., the general post office, which had been the scene of the Easter Rising in 1916. If she could get as far as the G.P.O., which she knew was right in the center of the city, at least it would be somewhere to start from. "Excuse me," she said to a man in a peaked cap, "could you tell me how to get to the G.P.O.?"

The man gave her directions but looked doubtfully at her suitcase: "Are you walking?"

"Yes."

"Well, it's a goodish walk. You'd be better off with the bus."

He told her where to get the bus and which number, but when she got to the bus stop, she had already forgotten which bus he had mentioned. Remembering his directions, she looked up the quays, jam-packed with hooting, honking traffic. At least it was a clear walk with no way to get lost. And it probably was not all that far. She decided to walk.

But after a few minutes, she wished she had taken the man's advice about using the bus. She hated the pungent, sweetish smell coming from the oily waters of the Liffey, which was at low tide; the black smoke belching from the backs of buses and trucks, the sodden litter that strewed the gutters and the sidewalks. And although she had turned up the collar of her coat, the cold drizzle was seeping uncomfortably down the back of her neck.

After ten minutes, the suitcase was dragging painfully at her shoulder and she had to put it down to rest. She seemed to have been walking forever and the city's center seemed as far away as ever. She could not walk any farther and looked around for a bus stop. Maybe she could take a taxi . . .

Then, just ahead of her, she saw a set of flags drooping on flagpoles from the facade of a gray building. A hotel! Whatever this hotel was, however much it cost, she would book a room. She picked up the suitcase again, walked the remaining few yards, and entered the lobby of the Clarence, small, warm, quiet—and laced with homely smells of cooking.

"May I help you?" The young woman behind the reception desk smiled, but Molly thought she detected a look of scorn in her eyes and wished she had taken off the too-short school coat before she had come in. Then she decided she was being oversensitive. She drew on all her willpower and courage: "I—I'd like to hire a room, please. Just for one night," she added, trying to sound firm and as though she was used to this kind of thing.

"Yes. Just yourself is it?" And when Molly nodded, the woman looked her directly in the eye: "That'll be cash in advance." Somehow, although the woman's voice remained pleasant, Molly immediately felt guilty. "Sure," she said, fumbling in her cheap shoulder bag, "how much, please?"

"Thirty shillings. One pound ten—but that includes breakfast."

Molly drew out Sorcha's envelope, and seeing the woman's eyes flicker toward it, castigated herself for leaving the money in it. And then she remembered the years of sacrifice that had gone into the gathering of it and raised her chin. There and then she decided she would never, ever, be ashamed of her mother or of her origins. Making no effort to hide the tattiness of the envelope, she extracted a pound and a ten-shilling note and passed them across the counter.

The woman wrote something in a book, then gave Molly a form to fill in. This time Molly had no hesitation. She wrote her name and address, in Irish, and passed the form back.

"Inisheer!" said the desk clerk, studying it. "My boyfriend's from Galway!"

"Is he?" Molly was almost taken aback by the change in the woman's demeanor.

"Yes. He's always at me to go out to Aran. I believe it's gorgeous—well, maybe next year!" She flashed Molly a smile of genuine friendliness, then hailed a porter who was hovering in the background: "Tony! Number twelve, please . . . I hope you enjoy your stay in Dublin. Shopping?"

"Y-yes, that's right. A bit of shopping!" Molly surrendered her suitcase to the porter—who did not seem all that much older than herself—and followed him up the stairs and down a short corridor lined with doors. He stopped in front of one of them and inserted a key in the lock.

Molly's only other experience of hotels had been the one night in the lodging house with her mam in Galway when she was five. Although this room was small and dark, it was clean, with a washbasin and a neatly made bed. Molly looked around and decided that it was grand.

"Will there be anything else?" asked the young porter. He seemed to be waiting for something. "No, thank you," said Molly. Then, remembering her manners: "Thank you very much for carrying my case." The porter again seemed to hesitate, but then smiled at her and left.

When the door clicked shut behind him, a wave of loneliness seemed to assault her from the wall opposite. No one cared what she did now. There were no nuns, no Sorcha, to tell her what to do. She was truly alone. She sat on the bed and concentrated on the fact that she must not feel sorry for herself. This had been her decision. She had to make the best of it.

She realized that she was very hungry. Good! Something to do. She would go and buy something to eat. She took out her money and counted it—still more than seventy-five pounds left. Although two days ago it might have seemed like a small fortune, she would have to be very careful with it. This money might have to last her for a very long time.

She tidied her hair in the mirror over the handbasin, then washed her hands and face and left the room. For a few seconds she was tempted by the smells coming from the hotel diningroom—and by the safety it offered—but then again raised her chin. She might as well get used to being on her own and in the city.

The desk clerk, who was holding the phone to her ear, smiled and waved at her as she left the hotel.

Outside, the traffic on the streets seemed to have eased a little, but although the drizzle had stopped, it was cold. She pulled the hood of her coat over her hair and buttoned the tabs under her chin. Unencumbered this time, she walked swiftly, and as O'Connell Bridge at last came into view, she began to feel almost adventurous, even slightly exhilarated. She had a base, a temporary home. She was embarked on—who knew?

When she reached O'Connell Bridge, she crossed it and, fascinated by the garish bustle, walked slowly up one side of the wide street and down the other. Everyone seemed to have somewhere to go. People got on and off buses and greeted each other and strolled arm in arm in pairs or in bigger groups. There were queues of couples outside the cinemas. She recognized the G.P.O. because of the posting slots and stamp machines and for a few minutes joined the dozens of people who, all dressed up and sheltering under its stone portico, stood swinging their gaze up and down the street watching for the approach of the people they were to meet. Almost happy now, Molly wondered how long it would be before she too had an appointment at the G.P.O.

She crossed the street. Clery's windows were plastered with red SALE signs and were crammed with goods. Molly had never seen so many goods in her life or such a variety—bed linen and dish towels and women's skirts, cardigans, underwear and bathing suits, men's suits, jackets and shoes, boys' blazers, girls' party dresses, luggage, tea sets and hurleys and tennis rackets, clocks, watches, kettles and cutlery. Sorcha would have loved it.

Farther down the street was a Cafolla restaurant. There were pictures in the window of plates of food, plump sausages and big chips, bright yellow eggs and massive, pastel ice cream sundaes. This was the place.

Although the meal was not as good as the pictures outside, Molly felt warm and fed after it and lingered over a cup of tea. Pleased to see she was not the only one eating on her own—plenty of the tables had only one person sitting at them—Molly felt that she would fit into city life just fine.

The streetlights were on when she went back out onto O'Connell Street. She wandered past Clery's again, then turned right, walking down North Earl Street and crossing onto Talbot Place. At the end of that street, there was another railway station—at least she assumed it was another railway station; there was a bridge running across the street in front of it. Two railway stations! Although she had often imagined how big Dublin must be, now that she was actually here, its size astounded her.

She was standing at the corner of Talbot Place, looking at the railway station, when she noticed, in the window of a pub on the corner, a small piece of paper. "Help Wanted," it said. Before she could second-guess herself, Molly went inside.

The bar was packed and noisy and there was a blue haze of cigarette smoke in the air.

A middle-aged man looked up from the row of pints he was pulling. He was balding and had a kind pink face. "Did you want something, miss?"

Molly's nerve almost failed her, but she forced herself to speak. "C-could I talk to the m-manager, please?" she stuttered.

"I'm the manager." The man waited but Molly seemed to have run out of words. What had she been thinking of? She imagined everyone in the bar was looking at her. "S-sorry," she whispered, and was about to turn on her heel to flee when the man called out: "Whoa! Hang on a sec . . ." He wiped his hands on an old dish towel and led her in through the connecting door from the pub to the lounge, which was also full but not half so noisy. He turned to her and smiled: ''Now we can understand each other.''

''It's—it's about the notice in the window . . .''

''I see.'' He seemed to be thinking as he lugged in an electric kettle behind the bar. ''Do you mind me asking how old you are?'' he asked.

''Sixteen—nearly seventeen, sir.'' Molly was astounded at her own daring.

''That's still pretty young—would you like a cup of coffee?'' Without waiting for her reply, the man spooned instant coffee into a cup. Molly had tasted coffee only twice in her life and had hated it, but she nodded.

He handed it to her and smiled, his head cocked to one side. Encouraged by his kindness, Molly threw caution to the winds: ''I really need a job. I'll do anything, sir. What kind of work is it you want?''

''Drink your coffee—do you take sugar, Miss—Miss—?'' He pushed a sugar bowl toward her.

''Ní Bhriain,'' Molly supplied, putting two spoonfuls of sugar into the coffee and stirring it.

Not knowing what to say next, she sipped the coffee, taking the smallest sips possible, while the manager busied himself transferring glasses from the countertop to the sink then running a noisy stream of water over them. At last he turned off the water. ''Ní Bhriain, eh? Are you from the Gaeltacht?''

''Inisheer,'' said Molly eagerly. Twice in one day! she thought. Inisheer certainly seemed to have a certain resonance for people in Dublin.

''Don't know Inisheer, but I know Inishmaan. John Millington Synge. I suppose you know all about him?''

Molly did indeed know the name of the playwright, not from the island, but from passing references in school. *''Playboy of the Western World,''* she said. ''And of course I've been to Inishmaan. Many times,'' she added.

''What's your first name?''

''Molly.''

''You look as though you should still be in school, Molly—but that's none of my business. Do you have any references?''

Molly's heart sank, but she gave it one more try. "Not yet, sir. This would be my first job, sir."

Again he cocked his head to one side: "I'll tell you what," he said. "Come back tomorrow evening about nine. I'll need help in the lounge. Would you be willing to stay late?"

Molly couldn't believe her luck. The coffee cup clattered in the saucer as her hand shook. "Of course I would, sir. As late as you like."

"That's it, then," he said. "See you tomorrow night, so! I'm sorry, but I have to get back to the bar. Mick'll crucify me!" Seeing her look of mystification, he giggled. Like a turtle retracting into its carapace, his ruddy face shrank into his collar, and his whole body shook with noiseless amusement. "Mick's the barman inside." Still laughing, he indicated the public bar with a jerk of his thumb. The effect was irresistible and Molly laughed too.

"My name's John Pius McCarthy, by the way," he added, holding out his hand, "but everyone calls me J.P."

Molly took the hand: "Thank you very much, Mr. McCarthy."

"Right-oh," said J.P. "See you tomorrow night." He showed her to the door of the lounge: "Mind how you go."

After he had gone back inside, Molly felt lightheaded. Only four hours in Dublin and already she had a job! And what's more, she had not planned it, it had just happened. She felt it was an omen. She was so elated she wanted to skip and run up the dingy street back toward O'Connell Street. Then she remembered. She had forgotten to ask about money! It did not matter, she told herself. She had a *job*—and already she trusted John Pius McCarthy.

The distance back to the Clarence seemed to be half what it had been when she had left the hotel. When she got into the lobby, there was a different receptionist on duty behind the counter; Molly informed her that she would be staying on for two more nights. She took her key, smiled at the young porter, and went up to her room.

But once in the room, her elation evaporated bit by bit as the events of the past few days crowded in. Too much had happened in too short a space of time. Three days, no, four days, no—six, seven days ago? Kathleen Agnes and Conor were the only two people on her mind; she had been down on the strand at Inisheer and Conor was coming ashore.

Now, a week or so later, her dadda was under the ground, Conor had vanished, maybe forever—and then there was what had happened to her that night with Father Moran.

She would not think about that, even here where no one could possibly know or guess what had happened. That was in the past. Something that had happened once and that would never, ever, happen again. Over. Forever. Resolutely she closed her eyes. She must get some sleep if she was to work effectively tomorrow.

Nevertheless, sleep eluded her and for hours she tossed and turned on the unfamiliar bed. She told herself that what was keeping her awake was just the night sound of the hotel, the small creepings and creakings and distant murmurs.

At one o'clock in the morning, she sat upright. What about school? She had abandoned school without a second thought. The nuns had had such high hopes for her. Maybe, she thought, plumping the single pillow and lying down again, she would take just this year out of school and go back twelve months from now. She'd save money and would have enough after this year to keep herself and pay the fees . . .

But although she tried to convince herself, somehow Molly knew deep in her heart that she was finished with school.

Next morning, bleary-eyed, she left the hotel at about nine o'clock. Seeing a church near the hotel, she considered briefly going in and going to confession, but almost as soon as the thought occurred to her, she banished it. What was the point? Priests stick together. Anyway, she really didn't have the nerve.

She marched past the church and went into the city center, where she spent the morning window-shopping and wandering around the huge department stores. She was loath to spend any of her store of money but decided that if she was to be respectable for her job, she should really have a new outfit. Clery's was jammed because of the sale, but it did offer the best prices. She selected a dress she thought would fit. It cost almost thirty shillings, the same as her bed and breakfast—but it was light gray, the same color as her eyes. The saleslady asked her if she wanted to try it on, but never having shopped on her own before, Molly was overcome with the strangeness of the experience and declined.

"No exchange on sale goods!" warned the woman as she popped the dress into a paper bag.

"That's all right, it's not for me, you see!" Molly lied. "It's a present."

The woman looked at her and then wrote something on a piece of paper: "Tell you what, dear," she whispered, "that's my name. If it doesn't fit you—I mean your friend—bring it back to me personally. All right?"

Her lie exposed, Molly blushed. At the same time she was very grateful—and pleasantly surprised at the kindness of Dublin people. First Mr. McCarthy, then this saleslady. She had always had the image of Dublin as an alien place.

She smiled at the woman and thanked her; then, carrying her purchase, she left Clery's. She found she was hungry again, so because it felt safe and familiar, she went back to the Cafolla's to eat her dinner. Afterward she walked back to the hotel, where she went to her room and tried on the new dress, which, as far as she could tell in the small mirror in her hotel bedroom, fitted her as well as could be expected. She took it off and hung it carefully in the wardrobe, then lay down for a nap.

Wearing the dress, she was at the pub shortly after eight o'clock. Mr. McCarthy was nowhere to be seen and no one seemed to be expecting her. But the barman in the lounge recognized her and allowed her to sit at the counter. He poured a Britvic Orange and plonked it in front of her.

Mr. McCarthy arrived in the lounge at a quarter to nine. "Punctual too!" he said when he saw her, then, standing back with his hands on hips, "My! Gray suits you, my dear, you should wear it all the time!"

"Thank you, Mr. McCarthy." The nuns had always told them to accept compliments gracefully, but Molly had always found this to be a difficult art and despite herself, felt a blush beginning. She looked away to give herself a chance to control it.

Mr. McCarthy ran the electric kettle under the faucet of the sink. "Call me J.P., please!" he said. "Everyone does. 'Mr. McCarthy' makes me feel like a teacher!" He giggled then—that extoraordinary retracting giggle—and at once she felt at ease.

As he made her a cup of coffee—Molly could see she would have to get used to drinking coffee—he explained what her duties were to be. Inexperienced though she was, she could see they were light: to assist the lounge boy if there was a crowd, to help with the cleaning up after closing time. Molly wondered if this job was a real one—or if he just gave it to her out of pity. And that made her feel uneasy all over again.

She could not think of any way to broach this, however. By this time, J.P. was explaining that not every night, but most nights, the pub played host to a small circle of special clients—actors, theater people, writers, artists—who stayed on after closing time. Part of Molly's job would be to serve them and to clean up after them. "But don't worry if it goes too late. We'll always arrange a lift home for you. Where do you live, by the way?"

When she told him her address was the Clarence Hotel, he was scandalized. "Living in a hotel? It must be costing you a fortune!"

Molly managed her work quite well that first night, and since no one stayed on after closing time, John Pius drove her home to the Clarence and she was in bed before one o'clock.

The next morning, John Pius, clutching a newspaper, arrived unexpectedly at the hotel. He announced he had found her a flat, a single room above a shop on Dame Street and had come to show it to her to see if she liked it.

Molly did. It was tiny and heated only with a single-bar electric fire, but it was clean and newly decorated and had everything she would need. They went back to the Clarence and checked Molly out. Then, while Molly was unpacking in the flat, John Pius vanished for a few minutes, and when he came back, pink and giggling, he handed her a large paper bag: "House-warming!" The bag contained a colorful wall calendar and a small table lamp with a pretty floral shade.

Molly was speechless at his kindness.

"And here's a plug!" he said, pulling it out of his pocket. He taught her how to wire a plug, using the blade of a knife he found in the cutlery drawer in the minute, curtained-off alcove that served as a kitchenette. The small single window in the flat faced north, but when they plugged in the lamp and switched it on, the whole place was flooded with warmth. "Oh, it's lovely!" Molly clapped her hands like a child. "Thanks a million, Mr. Mc—I mean J.P."

John Pius beamed back at her. "Now for the party!" he said, producing a small bottle of champagne from another pocket.

Molly felt more at ease with this man by the minute. She had never drunk champagne—nor any alcohol—and she was fascinated by the way it fizzed into the chipped glasses John Pius found in the kitchenette. When she took a sip, it prickled like holly on her tongue.

The actors came to the pub that night. They arrived at about eleven, and John Pius herded them into a corner until the rest of the patrons had left. Then he stoked the log fire in the lounge, turned the lights low, and brought bottles of wine from his cellar. While Molly cleaned up the counter area and made sure the actors had glasses, John Pius put Bach's Double Violin Concerto on his soft-toned hi-fi and then introduced Molly to everyone individually. She was sure she would never remember all the names.

John Pius went upstairs then to make tuna fish sandwiches for them in his own kitchen and Molly was left in charge of the lounge. She moved around as unobtrusively as possible. Following John Pius's instructions, she made sure the log fire was replenished and that she was always on hand to give out the drinks. Most of them were drinking wine, so it was quite easy.

For long periods that night she had little to do and she hung back in the gloom of the lounge, beyond the circle of light around the fire. But one of them, Macartan O'Toole, noticed her reticence and insisted she come for-ard to join them. She sat silently and in awe then while ʼe vivacious, glamorous people, keeping their resonant voices under control for fear of a raid by the Guards, drank quietly and reminisced and told stories. Molly was a new audience and they played to her. She adored them. She was enchanted by them.

Marcartan and his pal, Dessie Byrne, were the core of the group that came to the pub. On the fourth night he was there, Dessie made a point of talking to Molly. He was quick-witted, good-looking, and very charming. Molly had never met anyone like him before but to her surprise, she found it quite easy to talk to him as, gently, he quizzed her about her life story.

She did not reveal all of it but told him only the bare bones. She told them nothing about Conor or her dadda's death. But when he asked her why she had left school and come to Dublin so young, she felt bold enough to say "To seek my fortune!"

That gave Dessie an idea. The following morning, the Abbey was holding "extras" auditions for the crowd scenes in O'Casey's *The Plough and the Stars*. "You should come down and audition, Molly. Be a spear-carrier. It's how all the stars began their careers!" he said, slapping his knee at his own genius. And the audition will be as easy as pie—you'll see. They won't even ask you to read lines."

"Yeah, why don't you come along, Molly?" urged Macartan, who had been listening in, "it'd be a start and it would be great fun. You'd love it."

John Pius, also listening in on the conversation, encouraged Molly to agree: "Come on, give it a try, Molly, why not?"

"There'll be nothing to it!" said Dessie. "Honestly, Molly. Piece of cake! And we're both in it," he added, indicating himself and Macartan as if that clinched it.

"Don't be shy, Molly," said Macartan. "We're all shy, honestly!"

"Shy, me arse!" said Dessie. "The day you're shy, Macartan O'Toole, will be the day pigs fly! Seriously, though, Molly," he said, turning to her, "actors *are* shy. You know what they say, acting is the shy person's revenge!"

"I'm not all that shy!" Molly was very tempted. "I played Hamlet, you know."

"Oooooohhh! Stop the lights! *Hamlet* no less! Get

her, darlings!'' Macartan limp-wristed Dessie, who slapped him away: ''Shut up, Macartan, you'll put her off.'' He turned back to Molly: ''What about it, Molly? I'll set it up for you. Ten o'clock, Abbey auditorium.''

Molly looked at the circle of encouraging faces. ''Sure why not?'' she said recklessly.

For the rest of the evening her brain whirled with the heaps of advice she was given. Most succinct of all, just before he left to go home, was Dessie's: ''Forget everything we've just said. Just turn up and don't fall over.''

Next morning she arrived ten minutes before the appointed time. Only the working light illuminated the stage and the dark auditorium seemed cavernous, but she could just make out a small group, two young women and a young man, sitting together near the back. When she arrived, they stopped talking and looked across at her, but she did not have the nerve to join them and took a seat a few rows behind them.

The other three did not resume their conversation and Molly felt her confidence drain away as the seconds passed. Dessie's advice about not falling over did not seem so funny after all—she would trip over her feet and make an absolute fool of herself. She would open her mouth and nothing would come out . . .

Panic-stricken, she was standing up to leave the theater when a large, stooped man came onstage from the wings and clapped his hands like a schoolteacher. He shaded his eyes and looked out over the auditorium: ''One, two, three, four. This all?'' he said in a stentorian voice, ''I must say I was expecting more than four. Oh well—'' He sighed and took a pen from the side of a clipboard: ''Names, please?''

It was too late to leave now. Molly went to the front of the auditorium and, last to speak, gave her name.

Then the man called all four of them up on to the stage. The other three seemed to know exactly what to do. They exuded an air of experience and confidence. Molly stood a little way behind them and to the back. She had been mad to agree to this.

''Come on, come on, my dear!'' The man consulted his clipboard. ''Molly isn't it? Come on out here till we see you. Lovely, lovely,'' he said when Molly stepped forward. ''We'll have to hide that lovely blonde hair of

yours. Can't have you upstaging our stars now, can we?''
The other three laughed and despite her nervousness,
Molly found herself smiling along.

The auditions were easy—Dessie had been right. All
they had to do was to stand in the middle of the stage,
cheering loudly as if they were watching a football game,
and then they had to walk on and off a few times, using
different entrances and exits. "That's right," the man
encouraged, "your team's *winning*—try to look cheerful.
You, blondie!''—he addressed Molly—''cheer away,
happy happy happy . . . Good, good, good . . .''

At the end the man, whose name Molly did not know
because he had not given it to them, told all four candi-
dates that they were hired at two pounds a week for a
four-week run. Molly rushed back to the pub with the
good news and of course John Pius was thrilled for her.
He told her that during the run of the play, she didn't
have to come to work until after the final curtain each
night.

Then he took her out to lunch in the Gresham Hotel to
celebrate, just as though she were already a star.

Conor watched a little Arabic girl chase the pigeons in
Trafalgar Square. Again and again she rushed at them,
flapping her own small arms like wings, but the pigeons,
world-weary, were experienced enough to stay a few
inches ahead of her no matter how fast she moved or in
what direction. As her veiled mother watched dotingly,
her father, motordrive whirring, took photograph after
photograph of her.

Conor could not take his eyes off her. Although there
was nothing in the child's appearance that even vaguely
resembled his sister's, there was something about her
laughing and running that reminded him of his carefree
ramblings with Molly on Inisheer so many years before.

Resolutely he turned his attention away from the scene
and, hands in his pockets, watched the other tourists. He
had been to London on a few occasions, but those visits
had been made for pleasure: a football match or a weekend holiday. This time, instead of the joy of discovery
and carefree exploration, he found himself tramping the
London streets ridden by fear and a feeling of loss. He
had arrived in the city more than two weeks ago and had

spent his first night in a sleazy hotel in King's Cross. At
least, he thought, his attention caught by the sight of a
down-and-outer rummaging through a litter bin, he had
better accommodation at the moment, a small private hotel in Bayswater.

He watched the bum carefully unscrew a twisted piece
of newspaper and investigate the contents. The man could
well be Irish; Conor lived in fear of running into someone from home, since the first question was always,
"what county are you from?" and this inevitably led to
other questions. As a result, he avoided the conviviality
of the pubs. Even in the non-Irish parts of London, many
of the staff behind the bar were Irish.

So for the two weeks he had been in London, he had
haunted free museums and art galleries, eaten cheaply in
fish-and-chippers or in Chinatown, attended movies in
the afternoons.

The evenings were the worst, since he had nothing to
do except go back to his room.

He was running out of money fast. He had to get a
job.

The thought was daunting. He had to avoid anything
in the area of his expertise—botany, even gardening—
since he supposed that these were the areas the police
would check first.

He pulled out his address book. He had not yet telephoned the priest whose name Father Hartigan had given
him as a contact in case he needed help. His friend had
assured him that this priest was discreet, and he had also
promised to write immediately to him with an introduc-
tion.

He found the number and walked over to a telephone
box. He seemed to be hiding a lot under the skirts of the
clergy, he thought grimly as he dialed the number, but
he seemed to have created a trap for himself with no
other way out.

The priest, who was in and whose name was Frank
O'Hare, made it easy for him. "Oh, yes!" he said cheerfully, "Tom Hartigan's friend. I was expecting you to
ring. Now where'll we meet? I don't suppose you want
to come all the way out here . . . ." He lived in Willesden.

"I'll come anywhere you say, Father."

" 'Frank,' please! None of this 'Father' stuff over here,

not on my beat. I'd drop dead if any of my clients called me 'Father!' '' Father Hartigan had told Conor that Father O'Hare operated in some of the toughest parts of London.

"All right, Frank." But Conor found it difficult. Deference toward the clergy was very deeply ingrained.

"Now, what time is it?" continued the priest, then answered himself. "Just after two. Do you like fish? There's a lovely fish restaurant just off Leicester Square. Manzi's. Do you know it?"

Conor did not. "I'm sure I could find it, Father— Frank."

"All right. I could do with a good bit of fish. Once a month I treat myself. Suppose we meet at Manzi's at about seven?"

"All right, Frank, see you then. And thank you very, very much."

"Don't thank me yet; I haven't done anything for you yet. But I've been having a think since I got Tom's letter and maybe we'll be able to get you fixed up. I suppose you don't object to manual labor?"

"No, Father—Frank, I don't object to anything at all. Anyway, I'm hardly in a position to object . . ."

"Don't talk like that. Where there's life there's hope! All right?"

"All right. Thanks again."

"Until tonight, then . . ."

"Good-bye, Frank." Conor hung up. Expending nervous energy, he walked all the way to Cromwell Road and spent the afternoon at the Victoria and Albert Museum.

He found Manzi's easily that evening and went inside. He was too early, it was only a quarter to seven, but the restaurant was very busy and they could not guarantee him a table for at least an hour. "Perhaps we can accommodate you at the counter, sir?" The waiter was friendly but formal. Conor nodded, intimidated. He was virtually a stranger to good restaurants. There were a few in Dublin, but none was frequented by anyone in his circle of friends; his group tended to congregate in pubs or to eat celebratory meals in each other's home.

"May I have your name, sir?" The man held a silver pen over the reservations book.

"Molloy," said Conor, using the name under which he had registered at his hotel. "Seán Molloy."

"Thank you, sir," said the man, and looked over Conor's shoulder to where the next customer already waited.

Conor went outside and walked into Leicester Square. Although the theater rush-hour had not yet begun, the evening was quickening; couples peered at movie posters or scanned the entertainment pages of the *Evening Standard;* the tourists seemed to have left their shopping bags and cameras back at their hotels and strolled, unencumbered and ready for the night's entertainment, all around him. Their carefree demeanor shot knives into Conor; with all his heart, he wished the clock could be turned back, that the had not been so stupid as to take on his father. He looked at his watch. There was no use in feeling sorry for himself. The die was cast and he had to get on with his life as best he could.

He walked back to the restaurant and immediately on entering, was greeted by a blocky, sandy-haired man wearing a polo-necked shirt and gray jacket: "Hello there, looking for me? I'm Frank O'Hare."

"That's right—how did you know me?" Conor looked around nervously. Was he that obviously recognizable?

"Don't worry, son." The priest chuckled, "I got a good description from Tom Hartigan—and anyway, you're a pretty conspicuous specimen of Irish manhood!'

"What do you mean?" Conor felt sure that someone must be listening, but on checking again, saw that they were on their own in the tiny lobby.

"Fishing for compliments, are we?" answered the priest cheerfully. "Never mind. If you don't see what I mean, why should I turn your head! Now, shall we go in?"

"Yes—actually I was here earlier and I reserved a table."

"Good."

"But I could only get seats at the counter."

"Perfect. That way we can see what they're bringing us."

The man who had taken the reservation saw them come into the restaurant and after a moment came over to them. To Conor's relief he did not address him by name but merely showed them to two adjacent places at the counter. "This all right, sir?"

"Perfect," said Father O'Hare, picking up the menu. While he perused it, Conor watched him covertly; should he be the one to bring up the subject of their meeting? The opening sentence was on the tip of his tongue when Father O'Hare slapped the menu down on the counter with a grunt of satisfaction: "I do like a good piece of fish," he said. "This is a great idea. Now, tell me the whole story." He fixed Conor with his alert, pale eyes.

"The whole story, Father?" The priest's sudden shift disconcerted Conor. In the past two weeks, he had gone over the events on Inisheer so many times in his mind that they had become almost surreal; images of his father's glazed, lifeless eyes were juxtaposed with the eyes of the seagull he had encountered on the sea while rowing across to Doolin; the rosary beads dangling from the hands of his neighbors were intertwined with the net being mended by the old fisherman who had seen him struggle ashore. "It's—it's a very long story, Father."

The priest's gaze did not flicker. "Just the gist will do. And don't worry, this is not confession. I'm not here to forgive, absolve, or even understand; I just want to help, okay? Action is what we're about from now on." His air of calm acceptance was such a relief that Conor could have hugged the man. Instead, keeping his voice to a low murmur in case he could be overheard, he told the story as succinctly as he could, beginning with the history of violence between himself and his father and ending with his flight from the island. Throughout the short narrative, Father O'Hare listened without comment or question, and when it was finished, he said simply, "I see."

Their order was taken then, and after he had given it the priest continued, still in the same, matter-of-fact way: "What we need now is a breathing space. The police may or may not be after you—even if they are it takes time for them to catch up with people. I'm neither condoning nor condemning what you did, mind, I'm just helping, understand?"

Conor was distracted by the arrival of their soup. The priest picked up his spoon. "Now, I've been thinking since you rang me and I've a few ideas for you, but the first thing you have to do, Conor, is to change your appearance. Somebody who looks like you is too easy to spot . . .''

"What can I do? Should I grow a beard?"

"Mustache. But before that even, first thing tomorrow, get your hair cut really short. There's not much we can do about your height, but the head of hair is a dead give-away. Mmm''—he took a mouthful of the fish soup—"this is really good!"

"All right, Father," said Conor humbly, "I'll get it cut tomorrow."

"Really shaved now, mind!"

"Right. And I'll start growing the mustache right away."

"The next thing is, telephone that number tomorrow at eight o'clock. This man's reliable; he'll give you a start." He took a piece of paper out of his inside pocket and passed it to Conor, who saw, on glancing at it, that the name was Irish. "Who is he?"

"Subcontractor. Friend of mine. No questions asked. You've heard of the lump?" With gusto, Father O'Hare spooned up the remainder of his soup and patted his belly. "Delicious. Can't wait for the sole . . .''

Conor, who had barely touched his own soup, leaned forward anxiously: "I've heard of it. You get paid in cash and it's all under the counter, no tax involvement—but are you sure that won't get me into even more trouble?"

Father O'Hare laughed heartily. "If you do, my son, it'll be yourself and half the Irish community in certain areas of this town. That's the least of your worries—don't give *that* another thought."

Conor took a mouthful of his soup: "Do you think I'll be able to make a go of it, Father—building work, I mean? I've never done it before—''

"Of course you will, big fellow like you. There's nothing to it." Then the priest sat back and appraised Conor: "Pity, though," he said slowly, "pity it has to be like this. From what I hear you could have done really well for yourself. Still''—he looked appreciatively at the steaming sole being set in front of him—"can't be helped now. What we have to do from now on is get you on the road again."

With all her heart and soul, Molly threw herself into her new life. She wrote to Kathleen Agnes, although the

relationship between her and Kathleen Agnes, so close
at school, was fading as their lives took divergent paths,
and to her mam. To her mother she wrote:

> John Pius McCarthy, the man I told you about who's
> my employer at the pub, and all the people in the
> theatre, are being very kind to me and they all think
> that maybe I can have a career on the stage.
>
> It's much, much different to acting in school. I can't
> really explain it—it's just that everyone around you is
> so good at what they do and they all work so hard,
> Mam! It's sort of half fun, half the most serious thing
> in the world. Oh, I'm making a mess of this. I can't
> really describe it. You'll have to see it for yourself.
>
> Maybe yourself and Brendan, or yourself and one
> of the aunties, could come up to see me on the stage?
> I'd love to have you see me (although I don't have all
> that much to do, no lines or anything, but all the ac-
> tors say I'm quite good), and anyway I'd really like to
> see you. You could stay in my flat. It's small but I'd
> make you really comfortable. Oh, Mam, I'd love you
> to come. Please think about it.
>
> I'd love to show you around Dublin, too. I live right
> in the middle of the city so that I can walk every-
> where. I pass Trinity College, where the Book of Kells
> is, on my way to work every day. Think about it.
> Apart altogether from coming to see *me*, I could take
> you to a cinema—there are great pictures on in Dublin
> and they are on all afternoon, every day.
>
> Must close now as its time to go to rehearsal.
> *Rehearsal!* Doesn't that sound great?
>
> Love to yourself and all the aunties. I hope you're
> not too lonely, Mam, with us all gone now. But I
> know the neighbours will be looking after you. Have
> you heard from Brendan? I'll be home soon, don't
> worry. The only thing I worry about is where Conor
> is. But knowing him, he will be fine.

Before sealing it, Molly reread the letter. Where was
Conor? Hardly a day went by that she did not worry
about her brother. In her imagination, Conor sometimes
lived exotically, a nomad in the deserts of Arabia; some-

times mundanely on the building sites of Birmingham, of which she knew a little from Brendan. She never for a second, however, doubted that he was surviving.

He had written to her just once, a short note forwarded to her, via her mother, by his friend, Father Hartigan. In the letter he told her not to worry about him and finished by saying that, God willing, he would see her as soon as he could, even if it proved to be a long time.

She did miss him dreadfully, but every time she thought about him, that last dreadful scene of her father's death was superimposed on his face. No matter how tired she was, that image still haunted her every night as she lay in her narrow bed.

Well, she thought, it was early days yet. "Time heals all wounds" was one of the favorite sayings at the convent. She placed a five-pound note in the envelope and sealed her mother's letter. That was that. Now for her real life. She had been so lucky.

The thing now was she had to capitalize on the luck, work as hard as she could, keep her eyes and ears open. Then—who knew what might happen? The sky was the limit! She added a swift P.S. to the letter to her mother:

I nearly forgot, I'll be sending you a little bit of money very soon. And with my career about to take off, Mam, you'll soon be living in the lap of luxury.

She put the letter in her pocket for stamping and posting.

Molly continued to work for John Pius on a part-time basis and because she was so enthusiastic and willing, was taken on as an extra in the next show at the Abbey and the one following that. She became friendly with the backstage staff and when, in October, the run of her third play finished and there was no extra work needed in the following play, she was offered a slot as an assistant stage manager at the Peacock, the basement theater operated by the Abbey.

The routine at the theater was morning rehearsal, afternoon free, performance in the evening. Molly took full advantage of the afternoons, becoming an avid cinema-goer. Sometimes when the days were too fine to incarcerate herself at the movies, she explored the city, riding the buses out to their farthest terminuses in Tallaght and Stillorgan, Ballymun, Ballyfermot, Clontarf, Sutton, Finglas, Howth, and even Bray, just for the pleasure of the rides.

She loved Henry Street and the fruit vendors on Moore Street. Sometimes she bought a bag of apples for the pleasure of hearing the Dublin accent, so different from her own. She practiced the accent—which at night she heard regularly in some of the plays she worked on—and tried it out on John Pius. Laughing, he told her that for a country girl she was doing fine . . .

All the time there was the enchantment of her new job. Molly was amused but still fascinated at the bitchy, witty talk of theater people, even though she was now accustomed to it. She had come to the Abbey in a state of nervous anticipation, expecting a group of very special, dramatic, and high-octane personalities. She had expected uplifting discussions about art and that she would learn her trade at the feet of serious artistes who were on intimate terms with the language of Sean O'Casey and John Millington Synge . . .

What she found was a group of people who bitched and complained all the time about the cold, about drafts, about the shortness of their lunch hours, about the miserable effin' management which wouldn't give them the time of day; actors who read newspapers during rehearsals if not actually onstage—and sometimes when they were—who knitted, wore wooly hats and mufflers while rehearsing love scenes, and who drank endless cups of tea. She never ceased to be amazed each night when, from the wings, she saw this crowd of moaning caterpillars transforming themselves into elegant butterflies.

Her favorite time of the day was at around six o'clock in the evening, when the box office and day staff had left and the night staff had not yet come in. She was frequently alone in the theater at that time, and although the building was a new one, on the outside an uninspired concrete pillbox, Molly's vivid imagination clothed its interior with history and fantasy and peopled its huge open stage with traditional spirits.

She wandered about, loving the old smells, of venerable costumes, of flats repainted a hundred times, of sized wood and canvas; she listened for old whispers; she peered out into the tiers of empty seats which spread across the auditorium like a wide feathered fan of blue.

One evening, when she was absolutely sure she was alone, Molly stood very still, stage-center. She closed her eyes and imagined that she was an actress—a real actress, the lead in one of the Abbey plays: Nora Clitheroe in *The Plough And The Stars* or Deirdre in Synge's *Deirdre of the Sorrows*. In her imagination, the performance had been a triumph and she was taking her curtain calls while wave after wave of applause and cheering swept over her. "Well done, Molly!" said her costars to her as they held a hand on each side of her and took their bows at her side . . .

There was a sound of a door closing in the distance and Molly's eyes flew open in fright. Feeling foolish, shading her eyes against the single worklight, she peered into the auditorium, ready with an excuse—but there was no one there. She retreated into the wings and closed her eyes, continuing her "performance" where she knew she could not be observed.

Largely because of being adopted by Macartan and Dessie, she was accepted very quickly into the actors' pub circle, not only in John Pius's pub but in the bar everyone went to immediately after the performances. She listened to the outrageous character assassinations and with some fascination, began to notice the shifting romantic attachments.

Molly was so preoccupied with her new life and the possibilities of becoming a serious actress that she had not given sex or romance for herself much thought. And she was so pleasantly tired every night that even when the memories of the episode with Father Moran did intrude on her consciousness, she usually fell asleep before they could take hold.

One night, confident that Macartan and Dessie were already in the pub, she came in by herself to join them. But neither was anywhere in sight. John Chalmers, the visiting English director who had been imported to direct a production of Shakespeare's *A Midsummer Night's Dream* to be staged in the Peacock, was standing at the crowded bar, a pint of beer in front of him. "Hello!" he said on seeing her enter, "come and join me, Molly— I've been watching you!"

Although Molly was working on the production in her capacity as ASM, she had not had much social contact with the director, who was in his forties and formidably self-assured. She looked around to see if there was any help in sight, but everyone she knew was involved in a group. "Hello, Mr. Chalmers," she replied. "I'm actually looking for Macartan O'Toole. Have you seen him come in?

"Is he your boyfriend?" asked Chalmers.

"I beg your pardon?" Molly was startled at his directness.

"Is he your boyfriend? Macartan?"

Molly shook her head: "He's a colleague . . ."

"I see," said Chalmers. "I like to know these things." He called the barman. "Drink?"

Molly hesitated, then saw she had no option if she was not to appear rude. "Yes, please, a Britvic."

"Come on, have a real drink . . ."

"No, thank you. I'd really prefer the Britvic."

"Suit yourself." He ordered the drink and while they were waiting for it to arrive he pulled out a stool and indicated she should sit on it. "You were good this morning, Molly."

One of the actresses had been ill that morning and as was customary, Chalmers had asked Molly, as the ASM, to stand in at the rehearsal and to read the missing actress's lines.

"Thank you." Molly was genuinely thrilled. With no pressure on her to perform, she had moved about the stage quite naturally, taking cues, reading the lines from the promptbook without "acting." She had loved the experience.

"Have you had much experience onstage, Molly?" The barman poured half the orange drink into a glass in front of her and Chalmers passed a few coins across the bar. He poured the rest of the mineral water and handed it to her.

"Well, I was an extra in a few plays upstairs in the Abbey."

"Is that all? I would have thought you've done more than that."

"Well—school, you know . . ."

"What kind of things did you do there? Tell me." He

pulled out another stool and moved it very close to her. As he sat on it and looked directly at her, she realized his eyes were a deep brown. He was unnerving her. "Well," she answered, "you know how it is in girls' boarding schools—"

"No I don't actually." He laughed. "Midnight feasts in the dorm, bullying prefects, the triumph of Prue in the Lower Fourth—that would be my idea of a girls' school. Or at the very least, Edna O'Brien. *The Girl with the Green Eyes*. That sort of thing."

"What I meant was that when it's all girls, the taller ones get to play men's parts. I've played Malvolio and Saint Patrick and—and Hamlet," she ended lamely.

"I see." He laughed again. "Quite a spread. Seriously, though, I do think you have talent."

"Do you really think so, Mr. Chalmers?" Molly was unsure of how to react.

"I certainly do." He put a hand on her shoulder and brought his face right up to hers. "And I'll help you if you'll let me." The image of Father Moran's face exploded in her brain, but she forced herself not to flinch. This man was a *director*.

Over his shoulder she saw Macartan come out of the Gents. "There's Macartan now," she said gaily, careful not to seem as though she was rejecting Chalmers or being rude. The director looked around. "So it is."

Molly waved at her friend, but on his way over to the bar Macartan was intercepted by two women who had obviously been at the performance that evening; they were producing programs, which Macartan was proceeding to sign.

"That name of yours," said Chalmers, dropping his hand from her shoulder, "is it Gaelic?" He smiled at her and she noticed that for a man his age—he must be nearly forty, she thought—he had almost perfect teeth. In the habit of making instant decisions about people, she decided she liked him. His confidence and ease certainly made her feel quite confident herself. "Yes," she said, "it's O'Brien, really. If I was a man I'd be O Briain—the 'O' means literally 'from,' so it's 'son of . . .' Because I'm a girl, the 'Ní' is short for *iníon* and that means 'daughter.' So my name means 'Molly, daughter of Brian.' "

"I see," he said, still smiling. "Judging by the number of O'Briens I meet in Ireland, this chap Brian must have been quite a lad! May I buy you another drink? Sure you won't change your mind and have a real drink?"

"Oh, it's my turn!" said Molly, snatching up her handbag.

He put his hand over hers: "Put it away, my dear. By the standards of an ASM's salary, the Abbey is paying me a fortune."

"But—" Molly protested. She had already noticed that the tradition in the theater was that men and women, no matter what their status, bought their rounds equally.

"I insist," said Chalmers. "I'm thinking of it as an investment in your future." Again he smiled, and the expression in his brown eyes made Molly feel uncomfortable. "Thank you," she said, and when he turned away to order, she looked toward Macartan to appeal to him to come over, but he was still deep in conversation with the two theatergoers.

At that time of night the pace behind the bar was furious, but this man, Molly saw, had the knack of attracting instant attention. "Now," he said, after he had given the order, "what'll we talk about, Molly? Your career? What kinds of parts would you like to play?"

"Anything—anything at all. Well," she amended honestly, "anything good. I don't want to play rubbish."

"So young and so wise." He took her hand and, raising it to his lips, planted a grave kiss on the back of it.

Macartan joined them, but the director did not seem in the least embarrassed by being caught kissing Molly's hand. "It's my round, what are you having, Macartan?" He did not relinquish the hand.

"Thanks, John, pint of Smithwick's, please." Macartan never refused a drink. "How'ya, kid, how's she cuttin'?" He planted a kiss on Molly's cheek. He either did not notice what was going on, she thought, or he regarded it as perfectly normal that she was sitting in a public bar holding hands with an English director she did not know and who was more than twice her age. Her hand seemed to burn in Chalmers' as, raising his voice, he called the pint to the barman.

She did manage to extricate her hand when Chalmers had to use both of his to count some change out of his pocket. Macartan's arrival sparked up the conversation and she sat back and watched as the two men discussed details of the morning's rehearsal.

"And what did you think of our Molly here?" Chalmers put his arm around her shoulder.

"Powerful. Sure I discovered her!" Macartan grinned and gave her an affectionate thump. "This young one's going to go far, I'll tell you, John. Hope you won't forget your friends when you're a star, Molly!"

Molly felt absurdly pleased and excited. She agreed to go to a party Macartan had heard about and the three of them set off for Rathmines in a taxi. They stopped at an off-license on the way and the Englishman offered to go inside.

"Right, right, John!" said Macartan, "two six-packs should be enough. We won't stay long . . ."

"We should give him some money," protested Molly to Macartan when the director had gone out of the car.

"Nonsense," said Macartan, "he thinks this is great. He's on great money. Let him buy us a drink. It's our taxes that's paying for him anyway!" Molly was familiar with Macartan's logic. The National Theatre was subsidised; Macartan paid taxes; Macartan paid the salaries and fees for everyone in Ireland who did not pay taxes.

"You're absolutely awful." But Molly was laughing.

"Shut up, Molly, here he is, back. Hello, John. Good man, good man."

The party proved to be celebrating nothing in particular. The tiny flat was packed, with groups and couples either standing, or sitting on chairs and arms of chairs, on each other's lap, and on the floor. One group, ranged on two sides of a corner, made room for the newcomers, and Molly settled herself with her back to a wall, between John Chalmers and Macartan. She was wearing a miniskirt and took care to arrange her legs modestly to one side of her but noticed that the director was looking at them. One part of her liked it; the other wished she had worn jeans.

For atmosphere the host, another actor, had turned out all the lights and had set dozens of lighted candles in milk bottles and jam jars on the mantelpiece over the blocked-up fireplace. The candles threw long, dancing shadows and their waxy smell combined in the room with the cloying aroma from joss sticks. The Beatles' *Sergeant Pepper* album played softly on the record player, almost completely overwhelmed by the tidal wave of talk. Molly noticed that the stacking arm was out, meaning that *Sergeant Pepper* was the only record they would get to hear that night.

Macartan showed John Chalmers how to open a bottle of beer with his teeth. The director laughed: "That's very good, my friend. But where I come from, that's sissy. You've got to be able to do it on the wall. And with one hand. Don't worry." Noticing Molly's alarm, he put a hand on her shoulder. "I'm not going to give a demonstration tonight!" He handed Molly the bottle of beer Macartan had already opened and held out a second one for opening.

Molly hated beer, but not wanting to appear to be a party poop, she took a tiny sip from the bottle. Chalmers, she realized, was still watching her: "How old are you, Molly?" he asked suddenly.

"Eighteen." she lied. It was the first time she had ever done so and she was astonished. Immediately he slipped an arm around her waist. "You're very lovely," he said softly. For the second time that evening, the priest's face swam in front of her eyes. Chalmers sensed her rigidity: "What's the matter?" he asked.

On her other side, Macartan had felt her stiffen. He leaned forward. "Is everything all right, Molly?" he asked her, but looked at the director.

"Everything's fine," said Molly.

"Are you sure?"

"She's fine, Macartan," said Chalmers, who did not remove his arm.

After a while, Molly found she could relax a little. She even enjoyed the closeness. The Englishman was putting no pressure on her, but continued to chat easily about his career in the theater, about previous trips to Ireland. Macartan was absorbed in a passionate argument about the film *The Lion in Winter*, which was all the rage among the actors at that time, and Molly was left to her own devices as John Chalmers skillfully created an exclusion zone around the pair of them. Bit by bit, he drew her out, encouraging her to tell him about her childhood on Inisheer—it never ceased to amaze Molly how interesting people found Inisheer.

The director finished his beer, put the bottle on the floor beside him and, still keeping his left arm around her waist, took Molly's hand in his free hand so she was completely encircled. "Are you a virgin, Molly?" he asked softly.

Macartan, on Molly's other side, again felt her fright. He stopped in mid-argument and turned around. "Everything all right, Molly?" Again he stared hard at Chalmers.

"I beg your pardon?" The Englishman stared back.

"Did you say something to Molly? She seems to be a bit—*upset* . . ."

"I'm sorry, but I don't think this is any of your business."

"Oh, but it is. Did you know this girl is only seventeen?"

"She told me she was eighteen, but again, I don't see what this has—"

"Molly"—Macartan addressed her directly—"What did he ask you?"

Molly wished the ground would open up and swallow her. She was sure everyone in the room was watching.

"Look," said Chalmers, "whatever your problem is, Macartan, please don't make an international incident of it."

"Sorry, John"—Macartan's voice was rising—"but I'm not making an incident of this. I'm merely asking you what it is you said to her. You definitely said something. I know you said something, she's definitely upset."

"Please, Macartan, it's all right," said Molly faintly, "I'm all right, really."

"I think we should go," said Macartan decisively, standing up in one lithe movement. He leaned forward and crooked a hand under Molly's arm. "Come on, darling, let's go."

"Just a moment," said John Chalmers, "I think we should let Molly decide whether she thinks it is time to go or not. She's a big girl now. We were having a pleasant conversation, and I think perhaps it is up to her whether she wishes it to continue . . ."

"Well, Molly?" demanded Macartan, still with his hand under her arm.

Held between the two of them, Molly felt like a bird impaled on the spikes of a public railing. How on earth had this got so completely out of hand? "Every-everything's fine," she stuttered, "it's—it's all right, Macartan, really." He said nothing. "Honest. I'm not upset at all."

"See?" Chalmers' urbane tone had not changed at all during the exchange, and distressed though she was, Molly could not help but admire his composure.

"Well, if you're sure, Molly. I'm right here—remember?" Macartan released her arm.

"Thanks, Macartan, I'm fine. Honestly."

"Well, Molly," said Chalmers when Macartan had recommenced the argument about the film, "perhaps we could meet again sometime when your guard dog is on a Bonio break!" His smile was genuinely amused and Molly's tension snapped. She burst out laughing. "Oh, Macartan's a pet," she said, "don't mind him. And anyway, if it wasn't for him, I wouldn't be in the theater at all."

"Oh, I don't know," said Chalmers slowly. "I think that no matter by what route, you'd have made it all right, Molly Ní Bhriain. Totally unsuitable name for a star, by the way," he added, brushing a strand of hair off her face. "We'll have to put our heads together on that one!" He leaned over and very, very gently kissed her on the lips.

When, a little time later, he offered to give her a lift home in a taxi, Molly agreed. As she was leaving with him, however, Macartan pulled her aside and into a corner. "Watch out for him, Molly."

"I'll be all right, honestly, Macartan. He's very nice, really. And guess what! He really thinks I could be an actress."

"That's what I'm afraid of. That this is what he'll play on—Oh, I've no doubt he means it!" Macartan kissed the top of her head. "Just watch out, that's all. You are the most stunningly beautiful kid I've met for a long time—in my life, really—and you've got to be careful. There are millions of piranhas in this here fish bowl."

"What's a piranha?" It was all Molly could think of

to say. All these compliments, all in one night. It was all too much to take in. Macartan took her hand: "A piranha is a beautiful shining fish that will gobble you up and strip your bones before you even see him coming . . ."

"I see."

"I don't think you do. But people like Dessie and me, we're opportunists all right, but we're not piranhas. Stick with us, kid. We'll see you right."

Molly smiled. She felt warm and grateful, but she was very conscious of John Chalmers' lanky frame waiting for her by the door. "Thanks, Macartan."

"Thank me for nothing," Macartan said softly. "I could be a piranha too, with you, given half a chance. I watched you this morning. You'll go far Molly, farther than me and Dessie, farther, I think, than anyone in the bloody Abbey. But you've got to be careful. I wish I could go with you, but you're going to be too good for me . . . I just know it."

Molly kissed him on the cheek. "I'll never be too good for you, Macartan. You and Dessie will always be the ones who started me off."

"Watch out for Chalmers. I know I sound like a stuck record, Molly, but I've seen that type before. He's old enough to be your grandfather, for God's sake."

"Stop worrying. He's really nice. Honestly."

"Yeah, too nice! Well"—he gave her bottom a little pat—"I've done my best, off you go—good night."

"Good night, Macartan." Molly went across to where Chalmers waited. He held the door open for her: "What was all that about?"

"Oh, nothing. Macartan's a pet."

"So am I." He grinned. "I'm a real pet. You just wait and see."

All the way into town in the taxi, Macartan's warnings rang loudly in Molly's ears, but she need not have worried. John Chalmers behaved like a perfect gentleman. He told the taxi driver to wait when they got to her flat and got out with her, accompanying her right to the door. He kissed her as before, gently on the lips, but then he gripped her arms: "I warn you, Molly O'Brien, I'm putting you on notice that I think you are very, very attractive."

"Thank you, Mr. Chalmers."

"John, please, for Christ's sake." His brown eyes were very close to hers; they glistened in the yellowish light cast from the streetlamp nearby. He smelled of tobacco and aftershave. "I don't think you quite understand what I'm saying," he whispered. "What I'm saying is that I'm very attracted to you, Molly." It was on the tip of Molly's tongue to apologize, but she bit it back. How would a real actress respond? She smiled. "Thank you, John."

"Good night," he said, kissing her again. "Go in— go in before I carry you off."

"Good night, John."

"I'll see you tomorrow at the theater."

"Yes, John." He kissed her for a third time and let her go.

The next day, when she got to the theater at a quarter to ten, there were a dozen long-stemmed roses in the prompt corner.

6

Christian was bored, bored, bored. Almost for the first time in his career, he wished he was not a foreign correspondent.

At any other time, the two stories he was trying to cover—the vicious "cod war" between Britain and Iceland over the matter of national fishing limits and Britain's latest sex scandal in which a government minister had resigned—would have been meat and drink to him. But at present, all the action was at home where the U.S. Senate Watergate hearings were underway. The hearings dominated the world press, even in London, where he and Dick, becoming more and more frustrated by the minute, were cooling their heels.

He scanned the running stories, seeking new leads or anything out of which he could make capital: bow to bow, the Royal Navy had confronted the Icelandic fishing boats; protesters in Iceland had stormed the British embassy; Lord Lambton, the Defence Under-Secretary, while acknowledging his affair with a prostitute, was insisting that there was no threat to security. Nothing here, he thought with disgust, that could challenge Watergate on the front page of the *Chicago Sentinel*. He threw the newspaper aside and went to the house phone in the hotel lobby.

"Yes?" Dick's voice was groggy.

Christian did not waste time on preliminaries: "There's nothing new. All the action in the cod war is in *Iceland*, for Christ's sake—and I've just come off the phone to Tory headquarters; nothing doing so far." He had used every contact in his book, but up to now he had been unable to secure an interview either with Lord Lambton or with the other principal player in the scandal, Earl

Jellico, the leader of the ruling Tories in the House of Lords.

"Have you been drinking already, Christian? Do you know how early it is? Go back to bed, for God's sake." Dick was aggrieved at being woken for nothing, but Christian ignored his protests. "It's not early, Dick. Come on, let's go. We've got to get *something*."

"Any bright ideas? Want to hire a gunboat or maybe a helicopter?" The sarcasm was wasted on Christian. "Hey, a helicopter isn't a bad idea," he said, brightening. "No," he amended, "any helicopter we could get at this short notice probably wouldn't have the range. A plane! That's what we'll go for!" His voice was rising with enthusiasm: "That's a great idea, Dick. I can see it—it's a fight to the death out there. Ramming. That sort of thing."

"Christian, I was joking, I wasn't serious—"

"No, seriously, it's a terrific idea, really. We're not going to do shit on the sex story today, I can feel it in my bones. But we could do at least a decent feature out there,—and if you get a few good shots"—he paused for a second, his brain ticking off the practicalities of the situation—"we might be able to piggyback on television. I know a guy in production at ITN—"

"Christian, the Royal Navy is involved here. National security. How are we going to get permission? And what about the cost? The newsdesk—"

Christian cut across Dick's objections. "Stop seeing the hole in the doughnut, for Christ's sake!" He could already see Dick's pictures in his mind. "Television got pictures last night, didn't they?"

"Yes, but—" Dick was wasting his breath. Christian had hung up and was already thumbing through the classified telephone directory in search of a firm that would rent them a plane and a pilot.

Four hours later they were taking off from Gatwick airport. Christian had made a number of check calls to his contacts on Fleet Street and had discovered that the *Daily Express* was thinking along the same lines, had a plane lined up already and, not being in competition with the Americans, was only too pleased to share costs.

There were five on board in addition to the pilot and copilot; the *Express* had sent a writer and two photog-

raphers. Neither Christian nor Dick had met any of the
other newsmen before and the first leg of the flight was
largely silent except for the chatter from the cockpit radio. Christian sat in the seat behind the pilot, watching
through his window for anything at all he could use to
add drama and excitement to his story. As they crossed
the Scottish coastline and headed out into the Atlantic at
a height of twelve thousand feet, he was so engrossed in
his mental rehearsal of the scene below that, although
the aircraft was comfortably warm, he shivered involuntarily at the sight of the cold gray expanse of water. His
forte in writing had always been the creation of atmosphere. The reader of a Christian Smith piece always felt
at the end of it that he had been *there*.

"Here we are!" An hour or so after take-off they had
reached the disputed fishing grounds; the pilot, a lanky
young Australian, took the plane low and banked her in
a wide slow figure-eight pattern to give the photographers and reporters on both sides an equal view of what
was below. Christian, tape recorder at the ready, peered
eagerly through his window. The previous night's television pictures had led him to expect tight conformations
of trawlers with the gunboats prowling nearby. All he
could see, however, were three vessels, each presumably
fishing peaceably, each at least a mile from the other. Of
the Royal Navy, there was at present no sign.

"Want me to take you lower?" shouted the pilot over
the noise of his propellers.

"Could you take us father out?" Christian shouted
back. "Nothing much happening here . . . That okay
with you guys?" He turned to the *Express* men behind.
They nodded.

The Aussie shrugged and repositioned the aircraft,
taking her up and away from the three boats below.

They flew over the area for the best part of forty minutes, but it was not to be their day. Contrary to last night's
pictures, any boats they saw seemed simply to be minding their own business; even the sea, livid last night, was
rolling calmly in long, regular swells.

Eventually the pilot tapped his watch and his fuel
gauges and indicated it was time to return to base. "Let's
get a few stock shots, anyway," Dick suggested from
behind Christian. The *Express* men agreed and the pilot

gave them five more minutes, flying low enough for all three cameramen to take close-ups.

Christian threw his tape recorder into his kit bag and zipped it up, almost breaking the fastener in his venom. "What's the betting one or other of the interviews has come through while I was out here on this crap!" he shouted at Dick as the pilot headed back toward land. "Cool it, kid." Dick, hands busy in his camera bag, did not even look up. His calmness in such circumstances always infuriated Christian and he had difficulty in controlling the retort that sprang immediately to his lips; if they had been alone with the pilots he would have let fly; on the other hand, he had no desire to have himself and the *Sentinel* talked about up and down the length of Fleet Street. He contented himself with a poisonous glance at Dick and slumped back into his seat.

His apprehension had been well-founded, because when he and Dick got back to the hotel, there were several messages for them, two from Tory Central Office. "Oh, great!" Christian crumpled the notes. "What did I tell you? Thank you, God!" He pounded his fist into his other palm, "Now we've lost everything. We have zip! I knew this'd happen! Shit—I need a drink!"

"Hold on a minute—don't get worked up—how do you know it's happened?" Dick pointed out. "The interview might be for tomorrow—or it might be something completely different. How do you know until you call?"

"Sometimes it's difficult living with a saint!" But Christian crossed to the house phone and made the call.

His contact, Gillian Somerville, was still in her office. "I've been trying to get you several times," she said, so quietly that he realized she was afraid she was being overhead. "I can't promise anything, but I've put in a word and it's looking about fifty-fifty."

"You little darling!" Instantly Christian's mood changed. "You sweetheart! I owe you one!"

"You don't owe me anything—yet!" Gillian's voice nevertheless betrayed her pleasure. "The fact is that, as you well know, being a foreign publication helps. Most of them would perceive you as being slightly less, shall we say, biased?"

"You bet!" Christian was well aware of the politics involved.

"But if it happens—*if* it happens—you will have to share with one home-based publication."

"Which one?"

"Don't know yet. Probably the *Times*."

"That's okay. Which guy is it, Lambton or the other one?"

"I can't say."

"Make it Lambton if you can. Gillian, Gillian, I adore you! I'm your slave! What are you doing after work? Let me buy you a drink?"

"It's bedlam around here!" Her precise, Oxbridge voice wavered a little and became muffled, as though she was covering the receiver for a second or two; then she came back on the line: "Sorry, someone came in there—a drink, did you say?"

"Yeah. A barrel. A hogshead, whatever you English drink!"

"You know very well, Mr. Smith, that I drink white wine!"

"Yeah—white wine, anything you say. Tonight it's champagne . . ."

"Christian, don't get carried away, there's nothing guaranteed, I told you it's only fifty-fifty—"

"Fifty schmifty! We're halfway there. I've every confidence in you, my Miss Gillian. You're a genius. What time will we meet? Name a time and a place m'dear—anywhere. Wanna go to the Ritz?"

She laughed on the other end of the line. "Very well, then, I can probably detach myself from here around seven o'clock. Seven-thirty, Frank's?" Frank's was a Knightsbridge wine bar in which they had met before.

"Sure thing."

"I might be a bit late—"

"For you, Mizz Somerville, I wait until dawn."

She laughed again. "Until tonight, then."

"See you." He hung up.

Dick had been listening to his side of the conversation. "Heavy date, huh?"

"Yeah, you've met Gillian?" Dick shook his head. "Knows which buttons to push," said Christian. "She's a looker too, brunette, legs up to her neck. But who cares about that. We've gotten ourselves an interview." He punched Dick in the solar plexus.

"Are you sure?"

"Well"—Christian hesitated—"she said fifty-fifty. But I know my little Gillian. And after tonight, there'll be no way she won't deliver. I guarantee it!"

"I won't expect you for dinner, then? This time," Dick went on, "please don't involve me in any of your little playlets!" Christian's inventiveness when it came to snaring women frequently involved his friend. But Dick's admonitions were wasted; Christian was already walking away, his mind on a long, hot bath.

As she had predicted, Gillian was more than half an hour late that evening. She was as tall and slender as a model, and even dressed as she was in a plain tailored suit, she turned most heads in the wine bar as she walked in. Christian, already into his third drink, pursed his lips in appreciation as she slid onto the stool beside him. "Evening, Gillian. Well, you haven't changed. You're as gorgeous as ever."

She smiled at the compliment, then apologized. "Sorry," she said, "really sorry. I told you it was bedlam up there."

He covered her hand with his own: "Take it easy, sweetheart. You? You can be as late as you like. You just keep getting me my interviews and I'll happily sit here waiting for you till hell freezes over!"

"Christian—"

He cut off the warning, kissing her cheek: "I know, I know, nothing guaranteed . . . But I have absolute faith in you, my little darling. Now, what'll it be? Champagne?"

"I shouldn't—"

"Oh, yes, you should! It's not every day the *Sentinel*'s in such a generous mood."

"Oh, well, why not." She eased herself out of her jacket and settled comfortably on the stool. Underneath she was wearing a creamy lace camisole top, and Christian immediately noticed that she was not wearing a bra. Her only jewelery was a pearl on a fine gold chain; the pearl resting in the hollow of her throat. "Attagirl! I really meant it, by the way, when I said you looked gorgeous. Mind if I show my appreciation?" Before she could stop him he had leaned over and had kissed the base of her throat, his lips brushing the pearl.

"Everyone's looking!" But she was laughing.

"There's plenty more where that came from." Christian raised his hand to snap his fingers at the waiter, but she stopped him in the act. "Don't *do* that! Not in England, you goose. It gets people's backs up."

"Oh, yeah, sorry!" He grinned. "I forgot—well, *you* call the waiter then, okay? Let's see how equality works in England."

"Will we ever civilize you Yanks!" As she beckoned to the waiter, Gillian crossed one leg over the other and her skirt rode midway up her thigh. Christian whistled under his breath. "I never know why you're wasting all that on those stuffed shirts in the Conservative party."

"You know quite well I have a very good job—and they're not stuffed shirts! Well, not all," she amended, laughing.

"Whatever. I still think you could do better for yourself. Don't worry, I'm not complaining. If I may mix my metaphors, it suits me fine to have you squirreled away in there working like a beaver for li'l ol' me." He grinned again just as the waiter came to inquire about their order. "Champagne, my dear?" Christian asked.

"Thank you."

He ordered a bottle of Bollinger and they both watched as the waiter uncorked it and poured the wine into two flutes. "Cheers!" She raised her glass.

The wine Christian had already drunk was coursing like warm syrup through his veins. He locked his eyes on hers making clear his interest and measuring her response. To his immense satisfaction, he saw the answering flicker.

She took a sip of her drink, her own eyes merry. Christian waited until she had removed the glass from her lips, then he placed an index finger on one of her knees and slowly and deliberately slid it upward a few inches, stopping it just under the hem of the skirt. "Tonight," he said softly.

After a long, exquisite moment she broke the gaze and looked around the crowded wine bar. "A lot of people here tonight."

"Yes, quite a lot of people here tonight," he mocked.

"Stop it, Christian!"

"Stop what? I'm only agreeing with you."

"Stop—you know what I mean!"

"I don't know what you mean."

"Stop looking at me in that way!"

"I'm not looking at you in any way, Mizz Gillian. Sorry if I've offended you."

Again he waited until he had unnerved her and then lowered his eyes to her right breast. Within seconds the nipple hardened, a round button pushing at the thin lace over it. He kept watching it and smiled to see the flush rising toward her face across the pale skin of her chest. "More champagne?" Grinning broadly now, he picked up the bottle and held it out: "Nice blouse, Gillian, nicely filled, I must say!"

"Christian Smith! I swore after the last time that I wouldn't be susceptible to this kind of thing."

"What kind of thing?" Christian widened his eyes innocently. "I'm only saying what half the men here would say if they got the chance—which they won't, by the way, as long as I'm around."

"Don't step over the mark. Just because—"

"Just because what, Gillian? Remember the last time?" This time he put his finger on the inside of her knee.

"Of course I remember the last time!"

"I remember the last time, every second of it. Or should I say, every minute of it—"

"Every hour of it." He could see she was enjoying the game.

"Every inch of it, Gillian?" He grinned wickedly.

"You're incorrigible!"

"Aren't you glad?"

She paused for a few seconds and then matched his grin. "All right," she said, "I give in!" She slid off the stool.

"But we have a whole bottle of champagne, Gillian . . ." He stayed where he was.

"Bring the bottle."

It was his turn to make her wait for a moment or two. She was standing very close to him. He could smell her scent, fresh and flowery. "Well, if you're sure!" he said at last, as serious as a vicar.

"Jesus Christ. I'm going to walk out of here!"

"Ahh, don't do that, Mizz Gillian!" He got up from his own stool: "Where're we going?"

"You know damned well where we're going! I need my head examined! I don't hear from you for eight months and here I am falling into bed with you within five minutes of meeting you again!"

"I don't see any bed." Christian looked around the wine bar. Then he brushed his lips against the soft hair just over her ear.

"Come on before I change my mind!" She picked up her jacket and waited while he paid for the champagne, then walked ahead of him out of the bar. Christian's feeling of well-being and warmth increased still further when he noticed the stares that followed her exit.

Ten minutes later, hands on hips, he was surveying the disaster area that masqueraded as Gillian's tiny bedsitter. The flat, in a fashionable block in Mayfair, still looked exactly as he had remembered from the last time—as untidy and slapdash as a co-ed dorm at a junior university. "How you ever turn out of here looking like you do is a mystery, Mizz Somerville!" he said.

"None of your business," she answered, not at all insulted. "It's not home, it's only for sleeping in!"

"Or for other things!" Home, he knew, was a manor house somewhere in Dorset. "I've more than sleep on my mind, m'dear!" he shouted, flinging the champagne bottle, emptied during the taxi ride, into a corner and seizing her round the waist. He covered her neck with kisses. "Maybe you'll introduce me to your folks sometime!"

"You?" She laughed, closing her eyes and arcing backward in his arms. "To Mummy and Daddy, a journalist is a lower form of animal life than a rat catcher!"

"Mmm!" Christian ran his tongue under the pearl at her throat. "And that's saying something! Introduce me. I bet I could change their minds . . ." Not quite drunk, he was feeling giddy, as insubstantial as dust, so light, he thought he might almost fly. With one swift motion, he pushed the straps of Gillian's camisole off her shoulders and breasts; small and firm, they rose to his tongue and lips. "Say hello to King Rat!" He took one of the nipples between his teeth and bit gently into it.

"Ooh! That stings!" she protested, but made no effort

to get away or to stop him. She moaned a little and her hands searched at the buckle of his belt as he bit into the second nipple, his teeth still fastened to her, he helped her undo the belt and then guided her hands to his fly.

He had to let her go then as she took him in her hands. "Oh, Gillian, Gillian . . .''

"You called, Your Majesty?'' She bent and, just once, flicked her tongue on the tip of his penis. The touch sent multiple darts of pleasure straight to his fingers and toes: *"Gillian!"*

"Yes?'' She skipped back a pace. He reached for her, but she brushed his hands aside. "Uh-uh! You've got to sing for your supper, Your Ratness! I want to see you undress.''

Christian forced his fingers to obey him as he tore off his clothes. Luckily, he was wearing loafers and did not have to fiddle with laces. When he was completely naked, he collapsed backward onto a pile of what was presumably her laundry; again he reached for her but she continued to resist, slapping his hands away and standing over him, straddling his legs with her own so he could see, under her skirt, the tops of her stockings and the lace diamond of her crotch. "What's wrong?'' There was no play now. He wanted her now, immediately.

"There's nothing wrong, Christian.'' Her voice was husky, cleaned of all bantering: "It's just that I'd forgotten how beautiful you are.''

He reached up for her.

But she made him wait a little longer; unbuttoning her skirt, letting it fall as far as it could over her spread legs, unsnapping her garter-belt straps one by one so the tops of the stockings came loose and rippled downward a little on her thighs.

Christian could stand it no longer. He sat up and clasped her around the waist, burying his face in the front of her panties; reflexively, she grasped his head and pressed it closer to her. She smelled sweet and musky, like wild honey. She bent over the top of his head and ran her hands down his back as he pulled down the lace panties and kissed the soft, damp hair; urgently, his tongue sought the opening, and when it was reached, found it to be already wide and wet.

He levered himself to his knees and pushed the skirt,

stockings, and panties down to her ankles. With his tongue, he traced the dark line from the pubic bone to her navel and skilfully, without for a moment detaching his tongue from her skin, he stood gradually upright, continuing the line between her breasts, into the hollow of her throat, over her chin, until he reached her mouth. He kissed her then, deeply, tonguing into the back of her mouth so that she groaned and pressed herself along his length.

He stopped the kiss and scooped her up in his arms; surprised at the suddenness of the action, her eyes flew open as in four long strides he covered the tiny flat and dropped her onto the unmade bed in the corner of the room. Like a peacock's tail, her hair whooshed out on either side of her head as she looked up at him, her eyes opaque with desire and amusement. "Getting too old for the floor, are we?"

"I'll show you old!" Christian ripped the panties, stockings, and skirt from her ankles but left the camisole around her waist as he entered her.

When the ferry docked in Harwich, Conor, like most of the other passengers, followed the signs for the train to London. Unusually, because he was careful now by habit, he had struck up an acquaintance with an American backpacker, a young woman from Lubbock, Texas, with Texas teeth and broad Texas hips. She was "doing Europe."

"Irish, eh? How 'bout that. Y'all are certainly the first Irish guy I've met in Europe." She pronounced it "Yerp." Her name was Kirsty and Conor already knew she had spent Easter in Paris, had loved Amsterdam, had hated Rome, was dubious about Berlin. She had questioned him closely about Dublin, which was her last stop on her trip: what to see, where the guys were, how safe the streets were. Assuming he would never see her again, some streak of recklessness he now regretted had prompted Conor to direct her to the National Botanic Gardens and to say to any of the gardeners there that she had met Conor O Briain.

She was now giving him serious cause for worry as, extracting a notebook from a pocket in her backpack, she held her waterproof pencil over it: " 'Conor'—what a cute name! Is that with a 'C' or a 'K'?''

''With a 'C,' he said faintly. What had possessed him? She would undoubtedly head straight for the gardens. He consoled himself with the fact that after six years, the personnel would probably have changed. But he realized he had created a worse problem for himself when they docked, because she would undoubtedly stick to him like glue through the formalities of customs and Immigration. His passport, in the name of Seán Molloy, felt heavy in his wallet pocket.

When the time came, however, he managed to join a separate passport line and got through without incident. But he was sweating as he joined her again to board the train.

The episode was a warning to him. Seán Molloy, the itinerant laborer who had worked on building sites in London, in canning plants in Holland, in Volkswagen assembly lines in Germany, was second nature to him now—or so he had thought. It had been years since he had made such a slip.

Kirsty stowed her backpack inside the door of the train and joined him in his seat. Conor forestalled more questions. ''Would you mind if I tried to have a little sleep, Kirsty?'' he asked.

''Of course not, Conor. You go right ahead.''

The clacking of the train was soporific and Conor, who since he had begun his new life as Seán Molloy had taught himself to nap anywhere, was soon asleep. When he woke up, Kirsty was, in her turn, asleep, her cheek flattened against the train window.

He must be careful not to make the same sort of slip with his identity again. Ever-practical and pragmatic, in the six years since Conor had fled from Ireland, he had come to terms with his status and sometimes quite enjoyed the independence of his new life as an itinerant jobber. He missed Ireland terribly—and he mourned the satisfaction and even tenor of his former life as a botanist. But, strong and very fit, he had always managed to find work that was well-paid enough to ensure that he had plenty of leisure and to send money to his mother, always in plain envelopes with no return address. He was abstemious in his habits—although he still ate like a horse—and was not interested in material wealth. Consequently, while working, he had always managed to put money aside and then, when he had enough saved to buy himself some time, left his current job and moved on.

He used his leisure well. If he was in England, he utilized the library system to keep abreast of botanical developments; if abroad, he learned the vernacular of his temporary residence. He spoke French, Dutch, and German well enough to have a colloquial conversation and having acquired Latin in secondary school, found it quite easy to understand Spanish and Italian, although he did not speak those languages fluently. As a result, he never had any problem getting a job. Once or twice employers had sensed that this calm, self-possessed person was perhaps overqualified for the job he was seeking. Nevertheless, he always managed to reassure them that all he wanted to do was to make enough money to live.

Beside him, the backpacker stirred and rubbed her nose as though it tickled, but to his relief, she did not wake up.

Conor knew well that women found him attractive; and there had been women in his life, never serious and never for long. Many of the women with whom he had been involved had tried, in various ways, to prolong the relationship but Conor, knowing always that he was going to move on and being practiced in self-protection, never allowed himself to become emotionally dependant or attached.

There was another factor of which, up to now at least, he had been thoroughly frightened: when his defenses were down, Conor had had to admit to himself that all women, when placed against his image of his sister, were found wanting. From time to time, Molly invaded even his sexual fantasies, an invasion he found utterly appalling and which, each time he recognized it, he resisted as strongly as possible, batting her away from him as though she were a vampire. After that episode on his last day on the island—and those shame-producing images of her conjured in his lustful imagination—he had been so afraid of his own feelings that he had not even written to her save for one brief note.

Yet in the darkest, longest hours of the night, the memory of Molly, of how she had felt in his arms when he had wrestled her to the ground, of her long legs and pantied bottom when he had raised her skirt, still came back to tantalize him.

Idly, as the train now clacked on toward London, Conor glanced at the backpacker sleeping beside him; although she was plump and her hair was mousy, something about her childlike, relaxed face reminded him of the innocence he remembered in his sister.

What did Molly look like after all this time?

It had been so long, he thought, surely he was old enough and mature enough now to handle himself? Perhaps now was the time he should make a big effort to make contact again? The last he had heard of his sister, she was on the stage in Dublin. Finding her should be easy enough.

Conor decided he was too tired to make any decision at present. He would think about it after a good night's sleep.

The rest of the journey passed uneventfully. Kirsty did not wake up until the train pulled in to Liverpool Street and Conor found it quite easy to ignore her broad hints that they should get together while she was in London. Nevertheless, before they separated, he did accept her address in Lubbock, in case he was passing through, an event of as much likelihood, he thought as he walked toward the entrance to the Tube, as his passing the moon on the way to Mars.

He stopped at the bank of telephones to put in a call to Frank O'Hare. The priest was the only person in London with whom he maintained contact. It had been Frank who had told him of Tom Hartigan's death from lung cancer six months after Conor had arrived in London.

Father Hartigan's letters to Conor, sent General Delivery, gave no hint during those six months that he was so seriously ill. His last communication, the week before he died, was cheerful and optimistic and kind as always. By mid-February, he was dead.

Apart from the immediate aftermath of his flight, the days following that news were the worst of the six years since Conor had left Inisheer. He had felt appallingly alone, cut loose and adrift. He had even contemplated turning himself in to the police and facing the consequences, but an innate, island-bred distrust of the law stopped him from doing so.

The London priest had been kind and concerned, but he was run off his feet with his duties, and in any case Conor, fearing that he was simply transferring emotional dependency from the apron strings of one cleric to another, was angry with himself for his weakness and rejected the option. So although he kept in touch—and although the priest helped him with accommodations and jobs whenever he was in town—the two never actually became close.

Father O'Hare's telephone now rang unanswered. Conor looked at his watch. It was still before eight in the morning. The priest was probably out at early Mass. He would try his office in Camden town later on.

The morning rush hour was in full swing in the Underground, and Conor hesitated as the commuters flowed around him in a dark-suited tide. He needed a place to dump his bag until he found a flat. The last flat he had had was on a side street off Pentonville Road, but it was an area he did not like. He decided to take the Tube to Earl's Court.

The amplified wail of a busker's violin rose through the crowds as he descended to the trains. The busker was young—about twenty, Conor judged—and to his own untrained ear, highly accomplished. He felt around in his pocket until he found some coins, but as his step on the escalator was about to level out at the busker's feet, his eye was caught by a poster on the wall of the "up" side. It advertised a West End play, a revival of Noel Coward's *Blithe Spirit*. Conor was not a theatergoer. What riveted his attention were the pictures of the three stars, a man and two women. One of the women, the younger one, was his sister. He was sure of it.

He came off the escalator and joined the stream of commuters going up to the street. There were a number of the posters, spaced apart from bottom to top so that he could read everything on it. None of the names was his sister's, but the name under the younger woman's face was "Margo Bryan." There was no doubt about it. She was Molly.

Molly, as usual three hours early for the performance, passed under the marquee of the Wyndham's in London.

As usual, she could not resist glancing at the playbills on the front of the theater:

ANNABEL CRITCHLEY

in

BLITHE SPIRIT

by

NOEL COWARD

with Margo Bryan and Jeremy Forsythe

Six months into the run, Molly still did not fully believe that the huge lettering referred to her. Although she still had to pinch herself to ensure that she and not someone else was actually one of the stars of this show, she was, however, getting used to her new name. She saw herself now as two selves. Molly was the girl who had a history in Ireland and whose life was bound up in her childhood. Margo was an actress who happened to be Irish. She paused for a second to say hello to the doorman. "Lovely day today, Alf."

"Lovely, Miss Bryan. Great news about Princess Anne eh?" On her way to the theater, Molly had seen the *"Anne to Wed Mark!"* billboards on the newsstands. "Yes, Alf," she said, "I hope it stays fine for them!"

"Let's hope so!" The doorman seemed set for a chat, but she was anxious not to linger, and smiling a goodbye at him, passed around into the alley beside the theater toward the stage door. She went in, bidding another cheerful hello to the stage-doorman, climbed the stairs, and went along a corridor until she came to the small, scuffed door that led into her dressing room. Turning the key, she pushed open the door and, as she always did, inhaled deeply, feeling her way from the outside world into this closed, private world of backstage theater. She was usually the first of the cast to arrive, and this period before the other players came in was always her favorite part of the day: when the bustle and traffic outside seemed

very far away and when the theater all around her was
hushed and waiting, the smells and rustles of the past
undisturbed by the present.

The room was dark, lit only by a single shaft of gray
light from the barred window which faced over the alleyway behind the theater. She closed the door behind her
and switched on the lights. Naturally, Annabel Critchley,
who was playing Madame Arcati, had the Number One
dressing room, and looking around her own little hutch,
Molly sighed. In dire need of a coat of paint, the tiny
room was dingy and faded, the spaces between the floorboards packed with dust which probably dated back to
the last century and which had congealed over the years
to a substance resembling black mortar. Never mind,
Molly thought as she frequently did, someday soon she
would have the Number One . . .

She crossed to her dressing table and touched the mirror and then, in sequence, each of the small stones from
Inisheer she kept lined up on the surface of the table. She
had done this for luck before her first entrance on opening night, and it was by now a ritual, so deeply ingrained
that had anything happened to the stones she would have
panicked. Several letters and messages had been placed
on the table and she picked them up. The one on top was
from her agent, reminding her that an interview had been
set up for her with a talk show on ITV.

Her name change had been on her agent's insistence.
Dolly Mencken was Molly's agent, introduced to her by
John Chalmers. There was a message from him too; he
had left word he was coming in to the show again on the
following Tuesday night.

Again Molly sighed. She was guilty about John. After
all, she owed practically her whole career to him—if he
had not brought her to London and cast her in one of his
workshop productions . . . Her train of thought, weari-
somely familiar, was interrupted by the shrilling of the
telephone on the wall in the corner of the room. She
picked up the instrument. "Yes?"

"Call for you Miss Bryan, from Mr. Chalmers."

Molly hesitated. She was tempted to tell the doorman
that she could not take the call, but castigated herself for
being unfair. "Thank you, Alf," she said, "put him
through, please." She waited a second and then, as

Chalmers came on the line, forced herself to sound warm
and bright, "Hello, John! I got your message—you're
coming in again? You're a glutton for punishment!"

"Just wanted to make sure you got the message," he
said, "and to invite you to supper afterwards, if you'll
come."

Molly's heart sank. "Of course I will, John, that'd be
lovely."

"I'll come 'round afterwards, then, shall I?"

"Sure. See you then."

"How are you, Molly?"

"Perfect. Never better."

"How's Dolly? Haven't seen her for an age . . ."

Molly grasped at the opening. "She's fine, John. As a
matter of fact, I must get off the line, I'm expecting her
to call about an interview."

"Oh! Right-oh, then! See you Tuesday?"

"Looking forward to it."

"Have a good weekend, 'bye now."

"I will—you too! 'Bye."

Thoughtfully, she replaced the receiver. She really
would have to do something about John Chalmers. Right
from the start, the relationship had been unequal in every
way; it was not only the age difference between them and
their relative status in the theater, it was the way John
felt about her. At one point he had even wanted to marry
her, but eventually, had accepted that she could never
love him the way he, apparently, loved her.

Yet she needed him, and not only because of his influence on the London theater scene. Apart from Dolly
Mencken, he was the only person in London she truly
trusted. And so she kept seeing him, continued allowing
him to take her out. She despised herself for being so
utterly selfish as to string him along like this for her own
good. She was being most unfair.

Maybe she should ask Dolly's advice next time she
spoke to her. At least that was one relationship that had
worked out all right. She sat down at the dressing table
and transcribed the time of the interview from Dolly's
message into her appointments book.

Molly had been very unsure of Dolly at the start; on
first meeting her in a wine bar in Soho, all she had seen
was an overdressed, over-talkative little woman who wore

a lot of jewelery and who was far too bossy. Within minutes, Dolly was issuing edicts: "Come on, darling, your
name is nowhere. Old-fashioned. Not zingy enough.
What did Shakespeare say? 'What's in a name'? Was it
Shakespeare who said that, darling? Do you know who
said that, John?" Chalmers, who was present at the
lunch, merely winked across the table at Molly.

And Dolly had not wanted an answer. "What does it
matter, darling?" she had breezed on, waving one fat,
much-ringed hand, "what does it matter whether your
name is Hopalong Cassidy so long as they can *pronounce*
it and *remember* it and it has *zing*? It's *essential*, darling,
that it has zing! 'Molly' is at home sitting by the fire
knitting socks." She took a gulp of wine. "You go home,
darling, and have a little think and decide what
you could be called that's easy and that you like and
that they can *pronounce*. and *remember* and that has
zing . . ."

She paused for breath. "Now I think one-syllable and
two-syllable names are nice," she continued. "Jud-i
Dench! Dor-is *Day*! Get it? Got a nice, strong ring to
them, don't they darling? You certainly remember Doris
Day . . . !"

Molly, dazed before the gusty onslaught of Dolly's personality, felt bludgeoned. That night, after the show, she
and John Chalmers cobbled 'Margo Bryan' out of Molly's
real name. Next day she telephoned Dolly to suggest it.
Dolly was thrilled: "Now that's a *good* name, darling.
good and strong. Ten letters, five each one. Symmetrical.
Will look good on credits . . ."

Their next meeting was at a party in Dolly's Chelsea
home. Dolly organized the party specifically to introduce
her new client to casting directors and producers. An
hour into it, Molly, dizzy from introductions and fulsome
compliments—most of which she suspected were spuri-
ous—sought refuge in the kitchen. But Dolly came in
search of her and then, smiling brightly, took her firmly
by the arm and marched her right back into the party. At
least while Dolly was alongside, Molly had felt very little
need to shine in conversation; the agent's wall of words
left few gaps and all Molly had to do was to look interested and to smile a lot.

That party led to a small part in a BBC television play,

which in turn led to a bigger one in a play for Granada. Dolly then put her up for audition for the role of the bewildered young daughter of a forceful Scottish divor- cee in *Without Dad,* a new prime-time sitcom. Molly's nerve almost failed on the day of her audition—her prin- cipal worry was that she would not manage the Scottish/ English accent. But her quick ear stood by her, the di- rector liked her—and assured her that the sound of an Irish brogue sounded almost the same as the Scottish one "here on the mainland"—and much to her own surprise, she got the part.

The power of television was evident within weeks of transmission of the first episode. The show proved to be instantly popular and it was a shock to Molly how often she was recognized on the street. Dolly, naturally, seized on the opportunity, feeding the tabloids with selected tid- bits—leaning heavily on her client's "romantic" island upbringing—and quite soon, popular magazines like *Woman* and *Cosmopolitan* started to run features on her.

And within a short while, Molly had come to see that beneath Dolly's bombast and shrewdness, her agent was soft-hearted and kind. Dolly rapidly became a friend, a surrogate aunt. She helped Molly find a small terraced house near Bayswater, and since her new client's bank account was very new, Dolly cosigned for a mortgage, waving away all demurring and thanks: "Not to worry, darling, it's an investment in both our futures. I'll take it out of you before I die, don't worry!"

Dolly even took a hand in her client's social life, and Molly found that she was being photographed at various functions and that the photographs were appearing reg- ularly in the press. She learned when "on show" never to look bored or cross even if she was both; never to say anything inane. She realized very early on that talent was only one third of the ammunition, that a young actress also needed luck—and to be different. In a city crammed with eager young actresses who chattered and flirted in- cessantly and who would drop their grannies down a mine to get noticed, Molly developed a small but growing rep- utation for being not only beautiful and a very good ac- tress, but for being intelligent and committed.

And a good listener. At parties Molly never ceased to find it amazing how producers and casting directors were impressed with the sound of their own theories and insights and how frequently, in mid-flight, they credited her with being on the same wavelength.

With all that, it was not surprising that eyebrows had been raised jealously when she had been cast as Elvira in this revival of *Blithe Spirit*. Elvira, created originally by the incomparable Kay Hammond, was such an *English* part, said the other actresses who had read for the part. Molly was aware of the ripples, but she closed her mind to the outside world, an easy enough task while cocooned daily in the close family ambience of a developing production. She had worked hard, had watched and listened closely, had picked up lots of tips from Amanda Critchley—kind and, unusual for an actress, quite secure about her own stardom—and as a result, her notices for Elvira had been unanimously favorable. She was now, if not a full-fledged star, already well in the ascendant.

This was part of the problem with John Chalmers. Now that she was on her way, his proprietary grip on her had tightened, and because she was so fundamentally grateful to him, she did not quite know how to shake it off without mortal insult. And so she continued to go to parties and functions with him, to be photographed in his company.

She kicked off her shoes and eased her dress over her head. Yes, she thought, looking at herself critically in the mirror, she would have to make things more clear to John. The present situation was doing neither of them any good.

On the other hand, who else would sustain a romantic interest in her for so long? There was no one more mystified about her continuing virginity than Molly. Although she had long abandoned the practice of going to Mass, she sometimes thought her prudishness had to do with her Irish Catholic upbringing; sometimes she thought it had to do with the episode with that priest in the dunes six years before. Whatever its cause, here she was at twenty-two years of age, probably the only virgin actress in the city. Stripped to her bra and panties, she continued to study herself critically in the large mirror of the dressing-room. What was the matter with her?

Stop it, you *amadán*! she said forcefully to herself. She was thinking askew, falling into the trap of peer pressure. She put on her robe, tied her hair back in a pony-tail, and sat down purposefully to begin her makeup. There was nothing wrong with her, nothing at all—she simply had not yet met anyone interesting enough.

From now on she would be her own person, would cease envying the blithe self-assurance and ease with which her colleagues dealt with men, their assumption that sex went with the territory of dates and dinner par-ties. This would help her deal with John too. The very next time she met him—next Tuesday—she would tell him simply and clearly what she felt. . . . She would say she was very grateful to him, loved him as a friend, wanted to keep it that way; but if this would be too difficult for him, she would understand . . .

The telephone shrilled for the second time that evening and she jumped up to answer it. This time, the doorman told her that Dolly Mencken was downstairs with a re-porter.

"Put Dolly on, please, Alf."

The line crackled and then Dolly came on. "Margo!"

"Who is it, Dolly—I don't have any note of this, I'm not ready—"

"Certainly, Margo, Miss O'Connor and I will give you a minute, won't we, Una? Miss O'Connor is staying overnight in London and doesn't have to go back to Dub-lin until the morning, isn't that right, Una?"

Of course! Molly, picking up the signals, remembered that at least a week ago, Dolly had mentioned she had arranged an interview with the *Irish Record*. "Sorry, Dolly," she said, "bring her on up, but give me two minutes."

"Sure, Margo, sure!" Dolly hung up.

Molly used the two minutes to remove the headband from her hair and to brush it out. The skin of her face was shining from the cleanser and she slapped astringent on it. She was ready for the knock on the door. Making sure that the belt of her robe was tight, she took a deep breath and opened the door.

Dolly jangled in, kissing her on both cheeks: "This is Una O'Connor from *The Irish Record* in Dublin," she said, introducing the reporter who came in with her. "Hello, Una!" said Molly, smiling, taking in the other's appearance at a glance; the reporter was small, freckled, redheaded and, Molly estimated, about her own age or slightly older. She reminded her of Kathleen Agnes.

"Congratulations on the run and particularly on your notices, Miss Bryan!" said the young woman, seating herself on the scruffy chaise longue that ran along one wall of the dressing room while Dolly plonked her bulk on the chair in front of the makeup table. "I have a full set of them," the reporter went on, "they're really impressive. You must be delighted with them!" She had a pleasant voice, virtually accentless.

"Thank you very much. Yes, I am delighted. Would you care for something to drink?" Molly indicated the small refrigerator in one corner of the room.

"No, thank you, that's all right." She extracted a small tape recorder from her handbag.

"I've been trying to place your accent. Where are you from, Una?" Molly sat beside her on the chaise.

"Oh, Dublin," Una answered cheerfully. "But my mother is from Cork and my father's from the north, so I'm sort of a hybrid. I know you're pushed for time, Miss Bryan, so is it all right if we start?"

"Sure." Molly braced herself while the reporter switched on the tape recorder and checked the battery level. "Miss Bryan," she began, "I know a little about your background, your start in the Abbey Theatre and so forth, but one of the things which intrigues me is why you felt you had to change your name."

The implication was unmistakable: Margo Bryan had felt that her Irish name was not good enough for her. It was a bad start and Dolly jumped in. "Oh, that was my idea!" she said, patting her hair so her bracelets rang. "I felt—although Margo did not necessarily agree—that 'Molly' was just too old-fashioned for the type of market I could see ahead of her . . ."

"I see," said the reporter uncertainly, and Molly realized for the first time that she was nervous. She warmed to her; normally she hated giving print interviews because even when she was quoted accurately—which was rare—when she saw them in black and white, her words always appeared trite and not at all what she had meant to say. This young woman, however, did not seem to be one of the usual smart know-it-alls. She smiled to put Una at ease. "Well, it was really a joint operation," she said. "Dolly—Miss Mencken—wanted a new name, but it was I and John Chalmers who actually changed it. You've heard of John Chalmers?"

It seemed that the reporter had done her homework. She did know all about Chalmers' influence on her subject's career. From then on, both women relaxed and for the next twenty minutes, there were few problems with the interview.

Until they came to Molly's background. "I've read a few interviews with you before, Miss Bryan, and although you have mentioned your mother as being a great influence on you, I've never seen any mention of your father. Had he any influence on your career choice?"

Molly was off her customary guard. She hesitated and Dolly jumped in again, looking pointedly at her watch. "Time's getting on, Miss O'Connor. Don't forget, Margo has a performance in two hours' time and she likes to have a period to herself before she goes on. I'm sure you have plenty there. Anything else you need, you can always give me a call. You have my number?"

The reporter switched off the tape recorder and stood up. "Thank you, Miss Bryan," she said politely. "I really appreciate your letting me see you on such short notice."

Molly stood up too. "That's all right, Miss O'Connor, I enjoyed it." Damn it, she thought, she mustn't show she was flustered. "Of course I'd always do an interview for a Dublin paper! The home crowd is always the one to please. I'm sorry we have to stop it there, but I do have a lot of mental preparation to go through. I'm sure you understand. I hope you have enough there?"

"Plenty," said the reporter.

But as Molly saw her to the door, she had the firm impression that Una had made a mental note of the way the interview had ended. She might be inexperienced, thought Molly, but she was sharp. "I hope you enjoy the show tonight," she said as they shook hands. "I've arranged for a ticket—let me know if there is any problem with it."

"Thank you again," said the reporter, "I'm sure I will—enjoy it, I mean!"

"And come back afterwards for a drink?" As soon as the words were said, Molly wished them unsaid. She should be wary of reporters. But instinctively she liked this one and she had meant it when she said the home audience was very important. Respect in Ireland was important to her and she did want Una O'Connor to be on her side.

"Thank you, Miss Bryan," said the reporter, "I'd love to come back afterwards." Molly kissed her agent on both cheeks and saw the two of them out the door. As soon as they were gone, she sat at her dressing-table again and closed her mind to everything but the coming performance.

Four and a half hours later, she was taking curtain calls with the rest of the cast to wave after wave of applause. She enjoyed her role in *Blithe Spirit*. Elvira was a ghost, a troublesome one, who haunted her former husband and his new wife. The role called for lightness, wit, and a fine sense of timing, and tonight, Molly thought, her performance had gone particularly well. Some nights—entirely unpredictably—the audience seemed to gel with the action onstage, to become part of the feast rather than mere spectators at it, and tonight had been one such night. She applauded happily along as Amanda and Jeremy took individual calls, and when her own turn came, beamed across the footlights, surfing on the wave of love washing over her. She felt happy and elated and grateful for the wonderful gifts of this profession in which at will she could be someone entirely different from herself, have fun, be loved, and be paid for it.

Still high, she bounded up the stairs to her dressing room, and it was only when she was inside, with coconut oil all over her face, that she remembered she had invited the reporter for a drink. Oh well, she thought, at least she had to have enjoyed the performance. She tissued off the last of the makeup and went into the shower, hoping to be out and dressed before the reporter arrived.

But she was still in the bathroom when she heard her dressing-room door open. She turned off the water. "Hello, Miss O'Connor," she called. "Won't be a minute. Make yourself comfortable . . ."

There was a mirror in the bathroom, and looking at herself, she saw her face was blotchy and red from the removal of the makeup and the heat of the shower. To keep up appearances for the *Irish Record*, she applied

moisturiser and a light foundation of liquid makeup.
There was no sound from outside, except for the soft
clatter of hangers as the dresser hung up her costumes.
From the corridor outside, she could hear the voices of
the other actors, calling to one another through the open
doors of their dressing rooms. The theater was winding
down into darkness.

She removed the headband she used to protect herself
from grease and make-up and brushed her hair; then she
went out into the dressing room. "Sorry—" she began,
and then stopped dead.

The brightly lit room seemed to shrink. It was not Una
O'Connor but a man.

Now thirty-three, he had changed subtly since the last
time she had seen him six years ago. The face was deeply
tanned and, by contrast, the eyes seemed brighter. The
unruly dark hair was longer, curling over his collar; even
under the sports jacket and slacks he wore, she could see
his body had hardened. "Conor," she whispered.

"Dia Dhuit . . ." he said. He continued to stand,
waiting.

She had not heard Irish for six years. "My God,
Conor—*Cé'n chaoí 'bhfuil tú?* He had carried into the room
with him an air of purpose and energy and she became
supremely conscious of the surroundings. The theatrical
"Good Luck" cards, bright with black cats and green
horseshoes, which were plastered all over her walls,
seemed tawdry and unreal—so far from Inisheer and the
sea where she had last set eyes on him. She wanted to
rush forward to hug him, but she felt as though she were
physically paralyzed. Then, paradoxically, her mood
switched and she became angry with him. How dare he
turn up so casually after such a long time without a sign
or a sound: "Where were you? Not a word all these
years—and then you just swan in like—like—"

"Like a brother, you mean?" He smiled at her then
and her anger evaporated as quickly as it had risen. She
rushed to him and threw her arms around his neck. He
wrapped his own arms around her and hugged her back,
"That's more like it!" His arms felt strong and muscu-
lar.

They drew apart as the dresser, who had tactfully vanished into the bathroom during the little scene, stuck

her head out. "Excuse me, Miss Bryan, are you finished in here?"

"Yes, Joan, thanks," said Molly, reverting to English. "This, by the way, is my prodigal brother. Joan Thomas, my dresser."

"How do you do, pleased to meet you!" The dresser bustled forward and after shaking Conor's hand removed Molly's street clothes, which were draped across a small armchair, to leave space so he could sit down. He thanked her, settled himself as comfortably as he could for such a big man, and crossed one leg over the other.

"Mind you don't break it; all breakages have to be paid for!" Molly was still using English out of courtesy to the dresser. She turned toward the mirror and picked up a hairbrush. But when the woman vanished again into the bathroom, she broke again into Irish. "*Eist*—listen, Conor, I'm completely floored, I don't know what to say . . ." Although she had not lost her fluency, she stumbled on the Irish because her emotions were in such a jumble.

He, on the other hand, remained maddeningly serene. "What's to say? I died, now I am risen!" He smiled.

"Where were you, where have you come from, what were you *doing* all this time . . . ?"

"Now, Molly—or is it Margo—all in good time . . . I might ask you the same questions, by the way," he continued. He might have been chatting to a fellow-commuter he met daily on a train. "We both have a lot of catching up to do. As far as I was concerned, the last I heard you'd gone to Dublin to seek your fortune."

"That was a very long time ago—"

"Not all that long ago, when you think about it—"

"Six *years*, Conor—"

"Yes, well, maybe. I must say I had no idea that you had climbed to this exalted state until this very afternoon when I happened to be passing through a Tube station and something about the posters for this play seemed a little familiar!"

"Did you see the show?" She was momentarily diverted.

"No, I'm afraid I was a little late—but I will. And I did buy a program." He held it up: "I see by this that you're also a star in a hit television show."

She was not to be flattered. "Mam was very upset when you stopped writing," she accused.

"Yes, she must have been. I'm very sorry about that. I had my reasons—"

"For God's sake, Conor!"

"All in good time. Do you have, you know, a date or anything now?"

Dumb, Molly shook her head.

"Well, maybe we could go somewhere and talk?"

"I have all the time in the world," she said. "Let's talk now! Let's start with the missing six years, and with why you stopped writing to Mam . . . And how did you get to London? How did you live? Did the police ever find you?" The questions tumbled out, directionless.

"Whoa!" He laughed, holding up his hand. "One at a time! I stopped writing to Mam because I knew that sooner or later the Guards would be after her, asking her again had she heard from me—and I didn't want to put her in the position of lying for me all the time . . . And how is she, by the way?"

"She's a grown-up woman! You might have given her the option of deciding whether she wanted to lie for you or not," retorted Molly with some heat, but she was interrupted by a soft knock on the door. The reporter! She had forgotten all about Una O'Connor. Dismayed, she shot to her feet. "Sorry about this—it's a reporter. I invited her to the show after an interview she did with me this morning. I can't just turn her away . . ."

"Why should you? But remember my position." His expression was deadly serious now.

"I don't *know* your position, Conor!"

"I'll explain it all later. Just don't volunteer any information about me, all right? I can take care of myself. I'll make my own introductions—" The knock sounded again and he pulled in his legs so Molly could get to the door.

As she opened it to admit the reporter, Molly saw that Una had changed out of her afternoon clothes of blouse and skirt and was wearing a softly cut dress that flattered her full figure. It always moved Molly when she realized the effort people put in to attend the theater. "Hello, Miss O'Connor," she said warmly. "Won't you come in."

The reporter stepped across the door and then stopped. "Oh, you have company!" she said.

"It's all right," said Conor, standing up. "I'm nobody really, just an old friend from the old country. Seán Molloy!" he said, holding out his hand.

"Wha—" Molly began in surprise, but closed her mouth when she intercepted the look of warning he shot at her. She glanced at the reporter to see if she had noticed anything amiss, but Una merely accepted Conor's hand and shook it: "How do you do, Mr. Molloy, I'm Una O'Connor." Molly, trying to assimilate what was going on—*Seán Molloy*?—nevertheless saw the flash in the other woman's eyes as she looked up at him.

"Well, this is nice, isn't it? All Irish together!" Conor smiled. "Won't you sit down, Una? Did you enjoy the show?" He offered Una his chair and moved to the chaise, and since he seemed to have taken charge, Molly decided to keep her mouth firmly shut and to let him handle the entire scene.

"It was wonderful, really great!" Una turned to Molly: "Congratulations, Miss Bryan, you were marvelous. I must say you well deserved your notices."

"Thank you." Molly smiled as warmly as she could under the circumstances.

"Are you in the theater too?" asked "Seán," still addressing Una.

The reporter shook her head. "No, I'm a journalist, actually—with the *Irish Record* in Dublin."

"I see."

Molly was beginning to sense that in some way she was losing ground in some sort of battle, the spread of which she could not fully see. "Miss O'Connor interviewed me earlier today," she said.

"I see," said Conor again. He smiled broadly at her, then turned to Molly and included her in the smile. He folded his arms, seeming completely at ease. Molly could not think of anything to say. It was the reporter who broke the awkwardness. "Well, thank you for inviting me around," she said, and stood. "I'd better let you get on with it . . ."

Molly turned to the refrigerator in the room. "What am I thinking of! Please have a drink. What would you like?"

"No, really," said Una O'Connor, "it's getting late and you must be very tired after such a performance."

"Don't go—do have a drink! I'd like one too, Molly." Conor still wore a broad grin.

"Well, if you're sure." The reporter sat down again. She accepted a Perrier and Conor asked for a bottle of beer. Molly helped herself to a stiff whiskey. She felt she had earned it.

"And what do you do, Mr. Molloy?" Una asked when they were settled with their drinks.

"A little of this, a little of that. I travel."

"How interesting—are you a salesman?"

Conor laughed. "In a way, I suppose. I sell myself. No, I'm nothing special. I'm just a worker, itinerant— one of those who move where the work is. I'm just back from Germany, where I shot bolts into about nine million Volkswagens . . ."

Molly listened to the talk. This was a brother she did not know. Whereas the old Conor had been composed, the poise of this one was a revelation. And what was more, as she saw the way Una O'Connor responded to her brother as a man, she recognized with a shock that she was jealous—but as quickly as she recognized the feeling, she squashed it. "Would you like another drink, Miss O'Connor?" she asked, with Margo Bryan's sweetest smile.

At that moment the dresser, finished in the bathroom, came back into the room. "I'm finished, Miss Bryan," she said. "See you tomorrow. Nice meeting you, sir," she added to Conor, "and you, miss!" She nodded to them all and left the room.

Una stood up decisively. "I'm going too, Miss Bryan— I've overstayed my welcome as it is. Thank you very much for everything, I really appreciate it."

She shook hands with Conor. "It was nice meeting you, Mr. Molloy." Was Molly imagining it or did she stand a little close to him?

When the reporter had gone, Molly turned to Conor: "Now, what was *that* all about? Who's Seán Molloy?"

He was not put out. "Could we go somewhere for a drink or a meal or something? We've a lot to catch up on . . . I find it very hot in here."

"All right. Just give me a moment."

When Molly was ready, they left the theater and she directed the taxi to a restaurant she knew near Covent Garden. On the way, although they made small talk, they sat mostly in silence, a few inches apart in the dark vehicle. He still seemed perfectly relaxed, but Molly's confused mind raced. She was very conscious of his hands, one of which rested on his lap, one on the seat, palm up, between them. They were large and well shaped, with long, flexible fingers.

The restaurant, Italian, small, and intimate, was less than half full. "Good evening, Miss Bryan, lovely to see you again. Good evening, sir. May I take your wrap, Miss Bryan?"

"Thank you, George. This is my—er—friend, Seán Molloy." Molly surrendered her mohair stole.

"How do you do, Mr. Molloy. Any friend of Miss Bryan's is a friend of Luigi's. Tonight I have nice table for you, Miss Bryan." The headwaiter showed them to a table in a small alcove. She ordered a beer for Conor and a Bellini for herself. She looked around; although the restaurant was so quiet tonight, no one nearby was likely to hear or be interested in their conversation; only two tables near them were occupied, one by three men, all mustached, who were drinking champagne; the other by a soft-eyed couple who were gazing at one another, floating in a haze of love.

"All right!" said Molly when the waiter had taken their order, "let's get down to business. 'Seán Molloy'?"

"That's the name on my driving license. And on my passport and on my social security papers. Use your head, Molly! Why would you imagine I would want to be known by my real name?"

"How did you get those papers?"

"Molly, I can't believe you are so naive—"

"And *I* can't believe *you* just showed up like this!"

His surprised look made her realize how vehemently she had spoken, and with another unpleasant jolt, she realized she was behaving like this not because of his false identity but because of that look she thought she had seen in Una O'Connor's eyes. She tried to sound more conciliatory: "I'm annoyed because you must have known for months how to contact me, Conor! In fact, I haven't heard *one word* from you since you left Inisheer . . .''

"Is that a fact? I did write to you, Molly, before I left Ireland for England. I asked Father Hartigan to send it to you—"

"Oh, *that*!"

"Did you find it wanting?"

"It was hardly enough for *six years* . . ."

"Yes, well, I'm sorry. Will you accept my apology? I won't do it again—I promise! I'll write to you every other day . . ."

"Be serious, Conor!"

"All right, all right." He laughed. "I am serious about one thing. I'm not going to lose touch with you again."

"And what about Mam? Are you going to get in touch with her? Really, Conor, six years!" The waiter arrived with their drinks and she stopped. When he had gone again, she resumed her attack: "This play has been running for six months—there has been publicity in the papers—you must have known—"

"Where I work, we don't get the kind of newspapers your picture might appear in."

"Where do you work?"

"Like I told that girl, the reporter, I move around . . ."

"Yes, but where?"

"The north of England, Holland, West Germany . . ."

"Doing what, Conor?"

"Working."

"What kind of work?"

"Anything I can get."

"Like what?"

"Hod-carrying, digging tunnels, harvesting shellfish, packing frozen food in a warehouse; I told you about the work for Volkswagen . . ."

Her anger ran down again. "But your qualifications!" she protested. "What about botany and all the hard work you put into that?"

"Molly, botany is not exactly the profession of the masses. Those areas were obvious areas for the police to check—and even with my changed name, if I had tried to get work as a botanist—or even as a humble gardener—the police would have found me very quickly. You know as well as I do that the only choice I had was to disappear into unskilled labor and to keep moving.'' He lapsed into silence and looked steadily at her.

"Conor, don't. Why are you looking at me like that?''

"I'm not looking at you like anything.''

"Conor, you are. You're embarrassing me . . .''

He took her hand. "You have become very beautiful,'' he said simply. "I've missed you.'' Molly felt the tremor in his hand and was half exhilarated, half afraid.

In her hotel room, Una O'Connor ran the tape of her interview with Margo Bryan. It was all rather bland, she felt. There was some interesting stuff about the actress's exacting standards and her professionalism, but other than that, there was very little she did not know already.

She was intrigued by the woman's personal life. There was definitely something odd about the father and that relationship. Would it be worth it to do a bit of digging?

More to the point, she wondered about Seán Molloy. Was he a boyfriend? Una could not decide. There had been electricity pinging around that room when she had arrived, but she had not been able to decipher the signals. At one stage she had thought that perhaps they were in the middle of a row which she had interrupted with her arrival, but had changed her mind. He was too relaxed for that.

She found she could not get him out of her mind.

Una was in search of a man of substance. She could not have described the quality, or multiplicity of qualities that went to make it up, but Seán Molloy had it, whatever it was. His physical presence was immensely powerful; by closing her eyes, Una could recreate its impact on her.

She was sexually experienced, she had had several lovers, some she described as boyfriends, all of them nice and perfectly satisfactory in their own ways, but to date, all of her relationships had sort of faded away like the Cheshire cat's grin. Instinctively she felt that if she could organize this one, it could be different. Una had learned always to trust her instincts.

But however was she going to meet him again? There was only one legitimate line of communication and that was Margo Bryan. She had better not do anything to cross Margo. First, she had to find out whether she was trespassing on Margo's territory.

Una was honorable about things like that.

* * *

The next day was Sunday, and in a London pub, Conor sipped slowly at a pint of light ale while he perused his copy of the *Observer* in front of a log fire fed by gas. It was lunchtime and the pub, busy with chatter and decorated with chintzes and horse brasses to give it a homey atmosphere, was situated in a gentrified area along the Thames.

Conor found it difficult to concentrate on his newspaper. He tried to sort out his feelings. Although he had thought himself well prepared and in control, he had been more shaken by his encounter with his sister than he cared to admit; he had found her physical presence so disturbing that he wondered if it might not be a good thing to leave London again as soon as possible. All those feelings and desires—which defied logic and decency—had come flooding dangerously close to the surface when he had actually sat in the same room with her, breathing the same air. Would he be able to continue to control this desire? To keep it buried where it belonged? Should he torture himself this way?

On the other hand, he was relatively confident he had managed to carry off the meeting without frightening her or causing her to detect anything of his internal struggle. It was probably, he told himself, the shock of seeing her after such a long interval that had caused his internal self-control to waver. It would be easier next time.

The cool, muted voices all around him pattered and tinkled in a very English way—and as usual in such circumstances, Conor longed to be standing at a dark bar counter in Dublin, surrounded by the loud waves of talk, ribald, fatuous, even aggressive. The talk all around him at the moment was, he noticed, mostly about house prices. The colorlessness of the clientele and designer-created coziness of the decor was getting on his nerves. He looked at his watch—1:15. He supposed actresses were late risers, but this, surely, was a respectable hour.

She answered on the second ring, which meant that she was probably still in bed. Conor took a deep breath and found it surprisingly easy to inject a note of banter into his tone: "Not at Mass, I see?"

She laughed. "And what Mass did you go to, dear brother?"

"*Touché!* Did I wake you?"

"No, actually. I've already had a telephone call from a Miss Una O'Connor. Remember her?"

"Sure. Last night in your dressing room."

"Well, Miss O'Connor finds it necessary to turn her article on me into a 'profile,' and this apparently means that she has to talk, not only to me, but to others about me . . ."

"Yes?"

"And guess who she wants to talk to about me?"

"You tell me!"

"If you ask me, Miss O'Connor has a little crush."

"She couldn't have. We only met for ten minutes."

"How long does it take in Holland or Germany or the north of England?"

Conor heard the needle. "Well, it's out of the question. I can't talk to her about you."

"But, dear brother, I'm afraid I've already told her I'll pass on the message. Cooperation with the press and all that."

Conor sighed. Whatever was going on he had to divert it. "All right, we'll talk about it later. It's a lovely day. I wondered if you were interested in taking a walk by the river."

She hesitated. "What time?"

"Any time you say. I'm at your disposal."

"Fine, well, how about half-past three?"

"That's grand. I'll meet you at the entrance to Westminster Tube Station. All right?"

"All right."

"Good-bye so . . ."

"Good-bye, see you later."

He replaced the receiver and went back to the bar, where he ordered a small one. He brought the whiskey back to his table and attempted to concentrate once again on the magazine section of his newspaper. But he found he was reading the same sentence over and over again. He checked his watch. Two hours until he had to be at Westminster.

It was actually a few minutes earlier than that when he saw Molly emerge into the sunlight from the dark entrance to the Tube. She was simply dressed. It was a warm day and she wore faded jeans and a sleeveless buttoned blouse of primrose cotton. She had tied her hair into a ponytail, her feet were bare in a pair of thonged leather sandals, and slung over her shoulder was a light jacket in a shade of yellow deeper than the blouse. Except for her height and grace she might have been a teenager.

He had been killing time looking at the T-shirts and miniature Houses of Parliament and Big Bens in the souvenir shop a little way along the narrow sidewalk. His heart lurched when he saw her, but he gave himself a mental shake; out here in the busy sunlight, it was quite easy to be fully in possession of himself. And now he could be reasonably sure that his secret was safe. He would simply have to ensure that it remained so.

She saw him and waved, but before she reached him, was intercepted by a middle-aged couple, clearly seeking an autograph.

He strolled toward her, waiting a few paces away while she dealt with the couple, signing the back of an old envelope the woman had produced from her handbag.

"Hello there," he said, when the couple had left.

"Hello." She smiled at him and was about to take his arm but seemed to change her mind. "So here I am. All yours! What'll we do? It's such a gorgeous day, let's not hang around."

They decided to take a trip on one of the pleasure craft that ply the Thames as far as Greenwich and descended the stone steps to the level of the river, paid their money at a little booth, and with all the other tourists boarded one of the boats.

"Have you ever done this before?" She was gay.

He shook his head. "There's always a first time."

"Well, I've done it with Dolly—that's my agent, you'll have to meet her—she says that every visitor in London has to see the city from the Thames."

The boat, every seat occupied, chugged ponderously out from the jetty and set off. There was little opportunity for talk because as they slid along the great waterway, under one bridge after another, past barges, fire tenders, and pleasure craft, the barker kept up a running commentary through a loudspeaker.

As they chugged past, several two- and three-masted sailing ships moored behind one another were rocking heavily in the swell created by a pair of light speedboats racing one another in the waters beside them: "Far from currachs and the *Naomh Eanna*!" Conor shouted into Molly's ear. But his words were drowned by a tinny burst of "Tie Me Kangaroo Down, Sport!" from the pleasure boat's loudspeaker, followed by a ragged cheer from a small group of Australians seated just behind them.

They heard a condensed history of London as the barker indicated the features along the banks on either side: Cleopatra's Needle, the dome of St. Paul's, the gray bulk of H.M.S. Belfast, London Bridge and the Tower. It was breezy out on the water and when they got to Greenwich, Molly, who felt chilled, suggested that they disembark and have a cup of coffee.

This proved difficult. Sunday afternoon was a sleepy time, even along the tourist trail, and they had to walk through several streets before they found a little newsagent-cum-café which was open.

There was no one in sight, although through the doorway behind the counter they could heard the sounds of a cricket commentary on television. Conor banged on the counter, and after a minute, a small Indian or Pakistani appeared to take their order. They consulted the handwritten menu taped to the wall, ordered apple tart and coffee, then sat at·a little table near the fly-blown window. When it came, the tart was tough and doughy, topped with synthetic cream, and the coffee had obviously been made hours ago and repeatedly reheated. "Desperate!" said Conor, as he tasted it. He pushed it away and took a pipe out from the inside pocket of his jacket. "Mind?" He waved it at Molly.

"Go ahead. I didn't know you smoked a pipe," she said curiously.

"There's clearly quite a lot you don't know about me."

"So tell me! What don't I know?" Molly normally hated people to smoke anywhere near her, but she was fascinated to watch the deftness of her brother's hands as he unrolled a pouch and scooped tobacco into the bowl of his briar.

"Well, I've already filled you in on all the important stuff." He put the unlit pipe into his mouth.

"Tell me about the *un*important stuff, then . . ."

"Like what?"

To her alarm, Molly recognized what it was she really wanted to know. She stalled. "Let's see—tell me about Holland?"

"Holland? What do you want to know about Holland?" He seemed amused.

"I've never been to Holland."

"It's flat. And full of windmills and tulips just like the pictures, and Amsterdam's full of tourists."

"Come on, Conor. Don't tease me . . ."

"All right, I'll be serious then. Let's see, what can I tell you about Holland . . ." He considered, tamping the tobacco into the bowl of his pipe with the corner of a box of matches.

"All right, forget about Holland, tell me about you. Have you a girlfriend, for instance?" Molly couldn't help herself; the words seemed to fly of their own momentum from her unprotected mouth.

He struck a match and held the flame to the pipe: "No." He said it simply and she could not see his eyes.

"I see. Well, let's see, what else?" She tried hard to match his casual tone. "You're clearly healthy. Happy?"

"Enough."

"No girlfriend?" Again the words just came out. "That's odd, surely? Come on, there must have been someone! You're thirty-two years old . . ."

"Thirty-three, actually!"

"Don't quibble. Just tell me about the woman, or women, in your life . . ."

"Nothing much to tell."

"Conor O Briain! You're not going to have the nerve to tell me that you've got to this age and never been kissed."

"Oh, I've been kissed, all right!"

"I see." Molly attempted a light laugh. This was ridiculous. He must realize how oddly she was behaving. She looked out the window: "I suppose we should keep an eye on the time. Not to miss the boat back, I mean."

"We must, all right. Although I'm sure there's more than one boat on a Sunday."

"Anyone special?"

"Sorry?"

"You know, any special woman ever? That you might have married, for instance?"

"Umm . . ." He pulled heavily on the pipe and released a cloud of blue smoke.

"So there was someone special?"

"Not anymore, Molly, not that it's any of your business, I am, as you pointed out, over thirty, and I have had affairs with women." His mood had changed in a way she did not understand. He was still smoking the pipe, but suddenly he seemed tense.

Molly realized she had overstepped the mark. "Sorry," she said. "Let's change the subject."

He swatted at a fly which was hovering near his untouched and congealing apple tart. "Yes," he said, "let's."

Her blouse was gaping slightly and he was only too aware of the shadow that ran from her collarbone to a point between her breasts. He concentrated on his pipe as the silence stretched and stretched between them. Without thinking, he took another mouthful of the apple tart. It was inedible and he pushed it away. "I could ask you the same question, by the way," he said. "Anyone special in *your* life?"

"You made me change the subject."

"All right." He sat back, out of harm's way. "I'll tell if you will."

"All right," she echoed. "You go first."

But when it came to it, he could not maintain the level of lightheartedness. There had been no particular "special woman" in his life, he told her quietly. There had been several with whom, should he have pursued matters, might have become special, but he had not chosen to pursue matters.

"Why not?"

"For the same reason I don't use my real name . . ." He pulled at his pipe. "Your turn now."

Molly considered for a moment. What she said now was going to be very important. She had to keep it lighthearted. "Well, I'm not thirty-three years old yet," she said, flicking at her ponytail, "so *I* still have an excuse!"

"Come on! You mean to tell me that all the time you were in the theater in Dublin, even since you came to London, there has been no one interested in you?"

"I didn't say that . . ." Molly was confused. On the one hand she wanted him to think she was popular and had men lining up for favors, on the other she wanted him to know she was pure.

"What's wrong, then?"

"What do you mean, what's *wrong*?"

"You know what I mean . . ."

"I don't. Are you implying that there's something *wrong* with me?"

"Is there?"

She realized the conversation was again getting out of hand and sat bolt upright, gripping the table. "*I* wasn't interested in *them*!" She took a gulp of the awful coffee, now stone cold. "Let's leave this, Conor. I'm sorry we got into it . . ."

"It was you wanted to get into it—remember?"

"Yes, well, I've changed my mind." She sounded as if she were twelve years old.

"Anything you say, Miss Bryan. What do you want to talk about now?"

"I don't know."

"Well, are you not interested in anything else about me besides Holland and women? How about Volkswagens? Take your time, now. Don't want to rush you."

"What about Una O'Connor? Do you fancy her?" She had had no intention of bringing up Una O'Connor. What was happening to her?

"Molly, don't be ridiculous. How could I fancy someone I met for such a short time in such circumstances?"

"It happens."

"Well, it didn't. All right?"

"Well"—she rooted in her handbag—"I promised I would give you her number so you could tell her all about me." She handed over the piece of paper.

"But she's in Dublin," he said, looking at the number. "How—"

Molly snapped her handbag shut. "She said she'd come back over."

"Look Molly, do you not want me to talk to her?"

"That's up to you."

"I won't—all right?"

"Conor, of course you have to talk to her."

He sighed and put the piece of paper in his pocket.

Molly made one last determined effort to quash these disturbing, racing emotions which were prompting her to act in a way she had never before acted in her life. She drew on her acting talent: "Listen," she said brightly, "I've just had a great idea. I've a friend, she's an actress in the television show with me, she's having a birthday party tonight and I was dreading going alone. Why don't you come with me?" Perhaps, she thought, if she could get Conor fixed up with someone, if she could see it . . .

"I would really like you to meet her," she said. "She's terrific. You'd love her."

"I hate parties . . . What television show, anyway?"

"*Where's Dad?*, the sitcom you read about in the theater program."

"Oh, the reason you're *famous*!"

"Don't be so bitchy. It pays the rent. And anyway, I doubt if I would have been cast in the West End in *Blithe Spirit* without being so-called 'famous' . . ."

"When's it on?"

"Wednesday nights."

"How can you do that and still be onstage in the West End every night?"

"It's all shot in studio, Monday to Friday, bankers' hours! And they shoot around me when I have matinées. They're used to that. I'm not the only one who's playing at the theater at the same time. Dolly arranged it—"

"The famous agent?"

"The very one! Now"—Molly had the bit in her teeth and at last felt in control—"what about this party?"

"I told you, I hate parties."

"This one won't be too bad. It'll be crowded and noisy, so we won't have to stay long. We won't be missed if we leave early." To her chagrin, she realized that it had come out all wrong; it implied she wanted him all to herself, which, of course, if she was honest, was absolutely true.

Oh, God, she thought, unable to interpret his expression. She had to get out of here as fast as possible. "This girl's absolutely gorgeous, Conor," she said, refusing anymore to look him in the eye.

"So?"

"Maybe you'll like her."

"*So?*"

"Well, maybe you'll *like* her, Conor!"

"I said—*so*?"

Bravely she met his gaze. "For goodness' sake, Brother dear, don't be such an old fuddy-duddy!" She smiled her widest smile at him. "It's settled, then—you and me's going to a party tonight." She stood up: "For now, shall we go back to the boat? Come on back to the house—I'll give you a decent cup of coffee. Anyway, there's something I have to watch on television: I've recorded an interview for one of the more obscure arts shows here. I'm sure they'll only use a clip, but I'll have to look at it, if you don't mind. Dolly likes me to be in a position to criticize my own public appearances, to learn from them, d'you see."

"Delighted," said Conor, knocking his pipe on the side of the table and standing up too. "We'll see about the party, but I'd be delighted to criticize your public appearances with you."

Una paced the floor of her flat. She had arrived from the airport only fifteen minutes before.

There was no way in the world he was going to telephone her.

He might already have rung.

He might not have even got the message yet.

She had left the door of the flat open, just in case. Her flat was across the hall from the communal public telephone which served the house.

She went out into the hallway and lifted the receiver to make sure it was working. It was.

When she had telephoned Margo Bryan with the message that she was going to change the style of the interview, she had listened very carefully for nuances in the actress's voice. But her subject had seemed only marginally interested in the situation. Granted, she had woken the woman up and she was sleepy. But when, holding her breath, Una mentioned Seán Molloy's name, Margo Bryan had responded quite calmly and had taken down the telephone number.

Was the calm natural or acted? Una could not decide. And anyway, Una's request was so perfectly within the bounds of journalistic possibility that even if they were having a number together, Margo need not necessarily smell any rat in a bona fide reporter wanting to talk to her boyfriend about her. Una was no nearer knowing what the relationship between the two of them was. She would have to wait until she spoke to him.

If he rang.

The one thing Una could not stand was inaction. She was a bad waiter-arounder. She consoled herself with the knowledge that if she did not hear from him, she could call Margo again, on the pretext that since she was not always in attendance at her telephone, she must have been out when he called . . .

She put on the electric kettle to make a cup of coffee and then switched it off again, fearful that the noise it made might drown out the bell in the hall.

She stopped dead in the middle of the floor. She was behaving like a lunatic. Goddamn it, this would have to stop. She walked to the door of the flat and closed it firmly.

Immediately the telephone rang. She scrabbled at the door and ran out into the hall, but then stood in front of the instrument, letting it ring, while she caught her breath. It would not do to appear too eager.

"Hello," she said.

But it was her news editor. "Listen," he said briskly on the other end of the line, "apparently there's been a mass streak at a soccer match at Dalymount. Seven arrested—taken to Store Street . . ."

"I see," said Una, her disappointment acute. Already she was calculating how long it would take her to get to Dalymount, the soccer stadium on the north side of the city, and then to the Garda station at Store Street, which was in the center of the city.

She knew she did not want to go at all. Suppose he rang while she was out? "But I'm just starting on this Margo Bryan interview," she said.

"That'll keep," said the editor.

"It's for features," she protested, "they want it tomorrow—and you have me marked for the graveyard tonight . . ." Una was not normally scheduled to do the night shift but the paper was temporarily short-staffed.

"Oh, yeah," said the news editor. "Sorry. Forget it!" He hung up.

Una sighed. She went back into the flat, banged the door shut behind her, and switched on the kettle again.

Streaking, she thought as she made the coffee—that was this year's special offer. A bunch of adolescent male nudes with delusions of grandeur. In her own state of adolescent sexual tension, she wondered wryly if she could have been truly objective.

Placing the coffee within reach on the rickety table which doubled as a dining table and desk, she pulled her typewriter toward her. She set up the tape recorder beside the typewriter, and using the "pause" button on the machine to start and stop Margo Bryan's soft voice, she sat down to begin the transcription of the tape. It was funny, she thought, how most actresses, who could boom to the back of a theater at will, spoke so softly and intimately in normal conversation.

Having worked for about four minutes, Una got up, slunk toward the door, and again propped it open.

Pleasantly tired and relaxed, a large bourbon in his hand, Christian lay on the bed in his hotel room. No matter which channel he switched to—and there were not all that many of them here—he got something ethnic, arty, or religious. He hated Sundays in any foreign city. Sunday evenings were the pits.

It was still early and he did not have to meet Dick for dinner for another forty minutes. He debated whether he had enough energy to roll off the bed and go into the bathroom for a shower, but kept putting it off.

Christian's muscles were actually aching from the exertions of the previous night and morning. He smiled to himself as he took a mouthful of the bourbon. Gillian Somerville was something else.

Exhausted, they had slept until noon before going out for brunch—and then had cut the meal short to dash back once again to her flat. Christian had not had such good sex—or such a feast of it—for months. Not, in fact, since the last time he and Gillian had met. Whatever their schedules, he planned to see her at least one more time before he and Dick flew home.

He stretched his toes against the foot of the bed, wriggling them sensuously along its carved wooden curves; life was good and he had every confidence that Gillian would deliver on the interview—he was expecting to hear from her in the morning. He reached out and topped up his drink from the open bottle on the night table by the bed. Must watch the booze tonight, he thought. And must be in bed early, must be fresh for the work first thing in the morning.

He had been staring at the television screen without seeing it, but gradually, his mind began to focus on an interview with a blond woman. It was her voice that caught him initially, he decided—she had a strange, soft accent, Scottish, perhaps, or Welsh.

She was very beautiful, with fine bone structure and wide, expressive eyes. He began to pay attention to what she was saying. She was an actress, Irish it seemed—and apparently she was a hit in some English television show and a West End play. The more Christian listened to her, the more riveted he became. It was not really her beauty—Christian knew many, many beautiful women— it was something about the woman herself.

He put down his drink and, picking up the telephone, dialed Dick's room. "Dick?"

"Yeah?"

"Are you watching television?"

"Nope."

"Turn it on, will you—I think it's the BBC. There's an interview on with a blond actress." He could hear Dick sighing, but then there was a pause as the telephone was put down on Dick's end and his friend turned on the television, waited for it to warm up, and found the right channel. He came back on the line: "All right, I'm seeing it. What about it?"

"That actress—" said Christian slowly.

"Yeah? What about her?"

"Do we know her?"

There was another pause as Dick listened. "Not unless we've been to Ireland in our sleep," he said then. "She's Irish."

"Yes, but does she not look pretty familiar to you?"

Again there was silence as Dick watched for a little while. Christian was conscious of the voice of the actress sounding in both rooms, as if the program were being broadcast in stereo. "Can't say she does. Sorry."

"All right, never mind. See you in half an hour."

"See you."

Christian hung up and picked up his drink. Wondering if at the end of the interview they would use her name, he watched the actress for another minute or so and then the telephone rang.

It was his newsdesk. Christian got off the bed and turned off the television set.

Conor had not lied when he told Molly that he hated parties. He skulked in a corner of the little house, which he supposed the real-estate agents would have called a *pied-à-terre,* hating the noise and the mindless chatter, the smoke, the glass of cheap white wine put in his hand when he arrived. He hated most of all the prospecting, the sexual frisson that electrified the air. He had already had the same conversation with three women during which they assessed his exact degree of interest and availability. He was ill at ease for another reason, having to be watchful, careful to maintain the masquerade that he was a friend—and just a friend—of Molly's from the old days.

"Hello there! What's your name?" It was another one, blonde and skinny like most of them. He made an effort: "Seán Molloy."

"Is that an Irish accent I hear?" She raised an arch eyebrow.

"Yes." Conor had had enough. "Excuse me," he said to her as politely as he could, "I'll be back in a minute, I have to go to the bathroom." He moved away from her and out into the hallway. Squeezing past a couple locked passionately together at the foot of the stairs, he went up to what he presumed was the bathroom.

He knew he had been rude, and for Molly's sake, hoped that the woman was not important to her.

Mercifully the bathroom was vacant. He locked the door and sat on the edge of the bathtub, avocado, he noted, with gold fittings. Frilled bowls of potpourri on the windowsill. Typical. At least Molly's house showed a bit of taste and restraint.

The noise of the party swarmed up the stairs and nuzzled against the door and it was a while before he realized that it had been augmented by a timid knocking. "Yes?" he called.

"Oh, sorry!" said a female voice. "Will you be much longer in there? There *is* only one bathroom—sorry!"

"I'll be out in a second!" He ran water and flushed the toilet and then, bracing himself, opened the door. He apologized to the woman as she swept in past him. He looked down at the open hall door and wondered if he dared walk down the stairs and straight out through it but thought better of it. Molly would be very hurt. He went in search of her.

From the vantage point of his height, he spotted her easily, standing with a glass in her hand while a man, gesticulating, engaged her in earnest conversation. The man was about three inches shorter than she and she had inclined her head toward his mouth to hear him above the hubbub.

Conor pushed his way toward her. She saw him coming, smiled an excuse at the man, and crossed the floor to meet him. She led him toward the kitchen of the house, more crowded, if that were possible, than the tiny living room. "That's her!" whispered Molly, "that's Jenny, the one I was telling you about." Conor could barely see the hostess through the press of bodies; she was tiny, under five feet tall, and appeared to be dressed like a bird of paradise.

"Jenny!" Molly called, her trained voice cutting through the tumult.

Her hostess looked around. "Well, hello!" she called back, and threaded her way toward them. "Bedlam, isn't it?" She smiled happily when she got to them. "How are you, Molly—thought you weren't coming. You know everyone?"

Then she saw Conor. "Who's this, Margo?" she breathed, seeming to get tinier, looking up and up and up.

"Jenny, this is a friend of mine from Inisheer—Seán Molloy. I hope you don't mind that I brought him."

"Mind?" asked the bird of paradise. "Is he yours?"

It was too much. "Nice to meet you, Jenny," Conor said, then turned to his sister. "Molly, I'm afraid I have to go. I'll give you a call at the theater."

She looked from him to Jenny. "That's a pity, oh well, just wanted you two to get to know one another. Sorry, Jenny!" She shrugged her shoulders, smiled her wide smile, and took his arm. "Let me come with you as far as the door."

Conor was flabbergasted at her sophistication. And if he was honest, miffed that she seemed so ready to get rid of him. Was this the same person who had appeared so confused back at the café? "All right," he said, then repeated, "nice meeting you, er . . ." He had forgotten the bird of paradise's name.

They pushed their way to the front door and stepped out into the night. And as they did so he saw Molly was her real self again: "Are you sure you have to go?" she asked. "Was it really terrible?"

"Pretty awful."

"Sorry. Look, I'll leave too."

For a tantalizing moment, Conor wanted to agree, to sweep her away to a hideaway. "No, you stay!" he said. "They're your friends."

She looked uncertain again, but he kissed her firmly on the cheek. " 'Bye!"

"When will you telephone?" she called after him.

"Tomorrow."

"Promise?"

"Promise. Oh, and by the way, I meant it earlier when I said you were very good in your public appearances. You need have no worries about the famous Dolly. Television suits you!"

"Thanks." Dressed in a simple black sheath, she looked so beautiful he could have died. "Cheerio, see you soon!" he said, then, before he could say anything stupid, walked rapidly away.

Three streets farther on, he slowed down and inhaled a deep lungful of air. They had come to the party by taxi and he was not quite sure where he was. Looking around, he saw he was in a neighborhood of mews houses adorned with window boxes. There was a pub on a corner, The Slap And Tickle. It was quiet and half empty. He ordered a half of ale and sat in the corner. Searching in his pocket for change, he pulled out the piece of paper inscribed with Una O'Connor's name and telephone number.

He crumpled it and put it in the ashtray in front of him.

7

Christian's drinking bouts, which had worsened dramatically after his divorce, had begun to endanger his assignments.

Early in January, 1974, he and Dick sat in the huge lobby of the Addis Ababa Hilton, tiled and air-conditioned, furnished with soft couches and easy chairs and decorated with flowers and native art of the blander variety. The worn Muzak tape was meandering through a string version of the Beatles' 'Yesterday.'

Dick's patience was wearing thin and not only on account of the irritating music. For the third evening running, Christian was drunk. The front of the tracksuit he had bought at the hotel's gift shop on the evening they had arrived was now stained and his thick blond hair was tangled and unkempt; he was just on the verge of becoming belligerent and Dick wanted to avoid that at all costs. If it had not been so tedious, it would have been a constant source of wonder to Dick how his friend's personality changed so much with drink. "Come on, Christian," he said, "let's go to bed . . ."

"But we hav—we haven't discussed what we are going to do about the *story*. . . ."

"We'll discuss it in the morning, Christian."

"No! I want to discuss it now!"

Dick sighed and said as levelly as possible: "Christian, we've been here for three days now and you have showed no interest at all in this story."

It was all Christian needed. "Whaddya mean, *asshole*!" he bridled. "Whaddya mean? Thish—this is an im*por*tant story. We gotta be *thinking* right . . ."

"Yes, yes! For God's sake . . ." Privately, Dick was having serious doubts about whether they would get any story at all out of this trip. The telexes which arrived for

them several times a day from their newsdesk in Chicago
were becoming increasingly angry. Christian had refused
to answer any of them. "Tell them anything you like, Dick!
Tell them I'll contact them when I have the story . . ."
Since they had arrived in Addis, he had sunk into a state
of such lassitude, fed by a river of alcohol, that he seemed
incapable of making even the simplest decision.

But even more serious than his appearance was the
possible cause for it. Dick was worried that Christian
might have lost his nerve. They had come to cover the
famine, which, rumor had it, was about to rage out of
control in the north of the country, but so far, they had
not left the city. While he continued to telex back that
Christian was ill with tropical dysentery, Dick was seriously considering making his own arrangements, shed-
ding Christian and going out by himself, to send back a
picture story with extended captions. He knew from experience that there was no point at all in barracking his
colleague. He would, as always, simply have to wait until
Christian himself came out of the bender. They were
lucky in one area—so far, the newspaper had not succeeded in getting through by telephone, although Dick
knew this was merely a matter of time. He stood up.
"I'm going to bed, whether you do or not, Christian."

Christian had now fastened his attention on a huge fruit
arrangement just outside the main restaurant on the other side
of the lobby. "Look at that! The vul-vul-vul-garity of that
. . ." He attempted to rise from his seat but stumbled, and
Dick had to put out a hand to save him from falling.

"Christian, will you go to bed . . ."

"Go to bed? Go to *bed*?" Christian could not have
been more astonished had his friend suggested that they
grow wings and fly. He flopped back into his seat. He
clearly had difficulty focusing his eyes. "How can I
poss—" He hiccupped. Dick waited. "How can I posh-
possibly go to bed?"

"Why not, Christian?"

"Why not what?"

Dick gritted his teeth. "Why won't you go to bed?"

"Because I don't *want* to!" Christian's handsome features set themselves stubbornly.

"All right, Christian, see you in the morning—"

"Wait a minute, Dick . . ."

"What now?"

Christian's gaze had fastened again on the arrangement of fruit. "Do you not think it's vulgar, Dick?"

"Yes, I do—"

"Oh, so you *do* think itsh vulgar?"

"Yes, I do."

"Well, okay then!"

"Well, okay what?"

"You *do* think it's vulgar?"

"How many times do I have to say it?"

"Well, okay then!"

Christian sat back, satisfied. Even when sharp and sober, Christian had a peculiarly disconcerting lateral way of thinking, which Dick found especially irritating when he was drunk. He had had quite enough. "See you in the morning," he said, and walked across the lobby toward the elevators. Christian looked after him and shrugged. He closed his eyes and fell asleep.

Alerted by a scornful barman, the receptionist on duty woke him half an hour later and escorted him to his room.

When Dick came down to breakfast next morning, Christian was sitting in the restaurant in front of a Bloody Mary and an American-style bacon, lettuce, and tomato sandwich, held together with a plastic cocktail spear which flew a paper Stars and Stripes on its tiny masthead. His eyes were bloodshot and baggy and the lower part of his face was covered in thick blond stubble. At least, thought Dick, he was not yet drunk. "You look awful, Christian," he said as he sat down.

Christian pushed away the sandwich. "Don't rub it in."

"You've got to eat," said Dick. "You'll feel better then."

"I'm not hungry."

"You *need* food." Dick gave his own order, scrambled eggs and bacon. Then he sat back. "Look, Christian," he said, "they won't be put off anymore." He took the latest telex from Chicago out of his pocket and placed it on the table between them. "They want to know when they can expect copy and some idea of what it covers and how long it will be." Christian would not meet his eyes. "Christian?"

"I know, I've screwed up . . ."

"Don't give me any of that Uriah Heep, humble shit. The question is, what are we going to do about it?"

Christian shrugged, his head drooping, and Dick sighed, disgusted, but too fond of his friend to be angry. He had been looking after him all his life, it seemed. "All right," he said, "either we do something *now* or we cut our losses and get out of here. We can't spend any more of the paper's money hanging around here—anyway, your liver needs a break . . ."

"What'll we tell them?"

"We'll think of something," said Dick. "Stay here—don't move—and I'll go to the desk to see what the story is about our travel permits—and if they haven't come through, I'll ask about flights out of here."

"Yes, Dick," said Christian humbly, his contrition absolute. Dick thumped him on the shoulder with exasperated affection and went out to the reception desk. The receptionist had a message for them: they were to call the office of the interior minister and then the office that handled security; the permits which would allow them to leave the city had come through.

Dick hesitated. He thanked the receptionist and asked about flights north. The man made a telephone call to the airport: tonight there was an Alitalia flight to Rome. It was full but the standby chances were probably good.

When Dick got back to the dining-room, he saw Christian had still not touched his food. "Get your mouth around that sandwich!" Dick ordered. "We have to decide now; it's either piss or get off the pot. The permits are through—or will be in a couple of hours when we go to collect them. So it's up country today or alternatively, out to the airport by six-thirty. There's an Alitalia flight to Rome; no seats available, but apparently there never are at this stagè. We'd have to standby."

Christian held on to the sides of the table. "I think—I think I'm going to be sick—"

"Come on." Dick pushed the sandwich under his nose.

"I can't—"

"All right. I told them to prepare our bill, but let's see if we can keep the rooms for a couple of hours more. You, my friend, are going to take a nap and a shower."

"All right," said Christian meekly. "What time is it now?"

"Just after seven-thirty."

Christian closed his eyes: "Christ, Dick, I feel absolutely awful!"

"You look worse!" said Dick. "Now why don't you go up to your room. I'll call you at ten. I'll go up with you now and you can give me your room key. That way, I can get into your room and won't have to break the door down to wake you up."

Obediently Christian stood up, but as he stood he swayed a little, like a diseased tree. Dick looked at him ruefully. Getting mad at Christian was easy, he thought, staying mad was impossible. He felt like a mother hen.

Once in his room, Christian collapsed onto the bed, but before Dick let him close his eyes he found Alka-Seltzer in the bathroom. He fizzed three of the tablets in a glass and ordered Christian to drink. Then he forced him to drink two bottles of mineral water. "Come on, come on, you have to rehydrate yourself . . ."

"I'm going to get sick."

"No, you're not, mind over matter!" Dick waited until Christian had drained the second bottle. "Now sleep, and I'll see you in two and a half hours."

When he let himself back into the room almost three hours later, Christian was still unconscious. The windows were closed and the room still reeked of alcohol. "Christ," Dick muttered as he crossed to the window to let in some air, "how much did you have last night?"

He shook Christian's shoulder and woke him up.

Christian's powers of recuperation had always been strong and Dick actually enjoyed the receptionist's double-take when his friend, brandishing a concertina of credit cards, handed in his room key at about ten minutes to eleven. The staff at the Hilton obviously had had him pegged as a broken-down lush, but here he was, the picture of shining, clean-shaven American health. A close look would have revealed a network of red lines in the whites of his eyes, but in a replacement tracksuit, white with navy trim, which Dick had bought for him and which exactly fitted Christian's athletic frame, he might have been a tennis star on the international circuit.

* * *

Five hours later, Christian was regretting the decision to stay and cover the story, as, wilting in the afternoon heat, he and Dick were struggling to help their Ethiopian driver change a wheel on their jeep. The puncture had happened where the road ran on the crest of a little ridge, on each side of which stretched a brown, dessicated landscape swirling with dust devils.

They were surrounded by a circle of silent men, women and children dressed uniformly in brown rags. As the jeep was gray, the only colors for miles around were the red bandana Christian had tied around his forehead to keep his hair out of his eyes and the faded purple lettering that spelled out NOTRE DAME on Dick's T-shirt.

The only sounds in Christian's ears were made by themselves and a small crackling as the tindered stalks of what once was sorghum were stirred by a little breeze. "Notice anything?" he panted, straining at a wheel nut. "What?" Dick was not the strongest man in the world and hated unnecessary physical activity of any kind.

"No birdsong!"

"Thanks for the nature lesson," said Dick sourly. "I'll bear it in mind. These nuts must have been tightened by Hercules."

Christian straightened his aching back. His hangover had lifted in the past half hour, and for the first time in three days he was feeling almost human. What he wouldn't give now, he thought, for the sandwich he had rejected earlier that day. A woman in the crowd coughed, the phlegm rattling loudly in her chest. No one looked at her or moved, and ashamed of his piddling hunger in the face of such mass starvation, Christian bent again to the wheel.

Together the Americans leaned their weight on the tire iron, while the driver attempted to keep the head, the threads of which were worn, against the wheel nut. The sweat ran freely on all three men, cutting little channels through the dust caked on the skin of their faces, necks, and forearms. But despite their best efforts, the head of the tire iron kept slipping and the nut would not budge.

The fourth member of their group, their so-called guide, whom Christian knew well was really their "minder," sent along with them from Addis Ababa with explicit instructions about what they were not to see, did not help with the work. Dressed immaculately in khaki drill, the creases in his shirt and pants as sharp as blades, he patrolled in a little circle around the jeep and his charges, his eyes fixed on the crowd. He had tried at first to keep them all herded to one side, but, augmented all the time from the river of people that flowed toward the city, the crowd now numbered hundreds, and it proved impossible to keep them all together. So he prowled around the circumference of the no-man's-land he had created, from time to time brandishing his military swagger stick, in case any of the wretches was bold enough to take a step forward.

As he continued to strain on the tire iron, the skin on the back of Christian's neck began to prickle. He was unnerved by the profound silence, the still faces of the watchers. Out of the corner of his eye, he noticed a flash of white on the knees of an old man, where bare bone protruded through pressure sores.

The head of the tire iron slipped yet again and all three of the men working it almost fell to the ground. Christian vented his frustration, kicking one of the side panels of the jeep. "Shit, shit, shit!" He'd had it up to his tonsils with Ethiopia, with Haile Selassie, with dust and beggars, with broken-down jeeps, with miniature mountain ranges that appeared on maps as "all-weather-roads." It had taken almost seven months of negotiation, of personal interviews, of form-filling, of pulling strings, to get permission from the edgy Ethiopian authorities, who were not admitting to the famine, for himself and Dick to get into the country at all.

Staring at the dented panel of the jeep, he was regretting going to all the trouble. He and Dick were actually here under false pretenses: Christian had been tipped off that an archaeological expedition, led by a Dr. Donald Johanson of Cleveland University, had discovered what could be the anthropological find of the century, an intact fossil skeleton of a female hominid that could be three and a half million years old. If authenticated, it was one and a half million years older than the skull found by Richard Leakey in Kenya, which, until now, was thought to be the oldest living ancestor of man and could be the long-sought missing link between apes and man. It would also prove that Ethiopia and not Kenya was the cradle of man.

"Listen, kid, it's quite obvious this isn't going to work." Dick wiped his hands on the back of his jeans. Christian hated to be addressed as "kid." Scowling, Dick walked across to the minder. "How far are we from the nearest town, Samson?"

"Many kilometers, Mr. Spielberg," replied the man, who spoke excellent, if archaic, English.

"Yes, I'm sure. But how many?"

"I think, perhaps, twenty or so. That would be, perhaps, almost fourteen of your American miles." Anxious to appear cooperative in all respects, the minder smiled widely, showing three gold teeth in his upper jaw. Of the travelers, he was the only one who was not sweating. As well as his swagger stick, he carried a small plastic document case under his left arm. Christian and Dick, who were laden with bags and equipment, had noticed that his clothing for the trip, which was scheduled to last six days, was packed into one half-empty Adidas sports bag.

The front ranks of the crowd moved a little forward to hear the conversation, and immediately the minder raised the stick threateningly. One boy of about fourteen was not fast enough and to the Americans' horror, the minder brought the stick down on his head. The boy, cowering in the dust, did not cry out and no one came to his aid. Like all the others, he was desperately thin; the forearm he held to his bleeding head looked as though it could be snapped in two between two of Christian's fingers. "Look here!" Christian yelled at the minder.

"Easy, kid!" Dick put up a restraining arm. "Yes, Mr. Smith?" The minder was again smiling.

"Why'd you do that? There was no need for that—"

"I'm afraid I do not know to what you refer, Mr. Smith . . ."

"That, *that!*" Christian's tone was outraged as he indicated the boy, who was still hunkered down on the ground; a little blood had begun to ooze from a wound on his patchy head. "But Mr. Smith," protested the minder, "I am charged with your protection, and where these people are concerned, I act in your best interests. These people are unreliable. Trust me, Mr. Smith."

"For Christ's sake, man! This isn't a mob!"

"We may debate that, of course, Mr. Smith." The man's voice was silky, but Dick cut in before Christian could reply. "Look," he said, "we'd better not stand here all day. Samson, would you tell the driver to drain a little oil from the engine, and we'll try to loosen the nut with it."

"As you please, sir." The minder spoke to the driver in rapid Amharic and the man, sullen, with a pock-marked face, took a rag from under his seat. Lifting the hood of the jeep, he dipped it in the oil reservoir.

Dick snatched the rag from his hand and applied it energetically to the recalcitrant nut, squeezing the filthy, viscous fluid out of the rag and working it in. "Now let's try again." The three of them bent once more to the wheel and bit by bit, the nut began to loosen. "Thank Christ!" said Christian when finally it was off.

By the time the wheel was changed, the crowd numbered almost a thousand. Looking into those dark apathetic eyes made Christian feel desperately guilty and uncomfortable, and ignoring the warning gesture of the minder, he went over to the boy who had been hit. Smiling at him, he crouched down beside him and touching his own blonde head, trying to indicate sympathy and regret. "I'm sorry," he said slowly and very clearly.

"Sor-ree . . ." Obediently, as though they were a class and Christian a teacher, at least twelve people in front of him repeated the word. Then they all lapsed again into silence, waiting, it seemed, for the next lesson. The boy said nothing.

"Mr. Smith, Mr. Smith!" The minder was anxious. "We must proceed immediately, Mr. Smith . . ."

Looking around, Christian saw that the other three were in the jeep. But before he got in himself, he took an orange from a paper bag on the floor of the vehicle and walked back toward the boy with the orange in his hand. The silence in the crowd sharpened and he felt the skin on his neck prickle again as he offered the piece of fruit.

Delicately, as though it were a butterfly, the boy took the orange as behind him, Christian heard the urgent voice of the minder: "Go, go!" and the jeep crashing into life. Surprised, he turned, saw it was already moving, and had to sprint to catch it. As they drove away at high speed, he looked back through the window: the boy to whom he had given the orange was nowhere to be seen in a melee of dust, arms, legs, and flying rags.

That night Christian could not sleep although he was accustomed to sleeping outdoors and was comfortable enough in his sleeping bag. Part of the reason was hunger; although they had eaten a supper of fruit and cheese and had drunk thick Ethiopian coffee, his unsatisfied stomach rumbled all the time.

They were camping out because even allowing for the delay caused by the puncture, their progress had been slower than planned and darkness fell when they were still twenty-five kilometers from the small town where they had reservations in a hotel. Samson would not travel any farther but ordered the driver to stop in an open place, a good sentry position on the surrounding countryside. "Bandits, you see, Mr. Smith. Unfortunately, despite everything our emperor and the authorities do for them, there are ingrates and lawbreakers in our land who may attempt to steal our food and even our jeep. We shall not proceed any farther tonight. We shall camp here and I shall keep watch for part of the night and John Kebede, our driver, shall watch for the remainder."

It was cool and still, and although there was no moon, millions upon millions of stars glittered in the infinite African sky. Christian shifted onto his back and stared straight into its depths. What had happened to that boy and his orange? What a stupid thing to have done, to have brought out a single orange. Professional panic, never far from the surface, began to make itself felt. How was he adequately to write the story he had seen today? The story was too big and the responsibility was too much.

And he acknowledged he was afraid, not only that he would fail, but also of the story itself. Because somewhere up ahead, who could imagine what horrors waited?

Boneyards.

He looked across at Dick, sleeping so quietly. If only he could be like Dick. Dick never agonized, was never afraid of failure.

Easy for him, of course. Snap. One picture, take it or leave it. A job was a job and a good job was a good job and that was it. You win some, you lose some, that was Dick.

As far as Christian was concerned, he could never write a story *right*. He had never yet satisfied some standard he could not even define—and yet which was always tantalizingly out of reach. When people praised him or when he won awards, a little voice inside him always whispered: *"Okay—so you got away with it this time!"*

After a half hour or so, he fell into an uneasy, dream-filled sleep.

He was awake long before dawn and following a quick snack of fruit and Coca-Cola—they were laden down with Coke; the archaeologists on the dig had requested supplies—they moved on through the silence. At one point, Christian noticed a flock of birds, wheeling slowly high in the sky, too high for easy identification. Samson knew what they were, however: "Vultures!" he said succinctly. "But do not worry, Mr. Smith. Vultures will have no feast on our bones . . ." Christian and Dick exchanged glances. Each knew what the other was thinking: the vultures had given them ideas as to what they would like to do with the pompous little minder.

They had been traveling for almost two hours when the driver brought the jeep to a sudden halt and indicated that they should get out. Samson, smirking, led the Americans a few steps to the front of the vehicle. Suddenly, they could not walk any farther because it seemed they had reached the edge of the world. Even the placid and cynical Dick was impressed.

They were standing at the rim of the Rift Valley, the floor of which was six thousand feet below.

Samson, watching closely, was delighted with their reactions. "I thought you would like to see this for yourselves before we make our descent," he said. "Perhaps, Mr. Spielberg, you would like to have a few moments to compose some photographs?"

After Dick had taken his shots, they began their precipitous descent to the valley below. Both Americans were terrified and even the garrulous Samson, hanging on to the safety handle above his window, for once kept his mouth shut as, for almost an hour, the jeep roared and slithered at an angle of 45 degrees down the hairpin goat track that served as a road.

When they got to it, the driver set his wheels at their highest possible clearance, and for the next two hours they might have been the only living creatures in a pre-terhuman, broiling world. Although Samson had told them that bands of nomads sometimes moved herds of camels along this desert between Ethiopia and the Republic of Djibouti to the northeast, Christian, keeping his eyes peeled, did not see a single movement.

Samson decided that they should stop for a rest and some food when they reached the edge of a black lava field; the archaeological dig was near Hadar, still more than a day's travel ahead.

As the minder moved about, setting up a shade tent, Christian noticed enviously that somehow he had managed to retain his fresh, bandbox appearance. He distributed salt, admonishing the two Americans to add it to their Coca-Cola for rehydration and then, on a piece of cloth, spread out the meal of dates, sunflower seeds, and pieces of hard, dried fish as unyielding as nails.

After their meal they dozed, or tried to. Christian, propped comfortably on his rolled sleeping bag beside Dick, let his eyes wander over the baking landscape in front of him, flat in all directions and encrusted with the black scabs of lava. He fancied he could actually hear the sun buzzing and hammering against the rocks a few feet outside their tiny ration of shade. His skin felt papery, the sweat drying on it the moment it was produced.

When the minder decided that it was time to move, they gathered up the remains of their picnic while the driver opened the hood to check the oil and water levels. Christian saw immediately by the man's expression that something was amiss. "What's wrong?" He walked across and peered over the man's shoulder.

Disaster had crept up on them as quietly as a thief. The radiator was bone dry.

Dick and Christian returned to sit uneasily side by side under the shade tent while the two Ethiopians spoke together in rapid Amharic. "Let's take the worst case first," said Christian. "Worst case, we walk. Only debate is, do we walk forward toward the dig or back to the road, the way we came."

"How long do we walk?"

"Forward, I don't know . . . Back to the highway? We traveled in that jeep maybe two hours, ten, fifteen miles an hour. Plus climbing up that bluff. Maybe one day walking, including rests, then one day climbing—three days minimum we're back on the highway."

"Then what?"

"Then we hope that someone comes along . . ."

"Who?" Dick's logic was maddening. "For Christ's sake, Dick!" Christian took a slug of Ambo, the local mineral water, "the U.S. Cavalry! How do I know?"

"Suppose someone doesn't come along?" Dick persisted. "Suppose we walk back the way we came, how long to that last town we came through?"

"Maybe thirty kilometers . . ."

"So," said Dick, in his mercilessly reasonable way, "worst case is we get to the nearest town, all going well, in four days, maybe five." He got to his feet. "I'm going to check with that son of a bitch minder how much food and water we got . . ." Dick rarely swore.

Lethargy, induced by the heat, covered Christian like a blanket as he sat watching Dick talk to the two men inside the jeep. In a convoluted way, he was almost pleased at this distraction from the story. Fate had handed him a set of extenuating circumstances.

The two Ethiopians got out of the jeep and continued their discussion with Dick in front of the open hood. With an effort, Christian pulled himself to his feet and wandered over to join them. "How big is the hole?" Dick's tone was now businesslike.

"Mr. Kebede says the hole is perhaps as big as a child's fist," said the minder.

Dick walked around the jeep as the other three watched him. "What tools does Mr. Kebede keep in the vehicle?" After another rapid consultation, the minder answered. "Mr. Kebede wishes it to be known that he is not a mechanic. The tools he has are basic and not, he thinks, suitable for repair of a tear in damaged metals."

Dick walked around the jeep again. "Do we have a First Aid box?" he asked suddenly.

Samson extracted the tin kit from under a pile of supplies in the rear of the vehicle. Dick opened it and examined the contents. "Ask John to show me this hole," he said.

When he got to his feet again having examined the damage under the chassis of the jeep, he walked over to the partially dismantled shade tent and picked up a discarded Coca-Cola can. He turned it around and around in his hands. "Okay," he said, still addressing the minder, "please ask the driver to get under the jeep and to make the surface of the metal around the hole as smooth as possible." Obediently the driver got underneath and started to work with a screwdriver and the wrench.

Dick picked up a tire iron and proceeded to hammer the empty Coke can flat, using one of the rocks as an anvil.

"What are you doing?" Christian still felt detached.

Dick indicated the First Aid kit. "There's a large roll of adhesive tape in there; we might be able to rig up a temporary patch."

"But it won't be watertight!"

"Thank you, kid, for that brilliant and helpful observation." Dick did not look up from his task.

"Sorry."

"I know it won't be watertight, dummy, but it will, it *might,* buy us a little time . . ."

"How much water do we have?"

"We've a good deal of water, certainly enough for two tankfuls. And after that we have Coca-Cola."

"Can you use Coca-Cola in a radiator?"

"We're about to find out."

"But couldn't we damage the jeep?"

The irony of that was too much for Dick. "Would you go fuck yourself!"

"Sorry." Not in the least offended, Christian walked to the front of the vehicle where Samson was crouched, issuing instructions to the half-visible driver.

When Dick had four makeshift aluminum patches ready, he eased himself under the radiator with the first one and a length of adhesive tape. Then he told Samson to pour some water into the radiator, staying underneath with his hand on the adhesive tape. "It's damp, but holding," he announced after a minute or two. "Let's get the hell out of here before it all evaporates. And tell the driver not to tighten the cap on the radiator. We must let steam escape so that the pressure won't build up and blow the first patch too early."

They drove slowly back in the direction they had come, and within five minutes, steam was rising in great clouds in front of them. "Keep going! Keep going!" Dick

shouted, keeping an eye on the temperature gauge.
"We'll stop when we're completely empty and patch it
up again."

Darkness was falling when, five hours later, the fourth
patch blew; it had taken them that length of time to travel,
in a series of tension-filled hops, a distance that had taken
them forty minutes on the way out. The driver switched
off the engine and let the vehicle bump to a halt. "I
suppose we could make another set of patches." Christian did not relish the thought of walking.

"We will, but not tonight." Dick was decisive.

"Do you think, Mr. Spielberg, we should make camp
here?" asked Samson respectfully. Samson, Christian
saw, had abdicated leadership. "That's absolutely fine,
Samson," Dick replied. "We'll do that. Now I think we
should have a meal."

There was no fuel to build a fire, so the meal, once
again, was a cold one: dried fish, seeds and fruit. The
driver offered the other three a piece of *ingera*, a grayish
doughlike substance he carried with him in a canvas
pouch and which he dipped in a fiery sauce of chillis
called *wat*. Samson accepted, but Christian and Dick,
who had tasted the stuff in a restaurant in Addis Ababa
to the detriment of the lining in their mouths, declined.

Dick insisted that John Kebede and Samson take the
first sleep shift in the jeep while he and Christian,
wrapped in their sleeping bags, sat propped against the
side of it. "Thank you, Mr. Spielberg," said Samson.
"I would suggest that you and Mr. Smith should keep
your bodies well covered. There are few dangerous creatures in this part of the world, but the scorpion is one of
them."

"*Scorpions* for Christ's sake!" said Christian, looking
after the driver's back. "Now he tells us."

"Shut up, will you?" Dick was not altogether enam-
ored of the idea either.

"I wish I had a drink."

"I said, shut *up*!"

The two men huddled together in their sleeping bags.
Did a scorpion's feet click as he marched across rocks?
They were both delighted when at last their turn came to
sleep in the relative security of the jeep.

Next morning, after he had inspected the radiator, Dick

checked the state of their supplies. They had only one
two-gallon container of water left, but they did have a
complete case, twenty-four cans, of Coca-Cola. He
checked the First Aid kit and calculated that they had
enough adhesive tape for four more patches.

He removed the caps from eight of the cans and let
them sit awhile to allow the carbonation to subside while
he made his first patch with the tire iron. The radiator
took all eight cans of liquid and was still not completely
full.

Since the sun was not yet hot and the engine was starting from cold, they managed to travel for almost twenty
minutes before the first patch blew. Christian's neck
ached with tension as the sweetish smell of overheated
metal slowly permeated the jeep and the needle of the
temperature gauge on the dashboard crept inexorably upward toward the red "H." "Will we make it to the road
like this?" he asked Dick.

"I don't think so, but we'll give it our best shot. We
might make the base . . ."

But that forecast proved optimistic. The last of their
Coca-Cola evaporated when they were still some distance
away and Dick refused to use any more of their precious
water. But now that he knew that they were not actually
going to die in the desert, Christian, always volatile, was
at least in better spirits. Looking out at the six-thousand-
foot cliff they had to ascend, he thought of the mound of
gear he had brought with him, not only clothes, but a
portable typewriter, tape recorder, reams of paper, tapes,
packs of batteries, books. And then there was his medical kit, his bottles of Entero-Vioform, Kaopectate, io-
dine, oil of cloves for toothache, gentian violet for stings,
anti-histamine, insect repellant, his water-purifying tablets, Brook-lax, wide-spectrum antibiotics, and a variety
of painkillers, pills and tablets. Christian liked to be prepared for every eventuality. He even had a small bottle
of mustard-yellow liquid which he had acquired in Mexico and which was sold to him with a guarantee that it
drew venom from a snakebite.

"We'll divide up the essential supplies," said Dick,
"the food and water, First Aid box and so on. It's up to
each individual what he brings after that . . ."

Each of the white men jettisoned all of his spare clothes

and Christian dumped his paper, most of his batteries, and a few of his books. But neither could bear to leave behind any of his professional equipment. Dick insisted that all four men should be equally burdened, and before they set off, divided everything in four piles of roughly equal weight. And since each load was not equally easily carried, he dictated that they should be rotated every half hour. He included in the general pool of supplies a large number of oranges, as they were valuable sources of fluid and energy.

By the end of the first half hour, when Dick allowed them a five-minute break before they rotated their loads, Christian was already dead beat. The muscles of his shoulders, forearms, and thighs ached badly from lugging the container of water and his own typewriter. His feet hurt too, his shoes being more suitable for jogging on grass tracks than for trekking across this hot, rocky hell.

And by the time they got to the foot of the cliff, on their third load rotation, he was straggling far behind the others. "Fuck this!" he panted as he reached Dick and flung the aluminum camera case at his friend's feet. "I'm not carrying that thing another yard!"

"You don't have to until it's your turn next." Dick spoke crisply.

"Well, I'm having a rest here before I go on any farther."

"We're all having a rest."

"I want a drink."

"You can have an orange. I want to get a little farther up before—"

"You want! *You* want!" Christian raged. "Who the fuck gave *you* the stripes!"

"You are perfectly entitled to take charge if you wish and"—Dick emphasized heavily—"you can carry all your own stuff." He took Christian's typewriter, his medical bag, his tape recorder and bags of supplies and piled them up in a small, tottering heap. The two men glared at one another. Christian collapsed on the ground. He felt close to tears. "Sorry, Richard," he said. "I guess I overreacted a bit."

"We're all tired, kid," answered Dick. "Save your

breath for the climb.'' They both looked at the towering bluff above them.

"Right!'' said Dick, after they had each eaten an orange.

"Onward and upward!''

They set off again, not actually climbing, as such, but walking laboriously upward along the track which, the day before, they had careered down so fast. At least it was cooler and the higher they climbed, the better the ground was underfoot.

But Christian's entire body really hurt now, from the soles of his feet to the crown of his throbbing head. Suddenly his ankle turned on a small stone and he fell heavily to his knees.

"Please, Dick,'' he pleaded, "please can we camp here? I don't think I can go any farther today.''

"That's okay, kid,'' said Dick. "I was going to stop here anyway.''

They drank some of their precious water, passing around the single plastic cup they had brought with them. After an hour or so, during which no one spoke, they ate again and crawled into their sleeping bags. It was not yet dark but they were all asleep within seconds.

Christian again woke before dawn and lay quietly, unwilling to move any of his stiff, painful muscles. He found, somewhat to his surprise, that he was in relatively good spirits, even cheerful. The piece of ground on which they had pitched camp was quite level, and despite his muscles, which complained every time he moved, he was comfortable. The air around him was cool and sweet and he lay unmoving on his back, with his eyes wide open, watching the sky as it turned gold; Christian had always loved sleeping in the open air—it was something he had never been allowed as a child—and even in this situation, it honed his senses.

Although once again he was conscious that there was no birdsong, the very lack of it seemed to allow the more intimate sounds of the breaking day, the microscopic rustlings and scuttlings, to come into focus. Life was so unsentimentally simple out here, he thought. Whether you were a man or a microbe, you were born, you tried to stay alive, you died.

Just before the top of the cliff, Christian almost gave

up. he did not even have the energy to fight with Dick who denied him a drink of water on the grounds that there were only about two inches left in their water bottle. Somehow, half crawling, he managed to make it to the top with the others and collapsed under an acacia, withered but large enough to provide a little shade. His feet felt like raw meat; he removed his track shoes and lay spread-eagled on the hard ground. Dick, sweating profusely, sat beside him and removed his own footwear.

The two Ethiopians sat a few yards away, but not together. Now that they were back in the area where other people might lurk, Samson sat facing his charges like a small anxious Buddha, his legs crossed, lotus-style, his swagger stick held defensively across the front of his body with both hands. He need not have worried. They were entirely alone, it seemed, in the vast brown landscape.

The minutes ticked by and still the Americans did not move, but gradually, Christian became aware of a faint whining. Very far away, it came and went intermittently on the currents of warm air. "What's that?" He sat up. Immediately the minder shot to his feet: "I don't know what you mean, Mr. Smith—"

"That! That sound!" All four men listened hard and Samson walked to the middle of the road, looking north, shielding his eyes. "I—I believe it is a vehicle, Mr. Smith!" he said excitedly, "and it is coming in our direction!" Christian pulled himself to his feet and with the others, watched the plume of dust.

Fifteen minutes later they saw that it was not one but two, two white jeeps, traveling in convoy. "They mightn't stop!" Christian hardly dared to hope. "They will if I've anything to do with it," said Dick.

But although all four of them shouted and gesticulated, the first jeep, being driven by a man in some sort of uniform, did not stop.

Christian stared after it, open-mouthed. Then he realized that in their barefoot, filthy state, their clothes now as brown with dust as the rags of the Ethiopians they had seen on the road, the driver had probably not recognized them as foreigners.

The second jeep was bearing down fast and Dick wasted no time: "Grab hands!" he screamed.

The four men formed a chain across the road, blocking

the path of the vehicle, which skidded to a halt in the dirt, coming to rest a few feet from them. Dick walked to the driver's side. To his joy, Christian recognized the man, jet black, with a smile as wide and bright as a set of piano keys: he was a marine guard, whom they had seen only a few days ago when he and Dick had called to announce their presence in Addis Ababa to the American ambassador. The jeep belonged to USAID.

"Hi, guys!" said the driver, as the dust continued to settle all around them. He leaned over and opened the passenger door: "Wanna ride?"

That evening, after a sleep and a decent meal at the Hilton, they strolled down the hill toward the city, welcoming the cool, balmy air that wafted along the wide pavements of Churchill Road. This was the most affluent and westernized part of Addis Ababa, yet as soon as they had appeared they had attracted a small horde of beggars, many of them children. The crowd pushed and jostled amongst themselves as they walked along behind but never interfered with or impeded the Americans' progress; once again Christian found their very silence and politeness unnerving.

To escape, he and Dick went into a café, a bare concrete room, furnished with rickety Formica tables and plastic chairs and decorated only with a single picture of the emperor. There was no door, just a set of ancient and discolored plastic streamers drooping in the opening between the café itself and an area outside, where there were two further tables. Christian, not trusting his stomach, ordered Ambo, while Dick took a tiny cup of thick coffee. The respite from their camp following was only temporary. The little crowd settled down outside the café, some sitting on the ground, some leaning on anything handy—a car, a half-built wall. One adolescent draped himself across a tethered donkey. "Okay," said Dick, "we're agreed that we're going to abort the story. Let's discuss what we tell the newsdesk."

"Could we take a chance and tell them the truth?" Christian saw Dick's expression. "All right, all right, too original—let's tell them I died."

"Oh yeah, brilliant!"

"Seriously, we could say I was seriously ill."

"I've already told them that. All they wanted to know was when you were getting better."

"Well, in a way it's the truth. I am—was—seriously ill."

"Of alcoholic poisoning. You want me to tell them that? Better come up with something, kid, or your ass is in a sling."

Christian smiled his most enchanting smile. "I know you'll come up with something, Dick. You always do."

"Yeah," Dick muttered.

They finished their coffee, paid for it with a grimy five-birr note, and continued their stroll, leaving Churchill Road and crossing onto the unpaved side streets, lined with shacks and hovels, raw with human sewage. "Shit, I've had enough of this." Christian stopped dead. The crowd, which had swelled, stopped dead too.

They turned back toward the Hilton, which blazed like a casino across a hilltop. "Fortress American Express!" said Christian, stopping again and saluting, American-navy-style with one hand, *heil Hitler*-style with the other. The crowd cracked up as though he were a clown, wheeled out for their entertainment. "Oh, hell!" said Christian, and took all the money he had out of his wallet and the pockets of his tracksuit, distributing it note by note, birr by dollar, being fair, going around and around again until everything was gone. Then he shrugged, showed his empty wallet, turned out his pockets, and waved good-bye. Within seconds the group had melted away into the shadows.

"That was perfect!" said Dick as they walked back up the collonaded approach to the Hilton. "Wonderful. Now I've got to stake you to the taxi and everything else until we get back to civilization!"

They arrived at the airport early, but so, it seemed, had everyone else in Ethiopia. When they got through the considerable security checks and into the airport itself, it was Christian, by virtue of his height and demeanor, who took charge. When he put his mind to it, he could adopt an arrogant, commanding presence, and Dick watched in admiration as he cut a swathe through the heaving, gesticulating crowd, waving aside the protests of a woman with a walkie-talkie as though he were

Haile Selassie himself. They were called first from the standby list on the flight to Rome.

When they got to Rome early next morning, there was nothing going transAtlantic until much later, but they were just in time to make a connection to British Airways to London. Rather than check into a hotel in Rome, where neither spoke the language, they decided to crash out for one night in London.

On inquiry, the only accommodation immediately available was in a small private hotel in Belgrave Square. Exhausted, they took it, checking in just after noon and going immediately to their separate rooms.

Late that afternoon, having slept and showered, they took a cab into Picadilly. Christian, anxious to make amends to Dick for all the care lavished on him over the past few days, was on his best, most charming behavior. He did not dare broach the subject of the *Sentinel* newsdesk—which was still blissfully unaware that not only had they left Ethiopia and were in London, but that they had left with not an inch of copy.

The taxi let them off in the traffic flow that swirled around Picadilly. Christian's eyes lit on the Wimpy Bar. Dick held up his hand. "No, we're not going to Wimpy's or"—he turned resolutely away and began to walk toward Shaftesbury Avenue—"to McDonald's. Forget it, Christian!" Christian sighed. When he was hungry, he did not care at all what he ate, provided it was familiar and edible and available immediately.

They compromised on a Gallagher's Steak House and chomped their way through steak and Chicken Kiev, with mounds of English chips and a limp, ancient salad. "You still can't get a rare steak in this country," moaned Christian after the food arrived. He sawed savagely at his meat, which, to be fair, did show a single streak of faint pink deep in its tough heart.

"How many times have I told you that you do *not* order steak anywhere east of Rio de Janeiro or New York City?"

"Well, remind me again, next time."

"I reminded you just before you ordered."

"Yes, but how did I know things hadn't improved? How did you know, for that matter?"

"This is just silly, Christian. Just shut up and eat."

"The way you carry on, you'd think we were married!"

"Well, we are, in a way. We have to live together, don't we?" Christian laughed, and eventually Dick joined in.

They strolled toward Leicester Square after their meal. It was just after five-thirty and the streets were alive with office workers who hurried along, quite distinct from the tourists and visitors who looked vaguely lost, as though they could not find their mothers but were afraid to be babies about it. They came to a Keith Prowse ticket agency. Dick stopped to look at the posters in the window. "Want to go to a show tonight?"

Christian hesitated. He looked at his watch. Five forty-five. Theater was not his bag at all, but London was said to be its Mecca. Sir Laurence Olivier, all that. And, he reminded himself, he was being agreeable. "What's on?" he asked.

"Let's have a look."

They went inside and browsed through the leaflets and handouts at the desk. *South Pacific* (*"A smash!"*— *Evening Standard*) was playing at Drury Lane. Christian was amenable to *South Pacific*, having played a soldier, one of Emilio's sidekicks, in a production of the show in his sophomore year at Evanston High School. "At least I'll know the tunes." But *South Pacific* was sold out, except for single seats at matinées. "You could go along tonight, sir, and queue at the box office," said the clerk. "Sometimes there are returns."

"Nah!" said Christian. "That's okay, but thanks anyway—"

"What about this?" Dick was holding a flyer about a play at the Wyndham Theatre. "What is it?" Christian gave the leaflet only a cursory glance.

"A revival of a Noel Coward play, *Blithe Spirit*."

"What's that about?"

"I don't know, but I know about Noel Coward. And it's been running for months—must be good. As long as we're in England, we might as well see"—he read off the flyer—"'a quintessentially English play'."

"Is it heavy?"

"No, not if it's by Noel Coward."

"Are there seats available?" Christian asked the clerk.

"As it happens, sir, we've just had a release of a block of five seats."

Christian shrugged. "Okay. Noel Coward it is."

They took their seats five minutes before curtain. The old theater, with velvet seats and gilt on the boxes, smelled dusty and faintly sweet, and the audience, of all nationalities, spoke in hushed voices, as if out of respect for superior age. The muted lighting enclosed the space and cut it adrift from the outside world, and Christian, whose experience of theater had been limited to high school shows and The IceCapades, felt instinctively that he should walk on tiptoe.

But their seats were cramped and uncomfortable and he found it difficult to fit his long legs in the space provided. "Quintessentially English, huh?" he bitched. "Promise that if it's a dog, we leave at intermission, okay?" Then he spotted the little opera glasses fitted in their holder on the seatback in front of him: "Hey, look at this!" There was a slot for a 10p coin to release the glasses. Dick had one of the coins and Christian pressed it into the slot.

But the opera glasses proved to be a disappointment. No matter which way Christian twirled the little dial, he could not focus them adequately. "Leave them, Christian," said Dick. "When the lights are on on the stage you'll find it better." The lights dimmed then and the curtain went up.

Half an hour into the first act, all thoughts of leaving the theater at the intermission had left Christian's mind. He could not take his eyes off the actress playing Elvira. "It's her!" he whispered to Dick, digging him in the ribs. "Who?" said Dick.

"Sh-shh!" the disapproving hiss came from the row behind.

"It's the Irish actress," whispered Christian, "the one on the television last time. Remember?"

"Shh-shhhh!"

"Sorry!" Christian turned around and smiled at the woman behind him, then fixed his opera glasses to his eyes again. The image was fuzzy and distorted, but he was fascinated by the way she held her head, the way the lights played on the planes of her face, the way she seemed to float about the stage. She was different than she had looked on television where she could have been just any really beautiful woman. In the flesh, Christian thought Margo Bryan to be the most beautiful woman he had ever seen in his life.

He barely heard her lines, and cared not a fig about how she fitted into the plot. He lowered his glasses each time she made an exit and put them to his eyes again each time she came on.

He was in a state of high excitement at the intermission. While Dick attempted to order drinks for them through the crush at the bar, Christian perused the actress's biographical note in the program. "Don't you think she's really something?" he said to Dick when the latter came back bearing two teaspoonsful of liquor in two glasses.

"Who?"

"That actress, Margo Bryan, the one who's playing the ghost . . ."

"Yeah, she is, all right."

"And don't you think she's a knockout?"

"Christian, sometimes I can't believe you're the same age as me. You're incorrigible!"

Christian grinned, then searched again through the biographical note. "It doesn't say here that she's married."

"It rarely does," said Dick dryly.

"Well,"—Christian made up his mind—"I'm going backstage to see her after the show."

"And how do you propose to get in?"

Juggling his drink, Christian pulled out his wallet. He extricated his press pass and held it gleefully under Dick's nose. "These things have their uses . . ."

"You think she lets media people in to see her automatically?"

"She might let the foreign correspondent of the prestigious *Chicago Sentinel* in to see her, if I send word that she has just won the prestigious Foreign Actress of the Year Award from the prestigious Newspaper Critics' Association of Middlewestern America."

"The *what*?"

"You heard me."

"Somehow I have a feeling that I'm involved here. No,

Christian, no and no and no. You're on your own on this one.''

"Please, Dick, this'll be the last one—ever. I have a feeling this girl's special.''

"So was the last one. And the one before that. Why can't you just meet people in the ordinary way like everyone else?''

"Because I'm not an ordinary guy.'' Christian draped an arm around his friend's shoulder. "I promise, on my mother's grave, I promise, Dick, that I'll never ask you again!''

Dick downed his drink. "I need a shrink! What do you want me to do?''

"You're the photographer who will be taking pictures of the Foreign Actress of the Year while I interview her.''

"Why do you need me at all?''

"Please, Dick, it'll look a lot more on the level if we're a team.''

"Will she not be a little suspicious since there's the little matter of, like, I don't have a camera?''

"Dick!'' Christian stood back in mock horror. "You know the way I work on these important pieces for the prestigious Association of Midwestern Critics.'' He made a little gesture with his hand, flying an imaginary airplane. "Recon first . . . Little reconnaissance mission to spy out the land.'' He swallowed his drink. "Tonight we introduce ourselves. Tomorrow we do the interview. At least *I* do the interview, you take the photographs. A *few* photographs . . .''

"Wouldn't it be simpler to ask to see her and straight out ask for an interview? Most actresses like to see their names in the papers . . .'' But Dick knew he was wasting his time. For Christian, the elaborate side plays were part of the challenge.

The ushers had begun to call the resumption of the play. Dick drained the last millimeter of Scotch in his own glass. "And after I take just a *few* photographs, then I beat it?''

Christian put his arm around Dick's shoulder. "My friend, you are a prince among men.''

After the play, the two of them found their way around to the stage door. The theater was on a corner and to get to the stage door, they had to go around to the back of the theater, passing through a wide alleyway, picking their way through an overflow of drinkers from the pub on the other corner.

The lobby behind the stage door was an unwelcoming place, although it was stuffy with heat from an electric fire. There was a public telephone and a bulletin board fluttering with cast calls and Save the Whale literature. "Can I help you, sir?" At least the doorman was polite. "Yes," Christian answered with his most brilliant smile. "I'm sure you *can* help us. I'm the foreign correspondent of the *Chicago Sentinel*—that's in Chicago, Illinois, of course—and this is my photographer, Dick Spielberg."

He handed over his press pass: "We're on temporary assignment here in London and we have just heard that Margo Bryan, your actress, has won a very big award in America. My newspaper has assigned me to interview her for her reaction."

"This is the first I've heard of it," said the doorman. "Have you an appointment with Miss Bryan?"

"No," said Christian apologetically, "I got the call from the newsdesk about this award only at about seven o'clock this evening. And of course I knew there was no point in trying to call Miss Bryan so close to her show."

"Hang on a tick, I'll give her a call." The doorman picked up the telephone. "Is Miss Bryan available?" he said into the instrument. Then, after a minute or so: "Miss Bryan, there are two gentlemen here from an American newspaper. They say they want to interview you about your award."

He listened and put his hand over the mouthpiece. "What award again?" he asked Christian.

"Foreign Actress of the Year . . ." said Christian, sincere yet casual. Dick was carefully studying the bulletin board, staring at the fuzzy type on a notice advertising a forthcoming anti-vivisection meeting. "He says it's for Foreign Actress of the Year, Miss Bryan." The doorman listened again; then, replacing the receiver, told them they could go up to her dressing room. "It's the first she's heard of it too," he said, chuckling.

At the top of a short flight of stairs they had to pass along a brightly lit corridor, past other doors, through which came the sounds of chatter and water running. There was a profusion of competing smells, of sweat, of cats, of Jeyes Fluid, of concrete, of dust, and another one, which, from the days of his triumph as a soldier in *South Pacific*, Christian recognized as the smell of greasepaint.

Christian knocked on Margo Bryan's door. "I'm warning you, Christian, this is the very last time you're roping me in to your little scenarios," hissed Dick. But before Christian could answer, the door was opened by a rotund, bespectacled woman, who invited them in. "Thank you," said Christian, and stepped through the door. He stopped short; there was another man there, large and dark, but Christian barely had time to assimilate his appearance before the actress emerged from the bathroom, her face scrubbed pink and clean, her hair loose but secured by a headband. She wore a man's white terrycloth robe. "Hello!" she said, holding out her hand.

Christian's heart turned over and fell into his stomach. He introduced himself and Dick. "How do you do?" said the actress. Then she introduced the other man: "This is a friend of mine from Ireland, Seán Molloy." The man shook hands with the two Americans. Professionally, Christian assessed him: Competition? But Conor's face was open.

They all sat down.

"It's very nice to meet you, and I appreciate your interest," said the actress, "but what's this about an award? Alfred said—" Her voice, soft and accented, was entirely different from what it had been on the stage. It was Dick who answered "Miss Bryan—"

But Christian cut in: "We're very sorry to intrude like this, Miss Bryan, but you see, we've only just heard ourselves about this award. Perhaps you will hear officially later on tonight or tomorrow."

"This is the first award I've ever won!" she said, her face alight with pleasure. She turned to the other man: "It's wonderful, isn't it wonderful, Seán?"

Christian, all senses alert, had noticed an odd hesitation as she addressed the dark man. "Are you in the theater too, Mr. Molloy?" he asked.

"No." The man did not elaborate but Christian was not fazed. Americans, he knew, blurted their pedigrees and occupations within five minutes of new acquain-

tanceships. Other nationalities had different rules of social niceties.

"Would you like a drink?" the actress offered.

"No, thanks!" said Dick.

"Yes, please!" said Christian simultaneously.

She looked uncertainly from one to the other.

"We'd love a drink, Miss Bryan," said Christian,
smiling. "My photographer here is a little slow." He
aimed a slow wink at Dick, who clamped his mouth shut.

She gave each of them a beer from her little refrigerator and turned to the other man. "You, Seán?"

"Thanks, Molly, I don't mind if I do."

"Molly, is that your real name, Miss Bryan?"

"That's right. Now, tell me all about this award."

All three men were seated together on the small chaise
longue, and Christian felt hemmed in. In any event, he
liked to display his body to full advantage. He stood up
and leaned against the wall of the dressing room. "To
tell you the truth, Miss Bryan," he said, "we're almost
as much in the dark as you are. I do know, of course,
that it is prestigious and that it is voted on by the Association of Critics of Midwest America—"

"Who?" She looked puzzled.

"The Newspaper Critics' Association of Middlewestern
America."

"Is it only newspapers?"

"Oh no, it's television too—and radio," he impro-
vised.

"Why is it called the Newspaper Critics Association?" It was the man. He did not turn his head, but
addressed his question to Christian straight ahead,
through the mirror.

"Did I say that? I meant, of course, the Association
of Midwestern Critics . . ." said Christian, still smiling.
He took a sip of his beer.

The actress looked doubtful. "Please don't get me
wrong, I'm very flattered, but how did they see me, these
critics? I've never been to America."

"Who knows?" Christian shrugged. "I've never been
much for the theater myself. And I've never had to interview anyone connected with it before. I'll have all the
details before I do the actual interview with you."

The man cut in again: "Who got Foreign Actor of the

Year?'' Christian met his eyes in the mirror. "Sorry," he said simply, "don't know!" The dresser, who had been moving around, quietly tidying the dressing room, said a soft good-bye and left.

"Would I have to go to America?" The vista of escorting Margo Bryan to the United States, the two of them together for eight hours in the intimacy of the First Class cabin of an aircraft, spread itself through Christian's delighted mind. "You may indeed, Miss Bryan," he said earnestly, while Dick spluttered and coughed on his drink.

"Are you all right, Dick?" asked Christian, banging his friend energetically on the back with his free hand. Dick, whose face was bright red, coughed some more but nodded as best he could. Christian turned back to her. "Sorry, Miss Bryan. All will be revealed when I meet you for the interview. I promise I'll call my newsdesk the minute I get back to my hotel." He noticed that the man was studying his drink. It was unlike Christian not to be able to detect competition, but this man was inscrutable. Christian smiled again at the actress and decided to press his advantage: "When can we meet tomorrow, Miss Bryan?"

"Let me see—" She picked up a small green appointments calendar and opened it at a beribboned page. "Would sometime around lunchtime be all right with you?" She looked directly at him, so beautiful and fresh that again his heart turned over. "Perfect!" he cried, "I'll pick you up. Where do you live?"

She hesitated. "No, that's all right. I'll meet you somewhere convenient for you."

"Let me buy you lunch." He grinned. "Don't worry, it'll be on my expense account . . ."

"If you're sure."

"Of course. Where would you like to go? The Ritz? The Dorchester?" He was getting carried away and he knew it. She laughed, caught up in his enthusiasm. "Oh, no! They're far too posh."

"Where then?"

"What about a place called Kettner's in Soho—do you know it?"

"No, but I can certainly find it."

"All right, see you there at one o'clock. I'll make the reservation."

They took their leave then. Christian felt infused with gaiety and optimism. "Good-bye, Mr. Molloy!" he caroled, "I hope we meet again." Not waiting to hear if there was an answering good-bye, he let himself and Dick out of the room.

He bounded down the stairs two at a time. He felt like kissing Dick, the doorman, the actor who held the door open for them, the wino who stumbled aside when he burst out through the door. Outside again, he grabbed Dick's arm: "I'm in *love*! I'm going to marry that woman!"

"Right!" said Dick. "Now, how are you going to tell her about the award?"

As it turned out, there was no problem next day about the award.

The beginning was a little shaky from Christian's point of view. He arrived at Kettner's, in his opinion five minutes early, to find the actress already ensconced at a window table. It was Friday and the restaurant was doing a brisk trade, mainly from businessmen who sat huddled together over their soup.

"I'm really sorry, Miss Bryan. Have I got the time wrong?"

"No, that's all right. I'm always early for everything! I can't help it. It must be the boarding-school training." She looked over his shoulder. "I booked the table for three; where's Mr. Steinberg?"

"Spielberg. He was called out on another job." What he did not tell her was that Dick had already departed for Chicago, furious that he had been left to bear the brunt of the debacle in Ethiopia. "Oh!" She looked uncertain again.

"Don't worry, there are plenty of free-lancers in London. Everything'll be okay."

They ordered. Since she was playing that night, she asked for only a salad. He ordered a steak.

"Have you any more news about the award?" she asked when the waiter brought their drinks, Perrier for both of them—Christian was absolutely determined to turn over a new leaf; never would a drop of alcohol cross his lips again. He took a deep breath. "About the award Miss Bryan, funny you should ask . . ."

She looked puzzled and he plunged in the deep end. "There's no award, Miss Bryan. It was a ruse. I just wanted to get to meet you." He put on his most dazzling, most boyish smile. It had served him well with women all over the world. On tenterhooks, he watched as a succession of expressions chased across her face: bewilderment first, then annoyance, and finally, to his relief, amusement. "There's no award?" She said it flatly.

"Uh-uh."

"Is there such an award in existence?"

"Uh-uh."

"No Association of Midwestern Critics or whatever they are?"

"Uh-uh."

"I see." She took a mouthful of her Perrier.

"This is not to say, Miss Bryan, that you won't win every award going. Oscars, Golden Globes, Nobel Prizes for Acting—"

"There's no such prize."

"Well, at the very least, the prestigious award from the prestigious association of New York critics."

"Is *that* a real award?"

"I have no idea!"

For a brief moment he thought it was touch and go, but he held his nerve, eye to eye. "Why on earth did you simply not ask to meet me?" she asked finally.

"Because you might have said 'no'!" The waiter brought crudités, and as soon as he had left, she took a sliver of celery. "Suppose I stood up from this table right now and just walked out?"

"Suppose you do? I'm willing to bet you won't."

"Are you now?"

"Yep!"

"What's to stop me?"

"You are!"

"Why, may I ask?"

"Because you think I'm outrageous, and as well as that, you think I'm interesting, not to say good-looking. And you've never met anyone like me before."

"That's for sure."

She took a piece of cauliflower and chewed it in silence.

"Are you enjoying that, Margo?"

"It's delicious."

"I can show you where there's a great pumpkin!"

She laughed then and he was giddy with joy and relief. It was going to be all right. "I might marry you," he said.

She laughed again.

Late the next night, Father Pat Moran, snug in his temporary bed on Inisheer, stirred in his sleep. The resident curate on the island was laid low with a bout of flu, and not wanting to make more work for his elderly housekeeper, Father Moran, as locum, had accepted the offer of a spare room in one of the houses near the beach. He snuggled down into the warm cocoon of sheets and blankets, glad that he was cozy in here and not outside in the storm that battered its fury on the small window of the room and against the corrugated roof over his head. He was sleepily aware that the battering seemed somehow to be getting louder, more urgent. He half opened his eyes, then sat up suddenly. There was a continuous knocking on his door, accompanied by the voice of the woman of the house: *"A Athair, a Athair!"*

"Nóiméad amháin!" he called, but it was less than a minute when he got to the door, having put on the trousers that lay on the wooden chair beside the bed. The suspenders, still attached, dangled on each side almost to his knees.

The woman of the house stood outside in the main room of the cottage, dressed in her nightdress but with a shawl across her shoulders. He saw immediately why he had been awakened: behind the woman stood a disheveled Brendan O Briain, rivulets of water dripping off his oilskin as he twisted his wet cap in his hands. "Is it your mam?" asked the priest.

The man nodded without answering, his eyes large with fright.

"Give me a moment, I'll get dressed and come with you. Have you a lamp?" Again Brendan nodded.

The priest dressed quickly, putting a thick jersey under his black clerical vest. As a matter of course, he always

carried the Holy Oils with him on pastoral visits and he
retrieved them now from his valise, placing them carefully in the little traveling case. He knew that Sorcha had
been ill and had actually planned to visit her after Sunday
Mass, but he had had no idea that she was as bad as it
now seemed she was. The islanders were hardy people
and sent for the priest only at the end.

When he was ready, protected in his own oilskins, he
left the room and accompanied the silent Brendan out
into the storm. The wind, from the northwest, screamed
as it assaulted them and they were drenched instantly by
the driving rain and sheets of salt spray from the sea they
heard, rather than saw, crashing against the rocks about
thirty yards to their left. The night was so black they
could see nothing at all, just bolts of water driving
through the inadequate cone of light cast by Brendan's
flashlight. But Brendan, knowing every inch of the island, aimed his light at the ground a few inches in front
of his boots and walked on sure feet. Father Moran
tucked himself in behind, and single file they battled up-
hill against the wind, leaning into it at an angle of 30
degrees. Within minutes, the priest, who was running a
little to fat, was panting.

The storm was even worse up by the house. As Brendan pushed open the door, it was torn out of his grasp
by the wind which slammed it against the inside wall;
the wind rushed toward the chimney piece, plucking ash
and smoke from the fireplace and for a few moments,
while Brendan, coughing, struggled to close the door,
the kitchen was obscured in a swirling gray cloud of
ash. It settled slowly all over the kitchen when, eventually, Brendan did manage to engage the latch.

Both men removed their oilskins and then Brendan led
the priest to the back of the house and into Sorcha's room.

The O Briains had only recently got electricity, and
Father Moran saw that the new plaster was still unpainted
around the socket for the bedside lamp that burned, without a shade, on the table beside Sorcha's bed.

In the bulb's bare light, the lines of a hard life and a
harsher climate showed on the woman's spent face, adding many years to her real age, which the priest estimated
to be about sixty-five. Her thick gray hair, always so neat,
was loose and tangled, matted around her head on the

pillow. And although the blankets on her bed were augmented by extra coverings of shawls and greatcoats, she
was shivering. Her eyes were closed and she made no
sign that she knew there was anyone else in the room.
But when he placed a hand on her clammy forehead, she
opened her eyes.

When she saw who it was, she tried to struggle into a
sitting position but was too weak. "Don't be fretting
now, Sorcha," said the priest gently, kneeling beside the
bed and restraining her efforts with a hand on her shoulder. Her lips moved, but her voice was so faint he could
not hear what she was trying to say. He leaned forward,
his ear right above her mouth. "What is it, Sorcha?"

"You must be drownded, Father," she whispered in
English, each word costing her a great effort. "Would
you like a cup of tea?"

"No, Sorcha," he answered. "I'm absolutely fine.
Don't be bothering about me. Brendan can get me a cup
later."

She tried to struggle up again. "I'm sorry I don't have
a chair for you. Brendan—"

He restrained her and put his finger on her lips.
"Please, Sorcha, I'm fine."

She closed her eyes again, and to reduce the harshness
of its light, he moved the lamp to the floor. Then, putting
his lips close to her ear, he asked her if she wanted to
go to Confession. Without opening her eyes, she nodded.

He took the purple stole out of his inside pocket, kissed
it, and put it around his neck and then leaned toward her
again, so close he could smell the fustiness of the greatcoats that covered her. As if trying to beat its way into
the little circle of light and shadow, the storm outside
seemed to grow even louder.

She began her confession, making a tremendous, halt-
ing effort, but despite all his training in professional detachment, the priest found it difficult to concentrate on
this sad litany of wandering thoughts at Mass, of sins of
omission against her long-dead husband and the son who
lived with her. Of sins against an avenging, demanding
God.

As he often did in these circumstances he felt savagely
ashamed at their relative positions with regard to sin. But
in this case, the irony that she should be confessing this

childlike chronicle of pitiful transgression to him, of all people, was almost more than he could bear. He forced himself to be the representative of God that she so firmly believed he was, and tried to focus, not on himself, but on her words. "And is that all, my child?" he asked softly when, exhausted, she seemed to have finished. She did not respond and he put his hand on her shoulder: "Is that all, Sorcha?"

With an effort, she opened her eyes again. The look in them was so fearful that involuntarily he tightened his grip on her. "What is it, Sorcha? What is it?" The shivering, which had subsided, started again. Her head rolled on the pillow. "Sorcha, whatever it is, God forgives you. I forgive you in God's name . . ." But she kept her head averted.

Her lips were moving and he leaned so close that he could feel on his cheek her tiny puffs of breath. Still he could not understand what she was trying to say. "Say it in Irish, Sorcha, it'll be easier for you . . ."

He caught something. Something about Molly . . .

A cold fist in his stomach. He was afraid she sensed it. She had stopped trying to speak. He forced himself to be calm. "Take your time, Sorcha . . ."

She closed her eyes again. His body, lit from behind, cast a huge shadow over the bed and the ceiling. Despite the storm, their little circle in the room was quiet, now dangerously so. There were small sounds from the kitchen as Brendan moved around, and he noticed that the big alarm clock on the washstand double-ticked every second time. She waited so long that he thought she had fallen asleep and did not know whether he was glad or not. He was just about to make the Sign of the Cross to give her absolution when again she opened her eyes. The shivering had stopped. She seemed to have gained a little strength.

"Molly is not my child, Father . . ."

After keeping the secret for so long, Sorcha unburdened the truth of that morning years ago to the priest. . . .

After he left Sorcha and the dead child in the kitchen that morning, Micheál walked down to the beach. Still sunk in his own thoughts, he glanced out to sea as he walked, and stopped dead. There, in the small bay, bobbing across the breakers, was a little rubber boat of bright orange, luminous against the dark gray water.

It was not unusual, on the morning after a storm, that sea debris should be washed up on Inisheer. They got oars and lobster pots and planks of wood, cork life belts—even barrels of porter and preserved fish. Once, he himself had picked up three shoeboxes tied together with string. The fragile high-heeled shoes inside would have been entirely unsuitable for any island woman, since the heels would have broken off within minutes on the rough, uneven boreens and pavements. But Sorcha had dried them out and polished them and had taken them on one of her trips to the mainland where she had managed to sell them in the market. Several times in his memory, the island had drawn in an empty boat. And although he had never seen one himself, he had heard tell of boats like this one; they contained serviceable and useful goods: flashlights and whistles, radios, sometimes even food. And the rubber was good for patching, or for covering the winter ricks of turf.

He hurried the last few hundred yards down to the beach and across the soft sand to the edge of the sea. The tide was coming in and each wave brought the little orange boat closer. It was a peculiar shape. Square. He waited patiently. The collie stood beside him, watching his face so she could be ready for the next move.

Five minutes later the boat was almost on the beach. Micheál waited for a receding wave, and as it was bobbing away from him again, he leaned over and grasped the boat's edge, hauling it behind him, up above the waterline. He heard an odd noise, distinct from the sound of the sea, and looked around. He heard the sound again, like the mewling of a kitten. It was coming from a bundle on the raft, which, being the same color, he had not noticed earlier. The bundle was a life jacket, and it was moving. But it was not a kitten. There were small bare feet protruding from one end of the bundle, and from the other end, the back of a small blond head. To Micheál's astonishment, the life jacket, tied to the side of the raft, contained a baby and the baby was alive. As he stood, transfixed, the baby continued to whimper weakly.

Carefully he untied the string that bound the life jacket

to the side of the raft and then undid the life jacket itself. Underneath was a wool blanket, damp, but warm to the touch. Micheál, like all the fishermen and their wives, knew that wool, even when wet, was a good insulator. It was probably the blanket that had saved this child from dying of exposure. It was a girl, he saw, because she was wearing a pink smocked dress. He strained his eyes looking out to sea. There was no other flotsam to be seen.

He looked down at her again, surprising himself by speaking aloud: *"Céard as tú?"*

But of course the child could not tell him where she was from.

She opened her eyes and looked straight up into his own, and for a second or two they appraised one another. Her eyes were wide and of a clear blue and he noticed that although her hair was very fair, the lashes and brows were darker. He picked her up and she lay very still in his arms while she scrutinized him. Then she started to whimper again, but dry-eyed and exhaustedly, as though she had no more tears.

As he stood holding her, he conceived a terrible idea. Except for the eyes—Molly's eyes had not been so blue— the baby was of approximately the same coloring and weight as his daughter, so recently dead. Very few people had seen Molly in the last two months of her illness, not even her brothers, away at school on the mainland. At the present moment, no one except himself and Sorcha knew she had died in the night.

While the baby continued to whimper, Micheál argued the case to and fro in his mind. She obviously came from a ship or an airplane somewhere far away. Someone might even have set her adrift deliberately.

For once, thought Micheál, God might be on his side. If anyone on the island did suspect anything—for instance, if there was any malicious gossip about changelings—like everything else, it would be a nine days' wonder until something newer came along. They could just ignore it, he and his family.

But they must be careful. Someone would be looking for this child. His brain raced: If there was any gossip, it would lead to nothing. Certainly nothing outside the island. The island people kept their own business to themselves. He looked out to sea again. Definitely no evidence, only the small orange raft. When that was found, it would be assumed that all aboard had been lost.

The child had closed her eyes and appeared to be sleeping. Her peaceful baby face stirred a tenderness in him he had thought long lost, and for the first time, he felt the prick of tears for his own lost daughter. He knew that Sorcha was very lonely. This child could please Sorcha.

He took a final careful look, behind and all around him. Still nobody in sight. Then, quickly, he wrapped the baby again in the blanket. The collie, sensing excitement, began to make little yipping noises and ran ahead of her master, who hurried along the strand toward the rocks that bordered it at the far end. He went as close to the edge of the water as he dared, and first looking around to make sure that he was still unobserved, as far as he could with one arm he threw the life jacket out to sea. Then, preceded importantly by the collie, he turned and loped back up the hill through the vacant landscape toward his house. Behind him, the empty raft bobbed in the surf on the shoreline.

"I see, my child." Father Moran swallowed hard. He could see Sorcha's face was already smoother with relief. But he could hardly feel himself breathing. "When was this, my child?"

"The first of May, 1953." He forced himself to maintain the tones of a priest. "But Sorcha, how did you explain the child to everyone? Did no one get suspicious?" He took a deep breath and slowed himself down. "I mean, everyone on the island must have known that your child was ill. How did you explain it that she recovered?"

"There was talk, Father, but we keep ourselves to ourselves. The new child was about the same size and fair too. And I didn't care about the talk and I loved her like my own, God forgive me."

"Where is she, Sorcha? The baby? I mean your baby . . ."

"Micheál buried her under the potato drills."

He had a vision of the potatoes he had eaten that evening for supper. How many other little corpses sweetened the potatoes on this blasted island? He forced himself to continue listening to the weak voice. "I said prayers over her, Father, and she was buried with a rosary in her hands. I have prayed for her every single day of my life, Father.''

He lowered his head into one hand, assuming the confessional posture. ''Does Molly, I mean *this* Molly, does she know?''

''No, Father.'' The little puff of strength was nearly gone. He could hear cups being rattled on the dresser. In the kitchen, Brendan was making tea.

''Does anyone else know? Brendan? Conor?'' he asked urgently. He realized he was behaving more like a detective than a priest . . . She shook her head. Then she closed her eyes again. Automatically, falling back on ritual, he made the Sign of the Cross, *Ego absolvo te* . . . Even as he murmured the words, the revelation hammered at him: he was the only one who knew . . . He felt like an old old man as he got to his feet.

Looking down at her again, he saw she was now quietly asleep, her hands still folded together. He tiptoed out of the room and into the kitchen.

Brendan looked up from his task of pouring boiling water into a blackened teapot which stood on the hob by the fire. The O Briains' had a bottled gas cooker in the scullery, but like some of the others on the island, still used the hook over the fire to boil water. ''Would you have a cup, Father?'' Father Moran nodded and sat in one of the chairs by the fire.

They waited for the tea to draw. Brendan looked into the fire, but the priest looked away, toward the table. He focused his eyes on an empty sardine can, noticing that stuck to the oily surface of the metal lid, tightly rolled over its key, was a fine down of ash. The kitchen wore a forlorn, neglected look; with two unwashed plates on the dresser and a broom fallen across the doorway into the scullery which no one had bothered to pick up. He wondered what the house would look like after a few years in Brendan's sole care.

The storm outside was worse if anything. The wind howled in the wide chimneypiece, driving raindrops downward toward the sputtering, hissing fire; and they had to sit a little way back so as not to choke on the smoke that billowed all around them from time to time. But as the two of them sipped their tea, Father Moran was grateful for the din outside. It obviated the need for talk.

The longing to see her again was as strong as the storm outside. He felt that if he had been alone he probably would have wept. It was always dangerous for him to come to Inisheer, but he had managed to push her into a secret, unthreatening place in his mind. Nevertheless, he sometimes found it hard to breathe when he saw someone who reminded him of her, or absurdly, when he heard certain popular songs. The dead of night belonged solely to her.

Sorcha's revelation, in a way, was not so strange. Perhaps he had always known that Molly could not have been a child of this bare, tortured piece of battered rock. Staring at the ash-covered kitchen table, he saw again her pale, shimmering body in the sand.

He had to get away. He drank the last of his tea and stood up to leave. Brendan stood too, but Father Moran gently pushed him back down into the chair. ''I'll be off, then, Brendan,'' he said, ''but I'll be back early in the morning, before Mass.'' He shook Brendan's hand and turned away, but the man jumped up again and caught his arm. ''I'll walk down with you, Father . . .''

''No, Brendan. You stay here with your mother; she needs someone in the house.'' He saw then that Brendan was afraid to be alone with the dying woman. ''I know it's hard, Brendan, but you won't be alone for long. I'll be back soon.'' Brendan hung his head, and Father Moran touched him on the arm. ''Lend me your lamp, will you?''

Brendan walked across to the dresser and picked up the flashlight. He handed it over: ''Will you telephone Molly, so?'' The priest nodded and then had to wait while Brendan searched in a cracked milk jug on the dresser to find Molly's London number.

Outside, the storm sprang at him like a demon, taking his breath away, but he bent his head into its jaws and almost welcomed the black confusion of wind and water. He could lose himself. But the gale, now at his back, forced him headlong into a semi-run. Within yards he had tripped and fallen heavily. Pain shot through his shoulder.

With difficulty, panting, he pulled himself upright

against a wall, grazing his hand on the rough stone. In
an effort to catch his breath, he hung on to the wall,
standing as still as he could, but the wind, gusting, im-
pelled him on again. Despite the oilskin, the swirling
rain had streamed under his hood and was running coldly
down the hollow in the middle of his back. Holding on
to the walls, trying desperately to keep the light from the
flashlight trained on the ground in front of him, he moved
on.

Twice more he fell. The second time, the flashlight
went out and rolled out of his hand. He stayed on all
fours, crawling around in little circles, trying to find it.
The stones were slimy and freezing under his searching
hands and then he cracked his head hard against the wall.
The pain was intense, and for the second time in his adult
life, Father Moran lost control. He stopped searching for
the flashlight, and still on all fours, like a bull, raised his
voice, prolonging it, screaming his rage, his pain, and
his frustration, challenging the storm. He blasphemed.
"Fuck you, God! Fuck you!" He cried it twenty times.

He lowered his head in the blackness and let the storm
take him, allowing his body to go slack, until his back
hit the wall beside him. He lay quiet then, curled into
the lee of the jagged wall like one of the island collies
or a ewe sheep in his native Mayo.

Molly woke just before the clock chimed downstairs.
She was too comfortable to make the move necessary to
check her bedside clock, so she counted the chimes. It
was eight o'clock. The street outside was still, no traffic,
no delivery trucks, and the storm that had rattled her
windows in the early hours of the morning seemed to
have passed. She snuggled deeper under her comforter,
loving the warmth, the knowledge that it was Sunday. No
interviews, no press agents, no work, hairdressers or
makeup artists. She planned to spend the day pottering
around the house, reading Sunday newspapers, watching
television. In the meantime, she could stay in bed as long
as she liked.

Her mind drifted across the additions and improve-
ments she was planning to make to her house now that
she could afford them. Molly adored sunshine and light,
pale colors, freshness. Her bedroom was typical of the

rest of the house, with creamy sheepskin rugs on the polished boards of the floor, sepia prints on the walls, a glowing patchwork quilt over the duvet on the bed, a pottery jug filled with the drooping heads of early daffodils on the desk in the bay of the window. This coming summer, she was planning to add a conservatory to her south-facing kitchen—Conor would help her with it. She might, she thought, even include a small aviary.

Conor. Since he had come back into it, it was inconceivable to Molly now that Conor would not be in her life. Since childhood, she had pictured Conor analogously as different rooted objects—a giant oak, or a buttress on a bridge, or the tower of an ancient cathedral. She had often tried to imagine how he, in his turn, saw her and, on balance, thought he probably saw her still as a child, a small barefoot girl in a flowered frock, whose favorite pastime was searching for pink cowries on a beach.

She wriggled her toes on her smooth, warm sheets. Once, when she was about seven, she had tried to explain to him her personal vision of heaven. She had been puzzled by the concept of heaven being infinitely expandable and had asked her teacher how God managed to *fit* all those millions and millions of souls, more millions every day, into heaven. "God is a great organizer," her teacher had answered.

So ever after, Molly saw heaven as a sort of vast platform, floating along through eternal infinity, which was pale blue, with cottonwool clouds. On this platform were rows and rows of wooden school benches on which were balanced millions of identical white, stainless souls. The souls were triangular, balancing on one of their points and angled sideways so that as many as possible could fit on each bench.

Molly tried to explain to Conor about this and about God's job in heaven, always busy, welcoming gangs and gangs of new souls and fetching more and more benches for them to sit on. Heaven, in Molly's seven-year-old opinion, sounded dreadfully boring.

Conor had just shouted with laughter and tickled her and that was that.

Late last night after she had got home from the theater, he had telephoned, full of plans; he had just got a new job as a general attendant at the London Zoo, and although his wages would not be high, after paying for the rent on a small studio flat in Battersea, he would have enough money left to cover food and the fees for a night course in archaeology at London University. Molly had been delighted for him—and for herself. At least he would stick around for a while now.

She debated whether she should leave the delicious comfort of the bed—it was never the same when you got back in again—to make herself a cup of tea or coffee, and was still engaged in lazy debate with herself when the telephone rang. She stretched out an arm and lifted the receiver. "Hello?"

"Will you marry me?"

"Christian! Do you know what time it is?" Warm and secure in her bed, she laughed.

"Of course I know what time it is. The question is, will you marry me?"

"For goodness sake! We've had one lunch together . . ."

"Yes, but what a lunch!"

"Perfectly ordinary lunch, if you ask me. Salad, steak, nothing to set the world on fire . . ."

"It was the most extraordinary lunch in the history of the world. Marry me and you'll never have to eat salads again."

"Suppose I want to eat salads?"

"I'll buy you a lettuce factory."

"Christian, I'm going to hang up now . . ."

"Are you in bed?"

"Of course I'm in bed. It's Sunday morning."

"Oh, my God—can I come over?"

"No, you can't! I've things to do."

"I could think of a few things to do!"

"Christian!" But again she laughed. He had not lied when he had characterized himself yesterday as being outrageous, but to her surprise, Molly was enjoying it; this journalist was quite outside her experience of men. He was real, honest-to-God fun . . . "God, you're so *American*!" She stretched lazily and yawned. "Now go away and play! Go back to Chicago and write your stories—I'll see you next time you're in town."

"I'm in town now. I can't go home without some indication that you'll marry me. It's cruelty. I'll have to contact the association.''

"The same one which gave me the award?"

"No, this is a different association. This is the Association to Piece Together the Shattered Dreams of Smiths.''

"Oh, *that* association. Well, you'll just have to get on to your association then, won't you? I'm going to hang up.''

"All right, my darling Sleeping Beauty. I'll call you from Chicago."

"That'll cost a fortune, Christian."

"Oh, no, it won't, the *Sentinel* will pay—if I still have a job, of course!''

"Why would you not?"

"Don't worry your gorgeous head about it—just a technicality. Like I'm about three days overdue with no story . . .''

"Christian!"

"I told you not to worry, Beauty. It's my problem. You think about my offer. Best you'll get all day!''

"Good-bye, Christian."

"Good-bye, Beauty."

She had never been courted like this before, and although she did not take him seriously, the feeling was not unlike the feeling she got when she first drank champagne. This American's open, confident warmth and charm was like a bright breeze. She had never met anyone before who had laid his heart so readily on his sleeve.

If Conor was an oak, what was Christian? She tried for an image for Christian. Christian was a silver fish, always moving, impossible to pin down. She pictured Christian's body, lithe and athletic, with wide shoulders, long legs, and narrow hips. He was attractive, no doubt about that.

The telephone on her bedside table rang again, disturbing her reverie. She picked up the receiver: "I told you to go back to Chicago!" But there was a crackling on the line and then the faint sound of a woman's voice, very far away. She could just make it out. "Hello, hello, hello . . .'' said the woman, obviously shouting.

"Hello?" Molly answered, alarmed now. There was no reply from the woman, just more crackling.

"Hello?" said Molly again, louder. She had recognized the source of the static. She had never before had a telephone call from Inisheer so early in the morning. And it was Sunday. There was something wrong. Swinging her legs over the side of the bed, she sat upright on its edge. "Hello?" she said again, "who is this? Is there anybody there?"

She heard a man's voice now, also very faint, although she could hear by the tone that he, too, was probably shouting. "Hello, is that you, Molly?"

"Yes," she shouted back. "Is that you, Brendan?"

"This is Father Pat Moran," said the faraway voice, and Molly's body went rigid. "Hello! Hello! Are you still there?" the priest shouted.

She forced herself to answer. "What's wrong, Father?"

"Molly, could you come as soon as possible. It's your mother—" His voice faded away altogether. She gripped the receiver. "Hello, Father, hello . . . hello . . ." she shouted. He said something she couldn't catch, and almost crying with frustration, she put her mouth right down so that her lips were grazing the mouthpiece. "Can . . . you . . . hear . . . me . . . Father?"

He said something which again she could not catch.

"I . . . can't . . . *hear* . . . you . . . Father!" she shouted.

More crackling.

Molly spoke slowly and very clearly, calling on every ounce of her actress's training in articulation and voice projection: "Just answer 'yes' or 'no,' Father. Is Mam alive?"

She heard the faint "yes."

"How . . . bad . . . is . . . she?" She could make out the words "gravely ill" and again something she did not understand. "I'm coming on the first plane I can get, Father!" she shouted.

"All right, Molly," he shouted back. Then the line went dead. She sat, holding the receiver, staring at it. Then she replaced it. Automatically she looked at her clock. Eight forty-two. She got off the bed, walked into her bathroom, and turned on the shower. She was just about to step into it when she stopped.

Conor!

She turned off the shower again and went back to the telephone and dialed Conor's number. It rang four times before he answered.

"I had a telephone call from Inisheer," she said, trying to keep the panic out of her voice. "It's Mam. She's very ill. I'm going there straight away. Do you want to come?"

There was silence at his end of the line.

"Listen," she continued urgently, "why don't you meet me at Heathrow? I'll be there in less than an hour."

"All right," he said, "see you then . . ."

Since it was Sunday, with relatively traffic-free roads, the journey to the airport took only forty minutes, but he beat her to it. She saw him immediately when she entered the cavernous check-in hall shared by all the domestic and interisland airlines. He was standing by one of the Aer Lingus check-in desks, staring into space, unshaven and haggard, dressed in denim jeans and sweatshirt, over which he had thrown a duffle coat. Her instinct was to run to him and to throw her arms around his neck, but she checked the impulse. When she reached him, she merely touched his elbow: "Conor?"

His face was expressionless. She left him and walked the short distance across the hall to the ticket desk. She was lucky, there was a flight to Shannon at eleven. Using a credit card, she bought an open-return ticket and walked back to the check-in area where Conor stood, still staring into space. The clerk looked curiously at him. "Is your friend okay?" she asked Molly. "He doesn't look well . . ."

"We've just heard a friend of ours at home has died."

The clerk nodded sympathetically. "You have at least half an hour before you board. Why don't I see if I can get you into the V.I.P. lounge? You'll have a bit of comfort and privacy there." She made a telephone call, and within a few minutes another clerk came to fetch them. He took them upstairs and along a mezzanine, through a door and into the small lounge, furnished with a couple of sofas, an easy chair, and a coffee table. He asked them if they would like coffee, or tea, or something stronger— all of which they refused—then left quietly. As soon as they were alone, Conor put his head in his hands. "What am I going to do, Molly?"

"Would you not chance coming with me?" she asked. "It's Sunday morning; there certainly won't be many people about—and anyway, there's no Immigration on the Irish side." He shook his head. "For God's sake, Molly, have sense." He was so bitter he was almost shouting. "As soon as I step onto that island the Guards will know!"

"I know, I know, I'm sorry. It's just that I wish I could think of something that might help."

The tension crackled between them. The windows of the room were double-glazed. Outside, the airport bustle proceeded as if it were being projected onto the gray sky in a silent movie. "She mightn't die," said Molly eventually, although she knew she did not sound convincing. Again he just shook his head.

The minutes ticked away. There were copies of that morning's Irish newspapers on a small table in a corner of the room. Conor picked up a copy of *The Sunday Independent*, opened it, and bent his head into its pages. But after a while, he flung the paper onto a table and, rising, walked toward the window. "I wish—I really wish—If I hadn't—if he hadn't—If that thing hadn't happened with him—"

"Stop it, Conor!" she said, alarmed at their reversal of roles. He had always been the one in charge, the calm one. "It was as much my fault as yours," she said, appeasing. "I provoked him."

"Don't be ridiculous." He was really shouting now. "Of course you didn't provoke him. He was an awful, appalling human being—"

"But Conor—"

"You didn't fucking provoke him!"

Molly was really disturbed. Conor rarely swore. Her instinct was to calm him down at all costs but, seated on the sofa, she felt as though she were tied into a straitjacket. He clenched his fists and pounded one into the other. "You have no idea what I went through every time I saw him raise his hand to you and Mam . . ." She watched him pace up and down the small space between the two sofas. She had not felt this helpless since she was a small child.

There was a discreet knock on the door. It was the young airline clerk, back to see if they needed anything.

Conor kept his back turned to the door, facing out the window. Molly asked for coffee—anything to get rid of the clerk.

He left, leaving the door slightly ajar. Conor turned around when the clerk left and looked at her in a way that disturbed her even more and sent slithering fingers through her blood. The tension in the room, already high, stretched to breaking point. What was happening? Molly had never been more conscious that her brother was a good four or five inches taller than she.

In two strides he was beside her, pulling her off the couch by her shoulders, and for an extraordinary moment she thought he was going to kiss her. The prospect made her knees feel like rubber bands and she started to shake slightly.

But just as suddenly as he had come over, he dropped his hands and went back to the window; she saw his knuckles whiten as he gripped the windowsill.

An aircraft slid past the windows and the roar of its engines, muted by the double-glazing, filled the little room just as the clerk came back with the coffee, his eyes fixed on the little tray so he would not spill the liquid. "Sorry," he said, "but I'm afraid you'll have to drink it pretty quickly. We'll be boarding you in three or four minutes." Taking advantage of the moment, Molly collapsed silently onto the couch again. Her heart was beating like a trip hammer. Luckily, the coffee was cool enough to gulp.

Conor turned away from the window and picked up her coat from the arm of the couch. His face was as bland as a mask: "Have you got everything?"

She took the coat from him and nodded, afraid to look at him. The clerk took her overnight bag and the three of them left the lounge. When they got within sight of the security barriers, Conor stopped. "This is as far as I go," he said quietly. He kissed her on the cheek. Then he turned and walked slowly away.

Molly was the last passenger to board the aircraft, which was only half full, and the doors were closed almost immediately. She declined to take one of the sweets offered by the stewardess and closed her eyes when the aircraft began to roll out to its takeoff point. The memory of the extraordinary scene in the lounge was superseded by her terror of flying. As usual, when the engines roared for the takeoff run, her stomach began to churn. She clutched the armrests of her seat until her hands hurt, and although it had been many years since she had darkened the door of a church, began the silent childish litany: *Sacred Heart of Jesus, in Thee I trust; Immaculate Heart of Mary, pray for us; Our Holy Guardian Angels, protect us; St. Joseph and St. Jude, pray for us!* She recited it mentally over and over again as the plane raced along the runway and opened her eyes only when she felt the change in angle and vibration which meant that they had left the ground.

During the flight, she tried to blot Conor's face out by reading *Cara*, the Aer Lingus in-flight magazine, but his face floated over its glossy, colorful pages. She forced herself to think not of him, but of her mother.

It was a fine day in Shannon and she was grateful, as they traveled along the roads to the new airfield at Oranmore outside Galway, that the cabdriver was not inclined to talk at all. She leaned her head against the worn seat and watched as the countryside of County Clare sped by. Although the low January sun shone white, the storm of the previous night had left clear evidence of its passage. The poor land of the fields was waterlogged under the washed sky; many of the leafless roadside trees dangled half-broken branches, and several times the driver had to negotiate fallen trunks. The tires of the taxi crunched constantly on the litter of twigs. If it had been this bad here, twenty miles inland, thought Molly, what must it have been like out on the islands?

It was just after half past two when they pulled in to the airfield at Oranmore. She paid the driver and walked across to the tiny, one-story building, not much more than a shed, which served as check-in, assembly point, passenger waiting area, parcel office, and communications room for Aer Arann, the little airline that served all three islands.

Word had obviously spread about Sorcha, because the moment Molly stepped inside the hut, the young woman behind the counter, whom Molly recognized as one of the O'Flahertys from Inishmore, came forward to sympathize. "We were expecting you, Molly. We were all very sorry to hear about poor Sorcha." Faced with kindness and concern, Molly's self-composure was threatened, but she thanked the young woman and accepted a cup of tea which was produced for her from behind the check-in counter. "It won't be long now," said the O'Flaherty girl, "ye'll be going at three o'clock."

At five minutes to three, the six passengers were weighed one by one, holding their baggage, on a Berkel scale. The pilot himself did the weighing, chatting all the while he noted the weights on his manifest and then led them all out to the Islander aircraft, small and sturdy and specifically designed for island-hopping.

The flight was uneventful. They skimmed west, out over Galway Bay for fifteen minutes until Inisheer was in sight. It was Molly's first view of her home from the air—the Aer Arann service was new—and despite the tragic reason for her visit, she was fascinated at the bare, treeless landscape, almost entirely light gray in color, deeply scored with thousands of fissures and marked out in a crazy pattern by the drystone walls. The island looked like a limestone jigsaw on the surface of the dark green ocean.

It disappeared from her view as the pilot circled around again over the sea and lined up on the flat grassy promontory that served as an airstrip. She could see the tractor and trailer used to carry the freight and luggage and a couple of people standing on the grass, holding their hands to their eyes and looking upward. The arrival of the Aer Arann plane was always one of the highlights of island life and usually attracted a crowd, but today being Sunday, many people were still at their dinners.

Although it was dry and bright, it was obviously still very windy out here. The little plane see-sawed as it lost height and Molly's stomach started to heave. She realized she had not eaten all day, having had only the lukewarm coffee at Heathrow and the cup of tea at Oranmore. But before she got actually sick, the plane skewed once more and thumped onto the grass. She looked out her window and recognized one of the people on the grass. Older, fatter, but unmistakably Father Pat Moran. The priest's hair blew wild as he held the collar of his black clerical coat up around his ears. Preoccupied with other events of the day, this complication had not occurred to her. How could she have been so stupid—she should have realized that since Brendan was probably tending to her mam, it was inevitable Father Moran, being the one who had telephoned her, should meet her.

The plane bumped to a halt and the pilot unstrapped himself. He got out of his seat and opened the door, and immediately the cold air gushed through the tiny cabin. Molly braced herself for what was to come; not only with her mother but with this priest she had not seen since the awful and embarrassing events in the dunes. She unstrapped her seat belt and, carrying her overnight bag, struggled out of her seat.

The pilot said good-bye to her on the grass. She delayed until he had climbed back into his plane and then turned to face the priest. Walking across the short strip of grass, she extended her hand. "How are you, Father?" He took the hand but barely touched it before letting it drop. "I'm fine, Molly," he said. Then: "I'm very sorry about Sorcha . . ."

She nodded and the awkwardness beat between them. He leaned forward to take the bag from her and she noticed that his left hand was bandaged. "What happened to your hand, Father?" she asked as they walked toward the little opening in the stone wall that ran along one side of the airfield. "Oh, nothing much," he said. "I was out in the storm last night and just got a bit of a graze, that's all."

She could see he was avoiding her eye, but as he held the door of the car open for her, Molly, inexplicably, felt the weight of embarrassment lift from her soul. All that time she had wasted reliving the awful night in the dunes; when all that had happened was that a pathetic, overweight man who was facing into old age had in a weak moment yielded to temptation.

"Thank you, Father," she said as she squeezed herself into the vehicle. The car he had borrowed, one of the few on the island, was rusted and very small, and she had difficulty folding her legs under the dashboard, not least because there was a six-volt battery on the floor under her feet. As he muttered something about checking the water, she actually felt the first stirrings of sympathy for him.

They did not speak during the short, bumpy journey, and when they came within sight of the house, she saw a small group of men had gathered outside the front door, recognizing two of them, an uncle and his son, her cousin. All the men wore caps and all had their hands in the pockets of their Sunday suits. Two hens and a cockerel pecked around in the dirt by their feet. Molly told herself there was no reason to be embarrassed as the men stared at her obliquely from under their caps, but she did feel acutely uncomfortable and hesitated as she and the priest approached the door.

The group parted to let her pass, some going to one side of the door, two going to the other, so she had to pass through them as though they were a ragged guard of honor. As she walked into the house, first one, then another of them touched a cap. Molly kept her head high.

Father Moran followed her in, placed her bag against the wall of the kitchen, and went out again.

The kitchen was bright and clean, the fire banked, and there was a neighbor woman in the little scullery, washing dishes. Brendan was not in the room and she supposed he was in with her mother. She greeted the neighbor but put off going in to Sorcha, steeling herself to be calm, and while the woman prepared a cup of tea, Molly looked out the window. The heads of the men outside had swiveled after the priest, who had walked a little way along the boreen. He had stopped where two walls made a rough right angle and was leaning against them, pulling on a cigarette. The men, absorbed, did not realize she was watching them. She saw one of them snigger and was suddenly very glad she lived in a crowded, impersonal city.

Brendan came from her mother's room. *"Dia dhuit,"* he said awkwardly. He was thin and a little stooped; she saw with a shock that he had visibly aged.

She returned the greeting. They had never been close, she and this brother, and she knew that he resented her career in England and the success it brought her. Nevertheless, seeing his plight now, she felt nothing for him but pity. She had an impulse to hug him but knew better. "Is Mam asleep?" she asked.

He nodded, and indicating to the neighbor that she would have the tea later, she went into her mother's room.

There was a low hiss from a bottled gas heater under the window. The bed was neat, with fresh sheets and clean wool blankets, under a spotless white candlewick counterpane. Someone had draped a white dish towel on a makeshift frame over the top of the bedside light and the soft glow was kind to Sorcha's face where it lay on a white linen pillowcase. Sorcha's hands were folded on the counterpane, rising and falling irregularly as she breathed in shallow gasps. Her gray hair was loose to her shoulders, but neatly combed and kept off her face with an incongruously childish headband of red plastic. It was this detail that almost broke Molly's heart.

She sank to her knees beside the bed. For several minutes she gazed at the face of her mother, and then gently took one of the old hands in her own. The skin was hard and calloused and the thin gold wedding band had all but disappeared into it, but the hand itself was small and delicate. So little time now to tell her mother how much she was loved. Maybe no time at all. She stroked the fragile hand and then laid her cheek on it. It felt leathery and dry against her own soft, wet skin. Sorcha's eyes opened. "Is it you, Molly?" she whispered. She tried to struggle up but barely succeeded in moving her head.

"Rest, Mam, rest," said Molly. *"Suan!"* She leaned over and kissed her mother's clammy forehead.

"But after the long journey, you'll be wanting—"

"Stop it, Mam. Rest yourself, rest yourself . . ."

Sorcha succumbed. She tried to smile. "I'm glad you're come, Molly."

"Darling Mam, darling Mam!" was all that Molly could say in response, still holding the small hard hand in both her own. Then, almost to herself, burying her head on the counterpane, "What will I do without you?" With a great effort, Sorcha brought over her other hand and stroked her daughter's head. "Hush, *a chroí*, you will be the one now to look out for the family."

All Molly's great plans, all she had wanted to say to her mother, was no use now. There was no time, she could see that. "I will look out for them, Mam. You rest now. I'll mind them." There was a movement behind her. Brendan had crept into the room and stood near the bed, twisting his hands. His face was creased with misery.

When Molly turned back to her mother, Sorcha was looking straight at her. "I just want to say," she said softly, so softly that Molly had to lean close to hear, "that a mother knows more than a daughter thinks she knows . . ." Molly eased her arm under her mother's head so that she was cradling her and Sorcha's face was turned toward her. She brushed a strand of her own hair from where it had fallen across Sorcha's cheek and took one of her hands again. She barely heard the last faint words: *"Maith dom é! Maith dom é!"* Then Sorcha died.

"Whatever it is, Mam, of course I forgive you," whispered Molly against her mother's slack fingers.

Later that evening, the neighbor woman who had helped lay Sorcha out handed Molly a large manila envelope she had found under her mother's mattress. Opening it, Molly found it contained a large sum of cash; this must be, she thought, the money she and Conor had, over the years, sent home to Inisheer. Sorcha—and later Sorcha and Brendan—had clearly not touched a penny of it; they must have lived on what the state provided. And Sorcha had not trusted Brendan not to spend it, hence the hiding place.

More than her mother's death itself, the sight of the notes, so carefully folded into the envelope and so reminiscent of the dogeared £80 Sorcha had pressed into her hand that dreadful day she had left the island, caused Molly to break down completely.

The funeral was lashed with January rain and Una O'Connor shivered as she waited to offer her condolences to Molly at the graveside. She was the last to do so and saw the struggle to remember on Molly's face. "Una O'Connor," she said, extending her hand.

"Oh, yes," said Molly. She looked genuinely taken aback. "I'm sorry I didn't recognize you, but I didn't expect—"

"I'm very sorry about your mother," said Una. "I didn't know her, of course, but I know how it is to lose a mother."

"How did you know?" Molly still held Una's hand.

"My own mother died last year—"

"No," said Molly, "I mean, how did you know Mam had died?"

"The death notices in the *Independent*," said Una.

"Thank you very much for coming all this way, I really appreciate it."

Una was embarrassed. Her motives were, as usual, mixed. She had seized on the funeral as a way back into contact with Seán Molloy, daring to hope he might be present. But at the same time, she liked Margo Bryan and genuinely wanted to show her sympathy.

Molly dropped her hand. "You'll come up to the house?"

"Oh, no! That's for family only . . ."

"Of course you'll come. You've come all this way. This is Brendan, my brother . . ."

Una had presumed that the tall, stooped man, who looked old enough to be Molly's father, was the brother. Throughout the exchange between the two women, he had been standing quietly, hands clasped in front of him, as though waiting for someone to tell him what to do. Una was familiar with the type, inadequate and sad. She shook hands with him now. "I'm very sorry, Mr. O Briain."

"Yes, yes," he said, all in a rush, "come up to the house, come up to the house."

Una felt like an imposter. She wished with all her heart she had not come. She trudged after the rest of the mourners through the unrelieved gray of the streaming, rocky landscape as the waves and waves of rain beat at her city coat, useless against them.

How could anyone live in a place like this?

The little house was as she expected. She felt like a ghoul. Nevertheless, as the tide of Irish talk, so rapid that she could not understand it, washed around her, her professional eye noted and retained the features of the kitchen: the dresser and the blackened fireplace, the spotless starched linen on the table, the bottles of whiskey, piles of sandwiches, and barrel of stout, the assorted, borrowed glassware and rows of wooden chairs. She accepted a glass of whiskey from a woman who smiled at her with such friendliness that Una was doubly ashamed of her mixed motives.

Molly came and sat beside her, but they ran out of conversation fast. She moved across the kitchen and tried to talk to Brendan, but he kept his eyes fixed on a far corner of the room and answered all her questions in shy monosyllables.

"Did Seán Molloy not come to the funeral?" she asked him at last, when she was sure Molly was at the other side of the room.

His long, creased face puckered. "Seán Molloy?" he repeated as though thunderstruck. "Seán Molloy?" He threw his body backward in the chair and raised his eyes to heaven as though thinking, but it took Una only a moment to realize that the dumb show meant that Brendan was being polite to a stranger. He had never heard of Seán Molloy.

Not a boyfriend, then . . . she thought. But on the other hand, would Margo Bryan have confided in this brother?

She was no nearer. And the timing was hardly appropriate to ask Margo Bryan herself.

At least the actress would now look on her as a friend . . .

The moment Una allowed herself the thought, she felt like a worm.

8

There was too much wind and rain in this bloody country.

Father Moran shook his umbrella in the hallway of the presbytery in Tullyhalla and pulled off the plastic raincoat he wore over his ordinary coat. Despite the generous whiskey he had been given after completing the rituals of a sick call, he felt frozen through after the short walk from the sick man's house at the end of the village to his own bungalow. And his shoes were letting in the wet. He was sick of it, sick of it, he thought irritably, pulling the laces open and kicking the shoes into a corner. He looked at his socks. There were twin half-moons of wet around the toes.

February was by far the worst month in Ireland, he thought, padding into the gloomy front room, which smelled of polish. If it wasn't gales and sleet, it was rain, bloody rain. And as for it being the official beginning of spring, he had yet to see a set of daffodils in his back garden that could survive intact the blasts of February.

He glanced out the window at the village street. There was not a soul about. The lights of the small grocery shop on the opposite side of the street glowed cheerily, but through its steamy window he could see the owner sitting idly at the register, gazing out at the street. A young tree, planted by the Tidy Towns committee outside his front gate, jerked at its stake under the onslaught. He shivered. This was an awful country, he repeated to himself like a mantra, opening the press beside the fireplace and taking out the whiskey bottle and a tumbler. Not only was this an awful country, but this godforsaken village in the back end of nowhere, was its apotheosis.

He took the first sip of his whiskey. A draft, created by the open door, swirled down the chimney and blew

onto the floor a blurry snapshot of himself and a parish-
ioner which had been propped against a toby jug on the
mantelpiece. He looked at the snapshot with disgust.
How he longed right now for the sun on his bare back.
An awful bloody country.

He retrieved the picture from the hearthrug and replaced it on the mantelpiece, then, carrying his drink,
went into the kitchen. It was even colder in here, cold in
temperature with the drafts curling under the badly fitting
back door, colder in ambience. Not a cup was out of
place; the tiled walls gleamed in the wintry light from
the back garden. There was a note on the spotless drain-
board from Mrs. Conway. She had gone to visit her
mother in Galway and would be back in time to make
him his tea.

He stood there for a moment, indecisive, staring out
through the window at the sodden grass, forgetting why
he had come into the kitchen in the first place. Then he
went into the little dining room which adjoined the
kitchen and was his personal refuge. At least it was
warmer in here, although the fire had burned low. He
threw a log into the grate, raising a shower of sparks,
and turned on the television. There was racing on the
first channel, and when he pressed the button for the
second one, the air was filled with the sound of rico-
cheting bullets. He recognized Gene Autry and stood
watching for a moment, tuning in to the action; then he
sat down in his fireside chair and took the second sip of
whiskey.

He realized after five minutes or so, when his tumbler
was almost empty, that he had already seen this film—or
if not this one, one very like it—and his concentration
wavered. The decision he had been putting off for days
tugged at his brain. It had been half made already, the
day after Molly had returned to London following her
mother's funeral. It had been three-quarters made the day
he traveled the twenty-odd miles to the public library in
Galway to find the two addresses, of the Federal Aviation
Administration in Washington and of Lloyds of London.
He had not wanted to risk awkward questions from the
local librarian: *And what would you be wanting those for
now, Father?*

All that was needed now was the final push. A bit of

action. He would have to stop messing and just do it: it
was eating away at him, this knowledge about Molly
without knowing who exactly she was. It had to be easy.
There could have been only so many babies lost at sea
in the Atlantic at the end of April or the beginning of
May 1953. What he was going to do with the knowledge
after he acquired it was another story. Cross that bridge
when he came to it . . .

No point in waiting any longer, today was the day.
Mrs. Conway safely out of the house. Nothing on until
confessions after tea.

There was a small, cluttered bureau beside his chair.
Its leaded-glass front was jammed shut against a chaotic
pile of books and papers, but the desk part stood permanently open. It was territory forbidden to Peg Conway
and her polish. So was the bottom part of the bureau,
which was always locked and to which only he had a key.
In there were his most personal possessions—photographs
of his mother and from his childhood, books that had
belonged to his father, a missal given to him by his Jesuit
spiritual adviser when he had been ordained, a tin box
containing the medals, now rusted, he had won for hurling in his youth and another one that contained his father's old IRA medal.

In there was also a shoe box in which he had placed
over the years all the clippings and reviews of Molly Ni
Bhriain's work. He had been careful, always clipping the
material when he was alone, usually late at night, and
when he had done so, always burning the remainder of
the page. In summer, when there was no fire, he had had
to stand over the grate while it burned before raking the
ashes through the bars.

He unlocked the bureau and, reflexively, checked to
see that the box was still there. There was a surprising
amount of material in it—hardly a month went by but
there was something to be read about her in the chauvin-
istic Irish newspapers, whether in the gossip columns,
features, or arts pages. The box was now more than half
full.

On the writing surface of the desk was a pewter tankard, pitted with age and stuffed with old bills, rubber
bands, pencils without points, pages torn out of the *Sacred Heart Messenger* in the margins of which were pen-

ciled notes and telephone numbers. He put his drink
down and picked up the tankard, shaking it around until
he spotted the addresses he wanted, handwritten on a
crumpled page torn out of a pocket diary. He smoothed
out the page and placed it carefully to one side. Then,
replacing the tankard, he took up his whiskey glass again,
tipping the dregs up to his mouth. The whiskey stung his
lips, which were, as they always were in winter, chapped
and sore. He knew he was drinking too much but did not
care. More and more these days, he was finding he did
not care all that much about anything to do with himself.

He looked across at the television. Gene Autry was
still shooting it out with the bad guys.

Father Moran took a pen and a writing pad from another part of the desk and turned his chair around to face
it. The chair was too low for the level of the writing
surface and his back was uncomfortably strained. But
this was how he always wrote letters and he was too old
to change now.

Christian stared at the scarred surface of his editor-in-
chief's desk. The man was too thin. It was common
knowledge he suffered from a duodenal ulcer. The editor
was also meticulously tidy, Christian saw. Anal fixation,
he thought. No wonder the guy had an ulcer . . .

Although technology had caught up with the *Sentinel*,
the editor kept a supply of razor-sharp yellow pencils in
an old cigar box geometrically parallel to the edge of the
desk; the box, his two telephones, his computer terminal,
and a single manila folder, were all that were on the desk
at present. Although it was snowing outside, the window
of the editor's office was open, and Christian, through
the sounds of the downtown traffic, could quite plainly
hear the screeching of the El as it rounded a corner on
the elevated tracks above the Loop.

Although he refused to meet the editor's eyes, he was
conscious of the man's unwavering stare and that he was
picking his teeth with an open paper clip. Not wanting
to open the conversation, Christian looked out the window of the small office. The Chicago River, he saw, was
partially frozen, and the snow was beginning to lie on
the thin film of ice that looped along its side walls in
dirty opaque arcs.

Out the corner of his eye, Christian saw the editor throw the paper clip into a metal waste basket. Mentally, he braced himself; at the same time the irrelevant thought struck him that since the paper clip had landed noiselessly, the basket must be full.

"This is the last one, Smith!" The editor dropped the words one by one into the heavy atmosphere of the room. He opened a drawer and flung a card across the desk.

"Is that for me, sir?" Christian was careful to keep his voice neutral.

"Well, it's hardly for me!"

Christian picked up the card. Letra-Setted on it were the words: *If your mother tells you she loves you—check it!*

Christian knew all too well that for a while he had been living perilously close to his last chance at the *Sentinel:* his portfolio of work for the paper was impressive but his reputation for unreliability was growing. He had been given a warning after the Ethiopia debacle four weeks before, but the present blast was for, in his view, a relatively minor offense: a tiny error of fact—due to his taking a short-cut—which had led to the newspaper being sued by a state legislator and having to settle immediately to avoid going to court. "Thank you, sir!" He placed the card facedown on the desk.

"I think you get the message?" said the editor.

"Yes, sir," said Christian, and then something, that treacherous, reckless streak in him, broke through and rushed out before he could catch it. He heard his voice almost before he had thought of the words: "Well, I have a message for you—*sir!*"

He picked up the card again and tore it savagely into little pieces. Some of the Letra-Set resisted tearing and fluttered whole onto the editor's spotless desk. Christian paused just long enough to note with satisfaction that the man's eyes were bulging, then stalked out of the office.

Flushed with exultation, brushing off inquiries from colleagues, he cleared out his desk, scribbled a note for Dick, and pinned it on the bulletin board beside the newsdesk. Then he left the building.

He went straight to the Shamrock Bar and ordered a double bourbon.

Twenty minutes later Dick, breathless from running,

joined him. "For Christ's sake, Christian, what do you think you're doing? Go back right now and apologize. There's not all that much damage done yet—go back. He'll take you back if you apologize."

"When hell freezes over!" Christian's blood was up.

Dick argued and argued, but Christian would not budge. Rationalization had always been easy for him. Anything bad that happened to him could always be shown to be someone else's fault, and in this case, it was the troglodytes in management at the *Sentinel*—as personified by the editor. He had never been properly appreciated. He was too talented for such a Neanderthal organization. His resignation stood.

They had a few drinks and Christian went back to Dick's apartment for a few more. It was when he was finishing his fourth bourbon that Christian realized fuzzily that there were certain benefits from his resignation.

Like he could live anywhere in the world now. Like London. "Okay if I call Lon-London?" he asked Dick, his speech sounding slurred even in his own ears.

"Okay if you pay for the call!"

Before dialing Molly's number, Christian took a deep breath and shook his head violently from side to side to clear it.

The telephone rang six times before it was answered. "Christian!" said Molly, "you just caught me—I was just on my way out—I was out at the gate actually . . ."

"Nowhere special, I hope?" Christian's self-justification with regard to his abrupt resignation was still strong, but he was beginning to feel a little sorry for himself, and immediately, she picked this up. "No, just out to meet a friend for lunch. Is there something wrong, Christian? You sound odd."

"Do I?"

"Yes, you do."

"How are you, Molly?"

"Oh, so-so—you know. Working hard, that helps. Every so often, though, it hits me that Mam is gone. I know you've been in this situation for a long, long time, Christian—but at least you can't blame yourself for neglect. I'm feeling things like 'if only I went home to Inisheer more, I might have been able to'—oh, well. No use talking about that now."

"Poor baby!" said Christian after a long pause during which he could hear his own breathing.

"Are you sure you're all right, Christian? You really do sound a little peculiar . . ."

"I'm fine, I'm fine." Again he ran out of words. "Mol-Molly?" he said after a few seconds.

"Yes?"

"I might have a surprise for you in a few days."

"What kind of surprise?"

"Oh, just a sur-surprise."

She laughed. "I think you've had a few drinks, my friend. Will I like this surprise?"

"I sincerely hope so."

"Looking forward to it, then. Look, Christian, I really have to go; there's a taxi outside—"

"Do you love—do you *love* me, Molly?"

"Christian, we've been over this before. How can I possibly love you this soon? I don't even know you!"

"Well, do you love me a little—a little bit? Just a little bit?"

"Maybe a little bit!" She laughed. "Now *good-bye,* Christian! Go and sort out a revolution or something. I've got to run."

"Good-bye, my darling, see you soon."

" 'Bye!"

Christian crashed overnight on Dick's spare bed. Next morning, when he woke up, his head pounded with a hangover, but he was happy. He was free to go and see Molly.

Four days later, Cordelia traveled with him to O'Hare to see him off on the flight. He was still far more comfortable with his grandmother than with Malcolm, not least because her gentle presence acted as a buffer and intermediary in the prickly relationship between himself and his grandfather. Although in his more reflective moments he thought he would have liked to, Christian had never been able to bridge the chasm that had opened up between them during his teens.

Their good-byes had been formal. Christian knew that Malcolm was furious that he had chucked his job and was off on what he considered a damn-fool expedition to try his hand as a free-lancer in London. But they had not fought openly and Malcolm had limited himself to be-

having glacially in his grandson's presence. Christian was
relieved to escape. Nonetheless, it had occurred to him
that this might be the last good-bye and he found he had
been surprisingly emotional.

Malcolm was seventy-four now, as old as the century,
and although, to Christian, he had always been indestruc-
tible and still was, it was a shock to see his gnarled and
liver-spotted hands as they shook hands on the front steps
of Greentrees. "Grandma, I'm sorry," he said simply as
the Lincoln crawled along through the sleety rush hour
on the Kennedy Expressway toward O'Hare.

"I know, Christian," said Cordelia. "But it's all right,
honey. We all have one life to live and you have got to
live yours the way you see fit."

At that moment the Lincoln came to a complete halt.
"There must be an accident up ahead, ma'am!" said the
chauffeur over his shoulder. Sure enough, within minutes
the emergency vehicles, red lights flashing, screamed by
on the hard shoulder.

"Have you heard from Jo-Ann at all?" Cordelia asked,
wiping away the condensation on one of the side windows of the automobile. "No, Grandma. I hear from
Dick she might get married again . . ."

"That's good. I always liked Jo-Ann. I was sorry when
you divorced."

It was on the tip of Christian's tongue to present, as
usual, his side of the story, but he held it and contented
himself with a noncommittal "Ummm." The car started
to crawl forward again. "Tell me again what your plans
are, Christian . . ." said Cordelia.

Christian did not actually have anything concrete in
mind; his portfolio reposed in the trunk of the automobile with the rest of his luggage. He had done his re-
search—Britain was in the throes of recession, and
although he had faith in his own ability to get work, he
had no idea how much the general belt-tightening would
affect the newspaper world. He did hope, not without
justification, that his experience in disaster reporting—
for which there was never a lack of news appetite—and
his being American at this time in history, would be a
help. The world in general was still fascinated by the
soap opera surrounding the Watergate scandal; President
Nixon was on the run and he had good contacts amongst

the Democrats. "I have no immediate plans, Grandma," he said truthfully. But then, for her sake, he embroidered: "I've been offered several things, but I'm going to take my time. I need a break anyway . . . And . . ." He hesitated, but plunged on. "I've met a girl in London, Grandma."

"Oh, yes?"

"I've only met her twice, would you believe it, but we've talked a lot on the telephone. I'm crazy about her, Grandma."

"What's her name?"

"Margo Bryan. Well, actually, her real name is Molly, but she's an actress, a very good one, Grandma—and Margo is her stage name. She's Irish."

"Have you a photograph?"

"No, I'm afraid not. But Grandma, I know you'd *adore* her."

"How does she feel about you, Christian?"

"I—I'm not quite sure. She certainly hasn't turned me down, or anything like that. She's very upset at the moment because her mother's just died. Grandma, I've already asked her to marry me . . ."

"After two meetings and a couple of telephone calls?"

"I knew as soon as I saw her that she was the right one. I've never been more sure of anything in my life."

"I remember you said the same about Jo-Ann, Christian."

"I know, Grandma, I know . . ." He deserved that. He knew his grandmother did not mean to rebuke him, it was not in her nature.

Seeing his deflation, Cordelia patted his hand. "Christian, I wouldn't dream of interfering. I just want you to be a little cautious this time so you won't get hurt. But I do remember, believe me, I *do* remember, what it is like when you fall in love instantly, like summer lightning. It was that way for me and your grandfather. So I am sympathetic. Just take your time, won't you?"

"Of course I will, Grandma." He kissed her on the cheek. Even as he did so he knew he had no intention of following her advice.

"One more thing." She opened her handbag. "This is for you, but it's just between you and me, Christian, not for anyone else's ears or eyes, okay?"

Christian unfolded the check. He gasped. "Grandma!" The check was for ten thousand dollars. "It's from my own funds," Cordelia went on calmly, "and nothing to do with Malcolm or the family. Remember, the brewery was left to me." It was something which had never seemed to matter; Malcolm had dedicated his life so completely to the brewery that no one in the family ever thought about it as Cordelia's.

"Grandma,"—Christian felt dangerously close to tears—"I can't take this."

"Why not?" She was serene as always. "Well"—he searched for a reason—"I just can't, that's all!"

"You'll be getting all of it anyway, when Malcolm and I pass on, so what's the difference if you get a little of it now? I have a feeling you'll need it."

He was still holding the check when finally they pulled up at the international terminal. She would not come inside with him. "We'll say our good-byes here, my dear. I hate good-byes. Have a pleasant trip and, Christian, please call us when you arrive to give us your address. I know you don't think so, but your grandfather does worry terribly about you."

"I know he does, Grandma."

"And so do I, my dear. Take care now! And let us know what happens between you and your girl."

"I will, and Grandma—" She was getting back into the Lincoln and Christian noticed that although she was still elegant, she had gotten very thin. He wanted to say to her that he loved her—and Malcolm too. But when she turned around expectantly, he could not say it. "Thanks!" he said instead.

He treated himself to one last Business Class flight. For once, he did not sleep. Nor did he order a drink. All through the long flight, he sipped Perrier and orange juice. Since he had decided to go to London, he had a feeling that he was embarked on an adventure that was given to him on extra time, one last chance that he must not screw up.

He watched the flickering images of *A Touch of Class*. All around him people chuckled appreciatively into their headsets, but Christian, lost in plans and dreams, could not concentrate on the film, and after a while took off his headset. The engine note was steady and he was aware of the soft whoosh of the pressurized air system streaming cold air from the circular vent above his head. He closed his eyes, but his brain, fed by adrenaline, would not let him sleep.

When there were only two hours to go before landing, he did doze a little, but snapped awake when the captain came on the PA to say, "Good morning." The cabin staff was already coming through the cabin with trolleys laden with orange juice, coffee, and breakfast rolls. The captain went on to say that because of strong tailwinds, they were a good fifty minutes ahead of schedule, were therefore just over an hour out from London, and were at present about sixty miles off the northwest coast of Ireland.

Christian had flown this route on many occasions, but he never crossed this part of it without acknowledging that somewhere in the sea, thirty thousand feet below, lay his mother, his father, and his baby sister. As he strained to catch the first sight of land he was struck by an irony inherent in being in love with Molly. Should she agree to marry him—and he knew it was a very, very big "if"—he could look on it almost as cosmic compensation, as if fate, having used this region to decimate him, was now reusing it to give him joy.

There was no cloud of any consequence and now the jagged Irish coastline, fringed with white all along its length, was floating into view; they were flying so high that it was impossible to pick out individual landmarks, but he could count, dotted along the coast, seven or eight tiny islands; one of them could even be Inisheer . . .

As he sipped the orange juice, grimacing at its acidity, a memory of his mother, bright as a jewel, caught him unaware. He had run in from school, into the rec room. His mom was leaning over the bassinet and was picking up the baby, who was about three months old. She had turned and smiled at him and then, sitting in his grandfather's wing chair, had taken him on her knee and given him the baby to hold. They had sat there, the three of them, he safe in her warm arms while the sunshine from the lake bathed all of them through the open door. The baby had lain still, examining his face with wide, serious eyes full of surprise. He had been able to smell her, a clean, summery smell . . .

Carefully, Christian put the juice glass on the table in front of him. He turned his face fully to the window and stared hard at Ireland until he had his face under control.

One evening in the middle of March, Molly went out to dinner with Christian.

She had been seesawing between depression and normality since her mother's death. *Blithe Spirit* finished its run, heightening her sense of emptiness, and even the news that she had been nominated for a Laurence Olivier Award for her performance in the show had lifted her spirits only temporarily.

Although she had appreciated the support and formal expressions of sympathy from her friends, she had no one in whom actually to confide. Shortly after she came back from Inisheer, Conor, to whom she might naturally have turned for comfort, took a leave of absence from his job at the zoo and went to Israel on a dig in connection with his night course in archaeology.

And as far as Christian was concerned, the whole relationship was too new for her fully to trust him.

She did appreciate his attentiveness, however. As soon as he had heard about her mother, he had stopped off pressurising her into romance; she had been startled when he returned to London so unexpectedly, but more and more, found she actually enjoyed his company. A lot of the time he was busy with his own affairs, hustling work, of which there was no shortage at present; a grand jury in Washington had found that Nixon had been involved in Watergate, and Christian, having made himself an expert on this, was much in demand, not only for newspaper work, but as an interviewee on radio current-affairs programs. He was a talkative, interesting companion and most of the time Molly now felt comfortable with him; the only qualm she had was that from time to time Christian seemed to drink too much and to become quite volatile.

To celebrate her award nomination, Christian suggested dinner at La Vecchia Rizzione on St. Martin's Lane, a restaurant Molly loved. As her taxi pulled up, she saw him sheltering in the doorway from the rain, and she could not help but smile; with his trench coat, blonde hair, athletic frame, and a bunch of white roses in the crook of his arm, she thought he looked so—so *American*. "White roses—again!" She laughed as he held them out to her. "There can't be a white rose left in London—I'm thoroughly spoiled."

"These are special," he said. "I went out myself into the rose fields and gathered them at first light." He tipped up her face and kissed her gently.

Molly kissed him back; his mouth tasted of the rain. "Miles and miles of roses," he said, his voice husky. "There aren't enough roses in the world for you, Molly. You are looking unbelievably fantastic this evening, good enough to eat!" His mouth pressed harder on hers, but she pulled away from him. "Hang on a bit, not so fast. I'm not available for eating; maybe it's just as well we're going inside." Laughing, she linked arms with him as they went into the restaurant.

The evening was an unqualified success; the food, as always, was delightful, the restaurant packed, the decibel level cheerfully high as the diners competed with the ambient noise. The waiters bustled up and down the long room, speaking to one another in loud Italian, singing along with the operatic and Neapolitan background music, dancing with the female customers and sometimes with each other, dousing the lights for effect at a strategic point of the evening so that the fairy-lit mural that stretched the length of the restaurant on one wall could be seen to good effect.

When they were drinking sambuccas after the meal, Molly, feeling warm and relaxed, opened up about her fears concerning the film she was just about to start—her first. Although it was low-budget, with a shooting schedule of only eight weeks, it was prestigious, cast with real stars; it had been an honour to have been asked to test for the part, a triumph when she had got it. She was to play opposite Eugene Lothar, a handsome veteran, who had been voted "Sexiest Man in Britain" in a *News of the World* poll.

Molly's first appearance in front of the cameras was to be on the following Monday, but as the fateful day drew nearer and nearer, the insecurities common to all actors were becoming rife. She was terrified: she would not be able to handle it . . . it was an illusion that people thought she could act . . . everything else she had done and been

praised for was a fluke . . . she was a one-role actress
. . . she was too tall, too gawky . . . all the others in the
film were more experienced than she was . . .

"Molly, you'll slay them!" Christian took her hand
across the table. "And as for being too tall, they'll just
give your leading man a box to stand on. That's what
they always do."

"I know that—but it'll be so awkward!"

"It won't be awkward. Now, stop going on like a teenager going out on her first date. You're a brilliant actress—after all, what are we celebrating here tonight?
You'll be wonderful, I just know it. I'm no expert, but
as far as I can see, the camera loves you, isn't that the
correct phrase? It was where I first saw you, after all—
on camera—and you looked absolutely stunning!"

"You're biased! You would say that, wouldn't you?"
The candlelight sculpted hollows in the fine bone structure of his face, and as usual, the cowlick stood sentinel
on the crown of his head. Molly wondered then if she
loved him.

As though sensing her thoughts, he put out his other
hand and she took it. One of the waiters going by shot
them an indulgent glance; Molly caught it and smiled.
"We're behaving like kids."

"Yes, isn't it lovely! Marry me, Molly."

"Please, Christian." Molly withdrew her hands.
"Please don't pressure me—"

"Sorry, it just slipped out. Won't happen again—until
next week." He grinned, and she had to smile back. She
was feeling looser than she had in weeks.

They went back to her house for a nightcap. The telephone was ringing as Molly turned her key in the lock,
but by the time she got to it, the caller had hung up.
"Make yourself comfortable," she said to Christian, going toward the kitchen. "I'm going to have a cup of coffee; want one?"

"Got any whiskey?"

"Sure. Help yourself, you know where it is . . ."

When she came back into the room, he had switched
on the table lamps, drawn the curtains, and put Mozart
on her stereo. "Nice!" she said appreciatively, igniting
the gas fire in the fireplace. She sat in a chair opposite
him and smiled.

The street outside was absolutely quiet, and while they sipped their drinks, the little house drew closely in around the two of them and instinctively they lowered their voices while they chatted easily. "Mind if I have another?" Without waiting for an answer, Christian carried his glass over to the sideboard where the whiskey bottle rested.

"Not at all, go ahead!" Normally, Molly might have registered the fact that he had had a lot more to drink than she had, but tonight she genuinely did not mind; she was feeling so relaxed, nothing bad could happen tonight. The telephone rang again as he was filling his glass, and she went out into the hall to answer it.

"Hello, Molly?" She looked at her watch, half-past midnight. "Hello, John!" she said, her heart sinking. So much for feeling relaxed.

"Sorry to ring so late, but I did call earlier and you were out . . ."

"Yes, out to dinner actually—"

"With Smith?"

Molly took a deep breath. "Yes," she said quietly. "Christian took me out to dinner to celebrate my nomination for the Olivier award."

"I see!" His voice was aggrieved and Molly once again castigated herself for not having had the courage to be brutally honest with John Chalmers. Despite all her good intentions, she had not been able to tell him she did not want to see him socially anymore.

She realized there was a great deal of noise in the background. "Are you ringing from a party?" she asked, trying to keep her voice good-humored.

"Got it in one," he said. "I wanted you to come, Molly—there are a lot of people here who could help you in your career."

Bugger my career, thought Molly, but bit back the retort. She did owe John Chalmers a great deal: "Sorry about that," she said, "but you can't blame me for what I didn't know."

"No, I suppose not. It's not too late; why don't you hop in a taxi?"

"I don't think so, John."

"Oh, come on, what's to stop you? It's not even as if you're working tomorrow—"

"No, thank you, John, I don't want to go to any party."

"Is Smith there with you, is that it?" he asked after a pause.

"As a matter of fact, yes."

"I see."

The silence that followed lasted only a second or two, but during it Molly made a decision. "And also, as a matter of fact, we're celebrating something else to-night," she said firmly. "Christian has asked me to marry him!"

"Are you going to?"

"I'm thinking about it." By saying it, it suddenly seemed feasible. And restful. To have a companion, someone who was on her side . . .

Besides, she thought, her thoughts racing, being with Christian was fun. And he was beautiful, too. She could find no good reason to resist him anymore. "Yes," she repeated into the telephone, "I am thinking about it, John."

"I see. Well, do let me know!" To her joy she found that for once, his sarcasm, which usually upset her, had no effect. "I will, of course, John," she said warmly.

"I suppose there's no point in my saying I think you're making a mistake?"

"None at all, John." Molly laughed. Coming clearly into focus now, the idea of marrying Christian, so pre-posterous less than two months ago, was not only at this moment not preposterous but actually attractive, and get-ting more and more so by the second.

"I'll say good-bye then. And I suppose I should say congratulations."

"Not quite yet, John. Nothing's final yet."

"Good-bye, Molly."

"Cheerio." She put down the receiver and looked at it for a long, long moment. What had got into her? On the other hand, why shouldn't she marry Christian? What was to stop her, after all? She was in no doubt but that he loved her, and if being happy and feeling safe in an-other's company was love, well then, she loved him, too.

Then one of Kathleen Agnes's half-remembered phrases—*I wouldn't kick that man out of bed*—drifted through her head. Molly smiled to herself. Yes, she thought, by any standards, Christian Smith was a very attractive man and Kathleen Agnes would certainly not have kicked him out of bed. Would she? On balance, she did not think so . . .

She went back into the living room. Christian, sitting in a small easy chair, was staring into the flames of the gas fire, which flickered hypnotically in the converted fireplace. "Come here, honey," he said without turning toward her.

She crossed the room and sank to the ground in front of him, and he opened his legs so she could prop herself comfortably against the seat of the chair. He wrapped his arms gently around her and cradled his cheek on her hair. "Molly," he whispered, "please marry me. I can't live anymore without you."

Molly started guiltily. "Did you hear me on the phone?" She looked up at him, but his expression was puzzled. "No. Who was it? Not bad news, I hope?"

"No," said Molly slowly. "At least I don't think so." She turned around until she was on her knees and facing him. "That was John Chalmers," she said, "and I hope you don't mind—I told him I was probably going to marry you."

For a split second he did not react. Then he jumped to his feet, pulling her with him. "Mind? *Mind?* Do you mean it, Molly—do you really mean it? You'll really marry me?"

Caught up in his joy, she nodded.

"Oh, my God, oh, my God!" he whooped. "Oh, my God . . ." He brought his mouth down on hers, so hard that she almost lost her balance. His happiness and need of her was infectious and she found herself responding to his urgency, kissing him back, straining against him as his hands moved expertly over her body.

He pulled her down so they were both on their knees and then pushed her gently backward and rolled on top of her; all the time his lips and tongue were busy, his hands searching and caressing.

Molly wrapped herself around his firm body; one of his knees was driving insistently between hers, opening them; he brought the knee upward until his thigh was resting between both of hers, and instinctively she bore down on him, reacting to the sensations coursing through her blood. Seemingly of their own volition, her own hands started to explore, her fingers reaching under his belt, pulling up his shirt until they reached his skin, which was warm and smooth. He sat up quickly, shed his jacket and tore his shirt off so violently that the buttons popped, and then pulled at her satin blouse. "Steady on," she said laughingly, "don't ruin it!" She helped him undo the buttons and then herself undid the catch of her bra, releasing her breasts. This action stirred disturbing memories of what had happened with the priest, but the moment she recognized them, she put them firmly out of her mind. She was a grown-up woman now. Resolutely she took Christian's head and cradled it between her breasts. "My darling, oh, my darling!" he was moaning now, licking her breasts and sucking on them, feeding like a baby. Suddenly he raised his head. "I want to see you naked. Turn over!"

Gladly, laughing, she assisted him as he turned her over to unzip her skirt.

And then, when she was lying on her stomach and his hands were pulling up the skirt so he could take it off over her head, something happened in her brain, something unexpected and—as soon as she realized it—horrifying.

She found herself imagining it was Conor's hands that were baring her, fondling her, Conor's hands moving over her back and toward her buttocks.

She was so shocked she scrambled to her feet, away from Christian. "What's wrong?" Christian's face showed he was equally shocked.

"N-nothing." Molly stared at him, holding the unzipped skirt around her waist. "I don't know! Sorry. Just give me a moment, will you? I—I need a drink of water."

She zipped up the skirt and ran into the kitchen, where she gripped the edge of the sink, breathing deeply in an effort to calm her pounding heart. What the hell was wrong with her? How perverted could a person get?

She heard a sound behind her. Christian was standing in the doorway. "What's going on, Molly? Is it the Catholic thing?"

"It's nothing to do with that!" She was so shaken and so angry with herself that she had spoken more vehemently than she had intended. "Sorry, Christian, I'm really sorry." She ran toward him. "I didn't mean to snap at you. I don't know what happened to me, I can't explain it, but I'm all right now, really, I'm all right now." She pulled his head down and kissed him hard, as hard as he had kissed her. But he held her away from him a little. "Is it that I'm not attractive enough?" he asked.

"Of course not, Christian!" she cried. "You're probably the most attractive man I've ever seen."

"So what is it?"

"I told you, I'm all right now. It was just something I can't explain."

"Can't or won't?"

"Can't. Please, Christian, just kiss me," she said fiercely. "Kiss me and forget it. It won't happen again, I promise." Deliberately, she unfastened the skirt again and let it fall to the ground. Dressed only in panties and stockings, she stood in front of him, her head to one side. "There! Here I am. Now will you kiss me?"

"Oh, God," he groaned, taking her in his arms, "you're really beautiful, Molly—are you really going to be my wife? Could I be that lucky?"

"Lucky, lucky you!" she said, taking his head between her hands and bringing his mouth down to hers. They kissed until they were breathless and then Molly pulled away again, arching her back against his arms. He lowered his mouth to her throat and then tongued the sensitive skin behind one ear. The action sent shivers down her back and chest. "Could I ask you a big, big favor?" she gasped.

"What? Anything, anything, my darling darling darling." He turned his attention to the other ear. "Ask me anything."

"I know this will sound awful, but could we wait until our wedding night?"

"Wait for what?" He stopped what he was doing and looked at her.

"You know—" She was embarrassed because she did not quite know why she was asking. "To go the whole way, you know—"

"God, now she asks me!" His eyes glittered and she thought for a second or two he was going to be angry, but then he smiled: "So it is the Catholic thing! All right, but in return you have to agree to get married as soon as possible. Like tomorrow?"

She laughed, relieved he wasn't going to make a scene. "You know it's not possible so soon." And then she was upset with herself all over again. What difference did it make when they had sex?

"As soon after tomorrow as possible, then. Put your clothes back on before I go back on my word."

"All right, I promise." She kissed him again, but he took her by both wrists. "Don't, Molly, don't tease me."

"I'm not," she protested, although she was behaving in a completely irrational manner.

"Do you love me?" His blue eyes bored hard into hers.

"Yes, Christian," she said, "I do."

"Say it, then!"

"I love you!"

"Oh, God," he whispered, "I love you so much, my darling darling one." He hugged her tightly and then let her go. "Stop it, Christian!" He hit the side of his head with his palm and then looked at her, his expression wry. "No point in torturing myself. I'd better have another drink to cool down . . ."

It was on the tip of Molly's tongue to ask him not to drink anymore this evening, but she stopped herself; the way she had behaved, she was hardly in any position to take such a self-righteous stance.

She followed him into the living room, and when he had settled himself with his drink, she curled herself at his feet as before. She did love him, she told herself. What had happened before was a complete aberration. He was stroking her hair and she preened under his hand, lifting her face to his. "I can't wait!"

Bingo! Una pounced on the wire copy. Margo Bryan, Irish actress, formerly of the Abbey Theatre, had been nominated for a Laurence Olivier. Una knew that this award was the West End equivalent of a Broadway Tony, and as far as she knew, no Irish actor or actress had been nominated before. This was news. She brought the paragraph over to the news editor. "Have you seen this, Myles?"

348   DEIRDRE PURCELL

He scanned it. "This the one you interviewed before?"

"Yes. She's really good. She might even win. And I think there's probably a good background story there—if I can get it . . ." On tenterhooks, she watched him consider.

"Could you do it on the telephone?"

Una, adept at reading documents that were upside down, had already noted the latest circular from management lying on top of the editor's IN tray; it detailed measures to cut back on travel costs and expenses. "I'll make you a deal," she said swiftly. "I want to go to London anyway about something personal. If you pay the fare, I'll pay everything else. Even taxis!" She saw him hesitate.

"I have a contact in a travel agency, it won't cost that much—I'll go Apex!"

"You have to book Apex fourteen days before you travel . . ."

"I told you I have a contact in a travel agency."

The news editor shook his head priggishly. "The *Irish Record* does things legally."

"No one'll know. It'll be our secret."

"This 'something personal' must be some guy."

"He is."

The news editor pursed his lips. "Okay, you owe me one. It better be good!"

"It will," promised Una.

She walked back to her own desk, took out her address book, and dialed Margo Bryan's home number. There was no reply.

That afternoon she was assigned to cover a news conference about a new industrial initiative in the fledgeling Irish electronics industry. She looked at her watch—she would try Margo Bryan at the theater in two hours.

Five minutes before the conference was scheduled to start, Una, who firmly believed the only efficient mode of transport around Dublin was on two wheels, parked her bike at the hotel where the conference was being held. She signed in, accepted a glass of inferior wine, and a press pack, and scanned the room. They were all there, all the usual suspects—the obtrusive television presence of RTE, the Irish state broadcasting service, the suits from the "quality" press and business magazines, newsdesk hacks like herself who could be assigned to anything from a funeral to a bank robbery, a few live wires who she knew would try to excite a bit of controversy.

"Hi, Una. What's new?" Mark Trimble bounced across to her. At one time she had thought Mark attractive and went out with him a few times. But every man she met now paled into insignificance when set against the unattainable Seán Molloy. It was difficult for Una to believe that she could have a crush on a man she had met for ten minutes. The last time it had happened to her was when she was eleven years of age. She prided herself on her practicality and this obsession made no sense. In one way, she hoped that Seán would prove genuinely to be unattainable; then she could put herself out of her misery and work on something else. It was the not knowing that was killing her.

"Hi, Mark!" she said without enthusiasm, and continued to scan the gobbledygook and bar charts in the press pack. He was unabashed, and opened his own documentation. Mark was rarely still. He bounced and jigged now while he was reading, as if he might fall over if he stayed still. The habit had driven Una bonkers while they had been going out together.

The conference started, but Una could not muster interest. For once, she decided, she would stop being a perfectionist and would simply take the press release at face value. But for the sake of quotes in her copy, she went up to the podium after the formal conference had ended and asked for an interview with one of the Japanese who were opening the factory and with the Chamber of Commerce representative from the rural town in which it was to be located. She dispatched both of them in five minutes.

She all but ran to her bicycle to get back into the office, and was already dialing the Wyndham's Theatre with one hand while still pulling out the chair at her desk with the other. "Oh, no," said the doorman when she asked for Margo Bryan, "that run's finished, my dear. Got a musical in here now." Una hung up and dialed the actress's home number again. She was lucky. This time the telephone was answered on the third ring.

"Hello," she said, "this is Una O'Connor."

"Oh, hello, Miss O'Connor—Una. I'm sorry, I mean to write to you after my mother's funeral to thank you for coming so far. It was very good of you. I just didn't get around to it yet—"

"Please don't thank me, it was no trouble. I'm sure you're still very upset . . ."

"Well, life goes on, especially life in the theater."

She certainly did not sound depressed, thought Una. "I believe congratulations are in order," she said. "You've been nominated for an Olivier?"

At the other end of the line, the actress laughed. "News travels fast across the Irish Sea! Yes, I believe I have."

"That's wonderful, and no one deserves it more."

"Thank you."

"Which brings me"—Una took a deep breath—"to my reason for telephoning you. The newspaper, in the person of myself, would like to do a feature on you."

"*Another* one?"

"Well, if you remember, the last one was cut way back to quite a small article because of pressure of space in the news pages that day. I—we—would like to give you one with more prominence in the features pages." There was a pause and she held her breath.

"When would you want to do this?" said the actress at last.

"Within the next couple of weeks, if it suits you."

"It would have to be sooner than that. This is Saturday and I'm leaving on Monday to start work on a film."

"Better and better," said Una. "Our feature will be even more timely."

"Could we do the interview on the telephone?"

Damn, thought Una. The woman was learning. "Well, no," she said persuasively, "that would be really very difficult for me. I don't work well on the telephone. I think it would be far better for both of us if we could do it face-to-face."

"Well, all right," said Molly slowly. "I suppose we'd better leave it until I come back from the film, then."

"How about tomorrow?"

"Tomorrow's Sunday. My fiancé is taking me to Oxford for the day."

Fiancé? Shit!

"Who's the lucky man?" To her horror, Una heard her own voice actually squeak.

"He's an American. Actually he's a journalist. From Chicago."

All Una heard was the word "American." She felt like throwing the telephone receiver into the air and jumping up after it. "Well, double congratulations!" she cried, "that's wonderful!"

And although she could not persuade the actress to give up her day off, or even to come home from Oxford early, she was perfectly happy, in light of the great news she had just received, to leave the interview until Molly had fulfilled her film commitments. "We'll have more to talk about then anyway," she said, "and it will be nearer the time for the actual awards. It'll all work out for the best. Good luck on the film, and again, double congratulations! I'll telephone you when you come back in three weeks' time and we'll set it up."

She put the receiver down on its cradle, and the copy boy was treated to the sight of Una O'Connor throwing her arms around the news editor. "What's that for?" he said irritably, straightening out the copy she had crushed.

"I won't be doing that interview with Margo Bryan until three weeks from now."

"That's good news?"

"That's very good news!"

"What about the personal business in London—the contact in the travel agency, the Apex? It all seemed bloody urgent an hour ago!"

"That was before," said Una. "It'll keep for three weeks."

Three weeks wasn't long. She felt instinctively that if she could get him on his own, she'd have a good chance. Una hammered out her copy on the IDA initiative as though she were Michaelangelo who had hit a good streak while painting the Sistine Chapel.

She read over her copy but stopped abruptly before she got to the end. She had been so caught up with the idea of a relationship between the actress and Seán Molloy that it had never occurred to her that he might have another girlfriend.

* * *

Four weeks later, on a Saturday morning, Molly woke as usual at about eight o'clock, and immediately the dread of what she had to do today assaulted her. Her impulse was simply to pull the warm bedcovers over her head and go back to sleep, but somewhere, in some magazine article, she had read that if there is a difficult task to be done it should be the first one done in the day.

She had to ring Conor to tell him about her engagement, and she might as well do it right now and get it over with. Her brother had been due home from his archaeological dig late the previous night.

Before she could change her mind, she threw back the covers and forced herself out of the bed.

Still in her nightgown, she went downstairs and straight to the telephone in the hallway. But when she was halfway through dialing, she replaced the receiver and went into the kitchen.

Furious with herself, she slammed around, making coffee, squeezing oranges. Knowing it was irrational, she transferred the fury to Conor. How dare he make her afraid of him? What business was it of his anyway?

She marched back out into the hall, and before she could change her mind, dialed the number, the full number.

He answered on the second ring, sounding sleepy.

"Hello, Conor!" she barked, "still in bed?"

"Whoa," he said. "What's up with you? What happened to 'welcome home, Conor'; 'how did the work go, Conor?'; 'I've missed you, Conor!'; 'sorry I didn't write, Conor . . .'?"

She kept her spine stiff. "I'm ringing to invite you to lunch."

"I've had nicer invitations."

"Well, would you like lunch or not?"

"Yes, *sir*! How could a man refuse?"

"How about one o'clock at Kettner's?"

"Kettner's is too expensive."

"All right, McDonald's, then . . ."

"Come off it!"

"Well, where then? *I* like Kettner's. And in case you're still worried about the expense, I'm paying."

"Whoa again!" His own voice, which had been good-humored, changed. "First of all, women don't pay for me for lunch in expensive restaurants. Second, I don't think I want to go to lunch with you at all in your present mood.''

She knew he was right. "I'm a bit on edge, Conor—"

"I'll say!''

"I'm sorry. But I really would like you to come to lunch.''

"There's nowhere to park near Kettner's.'' Conor had recently purchased a battered Morris Traveller and was as proud and as careful of it as if it were a Rolls.

"It's Saturday, Conor. It'll be okay.''

"Okay. See you about one.''

She replaced the receiver and realized she was shaking.

Two hours before she was to meet him, she had a bath and dressed, a process that took three times longer than usual. All the while telling herself she was being ridiculous, she put on and discarded six different outfits. At the end of fifteen minutes, her bed resembled a stall in a jumble sale. Eventually she settled on a dress of pale blue silk with Fortuny pleating on the sleeves.

She arrived at the restaurant early. There was a brown, comfortable glow to Kettner's, and one of the reasons she liked it was that, compared to other fashionable places, the waiters did not harry or hurry the patrons, even when the restaurant was busy. As this was Saturday (an anniversary of her first lunch with Christian, she thought), there was plenty of space.

She was seated at a table in the bar area when Conor loomed through the door, dressed to match his Morris Traveller in old, sagging tweeds. He looked tanned and fit and his hair was shaggy. No one would have taken him for a humble zoo attendant, she thought fondly, temporarily forgetting her nerves and waving to attract his attention. He spotted her immediately and came toward her.

He stood off a little in mock fear: "Is it all right to kiss you, *mein führer*?''

"Don't be silly, Conor. I'm sorry about earlier.''

"Let's start all over again,'' he said, kissing her on the cheek and lowering himself into a chair beside her. "Hello! How are you today?'' He eyed her up and down. "My, don't we look smart!''

"Oh this old thing," she said, and drew on her acting skills to emit a light laugh. "Would you like a drink?"

"Let's get this straight," he said, taking off his coat. "I hate this. Drinks cost a fortune in this place."

"No more than anywhere else in central London," she protested. "But you're my guest and don't insult me."

"I'm sorry, Molly," he said, "but this is way out of my league."

"It's in my league now that I'm going to be a famous film star. So shut up, Conor, and just have a bloody drink."

"I hate this . . ." he repeated.

"I know. But think, when you're a famous archaeologist, you can invite me to your digs in the desert—and then you can be host and feed me ass's milk or whatever."

"It's unlikely I'll even pass my exams at the rate I'm going now."

She attracted the attention of one of the waiters and ordered a Bellini for herself. "And what'll you have, Conor?"

He fixed the waiter with a steely eye. "A glass of plain tap water, please."

"Really, Conor!" she said after the waiter had gone. "That was a bit unnecessary."

He ignored the rebuke and settled into his chair. "So what have you been doing with yourself lately? Tell me about the film."

"All in good time." She knew she should spit it out and get it over with. But she couldn't. She had not even had the guts to wear Christian's engagement ring, which was in a zippered pocket on the inside of her handbag.

He sighed. "Such suspense. Always the Sarah Bernhardt!"

When the drinks came, they talked about his work, what he now regarded as his real work, which was archaeology as opposed to his work at the zoo, which he used merely as a funding supply. There was a lot of work going on in Africa, he told her, where various expeditions in Tanzania, Kenya, and Ethiopia were pushing back the frontiers of man's birth on this planet. "You probably heard about the Leakeys, Molly, they're doing wonderful work, but there's another expedition working in Ethiopia, led by a man called Johanson. There are rumors floating around that he has found a full skeleton of a woman which might prove that man, as we know the species now, could be two million years older than we thought it was . . .''

They were called to their table and ordered their lunch. Conor continued to talk about his new vocation and tried to explain why it was so exciting. He peppered his conversation with technical jargon Molly did not understand. She realized she had not seen him so animated for years, but all the time, the flow of talk passed around the great dam of what she had to tell him.

She half listened, half rehearsed what she was going to say, while nodding at suitable junctures and asking what she hoped were reasonably intelligent questions. The more work and study he had to do, the better Conor liked it, it seemed. He told her that even though he had not got into Heathrow until ten o'clock last night, he had been up until four-thirty that morning working on a paper—hence the sleepy voice on the telephone.

After the food arrived, Molly found it difficult to eat and pushed her salad around on her plate. She had to tell him and soon. But there seemed no natural opening in Conor's flow of enthusiasm. Maybe she had been making mountains out of molehills and her news would not be a problem after all.

Oh, by the way, I'm engaged . . .

She watched him digging into his steak, thinking that it was one thing her brother had in common with her fiancé; Conor always ordered steak in restaurants. If there was no steak, he ordered chops. If there were no chops, he grudgingly ordered fish. Plain fish. He had it all planned, Conor was telling her now. As soon as he could earn his living as a professional in the field, he would give up his job and would offer his services as a researcher to one of the established digs.

"Of course I'll have to do a post-graduate course before I'm accepted in the real world of archaeology. I've already decided what it's going to be on—I won't tell you, it'd take me ten minutes to explain it—but I will be able to go on real digs. Imagine, Molly! I might be the one to fill a gap in what we know about our ancestors. I might be the one to find a new type of axehead used by *Homo Habilis* or even *Australopithecus africanus*!''

"Imagine!" Molly said dryly.

"Sorry!" He grinned, playing havoc with Molly's determination to be strong. She watched him mop up the gravy on his plate with the last piece of steak; he put the meat in his mouth then placed his knife and fork carefully together on his clean plate and sat back. "Now it's your turn. How was the film?"

"It was really exciting . . ."

"That's all you've got to say about it?" He mimicked her: "It was really exciting . . ."

"Well, it was."

"Come on, tell. What about this fellow Eugene Lothar? What was he like?"

No more procrastinating. Molly took a deep breath. "I'll tell you about it in a minute, but the real reason I asked you to lunch is that I've something to show you."

She reached under the table for her handbag and found the ring, slipping it on her finger before bringing her hand up to show him. The chatter and clatter all around seemed to rise in volume as he stared at it. His face seemed to close up, but although she watched him intently, Molly could see no trace of anger; she was having difficulty in analyzing her own feelings and realized that on one level she would have welcomed a scene. "Who's the lucky man?" he asked at last.

"It's Christian Smith, the American journalist you met in my dressing room the night he and his photographer came around. Do you remember?"

"That phoney!" She saw he was genuinely scandalized. She now regretted telling him about Christian's introductory ruse and the spuriousness of the award. At least this reaction was something real; Molly could with justification defend her fiancé. "Please, Conor," she said stiffly, "whatever else Christian is, he's not a phoney."

"I see," he said. His face was like granite. She must not panic, must stay in control.

"When did this happen?"

"Four weeks ago. What does it matter when?"

"I don't suppose it does really. What's the attraction. Is he rich?"

"That, Conor, is none of your business!" She was now genuinely angry at her own motives being impugned. "I think, brother dear, that you might, for instance, say, 'congratulations,' or wish me a happy life—or whatever is customary on these occasions.'' They glared at one another.

Conor was the one to give in. ''You're absolutely right,'' he said quietly. ''I'm sorry. I do wish you a very happy life, Molly, I really do.''

To her annoyance, she saw that during the exchange she had hidden the ring on her left hand with the fingers of the right. She uncovered it and laid the hand squarely in view beside her plate, which was still full of salad. ''I was hoping you'd come to Chicago and give me away at my wedding,'' she said.

''I can't afford to go to Chicago.''

''Your fare would be a built-in part of the wedding expenses.''

''Oh! And I suppose *he'd* pay . . .'' He was getting angry again.

''His name is Christian.'' There was another standoff. She reached down under the table to pick up her handbag. She put it on the table and took out a handkerchief.

''Don't tell me you're going to cry!''

She scrubbed at a nonexistent spot on the sleeve of her dress. ''No, I'm not going to cry. I'm not the crying type. I have no reason to cry. I'm not the one who is being irrational.''

''Have you told Brendan?''

''What has Brendan to do with it?'' she asked, astonished.

''He's your brother. The head of the family.''

''Come off it, Conor!''

He picked up his knife and began to chase a fragment of *mange-tout* around the plate. Molly knew Conor hated any vegetable that came only in French. ''You're my brother,'' she said, softly. ''As far as I'm concerned, you're the one who matters. Don't make this any harder than it is, Conor. I was afraid to tell you. I shouldn't have been.''

He continued to push the *mange-tout* around. ''I think you're making a mistake,'' he said. ''But clearly, anything I think or say will have no effect.''

Again it took all Molly's strength and resolve to stay firmly on the path she had chosen. Deliberately she conjured up Christian's beautiful face, his wide, wicked grin.

"I'm afraid not," she said. "It's all planned. We're getting married in Evanston, in Christian's house, on the second of May. And I hope you'll be there."

"You could have written to me."

That was easy. "I was genuinely too busy on the film."

"I see," he said slowly. "Well, the second of May is only a couple of weeks away. I have my exams coming up less than a month later. Even if I wanted to, I couldn't possibly take time off to go to America." He placed his knife and fork carefully together again. "And I don't want to. That's final. Now let's talk about other things."

Molly stared at him, her thoughts scrambled, disappointment competing with a strange relief at his decisiveness; not having him around the place during the wedding would take a certain tension out of the air. She wanted to get away now, as fast as possible. She felt too near to him; their table was small and she could smell the age of his jacket.

Nevertheless, she had to endure another quarter hour as they had their coffee. She forced herself to chatter about the movie, about Eugene Lothar and the goings-on between his wife and his mistress on the set.

He made monosyllabic responses and seemed to be paying no attention to the content of her chatter.

"Oh, how could I have forgotten, there are more congratulations in order!" Molly broke the news about her award. "I've been nominated for an Olivier." At least that drew a response. He looked up from his coffeecup: "Is that a big award?"

"The biggest in the West End!"

He seemed genuinely pleased. "That's brilliant, Molly!" Impulsively he seized her hand across the table and then, just as fast, dropped it, and she realized he had felt the ring.

"I've only been nominated, mind," she said desperately. "There are a few other contenders. Heavyweights! But it's a real honor."

"I'm so pleased, I really am." The phrase just lay there between them, and there seemed nothing further to say. "Bill, please, waiter!" Molly called, and took her credit cards out of her handbag. She made a great play of selecting the correct one.

"Where are you going now?" His tone implied that he didn't much care.

"I'm going to do an interview." She did not tell him that she was meeting Christian there, that Una O'Connor had persuaded her to bring Christian along to be interviewed too.

"I'll give you a lift."

"Not necessary, Conor!" Molly really did want to get away from him—and from her own treacherous feelings in his presence. "I can easily get a taxi."

"I'll give you a lift!" His voice was vehement.

"All right, if you're sure it's not too much trouble."

"It's not too much trouble."

There was silence between them for the next five minutes as Molly paid the bill and waited for her receipt. It was raining when they left the restaurant, and as neither had an umbrella, they had to run to the Traveller, which was parked about fifty yards away. Breathless as she got into the car, Molly was conscious all over again of his male smell, now overlain with the thick aroma of damp tweed.

Conor drove as fast as the traffic lights allowed and never once glanced across in her direction. She could not fathom his mood; was he angry? Upset? He was her brother, after all, why couldn't she just *ask* him . . . Try as she might, she could think of no suitable way to broach the topic.

When they pulled up outside the Cumberland at Marble Arch, Molly spotted Una O'Connor hurrying along toward the entrance.

"There's the reporter, Una O'Connor!" she exclaimed, and jumped out of the car.

"Una! Hello, Una!" she called.

Una heard her name called and turned around. Molly was standing by the door of a car, waving at her. She waved back and walked as far as the car.

"You remember, er, Seán Molloy?" said Molly, indicating the driver of the car. Una's heart lurched. He was leaning across the steering wheel to say hello to her—at least his lips were moving and she thought that must be what he was saying. She had the confused impression that his hair was longer than she remembered. "Hello,

Mr. Molloy,'' she answered, mustering every ounce of
sang-froid in her meager store, ''what a surprise! How've
you been?'' she added, mentally kicking herself for being so trite.

''I've been fine,'' he said.

''You've a great tan. Have you been away?'' Her smile,
she knew, was as cretinous as the remark, but again he
answered courteously. ''I was in Israel actually, on an
archaeological dig.'' If he was being sarcastic, it didn't
show.

Una became uncomfortably conscious of Molly standing behind her back as she leaned into the car. Damn.
She couldn't let this opportunity slip, it might be the only
one.

Desperate measures.

Egalitarianism between sexes and classes was one of
the few perks of her profession and now was a perfect
opportunity to take advantage of it. ''Would you like to
have lunch sometime?'' she blurted. She saw him glance
at Molly and registered the look for later analysis. ''I'd
love to!'' he said coolly. ''Here's my telephone number.
Next time you're in London, Miss O'Connor.''

''Una, please,'' she said faintly.

He fished a pen from his pocket and searched for paper. Flabbergasted though she was, Una was more aware
than ever of the actress standing behind her. ''Sorry,''
she said, turning around: ''This'll only take a sec . . .''
Her interviewee was staring off into the middle distance,
away from the car.

Una turned back into the Morris just as Seán Molloy
found an old playing card under the front seat. He scribbled a number on it and handed it over. ''Looking forward to it,'' he said. ''Becoming quite a habit, being
taken to lunch! Good-bye, Molly'' he called, leaning farther across so he could peer out. ''Thanks for the lunch.
Delicious!''

Una did not know what was going on and she did not
care. She clutched the precious playing card in her hand
and waved as he closed the door. ''Well,'' she said,
watching the receding rear end of the Morris Traveller,
''shall we go in?''

There was no mistaking the fiancé when they walked
into the lobby; he lit up like a Christmas tree when they

walked in. He was beautiful and charming and she could see other women in the lobby shooting glances at him. But, she decided, as early as ten seconds into the introductions, he was definitely not a man of substance.

She smiled brilliantly at both of them and walked ahead of them into the coffee shop to do the interview.

9

A few days later, on the twenty-eighth of April, it was a pet day in Tullyhalla, the sort of day that called a truce in Father Moran's long war of attrition with the Irish weather. The sun was as kind as summer and warmed the top of his balding head. There was only the gentlest of breezes, and it was so quiet in the village that he could actually hear the leaves rustling in all the new trees planted along the street by the county council and the Tidy Towns committee. He came out of the church after morning Mass and stood for a few moments, enjoying the air, listening dreamily to the whining of Silvie Cash's Honda 50 as, counterpointing the gentleness of the morning, it came up the street in fits and starts.

"Hello, Father!" the postman shouted as he approached the church. The man's relentless cheeriness usually got on Father Moran's nerves, but today he waved back as Silvie swerved into the churchyard, guided his red steed in a half-circle, and skidded to a halt in front of him, spraying gravel into the flowerbeds. "Not supposed to do this, Father!" he said, shouting above the nasal cough of his engine. "Not supposed to deviate from the proper route!" He pronounced "deviate" the local way, with the emphasis on the "ate." "But sure since 'tis yourself," he continued, sorting busily through his bag, "we can make an exception. Isn't it a lovely day, Father, thank God and His Mother! Lovely entirely! Great out!"

He handed three letters to the priest, tipped his cap, revved hugely, and shot out the gate. Father Moran looked at his letters and his heart jolted, making him feel nauseated. One of the letters bore an American postmark and the logo of the Federal Aviation Administration. His impulse was to tear it open right away, but he restrained himself, gripping it tightly, thinking that the letter must be blinking like a neon sign, thinking that everyone in the village must have noticed the delivery. There was not a soul within thirty yards of him, but across the road, the grocer was raising the blinds on his shop and carting in the stack of newspapers thrown on his porch by the driver of the Galway bus; everyone in the village knew that the grocer had eyes like a hawk.

The letter seemed to pulsate in Father Moran's hands as he stood, trying to decide whether to go to his house or back into the church. He remembered that it was a Fair Day in the nearby town of Toome and his heart sank. Mrs. Conway always wanted to get breakfast over with quickly on a Fair Day so she could be ready when her nephew called to drive her into town. She would know that Mass had been over ten minutes ago.

The envelope burned his hand as he walked the fifty yards to his front door. It would now have to wait until after breakfast. Before he went into the kitchen, he stuffed all three of the letters behind the glass of his bureau in the dining room.

He saw that Mrs. Conway, sitting on a stool in the corner of the kitchen, already had her hat on. "Sorry I'm a bit late, Mrs. Conway," he said with false heartiness. "Silvie delayed me . . ."

She sniffed. "That's all right, Father. It's none of my business, of course." Peg Conway had been widowed at the age of twenty-seven and had kept house for priests ever since. She had a brother, a bishop.

Father Moran attacked the rashers, eggs, sausages, and tomato she set before him, eating very fast, dying to get to the letter. But he was afraid to arouse the slightest suspicion by behaving in any way differently. So he ate the fry and two slices of toast spread with butter and homemade marmalade and drank two cups of tea, as he did every morning. Then he thanked Mrs. Conway as usual, and leaving her to clear the table, went into the little dining room, which he always referred to as his "study."

But it was not until he heard the horn of the nephew's car, followed by the bang of the front door as she left, that he dared to take the three letters out from behind the glass.

He took a deep breath and opened the one from America.

It was signed by someone called Philip Froelich, and informed Father Moran that sometime between the night of April 30 and May 1, 1953, a DC3 had ditched in the sea somewhere off the coast of Ireland, on a flight between Reykjavik and Shannon. The flight, which had originated at O'Hare International Airport in Chicago, had been chartered by a family named Smith, from Evanston, Illinois, and including the crew of three, had been carrying seven persons, six adults and a one-year-old baby girl. No bodies had ever been found, although several months after the accident, some pieces of wreckage had been washed up along the coast of the southwest of Ireland. An investigation had concluded that the aircraft had been caught in a bad storm, had gone off course, and had run out of fuel.

Now he knew.

Yet he knew nothing. Only that her name was Smith and she was from Evanston, Illinois, which he supposed, since the plane had taken off from there, was near Chicago. Her family had chartered an aircraft so they had probably been rich.

Not really knowing quite why he was doing it, Father Moran took a piece of paper and wrote, "Smith, Evanston" on it with a shaky hand. He folded the paper and put it in his pocket, then, unlocking the bottom of the bureau, took out the shoe box. Carefully folding the letter back into its envelope, he inserted it under the pile of clippings in the box, making sure it was completely hidden before replacing the lid; then he put the box back where it belonged and relocked the door of the bureau.

He stuffed the other two unopened letters, one that he recognized as a circular from his old school, the other a bill, into the pewter tankard on the desk part of his bureau. He looked at his watch, only nine-thirty. He wondered if he dared have a drink so early in the day; he had a funeral Mass, but since it was a Fair Day in Toome, the Mass was at eleven instead of the usual ten and he had nothing formal to do until then.

He went into the living room and opened the press that contained the whiskey, but immediately closed it again.

He had better not. Even if he ate mints, the mourners at the funeral were sure to notice the smell of his breath.

He stood looking out at Tullyhalla, at the wide street, the small single-story and two-story houses in varying degrees of order, some white, some colorwashed, some derelict, all leaning intimately against each other like the old, comfortable neighbors they were; at the chicken mesh erected by the county council around the boles of the sapling trees; at the two shiny new litter bins, against the base of which drifted a sea of lollipop wrappers, potato-crisp bags, and half-squashed soft-drink cans. At the far end of the street, a county council worker was alternately wheeling a pushcart and pushing a brush along the gutter. Directly opposite the house, the grocer was using a small paintbrush and a bowl of whitewash to paint the details of special offers on his shop window. The woman in the house beside the shop was cleaning the brasses on her door.

Father Moran took out the piece of paper from his pocket. "Smith, Evanston."

He tried to picture Evanston. He saw it as sunny, with good-looking American kids roller skating on the sidewalks or carrying tennis rackets slung casually over their shoulders. If it was anything like the richer parts of San Diego, where years ago as a young priest he had spent an idyllic ten months, it would be leafy, with wide streets and all the houses would be on separate lots, with no dividing walls. In the early mornings, women would drive husbands to the commuter train in station wagons, maneuvering past the large cars already parked neatly in the Park 'N Ride lot beside the tracks.

His Molly had been deprived of this sylvan, easygoing way of life and dumped into the wild barrenness of Inisheer. But now that he knew, the knowing was anticlimactic and he needed to know more . . . He looked again at the drinks press but turned decisively away. Like Scarlett O'Hara, he would think seriously about his problem tomorrow.

He went out the front door of his house, leaving it open after him, and crossed the road to the shop, where he bought two Cadbury's Flakes for which he had long had a passion, never chewing them but letting the slivers of chocolate melt slowly and deliciously in his mouth.

He picked up his daily copies of the *Irish Independent* and the *Irish Record,* and as usual he divided his change amongst the various charity boxes on the shop counter.

He went back to the house and into the cheerless kitchen, where he put on the kettle for a cup of tea, savoring his first Flake as he waited for the water to boil. He made the tea, poured it out, and carried it to the table. Then he opened the second Flake and spread out the *Independent,* turning first to the death notices, followed by the sports pages.

He was only halfway through the paper when he was interrupted by the telephone. After the call he hurried back into the kitchen, washed up his cup, rinsed out the teapot, and refolded the *Irish Independent,* taking it with the *Record* into his "study" for later perusal.

His pastoral work kept him out all day, and it was actually after six o'clock that evening before Father Moran got back to reading his newspapers.

It was well past his teatime when he let himself back into his house. Mrs. Conway was nowhere to be seen but, as a reproach, there was a plate of congealed lamb chop and chips set on the table in the kitchen, symmetrically placed between his knife and fork. The priest had already had a huge funeral meal with the mourners and could not face another mouthful of food. Feeling guilty, he dumped the unappetizing mess in the bin by the back door, put the plate and cutlery in the sink, and then went into his study via the cupboard in the front room from which he poured himself a substantial whiskey.

In the study, whiskey by his side, he opened the *Independent* and tried to concentrate on the news pages. The paper was full of the Beit art robbery. According to the newspaper, the paintings were said to be worth £8 million. *Eight million* pounds, thought Father Moran enviously. What he could do with that kind of money—what the parish, even the diocese, could do . . .

After a few minutes he threw aside the *Independent* and picked up the *Irish Record,* whose lead story was also about the art robbery. He checked the death notices on the back page, then, almost too tired to turn the pages, flicked from back to front through the rest of the paper.

She was there on page five.

Galvanized out of his torpor, Father Moran read Una

O'Connor's page-long feature with growing horror. Margo Bryan, local girl, successful actress and film star, was due to marry Christian Smith, heir to a brewery fortune in the United States. *Mr. Smith,* wrote Una, *has at last found happiness after a lifetime of tragedy. Born with a silver spoon in his mouth, his sheltered life was shattered when his mother, father, and baby sister were killed in an air disaster.*

Ironically, the piece went on, *although she was too young to have been aware of it, the DC3 in which her future husband's family was traveling ditched into the sea within a hundred miles of where Margo Bryan, whose real name, as is well-known in Ireland, is Molly Ní Bhriain, was born and reared . . .*

The rest of the page blurred in front of Father Moran's eyes.

Molly, his Molly, was about to marry her brother.

The paper rattled as his hands started to shake. He'd always known she would get married some day and had tried psychologically to prepare himself for the notion of her in some other man's bed. But even that awful prospect was superseded by the knowledge of this billion-to-one chance.

He railed at the unfairness of his dilemma. Of course he had to do something to stop this incestuous marriage, yet how could he reveal how he knew the truth? He was solemnly bound by the secrecy of the confessional. He had already betrayed that warrant by writing as he had to the FAA and Lloyds. And to whom should he confess? To Molly? How could he approach *her*? He felt weak and nauseated.

He made it up the stairs to the bathroom just in time to void the half-digested funeral meal. Again and again he vomited violently, until he was retching dry and the tears ran freely down his face. Exhausted, he flushed the lavatory and sank to the floor, resting his wet cheek against the smooth coolness of the bowl.

He struggled to his feet after a minute or so, washed his face, and went into his bedroom, where he sat on his bed and faced the truth. He had been weak all his life; now was the time, whether he liked it or not, when he had to behave with honor and courage, no matter what the personal consequences.

He went back into the bathroom and brushed his teeth to get the sour taste out of his mouth, then went downstairs and picked up the *Record* from where he had dropped it on the floor. He read the article again. There was no time to lose. The wedding, which was to be at the bridegroom's home in Evanston, was scheduled, apparently, for May 2. That was only three days away. Molly and this fellow—he could not bring himself to think of him as her fiancé, or even as her brother—were probably already in America, so that removed one option. It was not the type of news he could announce over the telephone and he could hardly arrive at their doorstep. He was relieved. At least he would not have to see her face-to-face.

Since there had been no bodies found, would the accident-investigation files on the air crash have remained open? Could he telephone the FAA anonymously, telling them he had certain information about the accident?

But if he did that would they act quickly enough? Would they contact Molly at all before they went through their files? And what possible reason could he give them for wishing to remain anonymous? They would think him a crackpot and dismiss him.

He looked at the article in the *Record* once again. This Una O'Connor—she would surely be interested in the story. And reporters were known to respect anonymous tipoffs and never to reveal their sources . . .

Father Moran quailed at the notion of talking to a reporter, especially on such a subject, but before his imagination could run too far with him, he used the phone to get the telephone number of the *Irish Record* in Dublin.

"*Irish Record?*" The call was picked up by a woman.

"Could I speak to Una O'Connor, please?"

"One moment, please."

He heard another tone and then, after the telephone had been lifted, a background hubbub: voices, typewriters, machinery. The sound was muted immediately. Whoever had picked up the extension had covered the mouthpiece. He could hear the muffled voice. Father Moran was now in an agony of impatience. He wanted to get it over with, whatever "it" was. At last a man came on: "Sorry for holding you—can I help you?"

"May I—may I speak to Una O'Connor, please?"

"Una's on a few days off. Can I take a message?"

"When will she be back?" Again the background noise was muted as the man obviously made inquiries. He came back on again. "Not till Wednesday, I believe."

"It's very important that I get in contact with her. Could you tell me where she is, please?"

"Is this to do with a story?"

"No, it's personal."

"I'm sorry, we don't give out telephone numbers or details about our staff."

"But it's a matter of life and death!"

"If you care to leave your name and number," said the man patiently, "I'll make sure she gets it if she calls in—*if* she calls in."

"No, that's all right," said Father Moran, and hung up abruptly. His heart was thumping. He looked stupidly at the silent black instrument, which seemed to leer back at him.

He would write anonymously to Una O'Connor and would hand-deliver the letter to her office in Dublin. It would be perilously close to the wire; her colleague had said she would not be back at work until Wednesday and Wednesday was the first of May, the day before the wedding. But once she read the letter, she would surely see the importance of urgent action. Miss O'Connor would also be morally obliged to do something about the information once it was in her hands. Indeed she would be happy to do so, since no doubt it would provide her with material.

He hurried to his desk, and before he could change his mind, pulled his writing pad toward him and took a biro out of the breast pocket of his black jacket.

He put no return address on the top right-hand corner of the page and began to write:

Dear Miss O'Connor,
Please forgive my intruding like this and the haste in which I write, but I feel I must inform you of a matter, arising out of your article in today's newspaper, concerning the actress Margo Bryan—Molly Ní Bhriain—and her forthcoming marriage to the American journalist, a Mr. Christian Smith.

Before I tell you of my concerns, please do not believe I am a busybody, or a gossip and please be assured that I write from the highest moral standpoint.

He reread the second paragraph and realized that it made him sound as if he were, indeed, a moral snoop. So he tore up the letter and began again.

Dear Miss O'Connor,

I am sorry for bothering you, but I read your article in today's newspaper and I think I have some very urgent information concerning it in which you may be interested. I have followed Miss Bryan's career with great interest and was at first happy to see from your article that she was going to be married. Unfortunately, I have received knowledge, I cannot reveal how, but believe me, the source for this knowledge is absolutely unimpeachable, that by a million-to-one chance, Molly Ní Bhriain and the American journalist, Christian Smith, are in fact brother and sister.

I know it sounds absolutely extraordinary, but if you write or telephone the Washington-based Federal Aviation Administration, they will confirm that on the night of April 30, 1953—the very night you mention in your article—a baby was lost at sea in an aircrash off the coast of Ireland.

Miss O'Connor, that baby was not killed in the crash but survived. She was washed up on Inisheer and was brought up by a poor family there named OBriain. I enclose a letter I received from the FAA confirming the crash, as I had reason to make this investigation myself.

I know that this is very difficult to believe, Miss O'Connor, but for professional, ethical, and moral reasons, I cannot reveal how I came by this information in the first place. It was revealed to me on an absolutely confidential basis and I have tortured myself since I received the letter from the FAA as to whether I should break this confidentiality. Were it not for this million-to-one chance, I would have carried the secret of Molly Ni Bhriain's true identity with me to the grave. But as I think you will see clearly, I am now taking this grave step only to prevent a greater moral problem and possible disaster for the two young people involved. As God is my judge, Miss O'Connor, I have nothing but their best interests at heart. For the same ethical and moral reasons for which I cannot reveal my source, I cannot myself approach the couple.

I am sure you will appreciate the significance of this information and I hope I can rely on your good sense to see, as I do, that this marriage cannot go ahead.

I took the liberty of telephoning your office and your colleague there informed me that you were not due back from holiday until Wednesday the 1st of May. But as you can see from your own article, which I also enclose, this marriage is to take place in Evanston, Illinois, on the 2nd of May. As you can see, the matter is one of extreme urgency.

I hope I can also rely on your discretion. And as an intelligent woman, you will possibly understand from the foregoing why I cannot sign my name.

Before he could change his mind, he unlocked the bureau, removed the FAA letter from the shoe box, and carefully tearing off the *"Dear Father Moran"* at the top, he folded it inside the letter he had written to Una O'Connor. He put the two letters in an envelope and addressed it to her, marking it "By Hand." Then, for reasons of security, he stuffed into his jacket pocket the fragments of the first letter and the "Dear Father Moran" piece he had torn off the one from the FAA.

There, it was done! He stared at the envelope on the desk. It mocked him. This was too dangerous. If and when she rang the FAA, they would have a copy of the letter to him in the Smith file, and he had no guarantee that his identity would not be disclosed.

He was being dispicably cowardly and selfish. How would Molly react to a reporter giving her such news, which wrecked her marriage prospects and exposed her to the possibility—no, probability—of public exposure?

There was only one other option open to him, the advice of the church; venerable as she was, there would surely be a precedent for this situation. He would have to confide in someone in ecclesiastical authority. Not his bishop, who was old and very conservative. That would

be too difficult and too galling. He decided to go to see
Ned O'Neill.

Father Edward O'Neill a Jesuit, had been Father Moran's spiritual adviser in the seminary in Maynooth. Ned,
who was now nearly ninety, was tolerant and wise, with
a bubbling sense of humor. Nothing, or hardly anything,
could surprise Ned. He had been confidante and friend
to hundreds of young seminarians, many of whom, including Father Moran, had stayed in touch. Ned would
know what to do. He had taken a few steps toward the
door into the hallway when he heard the key in the lock
of the front door. Mrs. Conway! He had temporarily forgotten Mrs. Conway . . .

He dashed back to the bureau and picked up the envelope addressed to Una O'Connor. Panicked, he looked
around. There was no fire in the grate. He scooped the
clippings out of the box and shoved the envelope under
them, replaced them, put the lid back on, and threw the
box into the bureau. He was locking it when she came
into the room.

"Good evening, Father," she said. To his horror, he
saw as he turned around toward her that one of the clippings had fallen out. "Hello, Mrs. Conway," he said
with phoney cheeriness, straightening up. He took a step
toward her so that he stood on the clipping. Had she seen
it?

She gave no indication she had. "I was down the village, Father, visiting Sarah Sheehan. She isn't long for
this world."

"Well, Mrs. Conway, she's a great age, God bless
her . . ." There was a corner of the clipping sticking out
from under his foot.

"I just came in to get my prayerbook, Father, I'm going over to the church to do the Stations . . ."

"Right, right, Mrs. Conway!" Still he didn't move. If
it had not been so fraught with danger, the scene, he
thought, might have been from a Marx Brothers comedy.
He was even tempted to giggle.

"Will I put down a fire for you, Father?" she said,
looking at the empty fireplace, "it's turning chilly."

"No, that's all right, Mrs. Conway. But would you
mind turning on the half-six news on the radio?" The
radio was in the kitchen.

"It must be nearly over, Father . . ."

"It's the weather forecast I'm interested in."

"All right, so!"

Mercifully, she left the room. He would never make a spy, he thought, picking up the clipping and mushing it in with the rest of the paper in his jacket pocket, which, he thought, was beginning to feel like a waste-paper basket. When Mrs. Conway came out into the hallway again, clutching her tattered prayerbook, he saw her to the door and closed it after her, then went immediately to the telephone.

He was in luck. Ned O'Neill was there. "Pat!" The old priest's voice, still strong, was filled with pleasure.

"Sorry for the short notice, Ned, but can I come to see you—this evening?"

"That urgent?" Ned's voice was cheerfully noncommittal. "Not thinking of leaving at this stage, I hope?" Father Moran laughed uneasily. "No, nothing like that, Ned, but it is very important."

"Well, whatever it is, can it wait for a couple of days?" asked the other man. "I'm invited to Maynooth tonight—in fact, you just caught me, my lift's just arrived—and one of my grandnephews is bringing me to Cavan tomorrow to do a bit of fishing . . ."

Father Moran clenched his fist on the telephone table. "I'm afraid it's a little bit more urgent than that, Monsignor!" He checked his watch. "It's only a quarter to seven and there's still an hour or two of daylight. How long will you be in Maynooth? I could be there in less than two and a half hours if you could see me there tonight. That's if I wouldn't be intruding on your dinner . . ."

Ned O'Neill's tone had changed subtly yet again. "I see. Well, Pat, certainly. And you certainly wouldn't be intruding. It'll be just a lot of old fogeys like myself, and I'm sure we'll run out of steam long before you arrive. I'm staying overnight in Maynooth anyway, and at my age, old bones don't need all that much sleep. I'll expect you so. I'll leave a message at the front where I can be found. Don't worry, I'll stay up for you—so don't kill anyone on the roads in your hurry!"

"I won't, Father!" promised Father Moran as he hung up. After he replaced the receiver, he again felt weak, and clutched at the edge of the telephone table to steady himself. He ought to eat something, he thought, since his stomach was now completely empty. Instead, forgetting he already had a whiskey in the study, he went to the drinks press in the living room and poured himself another one, which he drained in one long draft. The liquor warmed him all through, making him feel instantly better.

He poured himself a second, smaller one and took it with him into his study, where the television still laughed at itself in the exercise of a quiz show. He turned off the set and, decisive now, scribbled a note to Mrs. Conway, telling her he had been called away urgently overnight, but that he would see her around dinnertime tomorrow. It was the luck of God, he thought, draining his second whiskey, that she was out in the church and he didn't have to face any questions. If he got a move on, he would be well away before she got back.

He put the note on the draining board in the kitchen, put in a call to Wynn's Hotel in Dublin where he always stayed when in the capital, and took a clean pair of pajamas and underpants from the hotpress beside the Aga heater. Then he collected his toothbrush, toothpaste, and electric razor from the bathroom, and his breviary from the bedroom and, rolling the whole lot together, put them in a briefcase he pulled out from under the bed. Before he left, he went back into the living room, and watching out the window for Mrs. Conway's return, he poured one more whiskey, a small one, just to give him courage.

Luck stayed with him. He had started his car, a three-year-old Ford Escort, when he saw her leaving the church. Pretending not to see her, he gunned the engine and shot out the gate, roaring off up the street in the direction of Loughrea and the main road to Dublin. The roads were relatively clear and he drove fast, concentrating, aware that he had had a couple of drinks. There was a symphony concert on the radio, Beethoven's "Pastoral," a piece he had loved all his life.

It started to rain just outside Aughrim and he turned on the Escort's wipers. But their rhythmic swishing combined with the lush strings of the symphony so that by Athlone, despite having opened the side window of the car, the drinks he had taken earlier were affecting him and he was really having to fight hard to stay awake. He pulled into the parking lot of the Monarch Hotel to take a break.

The lobby was hopping and there were two separate sing-songs in progress, one in the bar, the other in a function room. As far as he could make out, Father Moran realized that there had been two separate wedding receptions in the hotel and that the guests were now intermingling in one huge party.

"Have a drink, Father?" Father Moran looked around. The man, enormously fat, with long strings of hair crossing his bald pate like a five-barred gate, was seated in an armchair in the lobby, holding up his own pint, which wobbled dangerously in his hand and threatened to spill over his gaping shirt front. "No, thank you," said Father Moran politely, and went into the bar.

The staff, two young women and a man, were running up and down along the bar, barely able to keep up with the demand. Half-pulled pints stood in neat rows along the counter. Father Moran found a vacant spot at a corner of the bar and managed to attract the attention of one of the women. "Could I have a sandwich, please?"

"What kind of sandwich, Father?"

"Anything you have," he said, in deference to the chaos.

"I'll have to go into the kitchen; would ham be all right?"

"Ham'd be fine!"

"Do you want a drink, Father?"

"Yes," he said, "I'll have a whiskey . . . Make it a double," he said then. It would be all right, he reassured himself, the sandwich would counter the effect. He had finished the whiskey before the sandwich arrived and ordered a half of beer to drink with it. Aware of eyes from all over the room watching him at the counter, he felt very uncomfortable and wished he had had the sense to change into civvies. He bolted the sandwich, gulped down the beer, and left as quickly as he possibly could.

It was a quarter to eleven when he reached Maynooth. But seeing the enormous gates, his courage failed him, and instead of turning right, which would have brought him into the seminary, he kept to the main road and drove through the town and out again on to the main road toward Dublin.

He thought briefly of getting out to have a walk to clear his head, but decided instead to have another sandwich in the next town of Leixlip. There was a pub on the main street, but each side of the road was choc-a-block with cars and there was nowhere to park. He drove on, turned right over the bridge, and saw that at the end of the bridge was another pub. This one did have a parking lot.

He pulled into it. He felt quite good now. It would not be long before Ned O'Neill would help him sort the whole thing out.

The pub was doing a brisk trade, but again he found a vacant stool at the bar. All that was available in the food line was yet another ham sandwich. "Anything to drink, Father?" asked the young barman.

"I'll have a beer," said Father Moran. "No, better change that," he amended. "Make it a mineral!"

"Britvic?" asked the barman.

Father Moran changed his mind a third time. "I'll have a coffee and a small Irish." The barman sighed and looked pointedly at his watch, but set the whiskey in front of him and then went off to get the sandwich and to put on the kettle for the coffee.

Father Moran saw, as he sipped the whiskey, that he was the only person there who was alone. People, men and women, sat in groups, laughing, chattering, enjoying each other's company. A blue cloud of cigarette and cigar smoke hung in strands in the air above their heads. On one side of him at the bar sat a group of three men, obviously well-heeled and old friends, who were guffawing loudly; the couple on Father Moran's other side were oblivious to everything except one another. Their drinks were untouched on the bar counter as they sat, his knees clutched around hers, gazing ardently into one another's eyes.

The priest stared into the golden depths of his own whiskey. He realized he had never felt so lonely in his life. He had come to this, he thought, sitting on a bar stool alone, half pissed. Everyone had someone, but no one cared for him. Through his fog of self-pity, he saw that the bar man had returned with the sandwich and the coffee and had asked him something. "What?" he managed.

"That'll be two pounds sixty altogether," repeated the

young man. Then: "Are you all right, Father? You don't look well."

Father Moran held up his hand. "I'm fine, son—I'm fine!" He removed the plastic wrapper and took a bite out of the sandwich, but it tasted like wallpaper and he could not face any more of it. Leaving the coffee untouched, he drained the whiskey and got off his stool. There could be no more running away.

In the parking lot, he switched on the engine, and the wipers, too, sprang into action, forward and back, forward and back. They made a little thunking sound on the "back" part before pushing aside the river of rain on the glass. He put the car in gear and drove out of the parking lot and onto the bridge, facing back into Leixlip.

As he got onto the bridge, his eyes were dazzled by the high beams of a truck that was just coming to the end of the bridge and had pulled out a little to negotiate the tight left turn. Father Moran put his right hand over his eyes to shield them against the glare and instinctively jerked the steering wheel to the left with his other hand. The truckdriver sounded his horn—a horrendous blast so close up—and Father Moran jumped in fright. As a result, his right foot gunned the accelerator.

The Ford Escort shot toward the ironwork of the old bridge and crashed through it.

More surprised than frightened, Father Moran was strangely relaxed as the car sailed through the air. Everything seemed to be in slow motion until, thirty feet below, it hit. The steering wheel cannoned into his chest but there was no immediate explosion of pain; winded, gasping for breath, he supposed the pain would come later; in his ears was a great roaring sound and he realized that his feet, which were trapped under his collapsed seat, were getting very very cold. He wondered if they were broken.

Water. There was water gushing in.

He fumbled for the door handle, but the car had come to rest at a half-sideways, half-forward angle, in such a position that he was lying heavily on the driver's door and, with the handle behind him, could not bend his arm to the angle required—although he did continue to try.

The water rushed farther up his body and the car started to spin and grind; Father Moran supposed he and

the car were impaled on a rock. He noticed that the water
was up to the level of his car radio, and, irrelevantly
wondered if a radio could survive immersion in water.
He was very cold and had started to shiver; still, however, he was not frightened. He just wished that the roaring would subside.

Father Moran almost never swore. He swore now.

"Ah, shite!" he said.

His last conscious thought, as the freezing, earth-
tasting water rushed down his throat and up his nose and
made his eyes opaque, was, absurdly, not of his immortal
soul, nor of Molly, nor of Ned O'Neill, who would by
now be getting concerned. He regretted that he had not
eaten his ham sandwich.

At the subsequent inquest, the coroner was unable to
determine whether Father Moran had made any effort to
get out of the car after it hit the water, which was in
flood. And since the priest's nearest living relatives were
all abroad, it was Mrs. Peg Conway who traveled to Dublin to claim his effects. Everything found in the car had
been packed into the briefcase.

"Here's his wallet," said the official, "and here are
his watch and the contents of his pockets." He gave Mrs.
Conway the wallet and a plastic bag containing the watch,
some coins, a pocket appointments diary, and some sodden pieces of paper.

At home that night, she opened the plastic bag. One
piece of paper had obviously been torn off a letter, the
heading of which showed it was from Washington, D.C.;
the second had Father Moran's writing on it; it was
smeared but seemed to say: "Smith, Evensong." The
third piece of paper was a piece of newspaper, soft as
tissue, but still legible. It was about Margo Bryan. Mrs.
Conway took all three pieces and burned them, setting a
match to them in the empty grate in the priest's study.
They burned slowly, but she stood and watched until they
had curled and turned to black ash. She went into the
kitchen then and sat at the table, lost in thought for a
while. Then she seemed to make a decision.

Although Father Moran's keys were in the briefcase,
she took her own set of keys out of her handbag and went
into the little dining room. She fitted one of the keys into

the bureau lock and opened the bureau, extracting the shoe box.

Mrs. Conway had not been shocked when she had discovered the contents of the shoe box several years before. He was not the first and he would not be the last priest to harbor such a passion. If anything, Peg empathized secretly, somewhere deep in a Celtic soul which no amount of Roman or puritan churchifying could entirely subdue.

She had decided out in the kitchen what she was going to do with the box and its contents. She could have burned the clippings, but she was superstitious about dead men's property. She was damned, however, if she was going to leave them for others to find, to paw over, to snigger and speculate and to sully his memory with inuendo about something they could not possibly understand.

She pulled a piece of Father Moran's unheaded notepaper to her and scribbled on it in capital letters:

FOUND AMONG THE EFFECTS OF FR. PATRICK MORAN
She opened the lid of the shoe box and put the note inside, on top of the clippings. Then, carrying the box and the lid, she went back into the kitchen, sat at the table, and taking them out one by one, read through three of the clippings until she found what she was looking for, a feature article that mentioned the name of a theater in which Margo Bryan had played. She copied down the name of the theater on another piece of paper and replaced the three clippings.

She pulled open the drawer of the dresser in which she saved wrapping paper, string, rubber bands, anything that might come in handy. She searched for a few minutes, then found a piece of strong brown paper large enough, smoothing out the creases as she brought it back to the table along with a ball of twine. She wrapped and tied the box into a neat parcel and wrote

MISS MARGO BRYAN, WYNDHAMS THEATRE,
LONDON, ENGLAND

on it in big lettering.

Then she made a cup of tea and went to bed.

Her nephew collected her next morning in time for the funeral, which was in Father Moran's home parish of Kilmacslea in County Mayo. She put the parcel on the

backseat of the car before settling herself in the front. "I
want to stop off in Tuam to post this," she said.

"But, Auntie Peg, the post office here is open!" he
protested. "We'll maybe have difficulty getting parking
in Tuam."

"Just do as you're told!" she snapped. At present, Peg
Conway trusted no one in Tullyhalla. Particularly post-
mistresses.

The church in her wisdom had given Father Moran the
benefit of the doubt with regard to suicide and allowed
him the full panoply of its funeral rites. The two shops
and three pubs in Kilmacslea closed for the morning and
the tiny stone church, which dated originally from the
twelfth century, was packed. There were thirty-one
priests and three bishops on the altar for the concele-
brated funeral Mass. Mrs. Peg Conway was the only one
in the congregation who wept at the graveside.

Molly had expected to be dazzled by the splendor of
the house in Evanston, but unexpectedly, the moment she
stepped into the wide entrance hallway, she felt immediately at home.

She stood for a few moments, looking upward along
the beautiful sweep of the grand staircase, while Christian fussed about with their bags and coats. Malcolm,
who had met them at the airport with the car, rushed off
to tell the housekeeper they had arrived, and Cordelia,
hearing them come in, came out of one of the rooms off
the hall, extending both hands. "You are very welcome
here, Margo," she said in her soft voice. "I hope you
will be very happy."

Molly liked her instantly. "Thank you, Mrs. Smith,"
she said. "I already feel welcome."

"I wish you would call me Cordelia. I hate Mrs. Smith.
If you call me Mrs. Smith, I'll call you the same!"

Molly laughed. "All right, Cordelia. And please,
would you call me Molly? Margo is only my stage
name."

"I much prefer Molly anyway!" Cordelia smiled.

Christian took Molly's arm. "Come on! I want to take
you down to the lake."

"Christian," protested Cordelia, "I'm sure Molly's
very tired and would like to wash up."

"Are you, Molly?" Christian was contrite.

"I'm not that tired, but I would like to change my clothes."

"Well, we'll go down to the lake first thing in the morning, okay?"

"Okay!" She laughed.

Malcolm, who had returned to the hallway, intervened. "Anyway, it's very cool out there. And dinner will be served soon."

She turned toward him. He had not yet removed his coat and she had the strong impression he was watching her closely. The impression did not diminish as, throughout supper, she continued to feel that he was scrutinizing her. He was the perfect host, chatting lightly, making her feel at ease—yet she could not shake off the feeling that behind it all, he was puzzling something out.

"Your show in London," he said. "I believe it's a hit and that you have been nominated for an award?"

"That's right," said Molly, "the run of the show is over, but I've been nominated for a Laurence Olivier. The ceremony is in ten days' time and the producers say I have to be there for it. That's why no honeymoon, I'm afraid."

Cordelia, who had had less than a month to plan the wedding in the house—"You didn't give me much time, Christian!"—explained to Molly what remained to be done. "Did you bring your gown?"

"To be perfectly honest, Cordelia, it was the last thing on my mind."

"Oh, good!" said Cordelia, "we'll go to I Magnin's tomorrow."

"Say 'good-bye' to your fiancée, Christian!" Malcolm laughed, but Molly noticed that Christian didn't. All through the meal, she had sensed an undercurrent of antagonism from Christian toward his grandfather, which she could not understand. Christian had told her many anecdotes about Malcolm's abrasiveness, but now that she had actually met the old man, she thought him perfectly accommodating and pleasant.

Christian, however, seemed to be resisting all his overtures. Could it be that Malcolm had mellowed with age and that Christian, still aggrieved at his earlier treatment, had not noticed? Or refused now to notice? She thought of the troubled relationship between her own father and those around him. Families were a puzzle.

As neither Christian nor she had wanted any fuss, the arrangements for the wedding were relatively simple. But Cordelia was apparently anxious about Molly's Catholic background.'' Are you quite sure, Molly,'' she asked now, "that you don't want a Catholic ceremony? I'm sure we could arrange it. Malcolm is on nodding acquaintance with the cardinal—aren't you, dear?''

"I'm quite sure, Cordelia,'' said Molly, before Malcolm could answer, "that even the cardinal couldn't fix things this quickly. There is really no problem, honestly! Whatever ceremony you have organized here will be absolutely fine.''

"And you're absolutely certain you're happy with getting married here in America? I'm sure Malcolm and I could have made the trip to Ireland.''

Molly knew that there was no way in the world that she could have got married to a divorced man on Inisheer. She had not bothered to go into the ins and outs of Catholic marriage law with Christian, telling him simply that on the island, it would have been thought outrageous that she was getting married less than four months after her mother's death. "Please, Cordelia, don't worry!'' she said. "It's no problem to me where I get married.''

"Well, if you're sure,'' said Cordelia, who went on to talk to Christian about where he was to pick up his morning suit.

Dick Spielberg, whom Molly had briefly met in her dressing room three months previously, was to be Christian's Best Man at the wedding, but there was still the problem of who would be Molly's bridesmaid and who would give her away. "It's such a pity,'' Cordelia said, "that none of your family is coming over.''

Molly knew it would have been a waste of time inviting Brendan—he would not have traveled even to London. And Conor had ruled himself out. "I've a very small immediate family, actually,'' she said. "I'm sure Christian has told you that all I have are two brothers, and unfortunately, even one of those is out of touch altogether, working abroad. But please, Cordelia, I'm just as happy that things are working out this way. I couldn't bear all the fussing that usually goes with weddings."

"And how about your friends, your colleagues."

"None of them could come, I'm afraid," replied Molly swiftly, refraining from adding that she had not asked anyone. "It's all been a little—well, *fast.*" She smiled at her future mother-in-law.

"And you're absolutely sure this is the way you want it?" Cordelia regarded her keenly.

"Oh yes, honestly." Molly wished the spotlight would move off her. She had not told anyone about this wedding because she had not had time—but also because she had meant it when she had said to Cordelia she did not want any fuss.

"Well, we'll have to find you a bridesmaid!" said Cordelia briskly. "And Malcolm will give you away, if that's all right with you."

"Of course it is! I'd be delighted!"

By the coffee stage, Molly was dropping with tiredness and asked to be excused. Christian got up from the table too, kissed his grandmother, and said that he, too, was going to bed.

They went up the stairs together and outside the door of the room she had been given, he took her in his arms and kissed her, holding her tightly: "You're very welcome, Molly," he whispered into her hair. "I've dreamed of bringing you here. I love you very, very much."

"I love you too," she whispered back. As she closed the door, the words rang with an odd resonance in her ears. *I do love him, I do,* she told herself firmly.

As she undressed, Molly thought back over the conversation at dinner, reflecting on how easily she had shed the practices and strictures of her church when she had gone to London. At the same time, she would always feel like a Catholic. What would Sorcha have thought? And would she be marrying Christian at all if Sorcha was alive? She was too tired to puzzle it all out, too tired even to unpack. That was what had caused the word "love" to ring so strangely, she decided. Tiredness—that was it.

She washed her face in her little bathroom and climbed naked into the cool, linen-dressed bed. Her room was at the back of the house, overlooking the lake. She had not

drawn the curtains and when she turned out her bedside
lamp, moonlight poured into the room, painting all the
furniture and objects around her in shades of gray and
silver. Floating in that state halfway between consciousness and sleep, Molly became aware of a sort of whispering sound, a continuous sigh as gentle as the lapping
of the lake; it cushioned her and made her feel extra
secure and comfortable. Just before she dropped off, she
had a strong sensation of déja vu; she knew this bed, this
room . . .

She woke next morning at four a.m., her body clock
still on London time. She could not go back to sleep and
was reading one of the books from the bookshelves in
the room when a maid brought her in a cup of tea. Shortly
afterward, Cordelia knocked on her door. "We're early
risers in this house," she said apologetically as she came
in. "I hope you don't mind my calling you so early, but
if we're to get all our shopping done, we should get an
early start. It will take a good hour to get downtown
through the rush hour."

Molly, who was not in the least interested in shopping
as a general rule, found she loved shopping with Cordelia. She saw that Cordelia was known and popular in
all the ritzy boutiques and shops on Michigan Avenue,
and to her surprise, she found she loved the unaccustomed feeling of fizzy recklessness as, under Cordelia's
prodding, she tried on gowns that were so expensive she
would normally have put them back untouched on the
rails.

Now, as thrilled as a schoolgirl going to her first
dance—or, she remembered with bittersweet fondness,
as excited as a five-year-old child going to Galway for
the first time in a borrowed dress—she whirled and
twirled for Cordelia's approval in clouds of silk and satin
and fichu lace before settling eventually for a simple,
elegant gown of cream silk jersey which draped itself in
sensuous folds against her skin.

"I look like Isadora Duncan!" she cried as she pirouetted in front of the floor mirrors in Saks. "What do
you think, Cordelia, do you like it?" She looked past the
saleswoman to Cordelia and immediately stopped her
prancing. There were tears in Cordelia's eyes.

"What's wrong, Cordelia?"

"It's nothing, Molly. It's just in that dress you remind me of someone else, long ago."

"Oh, I'm sorry. I wouldn't want to upset you. I'll take it off immediately. There are plenty more gowns."

"No," said Cordelia firmly, blowing her nose, "it was just a passing fancy. Of course we'll take that gown. You look spectacular, Molly!"

That afternoon, Molly was temporarily alone in the rec room, which the family seemed to use daily instead of the more formal and cavernous living room off the hall. Curious, she roamed around, examining the books in the bookshelves, the pictures on the walls. There was a piano in one corner, on top of which was a collection of photographs. There were several of Christian, in all stages of childhood—and of another baby, which she assumed was his dead sister. But it was a full-length photograph of a bride and groom that caught her attention. She saw why Cordelia had reacted the way she had in Saks. The bride was dressed in a straight white gown not dissimilar in style to the one that she had chosen. This woman was tall and slender, with broad shoulders like her own. The face was squarer and the hairstyle completely different. Nevertheless, the resemblance to her was remarkable. No wonder Cordelia had been taken aback. This must be Christian's mother. She heard footsteps approaching and guiltily, as if she had been caught spying through a keyhole, she put the photograph down.

The footsteps were Christian's; he had come to take her sightseeing. "And if you're not too tired, I've got tickets for the hockey game tonight. Dick'll come too. Would you like that?"

They flew happily around the city in a little Fiat Ghia which belonged to Cordelia. And for Christian's sake, Molly tried very hard to enjoy herself at the Chicago Stadium that night. But the noise and the violence of the game appalled her, as players skated deliberately into each other or tripped each other when they thought the referee was not looking. She spent a great deal of the time with her hands over her ears and with her eyes closed, and was exhausted when the game was over.

But next night, Malcolm and Cordelia took the two of them and Dick to dinner in the restaurant on the ninety-fifth floor of the Hancock Center, and the contrast with

the previous raucous evening could not have been greater.
When she emerged from the elevator, Molly gasped with
pleasure at the panorama spread below and all around
her, the floodlit skyscrapers set against the black lake,
the strings of lights along Lake Shore Drive, the streams
of car lights along the expressways, the coruscation of
stars, of lighthouses of airport control towers, of aircraft
warning lights on cranes, of the twinkling planes themselves moving slowly through the sky, landing and lifting
off at Chicago's three airports. Cordelia delighted in
Molly's reaction: ''I hope you'll be very happy in our
city, Molly,'' she said.

''I know I will,'' said Molly. She glanced at Christian,
who was beaming like a full moon.

All through the week before the wedding, Christian
continued to be an exemplary companion, gentle and loving. The only niggles in Molly's mind were his aloofness
from his grandfather and the fact that once or twice she
saw him reaching for the bourbon bottle a little too often.
It was just nerves, she reassured herself—perfectly un-
derstandable. Everyone got jittery as weddings approached.

And with regard to Christian's coldness toward his
grandfather, Molly told herself she was too new to the
family fully to understand the eddies and undercurrents,
and tried to put them out of her mind.

In any event, she had little time to brood, what with
wedding rehearsals and meeting Malcolm and Cordelia's
wide circle of friends and relations. A little girl, daughter
of Christian's second cousin, had been chosen by Cordelia as combination flower girl and bridesmaid, and
Molly found her enchanting.

The week passed in a whirl of activity until it was her
last night as a single woman. The house was a bower,
with white flowers everywhere, threaded through the
banisters of the staircase, framing the doorways, banked
in huge drifts in the corners of the entrance hall and the
living room, where they were to have their reception.

The ceremony itself was to take place in the rec room,
and the decorators had erected a floral arch of lilies and
white roses in front of the French doors. Molly would
marry Christian looking out at the lake.

The night before the wedding, Cordelia had insisted

that as a matter of tradition, Christian should leave the house to sleep elsewhere. Grumbling, he had gone to stay with Dick, and Molly went to bed early but she could not sleep.

As she lay in bed, looking at the patterns made by the moon on her bedroom wall, there was a soft knock on her door. She sprang out of bed to open it, certain it was Cordelia with some last-minute arrangement.

It was not Cordelia who stood there, but Malcolm. He was still fully dressed in his navy-blue pinstripe suit and breathing heavily, obviously from the exertion of coming up the stairs. Cordelia had confided to Molly that she wanted to have a chair-lift installed for him, but he steadfastly refused to ruin the aesthetics of the staircase. "I'm sorry to come up so late like this," he said, "but we haven't had much opportunity to talk and I would really like to have a chat, just the two of us, before the wedding. May I come in?"

"Of course," she said, opening the door wider and standing aside.

He sat in a small bucket chair by the window while she pulled the covers back over the bed and put on her robe. She felt she should be embarrassed, but was not. Malcolm was the one who seemed to be nervous as she finished tidying the bed and sat on it, looking at him expectantly. In Molly's experience, most of the old people she knew tended to fidget a lot, but Malcolm was an exception. He was always still and carried an aura of stillness around with him. He sat still now. "I suppose you're wondering what's so important that I should come barging in here like this." His tone was formal and she caught a glimpse of what he might be like in a boardroom.

"No, that's all right, I'm glad to have the opportunity to talk. Is it something to do with tomorrow?"

"In a way," he said, "in another way not. But I have been debating with myself whether to show you this . . ." From the inside pocket of his suit, he pulled out his wallet and extracted a small, passport-sized photograph and passed it across.

Molly studied it; it was a color snapshot of a young blond woman, with high cheekbones and a wide mouth. Apart from the eyes, which were round and bright blue,

Molly could have been looking at her own sister. "Who's this?" she asked.

"It's Jo-Ann, Christian's first wife," Malcolm answered. "When I saw you first at the airport, I was immediately struck by the resemblance. Jo-Ann was small, much smaller than you are, Molly, but outside of that, you bear a remarkable resemblance to one another. But that's not really why I brought this up. The point is," he went on, "when he first brought Jo-Ann home, I was worried about her too. You see *both* of you are . . . are very like Christian's mother, Maggie . . ."

Molly got the impression that this was so difficult for Malcolm that he had actually rehearsed it. "I've already noticed that particular resemblance," she said simply.

He put the photograph back in the wallet and took out another one, older and in black and white, a miniature of a studio portrait, preserved in a plastic wallet. Molly studied it. "I saw the wedding photograph downstairs on the piano," she said softly.

Malcolm was watching her reaction. "I just thought you should know," he said.

Molly was not as dismayed as perhaps he thought she should be. She had been present at many dinner parties where it was discussed, this male search for mother substitutes. And she was familiar with the subsequent consensus when, at one end of the table or the other, it was decided that this was a perfectly adequate psychological basis for a relationship.

"You're not upset?" Malcolm asked.

"No." She shook her head. "It's not surprising really. If what you're suggesting is true—*if* it's true—he's not the first and won't be the last to do that."

"You're a very mature young lady," he said. "Christian hasn't told us much about your own family background; your parents are dead? You have two brothers?"

She nodded. "Yes, they're both older than I am. One of them, Brendan, is at home still, he's the eldest of the family. Conor, he's the younger one, he was a botanist."

"Was?"

"Well, I don't know what he is now."

His eyes were in shadow, but she thought she saw his expression sharpen as though he detected something odd

in her tone. She realized that she had spoken as though
she felt guilty.

He got up from his chair and she stood up with him.
Then he took one of her hands and in a strange, courtly
gesture kissed the back of it. "I think you're a lovely
girl," he said, "and I am really looking forward to the
wedding and to having a new granddaughter."

He left the room then, turning toward her again at the
door. "Good night, my dear, and I'll see you tomorrow.
And I'd like you to know you will always be welcome in
this house." He hesitated. "No matter what happens."

Molly hesitated too. The phrase sounded as though he
was warning her, but it was far too late to tease it out of
him. "I already know that!" she said. But as he pulled
the door closed she experienced, as she had several times
since she had come here, that curious sense of having
been here, seen this, before.

Next day the ceremony went ahead without a hitch.
Molly enjoyed the attention, the way she looked, the
flowers, toasts, flattering and welcoming speeches. All
day she felt as though she were playing the lead in a
brilliantly successful play and that opposite her was a
leading man who never missed a cue and who moved
across the stage as gracefully as she.

Like the rec room, the dining room of Greentrees had
been transformed with flowers and ribbons and brilliant
white napery. As they sat down to the wedding meal,
Christian leaned across the small gap that separated them
and whispered into Molly's ear: "Careful with the drink,
m'dear, I want you fully alert for later!" Eyes glittering,
he raised a glass of mineral water in playful salute, and
such was the nature of the shiver that traveled across
Molly's shoulder blades that she did not know whether it
had been caused by fear or sexual excitement.

Conor, to whom she had given the Evanston address
in case of emergencies, sent a telegram: *Good luck to
both of you; long life and happiness.* He signed it "Seán
Molloy."

The bridal suite of the Palmer House hotel was every
bit as opulent as Molly had expected; she had never in
her life seen such an enormous bed. Although it had gone

so well, she realized now that the day had been stressful, and as she wandered around the room, checking closets and the bathroom, a profound tiredness dragged at her legs and the small of her back. She was not sure about how she felt, alone now with her new husband.

The bed, already so huge, seemed to swell alarmingly, to spread over the entire room.

Christian was supervising the placing of their luggage. He had ordered that champagne be placed on ice before they arrived, and as the door closed behind the bellboy, he crossed to the table where it stood and popped the cork. "At last!" he said, spilling the foam into two glasses, "at last, at last!"

Molly walked to the table and picked up her glass. "At last," she agreed. She gazed at Christian, gorgeous in a summerweight suit of pale linen; he was not wearing a tie and the skin of his throat shone golden in the glow cast by a table lamp beside the ice bucket. Her husband. The word sounded odd. Husband. "Sláinte," she said softly, raising the champagne in salute.

She could not shake off a feeling of unreality.

Christian had no such reservations. "Forever and ever," he said exultantly. "For*ever*!" He drained his glass in one gulp.

With an effort of will, Molly overcame her feelings of wariness and allowed herself to be caught on the hook of his elation. "Forever!" she said with him; then, playfully; "Forever's a bit daunting, don't you think?"

He leaned over and nuzzled her neck. "Hurry up and finish that," he whispered, "I have plans for you, my lady, big, big plans . . ." He placed a finger in one of the pleats of her silk skirt and moved it slowly upward toward the waistband. Molly, who was not wearing a slip, shivered at the slight pressure of his finger as it traced a line across her navel. He felt the response and hooked his finger into the waistband. "Hurry, Molly, I can't wait!"

Perhaps the champagne would help, she thought. She gulped it and filled second glassfuls for both of them. "Sláinte," she repeated, and again drank the wine as though it were water. Then, putting the empty glass on a table, she wound her arms around his neck and offered her lips for a kiss.

Christian responded eagerly, and with his mouth fastened on hers, moved her backward toward the bed. She felt its softness against the back of her legs and allowed herself to be pushed on to it. He did not follow her but stood over her, his eyes burning. "Will you undress yourself for me, Molly? I want to watch."

This was it. Molly closed her eyes in momentary panic—did she really want this?

Then she opened her eyes again. What kind of person was she? Of course she wanted it. This was her *husband*.

Hesitantly at first, watching him watch her, she unbuttoned her blouse and unzipped the skirt. Wriggling out of the garments, she saw his hands flicker and clench as though he had been about to grab for her but stopped. With a surge of confidence, Molly realized then that this could come easily to her—by acting out the situation as though she were onstage, she could even enjoy it.

She was playing the part of the seducer, he the seduced.

Deliberately, dressed now only in bra, panties, stockings, and garter belt; she elongated the process.

Keeping her feet on the floor over the side of the bed, she lay splayed on her back, her eyes fixed on Christian's face as her fingers slowly sought out her garter-belt straps. Cordelia had treated her to a prewedding manicure, and although she did not look at them, she was conscious of the visual effect of red nails against the creamy lace of the underwear as, one by one, using both hands, she undid the garters and allowed her stockings to fall to her knees.

"Oh, Molly," Christian groaned aloud and started to tremble.

"Yes, sir?" As an actress, Molly had never played such an explicit sex scene in her life, but this one, she knew, was going very well. "Something wrong, sir?" She smiled. Damn it, she thought, she was quite good at this.

She ran her nails along the inside of the garter belt and arched her back to undo the fastening; then, little by little, she withdrew from inside her panties the ribbons that held the garters.

Christian gasped aloud, then crouched down in front of her and parted her knees a little, kissing the soft skin on the inside of her thighs. Molly experienced a moment of fright; this had become too real.

But the tremor was momentary. She was so well into her role that she held on to her playfulness: "Now, now!" she said like a governess, pushing him away.

She maneuvered her legs upward out of reach and turned over so she was lying on her stomach in the middle of the bed. Quickly she undid her bra and slipped out of it, but before she could turn back again to see Christian's reaction, he was beside her on the bed, his hands simultaneously scrabbling at her panties and at the zipper of his own fly.

This time Molly did panic. She had lost control of the situation.

In an effort to regain it, she tried to push him away: "Hang on, a second, Christian, hold it a moment—"

But Christian had other ideas. He pulled her panties down, and although she resisted, managed to get them partially off over one of her feet. "Oh, Molly, my darling Molly, I've waited so long, we've waited so long, I love you, I love you—" The words were almost incoherent. He pushed his hand in between her legs and Molly's emotions rioted. She was afraid, excited, outraged, all at the same time. She managed to wriggle free." *Wait*, I said!"

Christian froze. "What is it?"

"Just don't *rush* me like this!" Quivering, Molly rolled off the bed and pulled some of the coverlet with her, enough to wrap around herself, covering her nakedness. With one foot, she kicked off the panties clinging to her ankle.

"What's the matter?" Christian's voice was icy.

Molly kept her eyes away from his crotch. "There's nothing the matter. You're just going too fast for me." She felt close to tears.

Christian stuffed his penis back inside his trousers and zipped up the fly. "What do you think you were doing just now on that bed?"

"*What?*" Molly's tears did spill over.

Instantly he was on his feet and had dashed around to stand beside her. "I'm sorry, Molly, I didn't mean it, it just came out—" He tried to take her in his arms, but she pushed him away.

"Molly," he said desperately, "please forgive me. I didn't mean it."

"It's not your fault," she sobbed, "it's mine. You absolutely—I had no right—" She knew she was being unreasonable but could not help herself. He had every right to expect sex from her. She had led him on.

She did not resist when, a second time, he tried to take her in his arms. Murmuring endearments, he kissed the top of her head, and her weeping gradually subsided.

"Sorry," she said, "I'm really sorry."

"I am too. I was rushing you. It's just that I love you so much." He kissed her, a soft kiss of comfort and affection, and she responded in kind.

"Don't be afraid, Molly," he said between kisses, "I won't hurt you—I'd never hurt you. We'll go as fast or as slow as you want." Gently taking her wrists, he pinioned them against the wall so that the coverlet she had been holding against her breasts fell away. He kissed her throat and when, almost despite herself, she was responding, moving against the linen of his suit, lowered his lips to her cleavage.

Molly gasped, and correctly interpreting that she was aroused, Christian freed her hands, caressing her sides, her waist. He moved his hands behind her waist and lowered them so that her buttocks were cupped.

Molly groaned and instinctively sat into the cup, bending her knees. Immediately Christian pressed one of his knees in between her legs so she was straddling his thigh, straining against it, the linen cool. "It's all right, my darling, my little darling, it's all right, it's all right." He crooned and kissed, and still holding her bottom with one hand, he stroked her breasts with the other; all the while he continued to cover her face and lips with his lips and tongue, now soft, now hard. In the middle of the confusion of emotions and instincts, Molly was conscious of individual sounds and sensations—of her own breath rasping in her throat, of the rough texture of the wallpaper against her bare back, of the wetness between her legs where she rode his thigh.

He bent his head to her naked breast and she arched her back, like a bow, to facilitate him. But he gave the breast only a token kiss and brought her face forward again to kiss her again on the lips. Almost involuntarily, she moved one hand to his penis. To her touch, its bulge felt, not long and thin as she had imagined, but full and round and surprisingly warm through the fabric of his trousers; it was moving slightly, pulsing.

The image of Conor flashed into Molly's brain, but desperately she flung it away as Christian took a breast in each of his hands, nuzzling and sucking them alternately. As he sucked first one and then the other, Molly felt as though he were tightening a piano string that stretched between the center of each breast and the center of her vagina. It was not Christian, it was not anyone; she felt now as though even her body were not her own; she lost all sense of objectivity, of danger.

Molly stretched both arms, cruciform along the wall, and surrendered to physical sensation.

Christian had begun again to murmur, "Molly, Molly, come on, darling, come on . . ." Suddenly he broke away and caught her wrists in both his hands. "Is it okay now? Are you ready?"

The shock of him stopping was great and she struggled to come to terms with reality, but again he pressed her to him. His arms tightly around her waist, he bent his head low, licking the undersides of both breasts. She stooped over his head and smelled the clean perfume of his hair but also something stronger, like horses. There were damp patches on his shirt, spreading out from under his armpit. "Come on, darling," he whispered, "I love you, Molly. Molly, oh, Molly . . ."

"I'm ready," she whispered back.

For the second time he pushed her backward onto the bed, this time rolling her over it until she lay in the middle. Still fully dressed himself, he knelt over her: "You are absolutely beautiful, Molly," he said huskily, "the most beautiful creature I have ever seen." She raised her arms to him, but he held them. "Just a moment," he said, "I have a treat for you."

He climbed off the bed and went into the bathroom, emerging again with a vial of bath oil. "All right, my darling," he said. "Close your eyes."

Molly complied.

Christian spilled the oil onto his palms and began gently to massage it into her skin. Starting at her knees, he avoided the pubic area, stroking sinuously along her flanks and across her breasts and downward again, but agonizingly for Molly, stopping just short of where her body wanted him to go.

She moved with him, pushing her stomach upward, trying to lure his hands to where she wanted them.

And when eventually his fingers found her vagina and caressed their satiny way into its warmth, she cried out.

She heard, rather than saw, the undoing of his zipper and then, momentarily, his penis was thrusting into her slipperiness.

Again she cried out.

As Molly and Christian woke on their first morning as man and wife, in London Una O'Connor was waiting nervously for her lunch guest in the restaurant of the Cumberland. She had been waiting for fifteen minutes. It was not that he was late—she had been twenty minutes early and there were still five minutes to go until their one o'clock appointment.

From her table, she could see the door but, determined he should not catch her looking out for him, kept her head down over the novel she had brought. Una, whose life was governed by the timekeeping habits of others, never left home without a book.

He arrived punctually, and once again she was struck by the power of his physical size and presence. He was absolutely unaware of it, she decided as they shook hands and he slid into his chair. She played the introductions very cooly. Una was always cool when she was not taken by surprise. She already knew the menu and, playing her advantage as hostess, pointed out various options.

"Do they have any steak?" he asked, looking at the long list in front of him.

"I'm sure they can cook you one," said Una. She raised her hand to a waiter, who padded over. "Is it possible that you can do steak?"

"There's steak on the menu, madame!" said the waiter.

"*Plain* steak," said Conor.

Una led the conversation, "interviewing" him. "Tell me about life at the zoo."

"Nothing much to tell," he said, shrugging his shoulders, "I'm a general attendant there, I can help out any-where."

"Do you actually like animals or is it just a job?"

"No, I like animals—but it is just a job. My real in-terest now is archaeology."

She caught the "now." "What was your real interest before?"

"Botany," he said.

There was something in his tone, a warning. She went back to archaeology. "I know absolutely nothing about archaeology," she said. It was like pressing a button. All she had to do was to sit, sipping her wine and toying with her monkfish while he ate his steak and poured out his enthusiasm for his subject. "I'm doing exams in a few weeks' time," he said, "I started my course late, only last January—and I'm up to my eyes trying to keep abreast of the class."

"When will you be qualified?"

"Probably never. I'll never learn enough, there isn't time in a lifetime—and as soon as you get caught up with what's going on in one area, another area leaps ahead. But I'll be accepted as a bona fide archaeologist, all going well, in two or three years."

Una was having difficulty in concentrating on his an-swer, although she felt as alert as if there were a high-tension wire passing through her body. This was all very well and he was totally at ease, but what on earth was the next step? She had no plan further than this lunch and she began to panic. He was finishing his steak and mop-ping up the meat juice with a piece of roll.

She became aware that he had stopped speaking and was looking at her expectantly. *Jesus. Had he asked her something?*

"Sorry," he said, "was I boring you? I do that a lot, I'm afraid . . ."

"No, you weren't boring me."

He looked at her without comment and then smiled. "It's your turn."

"No, I'd like to continue talking about archaeology."

Conor placed his knife and fork precisely where they bisected his clean plate. "Una," he asked, "why did you ask me to lunch?"

"Because you were there, like Mount Everest?"

"That's as good a reason as any, I suppose." Then he continued, his voice casual. "What do we do now?"

"What—what do you mean?"

"Well, I gather you didn't ask me to lunch because you thought I was fading away from hunger."

She gathered together the remnants of her self-possession. "If it comes to that, why did you accept?"

"Oh, for a variety of reasons, including the fact that I quite like red hair!" he said.

She saw he was still smiling, although for the life of her she could not interpret the smile. "Are you—are you on a day off from work today?" she managed.

"Yes. I should study of course."

"Oh, of course. Right!" She was gesturing to the waiter for the bill when he spoke again. "Why did you ask?"

"I was hoping you might be able to take me to the zoo!"

It was a brazen effort and he laughed outright. "All right, Una. The zoo it is!"

Molly inserted the key into the lock of the Vernon Street house while Christian paid off the taxi and struggled up the short walk with their luggage, including a trunk they had acquired to accommodate some of their wedding presents.

Molly's cleaning woman, Mrs. Sharma, had placed fresh flowers on the hall stand and had stacked a heap of mail neatly alongside it.

"I'm going into the kitchen, Christian," Molly called, and she went through the hall, taking the mail with her. She put on the kettle—always a reflex action when she walked into her kitchen after having been away—and sat at the table, sorting through the envelopes. She did not open any of the brown envelopes, junk mail or circulars, but set aside a heap of invitations, a letter from Brendan, and one in Dolly's flowing script. She opened this one first. It contained the shooting schedule for her film and a little scribbled note in which Dolly had written that she had received for her client a "very intriguing parcel," readdressed to her from the Wyndham's Theatre.

The kettle whistled. She could hear Christian humping

suitcases up the stairs. "I'm making tea, darling," she called through the door. "Do you want a cup?"

"Coffee, please."

"Instant all right?"

"Oh, all right," he said grumpily, heaving at the trunk. "I can't manage this up the stairs on my own. I'll need help."

"Why don't we unpack some of it down here?" she called. "It'll be easier to get it up then . . ."

"Oh, very clever! Just when I've nearly broken my back!"

"Christian! Don't be so crabby! You'd think we had been married for thirty years instead of three days . . ."

"Four days," he corrected, coming into the kitchen. "Don't forget the time changes." He came up behind where she stood filling the water out of the kettle into two mugs and squeezed her to him.

"Christian, I'll spill the water!"

He removed his arms from around her waist and raised both hands in the air: "Sorry!" He sat down at the table.

She brought the two mugs across to the table, determinedly bright. "Would you do me a favor?"

"What?"

"I've just had a note from Dolly that she has a parcel for me. She says it's intriguing, whatever that means. But I'm dying to see what's in it. Would you be a darling and take a taxi to her office to collect it?"

She saw he was not inclined to be helpful. "I'll do all the unpacking while you're gone, Christian," she said. "Then we can go to bed."

"For a sleep?" The sarcasm was unmistakable.

"Aren't you tired?"

"I suppose you are?"

"Isn't it normal to be tired after a transAtlantic flight like we've just had?"

"Yes, it's normal! Sorry, Molly, I'll go get your package."

After he had gone, Molly reflected ruefully that the sarcasm had been justified. After that first, abandoned sexual encounter on their wedding night, her body had seemed to close up shop. It was nothing to do with Christian, she felt, it was as if some switch had turned itself off. Now that they had returned to England, she would have to address the situation immediately.

She was in the bedroom, hanging up her clothes, when he returned with the parcel. She sat on the bed to unwrap it.

"It doesn't look like a script," he said curiously, sitting down beside her. He was right. When she had ripped the paper off, Molly found she was holding a battered old shoe box, the condition of which had not improved with the handling it had gotten from the post office. She took off the lid and found a note:

FOUND AMOUNG THE EFFECTS OF FR. PATRICK MORAN

The name, unexpected, came as a jolt.

Christian was looking over her shoulder. "Who's Father Patrick Moran?"

"Ah, it's just a priest I used to know," she said. "He must be dead."

"They're all cuttings about you," he said, reaching over and riffling through the top layer. "Was this guy sweet on you, Molly? A priest?"

"It's all a long time ago," said Molly, trying to put the lid back on the box.

"A woman with a past, eh? A *priest* yet!" He made a playful grab for the box, his customary good humor restored. "Let's see those cuttings!"

"Christian, don't!" she said, laughing, snatching the box to herself. She felt bashful about letting him read all that old stuff about her. But he grabbed for it again and they wrestled for possession on the bed. She eluded him and, keeping the box tight to her chest, ran out of the room with it, flitting down the stairs two at a time.

"Give it to me!" ordered Christian, thundering after her. "Wife! Listen to your master!"

"Master, me eye!" she said, and dodged out of his reach down the hall and into the kitchen. He caught her from behind, but she managed to hold on to the prize. "It's only a pile of old rubbish," she said firmly, "but it's mine. Nothing to do with you." Dragging him with her, she took a few steps across the kitchen, and while he continued to cling to her back like an oversized monkey, she reached up and put the box on top of the kitchen dresser.

"All right," he said playfully, nuzzling her back. "Come on, confess. Who was this guy, Moran?"

"Nobody that need ever concern either of us, Christian," she said, diverting him, kissing him on the mouth. He broke the kiss, gasping. "Molly, I warn you, kisses like that can have consequences . . ."

"So what? We're married!"

Christian struck his head with his open palm. "Now she tells me!" Then he stood back from her and took her hand. "You mean it, Molly? Everything's okay? I thought—"

"That's what thought did!" Molly was determined that in every sense she would be a good wife.

"Come on," he said, his voice tender. "Upstairs!"

10

I t's a little girl!'' cried the midwife triumphantly.

The tears poured down Molly's face as the baby finally slithered out of her.

She felt flattened and empty, exhausted yet exhilarated, all at the same time. Making a tremendous effort, she raised her head to see her daughter. But the baby had been taken to the other side of the room, to a table where they were huddled over her.

She lay back and held Christian's hand. She searched his face, but only his eyes were visible over the surgical mask he wore and his eyes were not looking back at her but across at the baby.

She was glad Christian was with her. She had really needed him to be with her.

There was another contraction. She closed her eyes and pushed out the afterbirth.

''Good girl!'' said the midwife.

Molly felt ludicrously pleased at the praise. The strong lights of the delivery room were hurting her eyes, but she looked up again at Christian. Although he was still holding her hand, his head was now swiveled around and he was looking away from her altogether, toward the door. There was some kind of hubbub at the door. There was a nurse running.

A young doctor came and sat on the stool at the end of the delivery table. She saw he was a West Indian.

''Just going to give you a little stitch,'' he said. ''You won't feel anything.''

''Where's the baby?'' she asked him. All she could see was the top of his dark head as he bent to his task of stitching her episiotomy wound.

''Easy, now,'' said the doctor softly.

"Where's my baby?" Molly felt panicky. Her body felt as delicate and stretched as the thinnest glass. She looked from the doctor to Christian. Christian's eyes were full of tears. There was something wrong.

"They've taken your baby to the nursery, to put her in an incubator, just as a precaution . . ." said the doctor, still without looking at her.

"What kind of precaution?" asked Molly, and her voice rose in pitch, but then a nurse came and gave her an injection.

"For the pain, my dear . . ." said the nurse. "And so you won't get sick."

Molly was unaware of any pain. And she did not feel sick. "What's wrong, Christian?" she asked him begging.

He did not answer, but he had stripped off his mask and she was terribly afraid when she saw the expression on his face.

"Is the baby dead?" Molly struggled to get off the table but she was still strapped into the stirrups and the nurse and the doctor rushed to restrain her. She thought she heard herself screaming, but her voice sounded very strange.

"There, there, my dear," said the nurse. "Everything's going to be all right. Just lie still and have a little rest."

The doctor said something that Molly could not understand because everything was suddenly so distant and she felt so, so tired, much tireder even than she had been before. The tiredness descended on her like a soft black blanket, so soft that it muffled all the words she was trying to say. She made an effort to fight, to throw it off, but it overpowered her, it was cutting out all the light and all the sound. She dropped into sleep as if she were falling down a deep well.

When she woke again it was dark, and for a few moments she drifted, full of delicious laziness, having no idea where she was. She had been dreaming, a very vivid, lovely dream in which she had been getting married all over again and the house in Evanston was floating on the lake like a flower-filled barge. Everyone was there in the dream, even Sorcha, her mother, looking beautiful, standing proudly as Molly walked up the short aisle. Jo-

Ann was there, blonde, in a pink dress, standing beside another lovely woman in gray, who smiled gravely at Molly as she walked by, and Molly knew that this was Christian's mother. She smiled back at the woman as she passed and the woman seemed very pleased. Malcolm was at the far end of the room, playing some sort of bouzouki-type musical instrument; he had multicolored ribbons and streamers pinned all over his navy pinstripe suit. John Pius, his pink face wreathed in smiles, was the preacher. Even Beauty, the little collie Molly had loved as a child, was an honored guest. She sat at John Pius's feet and wagged her tail, her ears pricked, as Molly approached. Beauty wore a tiny peaked clown's hat on her black and white head and a garland of flowers around her neck.

And when, after the ceremony, Christian lifted the veil off her face, it was not Christian, but Conor. And it felt warm and right, there had been no surprise.

She stretched in the warm, smooth bed, but when she moved, there was an uncomfortable tug between her legs. She remembered. The baby. She was in the hospital. She had had a daughter.

The filaments of the dream evaporated as with difficulty, her head swimming, she raised herself off her pillows and switched on the light over her bed. The room was clinically clean but bright with flowers. Someone had been in and had arranged them; they spilled all over the windowsills, lockers, and tables, even the television set, dozens of them—orchids, roses, dahlias, chrysanthemums, in baskets and vases and little posies. She had a sense of unreality, as if she had died and been transported in death to somewhere else. She had not seen anyone bring flowers.

She eased herself out of bed, feeling dizzy when she attempted to stand upright. Keeping her head low, she groped her way along the wall toward the window and pulled back the heavy curtains. Although the streetlamps were on outside, it was not really dark yet, but still dusky. Off on the horizon to the west, she could see the remnants of a red-gold sky.

She made her way back to the bed and collapsed onto it. There was a wire running from a wall socket under her pillow. She followed its length and uncovered a rubber bulb at the end of the wire with a red button in its middle. It was a call bell. She pressed the button and a light went on over her door.

Within seconds a nurse came in. "Good heavens, my dear. You shouldn't have got out of bed."

The nurse assisted her back under the covers and settled her down. "We didn't expect you to be awake for a little while yet! How do you feel?" She plumped the pillows behind Molly, professionally smoothing down the counterpane.

Molly felt more disoriented than ever. "Where's my baby?" she asked. Her voice sounded far away and very faint.

"We'll bring her in to you in a little while," said the nurse. "She's in the nursery now, the doctors are with her, we're running a few little tests on her . . ."

Tests. Through the fog, the word struck fear into Molly's heart.

"What kind of tests?" she managed to ask.

"Don't worry now, dear, the doctor will be in shortly and he'll explain everything. Would you like a little drink?"

The nurse poured some water from a turquoise-colored plastic jug into a turquoise-colored plastic beaker and held it to Molly's lips. The water tasted very sweet.

"Is there anyone here? Where's my husband?"

"You were asleep for such a long time, my dear, you were absolutely exhausted. He went home for a while, but he said we were to telephone him just as soon as you woke up."

"Will you telephone him? I'd like to speak to him, please."

"Certainly, my dear. We have the number out at the desk. You rest now."

"When can I see my baby?"

"Won't be long now, you rest now, dear!" The nurse left the room, the crepe soles of her shoes making a sucking sound on the parquet flooring. It was very quiet in the room after she had closed the sound-proofed door behind her.

Molly tried to hold thoughts in her mind but they kept slipping away. She knew there was something wrong with the baby. It was not just the behavior of the staff. She felt it in her bones. Where was Christian? Where were Malcolm and Cordelia? She tried very hard to focus. Malcolm and Cordelia had definitely been at the clinic at some stage; she was sure she remembered their faces floating vaguely somewhere above her own.

Or was that before? Had she only dreamt they were here? They were definitely in London—they had been staying in the Dorchester for the past week. Malcolm had insisted on coming for the birth of his first great-grandchild. He had been tremendously excited over the past few days.

She concentrated. Where were they all now? Christian should be with her. Cold fear assaulted her: he wasn't with her because he was drinking. He had promised he wouldn't. He was supposed to be on the wagon. He had promised.

She thought she heard someone at the door: they were bringing in her baby! But whoever it was passed on down the corridor.

Christian should be here with her. She would make it all right for Christian and herself. They would make a go of it now they had a baby.

Her thoughts struggled out of the fog, showed themselves, but slipped away before they crystallized.

Christian would cut down on the drinking. It was a girl, they had said. He would be able to cut down on the drinking because now he had a daughter.

On her side, she would make more effort to respond sexually.

After a relatively auspicious start, the sexual aspect of Molly's marriage to Christian had run into trouble. She had sincerely tried to open herself up to him but found his constant desire for her invasive; as a result, she had resorted to excuses—tiredness, her pregnancy, anything but the truth. Because the uncomfortable fact was that unless she managed to work up a fantasy—frequently about Conor—she did not enjoy sex with her husband at all.

Despairing, she had haunted libraries and bookshops, seizing on the latest self-help books and manuals, none of which, so far, had come to her assistance. Several of the books, however, had hinted that women did not mature sexually until after they had given birth.

Molly shifted in the unyielding hospital bed. She would really try harder. She had to, now that there were three of them. Now that they were a family.

They would all make a new start. As once again Molly sank into a half-conscious doze, a scene between herself and Christian, as vivid as though newly minted, reran itself in her brain. They had been back in London for more than two months and she had been chafing to get back to work; it had been her idea that they should take her colleague and friend, Jenny Baker, out to dinner. Dolly Mencken was being very cautious as to what roles she was putting Molly up for, but Molly felt that Jenny would have all the gossip.

It had been Christian who had suggested the Vecchia Rizzione. Unfortunately, he had met Jenny and her at the restaurant, having come from a press reception. And the moment she laid eyes on him, Molly had recognized he was in that state, betrayed by emphatic, too-careful speech and movement, which presages outright drunkenness. Her heart sank as he had given the order: "Chianti Classico!" and then had sunk even further as, noticing her reaction, he had amended it: "Two bottles! And a bottle of Soave too!"

Jenny, unaware of the undercurrents, had giggled. "Ooh! We *are* going to have a good time tonight!" As usual, she was attired in a bright, tight dress, this one of luscious cobalt-blue satin.

"You bet, gorgeous!" Christian had breathed, kissing Jenny's hand while Molly bent her head over the menu.

They had got through the meal somehow. Molly had given most of her attention to Jenny, fielding Christian's sarcastic interruptions—her husband's usual good manners always deserted him when he'd drunk too much—acting as though she were having a perfectly nice evening. By the time they had got to the Sambucca and coffee stage, it looked as if she and Christian might actually survive the occasion without a row.

But when, eventually, they had managed to flag down a taxi, Christian had become obstreperous, flirting outrageously with Jenny, ignoring his wife. "Excuse *me*!" he said loudly, insisting on positioning himself between the two women on the seat of the vehicle, and as the taxi had pulled away, he had dropped a hand on Jenny's knee.

Molly, although furious, had managed to hold her tongue.

Jenny, however, had shown no such compunction. "Keep your hands to yourself, my man!" she said pertly, removing the offending hand as though it were a particularly nasty species of spider. Leaning out so she could see beyond him to Molly, she had challenged her friend: "Can't you control your husband, Molly?"

From somewhere, Molly had summoned up a laugh. "Christian doesn't like the notion of being controlled."

Christian had not deigned to acknowledge Molly had spoken. Instead, he had attempted to plant a messy kiss on Jenny's cheek. "For Christ's sake!" Jenny's cool English voice had showed real irritation. "If you don't stop this, I'll clock you!"

"Aww, Jenny, gotta get it somewhere—don't I, *Margo*!"

Molly had gritted her teeth. She was not all that embarrassed in front of Jenny Baker—being an actress, Jenny was accustomed to dramas and scenes—but already she knew that when Christian was drunk and in a mood like this, there was little point in confronting him.

Luckily, Jenny's Chelsea house had been the first stop. "Good night all, thanks for dinner!" she had chirruped as she got out, adding, "Hope you have the Alka-Seltzer handy, Molly. Someone around here's going to need it."

For the next five minutes Christian and Molly had sat in silence. Then the taxi had swung unexpectedly around a parked car and Christian, unprepared, had slid off his seat and into a heap on the floor. It would have been funny, Molly had thought at the time, if it had been in a movie. And if she had not been part of the script.

But Christian had seen little humor in the situation. Scrambling to his knees, he had almost lost his balance again as the taxi wheeled around a corner. Furious now, he had banged indignantly on the glass partition between themselves and the driver. "What the fuck do you think you're doing?"

The driver, a small, wiry man with a thin face, had jammed on the brakes and pulled back the partition. "What the 'ell are you on about, mate?"

"I've a com—I've a com*plaint* to make here." Christian's kneeling posture made him sound pompously ridiculous.

"Is that right?" The cabdriver had clearly had a hard day. "Well, so do I, mate. You're drunk. Out of my taxi!"

"I beg your pardon?"

"You 'eard me. Out! You can stay, miss," he added, in Molly's direction.

"I've had *enough* of this," said Christian, but before he could remonstrate further, the cabbie had jumped out, pulled the passenger door open, and yanked him out onto the street. Christian had been too drunk to resist effectively. His jaw slack, he had stood foolishly on the pavement, gaping at the man.

The cabbie had slammed the door and had jumped into the driver's compartment. "I'm not 'angin around, luv. Do you want to go on?" He added, "I 'aven't been paid, by the way . . ."

Molly had known she was taking the coward's way out, but she had been suddenly very tired and felt unable to face any more aggravation with Christian. She had avoided looking out through the window to where, swaying slightly, he still stood. "Yes," she had said, "please take me on to Vernon Street."

It had been two hours later when, lying tensely awake in bed, she had heard Christian come in and tramp up the stairs.

"Sorry! Did I wake you?" His voice had dripped with venom as he had pushed the door open and snapped on the light.

"I was awake."

In two strides, Christian was across the room and had pulled the bedclothes off the bed. He had thrown himself on top of her, pulling at the hem of her nightgown, smothering her. She had struggled and struggled, but he had been too strong for her . . .

In her hospital bed Molly sat upright, her heart banging against her ribcage. For a few seconds, as the half-dream receded, she did not know where she was. Then she remembered.

Where was her baby?

She tried to remember the moment of birth, the cry of her baby. "It's a little girl!" someone had said. Then

there was that hubbub at the door of the delivery room.
She had not seen her baby; they had not given her her
baby to hold . . .

She rang the call bell and when the nurse came in, the
same one as before, Molly demanded to see the baby.

The nurse saw her agitation. "Yes, dear!" she said in
a soothing voice. "I'll go now and get the doctor for
you . . ."

Immediately after the birth of his daughter, Christian
accompanied his sleeping wife when she was wheeled
into the recovery room and from there into her room,
where it appeared that she would continue to sleep
soundly for hours. He sat in a chair in the room, feeling
useless and superfluous as the efficient staff came and
went, monitoring her condition. The doctor who had pre-
sided at the delivery, an elderly silver-haired man named
Sinden, came in at one stage and spoke to him in a low
voice. He was kind but not very informative, telling
Christian that he would return later, as soon as there was
any definite news.

Christian already knew that the news would be bad and
that it was now just a matter of degree. He had seen his
daughter, bluish and stiff in a nurse's hands as she was
rushed to the nursery incubator and had recognized that
she did not look at all like the newborn babies he and
Molly had seen in the training films at the pre-natal
classes they had attended.

As he sat in the quiet room, he tried to make sense of
his tremendous feeling of detachment. After the initial
trauma of the birth, his brain had seemed to slip out of
gear into neutral. He had the faraway sense that he should
be panicking, feeling sad or tragic or even fearful of the
future, yet all he felt was this great gray flatness. He
stared at his wife where she lay on her back, propped up
on pillows, her head fitted into a small hollow. Her hair
was tangled and unkempt and spread out in strings darker
than the white bed linen, made faintly luminous under a
blue nightlight above the bed. Her mouth was open and
she snored slightly as she breathed.

He had made a mess of this marriage too. Just as it
had with Jo-Ann, the successful conquest of Molly had
been the end of his desire. It had taken a while, of course.

His physical desire for her had been frenzied in the beginning, and the first time he had seen her naked in his
bed, he had felt like falling on his knees to worship such
perfection. He had been patient with her, knowing she
would need time to flower.

But as the weeks went by he had become irritated and
then frustrated. If he was to be fair, there was nothing
on which he could actually fault her; she was trying hard
to be a dutiful and loving wife; but somewhere along the
line, Christian knew he had failed to make some sort of
connection.

With hindsight he felt it had been a mistake that she
had given up her career—even for a short time. It had
been his idea, that she should relax for a while, get to
know her new family in America. She had seemed happy
enough about it at the time, and the stay in Evanston had
been blissful, at least he thought they had been. His
grandmother and grandfather adored her and the atmosphere in the house was happy, even gay.

But when, at her request, they had returned to London,
the situation had changed. He had become wrapped up
in work, and in any event, he seemed not enough for her;
she wanted badly to get back to work.

There had been one or two spectacular rows—with a
shiver, Christian remembered the aftermath of the night
he and Molly had taken Jenny to the Vecchia Rizzione—
but then she had got pregnant and the situation seemed
to improve a little. There had even been a side benefit,
an enormous leap for the better in his relationship with
his grandfather as Malcolm, overjoyed, took to calling
every day for news. At first Christian had been able to
rejoice in tandem, but little by little, as Molly, morning
sick and wrapped up in the pregnancy, shut him out, his
joy faded.

And as the months passed, their sexual life had dwin-
dled away to nothing.

He had tried to talk to her about it and she had always
participated politely, but each time, he had had the sense
that he was talking to someone buried deep in a secret
place, completely out of his reach. She had asked him to
be patient, promising him that this aspect of their lives
would improve as soon as the baby was born. But he had
felt with certainty that it was a promise she would not,

could not, keep. Nor, he now admitted, did he want her to . . .

He looked at her, now sleeping the sleep of the dead in her hospital bed. She was beautiful in repose, despite the untidiness of her hair and the dark shadows around her eyes, beautiful like an alabaster statue, he thought. The truth was, he reflected, Molly did not seem to need sex.

So, because he had loved her, or thought he had, he had tried to convince himself that sex wasn't everything and he had concentrated on work—he was now working free-lance for a number of publications all over the world. He had even imagined that if he worked hard enough at it, they might have some sort of chance of recreating the intimacy of their early time together. But Molly remained unreachable. They spent their days politely and, although separated by only a few inches in a large double bed, their nights apart.

Deep down, Christian admitted to himself that his drinking might be a contributory factor. She closed up on him when he had a few drinks, and although he tried, he really tried not to drink so much, he couldn't seem to help himself.

And although he might blame his circumstances, his early bereavements, her lack of appreciation—when he was low and sober like this, he knew that the blame was firmly with him.

All in all, Christian's sense of failure was enormous.

She sighed in her sleep and he leaned forward, ready for her to wake up. But she was merely changing position and he sat back again.

He had no idea what he felt about the baby. It was too soon and the scale of the difficulties ahead was unknown. But Christian's sense of self-loathing and failure was tempered by a feeling of deep resentment at the trick fate had played on him, on them both. *That* surely wasn't his fault. They were now in a trap, in a grotesque net that was tightening around them, binding them together.

Christian looked at his wife and all he saw was an eternity of dust.

She would be better off without him.

He stood up and went to the window, parting the curtains and peering out at the street below. There were people, ordinary people, shop and office workers, men and women with attaché cases, hurrying along the pavements. Cars nosed slowly into and out of parking spaces. A taxi picked up a fare.

Why him?

He glanced back over his shoulder at his unconscious wife. He had been sitting with her for nearly an hour now. There was no point in staying here. In any event, no one had seemed to care very much whether he was around or not, and it mattered least of all to Molly. He knew he should call Malcolm and Cordelia, who were probably getting anxious for news by now. He had promised that he would call immediately after the delivery. But it was hardly the kind of news a person could deliver on the telephone: *"Hey, Grandpa, guess what's happened to your first great-granddaughter . . . !"* He would have to go in person to the Dorchester.

He went back to stand again for a moment beside Molly's bed. The blue light from above reflected off her teeth and made translucent the satiny tissue of her eyelids. With a shiver, he realized she looked like a cadaver. Strangely, he felt an impulse to kiss her. He bent over her face and touched his lips to her forehead, which was cold and faintly damp.

He left the room, and writing the number of the Vernon Street house on the reporter's pad he always carried, tore out the page and gave it in at the nurses' station, telling the nurse on duty he was leaving for a while and would be home in about an hour and a half.

Outside, the heat was bleeding away from the May day, which had been unseasonably warm. Christian got a cab immediately and asked to be driven to the Dorchester. But when the cabby was taking a short-cut through Berkeley Square, on an impulse, he asked the man to pull up at the flower stall on the sidewalk. To the stallholder's astonishment, he bought fifty pounds' worth of flowers— orchids, roses, chrysanthemums, dahlias, all the showiest blooms the woman had on display.

Laden, planning to ask the taxi-driver to deliver the flowers to Molly after he himself got out, Christian climbed back into the cab.

As the taxi got nearer to the Dorchester and the moment when he would have to break the bad news to Mal-

colm and Cordelia, he began to funk it. Despite his
improved relationship with his grandfather, he felt that
somehow Malcolm would find a way to blame him for
this. He could not face it. Not just now.

He tapped the glass partition between himself and the
driver, and when the man slid it back, said he had had a
change of plan, that he wanted to be driven to Soho. The
cabbie threw his eyes to heaven and pulled his vehicle
through a screeching U-turn. "We're in Soho now, sir,"
he said a few minutes later, "Brunswick Street. Where
do you want to be let off?"

"L'Epicure Restaurant," said Christian. The restaurant, with its distinctive flaming torch, was, he thought,
as good a place as any.

It took another five minutes for the driver to get to the
restaurant. Leaving the flowers behind him on the seat,
Christian asked the driver to take them back to Saint
Catherine's. He scribbled Molly's name on a piece of
paper from his pad and paid five pounds over and above
what was on the meter. The cabdriver took the money.
"Whatever you say, guv. Have a nice day!"

As the taxi moved off into the distance, Christian looked
around; there was a pub kitty-corner to the restaurant.

It proved to be noisy and cheerful, full of young people, obviously workers in the nearby garment district.
There were a few advertising-agency types there too,
young men with ponytails and thin young women in very
tight dresses, with long painted nails and straight, expensively bleached hair.

Christian found a vacant space at the bar and ordered
a double bourbon on the rocks. When it came, he drained
it in one swallow, then, catching the barman's eye immediately ordered another. He took this one to a corner
of the room, where there was a free piece of windowsill,
and perched himself on it, sipping, thinking back over
the past few hours.

He had difficulty in thinking of that limp bloodied scrap
he had seen being rushed out of the delivery room of
Saint Catherine's less than three hours ago as his daughter, or even as a child at all.

He took a large swig of his drink. With the press of
bodies and the remnants of the day's heat outside, it was
getting oppressively warm in the pub. Christian loosened

his tie, drained his glass, and went to the bar to order another, finding himself beside another American, of about his own age.

There, however, the resemblance ended. The other man was small and tubby, with sandy hair and pale eyes. "Hi!" he said, "a fellow American eh?"

Christian, in no mood for pleasantries, felt he had to acknowledge the greeting. "Hi!" he said shortly, and fixed his eyes on the barman.

But the man was determined. "On vacation?"

"No," said Christian, hoping by his tone to deter him, "I live here actually."

It was a mistake to have admitted to any detail at all. The man fastened on it. "Well, how about that! Maybe you could give me a few pointers." He held out his hand. "Ferdy Cameron. It's a Scottish name. Professor of English at Modena in Oshkosh, Wisconsin. I'm on sabbatical here in England."

Christian took the hand. "Hi! Christian Smith. I'm a journalist."

"My God! Not the Christian Smith who wrote that great stuff about the convention in Chicago?"

It had been so long since this had happened to him that Christian was temporarily disarmed. "Yes," he said, surprised.

"Well, put it there, Christian!" said the other man. "I've used that article in my classes. That was some piece!" He seized Christian's hand again and pumped it enthusiastically. "This is great! Christian Smith! I gotta buy you a drink, Christian."

Christian, discomfited, saw there was no escape.

Three drinks later, he began to feel that old Ferdy was not such a bad guy after all and suggested they have a meal together.

Ferdy was delighted. He had been lonely in London so far, he confided. Londoners were cold fish. Christian, loosened by drink, was tempted to unload his current problems, but something, a sense of incompleteness, held him back.

He and Ferdy crossed the street and entered L'Epicure, and after a short wait, managed to get a table. They talked of America and their college days, and Christian managed to keep at bay the awful empty feeling in the pit of his stomach. He and Ferdy had a couple of brandies after the meal and ignored the flapping of the waiters around their table.

Just as the doctor was coming in the door of Molly's hospital room to tell her the truth about her baby, in another part of London Conor was in bed, beginning a row with Una O'Connor.

It had been a hot day for early May. The windows of Conor's tiny third-floor flat were open, but he was sweating as he lay on his back in the narrow bed, Una's soft, round body, also damp, snuggled against him. He wished he could get up right away, but tried to be patient as she cuddled him, making him feel even sweatier.

He stifled a yawn. Not for the first time, he wondered how he had got himself so deeply mired in this situation. He liked Una, she was an intelligent companion and sex between them was fun—or had been fun—but she took far more out of their relationship than he was prepared to donate and, increasingly, he felt she was a drain on him. She was able to manipulate her schedule so she could spend a great deal of her time off in London; he wished she wouldn't, but on the other hand, he felt ungrateful because he knew she spent all of her spare cash on airfares.

"Did you see the piece in the *Standard* about Margo Bryan?" she asked.

He used the opportunity to remove himself gently from her arms and to get out of the bed. "No. What piece was that?"

She turned on her back and stretched her body into a wide, sensuous X.

"Apparently, *Streams of Hope*, that movie she made with Eugene Lothar, has been nominated at Cannes—and Margo herself is an outside chance for an award. Of course, they called her a *British* actress!" Una, Conor knew, felt proprietorial about her journalistic protegée.

"Well, I suppose in a way they're right." He crossed to the sink and began to sluice some of the sweat off his face under the running faucet. "After all, most—all—of her success has been here in England."

Una raised herself on one elbow. "Seán Molloy!" she said indignantly. "How dare you! You of all people!"

"What difference does it make, Una?"

"It makes a great deal of difference to me—and I'm sure if Margo were here it would make a great deal of difference to her! How would you like it if you discovered some new fossil which was going to revolutionize the world's thinking on the origin of the species or something, and the papers all called you an Englishman?"

Conor continued to splash water on himself. Una, who tended to become vehement at the drop of a hat, was getting on his nerves. He knew it was unfair. "Uh-huh," he said, muttering into the water.

She would not be put off. "Well?" she demanded, and he heard the bedsprings creak as she sat up in the bed. He did not turn around, but he knew that her eyes would be wide with indignation. He was tired and fed up with the argument. He wanted to remove himself completely from the room, from her, from this stifling day.

Immediately he was ashamed. Una was a decent person, probably as decent a person as a man could find, and he knew that she was genuinely in love with him. She deserved better than this from him. He had never even told her what his real name was nor revealed his true relationship with Molly. Poor Una was still under the impression that he was simple Seán Molloy from Inisheer, old friend of Molly from the year dot. He dried his face and padded back to the bed, sitting down on the side of it.

She shifted to make room for him and wrapped her arms around his waist: "Well? You didn't answer me. Englishman!" She began to wriggle against him, arching her back, moving her thigh so it lay across both of his, pressing her breasts against his side. He was repelled. "Stop it, Una!"

He had spoken more harshly than he had intended and could see that she was hurt. He tried to make it up to her. "Sorry, I didn't mean it."

But she made a little 'hands-off' gesture, removing herself from him and getting off the bed. "Sorry, Una," he apologized, "I really didn't mean it. I'm hot and tired and I've had a really hectic week."

"So have I, Seán."

"I know. Let's go out and have a meal or something."

"No, that's okay. I'm tired too. I'll just have a

shower.'' She took the loose cotton dress that lay on the floor, slipped it over her head, and walked the few paces away from him toward the bathroom. After a few seconds, he heard the water running in the shower and sighed. This weekend was going to be tough.

He admitted to an acute longing to see Molly. Una was lovely, but she was no substitute. He had to see Molly. He knew her baby was due around this time. They had not met since her marriage to Christian—in fact, since she had told him about the marriage at that lunch. It would have been difficult for them to meet even if they had wanted to, because they were frequently on different continents. She had made several visits to America, and with the cooperation of the zoo, which continued to grant leaves of absence, he had immersed himself in archaeology and was himself frequently abroad, participating in various excavations.

On the other hand, he had mixed feelings about not seeing her during the past year. He missed her dreadfully and jealously and often woke up in the middle of the night thinking of her. But given her new status as Mrs. Christian Smith, he knew that if he did see her, he could not behave naturally toward her, in a manner befitting a brother—or even, if there were others around, as the supposed old friend, Seán Molloy. It was far easier on them both if they did not meet at all.

They had spoken, however. She had telephoned him to thank him for his telegram and his wedding present—a damask tablecloth of Irish linen—and on a few occasions since. But mostly they communicated by letter: stilted, formal epistles which might have been between penpals who had tired of the correspondence but who were still committed to it. From America she had written about the doings of her new family, particularly of the old man, Malcolm, of whom she seemed very fond. Her visit to Inisheer with Christian to meet Brendan was good for two months' letters.

But she had been already five months pregnant when she had broken that particular news to him.

In his turn, when he was abroad, he wrote her long involved descriptions of whatever desert or gorge he happened to be in at the time—and since there was every possibility his letters would be read by Molly's husband, he always signed his letters "Seán."

The sound of water running continued from the bathroom. He looked around at the tiny room, cluttered and claustrophobic, made more so by Una's scattered belongings and her half-unpacked overnight bag in the middle of the floor. Conor, who had been living alone for so many years, was meticulous and personally very neat and Una's untidiness was an additional source of irritation to him. He had to get out, and get some space . . .

He went to the bathroom door and knocked. Una didn't hear him at first and he knocked a second time. The sound of the shower stopped. "Yes?" she called.

"Una, I'm going out for a few minutes. Won't be long." He waited.

"Okay!" she said then, and he heard her resume her shower.

He threw on his clothes, which by habit he had folded neatly on a chair beside the bed, and left the flat, taking the three flights of stairs two at a time.

The Traveller was parked a short distance away, and as he walked rapidly toward it, he breathed deeply. He would have to confront the issue of Una once and for all; keeping the situation going like this was not fair to either of them.

He sat for a few moments with his chest pressed against the steering wheel of the little car, staring at the old-fashioned dashboard without seeing it. The feeling that he should go to Molly was growing more urgent. But how? How could he walk calmly into her life after an absence of more than a year—on what pretext?

This was ridiculous. He did not need any pretext to go to see his own sister. The imminent birth of her baby was the perfect opportunity to contact her; he was family, after all. He would be the baby's uncle. And if Christian answered the door, he would deal with that as it happened, say he was just passing.

He started the car and sped off in the direction of her house on Vernon Street.

When he got there, the street was as quiet as usual. He checked his watch—it was just after ten-thirty and the streetlamps were lit. Many of the houses showed lights in the windows, but there were no lights on in Molly's house. He rang the bell anyway, just in case she—or they—were somewhere in the back, perhaps in the kitchen. He was already regretting his impulse—what was he going to say?—and was almost relieved when there was no reply after his third ring. He was just about to leave when he heard the sash on the upstairs window of the adjoining house being lifted.

A head emerged, lit by the streetlamp below. "Looking for someone?" asked the owner of the head, a middle-aged woman with blonded hair escaping from a headful of curlers.

"Yes, I was looking for Mrs. Smith. Sorry to have bothered you," he called back. "I hope I didn't wake you up."

"That's okay, luv," said the blond head, "but you won't find Mrs. Smith there tonight. In the hospital, she is! Had the baby by now, I expect. She was taken off at about eight this morning."

"Thank you very much," called Conor, feeling silly. "You don't happen to know which hospital?"

"Saint Catherine's, I believe."

"Thanks again!"

"You a relative?" called the woman.

"Friend!" shouted Conor.

"Give her my love then, when you see her, dear—okay?"

"I will," he promised.

The window above him closed and he got back into his car. He drove out of Vernon Street and toward Earl's Court. The traffic was light and he risked parking near the Tube station, while he ran into the entrance where he knew there would be public telephones. He dialed 197 and got the number of Saint Catherine's private clinic from the operator. Then he called the clinic and said he was making inquiries about Mrs. Molly Smith.

"Just a moment, sir." The line went dead. When it came back, there was a different voice on the line.

"You're inquiring about Mrs. Molly Smith?"

"Yes," said Conor.

"Is this Mr. Smith?" asked the voice.

"Yes!" said Conor immediately, on instinct.

"I'm very glad you telephoned, Mr. Smith. We've been trying to contact you at your home, but there was no answer. Mrs. Smith has been asking for you; she is very anxious to talk to you. Can you come in as soon as possible?''

Conor's heart started to thump. "Yes, certainly I will," he said. Then: "Is everything okay with her?"

"The doctor is with her now," said the voice crisply. "I've just come on duty myself, but I know that things are under control. I'm sure the doctor will fill you in when you arrive."

"Thank you," said Conor. He hung up. He stared stupidly at the telephone, at the graffiti, at the little stickers that advertised the services of various "strict" head teachers and mistresses.

There was something wrong.

He had forgotten to ask for the address of the clinic. And he did not want to take time to call again or to go back to the car.

He ran out of the station and, not caring about the hazardously parked Traveller, flagged down a taxi. The cabby knew where the clinic was; getting there was a matter of only a few minutes through the light traffic.

Saint Catherine's proved to be one of a Regency terrace of houses in a quiet cul-de-sac. Conor paid off the driver and ran up the short flight of steps. The lobby, furnished with armchairs and coffee tables, was peaceful, with Mozart piped discreetly through the greenery that hung from a three-sided mezzanine around the stairwell. The only hint that this was a hospital and not a private hotel was the starched white uniform of the woman behind the reception desk.

"Mr. Smith!" he announced, "to see Mrs. Molly Smith." He felt like a criminal as he spoke; suppose Christian had arrived since he had made the telephone call? Suppose this woman had seen Christian earlier and remembered him? In his nervousness and guilt at the impersonation, Conor's voice was hoarse.

But the woman did not react—Conor supposed she was used to nervous fathers. She merely checked a Rolodex in front of her and directed him to the mezzanine and to the elevator there that would take him to the third floor and then picked up a telephone.

There were a nurse and a doctor waiting for him when the elevator door opened. The doctor introduced himself as Dr. Anderson and asked him to step into the office for a moment. Conor seized the doctor's sleeve. "Is Molly all right? Is she all right?"

"She's fine, Mr. Smith. She is a little agitated and we have given her a light sedative, but she is really fine. Dr. Sinden apologizes that he is not here himself to talk to you—we were trying to contact you for quite a while and eventually he had to leave, I'm afraid. But before he left, he familiarized me with the details of the case and asked me to fill you in when we did manage to get in touch." His voice was serious, urbane, soothing. As he spoke, he propelled Conor with him toward an office. The nurse came with them and closed the door after the two men, seating herself discreetly in a chair half hidden by a filing cabinet.

The doctor indicated that Conor should sit on a chair in front of the desk and himself sat on its edge.

"Is it Molly or the baby?" Conor asked, impatient with the man's scene setting.

"Your wife is fine, please don't worry about her. She's had a shock and she is naturally depleted and exhausted after giving birth, but in time she will come to terms with what has happened."

"So what's happened? What's wrong with the baby?" It occurred belatedly to Conor that he did not know whether Molly had given birth to a boy or a girl.

The doctor hesitated, then: "Your daughter may, I stress *may*, be suffering from a condition we call Cerebral Palsy." He put his hand on Conor's shoulder, a professional gesture that Conor immediately resented. He forced himself not to shrug it off.

"There is no easy way to say this," the man went on, "but your daughter is brain-damaged. It is too early to say how badly or how it happened, whether it is genetic or caused by something during pregnancy or labor. We will do our very best for her, of course, you can rely on that, but I'm afraid the prognosis is not good."

"You mean she's going to die?"

"Some people with this condition live to be quite elderly."

"But what do you think about *this* person?"

"It's too soon to tell."

"You think it's bad, don't you?"

The doctor nodded. "We always say there is hope in these situations, but yes, it's bad."

"What are the symptoms?"

"Each patient is different, of course, depending on the severity of the brain damage and where in the brain it has occurred, and in the case of your daughter, it is far too early to tell. We will have to watch her development . . ." He paused, giving Conor time to assimilate the information.

"In the case of your daughter, Mr. Smith," he repeated then, "it appears she might be a quadriplegic. In other words, she is largely paralyzed. There may be other problems as well. It is quite likely, Mr. Smith, that if your daughter survives, she will have to be institutionalized."

Conor had quite forgotten that he was not Molly's husband. He wanted to shake off this man, well-intentioned though he was. He stood up. "Can I see Molly—now, please?"

"She is probably sleeping," warned Dr. Anderson, "but of course you can see her."

He got off his perch and held out his hand. "I'm very sorry. You've had a shock, I know. And I'm sure you think it's easy for me to stand here telling you not to worry too much. But I can assure you that your daughter is in good hands at the moment. Everything which can be done will be done for her, please be sure of that. And we will arrange for a psychologist to see your wife, of course—" He hesitated. "I'm really sorry," he said again.

Conor took the man's hand and shook it briefly. All thoughts of Christian Smith had left his head and he no longer felt like an imposter. Their footsteps making no sound at all on the thick carpet, he followed the doctor down a corridor. Near the end, Anderson pushed open a plain heavy door, then stood aside to let Conor go in alone.

She was asleep on her side, breathing softly, her knees pulled up like a child's; the only light in the room was from a dim blue bulb directly over the headboard, and under its ethereal glow, her skin gleamed like fine china. Conor had to swallow. He thought her more beautiful than he had ever seen her. For the moment, he abandoned all questioning as to the propriety or morality of loving her. He loved her in every way there was to love another human being, so deeply at that moment that he was actually in physical pain.

Moving very quietly and keeping his eyes on her all the time, he carried a chair from a corner of the room to a spot beside the bed and sat in it, as close to her as he possibly could without actually touching her. A strand of her hair which had fallen across her cheek wafted on her breath and he longed to touch it, to brush it off.

He noticed that the room was full of flowers and became aware of the blend of scents in the room, in which the heady mixture given off by flowers fused with the hygienic hospital smell and with something else he recognized with surprise as the heavy bloody scent of parturition. During his island childhood, Conor had occasionally been present at the birth of a calf or a litter of puppies. This smell was not dissimilar.

And what of the baby—his crippled niece? Conor examined his feelings; could he stand passively by and watch his own niece be put into an institution? Again he had to swallow hard but forced himself to concentrate on immediate problems. First and foremost, there was Molly . . .

She slept peacefully on as he watched her. It was very quiet, so quiet that on the other side of the door, he heard a single clink, bottle against bottle or spoon against glass; the sounds from the street outside were muffled by double-glazing and heavy curtains on the windows.

After ten minutes or so, she opened her eyes. She looked at him for a moment without recognition and then smiled as guilelessly as a child. "You came!" she whispered.

He nodded. He thought his heart would split open.

She took her hand out from underneath the coverlet and held it toward him. He gripped it, warm and soft from its lair. "You know about my baby?" she whispered.

He nodded again. Her lovely face creased between her eyebrows as she tried to remember something specific. "There's something wrong with my baby, Conor . . ."

He tightened his grip on her hand and then relaxed it.

He was afraid he might crush it. "Molly, we'll face it together. We'll all help."

"Where's Christian?"

"I don't know, Molly, but after I leave, I'll find him for you."

"I don't know if he knows yet."

"I don't know either, but this is not something you will have to face on your own, I promise."

"Did you see her?" she asked, still whispering. He shook his head. "I did." she said. "I saw her. They brought me down to see her. She's in a little glass case. She's very beautiful, like a little delicate shell." She had difficulty getting her tongue around the words, and under the faint illumination, he could see that her eyes, which she held steady on his face, were opaque with sedatives.

"Have you decided on a name for her?" He felt instantly stupid. What difference did it make what this baby was going to be called?

But she answered. "Margaret Susanna," she whispered.

"That's a lovely name." he said. "Margaret Susanna Smith," he repeated, barely able to get the words out. "It's a lovely name."

"Yes," she said, "I know. It's a lovely name." She closed her eyes.

Conor cast around for something to say, anything but what was in his heart. "I was reading the *Evening Standard* earlier," he told her. "It says you're an outside chance to win an award at Cannes."

"Am I? That's nice." She did not open her eyes and Conor thought she had fallen asleep. But then her lips moved again: "Don't leave yet, Conor."

"I won't." Very soon after that, her hand slackened in his.

When he was sure she was soundly asleep, he disengaged himself, finger by finger, and stood up, not making a sound. Then, as though he were venerating a shrine, he bent over her and kissed her on the forehead.

He stood for a few moments looking down at her and left her, taking care to close the door without making a sound. From some other part of the building, a great distance away, it seemed, he heard the high, frantic mewling of a very young infant. Within seconds another one had joined in. He wondered with fleeting bitterness if either of them was Molly's, or if, indeed, Margaret Susanna could cry at all.

The dark-skinned nurse at the station in front of the elevator looked up as he pressed the call button, but he did not acknowledge her smile.

The night air outside was cool and fresh after the over-heated hospital. He remembered that in his haste he had forgotten to lock the Traveller. He hoped that it would still be there and went in search of a taxi.

Luck was with him, the car was still where he had parked it. He looked at his watch as he paid off the taxi, and to his surprise it was not yet midnight. So much had happened to him emotionally in the past two hours that had he been asked to guess, he would have put the time at nearer two in the morning. He discovered he was very hungry.

The next task was to find Christian, but before that he simply had to have something to eat. He saw there was a Wimpy Bar still open near the station. He drove the Traveller along Earl's Court Road and parked it on a small side street, then walked back to the Wimpy. He was the only customer in the glaring, garish shop, where he ordered two hamburgers and a bag of chips, eating them while standing at the counter, thinking furiously as he ate. He had no idea where Christian might hang out, knew none of his friends nor even his acquaintances. They had not a single mutual friend. He regretted bitterly now that he had not kept touch with his sister. Had Molly given any clues? Had the hospital?

That was it: *we've been trying to contact you at the number you left but there was no reply. . . .*

He finished the last of his chips and walked back toward the Traveller. There was a telephone booth on the corner of the street where he had parked. He had forgotten the number of the hospital and once more had to dial Information to get it.

The hospital answered on the second ring. Conor took a deep breath and feeling ridiculous, like an actor in a bad low-budget movie, did his best to assume an American accent. "This is Gerald Smith." he said, "I'm the brother-in-law of Mrs. Molly Smith, who has just had a baby there. I'm trying to get in touch with her husband, who is my brother, Christian. I understand he left a number with you?"

"Oh, yes, Mr. Smith," said the receptionist helpfully, "just a moment . . ."

There was a click and for a moment the line went dead. Then she came on and gave him the telephone number of Molly's house in Vernon Street. That was no use whatsoever. He thanked her and hung up. But at least he knew now that Christian intended to be at home at some stage. He dialed the number, but there was no reply. The best thing to do was to go home and to keep trying to telephone at intervals throughout the night. Christian was bound to turn up sooner or later.

Conor started up the car and sped off. He was crystal-clear now as to what he would say to Una.

The Friday night crowds in Soho swirled around Christian and Ferdy as they stood outside L'Epicure. Despite all the alcohol he had consumed, Christian had failed to fully anesthetize the horror. Now he urged his new friend not to go home just yet: "Come on, Ferdy, it's early. Let's go somewhere else!" If he could just have a few more drinks, he could postpone going back to the empty house where, alone, he would have to face his demons. Worse, if he did not have somewhere else to go, he should, in all fairness, go back to the hospital.

"I—I—don't know . . ." Ferdy's little face was doubtful. "Where would we go?"

"Plenty of places," said Christian. "London is full of nightclubs."

"No, I don' think so, Chrissian." Ferdy was slurring.

"Oh, all right!" Christian was tired of the man anyway. They parted from one another with exchanges of addresses and promises to keep in touch: promises which, in Christian's case, he already knew were empty. Then each went on an individual search for a taxi.

The street was so busy that it was twenty minutes before Christian secured one.

"Where to, sir?" asked the cabbie. Christian dithered. He should really go back to the hospital. He checked his watch, half-past midnight. She would undoubtedly be sleeping, he rationalized—his presence would again be superfluous.

The cabbie was drumming his fingers on the steering wheel and Christian made up his mind. He would salve his conscience by telephoning. And he would then go to the Dorchester to see Malcolm and his grandmother. No one could fault him then. "Would you take me to the Dorchester, please?" he said, "but stop at a telephone booth on the way."

When he called the clinic, Christian had to raise his voice to be heard above the traffic noise.

"Oh, yes, Mr. Smith," said the receptionist, "I'll put you through to the floor now."

"Hello?" said another voice, after a few clicks.

"Hello!" said Christian, speaking slowly and clearly, not only because of the traffic, but so as not to betray that he had had a few drinks. "This is Christian Smith, Molly Smith's husband."

"Yes, Mr. Smith?"

"I'm just checking on my wife."

"Well, there's been no change . . ." Even through the noise, he thought she sounded puzzled. "I see," he said. "Is she sleeping?"

"Yes, she is, and I'm sure she'll sleep now till morning . . ."

"I see. Well, will you take a message, please? Will you tell her when she wakes that her husband telephoned and sends his love and that I'll be in early in the morning . . ." The voice at the other end made no reply. "I'm sorry, there's a lot of noise here," said Christian. "Did you hear me?"

"Yes, Mr. Smith," said the voice slowly, "I'll see your wife gets your message."

"Thanks a lot," said Christian. He hung up and got into the cab again. "The Dorchester, please!" he said.

All too soon the taxi was pulling up outside the hotel. Christian crossed the lobby and asked the receptionist on duty to telephone his grandfather's room, and while the man made the call, tried to keep himself calm. He was dreading this encounter.

The lobby was so quiet that through the earpiece of the telephone, he could hear Malcolm's excited voice as he responded to the receptionist's inquiry and his heart fell still further. He almost turned tail and ran, but forced himself to walk toward the elevators and to press the ascent button. Suddenly he felt sober.

Malcolm, his expression happily expectant, was waiting for him in front of the elevator doors. "At last! We were getting worried, we really were—"

"Hello, Grandpa!" said Christian.

The joy died out of his grandfather's face: "There's something wrong?"

"Is Grandma here?"

"There's something wrong, isn't there? Tell me."

"I'm very tired, Grandpa—"

"You've been drinking!" His grandfather took a step backward but for once, Christian managed to control the retort that shot to his lips. There was nothing to be gained at this point by fighting. "I've had a few drinks, yes," he said unsteadily. "Look, can we go into your room? I don't want to tell you what I have to tell you out here in a corridor."

"Oh, my God!" After a few seconds, Malcolm led the way into the suite, the door of which was open.

As soon as she saw them come in, Cordelia half rose from her seat on a small chaise. Then, when she saw their expressions, she sat down again. "Oh, Christian!" she said, her eyes dismayed, "what is it?"

Christian walked across the room and kissed her. He could not bring himself to speak.

"What's wrong, darling?" she asked quietly, holding his hand and looking up at him.

"Can I sit down?" Christian felt as though his blood had thickened. weighting his arms and legs. Malcolm came and stood in the center of the room, jingling coins in the pocket of his trousers, and Christian sat on the chaise beside his grandmother.

Christian looked at the floor. "You're right, Grandma," he said, "there is a problem."

He was aware of Malcolm walking to the door and closing it and waited until he heard the click before continuing. "The baby is handicapped, Grandma," he said. "She's—its a girl—she's badly handicapped. Brain-damaged." He looked into the middle distance, the reporter in him noticing irrelevantly that the suite was decorated in the Regency style, with a profusion of pastels and stripes, tassels and furbelows. Then he felt

Cordelia's soft touch on his arm: "Have you seen her, Christian?"

"She's sleeping," he said. "They sedated her."

"The baby?" She was puzzled . . .

"I thought you meant Molly."

"No, I meant have you seen your daughter?"

"I saw her when she was born. She was blue. It was dreadful." He put his head in his hands. Now that he was talking about it, all the emotion he had been afraid to release threatened to overwhelm him. "Could I have a drink, please?" he asked through his fingers.

For once Malcolm did not object: "Is bourbon all right?"

Christian nodded and his grandfather went into the bedroom of the suite, returning with a bottle of Jack Daniels and a glass.

Christian poured a large measure of the liquor and gulped it in one mouthful. "Oh Grandma"—he looked at his grandmother as the tears finally came—"what am I going to do?"

Before he got to his flat, Conor stopped at a telephone booth and called the Vernon Street number, just in case. Still no answer. Then he rang the hospital yet again and said he was asking after Mrs. Molly Smith.

There was the usual click before the line went dead and then the woman's voice came back on. "Are you a relative?"

This time, he said it. "I'm her brother."

"Yes, well, Mrs. Smith is asleep and she is doing fine."

"Is there anyone with her?" he asked. "Should I come to sit with her?"

"Just a moment, sir . . ." said the voice and the line went dead again. After a minute or so, the woman came back on. "I've been on to the floor, sir, and the staff nurse believes that Mrs. Smith should be allowed to sleep."

"Yes, but is there anyone with her? She shouldn't be alone at a time like this."

"There are no visitors in the hospital at this hour, sir, only husbands, in exceptional circumstances and during labor and birth." She had obviously had to use these phrases many times before.

"Is her husband not with her?" asked Conor.

"Sir"—he could hear she was getting impatient—"Mrs. Smith is *sleeping*."

"Thank you, I'll call again in the morning." So he knew Christian wasn't there. Now he himself had to face Una.

Five minutes later he let himself into the house that contained his flat and climbed the stairs, making no effort to be quiet. Friday night was party night in the building. There was a fanlight over the door into his own bedsitter and he could see the light was on. Una was still awake. He realized that like a coward, he had been secretly hoping that she would be asleep.

"Hello!" she said, as he opened the door. She was sitting propped up on the bed, a book in her hands. Scrubbed and in her nightgown, her red hair curling around her face, she looked small and vulnerable as a child—and he felt that what he was about to do was despicable.

"You were a good while!" she said.

"Yes, sorry. Would you like a drink or a cup of tea or coffee or something?"

"I have some duty-free in the bag. I brought it for you, but when you were so long, I was going to open it myself."

"All right," he said, "I'll get the glasses."

While he rinsed out a pair of tumblers in the sink and filled a jug with water, she hopped out of the bed and rummaged around in the bag, scattering underwear, books and cassette tapes all over the floor. "Here it is! I always pack it in the bag. I hate carrying those yellow duty-free bags through customs at Heathrow. I feel they look at you with contempt, those officers. Ta-raa!" She held up the bottle of Paddy. Then she climbed back into the bed, smoothed the covers around her, and looked at him expectantly, the bottle still in her hand. "Well, come on, slowcoach!"

He brought the tumblers over and sat beside her on the bed. She filled them with generous measures and replaced the cap. He topped up each tumbler with water from the jug.

"Here's looking at you, kid!" said Una, raising her glass in a toast and then taking a sip.

"Are you not going to ask me where I was, Una?" he said quietly, without touching his own drink.

"That's your business. None of mine. We're not umbilically linked, you know."

She wasn't making this easy for him. He put his untouched drink on the night table beside the jug. "Una," he said gently, taking her hand, "we have to talk."

" 'Uh-oh! ' she said! I don't like the sound of *that*!" Despite the flippant tone, he could hear the seriousness.

"There's something I have to tell you."

"Don't tell me. I knew it all along. You've a wife in Clacton!" She withdrew her hand and took another sip of her drink.

"Una, I'm not married. But I have been deceiving you." She wrapped both hands around her tumbler and stared into it.

"Are you listening, Una?"

"Oh, no, I'm not listening. I'm singing. What do you think I'm doing?" She looked at him then, a straight, direct look. "You're trying to tell me you're in love with someone else."

He almost admitted it. The temptation was strong to tell someone, anyone. But not Una. "It's not that, Una. I'm not who you think I am."

"What?"

"My name is not Seán Molloy." He watched her while she digested this information.

"I see. Well, am I to know who you are?"

"Do you want to?"

"I'm not sure I'm going to like this, but we've come this far—" She made another little gesture which tried to be devil-may-care and failed miserably.

"My real name is Conor O Briain and I'm Molly's brother." Una looked genuinely bewildered. As well she might, he thought.

"I'm Molly's brother," he repeated. "I've just come from the hospital where Molly has had a baby girl. The baby is handicapped, Una. There are things I have to do now for Molly—for my sister."

He watched her face. To his horror, he realized he had made a mess of it; she thought it was going to be all right for them—and, of course, from her point of view, why not?

"Oh, Seán!" She put down her drink and hugged him. "I'm so sorry—I mean I'm so sorry about the baby, but I'll help! I'll do anything I can to help."

"No, Una." Gently he removed her arms from around his neck. "That's what I want to tell you. I don't want any help, not from anyone. I want to be on my own."

She lowered her arms and folded them, but he could see it took a while for his meaning to fully register. "I see," she said quietly. She picked up her drink again. "But why, Seán? What difference does it make to us? And by the way," she added conversationally, "why the deception? *Why* are you 'Seán Molloy'?"

"If you really want to know, I'll tell you, but it's a long and very complicated story. I have to find Molly's husband now. He has temporarily vanished."

"Why, Seán—Conor? I hate that name, by the way!" she said with some savagery.

"Why what?"

"You know—the real 'why.' I know you well enough to know you must have your own good reasons for changing your name—and for your sister to conspire with you. Are you IRA by any chance?"

He smiled in admiration. "No, you can take it that I'm not IRA."

"Thank heaven for that!" She attempted to laugh and again failed. "But the real 'why' is why should your name change affect us?"

"Again, that's a very long story. Let's just say that a lot of things have happened together to me and very suddenly and that I do, really, need to be on my own for a while."

She tried one last time. "For a *while*?"

"Una—"

"All right, all right!" She adopted a stage-Irish accent: "I know when I'm bet!" She tossed her drink off in one gulp and placed the tumbler with exaggerated care on the night table. Then, businesslike, she looked at her watch. "Do you want me to leave straight away? It's a bit late."

He thought again she looked like a child pretending to be grown-up. He took her in his arms. "Oh, Una!"

But she disentangled herself. "Now, now! Musn't be sentimental about these things!" Conor felt abjectly guilty as her mouth set itself in a parody of a smile. He stood up. "Of *course* you don't have to leave now, Una. And I hope you'll stay the weekend."

"*Please,* Seán!" She shouted it at him and picked up the book which lay discarded beside her on the bedcover. Turning away from him, she threw it with all her strength, not at him but away from him against the wall on the far side of the bed. The book was a paperback and it crashed harmlessly against the wall, falling with a soft thud on the carpeted floor.

Conor held up his hands in surrender. Although he was feeling so guilty about causing her such pain, the last thing he wanted was a scene. "All right," he said, "but please stay as long as you like. I have to go out now, to see if I can locate Molly's husband."

Una swallowed. "Yes, Molly. Well . . . Mustn't keep you from Molly!" Her voice was bitter. She swallowed again hard, and Conor saw that she was having difficulty with tears.

"Una," he said again, taking a step toward the bed, but it was her turn to hold up her hands. She kept her eyes fixed on one of the buttons of his shirt. "I really am very sorry about the baby. You know that. Please"— her voice wobbled—"please give Molly my love."

"I will."

"And," she said, again under control, "I'm putting you on notice that I *will* want to know about all the mystery. It's just that I can only handle one thing at a time . . . at the moment . . ."

Conor felt as though he were whipping her. He now wanted badly to get away. "You will know. I promise."

He looked back at her from the door as he let himself out. She was out of the bed, her back to him, picking up her book from the floor. He saw her shoulders were shaking and wavered for a moment. Then, resolutely, he closed the door.

He got to the house on Vernon Street just after one-thirty, parked a little way down the street, and turned the engine and the lights off to wait. He wished he had brought a coat; after the earlier heat, the night had turned quite chilly. He managed to doze a little, and it was after two when he became aware that there was a taxi turning on to the street.

The taxi stopped in front of the house, engine ticking quietly, and after what seemed like a very long time, the back door opened and Conor saw Christian stumble into the pool of yellow light cast by the streetlamp on the curb.

Even from a distance of twenty yards, he could see that the other man was in a state of advanced drunkenness. Christian's hair was disheveled and his shirt collar was open; his knees had buckled under him as he got out of the cab and he was leaning against the vehicle with both hands to save himself from falling. Conor felt the bile rise in his throat but took a firm hold on his emotions. He must stay calm and in control.

After the taxi drove away, Christian stayed where he was on the sidewalk, looking after it, his hands slack and hanging, knees still bent, head wobbling slightly on his neck. When it was turning out of the street he made a peculiar gesture in its direction, raising both arms in the air as though he were a victorious general saluting his victorious troops. Then he let his arms drop, shrugged at the now-empty street, and turned, aiming the crown of his head at his front door.

Conor got out of his car, closing the door very quietly so he would not startle the other man. He walked toward him. "Christian!" he said, when he had got within earshot.

Christian reacted without surprise, turning his head. "Oh! Who're—who're you?" he asked mystified.

"Good evening, Christian," said Conor. "I've been looking for you. Molly would like to see you."

"Molly?"

"Yes! Your wife, Molly!" Conor clenched his fists by his sides.

"Moll—Molly wants to—wants to see me *now*?" Christian staggered a little into the gutter. "But who're *you*?"

"You may not remember, but we met once," said Conor. There was no point in fudging now. On the other hand, the man was so drunk he probably would not remember. "I'm your wife's brother, Conor," he said crisply.

Christian gave the impression he was dredging through his memory. "I've never met you—wait a minute. You—you, you're the guy in the dressing room, Mallarkey . . ."

"Molloy!" said Conor. "But believe me, I'm O Briain, Conor O Briain, Molly's brother. Could we go inside now?"

But Christian was still stuck two sentences back. "Molly wants to see me *now*?"

"Come on, Christian." Conor took his arm. "Let's go inside and we'll have a cup of coffee. No point in talking out here."

Christian tried to shrug off his arm, but he was no match for Conor's iron grasp. "Okay, Okay!" He extracted his keys from his jacket pocket and Conor, whose impatience was getting the better of him, took them from him and opened the front door of the house.

He switched on the lights. The hallway bore the marks of a hurried departure. There was an empty paper bag lying on the floor and a single shoe abandoned under the coatstand. The mail had not been picked up from the floor.

He shepherded the shambling Christian down the three steps toward the kitchen at the back of the house, and when he switched the light on in here, there was further evidence that Molly had left in a hurry. There were dirty dishes in the sink and the lid was off the coffeepot, as if she had been about to empty the stale grounds but had changed her mind—or had been interrupted.

He found the packet of coffee and filters in a cupboard, rinsed out the old grounds into the sink, and measured out enough coffee to hype up an elephant. While he waited for the percolater to bubble, he glanced at Christian, and to his dismay, he saw that he was nodding off over the table. "Hey!" he called in a loud voice, "hey, Christian! Wake up! The coffee's just ready."

Christian opened one bleary eye. "What are you doing here, Mallarkey?" he asked in astonishment.

"I'm making you a cup of coffee, Christian. We have to go to see Molly."

"Molly?"

It was clearly no use. Christian would do more harm

than good tonight anyway. "All right, man," said Conor, "come on, I'll help you up the stairs." Christian shrugged and allowed himself to be helped up from his seat.

He cooperated willingly as Conor half carried, half frog marched him up the stairs, and when they got to the bedroom, Conor aimed his burden at the bed and heaved. Christian landed facedown, his feet dangling over the side.

He fell asleep instantly.

Conor drew back, panting a little. The other man was almost as tall as he was himself, and being deadweight, had been very heavy. He looked around the room: fresh flowers in a jug on a little desk under the window, soft sheepskin rugs on the bare floor—it had Molly's stamp all over it.

In one corner stood a wicker basket, draped with *broderie anglaise* and sprigged cotton; piled underneath and around it were unopened boxes, which, he could see by the illustrations on them, contained baby equipment. Beside the basket, an archway had been broken through the wall into the next room, which had been converted into a sort of dressing room. There were two huge Victorian wardrobes, two tallboys, and several chests of drawers in this anteroom and a dressing table in front of the window, the wooden frame of its mirror bristling with electric bulbs. There was also a wooden clotheshorse, now bare. The wardrobes both hung open. One, obviously Christian's, was disorderly, with suits, jackets, and shirts. There were ties strewn untidily on the floor in front of it and shoes stuffed any old way underneath its graceful arched front.

The other wardrobe was Molly's, hung neatly with dresses, blouses, and skirts in the soft fabrics and plain colors she favored.

Conor looked back at Christian, oblivious and snoring, hesitated a little, and then walked over to Molly's wardrobe. The dress of pale blue silk, with the pleated sleeves, which she had worn on the day she had told him she was going to be married, hung on one of the hangers. The rough skin of his hand snagged the fabric, soft as a cobweb, when he touched it.

He went back into the main bedroom and eased Christian's slip-on shoes off his feet, which still dangled over the side of the bed. Then, thinking to cool the room as a help in the sobering-up process, he crossed to the window and was leaning across Molly's desk to open it when his eye was caught by a silver-framed photograph.

It was of their mother.

And in a corner of it, tucked into the frame, was a blurry black and white snapshot of the whole family. They were all standing, stiff and unsmiling, staring straight at the camera. Micheál and Brendan stood in front of the cottage; Sorcha stood between them, her hand shading her eyes from the sun. Conor himself, in short pants, was looking away from the photographer toward the edge of the picture. He had one hand outstretched toward his baby sister.

Molly, about two years old, was standing, back to the camera and feet planted firmly apart. She held both hands clasped behind her back and her head to one side, obviously defying her brother's blandishments.

There was another photograph beside it, also framed in silver, a formal wedding photograph of Molly and Christian. He was looking at her, an expression of happy adoration on his face. She was solemn and very beautiful. Conor forgot his mission to open the window and, feeling he was trespassing, left the room, closed the door after him, and went down the stairs.

He hesitated at the foot of the staircase, looking at the telephone. Then he lifted it, and for the fourth time in five hours, called the hospital. When the phone was answered, he announced himself as Christian. "Would you give my wife a message when she wakes up?" he asked, hoping against hope that the receptionist was not one of those people who had a talent for recognizing voices. "Certainly, Mr. Smith," she replied.

Conor swallowed. "Please tell her that I love her and that I will be in to see her first thing in the morning."

"I'll see to that, Mr. Smith," said the woman, and to his surprise she chuckled, "but I already have your earlier message for her on my pad."

"Thank you!" said Conor abruptly, and hung up.

The aroma of coffee was thick in the kitchen. He poured himself a cup and added three teaspoonfuls of sugar to it. He opened the door of the refrigerator but could find no milk; in fact there was hardly anything at all in the fridge, just a small piece of cheese, a head of lettuce, and the heel of a loaf of bread. As ever, Conor was hungry. It was Friday, he thought—no, Saturday now. Molly probably did her shopping during the weekend.

He looked at the piece of cheese and, sighing, picked it up and put it on the heel of the bread. Then he carried the makeshift sandwich to the table. He pulled another chair out from the table, angling it so he could prop up his feet—it was going to be a long night.

He stayed at the table for what remained of the darkness, getting up now and then to walk around the kitchen, stretching his legs. Once, just before dawn, he went through the conservatory which led off the kitchen and out onto the miniature garden Molly had created on her flagged patio. It faced south and she had trained all sorts of creepers and flowering plants to grow on trellises fastened on to the whitewashed walls: clematis, lobelia, various ivies, old-fashioned climbing roses. There were geraniums and pelargoniums in pots and huge tubs filled with red and orange nasturtiums. The pearly light that precedes the dawn was not yet strong enough to make much of a differentiation in the colors of the different flowers—and many of them were still curled tightly closed, but their combined scent was already riotous. He remembered Molly herself, lying so still in her blue, flower-filled grotto at Saint Catherine's.

Conor stayed on the patio, breathing in the inert, moist air, watching the flowers come slowly to life as the sky flushed first salmon-colored, then gold, then the palest shade of blue, patterned with mackerel clouds of pink and white. It was going to be another warm, sunny day.

He went into the kitchen and brewed more coffee. If Saint Catherine's was a typical hospital, it would not be long before Molly was woken. He had promised her by proxy that Christian would be with her first thing in the morning and he was going to keep that promise. It was time to wake up Molly's husband.

He went to the front door: Luckily, the milk had been delivered.

11

Christian did not know what hit him. He was woken violently by a crashing noise and then, a second later, the pain descended on the top of his head like a pile driver. He risked opening his eyes, to find that the sound was of both windows in the room being raised. To his surprise, then outrage, he saw that they were being raised by a man he did not recognize. If the man was a burglar, why was he opening windows? But when he tried to remonstrate, to ask what the devil this man was doing in his private bedroom, the pain strangled the words in his throat. He closed his eyes again; he was too sick to care if there was a whole army of burglars in his room.

He was so sick he felt like crying. There was something cutting uncomfortably into his stomach, and he realized it was his belt buckle. He must have gone to sleep fully dressed. He could remember nothing of how he got home, nothing after he had gone to see his grandfather in the Dorchester.

Sick as he was, he was outraged when the burglar came over and shook him. He groaned into the bedspread under his face and tried to lift his head to tell the man to get lost, but the pain shot all the way down to his toes and no words came out of his mouth. His teeth rattled with the shaking; in his painful jaws they felt like electro-sensitized steel bearings. Even his ears hurt.

"Go away!" he managed thickly, but the burglar would not let up.

"Come on, Christian, come on!" The man's voice was like sandpaper on Christian's painful scalp: "You have to get up. I'm not leaving you until you do. If you don't get up I'll pour cold water all over you."

Christian was too sick to fight. It seemed far easier to do what the man wanted. He inched his knees upward, and without lifting his pounding head, sought the floor with his feet. Then he crept backward off the bed, leaving his head as the last part of his body to be lifted. He kept his head low, at right angles to his body, while he stumbled toward the bathroom.

His torturer was there ahead of him and the shower was running. "Who the hell are you?" he managed, but the effort caused him to retch.

"We met last night," said the man. "My name is Conor O Briain, I'm your wife's brother."

"You're in Aus—Australia or something."

"No, I'm not. I'm right here and you're going to take a long shower."

Too ill to resist, keeping his head low and sideways in an effort to minimize the pain, Christian stripped off his clothes and, leaving them where they lay in an untidy heap, stepped into the shower.

He screamed.

The water was as cold as ice and the shock made his heart beat so savagely that, to add to the pain in his head, he now had a sharp pain in his chest. He tried to step out of the shower again, but the man was there, a stone wall, blocking his way. "Get back in there!" he said.

Christian had had enough. "Fuck off!" Like a butting ram, he pushed his head upward under the man's chin. *"Fuck off!"*

The pain swelled and nearly split his skull.

The man did not move, nor did he seem in the least perturbed by the outburst. "We have to get to the hospital as soon as possible," he said. "Please get back into the shower. You are in no condition to go anywhere at the moment."

Christian made a canopy of his hands over his eyes as if by doing so he could tie the pain inside and stop it bursting out through his forehead. He glared at his enemy from under them. *"We* have to go to the hospital?"

"Christian, we're wasting time. Your wife has been trying to contact you. I happened to go in to see her last night. I promised her I would bring you in."

Chilled by his encounter with the cold water, naked and dripping, Christian started to shiver. From under the tent of his fingers, he stared at the man: he was standing in his own bathroom after all—the man was an intruder.

"Have we met before?" he said with as much hostility in his voice as he could muster.

"Yes, we have, the first night you arrived in London with that phoney story about interviewing my sister."

"Mallarkey!"

"Molloy! Now, are you going to get back in that shower or do I have to push you?" For a few seconds, they glared at one another.

Christian was shaking all over now, but he saw that there would be no quarter given, and in his present condition knew he would be no match for his implacable adversary if push came to shove. So he stepped back into the shower, taking care not to let the water hit him before he had turned the mixer tap to a respectable temperature.

He stayed in for a good twenty minutes, letting the water beat on his sore head, massaging its warmth into his face and the back of his neck. He felt marginally better when he turned it off and went back into his bedroom to dress. He could smell coffee from downstairs and the smell of something cooking. It turned his stomach.

When he got to the kitchen, the other man was standing at the sink with his back to Christian, clouds of steam around his head as he drained something out of a pot.

Potatoes. The man was cooking potatoes at this hour of the morning! "Are you crazy?" Christian managed to ask, before he found himself being forced by a strong hand to sit at the kitchen table, while a quantity of soft boiled potatoes were poured out of the pot on to a shallow dish already set between a knife and fork.

Christian looked with horror at the steaming, soggy mess; the potatoes had been boiled so soft they were almost mashed and were bleeding a substance like lumpy wallpaper paste at the edges.

Worse was to come. From a small pan, Conor poured hot milk into the dish so the concoction looked more like lumpy soup than solids; then he passed over the salt and pepper shakers. "Eat!"

"I don't want them, I couldn't eat them, I'll get sick!" Christian tried to muster some degree of self-righteous outrage. "Fuck off!" he said, pushing back his chair, which scraped horribly on the tiled floor.

"EAT!" thundered the other man, restraining him

from standing up. Christian looked from the plate to
Molloy and saw the menace in the man's eyes. For the
third time in half an hour, he gave in. He picked up his
fork and took a tentative mouthful. To his surprise, he
did not gag.

He shook a liberal helping of salt and pepper all over
the food and in a few minutes, had finished what had
been in the dish. Then Molloy poured out a cup of strong
tea and put it in front of him, while he poured coffee for
himself. Christian wanted to say that he would prefer
coffee, but he accepted the black tea and drank it meekly.

"If you're Molly's brother, how come your name's
Molloy?" he asked.

"It's a long story," said the other man, and Christian
did not have the energy to pursue the matter. Although
he was still feeling very sorry for himself, he had to
admit that in whatever Irish bog this man had learned his
hangover cures, they were effective. He was feeling more
human than he had forty-five minutes ago.

"Right," said the other man when he had finished his
own coffee, "I have my car outside. It's nearly a quarter
to seven. I'll have you at the hospital before a quarter-
past."

The horror of his situation was reborn on Christian.

They drove through the Saturday streets in silence and
Christian opened the window and held his face out to the
cool morning air. They got there all too soon.

If their mission had not been so serious, thought Conor
as he turned off the ignition, he would have enjoyed this
quiet part of London. The sunlight was filtered onto the
pavements through the branches of the plane trees, and
in the absence of weekday traffic, the chirping of sparrows was loud in their branches. He turned to Christian.
"Here we are."

The other man's face was haggard and Conor felt almost sorry for him as Christian opened the door and
swung his legs onto the pavement and said with some
dignity: "Thank you for the ride . . ." Then, with something approaching an appeal: "Are you coming in too?"

Conor shook his head. "I'll come in later. You'll need
some time alone with Molly."

Christian got out and closed the door. The Traveller

was parked about twenty yards beyond the clinic and Conor watched him in the rearview mirror as he walked slowly back toward it and climbed the flight of steps to the front door. Conor decided to get out of the car too, to get some fresh air. The end of the cul-de-sac was formed by one side of a railings which enclosed a small park, and not bothering to lock the car doors, he strolled toward them, letting himself into the park through a wicket gate.

It was a pleasant place, cool and green, boasting flowering shrubs and trees, flowerbeds, an expanse of daisied lawn, and a pond not much bigger than a large puddle. He had it all to himself and walked a slow circuit of the railings. Then he flopped onto his back on the grass beside the pond.

As his ears adjusted to the quietness, he could hear, alongside the birdsong, the minute paddling and scudding of water insects going about their business above and below the surface of the stagnant water, its smell warm and fusty in his nostrils. There were other insects at work too. Under his palm on the grass, he felt tiny movements, of ants, probably, and spiders. A cabbage butterfly fluttered across his line of vision, making him blink.

It was a relief to close his eyes. Thankful it was his Saturday off, he did not resist as he felt himself drift into a gentle doze.

As soon as Christian entered the hospital lobby, his queasy stomach began to heave again. He asked the receptionist where the lavatory was and she pointed to a doorway half hidden behind a flowering tree.

He got into the cubicle just in time to vomit.

He stood for a long time, knees quivering, before coming back out to wash his hands and face. There was a discreetly lit mirror behind the hand basins, and as he ran water over his hands, Christian studied his reflection. He thought of his wife waiting for him in the bed, of his first wife somewhere in Chicago, of his failed relationship with his grandfather. He thought of his brain-damaged daughter.

The conclusion was inescapable: although professionally competent, he was personally a loser.

His instinct now was to flee, but in all decency, he had to face this. He was trapped.

Going up in the elevator, he continued to argue with himself. Molly would be better off without him—even materially. If she never worked again, which, with her talent, was doubtful, she and the baby would have no material problems, his grandfather would see to that.

He braced himself and pushed open the door of her room. She was asleep, or seemed to be—but within seconds, opened her eyes. "Christian! Where were you?"

"What do you mean, where was I? I was here last night—don't you remember?" Christian bristled defensively. Molly had that effect on him recently. He had no freedom anymore.

"Yes, but since that—where were you since?" She was not being aggressive, he saw, her voice was tired and weak and he softened a little. "All right, so I had a few drinks. Would you blame me, Molly?"

She turned her head away, and like a thick fog, silence descended over the room. Christian pulled a chair up to the side of the bed. "How are you feeling anyway?"

"I'm fine." She kept her head turned.

"Did you sleep?"

"Yes, thank you."

"Molly, don't treat me like this!"

"Like what?"

"Like I'm a pariah. Goddamn it, I've had a shock—"

"So have I. How do you think I feel?" At last she turned her head toward him and he saw her eyes were cold with fury. Such a display of anger in Molly was rare, and Christian was taken aback. "I'm—I'm sure you feel awful. But so do I."

"Well, stop feeling sorry for yourself and grow up, Christian! Drinking does not solve one thing. You're only making the situation worse for yourself—and for me. We have to discuss this."

"I know, I know. But I can't discuss anything with you when you're—"

"Not through the bottom of a glass—no!"

He stared at her, grievance rising in him like sludge. How dare she? How dare any woman try to dictate how he should live his life? "I said I'm sorry!" he said coldly.

"No, you did not!"

"All right, I'm saying it now. I'm *sorry*!"

"It's too late for sorry."

He stood up, "I don't have to take this—"

"Nobody's asking you to!" She raised herself on one elbow: "Go back to the pub! By the way, did you have the guts yet to go and see your daughter?" Again Christian stared at her; he had never, not since he had known her, seen her like this, heard her use such bitter sarcasm—this was a new Molly. "I'm going now," he replied with as much dignity as he could summon, "and yes, I will go down to see our daughter. I'll come back and see *you* when you're in a better mood."

"Don't bother," she said, and with a bitter sob, she turned her head away from him. Christian hated to see women cry; his reaction was always to become confused. Helplessly, he watched her for a second or two and then turned on his heel and left the room.

He glanced at the direction board over the nurses' station; the nursery, he saw, was at the far end of the corridor.

Behind him he heard the doors of the elevator open, and turning around, saw, coming out of it, a man of about his own age, accompanied by a boy and a girl.

Christian made up his mind.

"Thank you," he said as the boy held the door for him.

Conor woke with the snuffling of a dog at his ear. The dog was an overfed Jack Russell and its owner, a small elderly woman dressed more for a winter drawing room than a stroll in a summer park, was calling it in a quivering voice: "Toddy, Toddy! Come back here! Come here this instant!"

Feeling lightheaded, Conor sat up. He patted the dog, which wagged its tail, barked, and then trotted busily back to its mistress, who leaned down and gave it a slap on the nose for its trouble.

Conor bent his head to his knees until the dizziness cleared and then looked at his watch. He had been asleep for nearly half an hour, he reckoned, and thought he might decently venture now to join Christian and Molly in the clinic. How he was going to handle the scene among the three of them he would just have to leave to instinct.

He felt scruffy and longed for a shower and a change of clothes. Luckily, since he needed to shave twice a day, he kept a battery-operated razor in the glove compartment of the car, so at least he could shave. He walked back to the Traveller and got into it, angling the driving mirror toward him. Although Conor used mirrors for his daily ablutions, his own face was of no interest to him and he rarely actually noticed how he looked.

But the morning sun caught his face obliquely through the car window as he scraped the buzzing razor over his chin, and he saw with some surprise that the bristle was now well speckled with gray. He was getting old.

When he had finished shaving, he ran his fingers through his unruly hair, smoothing it down as best he could. Then he got out of the car and walked toward the clinic.

There was a different atmosphere in the lobby this morning. The doors had been propped open to admit the air and sunshine; the Muzak was drowned by the whine of a vacuum cleaner being passed busily over the carpet by a woman in overalls; another woman moved along the mezzanine, using a can with a long spout to water the plants. Conor saw there was a different person from the one last night on the reception desk, but this time did not announce himself. He just smiled in her direction and passed up the stairs as though he belonged in the place.

He was not so confident, however, when he emerged from the elevator into the corridor. He had not thought out how he was going to explain his impersonation of last night, should he encounter any of the people he had met. Now that Christian was around, there could be no doubt in anyone's mind but that something fishy was going on. Christian and he bore not the slightest resemblance to one another.

He recognized the dark-skinned nurse he had seen the night before and braced himself for an awkward question. But she just smiled at him. "Hello, Mr. Smith," she said. He smiled back, relieved.

He was almost at Molly's door when he heard a man's voice call, "Mr. Smith! Mr. Smith!" What was he to do? It was the doctor, Anderson, who had spoken to him the previous night—obviously, the man had not yet met Christian. He waited while the man caught up with him. "Good morning, Mr. Smith," the doctor said, slightly out of breath. "I've just had a call from Dr. Sinden and he would like to see you when he gets here—he should be in at about nine o'clock."

"Thank you," said Conor. "How is the baby?"

"There is little change at the moment, although we should know more when we get the results of the tests we did yesterday. Normally, we would have to wait until Monday, but thanks to Dr. Sinden's status here, we managed to jump the queue in the lab."

"Thank you," said Conor. The doctor turned and went back the way he had come, and Conor proceeded to Molly's room.

The room, very different from the dim blue grotto he remembered, was bright with sunshine and colorful with the masses of flowers. She was sitting up, propped high against a heap of pillows, and was facing away from the door, gazing in the direction of the window and apparently so preoccupied that she did not hear him come in. Her hair had been combed, he saw, but there were dark circles under her eyes and the eyes themselves were puffy. He thought she must have been crying recently.

There was no one else in the room, which he thought odd. Perhaps Christian had come in and left again immediately? "Hello, Molly," he said softly from the doorway, not wanting to startle her.

She turned to him and her face suffused with pleasure. "Hello, Conor," she said. "You came again! I'm really glad."

"Has Christian left?" he asked.

"Yes." She looked down at her hands.

"Something wrong?" Then he could have kicked himself—of course there was something wrong. "Was Christian upset, is that it?" He sat on the side of the bed.

"It's nothing—"

"Molly, I can see it's something."

"We—we had a row." She was whispering.

Conor felt like running after Christian and beating him senseless. "I'm sure he's under a lot of strain." He managed to say it without choking.

"Yes. I know."

Grimly, Conor thought that if they continued to talk about Christian he would do or say something stupid. "Has the doctor been to see you this morning?" he asked.

She shook her head. "Not yet, but the nurse said he'd be in quite early." Conor got off the bed and walked to the window. "How are you feeling this morning?"

"I'm find, grand . . ." Then, hesitantly: "Would you like to see the baby?"

He turned to look at her. The appeal in her eyes was clear. "Of course, Molly," he said.

She got out of bed and reached for her robe. As she did so, he noticed that the nightgown she was wearing had a peculiar buttoned flap at the breast and realized that it was to facilitate breastfeeding.

As she led him toward the nursery, Conor tried to steel himself for what he was about to see. He had never thought of himself as squeamish, but he had never encountered a brain-damaged newborn baby before and did not know what to expect. He hoped that for Molly's sake he could make the right responses.

Margaret Susanna was the only baby in the nursery. The others, explained Molly, were all with their mothers, being fed. Her voice was matter-of-fact, too matter-of-fact, thought Conor as he looked at his only niece through two glass walls, the outer wall of the nursery and the wall of the incubator in which she lay.

She was naked, lying on her stomach, her tiny, flesh-less buttocks almost nonexistent. She had a thatch of reddish-blonde hair and her eyes were closed. There were rubber suction pads affixed to her back and arm; her face was turned toward him and he could see there were tubes in her nose and coming out of her mouth. The wires and tubes led to a variety of machines and monitors around the incubator, and trailing from a bag that hung on a stand, the end of yet another tube was affixed to one of her matchstick arms with a miniature splint. She was so puny and still, it was difficult to believe that she was alive at all, but he assumed that the blinking lights on the monitors attested to the fact that she was. Even at this distance and allowing for the tube, he could see that her mouth was misshapen.

Desperately he searched for the right words, but Molly

saved him. "Isn't she beautiful?" she whispered. She looked up at him.

"She is absolutely beautiful, Molly," he said. He felt once again that he would go to the ends of the earth, fight any foe, to protect his sister from further harm. He looked again at Margaret Susanna. Even this situation was not insuperable.

Where the hell was Christian? When he found him, thought Conor, he would give him a piece of his mind. The last things Molly needed now were tantrums from her husband.

They stood there for a while longer, but although the monitors continued their steady green vigil, the baby did not stir at all, and eventually they walked back slowly toward Molly's room. When they pushed open the door, the room was not empty. Malcolm and Cordelia were sitting stiffly, side by side, in two chairs beside the bed. "Malcolm, Cordelia!" Molly exclaimed, and crossed the floor, giving each of them a hug. Malcolm tried to stand, but she pushed him back down. "Oh, Malcolm!" she said. "Have you heard?"

The old man was older than Conor had expected from reports in Molly's letters. Even through that stilted, formal prose, Malcolm had appeared to be lively and full of energy. But this Malcolm Smith, although distinguished and aristocratic-looking, sagged in his chair, his knobbed hand clutched, clawlike, around the handle of a cane. In the bright morning sunlight, he was as pale as a tallow candle. His wife was a handsome woman who, Conor saw, was looking interrogatively toward him as he hesitated, unsure whether he should come in or not.

Molly looked at him too, and Conor walked toward the group, holding out his hand. "Good morning, Mr. and Mrs. Smith," he said. "Molly has told me a lot about you. I'm her brother, Conor." Molly gasped and he turned to her. "It's all right, Molly," he said. "All that's over and done with as from today." He was somewhat surprised to hear the confident tone of his own words and went on: "I've made up my mind that I'm going to sort things out." Then he turned back to Malcolm. "I'm sorry we have to meet in such circumstances."

The old man extended his hand and suddenly Conor wished he did not look so scruffy. The look Malcolm

gave him was almost an angry one, and Conor, afraid
that Malcolm might see through his defenses, turned away
immediately and introduced himself to Cordelia.

"This is the brother you told me about?" Malcolm
asked Molly, "the one who's the botanist?"

She nodded.

"I see."

Conor found himself explaining his present situation—
that his lowly occupation at London Zoo was a stopgap
to fund his interest in archaeology—and then realized he
was behaving as though he were somehow on probation.
"That's enough about me," he said abruptly, moving
away from the group around the bed and leaning his tired
back against the wall.

Malcolm turned to Molly and Conor felt himself dis-
missed from the conversation. "I feel really helpless,"
the old man said. "I won't go into the whys and where-
fores of how this could have happened, Molly—you've
enough on your plate. Is there anything I can do? Where
is Christian, by the way?"

Molly looked at the floor. "He was here earlier."

The old man's expression seemed to Conor to sharpen,
and as Malcolm glanced uneasily around the antiseptic
hospital room, Conor saw something else: as a self-made
man, Malcolm found it difficult to deal with failure, even
failure to which no blame could be attached. With a flash
of understanding, almost sympathy, Conor understood
something about Christian: growing up with this man as
a guardian could not have been easy.

Yet clearly he loved Molly. His hand tightening on his
stick, he appealed to her: "Please be sure that we, Cordelia and I, we'll do anything—"

A picture of Margaret Susanna's immobile, skewered
little body rose in Conor's mind and he knew in his heart
that with the best will in the world, there was very little
that anyone could do. He studied the carpet, which was
expensive and of a misty blue, like immature heather.

"I already love her, I really do," Molly whispered,
close to crying.

"I'll organize the best help," Malcolm went on desperately, "the best medical advice and the most advanced treatment that money can buy." He paused and

looked across at his wife, then back at Molly. "Do you think we could see her, my dear?"

"Maybe Molly's not up to it, Malcolm." It was the first time Conor had heard Cordelia speak. She had an attractive low-pitched voice.

"No, that's all right, Cordelia," said Molly. She took a tissue from a box on the night table and blew her nose. "Sorry for blubbering like this," she said, "I'll take you to the nursery now."

Conor felt that his presence was not needed for the moment. And he realized he was fired with new energy. Having made the first great leap, the admission as to his identity, he felt the urge now was to continue, to tie up all loose ends, to get rid of anything that was extraneous to this new certainty in his life. "Molly, I'll head off," he said, "but I'll come back again this afternoon."

She was in control of herself again. "I'll walk with you to the elevator," she said.

The elevator was halted on some floor below. They could hear a clanking noise as something big, probably a bed with a patient in it, was loaded. While they waited, she blew her nose again. "Sorry about that outburst back there, Conor," she said. "I'm afraid I don't know whether I'm coming or going."

"Don't apologize," he said, and lapsed into silence. He was disturbed by his consciousness of her physical nearness. Even if she were not his sister, in her present state his desire—even the thought of desire—was so unapt; he felt he must be some sort of monster. She was holding her arms crossed under her breasts, which, swollen with milk, strained the buttons of her robe. He could just make out the dark circles of the aureoles through the fabric, which was a thin cotton, and he had the insane urge to put his mouth over her nipples to suckle them.

The elevator came at last. Shaken, he got into it.

Una took a last look around the small bedsitter and picked up her bag. She stood for a second or two, deep in thought, then sat at the countertop which separated Conor's kitchenette from his living space and served as dining-room table and desk. Extracting a notepad and pen from her shoulder bag, she scribbled a note:

Dear Conor,

There is nothing so trite, I know, as "good-bye" notes, so I will make this as brief as possible. If you think this is a bit undignified (to write at all, I mean), I'm sorry. My motto in life has been "nothing ventured," etc. Strange as it may seem, I'm not used to being dumped. I'm tempted to tell you simply to fuck off. There are lots of really terrific bitchy things I could think of which would make your hair curl even more than it does already! But even if I did tell you to fuck off, I wouldn't really mean it. It would be pride speaking and I have found that pride is a very lonely virtue.

So, my dear, this is it, it seems. I want to think of something noble and Jane Austenish to say, but can't for the life of me. Some wordsmith I am!

I suppose I'm hoping that if I'm patient, we might sometime get together again. Anyway, I've enjoyed it. Can't say anymore without getting all smarmy.

Una

P.S. I think, actually, I'm brilliant to be taking this so calmly. What do you think?

Una did not reread the note, in case she changed her mind. She folded it, left it under Conor's tea caddy on the countertop, and replaced the notepad and her pen in her shoulder bag. She picked up the bag from the middle of the floor and without looking back, let herself out of the flat.

At the clinic, Dr. Sinden had left Molly, Malcolm, and Cordelia in a state of despair.

He had been very kind but had put no gloss on the facts. Margaret Susanna was a quadriplegic. She had a hole in her heart and a cleft palate and would be, as far as they could judge at the moment, profoundly deaf. It was too early to tell about her sight; although he had some of them, the results of all the tests were not available, so he had no definite explanations to offer as yet. The birth had been normal, with no significant deprivation of oxygen. It would possibly be weeks before it was known for sure what factor or combination of factors had caused the baby's multiple handicaps. "It could even be genetic," he had said, "and to eliminate that possibility, we will probably have to do tests on you, Mrs. Smith, and on your husband.''

After he left, none of the three of them spoke. Molly stood gazing out the window with her back to the other two. Malcolm and Cordelia sat side by side, and it was Cordelia who at last broke the silence. "Do you think we should pray?"

"No!" Molly and Malcolm had spoken simultaneously. Molly turned around. "Sorry, Cordelia. I didn't mean to speak to you like that." She crossed the room and got into the bed, arranging the covers over herself. She lay on her back, eyes wide open, staring at the ceiling. She had been on such a see-saw of emotions over the past twenty-four hours that she felt she should be hysterical by now. But all she felt was a great anger. And well-intentioned and loving though Malcolm and Cordelia were, she wanted to be alone. Several of her friends and theater colleagues had telephoned with enquiries but she had refused all calls; many had sent flowers—she would thank them as soon as she felt up to it. As the silence dragged on, she could hear the breath of the old man wheezing slightly in his chest.

"Where's Christian?" he asked out of the blue. "Christian should be here . . ."

"What time is it?" Molly, who up to now had felt the need to be loyal to her husband in front of his grandparents and others, did not care anymore.

"It's just after ten o'clock," said Cordelia.

"Well then, I know where he is," said Molly, "he's probably in some public house. Stands to reason, doesn't it?"

With difficulty, Malcolm stood up and Molly immediately regretted her rudeness. "I'm sorry, Malcolm, I didn't mean to talk to you like that—you of all people. But I feel so alone. Everyone is being so kind, but I feel so alone. I've never even held her, you know . . ."

Malcolm leaned heavily on his cane. "Would you like a priest to come to see you?"

She shook her head. "No, thank you. I'm very angry with God and the last thing I want to hear is about some Divine Plan."

Malcolm looked at her for a moment, then turned to leave: "Tell that grandson of mine, when he does turn

up, that he has me to answer to if he doesn't pull himsel?
together!''

Cordelia hugged her, and to Molly's relief, she and
Malcolm left the room. But she was not to be allowed
her solitude, because almost as soon as the door closed
behind them, it opened again to admit two nurses, who
announced that they had come to take her for her bath.
She protested that she could happily bathe herself, but
the older of the two nurses, who seemed to be in charge,
would not hear of it. "Part of our job, dear, first baths
always to be attended—and you'll be surprised how tired
you'll be after it. We don't want you conking out on us
and drowning! It'd look bad on our records now, wouldn't
it?'' Molly was grateful to hear an Irish accent, even one
overlaid with many years of London.

She went with them into the bathroom attached to her
room, and while the younger nurse drew the bath and
shook Dettol and a handful of salt into it, the Irish one
wrung out the washcloth on the sink and proceeded to
wash her face with gentle but firm strokes. Molly, who
was much taller than the nurse, had to lean over so her
face could be reached properly. Nevertheless, she felt
like a child and, to her surprise, found it to be a comfort.

She surrendered herself to them as they removed her
nightgown deftly and helped her into the milky water. It
stung a little between her legs at first, but not for long.
They sponged and washed and soaped her, and one of
them combed her hair. Soon the water was like balm.

Her breasts felt very heavy and seemed to be getting
sorer all the time, and she asked them if this was normal.
"Have you had your injection?'' asked the nurse with
the Irish accent.

"I've had so many injections,'' answered Molly, "I
don't know which one you mean.''

"Well, you would have been told about this one—it's
to dry up your milk.''

"I don't know. I can't remember. Such a lot has happened.''

"You poor darling!'' said the Irish nurse, whom Molly
saw from a badge pinned to her ample chest, was named
Mrs. Bridget Slevin, S.R.N. "I'll go and check when
we've finished here and we have you all dry and comfy
in your bed,'' she continued. "We'll sort you out, never

ear.'' She soaped Molly's back. ''Yes, we'll sort you
ut.''

For the first time since the birth, Molly consciously
elaxed as she floated in their competent and kind ministrations. The nurses had been right about the bath pro-
moting relaxation; there was a languor coming over her
and she longed for her bed and a long sleep. ''Sit back
there now and take it easy,'' said Bridget Slevin, ''while
we make your bed. We'll leave the door open, though,
so we can see you.''

Molly lay back in the water and watched as the whiter
strands left by the soap pooled and separated and joined,
then separated, then pooled again, like rivers in a delta.
She heard the nurses moving around the bed and the
shirring and plumping as sheets and pillows were removed and replaced. They talked quietly as they worked,
but she could not hear what they were saying. Lulled by
the warmth and comfort of the bath, she was drifting,
ever so peacefully, toward a misty sleep.

''Are you all right in there?'' It was the Irish nurse,
popping her head around the door.

''Yes, I'm fine.'' Molly came to and straightened up a
little.

''Don't want to lose you! Important lady like yourself!''

''Not that important.''

''Oh, come on now. Such modesty! Aren't you on the
television and don't you have your name in the papers
and everything? Margo Bryan, the famous actress!'' The
accent was pure Galway, absolutely familiar to Molly.
''Come on now, darling, time to get you back to bed.''
Mrs. Slevin helped Molly out of the bath and threw a
towel around her, drying her with it energetically until
Molly's skin tingled. Then she handed her some clean
underwear and pads. ''Have you got a fresh nightgown?''

Molly indicated the locker beside her bed and Mrs.
Slevin opened it, pulling out one of the beautiful new
maternity nightgowns made of lawn that Christian had
bought for her in Harrod's. ''Isn't this absolutely *gorgeous*!'' She held it up to her nose, smelling the new-
ness. ''What a lovely thing!'' She gathered it up and
popped it over Molly's head. ''There we are, darling, all

nice and clean. In you get!'' Molly noticed that the othe
nurse had left.

Bridget held the crackling sheets apart so Molly coul
slide in between them; then, when she was settled, tucke
them in around her. "Annie's gone to check about tha'
injection," she said. "I'll be back in a little while. You
rest now and have a little sleep if you can.''

Molly responded to the mothering like a blind, starved
thing. She felt warm and snug and cared for and somehow safe. "You know about my baby?'' she asked.

"Musha, I do!'' said Bridget, plumping pillows already as fat as Christmas geese. "You poor old darling,
you're having a time of it, aren't you? But try not to fret
too much, God is good!'' In her mouth, the aphorism,
familiar from her own childhood, sounded fresh and new
and Molly did not resent it. She closed her eyes and the
nurse left.

She must have slept then, because the next she knew,
there was a sort of muted commotion around her bed.
Molly opened her eyes. It was Bridget Slevin again, but
her kind face was creased with concern. "Mrs. Smith!''
she was calling softly, "Mrs. Smith!''

There was another nurse behind her, and in the doorway Molly thought she saw a male figure in a white coat.
She groped for consciousness. "What is it?''

"You're wanted in the nursery, Mrs. Smith,'' said
Bridget, coming to the head of the bed. "Come on, darling, I'll help you.''

She reached under the bed and, taking Molly's slippers, turned them toward her so Molly could slip her feet
into them. Molly's robe was hanging up on the bathroom
door and Bridget took it off its hook and held it out.

"What's the matter?'' Molly asked as, helped by the
nurse, she put her arms into the sleeves and tied the ribbons that fastened the robe down the front. Bridget's face
gave the answer away and Molly stood as still as a stone.
"How bad?'' she asked.

"I don't know, darling,'' answered the nurse.

The short walk to the nursery, with Bridget beside her
and the other nurse walking behind them, passed as
though in a dream. Molly felt her heart had stopped beating and she was somehow flying. Her head felt light and
she could not feel her own breath.

As she entered the nursery, she heard one of the infants in the corner of the nursery crying, making tentative little yelps, but there was silence around her own baby's incubator. There was a little crowd around it and they seemed to be doing something, but the monitors told the story. Instead of blinking and bleeping, they were quiet and dark. Margaret Susanna, less than twenty-four hours old, had given up her fight.

Molly moved toward the incubator and stood beside it. It was open. A doctor was removing the suction pads from the baby's back. They made little plopping noises as they came unstuck. The tubes were already gone from her mouth and nose and her tiny arm was free of the feeding drip.

The doctor, a young West Indian (the same one who had stitched her up? Molly could not tell) completed his task and stood aside respectfully. "We are very sorry, Mrs. Smith," he said. "We did all we could."

"Can I pick her up?" asked Molly.

He nodded. The others around the incubator left, and after a small hesitation, so did the doctor. Molly reached into the transparent box and carefully picked up the little body. She was still warm to the touch, since the temperature within the incubator had not yet cooled. Her head flopped on her neck and instinctively Molly caught it.

She felt someone at her side—it was Bridget, who was holding out a soft nursery blanket. "Here!" she said, "let me wrap her for you." She took the corpse and with expert hands swaddled it in the blanket, then handed the little bundle back to Molly.

Molly cradled her daughter for the first and last time. With her forefinger, she traced the line of her eyelashes and the curve of her tiny cheek and leaned her own cheek against the damp thatch of hair. One of the baby's hands protruded a little from the fold of the blanket and Molly touched the fingers, as delicate as the stalks of the wildflowers that grew in the crevices of the limestone on Inisheer.

"Would you like to baptize her?" It was Bridget, whispering. Molly nodded.

Bridget left on soft feet and returned a few moments later with a pitcher of water. She poured a few drops over the baby's head and said in a low voice: "I baptize thee in the name of the Father and Son and Holy Ghost.'' The water ran off the baby's head and down along Molly's side, wetting her.

    Mrs. Slevin moved away again and picked up the baby in the corner of the nursery, who had discovered his voice and had started a full-throated, despairing roar. She came back toward Molly. "I'll bring this fella down to his mother and then I'll be back,'' she said quietly. "Sit down, darling.'' With her free hand, she led Molly to a little stool set against a changing table in the room.

    There was another nurse present, writing at a little desk, but she did not look up and kept her head bent tactfully over her task.

    Molly felt very calm. She sat and gazed at the peaceful face of her baby, committing every line of it to memory. Margaret Susanna weighed as little as a bird and the little head felt snug in the crook of her arm and pillowed on her breast. She wished she could open the eyelids to see what color her eyes were but contented herself with smoothing her hair, which, having been wetted, was now springing back over the soft fontanelle.

    "The poor little creature,'' said Bridget softly at her elbow. "Isn't she beautiful!'' Being Irish, Bridget had none of the reticence about death that sometimes characterized her English colleagues. "You can be sure of one thing anyhow,'' she continued, herself stroking the little head, "you have a little angel up there now to look after you.''

    The tears began then, but they began in Molly's heart, big tears of mourning and grief, cleansing her of bitterness. She made no attempt to stem them or conceal them as they poured up from her heart and down her face.

    "You poor darling,'' murmured Bridget, putting her arm around Molly's shoulders. "There, there! Poor old thing . . .''

    The other nurse got up quietly and left the room while Molly pillowed her head on this kind woman's breast and wept for herself and her baby.

    That afternoon Conor searched the city for Christian. He toured the pubs near the hospital and Molly's house, around Fleet Street and in Soho, but drew a blank. Then, assuming again that sooner or later Christian would show up at the house, that night he went back to the hospital and got Molly's keys. He let himself in and settled down in the living room to wait.

He was asleep on the couch when he heard Christian arrive. He had left a table lamp on and looked at his watch: two o'clock in the morning.

Then, to his horror, he heard Christian's voice and realized he had not come home alone. "Christian!" he called, before he could think.

Christian came to the door of the living room, and although his eyes were bloodshot and his clothes were rumpled, Conor saw that he was not completely drunk. "What are you doing here?" he asked in astonishment. Then the surprise turned to hostility. "And how the hell did you get in?" Over his shoulder, Conor saw the startled features of a tall young woman. Christian intercepted the look. "This is a friend of mine," he said insolently, "Gillian Somerville."

Conor's anger was so complete that he felt absolutely calm. He stood up from the couch. "Christian," he said, "I have a message for you from the hospital—"

Ignoring the gasp from the woman, he continued, "—from your wife. Your daughter died this afternoon. If you are interested, the funeral is tomorrow afternoon at two o'clock in the convent of Our Lady at Willesden. Good night." With so much force that they hopped a foot off the floor, he threw Molly's keys at Christian's feet as he pushed past him in the doorway.

The funeral in the convent had been facilitated by Bridget Slevin, whose aunt was one of the community.

There was little pomp. Mass of the Angels was celebrated by the convent chaplain, who, like his charges, was too old to be on more active service; it was sung by one of the nuns with a wavery voice that had once obviously been quite good and who was accompanied by another nun whose arthritic fingers did not always make the octaves on the cracked harmonium.

Throughout the Mass, Molly, who was tired almost beyond endurance and whose body ached in every pore, was nevertheless very calm. With its cleanliness, simplicity, and ambience of women at peace together, its tiled black and white floor, the oratory reminded her of

her schooldays. The sunshine splayed through plain glass
windows over plain furniture; and rendered almost invisible the flames of the Paschal candle and altar candles
that had been lit for the Mass.

Other than the candles, the oratory was decorated only
with sprays of white lilies on each side of the white infant-
coffin which reposed on a low step at the entrance to the
sanctuary. Free of all ornamentation except a plaque of
sterling silver on which were engraved the names, *Margaret Susanna Smith,* it pulled Molly's eyes like a mag-
net. Nevertheless, although she had not been in a church
since her mother's funeral, Molly found herself soothed
by the gentleness of the service in such surroundings.

She was also conscious of silent support from Malcolm
and Cordelia behind her and of the solidity and strength
of her brother by her side. Conor had arrived at the hospital with the news that he had found her husband. They
had waited until the last moment, and when Christian
did not arrive at the hospital to accompany them to the
funeral, something seemed to give way in Molly. At present, she did not care whether or not he ever turned up
again.

When the Mass ended, she would not let anyone but
herself handle the white coffin, but as she turned to carry
it down the aisle, she saw Christian at the back of the
chapel, and for a second or two, her composure slipped.
She wanted to scream at him, to strike out at him. Then
a great indifference replaced the anger, and avoiding his
gaze, she carried Margaret Susanna's coffin past him and
out into the convent grounds.

It was another hot, sunny day and the sun temporarily
blinded her. She was conscious of the beginnings of a
headache.

It was a short walk to the cemetery. Molly carried her
burden behind the stooped chaplain and the nun who had
assisted at the Mass; she was aware of Christian falling
into step beside her but as far as she was concerned, he
might have been at the other side of an ocean. She concentrated on her task, on the sound of feet scuffing the gravel as
the baby's funeral procession, which included the community of seven nuns, made its slow way toward the grave.

The old priest, stole and surplice drifting in the breeze,
could walk only at a snail's pace, and after a few min-

utes, Molly's arms ached under their burden and she tried
to shift the coffin to a more comfortable carrying position. Conor, walking just behind her, noticed and made
a gesture as though to take it, but she refused to let him.
As her eyes met his, she saw they were filled with tears,
and her calm wavered.

She schooled herself. She must stay strong, at least
until the burial was done. She closed her eyes briefly to
prevent tears, and as she did so, stumbled a little on a
stone. Instinctively Christian put out a hand to save her,
but with her elbow, she shook it off, her savagery surprising her.

The graveyard, neatly tended, with rows of plain white
crosses, was in a corner of the nuns' small apple orchard,
which buzzed with bees and butterflies and which in
hands other than theirs would have been, in this part of
London, a priceless piece of real estate. The little procession halted in a place, a little apart from the lines of
crosses, where a high hedge of fuschia screened the nuns'
property from the surrounding houses. The hedge had
been trimmed recently, and in the process, a profusion
of the deep pink and purple bells had littered the ground
like gay confetti around Margaret Susanna's grave.

Molly did not relinquish the coffin while a decade of
the rosary was recited by the chaplain and the nuns. Not
hearing the prayers, she stood between her brother and
her husband, feeling the ache in her arms and the sun
beating on her bare head. It was as though she had taken
root; as though her whole life had shrunk to a pinprick
of sensation, all centered around the small hole into
which, shortly, she had to put her daughter.

When the time came, she did it carefully, bending her
knees until she was squatting by the grave, taking care
not to jolt the coffin or bump it against the earth.

The chaplain sprinkled a few drops of holy water on
the coffin and said some more prayers. When she realized
he was finished, she stepped forward, and Christian,
misunderstanding, stepped forward with her, but with a
gesture she warned him off.

Molly wept at last as she pushed the soft earth back
into the hole until the coffin was covered and the hole
was filled.

Wordlessly, Christian watched his wife at work on his daughter's grave. The birds sang and an aircraft, very high, passed overhead, its sound as soft as an echo. Behind him Christian could hear his grandfather's wheezing breaths. His overwhelming feeling was one of utter, abject failure.

He saw Molly was finished and was straightening up. He took a step toward her. "Molly?"

But she turned away to her brother and took her brother's arm.

12

In October, four and a half months after her daughter's death, Molly started preproduction work on her second film.

The first, *Streams of Hope,* had been successful at the box office. Despite British newspaper speculation, it had won nothing at Cannes but did win two Oscars—Best Supporting Actress—for a newcomer, Tracy Sullivan, and Best Score for the composers—the rock band Morgan La Fay. Molly's own work in *Streams* had won almost unanimously good reviews from the critics both in Britain and the United States, and with some Oscars under its belt, the movie attracted great attention, so much so that Dolly Mencken was up to her fat ankles in offers for Molly.

Taking Dolly's counsel, Molly took her time about accepting any of the offers and chose for her second foray into the cinema *Emerald Night,* a semifantasy, based loosely on a children's fairy tale. It was another low-budget movie, and probably because of her West End success in *Blithe Spirit.* she was cast as a mysterious otherworldly creature who casts a spell on a middle-class, conventional professor of mathematics at Liverpool University.

Although she loved the part, she was wary of type-casting and went to have a chat with Dolly about it.

Dolly, however, had no such qualms. "Listen," she said from behind mounds of paper on her desk, "when you've nothing else on your plate except an offer to play your *fourth* ghost or fairy or mermaid, then we'll worry." Bracelets jangling, she opened a drawer, took out a compact, and applied rouge to her wrinkled cheeks. "Margo, this is tailor-made for you. And listen, darling, they didn't ask you to *test* this time. That means we're really on our way. After this one, if you like, we'll get you something where you'll stomp around in handknits and tweeds followed by a pack of dogs. All right, darling?'' She snapped the compact shut. "All right?"

"All right," agreed Molly.

"And you'll be playing opposite David Croft, darling . . ." David Croft, who was to play the professor, was an international star.

Molly went off reassured, but as the first day of shooting approached, she became sick with nervousness. The night before she had to travel to the location in Liverpool, she came down with pains and aches and had to go to bed.

At about eight o'clock in the evening Conor, who was now living at the house on Vernon Street, knocked at her door. "I've made you a cup of Bovril, Molly."

"Thanks, Conor, but no thanks. I couldn't face it."

He opened the door. "You have to have something. Anyway, hot liquids are good for pains and aches."

"Who says?" She felt really miserable.

"I say. Now listen, Molly, I think you should try to pull yourself together."

"What?" Miserable as she was, she was outraged.

"You know what I believe?" he went on. "I believe you're just scared of tomorrow and your body got sick on purpose to give you an excuse not to go. I think your pains are psychosomatic."

She struggled to a sitting position, tears of rage in her eyes. "How dare you! I'd like to see *you* cope with what I have to cope with."

"And just what do you have to cope with, Molly?" He remained infuriatingly calm. "I know you've had a rough time emotionally—but you have a good career, people clamoring to hire you, a nice house, plenty of money, even a live-in houseboy who puts up with your nerves and brings you hot drinks when you, as you put it, 'can't cope'!'' She glared at him but it had no effect. He held out the steaming mug. "Are you going to take this drink or shall I just leave you to your misery?"

She took the drink. "As long as I don't have to have lectures with it!"

"Lecture's over!" He bowed like a mandarin and left the room.

Molly, propped on her pillows, sipped the Bovril. He

was probably right, she thought grudgingly. He was nearly always right about everything to do with herself and her life. After Margaret Susanna's funeral, she had accepted his suggestion, tentatively made, that to keep her company he should temporarily move to Vernon Street. He had not disposed of his own flat and continued to pay the rent there, but had moved a few clothes and personal belongings into the spare room of her house. Four months later he was still here and the arrangement looked like continuing.

Life ran on an even keel in the house as both of them came and went and became reimmersed in their own lives. Each had a separate circle of friends—the more discreet of whom now knew who Conor really was—but when they were home together, they spent the time quietly, reading or, in Conor's case, studying. They watched quite a bit of television.

"Like two old frumps!" Molly joked whenever her friends asked how she and her brother got along. "Typical Irish bachelor brother and sister setup!" This was not strictly accurate, she knew. For brother and sister, they were unnaturally respectful of one another's privacy, and if by chance one touched the other while passing in a room or in the narrow hallway, there were elaborate apologies. But by and large they were both calm and even happy, and the frisson between them became a part of normal life in the house, shimmering but under control. Molly felt cherished and cared for, and from time to time, she had the strongest impression that she was a child again and she and her brother were playing house.

She found she could talk freely to him about her grief and sense of loss about the baby.

They also discussed Christian, but not a lot. Although she had spoken to him twice on the telephone—stilted, awkward conversations—she had not seen her husband since the funeral. From time to time she saw his byline in a newspaper and got a jolt, but her feelings about him now were rapidly approaching indifference.

Nevertheless, she knew that her marriage was unfinished business and was annoyed with herself for ducking a confrontation.

Conor's strong advice in this matter never varied; he

believed she should do nothing immediately but should, in the interim, take legal counsel.

She finished the Bovril. Was she imagining it or had the aches in her joints lessened? She tested her legs: they were as stiff and painful as before, but she decided to try to ignore them and to think positively. She got out of bed, put on a bathrobe and, carrying her empty mug, went downstairs. "Thanks, Conor," she said when she went into the kitchen. "Sorry I was crabby!"

"You're welcome. Feeling a bit better?"

"A little," she admitted.

"Dr. O Briain's magic potion again!" He was writing a letter at the kitchen table.

"Who's the letter to?"

"The usual."

"I see. How's it going?"

"Pretty well, I think, but we can be under no illusions, it will be a long haul, Molly." She clucked sympathetically and rinsed out her mug at the sink.

Conor had begun negotiations with the representatives of the Irish law. Caution had become a byword with him, however, and he approached the problem by a circuitous route. He had telephoned a friend in Amsterdam who had hired a Dutch solicitor. This solicitor was briefed by the friend and approached the Irish embassy for advice. The embassy there had made inquiries of the Department of Justice in Dublin and had come back to the solicitor with the information that the file on the case was still open— and technically Conor was still being sought.

He was now engaged in tripartite negotiations with the Dutch solicitor, an English solicitor, and the Department of Justice, via the embassies in both countries. In the meantime, as a precaution, he had ceased to travel outside England and continued to work and to maintain his documentation under the name Seán Molloy.

"That reminds me"—Molly finished at the sink—"I must write to Malcolm and to Brendan. Anyway, it'll take my mind off tomorrow . . ." Opening a drawer of a small chest against one wall of the kitchen, she took out her writing materials. "I'm still sore, you know, still full of aches and pains!"

"Of course you are," he said without looking up from his own writing, "why wouldn't you be? You'll see, though, once you get on that set tomorrow, you'll be fresh as a daisy!''

Conor had been right as usual, Molly thought next afternoon, as she sat with the director and David Croft in the latter's trailer to discuss the first scene they were to shoot together. Both she and David were made up and in costume—since the budget was so tight, rehearsal time was limited—and Molly found there was not a trace of an ache or pain in a single bone.

David Croft paced around the trailer, talking like a machine gun. A chain-smoker, he was large, lithe, and thin as a whip, perpetually cast by the media, particularly the tabloid press, as an impatient, volatile hell raiser who was as likely to throw something and walk off the set as he was to turn in a good performance.

He also had a reputation as a lady killer, and Molly had vacillated between worrying that she would not be able to handle him and shame that she should have the arrogance to think that he might be interested in her in the first place. And even if he was, would she be interested in him? The truth was that she was perfectly happy to be celibate and unattached. Her brother was the only person, male or female, who could penetrate her emotional defenses, and since he was out of bounds sexually, she had accepted their companionship in lieu.

Croft lit one cigarette from the butt of another as he suggested script changes that would accommodate what he saw as his character's motivation in certain scenes. Watching his clever animated features as he paced and expounded in the trailer, Molly found her nervousness about him easing; his very agitation contributed to her relaxation and she could clearly see why he was considered to be so attractive.

Seeing how vulnerable he was beneath all the noise and aggressiveness, Molly empathized with him and recognized that, experienced star though as he was, David Croft was as terrified about this first leap into the film as she was. As he continued to bombard the film's director with questions and theories, answering the questions before the director had a chance to do so, Molly's instinct was to wrap him up in a blanket and to say ''there, there!''

Finally, when his star ran out of steam, the director, who was Welsh, stood up. "Some of those suggestions are really excellent, David and I'll talk to the scriptwriters. But I have to see to the setup now. Maybe you would run the scene as scripted just for the first time, so we see what we can improve on?"

Croft was left with no option but to agree.

"I'll see you on the set for rehearsal, then." The director exited the trailer and Molly was left alone with her costar. "Want one of these?" He offered Molly a cigarette.

She shook her head. "Would you like me to leave too, David?"

"No, stay, darling, stay, please. You're a good influence on me!" He lit a cigarette and threw himself on his daybed. He looked consideringly at her. "Have you met Tammy yet?"

"No." Tammy Simms, who had won an Oscar nomination for previous work, had been cast as Croft's wife. "Well, watch out for her," he said now. "She's actually quite sweet, but she's insecure. She doesn't like competition."

"But why?" Molly was genuinely astonished. "We're different types and we have completely different roles—"

"Yes, darling, but like you, Tammy's blonde, or was, is fifteen years older than you, and is at her peak now. You're only starting. And just *look* at you!"

Instinctively Molly looked in the mirror a few feet away from her and became instantly embarrassed. "I think Tammy is beautiful," she said.

"And what do you think you are?" His eyes were green, she saw, flecked with brown. Her embarrassment increased. "You're a strange one," he said curiously. "I saw *Streams of Hope*. Did you enjoy making it?"

"Yes, very much."

"The camera likes you . . ." Molly recognized the come on, a certain look and tone of voice with which she had become familiar since becoming an actress. The fact that David Croft was no different from any of the others gave her confidence; she was not going to be a notch in his belt and diversion was the name of the game. "If we're to be friends, David," she said boldly, "you should call me by my real name, which is Molly!"

"Molly," he said, repeating it, drawing out the "L"'s, "Mol-llll-ly. That's nice. Soft. Like you."

"I'm not soft," she retorted. "Don't ever think I'm soft!"

"Great!" he said. "A toughie! I hate soft women!" Again he gave her that long, raking look. But before she could think of a suitable riposte he jumped up from the daybed, resuming his pacing. "What do you think of this script? Do you like your character? Do you think he's overwritten, my professor?"

"I think it's a very good script," said Molly.

"Do you, indeed?" He rounded on her. "And how many scripts have *you* read in your lifetime?"

"What do you expect me to answer to that?"

"Just answer me—how long have you been in the business?"

"Oh, my! A touch of tetch?"

"I'm sorry, darling!" He was instantly contrite. "Don't pay any attention to me. I'm always like this on the first day of shooting. You'll get to know and love me . . ."

"Maybe I will, maybe I won't."

"Yeah, no softie!" he said, throwing himself again on the daybed. "How do you feel about this love scene we're about to do in fifteen minutes?" It was a fact of life that since films were not shot in sequence, people who did not know one another sometimes found themselves making love within an hour of meeting.

"I'm nervous about it." Molly decided there was nothing to lose by being honest, although she knew this particular love scene was relatively innocuous. According to her script, she visited the professor in his sleep, hung above his bed, and in close-up, kissed him languorously, leading him to wake in fright.

"It'll be all right." he said. "You really are a beauty, Molly. Can't wait to kiss you." But she saw he was looking past her at his reflection in a mirror. "Hope you're not disappointed," she said lightly, and was saved from further answer by the second assistant's knock. They were wanted for rehearsal.

Croft put out his cigarette and took a vial of breath spray from his makeup table. "I've been shredded by hundreds of leading ladies for kissing them with cigarette breath. Never travel without my Gold Spot!'' He sprayed two puffs into his mouth. ''Ready for anything now, ducks.'' He grinned and Molly decided that she liked him.

For the next six weeks, she threw herself into the work and, from the beginning, had fun. Her first meeting with Tammy Simms was a delicate affair, but forewarned as she was, Molly behaved demurely, the neophyte at the feet of the Great Actress—and Tammy Simms was reassured and then charmed.

It was a very happy set, and cast and crew melded around the director to become a unit. Shooting went smoothly and they were all working so hard that there were few opportunities for offscreen dramas. David Croft, who was going through his third divorce, laid a halfhearted romantic siege to Molly throughout the schedule, although his sense of humor saved the situation from being embarrassing and allowed it to become a running gag on the set.

He grabbed her and kissed her frequently—to the great frustration of the makeup crew—and when she wriggled from his grasp, would appeal to the assembled gallery of technicians, continuity girl, assistant directors, and gofers. ''Look, look! See what I have to put up with!''

He sent her drifts of flowers. Every morning, when the car came to collect her from her hotel, there was a fresh bouquet of white roses on the backseat. There were white carnations on her pillow when, dog-tired, she got back to her room at night.

Molly enjoyed all the attention. She was laughing more than she had in months. But toward the end of the shooting schedule, she began to worry a little. It was too much fun. Christian, too, had courted her like this.

When they met on the set for the first day of the last week's shooting. Molly carried the latest bouquet, of baby's breath and white freesia, in her hand. ''Listen, David,'' she said, ''I really think this has gone far enough. I have enough flowers to fill a florist's, and while I love flowers and I'm really grateful to you for everything, you've got to stop it now.''

He looked down at her and she was conscious that he was probably the first actor she had ever worked with who was a good head taller than she. In some respects,

his imposing physical presence reminded her of Conor's.
"Why?" he asked.

"No why. You know why!" she said, her resolve tee-
tering. "Just *because*!" she finished lamely.

"Because why?"

"I told you. No why—just because."

"Is that some sort of Irish reason? Do you not like
flowers, Molly?"

"I love flowers—I told you that a million times. But
I've also told you a million times that I had enough flowers to last me a lifetime. And, and—"

"And what?"

"And I don't need any more flowers."

"But I love sending flowers."

"Look, David—" Molly was stuck. After all, he had
never said explicitly that he was serious about her.

"Yes, Molly?"

She became aware that one of the unit drivers and a
boom operator were standing together close by and were
obviously listening to the exchange. She took David by
the arm and led him behind a cyclorama. "*Why* are you
sending me all these flowers?" she asked. "Why me?"

"You know why—or have I lost my touch?"

The green eyes were, for once, very still. She wavered
for a split second. It would probably be great fun to have
a full-blown fling with this attractive, amusing, and talented man. But as she wavered, the expression in his eyes
changed to one of tenderness and she retreated immediately into her stockade. "David," she said, "I like you
very much. But that's all."

"The lady's wish is my command . . ." He bent low
over her hand and kissed it.

"I—I hope you don't mind . . ." she said hesitantly.

"My dear Molly," he said, "never has a man been
rejected with such finesse!"

"I'm not rejecting you."

"Please, my darling, no remonstrations of innocence.
Wish I could be the man, that's all."

"There's no man; don't think that!"

"Oh, no?" He raised his eyebrows. "Must dash—
pity!" He added, turning away, "It might have been good
fun!" Molly was almost tempted to call him back. Why

the hell shouldn't she have an adventure? What was the matter with her?

There were no more flowers and Croft behaved impeccably during the last week of shooting. Luckily all the love scenes were in the can, and in the scenes they did have, mainly shot in filthy weather on the Mersey ferry, both of them were so preoccupied with rain and makeup and wet costumes and keeping on their marks on the rocking vessel, the week passed quickly.

The unit had a party on the final night and they all had a great deal to drink as work tensions unwound and spirits heightened. David, who had been sitting opposite Molly at the dinner table, paying a great deal of attention to the continuity girl, leaned across when the young woman went to the lavatory. He took her hand. "Are you really, really not going to sleep with me?" He was a little drunk, she saw.

She had been drinking champagne and was herself feeling loose and warm, and for a wild moment was tempted. But the moment passed and she shook her head. "David, I'm really, really not. Anyway, you seem to be getting on very well without me."

He dropped her hand and patted it. "If you ever change your mind—" he said. "I know where to find you!" she finished.

Kissing him on the top of the head, she left the party shortly afterward, and next day, when she woke, there was a final message from him, slipped under the door of her room sometime during the small hours of the morning while she slept. Written on a plain white card in his uneven large handwriting, were two words: *Forse ancora.*

Molly smiled. She knew what *ancora* meant— "again"—and could guess, having studied Latin in school, what the first word was. "Perhaps again." He had signed it simply "D."

The film company had reserved a First Class corner seat for her on a mid-morning train to London, and to her relief, her coach was half empty. Two middle-aged housewives, who recognized her from the television show, approached her shyly for autographs before the train left Lime Street Station, but she was left in peace for the remainder of the journey.

As the train clacked smoothly along, Molly took David Croft's card out of her handbag, contemplating his message and another lost opportunity. It was time, she knew, seriously to examine her present life, her constant rejection of emotional ties. She had read as many pop-psychology articles as the next person, and from what she had understood from them, many of the problems of this nature were experienced by people who had been abused, traumatized, or neglected in their childhood. She had no such excuse. Up to the time her father was killed, she had had a relatively normal life.

On the other hand, only onstage, or in creating a character not her own, did she feel in any way whole. Because whatever the cause or character defect, she seemed somehow to be a spectator in her own offstage life. No matter what effort of will she made, she continued to feel displaced, a partial person, a mother without a child, a wife without a husband, a child without a mother or father, a woman without a man. Yet every time a lifesaving line was thrown to her she threw it back.

She continued to wonder about that episode with the priest in the sand dunes. Had she suppressed some aspect of it in some way? Was this a contributory factor to her sense of detachment? In her mind that experience had been insignificant and ethereal, a minor thing which might even have happened to someone else. If it was a cause of her adult problem with men, surely she should feel Father Moran had done something awful to her. But she did not. The memories of that eventful period of her life, which had spanned only a few days, were dominated, not by Father Moran and his clumsy attempt at seduction, nor even by her father's death—but by that mental picture of Conor pulling away from her in the black currach.

She watched the undulating, tidy landscape rolling past her window as she traveled home. Home. London was not her home, she thought, but then, neither anymore was Inisheer. She tried to conjure up her childhood, the storms and sunrises and harshness of that place of stones, her taciturn father and gentle mother. But they were all shrunk, like framed pictures on the walls of a gallery.

Except for Conor.

Guiltily, she admitted to furtive excitement that she

was going home to Conor, and wondered, not with any real intent, if she should consult a psychiatrist.

Decisively, she abandoned all this self-analysis—which anyway, she had been taught in school, was pure self-indulgence—and opening a magazine, tried to concentrate on an article about the queen mother. But the excitement and anticipation of seeing Conor again grew in the pit of her stomach as the train neared London.

To her disappointment, the Traveller was not outside the house, and when she let herself in, the hallway had the forlorn, musty smell of emptiness. There was some mail on the mat inside the door and she picked it up, adding it to the neat pile on the hall table. Then, when she went through to the kitchen to put on the kettle, she found a note from him on the dresser; he had gone away for the weekend to York and was not due back until the following Tuesday.

Molly, feeling as empty as her house, collected her mail and opened the envelopes at the kitchen table. In her absence, she saw, Dolly had been busy and had organized several meetings about future work and press interviews.

She telephoned Dolly. The agent, who recognized post-work anticlimax when she heard it, immediately invited her out to dinner.

As the first anniversary of Margaret Susanna's birth and death neared, Molly, playing Ophelia, had completed a limited run of *Hamlet* in an art house on the outskirts of London. Dolly had thought it would be good for her reputation; the critics, luckily, had agreed.

And one morning in May, Molly was invited to see a rough cut of *Emerald Night* in an art house hired for the occasion.

The director had begun the process of hyping his movie and had invited, as well as cast, crew, moneymen, and friends, a carefully selected group from the press: five critics whom he respected and knew personally. When the house-lights came up at the end of the screening, cast, crew, moneymen, and friends stood up in their seats and applauded and cheered.

The critics, Molly saw, were applauding too, but discreetly. They had chosen single seats, apart from everyone else and apart from each other. Islands of gravitas in a sea of enthusiasm, each watching the other four out of the corner of his eye, they clapped slowly and reflectively, none wanting to lose face by revealing immoderate liking. Of course, they had all agreed in advance to be bound to secrecy until the actual release of the film, a promise that the director well knew was about as reliable as a twopenny watch. He had utter confidence that not one of them would be able to resist leaking little hints and innuendos and that each would rush to score against the others, to be the first with the news, to be seen by the public (and most of all by rival critics) as an insider.

After the screening, the director threw a lunch in the upstairs room of a pleasant restaurant in Covent Garden, to which the critics, as befitted their independence, did not go. But Molly did and enjoyed herself thoroughly. She had been pleased with her work and found to her surprise that she was able to suspend disbelief and watch her performance as a character rather than as herself. Because they were both abroad on other projects, neither of the leads could be present at the screening, so Molly was the highest-ranking cast member at the lunch and was treated accordingly.

She drank some champagne, and after the second glass, felt as light and insubstantial as a feather. Her habit was to alternate alcohol with Perrier, but today she allowed herself to be wafted along in the flow of the general good cheer and high hopes and drank glass after glassful of the champagne. She was going to be busy with publicity and interviews over the next few days, but she had nothing else to do today. The hell with it, she said to herself after her fourth glassful, it's not often a woman gets to see herself in her own movie. "Thank you!" she said graciously as her glass was filled again by an attentive waiter.

The more she drank, the more tender grew Molly's affection for cast and crew, the more brilliant and entertaining she found their conversation. She loved *everyone*, she decided. Without waiting for someone to offer her the bottle she filled her glass, spilling a little of the wine on the tablecloth, but everyone told her it was okay—not to worry . . .

Such lovely people!

Molly loved acting, movies, the continuity girl, who was seated to her right. "And how's David?" she asked, aiming her chin on to her hand and missing slightly. "David who?" asked the continuity girl with a little frown of puzzlement creasing the space between her eyes.

"David!" said Molly. "David, you know, David Croft, our star! *Your* David . . ."

"Oh, *that* David!" said the young woman with a laugh. "He's not my David. Why would you think he's my David?"

"Ohh!" said Molly, her elbow slipping off the table "Oops!" She giggled and turned to the lighting cameraman, an Australian. "Of course! He's not her David at all—he's nobody's David. *Forse anc-ancora!*" She waved her hand across the table like a benediction and bowed her head. "How are you, Bluey?" she asked the cameraman, blowing him a kiss.

"Who's Cora?" asked the continuity girl.

It was Molly's turn to be puzzled. "Cora? Cora who?"

"Never mind, dear," said the continuity girl, patting Molly's shoulder. "I'm fine, Margo!" said the cameraman to Molly's left, and she swiveled to look at him. He was supporting, Molly knew, at least two wives and about seven children.

"And how're, how're all the chi- children?" She was hit with a bout of hiccups.

"They're fine, Margo, ace!" said the man, chuckling. "Have a drink of water—maybe you should go home?" Molly decided that this might, indeed, be prudent. She looked at her watch and was amazed to find it was almost four-thirty. She bid a sentimental good-bye to the director, who called a taxi and stood with her in the entrance to the restaurant until it arrived. Before getting into the taxi, she embraced the director and told him she loved him *dearly*.

All the way home, Molly, who had never been so drunk before, reveled in the frivolous, mellow feeling. She thought sentimentally about all her dear friends in the cast and crew. David, dear David. She would have to send David a card. As the taxi wheeled around corners and darted in and out of the traffic, Molly, utterly relaxed, rolled from side to side in her seat and giggled.

"You all right, luv?" asked the driver indulgently, shouting over his shoulder after a particularly daredevil turn.

"Never better—I'm—I'm in a movie!" She felt loving and loved and airy as swansdown. When the taxi pulled on to Vernon Street, she was cheered to find the Traveller was parked outside her house. Conor was in. She paid the cab fare, tendering a ten-pound note and telling the driver to keep the change.

"I'm home!" she caroled as she turned her key in the lock. "They loved it, they loved it—and I was *terrific!*" she continued, dancing into the kitchen. "Meet Mar-go-Mar-go-Mar-go Bryan!" she sang. "I'm going to be a *film* star!" She pirouetted around the room, picked up a vase of flowers off the kitchen dresser, and using it as a particularly large microphone, sang a chorus of "What a Wonderful World." Her singing voice had never been Molly's strongest attribute and she cracked on a high note. "Oops! Sorry!" she giggled, putting her hands over her mouth like a child.

Conor, who was sitting at the kitchen table, smiled at her happiness. "Carry on. And anyway, film stars can sing in their own kitchens anytime they like."

"Anytime?"

"Anytime," he assured her.

"Whee!" she said, and scattered the flowers all over the kitchen in handfuls.

"You're drunk, Molly!" He was amused rather than scandalized.

"Yep! And issa lovely feeling. She was off again with a song from *My Fair Lady.*

Conor waited until she had finished the last chorus of "Wouldn't It Be Loverly" before telling her his own news. He had had a telephone call from his solicitor; he had to travel to Dublin to attend a formal interview at the Department of Justice, in the presence of the solicitor, next Monday. "I'll go a couple of days early," he said. "I might even go out to Inisheer."

Molly saw his pleasure and excitement. "Oh, that's wonderful, *wonderful!*" Replacing the vase, she crossed the kitchen and threw her arms around Conor's neck. Then, hiccuping, she withdrew hastily. "Sorry!"

"That's all right," he said wryly. "It was nice. Don't apologize."

An hour later, Molly was sound asleep in her bed when Conor woke her to take a telephone call.

"Who is it?" She felt groggy and disoriented.

"I wouldn't have woken you," Conor apologized, "but it's Christian and he was very insistent that he should speak to you."

Molly struggled out of bed and went downstairs. "Hello?"

"I gather you were asleep." Christian's voice was distant and formal. "I'm sorry, but I have to come and see you."

"When?" Molly was too sleepy to argue.

"As soon as possible."

The way she was feeling now, Molly knew that although she had free time, she could not face him today. "Today's out of the question," she said, "and I'm working over the next few days. How about next Sunday?"

"Fine—if that's the earliest you can manage."

"It is," Molly said coldly. Her head was clearing.

"What time?"

"Eleven o'clock. What's this about that's so urgent after all this time?"

"I'll tell you about it when I see you. We have to talk."

Molly went back to bed, too lightheaded to worry yet about what was in store for her. Anyhow, the interview with her husband was days away yet, she thought, as she slipped into a deep sleep. She'd think about it nearer the time.

The director of *Emerald Night* had chosen his critics well. Within two days, columns with titles like "Under the Arcs" or "Cyclops" began to bristle with sentences and paragraphs mentioning—in passing—that the eagerly awaited *Emerald Night* was now in the can.

One critic, Clive Treethorne wrote in an "I hear"-style paragraph that newcomer Margo Bryan, who had "so impressed" in *Streams of Hope*, had fulfilled all that promise and was "one to watch" in the Oscar stakes. Another, Trilby Owens, wrote that he had heard from reliable sources that the on-screen chemistry between David Croft and film newcomer Margo Bryan ("one to watch for an Oscar?") was "truly electrifying."

A third, Derwent Reed, did not bother to disguise the fact that he had had a preview of the film and thus infuriated the other four. He wrote that while Tammy Simms turned in "her usual sterling comedy work," it was "fey, willowy newcomer Margo Bryan who appeared from nowhere like a shooting star in the firmament to impress greatly in *Streams of Hope* (as this reviewer pointed out at the time) and who now fulfills that promise by carrying off the acting honours in *Emerald Star*. This is no mean feat when one considers that she is up against old hands like David Croft and Tammy Simms. Watch out for Bryan for an Oscar early next year . . ."

All this hype did not pass unnoticed through the sieves employed by the British wire services, and a small paragraph on Margo Bryan, rewritten with an Irish emphasis by a showbiz stringer, was transmitted and received in the wire room of the *Irish Record* in Dublin, was ripped off the machine, and was placed with the other copy in the news editor's basket.

The news editor, having read the telex, took it across to the desk of one of the reporters. "Isn't this one your baby?"

Una O'Connor read the paragraph. "Do you want anything on it?" she asked.

"You don't sound all that enthusiastic."

"If you want something on it, I'll do it."

The news editor considered. They were coming up to the slow summer season and the features area of the paper was always on the lookout for personality pieces. Even if that did not work out, if this woman Bryan did get an Oscar nomination, it would be as well to have established a prior relationship with her. "Yes," he said. "See what you can do with it."

Una took a deep breath. She got Molly at home on her first telephone call. "Hi!" she said brightly. "Remember me? Una O'Connor, *Irish Record*?"

"Oh yes, Una, of course I remember." Molly hesitated and Una knew what she was thinking. Seán.

"Look," she said, "this is probably as embarrassing for you as it is for me and I'm sorry, but this is a professional call. My newsdesk wants yet *another* piece on you because of all this speculation about you and an Oscar and your film."

"But the film hasn't even been released yet!"

"I understand it's imminent, though. The piece on you would run to coincide with the release here . . ." Again Una heard the hesitation. She would just as soon not get entangled in anything to do with Seán Molloy again, but this was work. She appealed to the actress's sense of duty. "I'm sure that the article will help the film attendance here. We'll give it a good spread."

"What kind of piece would you do?"

"Well, it would be another personal piece, catching up on what you've been doing over the past year—which I understand has been considerable."

"Would you leave my personal life out of it?"

"You mean your marriage?"

"No," said Molly quietly, "I mean the death of my baby."

It was Una's turn to hesitate. "I think you know by now that you can trust me not to let you down."

"All right, so, but I will be busy from lunchtime tomorrow until the following Monday."

"If I could arrange it, could I see you tomorrow morning? I promise I won't take up too much of your time."

"Fine."

Una told the news editor that she had secured the interview. "All right," he said, "but do it immediately. Abbey Street and Burgh Quay get the wires too." The offices of the *Irish Record*'s rival newspaper groups were located at Abbey Street and Burgh Quay. "What about photographs?"

"I don't want a photographer with me on this one," answered Una immediately. "We can pick up the photographs later." She telephoned Molly a second time and they arranged to meet, this time in Molly's house, at ten o'clock the following morning.

When she was in London, Una always stayed at the Regent Palace, not for its luxury—it was far from luxurious—but for its location. It was right beside Piccadilly Tube station, across the street from a Boot's Chemists and with several fast-food restaurants nearby. All a journalist needed.

She was up at seven and by nine, breakfasted and alert, with new batteries in her tape recorder, spares in her pocket, and new cassettes broken out of their plastic

wrappers in her handbag, she was out in the rush hour,
flagging down a taxi. She had received directions from
the actress as to how to get to Vernon Street by Tube,
but on an assignment where she did not personally know
the interview venue, always took the most reliable form
of transport, which in London was the taxicab.

On the way, she resolutely refused to think of Seán
Molloy—she had never been able to think of him under
his real name of Conor. In the long nights alone in her
bedsitter, Una knew that he had ruined her for other men,
but she was resilient and fatalistic. It was her own fault
that she had got herself into this situation. She had
pushed, she had used Margo Bryan, but she had failed in
her primary objective. Her secondary objective, the continuing professional relationship with the actress herself,
was independent and must be preserved.

The cab deposited her at Molly's front door with twenty
minutes to spare, so she walked out of Vernon Street
altogether. It was worse to arrive too early for an interview than too late, since the interviewee, particularly one
who was uneasy and who had to be seduced, would probably be found at a disadvantage. If they were to open up,
he or she had above all to be made to feel secure.

Vernon Street, which she saw was a street of well-
maintained terraced Victorian houses, was in a very quiet
part of London, but there was a corner shop on an adjoining street, and more to kill time than because she
wanted it, Una went in and bought a Mars Bar. It was
nearly ten minutes to ten. She walked back to Vernon
Street slowly, employing her observer's antennae to the
full, in case she would need to pad out the piece, noting
the types of houses, gardens, cars.

She stopped dead when she turned the corner. The
Traveller was parked outside the door. It had not been
there when the cab dropped her, she was positive about
that, she certainly would have noticed. Her heart raced
with all the old feelings and nerves. What was she going
to do? She tightened her lips. She was going to do an
interview. That was what she was going to do. It was one
minute past ten when she rang the doorbell.

To her relief, Molly herself answered. Automatically
Una noted what she was wearing (jeans and a man's shirt)
and how she looked (older but more relaxed, still spec-

tacularly beautiful). During the hello's, she took a mental photograph of the hallway (red and white tiles, one small watercolor—an abstract—antique hall table, small bowl of white roses) and registered the smells and ambience of the house (coffee, brightness, warmth, coziness).

Molly brought her into a small room off the hall, beautifully and simply furnished, with smallish chairs and tables, appropriate to the scale of the room and a lovely old Victorian fireplace that now housed a gas fire. Again there were bowls of white flowers everywhere.

"You're welcome, Una. This is becoming quite a habit, isn't it?"

"Well," said Una, "some journalists specialize in the Iron Curtain, some do flower shows, I do you!"

Molly laughed. "Would you like coffee? I could do with a cup myself. Feeling a little fragile this morning."

Una nodded that she would and the actress left the room. Where was he? In the kitchen? Would she see him at all? Her fear of seeing him and her longing to see him flip-flopped, distracting her. She stood up to take a look at the titles of the books in the glass-fronted bookcase that occupied an alcove beside the fireplace. She shouldn't have. The bookcase contained a mixture of plays, paperback novels, and tomes on botany and archaeology.

Was he living here?

"I've been looking at your books," she said when Molly came back with the fragrant coffee and a plate of biscuits.

"Nothing brilliant there!"

There was no help for it, she had to ask: "Is your brother here?"

Molly flashed her a quick look. "He is actually. He lives here now—but he'll be leaving in a few minutes," she added quickly, "he's going to Dublin."

"Right, shall we begin?" asked Una, busying herself by taking out her tape recorder.

She began briskly, bringing herself up to date with the actress's career development since they last spoke— mainly the filming of *Emerald Night*. She concentrated fiercely, and although now and then she thought she heard noises from other parts of the house, managed successfully to conduct the interview on two levels. Trusting her tape recorder to take the narrative of the questions and answers which were relatively standard, she was also listening intuitively to the subtext, watching her subject's changing expressions and hearing the tone of her voice, the little pauses, hesitations, and rushes. All the time she was waiting for the right moment when it would be opportune to lead Margo into the area of her personal life.

It came quite easily and naturally. Molly had been talking about scenes she had particularly enjoyed filming, in the two films she had done, and Una was following along gently, eliciting information about acting techniques and why one particular scene was more enjoyable than another, when the first side of the first cassette tape clicked off in the tape recorder. Una, who had worked hard but unobtrusively to weave around the two of them a warm cloche of intimacy and understanding, reached to turn it over. While she did so, keeping her eyes on the tape recorder and making her movements more elaborate than necessary, she asked casually: "Was it difficult to get back to work after the death of the baby?"

Molly did not answer, but Una kept fiddling with the tape recorder as if there were a problem fitting the cassette back into its compartment. Eventually she seemed to get it working again and put it back on the little table between them which held the remains of the coffee and biscuits. She leaned forward and looked expectantly and emphatically at her subject.

Very few people can withstand a long pause in a conversation and Molly was no exception. "It was a bit," she admitted eventually.

"Did you find everyone else sympathetic?" asked Una, dropping her voice to match Molly's tone exactly. Again she waited. Molly hesitated, but Una did not lose her nerve.

"Yes, they were," said Molly, "but I don't think anyone who has not gone through it could understand how bad it is."

Una knew she had struck gold.

For the next half hour, Molly spoke about the birth and death of the baby, in fits and starts at first, but then headlong. She had the actor's sense memory and eye for detail, and Una felt that prickling sensation at the back of her neck that told her she had good material. In any terms, she had a great story. When the second side of the first tape ran out, she did not immediately change it, but kept her eyes on Margo, who was telling her at that point about the kindness of Bridget Slevin. She was crying. Una threw a switch in her brain that acted as a substitute recorder, memorizing the quotes while slowly reaching into the handbag at her feet, extracting a second tape by sense of touch. She succeeded in substituting it for the first one in the recorder without jolting Margo out of her narrative. She switched the machine on and relaxed again, letting it do its job while she concentrated on keeping the story going.

It came to an abrupt end when Conor opened the door. "Sorry to interrupt, but I have to leave now or I'll miss my plane." He walked over to Una. "I couldn't leave without saying hello," he said.

Una stood up. Molly had obviously told him she was coming. "Hello!" she said. To her fury, she felt her heart start to thump.

Conor looked across at Molly, whose white face was tear-stained: "Is everything all right?" Seeing her subject through Conor's eyes, Una now felt absurdly guilty. But Molly was generous: "Yes, yes, everything's fine!" she said. "Honestly! I was just reliving a few old memories."

Conor turned back to Una. "How've you been, Una?"

"I've been fine."

"Thanks for your letter, by the way." Many was the night Una had clenched her toes in bed at the memory of what she had written in that letter, not regretting or repudiating it but because she had no idea how it had been received. "I've saved it," he said now, "and I'm sorry I didn't reply. I will someday, I promise."

Una nodded, speechless.

"Well, I have to be off, cheerio! Wish me luck, Molly."

"Of course I do, Conor!"

He kissed each of them on the cheek and went out the door.

Una realized her recorder was still running. She switched it off. In the silence they heard the door slam and the engine of the Traveller start up.

Una was, unusually, at a loss. She had to maintain the

intimacy she had built up between herself and the actress. She wanted Molly to be secure, to feel easy that
the personal stuff would be in context, but at the same
time, she herself was still trembling inwardly from the
contact with Conor. She had to force herself not to touch
her cheek where he had kissed it. "Have you any cuttings
about your career to-date which I could refer to for the
piece?" she asked; it was safe, neutral ground.

Molly looked almost startled to be brought back to the
subject of acting. She frowned in concentration. "I don't
think so," she said. She thought. "Dolly has files of
them, though—you know my agent, Dolly Mencken?"

Una nodded. "I'll contact her when I get back to my
hotel." Privately, she eschewed any notion of going anywhere near the old battleaxe. She stood up. "Thank you
very much, I'll leave you in peace." The priority now
was to get out before the actress realized she had said
too much and started imposing conditions.

"Would you like more coffee?" Molly had recovered
her composure.

"No, thank you. But you mentioned you like gardening—I'd love to see your garden," Una answered quickly,
not wanting to betray her eagerness to leave.

Molly seemed genuinely pleased at the request. "Certainly. It's lovely at this time of year." They went down
the hallway and out toward the conservatory and the little
patio.

"What a lovely kitchen!" said Una, admiring the big,
sunny room that was one of the best features in the house.
"It is nice, isn't it?" Molly agreed. "I brought some of
the furniture from Ireland, to remind me of home—that
little chest there, that dresser—Oh!" Molly, spotting
something on top of the dresser, interrupted herself. "I
forgot about these—you asked about clippings?" She
reached up and took down from the top of the dresser a
battered old shoe box and blew dust off the top of it.
"Sorry about the dirt! I guess my cleaning lady doesn't
reach that high.

"I haven't actually read through these," she went on.
"Dolly has a clippings service and she keeps everything
anyway—but there is probably some early stuff in it.
Would that be any use to you?"

"Thank you very much, that'd be great!" Una took the box.

"Just get it back to me sometime at your convenience . . ." said Molly, and then she seemed to remember something. She took the box back from Una, opened it and extracted a piece of paper from the top of the pile inside and, crumpling it, put it in the pocket of her jeans. There had been writing on it in big capital letters but Una had not been quick enough to decipher what it was. Molly replaced the lid and handed the box to her, then led her outside through the conservatory.

The patio was indeed lovely, with all sorts of flowers that Una could not name in planters and tubs and pots—although she did recognize the beautiful blooms of a rhododendron. It was only May, but out here the sun was hot and there were bees making a racket, clustered around some sort of bush with bluish-purplish flowers.

They stood together in the sun and made small talk about the possibility of its being a fine summer this year. Una admired the patio and the flowers and then said she really had taken up enough of Molly's time and that she must be going. Juggling the shoe box, her tape recorder, and her shoulder-bag, she shook the actress's hand at the front door.

"I'm sorry I got emotional," said Molly. She hesitated, then took the plunge. "I'm not going to say you can't use that stuff about the baby, but I'm trusting you not to make it sensational." There was an appeal in her voice and Una's heart went out to her. Now that the stuff was safely on tape, she could afford the luxury of humanity.

"Don't worry," she said, and really meant it. "I promise that it will be okay. Anyway, I'm sure that what you said will be a great help to other women in the same situation."

"Yes, there is that," said Molly, but Una could see she was unsure. "Please believe me," Una said, "you *can* trust me!" Again she meant it. There would be no future for her or the paper in betraying the woman by cheapening the piece. They might need her again. As she walked away from the house she was already composing the opening paragraphs in her head. At the same time, she wanted to be alone to think about Conor.

She longed to be safely back in Dublin. Where was he going to be in Dublin? That was a treacherous thought with no future. She squashed it.

By the time she had got back to the hotel, from which she had already checked out, she had calmed down. She retrieved her overnight bag from the porter and stowed the tape recorder carefully inside it. She tried to stuff the shoe box in too, but it would not fit. *Blasted nuisance!* she thought, sorry now that she had asked about the clippings. She'd have to nurse it all the way back to Dublin and then she would have the bother of parceling it up again and sending it back. She considered briefly posting it on right now, from London, but then thought it would look ungrateful.

In any event, there might be something in it she could use, although she already knew she had more than enough on tape to write one of the best human-interest stories of her life.

But when she got back to Dublin she was not able immediately to start; the news editor informed her that Margo Bryan could wait for the features section of the following weekend and that said, assigned her to another story in Limerick.

She did not let herself into her untidy, decrepit bedsitter until late the following evening. She felt restless and full of energy, and decided to postpone work on the more recent story and to make a start on the Margo Bryan feature while its subtleties were still fresh in her mind.

Extracting the shoe box and the tapes from where she had stashed them in her closet, she threw the box on the bed and brought the tapes over to the worktable in the center of the room that served for typing, dining, and preparing food; one leg was shorter than the other three and was supported on a small block of wood, but it was big enough to accommodate all the functions Una cared to throw at it. She had not planned to live in such circumstances for as long as she had—she could certainly have afforded better—but there had always been something more interesting than flat- or house-hunting to occupy her mind and her time.

Una debated for a few moments whether she should telephone the news editor to determine what length she should aim for with the Bryan story, but then decided not to. There was always a possibility that the editor's input might be negative. She would deal with that, if and when it happened, after she had finished; she knew all too well that the worst thing that could happen to a journalist's conviction about a story was an argument about it before it was written.

She clicked the first cassette into the recorder, but before switching it on, she typed the quotes she remembered from the time she was changing tapes. Then, omitting only her own questions, she transcribed the interview, a task that took almost five and a half hours. It was after eleven when the sound of Molly's drawing-room door opening, followed by Conor's voice, filled Una's flat.

Abruptly, Una switched off the tape recorder and stood up. She realized she was very hungry. She went to the refrigerator in her "kitchen," divided from her "living room" by a curtain strung on sagging wires. There was nothing in the fridge except a carton of milk and two moldy tomatoes.

She left the flat and walked the few hundred yards on to Rathmines Road and the local Kentucky Fried Chicken, which always did a roaring trade at this time of night, after the pubs closed. She had to line up for her Snack Box and Coke, and since all the tables were full, decided to bring it home with her. She let herself into the flat again and still carrying her Snack Box, crossed to her bed to turn on the radio that stood on the bedside table. Her glance fell on the shoe box and she sighed. She had more than enough material, but a sense of duty and her own perfectionism prodded her. There might be something here she did not know. Anyway, she had dragged it all the way from London, she might as well get some value out of it. She turned on the radio, tuned it to the national pop station, RTE Radio Two and eyed the shoe box with distaste.

Sighing again, Una sat on the bed, opened the Coke, opened the Snack Box, and put a chip in her mouth. Then she took off the lid of the box and shook it upside down so that the clippings would fall on the bed beside her. They were soft and graying, some were even yellow, but they had been carefully folded exactly to fit the dimensions of the box and were slow in coming out. Wiping

...er greasy fingers on her dress so she would not dirty the
clippings, Una prised out the ones that were stuck. There
were more than clippings in the box. There was an envelope. The envelope had her name on it. Was this some
kind of joke played on her by Molly?

Her heart stopped. Conor! He had said he would reply
to her letter "sometime" . . . Before she opened the envelope, as though to slow herself down, she took one
more chip.

Una did not know whether she was disappointed or not
when she saw the heading: Dear Miss O'Connor . . . It
wasn't from him, then. But from whom? She began to
read.

> Dear Miss O'Connor,
> I am sorry for bothering you, but I read your article
> in today's newspaper and I think I have some very
> urgent information concerning it in which you may be
> interested . . .

Una had to read the letter twice before she had fully
comprehended it and its enclosure.

However this letter had got mixed up with Margo
Bryan's clippings, the implications were unmistakable:
the woman had married her brother. Did she know? The
questions hammered in Una's brain. Answers too. This
probably explained the handicap problems with the baby!

Her brain clicked into automatic. One thing to check.

She went to her own "filing system"—a series of canvas sports bags under the bed, but kept loosely in order—
and searched through it until she found her own story on
Molly and Christian. She checked the dates with the dates
mentioned in the FAA letter.

They tallied. There could be no mistake.

If she thought she had had a good story before, this was a
story to beat all stories. And if Molly got an Oscar . . . !

Steady, steady, she thought, she should not anticipate;
this one had to be taken logically, one detail at a time.

Who could have written the letter to her and why to
her?

She read the letter again. The latter part of the question
was easy: *I read your article in today's newspaper* . . .

That was why. But who?

I have followed Miss Bryan's career with great interest . . .

That explained the clippings.

I had reason to make this investigation myself . . .
Why?

The only reason for making such an investigation could have been personal interest. This man, or woman, was personally interested in Molly. It was too much of a cliché to imagine that it was a man in love. The more logical thing must be that it was a woman. Molly's real mother?

She checked her own article again. The Smith baby had been from a wealthy family, lost at sea in a chartered aircraft. The mother's body had never been found. Even if she had survived somehow, unknown to her family, would it have been likely that she would have known where her daughter was, followed her progress, and not come forward?

This was all too far-fetched. She was thinking rubbish, Una decided. To steady her thoughts, she crossed the room, threw open the single, rickety window, and put her head out into the night air. It was drizzling, but she closed her eyes and allowed the mist to cool her hot cheeks. There was only one explanation. The letter had been written by a man who loved Molly but who could do nothing about it.

Married?

She remembered something from the end of the letter. She withdrew her head, closed the window, and went across to the bed, from which she picked up the letter again.

. . . revealed to me on a confidential basis . . . revealed . . .

Revealed . . .

Confessed! The man was a priest.

Una's knees went weak and she sat down on the bed. She rooted around in her bag and took out the Mars Bar she had bought the day before, unwrapped it with shaky fingers, and bit off a huge mouthful of it.

What to do?

The first thing to do was to contact Margo Bryan. She looked at her watch. It was a quarter to one in the morning. It would have to wait—she could not wake the woman

vith this kind of information. In fact, she should not tell
ner on the telephone at all. She should go to see her again
as soon as possible.

She stuffed most of the rest of the Mars Bar into her
mouth, turned up the radio, and chewed furiously. Forever after, when Una thought of Margo Bryan, she as-
sociated the actress with a mouthful of glutinous
chocolate and toffee and the sound of The Average White
Band.

She threw off her clothes, turned out the light, and
tried to go to sleep. The situation begged other questions.
Conor? He was not Molly's brother after all, it appeared.
Did he discover this somehow? Was this the reason for
his very sudden disengagement from herself?

Una tried not to think of that aspect of the problem. It
would serve only to complicate the already complex journalistic task she now had.

Try as she might, she could not go to sleep. At one
point she turned on her bedside light and reread the letter. Could she dare ask Molly about Conor?

At about four o'clock, Una gave up on sleep. She took
her coffee jar, full of tenpenny pieces, and crept down
the hall to the communal bathroom. It was cold and
damp, but in her feverish state she welcomed its coldness. She fed the meter, turned on the gas, and took a
long, hot bath.

She was at the airport just after seven o'clock. She
used her American Express card to buy a ticket on the
first flight to London, due to take off just before eight
o'clock. She had only a short time to spare before boarding, but she went to the public telephone and dialed Molly's number.

The telephone rang for a while before Molly answered.
Her "Hello?" sounded sleepy, and Una's stomach danced
with nervousness while the coins fell into the slot. She
was afraid the actress would have hung up. "Hello?" she
said as soon as the last coin had clinked in.

"Yes? Who is this?"

"Molly, it's Una. I'm awfully sorry to wake you up—
I really am—but something very, very urgent has come
up in connection with the piece I am writing about you."

"Do you know what time it is?"

"Yes, I do, and please believe me, I would not disturb

you if it wasn't extremely urgent. I'm at the airport—I'm actually on my way to London to see you.''

"What?" Una could hear the annoyance in the voice at the other end of the line and rushed on. "I have some information for you."

"What kind of information?"

"It's about your husband," said Una, inspired.

There was a short pause. Another coin fell into the slot.

"What about my husband?" Molly's voice was wary.

"I can't tell you over the telephone, I really can't—but I do really, really think you should let me come to see you." Una heard the "last call" for her flight being boomed over the public address system of the departures terminal.

"Well, it does seem you're on your way already!"

"I'll come straight to your house from the airport . . ."

"All right."

"Again, I'm sorry for waking you, Molly."

"That's all right."

Una hung up and raced for her plane. She was the last to board and flopped into her seat, panting. As soon as the aircraft took off, her stomach began to churn with nausea and nerves. *What am I worried about?* she repeated to herself, but it was no use. Although professionally she was still excited, she dreaded the coming scene and projected it a hundred ways: Margo incredulous, angry, indignant, threatening, weeping, violent, hysterical? All of those? How would she herself feel or react if someone, if a *reporter,* arrived out of the blue with proof that her husband was her brother?

Behind it all was the insistent, thumping question of her own personal interest—where did Conor now fit in? First he was the friend, then the brother, now what? Una refused to think about Conor. She would think about him *after* she had done what she had to do with Molly . . .

She wondered if she should take flowers—there was a flower stand in the arrivals hall at Heathrow—but rejected the idea as being too schmaltzy and insincere.

She had the shoe box with her in, of all things, an ancient string bag, and as she traveled on the Tube into the city, she was conscious of how incongruous it looked.

The anonymous letter was stowed in her handbag, which she clutched under her arm and the overnight bag, which she had not unpacked from the previous day, again contained the tape recorder, fitted with a brand-new tape and another set of new batteries. She had no fixed idea about how she would handle the situation as a story. She could not, in all decency, whip out the tape recorder immediately.

The central problem remained: how would she break the news? Should she just go ahead and do it, or pussyfoot? She had still not decided when the taxi dropped her on the corner of Vernon Street. She paid the driver and walked, heart thumping, toward Margo Bryan's bright yellow door.

Molly's heart was thumping too as she waited for the reporter's arrival. Enemies do not wear horns or carry tails, but speak in soft, beguiling voices, and she had developed a foreboding about this Una O'Connor, with her open, freckled face and mop of bright red hair.

There was another problem. She had been half asleep when she had taken the call and had forgotten to mention that Christian was coming. Well, she would just ask Una O'Connor to state her business as quickly as possible and then to leave.

She felt so wound-up and jittery about the confluence of events that in an effort to calm her apprehension she had taken a scented bath and had dressed in one of her favorite, most comfortable outfits, a jumpsuit of white cotton.

But now she could not rest easy as the minutes dragged into hours. She looked at her watch: it was nearly half-past ten. Who knew what time the woman would come—it would be just her luck, she thought, for the two of them to arrive together. Well, she thought, working herself up, if that happened, she would just bloody well ask the reporter to leave and to come back at a more convenient time.

She tried to read a script that Dolly had sent her with a recommendation that she should consider it favorably. This one was to be filmed in Argentina and was a high-budget, star-cast project from one of the major studios. Dolly's covering note had advised that the part envisaged for her was ideal, but had warned that since the budget—and therefore the risk—was so high, she might have to test for it. She tried to concentrate on the print but found she was reading the same page over and over again. She threw the script on the kitchen table, but then picked it up again and brought it back into the living room and filed it neatly away on the bookshelf. She turned on the radio, but could find nothing that had no religious overtones—except on Radio Three, which was playing music she did not like. She turned the set off again and continued her pacing of the house, straightening cushions that did not need straightening and wiping down the already immaculate work surfaces in the kitchen.

She went out onto the patio. After a succession of glorious warm days, the weather had changed overnight and the morning was overcast, with a wind from the northeast that had torn petals from the early-flowering roses and some of the more delicate of the pot plants, discarding them to drift like pastel snowflakes around the flagstones. She shivered and went back into the house, moving again from room to room in search of something productive to do. Everything was gleaming, Mrs. Sharma had been in the afternoon before, so there was not even a speck of visible dust to be banished. She got a cardigan, pulled it around her shoulders, and went back out to the patio. She swept up the petal debris, and when that was done, began to dead-head the potted geraniums and pelargoniums. The wind stung her face, but the steady work settled her down a little.

Having thought about it, she had narrowed down the possibilities as to what Christian wanted to discuss—either a reconciliation or divorce. The former was out of the question, as far as Molly was concerned. As for divorce, she would probably agree.

But what could this woman have discovered about her husband—other than what Molly herself had told her in the interviews? Could it be something to do with his drinking?

She would hardly come all the way over from Ireland for a second time just to discuss that. Could Christian have contacted her?

Molly vacillated wildly between wanting to know what

this information was and not wanting to know. She had a premonition that whatever it was, it was going to affect her radically. Or was she panicking unduly, mistaking fear for foresight?

For the past few months she had been living in a fool's paradise, playing house with Conor, burying Christian's existence at the back of her mind. But she saw now that she had been a coward. Christian was her husband, her responsibility. She should not have left things slide.

When she had hung up after Una's telephone call in the early morning, her instinct had been immediately to telephone Conor. She knew the name of his hotel in Dublin. But she resisted the urge. He had enough on his plate without hysterical calls from her about information, as yet unspecified, which was threatened by a reporter and which might or might not prove to be important or even true.

She heard the doorbell ring and her stomach gave a great lurch. Twenty minutes to eleven. Una O'Connor would get short shrift.

At least the waiting was over.

Forcing herself to move at a normal pace, Molly went into the kitchen and removed her cardigan, hanging it over the back of a chair. Before opening the front door, she stopped in front of the mirror over the hall table to check her appearance and to compose her features; when she opened the door, no one would have known she was feeling anything but her usual self. "Good morning!" she said, "won't you come in?"

As Una stepped into the hallway, Molly noticed that the woman's skin was blotchy and that there were dark rings under her eyes. She also seemed nervous. A wild suspicion flashed through Molly's mind that this woman might be having an affair with Christian and had come to confess—but the idea was so ludicrous, she almost laughed out loud and her own confidence increased. "I'd offer you a cup of coffee," she said, "but I'm expecting someone else in a few minutes. I hope this won't take too long."

"No!" Una gave a half laugh. "Anyway, I'm up to here with coffee"—she made a gesture to indicate a line somewhere between her collarbone and her chin—" my own and the airline's. I've been up all night."

Molly hesitated, then: "We might as well go into the kitchen anyhow—" The reporter followed her into the kitchen and stood awkwardly as though not knowing where, or if to sit. Molly indicated one of the chairs at the table.

Una sat down. "Before I forget!" she said, taking the shoe box out of the string bag and handing it over.

Molly took the box and put it back on top of the kitchen dresser. She sat at the kitchen table, facing Una. "Let's get this over with. What is it you want to tell me about my husband?"

Una stared hard at the table and Molly waited, for an age it seemed to her. Finally Una looked her straight in the eye. "I've rehearsed how to say this over and over again, all last night and coming over in the plane, but I still find it very difficult."

Molly would not help her. She continued to wait.

"I have something to tell you about your husband and yourself . . ."

"Yes?"

"Molly, it will be a terrible shock to you!"

"For God's sake get on with it." Molly's nerves were strung tight.

"Yes, well, but before I tell you there is something else I have to say . . ." Una took a deep breath. "You must remember I am a reporter—and my job is to cover stories."

Molly's nerves could stand no more of the preamble: "*Please*, will you tell me what's on your mind?" With that the doorbell rang. "Oh, my God!" Molly sprang to her feet. "You won't believe this," she said, "but that'll be my husband. He was due to call at eleven. He's early, damn it—this is what I was afraid of!"

Una was staring at her with a peculiar expression on her face which, if she were not so agitated, Molly might have interpreted as fear. She had no time or inclination to figure it out, however, as she walked toward the hallway. "I'll go and let him in," she said. "I'll put him in another room. You'll have to go, I'm afraid. Maybe you can come back later, but this is something I have to deal with."

She left the reporter and opened the door to Christian. "Hello, Molly," he said quietly. He had heavy bags under his eyes, but his hair was groomed and he was spruce in his pale trench coat; he had clearly made an effort.

"Come in, Christian," she said. As he stepped across the threshold, she got the strong smell of alcohol. "You've been drinking!" The accusation was out before she could stop it. She wanted to hit him.

"Yes—so what's it to you?" Although he thrust his chin out belligerently, she realized he was as nervous as she, and the impulse to strike him receded. "Never mind, come in," she said, closing the door behind him.

"There's one thing I've got to tell you," he said, looking at the floor. "I'm here because my grandfather insisted. I wouldn't bother you otherwise."

"I see." Molly's agitation changed to anger. Some husband he was. "I'll be with you in a moment," she said as coldly as she could. "There's someone in the kitchen who's just leaving." She showed him into the small room off the hall and went back to the kitchen.

The reporter was where she had left her, but standing. "I'm sorry, Miss O'Connor—" Molly began, but then saw that the woman was holding out a white envelope to her. "What's this?" Molly looked at it. "This is addressed to you."

Una nodded. "This is why I came. It concerns you and your husband. I think maybe your husband should find out about it at the same time."

Molly bit back a retort: something about the reporter's expression struck terror into her. In silence, she left Una and went back to the other room. Christian rose when she entered. "Would you come to the kitchen, please?" she asked. "This person I said was here is a reporter; she says she has something about us we both should see."

"My business is with you, Molly—"

"Come into the kitchen!" The ferocity of her reply caused him to comply and he followed her out of the room.

Molly performed the introductions. "This is my husband, Christian Smith. This is Una O'Connor."

"We've met before!" Both spoke simultaneously, and an awkward silence descended on the kitchen.

Una again held out the envelope and Molly took it. Opening it, she withdrew a handwritten letter and another one, typed, with the top torn off. She read the handwritten one first and as she read, time stopped. The refrigerator, which had been humming quietly, clicked off, and the silence that took its place seemed as loud as rushing water. The second letter confirmed what the first one said.

"Who's the second one from?" she asked, whispering. "The top is torn off."

"Yes," said Una, "but as you can see, the name under the signature shows that whoever wrote the letter belongs to the FAA—that's the Federal Aviation Administration in America."

"What—what is it?" Christian was still as a stone. Wordlessly, Molly handed him both letters, but she could not bear to watch his face as he read. Halfway through the second one, he collapsed onto a chair.

Molly hardly noticed; her face felt cold as ice. "This can't be—" she pleaded, to whom she did not know. This had to be some sort of mistake, some sort of practical joke.

Una spoke first. She put a hand out, but retracted it and looked from one to the other: "I'm really sorry to be the one to do this to you, I really am." She was whispering. "Could I get you both a drink, a brandy or something?"

"Fuck this!" Christian stood up and threw the letters against the wall. "I don't believe this. Some people will do anything for a story!" He came back to Una and thrust his face into hers. "Nice try, Miss O'Connor, but it won't work!" He went to the kitchen dresser, where he knew Molly kept brandy for use in cooking. Pouring himself a large measure, he tossed it off in one gulp and poured a second one.

Molly stared at the two letters lying on the floor. As though moving in a dream, she walked across and picked them up. "Where did these letters come from?"

"From the shoe box you gave me with your clippings." Una's voice was stronger now. "I don't know why the person who wrote me that letter didn't send it."

The shoe box. Father Moran. FOUND AMONG THE EFFECTS . . .

Molly stared at her. "How could this be? It's impossible. That means that if he's my brother, then Malcolm is my father, no, my grandfather.''

''Shut up, *shut up*!'' Christian drained the second glass of brandy. ''This is a setup. It's a setup, I tell you.''

''It's not a setup.'' Una was clearly restraining herself from shouting back. ''That letter was addressed to me a long time ago. It came into my hands by accident. I could have used it but I didn't. I'm being responsible here.''

''Yeah, some responsible . . . !''

Molly ignored the exchange. ''Conor,'' she whispered, ''he's—he's—'' She had never before fainted, but the room began to spin around her and she felt as though she was going to. The letters in her hand began to rattle as she started to shake.

''Perhaps you should have a drink too,'' Una suggested.

Molly sank into the nearest chair and pillowed her head on her arms on the table in front of her. Una took a glass off the dresser, filled it with water, and brought it back to the table. Molly picked it up, but she could not hold it, and some of the water slopped out. Una helped her to raise it to her lips.

''I'm sorry, Molly.''

''Sorry!'' Christian raged, ''sorry doesn't even start to come into it!'' His glass followed the letters against the wall with such force that it shattered into hundreds of pieces.

''Put your head down to your knees.'' Una was concerned with Molly. The letters had slipped out of her grasp and lay on the floor underneath the table, and as she put her head down, Molly was aware of Christian rushing over to pick them up again. ''There!'' he shouted, ''there! That's what I think of your fucking letters!'' Violently, he ripped the paper crosswise and dashed the pieces to the ground. Molly felt Una's hands tighten on her shoulders: ''The fact that you've torn them up does not alter the facts in them, Mr. Smith.''

''Molly is not my sister, she's not!'' Christian's voice wobbled dangerously.

''I know you've had a shock, Mr. Smith—''

''Oh, that's nice, that's really lovely . . .'' He mimicked her: ''I know you've had a *shock*, Mr. Smith. Easy for you, Miss tweety pie reporter.''

"Don't shoot the messenger, Mr. Smith. I think you should have some regard for your wife here—"

"My *what*?" Christian's voice was suddenly full of menace. "I thought your garbage here"—he indicated the letters "—is insinuating that this woman is not my wife but my sister."

Mustering all her strength, Molly raised her head. *"Stop it, Christian!"*

Christian pounded one fist into the other. He strode to the sink and gripped its edge, glaring out through the window. Molly stood up and retrieved the letters, now in four pieces. With shaking hands she fitted the pieces together. The other two in the room receded from her consciousness as she reread Father Moran's letter:

I have received knowledge, I cannot reveal how . . .

for professional, ethical and moral reasons, I cannot reveal . . .

revealed to me on an absolutely confidential basis . . .

With sudden clarity she saw there could be only one conclusion. Confession. He had to have learned it in confession. And it had to be from someone who was involved. Her father? Sorcha? She would never know now.

She raised her eyes to Una. "I know these letters are yours, but could I keep them for a few days?" she asked, trying to keep a tight rein on herself. "Obviously I'll have to—there are some things that I—that we have to—"

"Fuck this!" Christian walked rapidly to the door. "I'm not sticking around for this. You can take your garbage, Miss O'Connor, and stuff it!" He disappeared and a few seconds later, the front door slammed.

The two women looked after him. Molly's head was reeling. There was too much to take in in one go: Christian her brother? That meant Malcolm was her grandfather.

It also meant that Sorcha and Micheál were not blood relatives at all and Conor—With a great effort, Molly postponed thinking about Conor.

She was aware that Una was pulling her chair forward until she was very close. "Keep the letters as long as you like," she said. Then she paused, and devastated though she was, instinctively Molly knew she would not like what was coming next.

Her instinct proved correct. Because after clearing her

throat, the reporter launched into a speech she had, Molly realized, clearly prepared: "I've said already that I'm a reporter, doing my job," she started. "Now, I've no wish at all to make life difficult for you—more difficult than it is going to be. But if you put yourself in my shoes, you must see what a big story this is. In a sense, because the information was sent to me, it is my story now as much as yours."

Despite her own shock, Molly saw that Una was finding this difficult, that she was embarrassed. But she was damned if she was going to help her out. She pulled around her what shreds of self-possession she could grasp. "And maybe you'll appreciate, if *you* put yourself in *my* shoes—" she started, but Una cut her off.

"I know how you feel," she said, "I really do—and of course I'll wait a few days . . ."

She paused now and Molly noticed that her freckles joined over her nose. "Really?" she said, trying to force irony into her voice.

"I can't just do *nothing* about this story, Molly."

"I'm sorry, but I think you can." Molly tried to be strong, but the voice that came out was high-pitched and weak.

"Listen," said Una softly, after a pause, "I'm sorry for being the messenger, but I didn't ferret out this information, you must know that. I didn't look for it—it was written to me unsolicited by someone who, if I may say so, really seemed to have your best interests at heart. Whoever wrote me that letter trusted me to do the right thing. Well, I think I've done the right thing in coming to you, but as I said, I'm a reporter—"

Molly could see that Una's confidence was growing. She felt trapped. She was also worrying about Christian, where was he—in what pub? They had to talk . . .

She forced herself to concentrate on what the reporter was saying. "What I'm suggesting," Una continued, "if this is okay with you, is that I do nothing at all with this story for a month, to give you time to sort out what you need to sort out. And I'll help you—honest! If there is anything I can do, I'll do it. My paper has considerable resoources and contacts."

"But the publicity—"

"Believe me, I'll make it all right. You will not be

ashamed of anything I write. I never, ever do this, and
my editor would probably kill me if he finds out I'm
even breathing this—but if you like, I'll let you see the
stuff before it's printed. There will be no guarantee that
I'll change anything, mind you, but it should put your
mind at rest. And if there is something that I've got
wrong or something that really causes you or your family terrible pain or embarrassment, I'll have a rethink
about it. If you cooperate with me, I'll cooperate with
you, and I *promise* you that things will work out all
right!''

It was all too much. The aftershock of what she had
just heard started to rattle around in Molly again as she
looked at this woman with her carrotty hair.

On the other hand, the urgency of Una's argument
had wiped the veneer of sophistication from her speech
patterns and the accent had reverted to its Galway
origins, and Molly was reminded a bit of Bridget Slevin,
another Galway woman who had helped her in an hour
of need. She decided that in any event, she had no
choice but to depend on this woman. ''Are you sure I
can trust you?''

''Yes. Mind you,'' added Una, who suddenly became
conscious that for someone who was only a base grade
news reporter, she was promising quite a lot on behalf
of the *Irish Record,* ''I'll have to check all this out with
my editor. After all,'' she continued, ''none of this is
your fault, any more than it's mine. You can hardly be
blamed for an air crash that set you adrift in the Atlantic
and for the deception which was perpetrated on you when
you were one year old!''

''Has this ever happened before?''

''I've heard of it happening before.'' Molly felt Una
was operating on instinct, but had no choice but to follow
her.

''In Ireland?''

''No, I think there was a case in America that I read
about recently. I'll find out for you.''

Molly looked at her, only half believing. On the other
hand, the reporter had promised her time. ''If you
could,'' she said, ''maybe I could get in touch with those
people, find out how they coped . . .''

''I'll do that!'' Una promised. The conversation petered out. Molly did not resist when Una touched her arm. "Have you anyone you could go to for the rest of the day? I don't think you should be alone."

Alone. The word sounded funny.

"Al-one." What did it mean? Again she forced herself to concentrate. There was no one at all she could go to, flopping onto their shoulders with this thunderbolt. At least there was no one in London.

Conor.

She could go to Conor in Dublin.

No. The subject of Conor was something to be considered in isolation. She thought of John Pius, also only a plane ride away, but then remembered that John Pius was on holiday in Mauritius.

That left Malcolm and Cordelia, so far away in Chicago. And although they would have to be told, the telephone was certainly not the proper medium for such momentous tidings.

Yes. She would go to Chicago. She had no work to hold her here for the moment, and Conor was planning to go to Inisheer to visit Brendan if the interview in Dublin turned out as he hoped.

Thanks to Dolly's shrewdness, she had quite a healthy bank balance and she could afford to fly to America at will. "I'll go to Chicago to see Malcolm, my—my grandfather," she said to Una, the words again sounding strange. Molly had never had a grandparent, since both Sorcha's and Micheál's parents had been dead when she was born.

Or had they? Things were becoming more and more confused.

They would not have been her grandparents anyway. She had not been born on Inisheer. Sorcha and Micheál were not her parents. All along she had had no parents, just like Christian, but she had had a grandfather. She did have parents too, they were Christian's parents, but they had died in an air crash as Christian's parents had.

"So my real name is, is—" she thought of the array of photographs on the piano in the Evanston house. The photograph of the baby—of herself. She could hardly bring herself to say the name "Susanna."

"Susanna?" said Una.

"Susanna!" repeated Molly, barely audible. And then

she thought of her own baby Susanna, the still, warm little body she had held in her arms in the nursery of St. Catherine's, the head downy against her cheek.

Una let her cry. It was probably very good for her, she thought. She stood up from the table and did what all Irishwomen do in a crisis—she made a pot of tea.

13

When Molly took a mouthful of the tea she almost gagged.

Una ordered her to drink it. "I put four spoonfuls of sugar in it. You need it!"

As Molly sipped at the sweet liquid she felt surreal, as though she were at one and the same time in a movie and watching it.

Gently Una suggested they travel together out to Heathrow, so Molly went with her up the stairs to her bedroom and sat on her bed while Una went into her dressing room.

Then Una opened the wrong wardrobe, "They're Christian's," said Molly. "I never had the courage to get rid of them." She watched Una select some clothes from the correct wardrobe and pack them in a suitcase and then go into the bathroom and come out with armfuls of cosmetics and toiletries. The whole operation took less than ten minutes.

Una called a taxi and turned to Molly just as they were about to leave the house. "Have you got your credit cards?"

Molly picked up her handbag from the hallstand and, obedient as a child, nodded. She was still dazed. It was nice to have someone taking care of her.

"Passport?"

"No, sorry—"

"Where is it?"

"It's in the little chest in the kitchen."

"I'll get it. Don't move."

"Thank you, Una."

Una came back with the passport, looking through it. "Are you sure your visa's okay?"

"It's fine, it's a five-year one."

Una took Molly's handbag, opened it, put the passport in, and closed it again. She hesitated. "Are you sure you're all right?"

"Yes, really," said Molly. Una asked her twice more in the taxi if she was all right, and twice Molly said she was.

Although it was Sunday, the noise was frightful when they got to Heathrow; Molly had not shaken off the surreal feeling and left all the arrangements to Una. Since there were no seats on a direct flight to Chicago, she agreed to go via New York. Una took her credit card to pay for her tickets; all Molly had to do was sign her name. She did notice that the tickets were red. "First Class!" said Una shortly. "You can afford it—and you deserve it. You'll need looking after and a bit of sleep."

Molly was grateful for all Una's care and attention but suddenly afraid of traveling alone. "Would you not come with me?" she asked. But Una shook her head, "I can't, I wish I could, but I really can't. I have a job, you know. As a matter of fact, I'm supposed to be in the office in two hours' time."

"Of course, I'm so sorry."

"Molly! Please don't apologize like that! I hate myself for what I've done to you!" They were still standing at the ticket desk.

"Could you stay for a little while?"

"Yes."

Molly again watched as Una, showing her press card and smiling a lot, wangled it so she could go into the First Class lounge with Molly. And when they got there, she held on to Molly's hand.

"It's a little difficult to take it all in, you know," said Molly.

"It will take a bit of time," said Una. "I think you should go and see a doctor when you get to Chicago. Give me the telephone number of the house and I'll call ahead and get them to meet you."

"Would you do that? You're very kind."

"Stop saying I'm very kind! I'm not very kind. I feel like a shit at this very moment. Now give me the number." She copied the number into her own address book. "Now remember, I won't have told them anything. I'll just alert them to the fact that you're coming and that they're to meet you.''

''Maybe they won't be able to meet me.''

''So what! Have you money? You can get a taxi.''

''I'll change money in New York.''

''Atta girl!'' said Una. She got coffee for them then.

''Do you think I should telephone Conor?'' asked Molly.

Una looked at the floor. ''That's one area I can't help you with.''

''Sorry . . .''

They sat there, Molly still holding Una's hand. Then Molly said, looking away from Una toward a painting on the wall of the room, ''I think I love Conor.'' She said it not to Una but to herself.

Una said something, so low that Molly could not catch it. She had her head down so Molly couldn't see her face.

''I beg your pardon?'' she asked politely.

''I said, 'of course you do, Molly!' '' said Una quite loudly.

When she had seen Molly safely off, Una walked slowly back toward the main hall. Since Molly's need had been greater than her own, she had reacted instinctively by playing nursemaid. Now that Molly was gone she had time to think about herself. First things first— she realized her stomach was rumbling—she had not eaten since the night before.

Although she knew she should check to see what time the next flight to Dublin was due to take off, or if there were even seats on it, she decided that for once she would be good to herself. She climbed the stairs to the restaurant and, seating herself at one of the tables, ordered a large steak and chips.

But when the food came, although there was nothing wrong with it, she found she could not eat it. She took a few mouthfuls, but her earlier hunger had disappeared.

She had lost him irrevocably now.

She stared at the food. And then she realized clearly that whatever she had told herself when he had broken it off with her, she had not told herself the full truth. She had been secretly hoping against hope that somehow she would find a way to get him back again. Una despised herself for that self-delusion.

She had to face the fact that she had truly lost him.

"Is everything all right, madam?" The waiter was indicating the almost untouched food. Una raised her eyes. Through her tears his Oriental features were blurred. She attempted to smile. "Yes, it's just that I was not as hungry as I thought—"

The waiter picked up the food and took it away.

Una picked up her bag and shook her head angrily to remove the tears. It was all such a big cliché, the great empty space inside her, the pain . . . She had always prided herself on her toughness and invulnerability and here she was crying her eyes out. He was only a man, after all.

She would concentrate on her story.

She paid for the uneaten meal and went down the stairs to the Aer Lingus ticket desk, but every step drummed in her head. She had lost him, lost him . . .

Halfway across the Atlantic, Molly became irrationally convinced that Malcolm would die before she could tell him the news.

The First Class cabin of the jumbo was only half full and she had a window seat but no seat companion, and as her panic mounted, for that at least she was grateful. Her earlier mood of calm acceptance, when she had let Una run her as though she were a clockwork toy, had evaporated during the horror of the takeoff and, since then the implications of Una's discovery ran around in her head as though on a train track, flashing by each time before she could fully see them.

Christian was her brother.

Conor wasn't her brother.

Sorcha wasn't her mother.

Micheál wasn't her father.

Malcolm was her grandfather.

Cordelia was her grandmother.

Her mother was Maggie, her father was Cal.

Her mother was Maggie—that grave woman in the wedding photograph.

She had grandparents and cousins in America.

She knew that she would be making discoveries about

herself now for the rest of her life. All that time lost, but was it?

The chances were she would never have met Conor.

She understood Una's reticence now about Conor.

Poor Una.

But once, when the thought of Conor came around again, it broke her through into the sunshine. She smiled so widely at the stewardess who was serving her with canapés at the time that the woman smiled back but looked puzzled.

Now Molly willed the plane to go faster. She pushed it on with all her might. She wished she had taken Concorde. She had to get to Chicago to see Malcolm, but more urgently than that, she had to get to a telephone in New York so she could talk to Conor.

She called the stewardess and ordered champagne. Her excitement was mounting to such a feverish pitch that she thought her head would fly off.

She changed her mind about the champagne when it came and ordered beer instead. Champagne would fizz inside her; beer might slow her down. She needed to be slowed down.

"Certainly, ma'am," the stewardess said, taking away the champagne. Although the woman's professional smile did not slip, Molly could see that again she looked puzzled. The stewardess must think she was on drugs. That was the way she felt, Molly thought—as though she were drugged.

She picked at the rich First Class food but drank all her beer, and the combination of it and the soporific sun on her face through her window calmed her. She managed to sleep when they still had more than two hours to go before landing.

The stewardess woke her gently with a hot towel.

Kennedy airport was bedlam and Molly, disoriented, muzzy from the sleep and the traveling, found that her urgency about telephoning Conor had ameliorated. What would she say to him, anyway, on the telephone? It was something she had to tell him while she watched his eyes.

She let the airline people shepherd her gently through the First Class transit procedures and into another aircraft to Chicago. This flight took another two hours, but it seemed no time at all before the familiar streetscapes along the lake appeared beneath her window.

Cordelia was waiting for her at the exit gate.

Darling Cordelia.

Molly burst into tears and flung her arms around Cordelia's neck.

"Molly! What is it, what is it? My poor Molly. What is it?"

The other people in the arrivals area gave them space. Molly continued to sob, laughing and crying alternately.

"Come on, Molly," said Cordelia at last. "Come on—you can tell me all about it in the car."

It was dark in the recreation room. Malcolm was sitting in his wing chair, which was now showing its considerable age. The brocade was rubbed shiny at the corners and threadbare along the padding where his head had rested for so many years. The only illumination was cast by a tall floor lamp, almost as venerable as the chair, but as it was a warm night, the French doors stood open and the lake, like a thin sheet of pewter, gleamed beyond them through the screens under a three-quarter moon.

Cordelia came with Molly into the room. "Malcolm, look who's come to see us!"

He might have been sleeping because he started, making a small guttural sound, before attempting to push himself upright, leaning heavily on the armrests of the chair. "Molly! My dear! How lovely to see you!"

"No, please don't get up, Malcolm," cried Molly, rushing forward and restraining him. "I'll sit here." She fetched a tapestry stool from its place in front of another chair and placed it in front of him.

Cordelia made for the panel of light switches just inside the door. "Let's turn on a few lights in here—"

"No, it's okay, I like it like this," said Molly.

"All right. I'll leave you two alone. I'll get coffee."

"I'm sorry I didn't go to the airport with Delia to meet you, my dear. I was a bit tired today." Half of Malcolm's face was in shadow, but Molly saw that whereas in repose the face showed her grandfather's years, when he was talking he looked like a much younger man. "Oh, Malcolm," she said, "of course you didn't have to come to the airport. I—I have something really extraordinary to

tell you . . .'' Then she did not know how to continue.
It had been easy with Cordelia. The words had un-
dammed on the flood of tears.

"Is it getting a little cold in here for you?" she asked.
"Should I close the doors?"

"No—it's not cold and I'm not cold. What is it you
have to tell me that's so extraordinary?"

"You're going to find this very, very hard to believe,"
she said hesitantly,'' and I hope it won't be too much of
a shock . . .'' She leaned forward and gripped his hands.
"A reporter came to see me today—yesterday—no, today, with a story about myself. She had absolute proof—
I know where she got it and who supplied it and I think
I know how *he* got it—with proof that I'm not who I've
thought I was. I'm not Molly Ní Bhriain from Inisheer."
She stopped. "This is very hard . . ."

"Go on, please go on . . .'' Malcolm had stiffened,
tense as a cat.

"Malcolm, I'm your granddaughter. I'm Christian's
sister."

He didn't move.

"I know it's very hard to believe. But that air crash,
that plane that went down. Apparently, I survived and I
was washed ashore on a life raft, on Inisheer. I don't
know the full details about what happened, but I was
found by my mam and dadda—at least, I mean, by the
people I thought of as my parents. But I wasn't theirs.
I'm yours—'' She dropped his hands in despair. "Oh.
I'm making a mess of this!"

Very slowly he folded his hands in his lap. "I think
somewhere deep down, I've known this all along," he
said very calmly, but the effort to control himself was
showing. "It will take me a while to adjust, but I don't
need convincing that you're who this reporter says you
are."

"I really am your granddaughter!"

The old man continued to sit very still, but the expression on his face was one she was to remember for
the rest of her life. He began to talk as though to himself.
"When you came out of customs that first day with
Christian, I could have sworn you were Maggie in the
flesh. I think I must always have known something like
this. But it was just so improbable. It was not only how

you looked, it was something about the way you walked
and held yourself—''

He banged his fist on his knee. ''When we were told
about that empty raft, we should have searched those
islands. I should have gone there myself, house to house;
I would have recognized you immediately . . . all those
years . . .''

Cordelia came back into the room and saw his agitation. ''What about Christian?'' she asked quietly.

Malcolm looked across at her over Molly's head and
then stood up. ''I'll go to London.''

''No!'' Molly had spoken instinctively but then
changed her mind. ''Sorry, Malcolm, I didn't mean to
sound so abrupt. But Christian already knows. He was
with me when I found out.''

''How did he take it?'' Cordelia's face showed she had
a very good idea how Christian had reacted to the bomb-
shell.

''I'm sorry.'' Molly stood too and took her grandmother's arm. ''He'll need time—''

''We'll all need time.'' Malcolm sat again in his chair.
He looked for a long time at Molly. ''You're my Susanna?''

''I'm your Susanna, Grandfather—but it's going to take
me a while to think of myself with that name!''

''Names, names,'' said Malcolm. ''You're back!''

Molly did a childish thing that night. She took a lip-
stick and wrote ''MY NAME IS SUSANNA!'' in scarlet
block capitals all over the mirror of the dressing table in
the guest room. Although she had turned the lights off,
she had not pulled the curtains, and from where she lay
in the bed she could dimly make out the letters on the
mirror, which gleamed in the moonlight. It was the first
opportunity she had had all day for reflection.

She placed her left hand in the path of the pale light
that slanted from the window across the room and onto
the counterpane; the diamond of her engagement ring
caught it and flashed. She could hardly continue to wear
it now. Or her wedding ring.

For the first time in her life, she wished she was a
writer or, more likely, a composer or a painter. She tried
to imagine what her painting would look like. Swirling

circles. On the periphery it would be full of yellows and oranges and bright reds for the highs: for the good work she had done, for her lovely, bowered wedding day, for the moment of happiness when her baby had been born. But these brightnesses would whirl around a central vortex, menacing with mustard and vile greens and dirty browns, the instant snatching away of her baby, Christian's drinking and desertion. And right in the middle would be a white circle that represented the unknown. Her future.

Conor. It must be six o'clock in the morning in Ireland, she thought. His image had hovered all day just out of the span of her attention, but she had refused to grasp for it. The implications were too new, too exciting, and in a way too terrifying, to examine.

She laughed aloud in her bed. It was ironic, she thought, that just as he had come out of the closet to declare he was her brother, she could tell him he was no such thing.

She sat up suddenly. That was something that had not occurred to her until now. How did Sorcha and Micheál explain the sudden arrival of a one-year-old baby in their midst? Had Conor and Brendan known all along that she was a foundling?

It became imperative that she ring him. She jumped out of bed and as quietly as her urgency would allow, hurried down the stairs and into the living room, which was little used but was far from any of the bedrooms. She did not turn on the lights; the moonlight was bright enough to see the telephone, which was conveniently on a little side table by one of the floor to ceiling windows. She pushed the buttons for the long-distance operator and, giving the Dublin hotel name, asked for the telephone number.

"Is that north or south Ireland, miss?"

"The Republic!" she said. Normally that kind of question irritated her, but not tonight. Illinois Bell, despite its ignorance of the capital cities of the world, operated with its usual efficiency, and she had the number within thirty seconds. "Thank you!" she said politely to the operator, and before she could forget them, punched out the digits.

The phone rang and rang, for so long that she was in

despair and was about to hang up when it stopped and a male voice, not exactly the product of a charm school, came on the line.

"Yes?"

"May I speak to a Mr. Conor O Briain, please? He is staying there."

"Hold on . . ."

To her relief, she heard Conor's voice a few moments later. "Hello?" He did not sound sleepy.

"Hello, Conor."

"Is that you, Molly?"

She felt giddy. "Well yes, in a manner of speaking!"

"What?"

"Yes, it's me, Conor."

"Molly, are you drunk? Where are you calling from? You sound as if you're on the far side of the moon."

"I sort of am—I'm in Chicago, well, not Chicago, Evanston, actually."

"What are you doing there?"

"Oh, I'm here on a sort of mission!"

"I see!" Now he sounded impatient. "Look, Molly, why are you ringing me at this hour of the morning? This is a very important day for me and I've been up since five o'clock, going over and over what I have to say in less than four hours' time!"

"I'm not playing games, Conor."

"What?"

"I'm not playing games! I have a very important question to ask you. Now you might think it is very odd, but it is part of the reason I'm here. It's a matter of life and death, Conor and, I'm half afraid to ask you."

"What is it, Molly, for God's sake!"

"Do you know anything about my birth?"

There was a pause, and when he answered, she could hear the astonishment in his voice.

"Your birth?"

"Yes, my birth."

"Well, I wasn't at it, if that's what you mean. I was away in school at the time."

"What age was I when you first saw me?"

"Oh, Molly, for crying out loud, what's this all about?"

"I'll tell you when I see you, Conor. Now will you just answer me? What age was I when you first saw me?"

"You must have been about two months old or something like that. I came home from school at Easter with Brendan and there you were."

"Are you sure you saw me that Easter?"

"Of course I'm sure. You wouldn't remember, but I was the one who brought you down to the beach for the first time. And it was definitely Easter Sunday because we had chicken for dinner."

She laughed. Dear Conor. Always food. "Are you sure you couldn't be mistaken?" she asked. "Could I have been one year and two months old, d'you think?"

She could hear him sighing.

"You were a very small baby when I brought you to the beach, Molly. You couldn't walk, or talk or sit or even babble. Now does that answer your question?"

"Yes!" said Molly, happiness beginning to bubble in her veins.

"And now can I get back to preparing for my interview with the massed ranks of the hierarchy of the Irish police force?"

"I want you to listen to me very carefully, Conor. I've to stay here for a couple of days, there are a few things I have to do, but I'll be coming back to Ireland later in the week. I'm going to go over to Inisheer and see you and Brendan."

He paused again, then said carefully: "Are you over there with Christian? Will you be bringing Christian with you?"

"I have no notion of where he is at the moment. And I won't be looking for him, at least not yet. I will not, repeat, will not, be bringing him with me."

"I see."

"Conor, something really extraordinary has happened, but I want to tell you in person and I want to tell you on Inisheer."

"Just tell me one thing—is it good or bad?"

"You'll just have to wait and see, but I think you'll be impressed!"

"You've been nominated for an Oscar!"

"For goodness' sake! That doesn't happen for months and months. Anyway, it's better than an Oscar—"

"So it's good, then."

"Just wait and see. **And good** luck today. I've a hunch nothing at all can go wrong today."

"Good-bye, Molly." She could tell he was smiling.

"Good-bye Conor!" She sang it.

She raced back up the stairs to her bed. He had seen her when she was two months old. That was a mystery they would have to unravel together. It must have been a different baby. Poor baby. But her brain couldn't deal with that now. Nothing could dampen her exhilaration now.

Malcolm was already fully dressed when she came downstairs early in the morning. The rolltop desk in his den was open and he was sitting at it, notepad in front of him. He slammed down the telephone receiver in frustration when she came into the room: "Damned answering machines!"

"Malcolm," she protested, "it's only seven-fifteen in the morning. Who are you trying to call?"

"I was trying to get through to Christian," he said. "Anyway, good morning, Susanna."

"Susanna, Molly, Margo—I think I'll just call myself 'Fred' and be done with it!" She walked across and kissed him on the cheek. "Good morning, Grandfather."

Although Molly and her grandfather did not know it, Christian was already in the United States but not in Chicago. He had had every intention of going home to Evanston when he had—a few hours later than Molly—taken the transAtlantic flight, but when he landed at O'Hare, his nerve had failed him.

He took a taxi into the city and phoned Dick Spielberg, but Dick's answering machine was on. Christian did not leave a message. He had been drinking a lot in the days before the interview with Molly—and on the flight across the Atlantic; his thought processes were now blurring as he tried to weigh up his options.

Briefly he considered telephoning the Evanston house, but the events of the past sixteen hours had been so confusing that he had no idea what he should say.

Christian went into a bar and ordered a double bour-